A KINGDOM OF NOMADS

Book 2 of the Outcast Series

S. B. NOVA

Copyright © 2023 by S. B. NOVA.

Published by Night Owl, 2023.

The right of S.B.NOVA to be identified as the Author of the Work has been asserted by her in accordance with the Copyright, Designs and Patents Act 1988.

All rights reserved.

This book is sold subject to the condition it shall not, by way of trade or otherwise, be circulated in any form or by any means, electronic or otherwise without the publisher's prior consent.

This is a work of fiction. Names, characters, places, and incidents either are the product of the author's imagination or are used fictitiously. Any resemblance to actual persons, living or dead, events, or locales is entirely coincidental.

For Beren,
Thank you for believing in me. You brought light into a very dark place.

And to the readers who've stayed with me over the years—this one's for you.

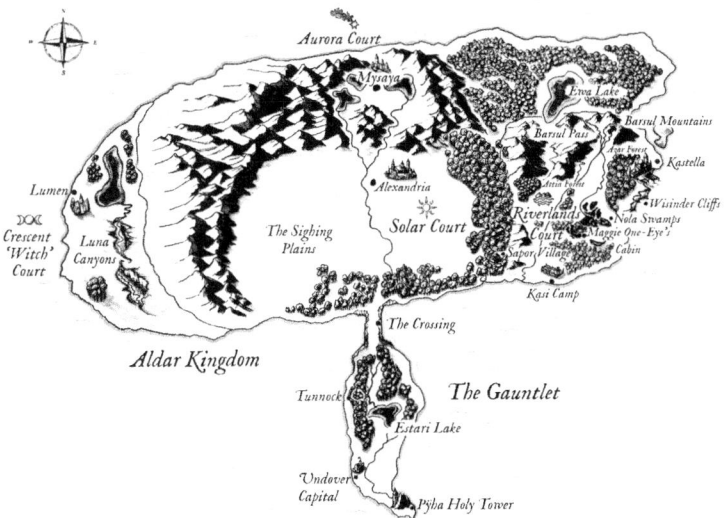

PROLOGUE: TO DEFY A QUEEN

-WILDER-

Over the tortured screams haunting Alexandria's dungeon, I detected a set of rapidly approaching footsteps.

Click-clack, click-clack, click-clack.

With adrenaline firing into my cold and tired body, I pushed off the hard slats that served as my bed and faced the sole source of illumination that was the torch light spilling in through the crack under the door.

I felt sure *click-clack* had come for me. Hours ago, soldiers had arrived with a standing bath and fresh clothes. Their sudden concern for my poor hygiene suggested my situation had changed.

A clunky key turned in the lock. My jailor set the door wide but stood off to the side. "The Queen demands your presence."

And there it was.

I quickly left the cramped cell, ducking out into the corridor. My vision turned yellow, assaulted by the flickering torch-flames. I threw up my arm to shield my eyes—eyes that were accustomed to the darkness of a prison.

"Hello, Wilder."

The fire-colored spots that swam in front of me faded, revealing a male with black hair, gray wings, and dark eyes. A familiar face.

A growl escaped me. "Hunter."

His lips pressed together, forming a thin line of misery.

I raked my eyes over him. Last we met, he had served in the Wild Hunt. Now, he wore the uniform of Morgan's personal guard, the spiders. A unit infamous for their brutal tactics and bloodstained hands. "You didn't escape, then."

He frowned, confused. A reminder was needed.

"Serena said you'd planned on fleeing to the continent with her." My wings flared aggressively when I added, "You told her that she should forget about me and let me be captured by Morgan."

"An apology would be meaningless at this point, but I'll say it anyway. I'm sorry. For that, and for bringing you to Alexandria," he said in a dead-sounding voice.

"You helped Goldwyn and Dimitri capture me?"

His throat bobbed. "Yes."

I stressed at the holes in my memory. Goldwyn had shown up at the arena where our recruits were fighting. She spat lies to lure me away from Serena. Like a faeling fool, I followed her. The next thing I remembered, I woke up underground and recognized the palace dungeons from their scent. They had always reeked of shit, stale sweat, and fresh blood.

"You drugged me," I said, guessing aloud.

Hunter bobbed his head, unable to meet my eye. "Just during the flight, so you wouldn't wake up and try to escape."

"If you really are sorry for what you've done, then tell me about Serena," I said, struggling to keep my desperation from showing in my voice. "Have you seen her? Is she in Alexandria?"

In my seclusion, I'd tried to use our bond to see if she was in pain or facing danger. I'd felt nothing. So either she was fine, or more likely our guardian bond hadn't developed enough for me to sense her yet.

"The last I saw of her, she and her friends were facing off with Dimitri, Tysion, and Goldwyn in an attempt to rescue you," Hunter said.

Panic clutched my heart.

Hunter went on in an undertone, as if worried the walls had ears. "But the rumor going around court is that Goldwyn and Tysion returned to the palace in disgrace. I haven't heard anything about Dimitri."

I saw no lie in his eye. The relief I felt almost brought me to my knees. For too long I'd dwelled in the dark, my sanity hanging by a precarious thread, terrified they had taken Serena, too—that she suffered at Morgan's hands.

"We have to go, Wilder. We can't keep the Queen waiting."

There was that dead, resigned tone again. I studied the way his arms were relaxed at his sides. He hadn't reached for the daggers at his hips to threaten or coax me. He carried a listless, muted air about him. I'd seen the same hopeless look on other soldiers' faces before. It was the look of somebody ready to die.

"What would you do if I tried to disarm you?" I asked, testing him.

Hunter didn't even flinch. "Try if you want, but my death won't change anything. You can't escape Alexandria."

Temper shortened by captivity, I spoke harshly. "I was stationed in the capital for centuries. I'm well aware of how difficult it is to leave the palace. Morgan knows it, too. That's why I'm not shackled." I roughly pushed past him. "Let's just get this over with."

I started along the stone passage where, if memory served, a curved staircase would be waiting to take me topside. Hunter hurried alongside me as I marched past a row of cells. Few prisoners languished on this level, but those that did begged and howled as we passed. I wasn't surprised by the lack of people. Morgan preferred her subjects to be punished in brutal public displays. I'd likely experience such a thing for myself soon enough.

"How long have I been here?" I asked Hunter.

"Almost two weeks."

That wasn't a shock. It had felt longer.

We met the stairs. Hunter went up first.

Once we had ascended into the palace proper, I dragged the fresher air into my greedy lungs and savored the sunlight that beamed in through the corridor's wall-to-wall windows.

Head clearing a bit, I watched the people passing by. Most of them didn't spare us a glance. Those that recognized me from my days at court didn't approach; they reacted with everything from hostility to curiosity to pity. It just depended on the person.

A minute or two later, we reached a pair of doors guarded by two armored males and a male page who fit Morgan's preferences for her household servants perfectly. He was elegantly dressed and uncommonly pretty.

"Wait here," the page said to Hunter in Kaeli, the fae language. He turned and hurried through one of the doors.

Tension bolted through my already stiff limbs as our names were called out by the servant.

Then the voice that had conquered kingdoms rang out in Kaeli. "Send them in, then go to the Endora Suite. Tell the cripple to bring *her*. But they must wait outside the doors until I'm ready to permit them an audience. Dismissed."

The page backed out of the room, his body bent in a retreating bow. Reaching us, he gestured inside with a well-practiced smile. "Her Majesty will see you now."

Steeling my spine, I walked through the door with Hunter. As we crossed the throne room, our steps sounding loud on the hard floor, I observed the space. It appeared much the same as it had before I'd left this accursed place.

Regal pillars still bordered the room and supported a high ceiling decorated with paintings, each an ode to nature. On either side of me stood statues of the benevolent gods. Ironic, considering the alabaster marble used to make them could only be found in one quarry—a hellish place. Death visited it so often, the overseers threw the bodies of the slaves down the pits rather than bother with graves or pyres. Such horrors were commonplace in the Solar Court. Sorrow had found a soft place to land here.

I stopped ten feet from the throne. Lucinda, a mad but powerful seer, lingered at the bottom of it, turning a spinning wheel, humming happily.

Checking my mental defenses were solid, I moved my gaze up the throne's staircase. There, sat atop a throne crafted for its likeness to the sun, was Morgan Yves. The fae who had fractured Aldar and filled the cracks with her venom.

A gloom settled over my bones. I found her thin frame, wicked features, and waist-length ebony hair unchanged. But her olive skin looked pallid, and the dark smudges under her charcoal-lined eyes stood out. Had something been keeping her from sleep?

Morgan stared down, expressionless, waiting for a show of deference. Her sharpened fingernails drummed against an arm of her golden throne.

I did not bow.

"Wilder."

"Morgan," I shot back.

That open display of disrespect—my informal address—had her rising from her throne. The crown of monarch butterflies atop her head seemed to move as she glided down the staircase in a sleeveless dress that fanned out behind her in red silk rivulets. Her only weapon was a bejeweled knife tied around her waist via a fabric belt.

Morgan paused on the bottom step, unveiling her wings. Their insect-like membrane and their black-red pattern were similar to a cinnabar moth. And I wanted to spit on them.

For a few cold seconds, the silence stretched. Grew bigger.

Hunter nervously shifted his weight.

"I've given you endless opportunities to return to my court of your own free will," Morgan told me, changing to the common tongue. "If you had done that—if you had put aside your pride even for a moment—you could've taken your post up again with your dignity intact. But you've exhausted my patience." Her garnet stare sharpened. "No more chances. No more delays. You will become my bloodsworn. Today."

My mind stumbled over the archaic term for a guardian. Morgan preferred it, probably because the word "guardian" implied she needed to be protected.

"You made the same threat years ago," I reminded her, sweat gathering on my top lip. "I told you then I won't submit to the bond. I'd bite out my own tongue before that vow ever passed my lips."

Morgan baited me with a slippery smile. "Stubborn to the end. I should actually thank you for it. Your refusal back then presented me with an interesting problem, one that I've since overcome."

Morgan left the dais. Hips dipping, she prowled toward me.

My breath escaped in clouds as the temperature dropped.

Not breaking from my gaze, she stopped a few feet away. There, a frost bloomed, darkening the skin of her hands and forearms. I knew

Morgan possessed mastery over air and ice. But when I resided in Alexandria, her magic had manifested in a crystalline-blue form. Not this lifeless gray that smelled wrong. Unnatural.

The hairs along my arms prickled in alarm. "What have you done to yourself?"

A dark chuckle sprang from red-painted lips. "I've evolved. Become something greater." She raised her hand and summoned ash-colored snowflakes to float above her palm, staring at them as one would a lover. "The monarchs of the past were lazy, entitled. They never had what it took to rule the fae."

"But you do?" I said sarcastically.

"Yes." Her eyes sparkled with impassioned pride as she raised her chin. "Not only that, but as of yesterday, I've become the only witch in our long history who can bind a guardian without the oath taking. I don't need to break into your mind. I don't even need you to speak to make you mine."

Shock ensnared me. If she really could circumvent *myena*—the vows used to create bonds—then fae culture would be irreparably altered. And not for the better.

"If that's true, then you've forfeited your soul to the darkest of magics, if you ever had one to begin with."

"Say what you want. It won't change your fate." Before I could assume a fighting stance, Morgan trilled, "Lynx, bring him down."

Hearing that name, my bowels turned watery.

Lightning blasted into me, too fast for the eye to comprehend. My attacker remained unseen, but his magic drove me to my knees. I folded in on myself as if my body were a vessel that could bottle my agony.

Through the ringing in my ears, I heard a muffled voice. "Hunter, hold him upright. But make sure he stays on his knees where he belongs."

Too weak to resist, I was forced into a straight-backed position by Hunter. Morgan brought the cool steel of her dagger up to greet my throat.

Meeting her pitiless gaze, I lined my voice with all the hate I bore her. "You can force a collar around my neck, but I'll never be yours, you crazy bitch."

"We'll see." Such hateful joy.

She sliced my palm with a deft flick of her wrist. I was thrown off when she cut her own and linked our hands. What the fuck was happening? A normal guardian bond demanded that she drink my blood, not intermingle it with hers.

My entire arm went numb as her vile magic moved through my body like an infection. The fires of hell crept into my bones and flamed my insides. I fought with what strength I had left. Hunter kept me locked in place until Morgan said, "It's done."

Just like that, I'd been locked into a bond with a tyrant.

Morgan's hand left mine to trace the scars on my cheeks, scars that she had carved into my face many moons ago. My stomach convulsed at her caress, at this perverse intimacy.

"Shall we start?" she purred, lightly scraping my stubble with her frost-tipped fingertips. "I order you to tell me everything you know about Serena Smith."

The compulsion to obey had my mouth popping open. Hysteria ballooned beneath my breastbone, and I quickly swallowed words that would make me a traitor.

Morgan dug her icy nails into my chin. "Speak."

No. *No.*

I ground my teeth until my jaw ached. My defiance cost me. She pulled up on our connection, shortening my leash as one would a dog. I felt her pushing her will upon me, trying to force me into providing answers.

The image of two faceless fae formed in my mind—one was white and glowing, the other red and pulsing. I recognized the shapes were just symbols for the magic powering both of my bonds. They grappled for dominance, seeking to claim my loyalty.

Seconds turned into minutes, but neither side won.

That battle of the bonds triggered a pounding headache. I thought my skull would surely crack open from the mounting pressure.

Finally, Morgan relented. She had failed.

"What did you do?" she asked, baring her teeth.

I chuckled hoarsely through stuttering breaths.

"You swore to be Serena Smith's guardian, didn't you?" A soft ask. Lethal.

"Yes," I spat out, wrenching my chin from her cold grip.

Straightening up, Morgan stared down her nose at me. The flesh of her arms started returning to its olive hue as the magical frost left her body. "Why would you do such a thing?"

"To protect her from you."

Betraying Serena violated the magic governing a guardian. I couldn't do it even if I'd wanted to. That was one of the reasons I'd sworn myself to her—to ensure her secrets would be safe if somebody got into my mind. I hadn't foreseen becoming a bloodsworn, though. Thank the ancestors, our bond had still shielded Serena.

"Why do you want to protect her?" Morgan's voice dipped, becoming as bitterly cold as a Riverlands stream in winter. "Tell the truth."

That command couldn't be denied. "I love her."

Regret soured my stomach. Serena should've been the first person to hear that.

"Fool," she hissed. "I didn't know that you'd fallen so far as to love even the dirt beneath your boots. A human, Wilder. Really?" Morgan's nose and lips wrinkled in disgust.

Anger beat like a wild thing at the bars of my ribcage. It wanted out. To strike at her. To kill.

"Get up," she barked at me. "This position is putting a crick in my neck."

Another command. Another compulsion. I staggered upward until I stood tall in the peasant clothes I'd been given.

"I trust you'll come to your senses soon enough," she said, her expression laced with violence, her tone threatening. "Time we moved on." Morgan's gaze drifted to Hunter. "Wilder's gift should've arrived by now. Let them in, and after that, report to Sinjin."

Hunter showed his respect before hurrying out.

I rounded on Morgan. "I don't want anything from you."

Her dark eyebrow jumped. "My Queen."

"What?"

"You will address me as 'my Queen.' Say it. *Now*."

The words were ripped from my mouth. "Yes, my Queen."

Her insipid smile edged toward something dangerous. "Good boy."

I bit back the curses I longed to hurl at her.

The sounds of people entering the throne room made me glance over my shoulder. Tysion—a former recruit of Kasi—dragged Goldwyn behind him. Both had sustained heavy injuries. Tysion's left wing was gone, replaced by a sheet of shimmering fabric stretched taut over a wooden frame. Goldwyn's face appeared mangled. Bruises blotched her skin, her nose looked broken, and she had numerous cuts that had festered.

When they reached us, Tysion yanked Goldwyn down into a bow.

"Stand." Morgan made an upward motion with her hand.

As soon as their backs were straight, Goldwyn started. "My Queen, *please*—"

"Who gave you permission to speak?" Morgan said, refusing to look upon her pleading subject.

My brow pinched in confusion. "Goldwyn captured me. Why are you punishing her?"

Surprisingly, Morgan deigned to give me an answer. "Because she allowed Dimitri to be killed and for his son to become a cripple."

She shot Tysion a look devoid of sympathy.

Dimitri was dead?

"I could've forgiven such mistakes. But I can't abide cowards." Morgan's punishing gaze pinned Goldwyn. "This worthless worm fled when she encountered a witch who could use light magic."

"My Queen, forgive me! Please—"

"Tysion." Morgan spoke louder, drowning out Goldwyn. "Silence her flapping tongue for me."

He grasped a handful of Goldwyn's matted hair. In a move reeking of undiluted aggression, he yanked her head back and placed a blade at the seam of her mouth.

Goldwyn whimpered.

"Any guesses on who made the coward flee?" Morgan glared at me, her eyes wide and filled with the fires of madness.

Serena? It had to be. She must've tapped into her magic.

I removed emotion from my voice. "No."

"No guesses? No opinions?" Morgan's expression was that of a spider stalking a fly. "Is that because you already knew it was your whore?"

I pulled an innocent face that said I was bemused, not guilty. "I've no idea what you're talking about. Serena isn't a witch. Even if she was, humans can't wield light magic. Their bodies are too weak to handle it."

Goldwyn made a noise to get attention.

Morgan flashed her teeth. "What now, worm?"

Tysion removed the blade from Goldwyn's mouth. Not stopping to wipe the drool from her chin, she rushed out, "Wilder's telling the truth. Serena never had a magical signature. I would've sensed it."

My mind paused at that. I knew certain individuals could detect witches with unerring accuracy, and even track them through their power. I hadn't thought to look for such a skill in Goldwyn, though. I'd been an idiot. A blind idiot.

"She must've used a spelled stone to destroy my trap," Goldwyn babbled. "That's the only thing it could be."

Morgan's red and black wings twitched. "A human, without a coin to her name, just happened to be carrying a stone powerful enough to destroy your trap—that's your conclusion?" The whites of her nostrils showed. "I'm tempted to pull your fangs out for speaking such nonsense."

I cringed as Goldwyn trembled.

"But as it is, you're not even worth the time it would take to torture you." Morgan tossed her dagger at my feet. "Here. I give you permission to kill the female who betrayed you."

"Do it yourself," I shot back.

Her darkening mood leaked out into the air, creating a blistering cold spot. "Don't test me. I can make you do anything—*anything* that I wish. I merely have to want it enough, and I could have you carving your own eyeballs out with a spoon."

I was struck silent. Not from fear. From a silent command.

My unwilling obedience seemed to put her in a better mood. Her facial muscles relaxed into smugness and her mouth sketched a sly line. "Goldwyn's death is your gift, to celebrate our union. End this coward, and do it with a smile."

Even as my soul rebelled at the prospect, my legs bent; my hand secured the knife, and a grotesque smile tightened my cheeks. With a heavy heart and leaden feet, I started toward Goldwyn. She went berserk, screaming and fighting against Tysion's hold.

"Tysion, release her," said Morgan.

He obeyed.

Before Goldwyn could flee, Morgan froze her body in a gray frost. Only Goldwyn's head retained any movement.

I planted myself in front of her.

"Don't do this," she begged me, her eyes popping in fear. "Fight it."

"I'm trying," I said, hard and rough. "I can't."

"Hurry up, Wilder," Morgan said in a tone pitched with mounting bloodlust.

Goldwyn's face slackened, draining of color and hope. She hadn't earned kindness from me. All the same, I said, "Close your eyes."

"Fuck you," she snarled. But when I moved to her side, she lowered her lashes. A single tear fell.

I aimed for the base of her skull, a spot that granted a quick release. The force of slamming the dagger through muscle and bone vibrated through me.

Morgan released her frost-freeze over Goldwyn. Life extinguished, the body collapsed and blood puddled on the floor. It made me sick.

"Tysion, dispose of the body, and then find something useful to do. We're done here," Morgan said flippantly.

Tysion hauled Goldwyn back through the throne room and out the doors.

"Now that's taken care of, it's time we dealt with Serena Smith."

That wrenched my mind from what I'd just done. I spun around, confronting Morgan. "If you hurt her—"

"What?" she snapped. "What are you going to do about it? You can't do anything except pout and glare."

I strangled the sullied blade in a death grip. Morgan was a threat to Serena's life. If it were anyone else standing before me, I would've put them down instantly.

Two forces, two bonds collided again. The instincts of one lay in direct opposition to that of the other. Another stalemate was reached.

"Drop the knife," Morgan said, sounding bored.

I didn't bother to resist that command. We both knew I couldn't kill her. Disgusted with myself, I cast the knife aside. It flew across the room, landing with a *clink*.

"Lynx, reveal yourself," Morgan called out.

Lynx Johana chased his shadows away, materializing closer than I expected, just beside the throne's dais.

My wings clenched, pressing in closer to my spine. He was a giant, an ox of a male, but that wasn't what unnerved me. Fae could identify witches through their use of magic—unless they were weak or knew how to hide their power—because it had a unique taste and scent. Like the air right after it rains. But Lynx's magic was so potent, it made everyone in the vicinity want to run in the opposite direction. I'd felt its likeness only once: when I was young, I'd witnessed the skies above my home thrash and turn a violent green. A sign of an incoming storm.

Morgan moved up two steps of the dais staircase. As if she was wary of being dwarfed by such a male as Lynx.

Dressed in black and red armor, he faced the throne and knelt. Morgan fixed her sights on his lowered head. "I want you to join in on the hunt for Serena and her rebel pack."

Fear struck me like a physical blow, one worse than enduring twenty lashes to the wings.

"Of course, my Queen," Lynx said without inflection. "I shall leave tonight."

"There's something else." She crossed her arms and smoothly drummed her fingers against her bare bicep. Not a nervous action—more restless. "Dimitri told me that Serena had a lover in the training camp. It turns out that this male also fled with her."

Morgan side-eyed me, looking for a reaction to her news. I'd no desire to correct her assumptions about Serena's "lover," so I pasted on a pained look and pretended to be jealous.

"The problem is, nobody could tell me where this male hailed from, not even his family name," Morgan said, her attention drifting back to Lynx. "It wasn't until I searched Tysion's mind that I discovered the male's identity. Imagine my surprise when I recognized him from *your* memories and that it was none other than your old friend Frazer Novak."

She took a deliberate pause.

"What say you, Lynx?" she asked, her blood-colored eyes glittering strangely. "Are you pleased to hear the traitor is alive and well and rutting a human?"

"I have nothing of value to say, my Queen," Lynx said softly.

She frowned lightly at his lack of reaction. "You are being obtuse, and I won't have it. Do you hear me?"

"I do, my Queen." Lynx continued in barren tones. "I simply meant that I haven't spoken to Frazer Novak in eighteen years. We're strangers to each other, and I don't have any opinion on who he spends his time with."

The only thing missing in Morgan's irritated demeanor was the swish of a cat's tail. "I'm glad to hear it because if the girl actually cares for her fae lover, he might be the key to bringing her to heel. If I learn you've been neglecting your duties in hunting him and the others down out of some misplaced sense of loyalty, the consequences will be severe. Do you understand?"

"Yes, my Queen," was all Lynx said to that.

"Good. We'll talk more before you leave."

"Yes—"

"Go away."

Not wasting a second, Lynx turned and strode off. Now it was only Lucinda, Morgan, and me.

"I'm appointing you as Prime Sabu," Morgan declared.

My heart dropped, but I nodded. That was the last thing I'd wanted. But it wasn't unexpected.

Descending the steps, she settled opposite me again. "And when I've caught this pack—and I will." Her long fingernails traced a line down my shirt. The trail she laid ended on my lower stomach where she crooked her index finger into the top of my drawstring pants. I suppressed a shiver, hating her proximity. "I'll take you into my bed and make your whore watch us."

I sneered openly. "I'd sooner cut my own dick off."

With a pitiless yank, Morgan tugged on my leash, silently enforcing her will upon me. I found myself glued to the spot, frozen and helpless.

"You'll do no such thing." She stepped closer, brazenly shoving her hand down my pants and scooping up my private parts. "I've seen your cock, and it's a thing of beauty."

I winced. "Don't remind me."

It was true she had seen me naked; she had ordered me to undress on numerous occasions. To my shame, I had gone along with it. Back then, her blatant threats against the few people I'd cared for had been enough to forgo my pride.

She gave my cock and balls a squeeze. "I never asked you ... Does the human whore love you back?"

I felt compelled to answer. The bond mustn't consider that information a danger to Serena. "She did. I don't know if she still does."

Morgan smiled. It was a bland, empty thing. "Her regard for you will fade. It is the way with humans—their fickle natures are as predictable as wind on the plain."

I wished to speak but couldn't. She had muzzled me.

Morgan rose onto her tiptoes and whispered in my ear, "I always get what I want, Wilder. And you are mine."

That possessiveness set my skin crawling with an itch I couldn't shake. I wished for a hot bath—to scrub myself clean a hundred times or more.

Her hand left my groin. She reached up and pushed her finger past my lips. "Suck."

I almost gagged at the intrusion.

A captive in my own body, I sucked her finger, hard.

"See, little pet?" she crooned, batting her lashes. "See how I've laid claim to you?"

Fury stuck in my gullet.

She removed her finger with a *pop* and tweaked my nose. "Good boy."

An addled laugh burst from Lucinda. "Such fun we'll have when light meets dark, and dark spreads far and wide! Wheeeeheeeee!" She set her wheel spinning around and around.

Fuck me. I'd landed straight back in the madhouse.

Morgan's grin was that of a wicked-hearted lunatic. "Hear that, my Sabu?" She looped her arm through mine. "We're going to have lots of fun, you and I."

I stayed mute as she steered me out of the throne room. Morgan's taunts couldn't erase the truth: Serena was free and bound for Lake Ewa, destined to become a fae. The thought of her growing stronger bolstered me. It inspired me to endure, to think ahead. To be a Sabu. For I might be enslaved to Morgan, but I also held a position of power in her court. I'd use that influence. I'd scheme and plot and deceive. I'd look for every and any opportunity to help Serena. If I could do that, I would honor my bond with her ... I would protect the woman I loved.

CHAPTER 1
SEPARATED

Who is the devil, but my own choice,
A capture and her strings?
Who is the devil, but my own voice,
The one who never sings?
—Chris-Anne—

F*razer? Can you hear me? Brother?*
My desperate calls went unanswered. I hadn't seen or heard from him in hours, and I was becoming undone by our separation.

Cai doubled back. "I know it's hard, but we can't stop."

"Sorry," I mumbled as his hand went under my elbow. "I didn't realize how slow I was going."

Body heavy with exhaustion, I matched his faster stride on aching legs. Liora had waited up ahead, and once we rejoined her, our trio hurried through the tangle of forest connecting Aurora and the Riverlands.

"Are you all right?" Liora murmured as she studied me.

I was definitely, absolutely, not all right. The worst of Morgan's warriors—six of her spiders—had almost captured us. In the mayhem, Cai, Liora, and I had become separated from Frazer and Adrianna in the early hours of the morning.

Now, we traveled along a nonexistent path thick with bracken, sorrel, and ground ivy. The sun loomed overhead, but we were no closer to reuniting with the two fae in our pack. The only thing that kept me from panic was that I could track Frazer through our kin bond, a connection that ensured we would always find each other.

"Serena ..."

Liora's prompt pushed me to give her a halfhearted answer. "I'll be okay once we've reunited with Frazer and Adi."

"Frazer's still headed northwest, right?" Cai's hazel eyes fixed on me. "Toward Lake Ewa?"

"Yes."

"Then they're good," Cai said with all the confidence of an optimist. "If the spiders had them, they'd be going southwest to the Solar Court."

He'd pointed out that fact twice already. My anxiety refused to shift. "I just wish I understood why they keep moving. Frazer knows where I am, but he's not slowing down or moving in our direction."

Cai's eyes showed the effort of his smile. "They might be worried about being followed." He slipped his arm over my shoulder. "He's probably just being overprotective and not wanting to lead any spiders back to us."

I slid my arm around his lower back. "Thanks."

"For what?"

I jostled him in our side-hug hold. "For trying to make me feel better even when you're tired and stressed."

He ruffled my hair. "Don't be stupid. You don't need to thank me."

"Yes, we do," Liora said quietly on my left. "You've kept us going."

I snuck a peek at Liora. Fatigue shadowed her lower lids; her fevered complexion made her freckles look garish, almost pox-like. She had gone from looking bad to awful these last few days. The knowledge of why wasn't a comfort.

In an effort to prevent Morgan from recruiting her, Liora had left her home and bound her powers. But her magic was too strong, too wild to be contained. It lashed out against the binding—the cage surrounding it—and weakened her, bit by bit. Our pack hoped Hazel, the witch who had promised to transform me from human to fae, would have answers. That she could free Liora from the binding. From the noose around her neck.

"You're giving me too much credit," Cai said, interrupting my thoughts. "I'm likely the reason we were ambushed in the first place."

Wait. "Why would you think that?"

He tossed me a look that seemed to say *Isn't it obvious?* "I must've messed up with the concealment charm. Maybe I didn't charge it right or something."

"If it's anyone's fault, it's probably mine," I said, shame heating my face. "If Morgan's broken into Wilder's mind, she'll know where we're going. The spiders might've found us because she ordered them to watch the border."

My choice to confide in Wilder had kept me up most nights, as had my decision to tell Hunter about my parental figures, John and Viola. He even knew where they lived in the human realm—in the Gauntlet. I would never forgive myself if Morgan hurt them because of me. Because of my poor decisions.

"Our location could've been discovered in lots of different ways, many of which have nothing to do with us and everything to do with bad luck," Liora said, her lilting voice easing my guilt, somehow convincing me.

"I just wish my magic hadn't abandoned me." I went on, frustrated. "If I could still use it, I might've stopped the spiders before they separated us."

"You also might've hurt yourself in the process," Liora countered tensely. "You almost died using it to break Goldwyn's trap. That's not something I want to see repeated."

Cai cringed, not disagreeing.

For Cai and Liora's sake, I refused to give breath to my thoughts. But inside I was in knots. Even without using my light magic, I was fading like the waning moon. Frazer sharing his strength—his life-force—kept me vertical, but our month-long trek up the Riverlands had tested us both. We relived the same pattern day in, day out, until every day was a poor copy of the last; we slept rough, ate poorly, avoided hungry devos sprites, and lived in constant fear of capture. That stressful, limb-aching sameness had exacerbated my decline, turning my future into a blank space. A formless shape.

I pawed under my long-sleeved shirt, seeking an old comfort. The small stone in the middle of my necklace felt warm to my touch, but no voice filled my mind. I missed Auntie—the mysterious entity who had guided me from inside the pale blue gem. After she erased the barrier that had kept me from my magic, she had fallen silent, leaving me with questions and the dying embers of my strength.

Instinct said I'd brooded long enough. In the end, I had no choice but to ignore my failing body. To deny death. If I didn't, I'd pull Frazer into the afterlife with me. I would not, could not accept that.

An hour or so dragged by, unmarked and uneventful. The mindless monotony was shattered by a suspicious birdsong. A melody that went back and forth, like a call and an answer.

Cai, Liora, and I ground to a halt. We traded fleeting looks lined with caution. Acting as one mind, we peered up at the trees' summer crown.

The canopy trembled in several spots causing my adrenaline to surge. Then came the creak of branches and the telltale hum of fae in flight. Cai called out in a battle cry, "On me!"

He sprinted forward. A pack mentality, sharpened by weeks on the run, clicked into place. Liora and I rushed after him, two arrows to his bow.

In the flutter of a stunned eye, two unfamiliar males dropped from the sky. They landed directly ahead, blocking us with outstretched wings.

Magic stirred in the air. I recognized it by the thrill that blasted down my spine. With an outthrust palm, Cai turned a sighing wind into a roaring weapon. His signature air magic slammed into the males. The fae's bodies spun up and away, like milkweed seed in a hurricane.

We ran past them. I didn't look at their faces. I didn't listen to their calls to stop.

Somewhere under my third rib, I felt a tug. Frazer was hooking and reeling me in as one would a fish. Likely, he had sensed my alarm.

"This way," I called out to my friends.

I took the lead northwest, rushing like a river to its source. Liora and Cai stuck close, no questions asked. We raced over mosses and mushrooms; we sped past ferns and brambles.

Over my hummingbird heart, I heard more fae gaining on us. They circled above like vultures eyeing their next good meal.

Aiming wildly, Cai air-blasted the canopy again and again. A valiant effort, but the targets weren't clear. The fae were veiled by leaf and twig, resigned to loom, as threatening as thunderclouds.

A whistle cut through anxiety-thickened air. Courts, what now?

On our left, an arrow slammed into the trunk of a tree. The next arrow landed closer, striking the forest floor.

"They're trying to herd us," Cai puffed out.

Arrows rained down.

I pumped my arms and long legs faster. Sweat slicked my skin, my muscles suffered, and the weight of my rucksack and sword aggravated me. I was near collapse.

A second whistle, shorter than the first, blew out. Fae landed in more numbers this time.

Cai, Liora, and I skidded to a stop. We drew our weapons: a longsword, a rapier, and an Utemä. I mourned the absence of my kaskan bow, a weapon that when used by me would always hit its target. But Frazer had carried it for weeks, sparing me the extra burden on my back.

Through sheer will, I battled the tremors in my weak flesh and lined my sword up to the first fae in my sights. Even as I did that, I knew it was pointless. Too many fae encircled us, bows drawn. Cai could blast a path through their twelve-strong formation, but we wouldn't get far before their arrows found us.

Trapped, I looked these fae over for clues as to their origins. They wore inky-blue tunics and shirts of fish-scaled armor. Such bright, brilliant outfits were far removed from the naked aggression of the spiders' uniforms.

"Who are you? What do you want?" Cai challenged.

"I'll answer your questions after you lay down your weapons," said the male in front of Cai.

"I don't think we will, but thanks for the offer," Cai said, the veins in his hand standing out as he gripped his sword tighter.

The same soldier, presumably their mouthpiece, spoke again. But his words went out of my head as soon as my brother's call ricocheted around my skull. *Siska! Are you there?*

Yes! I'm here. I can hear you.

What's going on?

Fae chased us down. We're surrounded.

Show me.

Our minds fused as iron filings would to magnets. I sent him a visual of our predicament through our mind-to-mind connection.

Frazer cursed. *Those are Riverlands soldiers. Don't let them take you anywhere. We'll be there soon.*

I hesitated. I wanted him here, but I hated the idea of him in proximity to pointy-looking arrows and violent-looking fae. The latter instinct won. *You should hang back. We don't know what they want with us.*

Nice try, siska. We're already on our way.

Rutting hell.

I focused back on the conversation between Cai and the group's mouthpiece.

"Look, we have no desire to hurt you," said the lead soldier. He had a punctuated monotone. A pauper selling diamonds would've sounded more sincere. "But if you don't disarm, we'll have to force you."

"I wouldn't if I were you," Cai threatened. "Not unless you want me to send your arrows into your friends' throats."

Cai charmed the wind with his available hand. His power became visible when dirt and fallen leaves rose, turning the air brown and green. I saw it for what it was: a bluff. A piece of theater.

"Stop this or we'll attack," said the mouthpiece.

Another whistle sounded, but this one was low-pitched, almost pacifying.

Beyond the circle of fae, another person glided down from the treetops. Cai's wind promptly died at the sight of her.

Diana Lakeshie marched into a gap in the fae-ring and stopped there. She was tall and slender with smoky-blue eyes. Her wardrobe was neat and reflected the power of a queen. She wore tailored trousers, a black velvet jacket adorned with gilded chains and buttons, and a stunning dagger at her waist belt.

As I looked her over, the image of a foxglove sprang to mind. For such a flower also demanded attention and respect; it was arrogant in its bearing, beautiful in its bloom, and lethal in its roots. Diana seemed to be all those things and more.

"Do you know who I am?" she asked, her rich accent reminding me of her daughter's.

Liora, Cai, and I had seen her once before, at Kasi.

Spine knife-straight, Cai replied, "You're Diana Lakeshie, Queen of the Riverlands. To what do we owe the, *errr,* pleasure of your visit?"

"I would have thought that were obvious," she said, blunt and formal. "I'm here for Adrianna. I know she's traveling with you. Where is she? I wish to speak with her."

My palm twitched; my sword quivered.

"Why would we tell you anything?" Cai deflected. "Your people are holding us hostage."

Her head of netted ebony hair canted to the side. "These warriors are my personal guard. Their duty is to neutralize any threat toward me. I'm sure you can understand why I won't usually speak to anybody armed." A tense pause was followed by, "How about a show of good faith?" She turned to her guards. "Lower your bows."

Every fae complied in one synchronized movement.

Diana nodded at our trio. "Your turn."

Cai, Liora, and I sheathed our swords.

"Now that that's sorted, will you tell me where my daughter is?" Diana asked.

"Up to you." Cai nudged the back of my hand with his knuckles.

I eyed him, a frown forming in the center of my brows.

"You're the only one who knows what Adrianna would want." A tiny wink.

A line of understanding passed between us, and it clicked.

I tuned in to my brother. *We've got a problem. Diana's here. She wants to know where Adi is. What should I say? Can you ask Adrianna?*

A handful of toe-tapping seconds passed.

Tell her Adrianna will be there soon.

Nerves hopped around my belly. *Are you sure about this? For all we know, Diana might be planning to sell us out, including her own daughter.*

If she tries anything, I'll rip out her sparrow's heart. Direct, dark, dry. Typical Frazer.

I hastened to stem his murderous musings. *If you attack her, we'll have the whole of the Riverlands baying for our blood, and we've got too many enemies as it is.*

She betrayed your kin. She deserves it.

That explained the rage and resentment sparking in him. Frazer despised disloyalty, and Diana Lakeshie had chosen to remain neutral after Morgan rose to power instead of supporting and securing her friend's position on the Solar Court throne. That friend also happened to be Sefra, my long-lost half sister. It begged the question, if Diana could betray her friend, could she betray her daughter?

I regarded the female in question, weighing her. She'd made no call for us to speak, as if her patient stare was enough of a demand. In the end, it was faith in my brother's judgment that made me tell Diana, "Adrianna will be here soon."

If she questioned how I knew that, she didn't say. Diana clasped her hands over her lower belly, and said, "Then we wait."

I groaned silently. It would be a miracle if this ended well.

CHAPTER 2
A PACK OF OUTLAWS

The fae in our pocket of space soon detected their princess's approach; their gazes locked in one direction. As a human, I had learned to trust in their superior hearing. I set my focus where the fae did and waited.

A minute lapsed, maybe more.

My first glimpse came from up ahead. Relief rushed through me like meltwater at the sight of Adrianna flying, weaving skillfully between the trees. Frazer had allowed her to carry him. That alone shouted of his concern for us.

Adrianna landed and set Frazer down. They were too far away for me to overhear their conversation. I could only see their mouths moving. After a brief exchange, they started toward us, their pace measured but assured.

I focused on my brother. *What happened after we got separated? Why didn't you come find us?*

I'll show you.

An invisible hand brushed the edges of my mind. Realizing his intent, I reached out with a tendril of thought. He lifted his mental-shield like a curtain near an open window and linked our minds as surely as if we had grasped hands.

Memories were shaken loose by our contact. Everything we had seen, done, and felt this morning flowed between us.

My recollections traveled along the bond in chaotic rhythms. Sometimes quick, sometimes slow. There wasn't much structure to them, but the colors were vivid, the sounds sharp, and the emotions intense.

Meanwhile, Frazer's stories came in thick and fast, without embellishment. Everything was neatly presented in chronological order.

I saw again the six fae who had tried to ambush our pack. I witnessed Cai's power giving us an escape route, and how in the chaos we'd gotten separated.

Through my brother's eyes, I learned that three of the fae had targeted him and Adrianna. They had fought, and the spiders had fled after suffering a defeat, vanishing into the thick of the forest.

Frazer and Adrianna had decided to stay away from the rest of us until they could confirm they weren't being followed. I sensed my brother had also hoped that by laying another set of tracks, any pursuers might be tempted to go after him instead of me.

The stream of memory stopped. We untangled ourselves from each other's minds. Frazer's mental-shield dropped down in a final act of separation.

I was left with my own thoughts and concerns. The most pressing was whether we had actually evaded the spiders from this morning or if they were working with Diana—had she found out our general location from them?

Adrianna and Frazer reached our hostile party. They stalked past the soldiers, not sparing the queen in their midst a look.

I drank them both in, scanning for signs of their fight with the spiders. I found none. The only damage done to my brother was because of me. Frazer, twin to my moon-pale skin and raven-wing hair, looked almost as bad as I did.

His midnight-blue irises, encircled by a clever flash of silver, had dulled this last month; the hard angles of his face had sharpened, shifting from intimidating to downright frightening. His features had always married light and shadow, but the strain of our twining had made him more night than day.

Guilt became my master. He suffered, and it was my fault.

He threw back, *It was my choice. Stop blaming yourself.*

It wasn't unexpected that he'd reacted to thoughts I hadn't shared. I was working on my mental discipline, but I inevitably did a lot of what my brother called loud and noisy thinking in his direction, especially when emotional. A problem for another day, if we lived that long.

Liora stepped away from me, making space for Frazer. He took his place at my side, on my left. A sense of calm washed over me.

He was here. He was safe. We were together.

Frazer didn't look at me. He studied the soldiers surrounding us as if they were the teeth of a bear trap.

I glanced at Adrianna, who had placed herself between Cai and me. Her gaze swept over the soldiers as if searching for people she recognized. When she was done eyeing them, she bowed to her grim-faced mother.

An emotionless mask glued to her face, Diana addressed the male to her left. "I wish to be alone with my daughter and her friends. Go, secure the area. Ensure we aren't overheard. Then deal with the bodies."

The same male asked, "What do you want us to do with them?"

Bodies? What in the courts was that about?

"Weigh them down and drop them in the Eastern Seas."

"Understood." He faced the eleven other warriors and barked out a command. "You heard your Queen. Wings out."

In perfect formation, a dozen fae took flight. Their wings conjured a breeze that fanned my sweaty brow. My eyelids drooped in momentary bliss. When I opened them again, I saw mother and daughter staring each other down.

Adrianna broke the impasse. "Why are you here?"

Diana's smoky-blue eyes held reproach. "To protect my fool of a daughter. Morgan has charged your pack with desertion, the murder of Dimitri Kato, and the mutilation of his heir, Tysion."

Shame whispered in the dark. *That's right. You killed Dimitri. You're a murderer.* I pushed away memories of sightless eyes and the life I'd taken.

"I never asked for your help," Adrianna said, sounding colder than iron in winter.

"No, but you need it." Diana's full mouth thinned. "Morgan threatened our court with war if I didn't pay a huge fine, name you as an outlaw, and assist in your capture. I agreed to help in the hunt because it gave me an excuse to send my soldiers to the same areas as those tracking your pack. I had a soldier monitoring the spiders who spotted you this morning. His report made it possible for me to find and eliminate them before they could reveal your location."

A stunned silence settled in as everyone absorbed that.

"The bodies you spoke of were the spiders?" Liora guessed.

Diana's answering nod had a lock of black hair escaping her velvet hairnet. "And there'll be more where they came from. Morgan is obsessed. I dread to think what she has planned for each of you."

A nasty jolt hit my midriff at the thought. Our pack had stood on shifting sands for weeks, but with talk of war and bodies, I felt the tide rolling in, threatening to drown us.

"You didn't chase us down to say you'd killed the people following us. What is it that you want from me?" Adrianna's voice was as sharp as it was suspicious.

"I want to help you," Diana said.

I couldn't detect a whiff of insincerity in her answer. Adrianna, however, snorted in disbelief. "You've spent years appeasing Morgan in order to avoid war. But now you're willing to risk everything? Do you really expect me to believe that?"

"Everything I've done is to protect our court." Diana's stare was direct, unapologetic. "But I won't stand by and watch my only child become a political prisoner, especially not to someone like Morgan. She would make your life unbearable."

Those words made my chest feel stuffy, panicky.

Diana's gaze moved over our group. "Tell me what your plan is. Then we can figure out if there's anything I can do to aid you in it."

Adrianna rested her hand atop her sword's pommel. "Who says we have a plan?"

That earned an irritated look from her mother. "I do. Your choices have hurt the Riverlands, and whatever your feelings are about me, you've always taken your duty to our people seriously. You would not want them to suffer needlessly, I think."

Adrianna's face contorted in a bee sting flinch. "Our people have been in danger since Morgan conquered the other courts. My *duty* has always been to do something about that, not cozy up to a tyrant and betray my allies."

"How many times must we go through this?" Even as frustration pinched Diana's features, her tone remained cool and polished. "These notions of nobility belong to the warriors and the poets, not the ruling classes. We don't get to be heroes or slaves to our emotions. We're leaders—we must be brave enough to make the hard choices and act in the interests of our country."

An animal wounded, Adrianna spat out around emerging fangs, "You lecture me on putting politics before everything else, and yet you still want me to trust you with our plan?" She didn't wait for a reply. "You betrayed Sefra Lytir, a friend and ally, in order to placate Morgan. What's to stop you from doing the same to me?"

The reminder that my half sister had been abandoned by the female in front of me proved as unwelcome as pins in the skin. Frazer's suspicions of Diana were also uppermost in his mind. They gathered there like a murder of crows perched in a withered tree, their sharp eyes leveled at Diana in quiet judgment.

"If you won't trust me as is, it seems I'm left with no choice." Diana lifted her chin and linked her hands behind her back beneath her scaled wings. An elegant pose strengthened with resolve. "I can't let you go knowing my resources might keep you safe and that you might accept them if I tell you the truth." She spoke as if to convince herself of something.

Adrianna folded her arms across her chest, fortifying herself. "What truth?"

"I never betrayed Sefra Lytir. To this day, I remain her friend and ally."

Everything stopped; everything realigned. The experience felt jarring; my mind groaned under the effort of shifting perspective so quickly.

Frazer recovered first. "Explain."

Diana's smoky-blues unfocused as if she'd retreated inward, into the past. "Eighteen years ago, Sefra and I met to discuss the future of our courts. Morgan had just conquered the Crescent, and our spies reported that she intended to strike the Solar Court next." A long sigh slid out of her nose. "The King of Aurora refused to take sides. That left Sefra and me to fight the largest witch army in Aldar."

Frazer crashed into her explanation with an accusation. "If you'd sided with Dain Raynar back when Morgan was fighting for control of the Crescent, you might've stopped her from becoming so powerful."

My heart grew sore at the mention of Dain, my birth father.

"The witches won't stand for others interfering in their politics," Diana told Frazer. "Dain knew that, which is why he refused our help when we offered it. If Sefra and I had joined forces with him, he would've lost the support of his loyalists."

But what if they had helped him? Would they have defeated Morgan? Would I have been raised by Dain instead of Halvard?

I didn't give air to such sad thoughts, but they sat like a bag of rocks in the bottom of my belly all the same.

"What happened during your meeting with Sefra?" Liora asked, getting the conversation back on track.

"She told me that she wasn't going to fight Morgan," Diana said while staring at Adrianna. "Sefra didn't want to subject her people to war when the chances of her winning were so slim. So I offered to help her go into hiding. By her leaving, the outlying regions of the Solar Court surrendered almost immediately. The capital was taken a few months after that."

Diana's wings and shoulders dropped a bit. The only sign of grief she allowed to show. "From there, I did what I could to keep my throne. I've protected the people I needed to, but I never lost touch with Sefra. Both of us want Morgan's stranglehold over Aldar to end. That's our goal."

Frazer confronted Diana. Interrogated, really. "How have you kept your defiance hidden from Morgan? She must've tried breaking into your mind."

"Of course," she said, her mouth a grim line. "But she only saw and heard what I wanted her to."

"That's possible?" I questioned.

"Yes." Pride pushed her shoulders back. "I've trained extensively in mental defense. I tutored Adrianna; she can attest to my skill. I'm also warded against magical interference, which protects me from witches who can divine when somebody is lying."

I side-eyed Adrianna. Her face was drawn, concentrated. She had the look of someone walking a tightrope over a snake pit. I didn't blame her. This confession was bending my mind around some steep corners. It had to be a hundred times worse for her.

"What do you think?" Cai asked Adrianna. "Is she telling the truth?"

Diana became a tower of ice. Adrianna, a pillar of stone.

A painful minute dragged by.

Adrianna finally unglued her clenched jaw to punch out a hard, "Yes."

Hope sprouted wings in my chest. It seemed that Diana might be the key to our plan to find Sefra. That goal had developed a month ago, when my mother's spirit had said I needed my half sister and my yet-to-appear mate to save these lands. My pack had decided that she meant we must stop Morgan—what else did Aldar need to be saved from? But in the end, my mother had only instructed me to seek Sefra across the sea, in the east, where the sun shines brightest. The eastern continent was vast—we could search forever and never find her.

With that worry in my heart, I addressed Diana. "Can you tell us where Sefra is?"

"I could." Diana angled her head in the small and graceful way of someone accustomed to a crown. "Why do you want to know?"

Tension ran through my pack. I felt it in the shifting of Cai's feet, in the fussing of Adrianna's wings, and in the tensing of Frazer's muscles.

"Because we need to speak with her," I answered.

"Why?" Diana asked, her gaze roaming, taking the measure of each of us.

"Tell me where Sefra is first," I said. "Then I'll explain."

Siska. A warning resonated in Frazer's mental voice.

I met his waiting eyes. *I know you don't want me revealing anything to her, but it's worth the risk. Besides, we already know Sefra's on the continent. If Diana can confirm that, we'll know she's been telling the truth.*

Fine, but keep it simple. Don't say anything you don't need to.

My silent agreement shone through the bond.

"Do you really have to know her location?" Diana asked Adrianna.

"Yes." A cold, definite answer.

Diana frowned. I wasn't sure if she doubted her daughter's word or if she was simply thinking it over.

My impatience caused my toes to itch in my boots.

"Sefra is on the continent, somewhere in Asitar. That's all I know."

I guess she's not totally full of crap, Frazer conceded.

Indeed.

"It's your turn," Diana said, her queenly gaze centered on me. "Why did you want this information?"

"Sefra's my half sister. I need to meet with her so that I can get her help with something." I left it at that.

Diana's lips parted a bit. Had she been slightly less practiced at hiding her emotions, she might've gawked at me openly.

"That's not possible."

"I'm not lying." I added, "Sati and Dain were my parents."

"You're a human—how can they be your parents?"

Frazer shut that down. "You don't need to know that."

"Agreed," Adrianna said.

Refusing to back down, Diana asked me, "How old are you?"

"Eighteen."

Something clicked into place behind her stare. "Then Sati must've had you after she disappeared ... I had assumed she'd died when Dain had—that's often the case with mates. Did she pass giving birth to you?"

A direct ask, one that tore at a fraying wound. "No, she didn't. And don't ask me how she died."

Diana's eyes narrowed on me. Evaluating and calculating. "You do look a lot like Dain. You've got his scowl for one."

If I'd had fangs, I would have bitten her.

Want me to do it for you? Frazer asked, perfectly serious.

Maybe later.

"I suppose if your parents were both powerful witches, it would go a long way to explaining how a human could wield light magic," Diana said, surprising the rest of us with what she knew about me.

Alarmed, I leaned away from her. "Why would you think I'm a light-wielder?"

Diana's face cleared. "Maggie OneEye wrote to me after your pack left her cabin."

Maggie, a witch and a seer, was the first person to recognize my capacity for light magic. I hadn't expected her to keep my secrets, but still ... how many people had she told about me?

"That gossiping swamp-hag," Cai exclaimed.

Frazer's thoughts accelerated. I witnessed several plans take shape in his head, all of which revolved around the untimely demise of Maggie

OneEye. He was particularly partial to the idea of stuffing the witch up her own chimney. I didn't try to dissuade him.

"Don't think too harshly of her," Diana advised me. "Maggie wanted my help to protect your secret. But I'm afraid I've failed you in that regard. My informants tell me that Morgan has discovered you're a light-wielder."

I'd expected that, but it didn't make the knowledge any less burdensome.

"Fucking Goldwyn," Cai spat.

"It was her, then?" Diana directed that question at me. "She discovered your secret?"

I nodded as heart-hurting images staged an invasion.

Wilder being taken away.

Tysion's wing being severed.

My arrow in Dimitri's chest.

Goldwyn slicing into Liora's skin.

Spitting out blood as light magic tore out of me.

I wanted to erase those images. To forget the past. To forsake memories that acted like demons lurking in the depths of my mind. Such restless monsters were ever-keen to pop up and haunt me. Unlike the good memories. Those were buried gems, gems that I had to go looking for.

"Did you know Goldwyn was spying for Morgan?" Adrianna asked Diana.

"No." Diana's expression darkened. "I only learned about her true loyalties when she fled my lands and showed up at the Solar Court."

Cai let out a derisive snort. "I bet Goldwyn couldn't wait to squeal. She probably dropped to her knees and licked Morgan's—"

"Stop right there," Adrianna snapped, holding up a palm. "I don't want whatever image you're about to put in my head."

Cai lifted his shoulders innocently. "I can't think what you mean."

Adrianna rolled her eyes.

"Whatever Goldwyn said or did, it wasn't enough to save her life," Diana said in a blunt, unfeeling tone. "Morgan had her executed. I'm assuming it was because she failed to capture your pack."

Cai crossed his arms. "Well, I won't mourn the treacherous snake."

"Neither will I," Liora said, her features wooden.

Agreed, I thought savagely. Not only had Goldwyn sold us out, but she had held a knife on Liora and used that to blackmail the rest of us into surrender. Liora's cuts from the incident had faded. The memory of Goldwyn's betrayal hadn't. For any of us.

"You should know her execution was carried out in Alexandria about a fortnight ago." Diana's mouth pursed slightly before she continued. "Your old mentor Wilder Thorn killed her on Morgan's orders."

My body flashed hot and cold within the space of a breath. *Whatwhyhow?*

Adrianna got straight to the point. "Why would he do what she asked? Wilder hates Morgan."

"Because she's discovered how to bind a guardian without their consent." Diana slipped her hands into the pockets of her velvet jacket. "Wilder had no choice but to follow her orders."

Cai and Adrianna cursed. Liora gasped quietly. Speech abandoned me completely.

For four long weeks, I'd clung to the hope that Wilder might've escaped before reaching the Solar Court.

There was nothing left for me now. No relief to be found. My guardian was enslaved to that monster. Forever.

Heartbeat quick, my legs wanted to give way.

Frazer's arm wrapped around my waist. He wasn't comfortable with touch, so I appreciated the gesture all the more.

Steady, siska. Breathe with me.

My chest rose alongside his. In. Out. In. Out.

All hot steel and cold fire, Adrianna demanded, "How is that possible?"

"I don't know," Diana began, "but Morgan was always ready to learn and do things that no sane individual would." Blue eyes flitted from me to Liora to Cai. "I'm not sure how much the three of you know about the guardian bond—"

"A guardian can sometimes sense when their charge is in danger." I went on in a daze, repeating what Wilder and Frazer had taught me. "The charge can also give their guardian an order and the bond will push them to obey."

The thought of Morgan doing that to Wilder sickened me.

Diana nodded. "That's all true. But the reason I raised the subject was because the rumors coming out of her court suggest there are limits to what she can compel him to do. There also aren't any signs that she's broken into his mind yet. Take that for what you will. I believe it's a sign that her grip over him isn't absolute. Not yet, anyway."

Frazer gave me a mental nudge. *If he can resist certain compulsions, your bond might be the reason.*

What do you mean?

Wilder swore to protect you when he became your guardian. So what would happen if Morgan ordered him to kill you? I think the two compulsions might cancel each other out. The same principle would apply if she wanted him to reveal information that could be used against you.

I brooded on that. *He's still protecting me then ... Even after I failed him.*

You did not fail him, Frazer argued.

I didn't go after him. If I had—

Hunter flew away with him. We couldn't have tracked them through the air. And we would've all died if we'd tried to sneak into Alexandria. Let it be, siska.

Guilt still stalked me. It paid no attention to my brother's logic.

"What if Morgan tries to force you into a blood oath?" Adrianna said to Diana. "How are you going to stop her?" More of a demand than an ask.

"I'll do whatever is necessary."

"Meaning?"

Diana removed her hands from her pockets and palmed her dagger's hilt. "When the river shifts—"

"We must bend with it," Adrianna ended.

"That's right." That controlled facade slipped, and her features blazed with a cold ferocity. "So if she makes moves to take the Riverlands, I'll fight. I'll declare war. But if I am taken, you cannot allow Morgan to use me as bait to lure you out. If she has me, I am already dead and you must claim the throne. Agreed?"

Adrianna replied with a tiny nod. A reluctant yes or a lie, I couldn't tell. By the look on Diana's face, she wasn't sure either.

An uneasy quiet fell. That ended when Diana said, "It occurs to me that I haven't done much to help you, aside from passing on information. But if your goal is to speak with Sefra, then there might be something else I can do for you." Her focus shifted to me. "Are you still determined to meet with Sefra knowing she's on the continent? If not, I can work on getting a message to her. I don't know how long it'll take, but the option is there—it's that or sail east, which brings its own problems."

That offer hung in the air. My mind wrestled with it. Our pack had already decided to head east after Lake Ewa. But I hadn't planned on being able to message Sefra. If I asked her to return to Aldar—would she come?

I faced my pack. "This decision effects all of us. I can't make it alone."

"How will you contact Sefra if you don't know exactly where she is?" Frazer asked Diana.

"We have a mutual friend who we communicate through. If anyone would know where to look for her, it would be him."

Adrianna's eyes tapered into triangles. "Who is he?"

Diana parried that sharpness with a smoothness. "His name is Zeke. He's helped Sefra and I more times than I can count. I trust him implicitly."

A beat later, Adrianna turned to me. "Trustworthy or not, I don't like the idea of waiting around for someone else to find her. And while the continent has its issues, we won't be outlaws there. I say we go east."

"Both options have their downsides," Liora said, wearing a light frown. "But my instincts say we should get out of Aldar. At least for a while."

"If Li can sail, I'm in," Cai added.

Anxiety gripped me. Liora's voyage depended on whether Hazel could free her magic. If that failed, the siblings had planned to sneak back to the Crescent and search for a witch who could undo Liora's binding.

I looked at Frazer. He shrugged. *What's the alternative? We hide under a rock until Sefra arrives? That could take months.*

That settled it for me.

I glanced at Diana. "We'll go east."

Her serious gaze passed over each of us again. "Then you'll need a ship that can get you past Morgan's coastal blockade."

Our pack had known this and discussed it.

Frazer interjected. "We've heard of smugglers taking people to the continent for a fee. We'll make inquiries at some of the port towns and go from there."

"There's no need for that," Diana declared. "An associate of mine has command of a ship called *The Eye of the Wind*. He's a great smuggler and more importantly, he can be trusted to honor agreements. He typically sails out of Nasiri Port and docks at Casatana, Asitar's capital. Is that an acceptable option?"

Our pack of five exchanged similar looks.

Cai assumed responsibility. "That'll work for us."

"I'll arrange with Captain Armstrong to meet you in Nasiri," Diana said brusquely. "When you see him, repeat the phrase *aurinka perista itän*. He'll use that to confirm I sent you. Repeat the words back to me. All of you."

We did.

Diana nodded, approving of our efforts. "You'll also need a guide in Asitar, and there's no one better for that than Zeke. I'll send word so he knows to watch for your arrival at the docks. If he doesn't show, head into Casatana's Sashkan Market and ask for him at a place called The Oasis Lounge. It's popular with the locals, so you can get directions. You'll know Zeke by the bird inked on his shoulder, and you'll need to repeat the same phrase to him. What was it again?"

Frazer growled, hating to be patronized. I wasn't keen on it either, but I repeated the phrase along with Cai and Liora.

"How much will these associates of yours want for helping us?" Adrianna asked.

Problem. Our pack hadn't much money.

Diana reached inside her jacket and pulled out a leather pouch. I heard the distinctive chink of coin as she held it out to her daughter. "Poor outlaws don't last long." Diana's mouth twitched. A joke, or a reprimand? Before I could confirm an actual sense of humor, she went on. "There's florén and gold in there, enough to pay for Captain Armstrong's fee and to support you while you're in Asitar. Zeke won't ask you for money."

What's florén?

It's our paper money, Frazer answered.

Adrianna hesitated.

Impatience biting, Diana clucked her tongue. "Are you so used to arguing with me that it's just a reflex now? Take the money, Adrianna."

She tossed the bag to her daughter. Adrianna caught it deftly and weighed it in her hand.

"There's also a concealment charm in there." Eyeing the coin-purse Adrianna was currently tucking into her rucksack, Diana continued. "That will stop you from being tracked magically."

Cai cut in. "We already have one, and the spiders still found us."

"The spiders are patrolling the borderlands. They might've just gotten lucky finding you when and how they did," Diana said. "As for the charm, keep both. Mine doesn't require charging with magic, so you won't have to expend your energies on that at least."

"Then what powers your charm?" Cai asked.

"You'll have to ask Sefra when you meet her. She was the one who sent it to me."

The thought that my sister was in some way protecting us was a strange comfort to me.

"It's time we went our separate ways." Diana slowly fanned her blue wings, not enough to take flight, just enough to get the blood flowing. "More spiders will head to this area once the others fail to report back, and we've already tarried too long in one spot. Stay vigilant, even when you reach the continent. Morgan has people there, too, and she'll almost certainly send your descriptions to them. Too many outlaws have attempted the crossing for her to not consider the possibility that your pack might do the same."

There was a moment, a breath, where she looked at Adrianna and seemed to be searching for what to say.

"May the rivers guide you to safety." That was how she said goodbye to her daughter. A stiff, impersonal farewell.

Adrianna's features were emotionless, closed-off.

"And may the moon's light guide your feet, Queentina." Liora was politeness personified as she bobbed in a small curtsy.

A bland smile lifted Diana's cheeks. "Thank you."

That word, though. *Queentina?*

Frazer answered my question even though I hadn't asked him for an explanation. *It means "acting queen." You use it when addressing rulers of foreign courts.*

"Thanks for your help, Queentina." Not wanting to be ignorant, I attempted my own curtsy.

Amusement trickled in through my kin bond. I side-glared at Frazer.

He ignored me, assuming a noble air.

Diana pulled my focus. "Blessings to you, Serena Raynar-Lytir."

A quiver of uncertainty stirred my insides. I hadn't acknowledged or accepted that shift from Smith to Raynar-Lytir. Soon, perhaps.

"The rest of you, go ahead. I'd like a moment alone with my makena," Adrianna announced, her eyes never leaving Diana.

Cai didn't hesitate. "Sure."

He sketched a bow to Diana then left at a quick march.

Liora trailed after her brother.

I walked behind them with Frazer. He stuck close, as if he feared one good gust of wind would knock me over.

So ... that was a lot. I found Frazer's veiled gaze.

He huffed flatly before falling silent.

A minute or two later, Adrianna landed nearby, face riven in anger.

Our pack huddled so we could walk and talk. "Did you say what you needed to?" Cai asked lightly. Nonthreatening.

"Yes," Adrianna said, voice tight. "Not that it did any good."

Empty silence.

"I know what you're thinking, but you're not abandoning your people," Liora said, staring at Adrianna. "If you went back to your court as an outlaw, you'd put your makena in an impossible situation. You might even trigger a war."

Adrianna flashed Liora a leave-it-alone look.

Liora caught my eye, seeming to say *Well, I tried*.

I traded her a closed-lipped smile.

The five of us settled back into a well-established routine. We put one foot in front of the other and warded off boredom with idle chatter, Cai being the main creator of conversation.

Mind in a muddle, I exchanged the odd thought with Frazer over Diana's revelations. But as the day wore thin, my adrenaline long since dead and bone-melting exhaustion returning, there was no energy left to think about anything except walking.

At some point, my hand floated up to where my necklace sat on my chest and it stayed there. My mother had gotten it from the undines—

water sprites and residents of Lake Ewa—and the heirloom was now as much a part of me as the heart beating beneath my breastbone. But its solid presence couldn't do anything to still my inner death-clock. *Tick-tick-tick* it went, making me think I'd finally entered delirium. *TICK-TICK-TICK* it went again, each chime a second lost and a second closer to silence.

CHAPTER 3
THE DEAD AND THE DYING

Yesterday, we fled from spiders. Today, we awoke to a suffocating heat, one that closed in and made the world oppressive. To move was akin to passing through treacle, the air mist-kissed and sticky with birch sap. But all of us were like-minded, bound and determined to reach the lake as quick as could be.

With that in mind, we shouldered summer's humid shroud, striking out through the thinning forest, marching uphill to the beats of buzzing insects. The mountain range that barred our crossing into Aurora towered up, nearer and nearer.

After hours of hiking, we left the forest and arrived at the mountains' roots. My first unobstructed view of the giants' faces revealed that snow glorified their heads, skinny streams marked their pitted bodies, and clouds of vapor gathered at their feet.

"Let's take a break," Cai called out.

Exhaustion was a chain snapping around my wrists and ankles, dragging me down to dry earth. On my knees, I slipped off my backpack and rolled onto my back. Liora copied me.

I rested my glass bones where grass, crocus, and ample buttercup grew. In this fatigued state, I watched the three of us still standing.

"This pass of yours is nowhere to be seen," Adrianna said, shielding her upturned gaze from the afternoon sun as she surveyed the mountains ahead.

"It can't be far." Frazer's eyes swept the area. "I recognize the curves and lines of the land."

"Maybe your path was destroyed by an avalanche," Cai suggested.

"It's possible, but I only used it this past winter." Frazer gripped the limb of the bow he carried for me. "We should keep looking."

"You and Serena get weaker by the day, and spiders are hunting us like hounds after the fox," Adrianna said, as straightforward as ever. "We don't have the luxury of searching for a path that might or might not be there." She squared off against the lofty peaks. "I'll have to fly us over, one by one."

Frazer confronted her. "If you do that, any spider with a clear eye to the border could see you. You also haven't flown at high altitude for a while. Even the wind's against you." He gestured to where mist, propelled by strong currents, billowed down the giants' sheer sides and landed in the forest's vast basin.

"Maybe the spiders see us, maybe they don't. What's certain is that our time is running short." Adrianna faced Frazer. "As for my ability, I've trained in all conditions. I can get us over them. I wouldn't say it if I couldn't. And if you're worried about my wing, it healed weeks ago."

I glanced at the wing in question. It had been cut right before we'd fled Kasi. The incident had left behind a scar and a few deformed scales.

Frazer slipped on a cooler mask than usual. "This isn't about your injury—"

"It was barely that," Adrianna snapped, her wings flaring.

Tension swirled, magnifying the stifling humidity. Worried they might fight, I sat up on my elbows. Totally pointless, I realized. I couldn't stop them from fighting. I'd be a cub swatting at two angry bears.

Cai rescued us from fae posturing and aggression. "Why don't we walk awhile and see if we can spot this path? If the gods shit on us and we can't find anything, we'll fly. Agreed?"

I stifled an inward groan at the thought of more walking.

"Fine," Frazer said.

Adrianna shrugged, pride stealing her voice.

"Let's head farther west," Frazer added.

Motion on my right caught my eye. Liora was rocking up and extending her hand to me. My gut sunk with dread when my palm greeted a blazing forge. She was burning up.

I rolled up with her help. "You've got a fever."

Her bloodshot gaze danced away. "I'm okay."

She wasn't. "It's okay to say if you're not."

"Resting won't help me," Liora said, pulling her clammy hand away. "Finding Hazel will."

Stars, please let her be right.

Liora and I grabbed our rucksacks and our pack moved off. What little energy I had to spare soon dried up. Just before my legs went out from under me, Frazer scooped me up.

"Put me down," I murmured as he stalked onward.

He said, "No," and that was it.

"You're tired—"

"Hush," he replied, not sharp, but firm.

I flushed with shame. His strength ebbed alongside mine; my magic was a burden around both our necks. How I despised the thought.

As we covered more ground, the suspense made me restless, almost itchy. Any reservations I'd harbored about becoming a fae were long gone. I wanted to change. I wanted to stop feeling so rutting weak.

Frazer picked up on my frustration through our bond. "You aren't weak. You never were."

He pinned me with a stare intense enough to make a monster quail. I didn't shy from it, though. "Said the person currently carrying me."

"You're sick. That's not something you can help," he said, his voice sounding strained.

A breathy but real laugh escaped me. "All right. I hate feeling ill. Better?"

He nodded, a curt dip of his chin.

In the next breath, a breeze tickled my ears and brought with it a faint humming. I arched up in my brother's arms, casting an eye in every direction.

Frazer stopped. "What is it?"

"Can't you hear that?"

Wariness lined his voice. "Hear what?"

"There's a humming."

"No there isn't." Adrianna frowned, her silver-inked forehead knotting up.

I didn't blame her for doubting me. Humans didn't pick up on noises that fae couldn't.

Frazer glared at Adrianna. "Don't look at her like she's mad."

"I'm just worried about her, you korgan's ass," Adrianna sniped.

Liora interceded before more cross words could be bandied. "Where's it coming from, Serena?"

Frazer arrived at the borders of my mind. *Let me listen.*

I linked up with my brother. Together, we heard the *hummm*.

Frazer followed the noise until it got louder, nearer. When the sound resonated as clear as a bell, he halted. Frazer and I spoke as one. "It's coming from the mountain."

Wide-eyed gazes lifted to the craggy giant before us.

"Brata, let me down," I said.

He gently set me on the ground. Belly fluttering, I walked up and pressed my ear against the mountainside. "It sounds like there's a bunch of angry bees stuck inside."

The humming dropped out, and an amused voice interjected. "Not quite."

All five of us whirled around to confront this new threat.

Frazer drew his blade. Cai summoned a breeze. I smiled without restraint.

Hazel Greysand was here. Where she'd come from, I'd no idea.

I soaked in her appearance.

Country clothes, a wide-brimmed hat, and the mud on her boots gave her a humble aspect. On the other hand, her high brow, dark purple wings, and silver-streaked ebony hair made her seem a touch distant, a bit mysterious.

I placed a hand on Frazer's hunched shoulder. "It's Hazel."

Cai and Frazer relaxed. They sheathed their respective weapons. Both magic and sword.

"Serena, Adrianna"—Hazel inclined her black hat in our directions—"it's good to see you both again."

"Likewise," I said.

Adrianna didn't react. Not a word. Not a nod. I suspected she was remembering her previous meeting with Hazel. Like many fae, Hazel considered the Queen of the Riverlands to be a traitor. Seeing that Adrianna was Diana's daughter, Hazel had initially treated her with contempt and suspicion.

Overlooking Adrianna's silence, Hazel spoke to me. "The humming you heard comes from the undines—they're calling you to the lake." I thought to ask her how water sprites could sing through stone, but her gaze was already moving to the members of our pack that she hadn't met yet. "May I have your names?"

Cai introduced himself, then added, "Merry meet, Priestess."

Hazel smiled politely.

Liora gave her name, but any further witchy greetings were cut off. "I'm Frazer," he said. "Serena's kin."

Hazel blinked, startled. "You've bonded?"

"Yes, and we've twined our life-forces. Her magic had started to kill her, and it was the only way to slow down the process." Frazer continued, a sharp edge slicing into each word. "So we don't have time to stand around exchanging pleasantries. Just take us to Ewa."

"Please," I tacked on to soften his demand.

Hazel's gaze skipped to me, darting over my features. I'd looked upon my watery reflection enough times to know that she saw a sickly complexion.

Concern deepened the lines on Hazel's forehead. That touch of earthly years reminded me that fae weren't immortal. Not really. I'd learned that fae could live for centuries, millennia even. But once their souls wearied of life's cycles, once they no longer fit, their links to the natural world were severed. They aged and died as a human would.

"Rest easy," Hazel said to me. "We can do the spell today. You have the ingredients—yes?"

I nodded, thinking of the objects we carried: the nightshade, dragon fire, white-tiger claw, and phoenix feather. They were key to the spell to change me.

"Then let's not wait for the leaves to turn." Hazel waved at the mountainside. "Ava käskistini." That banished a glamour and revealed an archway. "Follow me."

She walked up to the mountain and through the opening. Frazer and I joined her, entering a tunnel with no end in sight, wide enough for three people to walk abreast.

Adrianna and Liora came up behind us. Then Cai, who stood at over six feet and had to stoop to keep from hitting the stone ceiling. With the six of us in the tunnel, the glamour behind us blinked into view again, veiling the outside world.

Firelights bobbed above our heads, lending their warm and golden glow to the long passageway. I glanced around: the walls were rough, the floor was smooth, but it was the tombs lining the sides of the tunnel that demanded attention, as did the words and pictographs dressing them. They looked freshly carved yet ancient in their unfamiliarity. That combined with the scents of old dust and older bones lent context to this passageway. A weight. As if time was frozen here and history had claimed it.

"What is this place?" Liora asked quietly, reverently.

Hazel talked and walked. "It's a path that also happens to be a crypt." She studied the tombs and writings with scholarly interest. "Most of this script belongs to languages long since dead. But from the snippets I can read, I'd say the bodies here belonged to soldiers—fae *and* human."

"Isn't it more traditional to entomb warriors in a public place so that they can be honored?" Liora voiced, her curiosity clear.

"Maybe this lot did something naughty," Cai teased.

"Perhaps they did," Hazel said in a droll way. "Barring that, I don't know why the dead were buried where no one would think to look. But there's a protection spell embedded in the rock, hidden in among everything else." She lightly brushed the carvings as we passed, tracing their lines and whorls. "Someone obviously thought this place was worth concealing."

The tunnel suddenly felt crowded, watchful. My mind wove its own tales, its own possibilities. Was I sensing the Dead? Could the spirits tell I was dying—that I was close to joining them?

I shook from a sudden chill.

Frazer interrupted my grim musings. *Don't become as morbid as me. It won't do either of us any good.*

I offered him an appeasing look, but fear hid under my ribs and made a captive of my heart. I was on the brink of my—our—endurance, and I needed a distraction.

Hazel was right here, and she seemed approachable for an elder fae.

I pushed through my awkwardness, asking, "How are you? How have you been?"

She met my interested gaze with a faint smile and tired eyes. "I'm relieved that you're here. Relieved that *I'm* here." A sigh passed her lips. "As you saw when you visited my house, Morgan keeps an annoyingly close watch on me and on any witch she deems a threat. I wasn't entirely sure if I still had it in me to evade the spiders. I had to be careful. So careful that it took over a month to get here. I only reached Ewa a week ago. When I saw you hadn't arrived, I debated setting out in search of you. But the undines saw that your pack would arrive today. They showed me the tunnel so I might bring you to the lake."

"How did they know we'd get here today?"

"Undines are gifted with the Sight."

No one questioned that. I guessed that it was common knowledge for people who'd grown up in Aldar.

Hazel flipped the conversation. "Anyway, enough of that. How are you? Tell me everything."

Memories stirred and spiraled up from the depths of my mind, like sand disturbed from a riverbed.

I caught her up on what had happened since we'd last spoken. The others chimed in when my exhaustion made me fumble in my recollections. I ended by recounting our decision to look for my sister and what we'd learned from Diana.

Hazel's first reaction was to push out a short laugh that reminded me of a teaspoon clinking against a cup. "I must say, that's a lot to take in."

Straight to it, I asked, "Do you know why my magic has refused to work for me these past weeks? Is it because I'm human?"

"I'd say so." A careful nod. "You likely only survived using magic to destroy Goldwyn's trap because you had Frazer's strength to draw upon. But after channeling so much so fast, his energy must've been drained. The strain of supporting your life up to this point might be what's preventing him from fully recovering."

I side-eyed Frazer.

Stop feeling guilty.

Yes, sir, I sent back.

Frazer gave me a flat look.

"There is another possibility," Hazel said, drawing my attention. "Your magic could be evolving."

My heart jumped. "What d'you mean?"

"A witch's power keeps growing until they reach maturity. That could be what's happening to you. And if you are getting stronger, it'll be putting more stress on both of your bodies."

I wasn't sure what to do with that. Blankness prevailed.

"But she'll be okay once she becomes fae, correct?" Frazer leveled that sharp question at Hazel.

"I believe so," she said, a bit vague. "But there is another factor we need to discuss. Since arriving at the lake, the undines have told me that we'll need more power to fuel the spell. The ingredients you've brought won't be enough."

My lungs seized. Breath halted.

"I thought they would be," Hazel added, an apology shining through in her expression. "But what I didn't account for was that when you became human, I would be making you weaker. At least physically. To do the reverse meant creating a more powerful vessel, which in turn—"

"Requires a fuckload more magic," Cai guessed, his spirited timbre tightened by worry.

"Indeed."

I struggled not to lose hold completely.

Hazel's nut-brown eyes were kind as she viewed me. "Don't despair. The undines have a source of power we can draw upon at the lake."

Faint-headed with relief, I drew in a shaky exhale.

"What source?" Frazer stabbed out at Hazel.

"The undines are better suited to answer that question."

I'd neither the will nor the energy to push for a more direct answer. Besides, Frazer was annoyed enough for the both of us.

She shouldn't have been ignorant of something so critical. There was more he wouldn't voice, mentally or otherwise, but the doubt was clear in his eyes. They said *What else has she got wrong?*

I shoved that fear down. It would do no good to brood on it.

"I'm sorry for what happened to your friend Wilder," Hazel remarked, shifting the topic. "What Morgan is doing—what she's done." Her upper lip curled. No fangs, though. "There aren't any words horrible enough to describe it."

Mouth sticky, I made a noncommittal noise.

As I traveled along in a reflective mood, isolated from the world's daily rhythms, I lost time. Fifteen minutes or an hour might've been spent in that tunnel.

"How much longer until we get out of this infernal place?" Adrianna asked from behind me.

"Soon," Hazel replied.

Insistent and grumpy, she added, "How soon?"

Hazel breathed out a laugh. "Soon enough."

We rounded a curve, and there I spied daylight.

"I hope that answers your question," Hazel said, her amusement ringing like silvery bells through her words.

Adrianna was cranky in her silence.

I became fixated on the opening in the rock. Was Lake Ewa on the other side, or would we have to cover more miles?

Every step taken had me holding my slumped head a bit higher.

Fifty paces.

Thirty.

Ten.

My eyes started watering, streaming from the brightness. I squinted to keep from being blinded as we left the dim passage, the tombs, and the firelights behind.

I took a few bleary-eyed steps forward. As my sight adjusted, I stopped and absorbed my surroundings. The lake was up ahead, a short walk away. It was large enough that I couldn't see the entirety of it, and its teal waters were edged by a stony beach, beyond which was a silver-barked forest. The trees there were the tallest I'd ever seen, and their branches carried pearl-colored leaves and snow-bright blossoms.

Lake Ewa: we had made it against the odds. Excitement and relief traveled the length of my spine, setting my toes a-tingling. I felt like kissing the earth.

From the back of our group, Cai whistled a *tweet-too*. "Well, it ain't ugly, we can say that."

Liora softly snorted a laugh. "Bit of an understatement."

I glanced behind me to check that the six of us had come through. We had. The tunnel's mouth had also vanished, replaced by a stony hill that backed onto the mountain range we had passed through.

"Ready?" Frazer muttered beside me.

I nodded.

The two of us led our group to the water's edge. As we did, a person rose out of the lake. She looked human but moved with an *otherness*. That, and the fact her mint-green dress dried upon reaching land, made me assume that this must be an undine—a water sprite.

We quickly reached the undine waiting for us shore-side.

Hazel introduced us, then added, "This is Merida. She currently speaks for the undines."

The sprite bowed her head. The white lotus blossoms adorning her copper hair fluttered, waving at us in the sweet warm air. "My heart grows light seeing you've all arrived safely. Before we can go any further, my sisters and I have to release Sandrine." Merida extended her palm out to me. "I'll need the necklace."

I reached beneath the neckline of my blouse. There, I grasped a glass-smooth gem suspended on a delicate silver chain. "The voice ... the person inside my necklace, she's called Sandrine? Who is she?"

"She's one of us. An undine," Merida replied.

I blinked twice at her.

Frazer bumped me with his elbow, bringing me to my senses. I unclasped the chain, lifted it free, and handed it over.

"This will take a few minutes," Merida warned us.

Adrianna shifted into a tense stance with shoulders back, chin raised, and a grip on her sword. "We almost got captured at the border by Morgan's people. We lost them, but more might be in the area. Can the undines fight if they discover us before the ritual is completed?"

"There won't be any need for that. This section of Ewa has long been hidden from prying eyes and ears, for reasons that will soon become clear." She continued, her voice a lullaby, "Shed your fears and your weapons. It'll do you good to put down your burdens and rest awhile."

Merida turned away, gliding across the rounded pebbles underfoot, not making any noise as she went.

Frazer sent me a growly sort of thought as she descended into the lake's cauldron. *She's too mysterious. It's annoying.*

I smirked at Frazer. *You get the irony of you saying that, right? You, who are made of secrets?*

He grumbled with reluctant acceptance. Ha. Ten points to me.

Cai stepped out of our group's huddle. He paced over to a fallen tree and dumped his things next to the log. The rest of us echoed his example, stacking our weapons and rucksacks in one neat pile.

Cai, Liora, and I perched on the log, avoiding the flat-headed mushrooms and the saplings drunkenly sprouting out of the cracks.

The fae among us stayed standing. Adrianna seemed agitated, her feet shifting, and her eyes darting over everything. Hazel and Frazer quietly observed Merida, who stood waist-deep in the lake with her back to us.

Left to sit and dwell, my leg started to jiggle. Liora gently placed her palm on my knee, stilling the movement. I knew she'd done it to comfort me, but when I met her eyes, I could only think of the exhaustion in them. That pushed me to say, "You should ask Hazel about the binding."

Everyone looked at us.

"What binding?" asked Hazel.

"After," Liora mumbled, removing her hand from my knee.

"Why not now?" Cai questioned.

Expression pained, Liora hung her head slightly. Was she scared to ask? To find out that Hazel might not be able to do it?

Cai faced a puzzled Hazel. "Can you remove a witch binding?"

Hazel's face cleared. She looked down at Liora. "Your magic is bound?"

A small nod.

"I can do it," Hazel said, and Liora's head went up at that. "But the spell to free you will take weeks to prepare, and there's no guarantee you'll be as you were. Bindings can be tricky things."

The five of us paused. That sounded neither hopeless nor hopeful. Did Liora even have weeks? If she died … No, I couldn't go there.

"We can talk about this after Serena's changed," Liora said, loyally.

Love and fear mixed together.

A minute lapsed. My fidgeting caught on. Adrianna knocked out a rhythm on her pommel. Liora fiddled with her thick plait. Cai rummaged for what I guessed was food since his appetite could've rivaled even mine. He proved my suspicions correct when he produced a strip of dried meat from his bag. Looking like a starving lion, he bit into what was essentially spicy cardboard and made a face.

Then it happened.

A lively wind whipped up, cleaving humid air. This fresh breeze carried a chorus of feminine voices that sung to the bees, the birds, and the trees. They called out to the creatures of the lake, land, and sky.

Cai, Liora, and I stood as thirty or more undines rose out of the lake. They brought with them a fog that settled over the water like smoke over glass, and a bridge of giant water lilies that connected the shore to an island not far out. On that island, a magical-looking tree was revealed. Each of the four seasons decorated her branches: the cherry blossoms of spring, the rich greens of summer, the russet golds of autumn, the stark bareness of winter.

Hazel pulled our focus. "That's my cue to prepare the spell." She unbuckled her holster bag from around her waist. "I'll be needing those ingredients now."

Frazer grabbed my bag before I could. He rooted out the pouch that held the nightshade and handed it to Hazel. Adrianna, Cai, and Liora added their ingredients to her leather bag.

Quietly, I asked Hazel, "Will it hurt?"

Her lips parted in a tentative way. "I wish I could answer that, but there's no precedence for this."

I nodded, looking down at my feet. It had been stupid to ask, I told myself. I had to go through with the change—what good would it do to know if it was painful?

Our pack grouped at the lake's edge.

Hazel stepped onto the water lily bridge. I watched as she walked over the lake, stopping halfway to the island to converse with Merida and a few other undines, who stood waist-deep in the water. Was one of them Auntie? Would she acknowledge me?

I think that's her, in the pale blue. Frazer jerked his chin toward a sprite who had left the crowd of undines to drift toward us, effortlessly slicing through the water.

She stepped upon the shore in woven sandals. A diadem of pearls rested upon her brow, and her floor-length gossamer dress sparkled when it caught sunlight.

"Are you Auntie?" I corrected myself. "I mean, Sandrine?"

She nodded, her expression complex, as intricate as a tree knot. Grief-tinged joy was the best I could fathom. That irked me, as did her appearance. I'd imagined some wizened crone, but Sandrine didn't look much older than me. She also happened to be beautiful, with fine bones, brassy locks, and flawless skin. Then there were her jade-green eyes. All too familiar.

I was staring at a ghost.

The skin along my arms erupted in goosebumps. "You look like my mother. Who are you?"

"My name is Sandrine Lytir. I was Sati's older sister." Nerves threaded through her notes as she continued. "I'm your aunt, or atierä in Kaeli, if you'd prefer."

My mind was pulled apart. "How can you be my mother's sister when you're an undine?"

"Because I'm only half undine," she explained. "I inherited the Sight and the characteristics of our sprite mother, but my father was fae. Sati took after him. She got the fangs and the wings."

Cai's punchy laugh cut through my inner chaos. "Well, there we go! Never short of surprises, are we." He side-jostled me. "And there's nothing wrong with your instincts. You called your actual aunt, Auntie. Who'd have thought it, huh?"

A weak laugh whispered past my lips.

Cai directed his disarming grin at Sandrine. "Well, it's nice to finally meet you. You're looking very solid."

Sandrine's smile reached her eyes. "I'll miss listening to you, Caiden. You always could make me laugh."

Gods, this was so *weird*. She gazed upon the others with affection, but she had never seen them before, except through my eyes. Nor had she spoken to them, except once with Frazer. That line of thought conjured up more memories of the last few months, and my mind halted. The things she had witnessed ... My intimacy with Wilder.

I felt an over-boil of embarrassment. "Why didn't you tell me who you were?"

"Because I was just a voice inside a necklace. I wasn't sure whether you'd believe me at first." She wrung her hands. "I thought about telling you once you'd discovered your parents were fae, but I was afraid you'd resent me for not saying something sooner and cast the necklace aside. If you had done that, you would've died."

"Oh." I deflated. Adrift. Confused.

Regret shone in her jade-greens. "I'm sorry, alätia. I've been made cautious by centuries of visions and seeing firsthand how dangerous information can be when shared at the wrong time."

The translation of "alätia" trickled in through my kin bond. *It can mean a few different things. But in this context it would mean beloved.*

I swallowed the last of my discomfort and asked, "How did you end up in a piece of jewelry?"

"Sati intended to return to Aldar with you when the time was right, but we knew you'd both have to make the journey back as humans," she explained, her arms slackening at her sides. "Aldar is a dangerous place for humans as you well know. I bound my spirit to the stone so that I could slowly return your magic and a drop of your mother's blood to you. That way, you'd have the power to protect yourself should the need arise."

I frowned. "What was the blood for?"

"It strengthened your body." She paused, her brow furrowing. "But fae-blood wasn't enough to keep your vessel from combusting. I had to borrow the necklace's power to put a dampener on your magic, both to protect your body and to stop fae from sensing it."

I flashed back to when she'd told me about the leylines of salt, iron, and obsidian in my body. Before she had removed those barriers, they had voided my magic and kept me from using it.

The past grew clearer. I glanced at it through a new lens. "Is that why Hunter and Wilder threw up when they drank my blood? Because of the extra salt and iron in it?"

A sober nod. "That's right."

"You must've really loved Serena to live inside of a stone for years," Cai said, staring at Sandrine with bemused respect. "It's the size of a rutting thimble."

My thoughts fell out of my head. "How did you fit inside?"

"How did you stay sane?" Adrianna added incredulously.

Sandrine's lip thinned, not from disapproval but from smothered laughter. "I had to embrace my true form. In such a state, size isn't an issue. The gem in your necklace contains water. That was enough for me to inhabit it. As for my mind, I avoided decay by entering a meditative state common among my kind. I could dream though." My aunt seemed to diminish before my eyes, and she was already a petite creature. "That was how I learned Sati had died."

Sadness stuck in my craw. "You dreamed about her dying?"

"Actually, I saw you." Grief clouded her face. "You were so young, but you still snuck out on a winter's night to visit her grave. I was terrified you were going to freeze to death."

"I almost did." I could live ten lifetimes and never forget that night. Younger me had bashed the icy ground and screamed at the stars to bring my mother back. I'd fallen asleep by her graveside when my pleas went unanswered.

The wind became a hundred voices, whispering, "*Sandrine, ready the girl.*"

Our group stiffened.

Sandrine peered out at where Hazel and the undines gathered. "They're calling us." Focusing on me, she continued. "Before we go, I need to prepare you for what you're about to face, and to do that, I should explain something about the spell."

I did not like her expression. Not one bit.

Gathering her wavy locks over one shoulder, Sandrine reached behind her neck and undid something. From out of her star-studded dress, she produced my necklace. "I know you've heard that we'll need more power to fuel your transformation."

"You're going to use the necklace?" Frazer guessed, a step ahead.

"In a way, yes."

Nearing me, Sandrine twirled her finger. I spun around and crouched. My aunt fixed the chain around my throat, careful to miss tangling it up in my shoulder-length hair.

I pivoted back around.

Sandrine eyed the gem in the center of the flowery chain, her expression hard to read. "That is more than water sustained in gemstone. It's a source of waterlight, the branch of magic responsible for the Sight in all creatures, including undines. That's why I could use its power to void your magic—our core natures are the same."

Her gaze moved up, meeting mine.

"Another property of waterlight is that it can dilute other forms of magic. That's how we're going to weaken a spell that's kept a gate locked for almost a thousand years. The gate is the tree." She lifted her chin toward the island—an island that the undines had partially encircled. "And the light court lies beyond."

Our pack was quiet. Snails would have been louder.

My thoughts were mayhem when Adrianna snapped. Badly. "You can't expect us to believe that. The gods haven't been seen for eons, if they were even real to begin with." Expression furious, she ended with, "This is madness."

Sandrine looked resigned, as if she'd predicted her words might be treated like an autumn wind passing by our ears. "The gods are real. They've just been locked away for a very long time." I was short on breath when she faced me. "The spell over the gate is too powerful for us to break, but we can knock a few holes in it, temporarily. That should be enough for the firstborn—or gods, as you call them—to open a portal from their side. They won't be able to enter our world, but they can send their power through to help restore you."

A sound of disbelief escaped me. "So, this extra fuel you need for my transformation is coming from the gods? And you expect them to show up? Why in the courts would they help me or even care about me?"

My aunt's stare left me for the lake's calm surface. "The light gods can speak to undines through the waters. It's a difficult method of communication and much can be lost between worlds, but my sisters are certain the firstborn will show for us." She pinned me with a confident stare. "As for why they would help you, your mother's already answered that question. Because you can save these lands. Because you're important." Before I could ask her to clarify, she went on. "Now, we really must start." Her jade-greens slid to Frazer. "Given your quick mind, I imagine you've guessed this spell might affect you, too."

Alarm banged into me. "Affect him how?"

Sandrine shot glances between me and Frazer. "We can't remove the twining prior to the transformation—not without killing Serena. And then, there's your kin bond to consider. Having such a close connection might mean the spell won't be able to differentiate between you two. Your minds are mirrors, after all, and sometimes mirrors cast reflections."

I gaped at her. Did she think that made sense?

"I don't care. Let's just do this," said Frazer.

I gave him a sidelong glance. "You should care."

"Why?" He raised an eyebrow. "It's not as if I can become a fae again."

I arched an eyebrow too, matching him for sarcasm. "No, but you might grow boobs."

A rare smile curled upward, inciting his midnight eyes to glitter. "If that happens, I'll just borrow your bras. I didn't happen to pack any."

"I'm not sharing my underthings with you," I snapped, annoyed at how lightly he was taking this.

He chuffed a dismissive sound. "Yes, you will."

Frustrated, I clenched my jaw. He was crazier than a land-loving fish.

"I'll bet five florén on Frazer growing breasts," Cai said cheerfully. "Li—you want in on this?"

Liora and Frazer sent their eyes skyward at the same time.

Our silly moment popped like a bubble when Sandrine slipped her hand into mine. "It's time, alätia. I have to stand with my brethren in the water, and you must join Hazel on the island. Walk over the lily pads. Don't go into the lake if you can help it."

Frazer confronted Sandrine. "I'm going with her."

"I know." Sandrine smiled softly. "Thank you for always sticking by her side. I owe you a debt that can never be repaid."

"There is no debt. Just save her life."

Smile gone, Sandrine nodded. "We will."

I quickly searched my friend's faces: Adrianna looked so uncomfortable, I thought she might throw a dagger at someone; Liora had a shattered glass expression, her anxiety painted clearly over her heart-shaped face; Cai's smile was too strained, and his tone too upbeat when he said, "Can't wait to see your new wings."

His wink made me feel like my chest might implode. But the fear constricting my ribcage didn't stop me from attempting a reassuring smile. "See you soon."

Rain started to fall from the heavens. The droplets hitting the lake went from a steady *drip, drip, drip* to a chaotic *thud, thud, thud* in mere moments. A storm had arrived. I prayed to the gods beyond the gate that I survived it.

CHAPTER 4
THE END AND THE BEGINNING

Sandrine was the first to move. She waded out into the lake, leaving our pack on the shore. Away she went, seeming to fly through the water to where the other undines waited for her.

I eyeballed the fragile-looking path of lily pads. I'd seen Hazel cross over it, but I was still skeptical it could carry my weight.

Frazer grasped my hand. He pulled me after him onto the bridge, and it proved as solid as a stone road. I didn't feel relieved, though. My anxiety about what lay ahead was too intense for that to be possible.

We crossed the bridge with mist lapping around our feet, and summer-warmed rain falling atop our heads. It wasn't long before we passed by Sandrine where she waited in the water. She and the other undines had gathered in front of the island.

Frazer and I stepped off the path onto the grassy hillock. That moment struck my very bones, and I stopped. There was no going back after this. This island was where Serena Smith would die.

Come on, siska.

That mental nudge from my brother pushed me to breathe and start forward again. We moved toward the center of the island, to where Hazel had lined up the spell ingredients under the tree. Once we'd reached its protruding roots and halted, white-as-bone branches shook overhead showering us with rain, autumn leaves, winged seeds, and cherry blossoms.

Grumpy-faced, Frazer picked foliage out of our hair. I pulled my sleeve down, wiping the rain from our faces.

Hazel turned toward us, her face perfectly dry thanks to her wide-brimmed hat. "Stand here." She maneuvered me a few feet from the trunk. Before she released me, she grasped my wrist. A reassuring touch. "All will be well."

I nodded, afraid to speak for fear gibberish would spill out.

"I'm going to begin the ritual, but your transformation won't trigger until we've opened the portal and the gods have added their power to the spell," Hazel said, and my guts twisted up. "Okay? Ready?"

My heart raced faster than a bolting rabbit, but I still said, "Yes."

Hazel spun around. She held her hand out to the ingredients on the ground and muttered a few words in a foreign tongue. I guessed Kaeli.

What is she saying? I asked Frazer.

It's an archaic form of Kaeli. I only understood the word "transfer," or maybe it was "vessel."

Whatever was said, it turned the ingredients to smoke and ash and wind. Hazel faced us, her palms glowing with power.

Frazer clasped my hand again. That lent steel to my spine, even as fear seeped through my veins.

Face set in concentration, Hazel chanted in the old language and drew a large, complex shape in the air with her shining hands. Every stroke of her finger left behind a glittering trail of golden ink.

A minute or two later, the sigil done, Hazel pushed her palm toward me. The spherical mark shot straight into my chest. I flinched.

Frazer gripped my shoulder. "Are you all right?"

"Yes." I rubbed the spot over my heart. "It just burns a bit."

Lies. It was five times worse than heartburn.

The light in Hazel's palms died. She dropped her arms to her sides and moved closer to say, "The next step is to open the gate, but that's undine territory. My part is done." Her voice sounded raspy, fatigued.

"Thank you," I said, meaning it.

A nod and a smile. She walked past me toward the lake and the undines. "It's time," she called out to them, pitching her rough voice over the rising wind.

I glanced behind me and saw the undines clasp hands above the surface of the water. Each of them started to sing, their voices harmonizing in a chant. The words held no meaning for me, but the melody conjured head-to-toe shivers and heated the gemstone at my chest.

Thunder drummed out overhead. Through wisps of windblown hair, I stared up at a violent sky, a wretched gray-green canvas. A witch's brew was happening up there. A warning of imminent devastation. Where had this storm sprung from? Was it magical?

The undine choir pitched their voices higher, ascending into the soprano range. Their song was life and light. An external heartbeat.

Coal-black clouds billowed across the sky. They seemed to sweep my mind clear of thoughts. All I could do was feel: the panic beneath my breast, the knots in my stomach, the sweat at my palms.

As the undines' tune peaked in a dramatic crescendo, thunder rang out above like heavenly cymbals. Flocks of birds erupted from the surrounding forest, sending out throaty calls of alarm. That was a prelude. Only the beginning.

Fast and quick, lightning rode the skies. It struck out like a wounded beast, hitting the tree in a dazzling display.

I threw my arm up in front of my face, shielding my sight from the blinding light. The air suffused with a sweet *zing* that reminded me of the smell of a barn after an animal had given birth. The promise of creation, perhaps.

I peeked through wary lids, finding a long, narrow rip had formed in the tree's trunk. Beyond this danced a pure, cold light. A door cracked ajar. That's what it looked like.

As one, the undines quieted. Then a ray of light bled out from the trunk—from the doorway into another world. It touched my chest before splitting apart and unraveling like sun-kissed spider-silk toward Frazer, and back on the shore, Adrianna, Cai, and Liora.

Fear bridled me as the cobweb of light connected all of us. Why was the spell also focusing on them? Would it hurt them? Should I stop this?

Frazer squeezed my hand. *There is no stopping this, siska.*

I looked into his night-blues. He was sure where I wavered. So I nodded. Accepting his judgment.

A voice wearied by age echoed inside of my head. *Is it her?*

Who else would it be, Oryas? An exasperated reply.

Wide-eyed, I stared into the doorway. I could see nothing, but those voices had certainly come from the other side. From the light court.

Someone sniffed. *I must say, the girl seems rather frail to take on such a great task.*

Shut up, Aeryn, said a fierce-sounding female.

There's no need for that attitude, young lady.

Go stuff your hole.

A masculine voice boomed out, *Enough! Zola, Thea, are you ready?*

Holy fire. I recognized those names: Zola and Thea were daughters to Balor, King of the Light Court.

We won't let you down, said the fierce female.

A gentle-sounding person chimed in. *We'll watch over her, father.*

That booming voice returned. *Sati, Dain, you can speak to them now. But be quick.*

I'm here, Ena. So is your father.

Hello, tilä.

I seemed to die twice over hearing my mother and what I presumed was my birth father. *Mama ... is it really you?*

It's me, she said in a sweet, sad timbre.

There's no time to say everything we wish we could, so we're going to have to focus on what you and your brother need to know, Dain added. *To start, the firstborn have to make the twining between you permanent. We know you won't like it, Ena, but it's the only sure way you can survive. A power like yours can't be borne by one person alone, not even by a fae.*

The world turned on its head.

Frazer? Mama called his name softly. *The firstborn need your permission to do this.*

He didn't hesitate. *You have my permission.*

"No." My head turned sharply toward Frazer. "Brata—"

"What would you do if the situation was reversed?" Frazer glared at me, eyes lit with a dark inferno. "Would you do it for me?"

He knew I would. But ... "This isn't right. It isn't fair on you."

Frazer's gaze flickered. "You've got it backward, siska. To watch you die wouldn't be right. For you to leave me to walk this world alone wouldn't be fair."

His words were a knife in my heart, silencing me.

Softer now, he added, "This is what I want. Respect that."

The fight went out of me. "Okay."

Dain picked up the conversation. *It's important you both understand what this means. This new twining will be unbreakable. There'll be no end to it, in this life or the next. And if one of you should die, the other will fade away until their strength is spent and they also die.*

I understand, Frazer answered, sober and certain.

A tear rolled down my cheek. *Understood.*

Ena, two of the firstborn—Zola and Thea—have been chosen to train you in light magic, Dain said. *They're going to fuse their spirits with the stone on your necklace and use it as a conduit to speak with you.*

I hadn't gotten my head around that when he went on. *And one last thing: grant your birth father this request? In the coming months when the blood spilled feels unbearable, remember that their deaths are not yours to bear. They belong to those who'd murder the world just to wear a crown.*

The rasping, ravaged notes of a god interrupted. *We must begin. Keeping the portal open tests our strength. Others will have to explain about the mark.*

What mark?

Ready yourself, Serena, warned the booming, commanding voice from before. *Firstborn—now!*

Consumed by this back and forth, I'd almost forgotten what was about to happen.

A wave of blue light crashed into me. It pulled me apart as if I were caught in a riptide. My windpipe filled up with water or blood—I couldn't tell which. I dropped to my knees, gagging and heaving, but nothing came up.

Frazer crouched to hold back my hair. His mouth was moving, but my ears weren't working. I was underwater. I couldn't breathe.

A silver arrow flew out of the gate and struck me. The arrow and the sensation of drowning vanished, replaced by the feeling of countless ice-shards stabbing into my flesh.

I screamed, bloodying my throat. But the gods showed no mercy. They delivered a third blow in the form of a golden spear. I saw red as it set fire to my nerves.

Convulsions. Knives behind the eyes. Torture.

Frazer wrapped his arms around me. I peered up at his pained face through a haze of sweat, rain, and tears.

The next blow would surely end me—end us. My brother held me tighter as if he'd heard that thought. As if he could shield me from what would happen next.

Star-white lightning bolted outward and jolted me. It froze the air in my lungs, turned my blood to ice, and slowed my heart.

Faintness circled. The last of my strength bled out.

I was cut from my skin. From all mortal chains. Spirit freed, I moved for the doorway. Toward the light court. I sensed a place of never-good-byes. A place without sorrow or death or disease. Paradise.

But the primal instincts of my phantom form were denied as something or someone grabbed onto me. I glanced back to see the cause. Frazer supported my dying body, his face wracked with torment.

It isn't time for us to die, siska, he said, his mental voice sounding distant. *Fight it. Fight this.*

That shook something loose, something that shouldn't have been forgotten. If I died, I'd drag him with me. But for whatever reason, I still struggled to return to him.

The gate was calling me, its allure potent.

Mama was firm as she said, *Ena, stay with Frazer.*

Divided by love and instinct, my spirit stayed stuck. To and fro.

Stay or go?

I straddled this world and the next, somewhere in between human and fae, between life and death. Just a cusping moon.

An invisible hand touched my cheek. Through that touch, I felt my mother's love, unconditional and eternal. *We'll always be with you, Ena.*

I wavered, drawing out our closeness. I missed her so much. And Dain—I'd never gotten the chance to miss him.

Frazer's panic cut through me. *I can't hear your pulse anymore. Please, siska, come back.*

His plea echoed through my bones louder than clanging bells. It drowned out the light court's call; there was no room left for death. *I love you, Mama. I love you both.*

We know.

Be well, tilä.

Bracing myself, I clawed my way back into flesh and bone. Back to my anchor. Back to my brother.

I recoiled at the soul-ending agony awaiting me inside of my broken vessel.

The sky thundered, and a deep voice sounded alongside. *Hear me, child. Your new life as a fae will test you, but those reborn in the midst of a storm are the strongest of us all. Do not doubt yourself.*

A shadow in the shape of a giant sword flew out of the doorway. It pierced me through my chest. With that, the candle flame of my human existence was snuffed out, consumed by the darkness lying in wait.

Muscle tissue was destroyed.

Organs became jelly.

Skin sloughed off.

I became agony. Torn apart, the threads of my existence were unpicked, unraveled, and scattered to the four corners of the universe.

I was shadow and stardust—the stuff of primordial creation. There, I felt the bond between Frazer and myself re-form into a single strand of glowing white light.

Bound to the life-force of my brother, I was stitched back together.

Human to fae; new bone, new muscle, new skin formed.

Fangs sliced through raw gums. Terrible pain crawled up my spine as wings burst out from between my shoulder blades, shredding the back of my bra and top. With a lolling head, I looked over my shoulder at white feathers fringed with a golden shimmer.

I'd emerged, like a butterfly from a chrysalis.

Frazer screamed violently. Ash-gray wings spread out from his shoulders and splayed wide. Shock, wonder, and a fear so bright it would shame the sun flooded my brother.

I hadn't a second to process any of it. My ribs, hands, and forearms heated as if I'd been cattle-branded. Voices from across the sea, sky, and land flooded in, overwhelming me. My wings retracted, disappearing as though hiding from the sound.

At that, my mind reached every limit it had. I sped toward the darkness, and the world dropped out of view.

CHAPTER 5
TO FLY, ONE MUST FIRST GROW WINGS

Should I start yelling?

No, Zola. Be patient. She's been through a lot.

Those poor attempts at whispers roused me. I rose out of the darkness and stretched out into a body that felt weightless yet full. A glass bottle with sunlight inside.

My lashes were a fledgling's wings, struggling to open. Bright light immediately stabbed at my eyes. I groaned, and the noise was loud in my ears. Other sounds rushed in, bleeding into one another, becoming an assault on my sensitive hearing.

"I'm here, siska," came a murmur from nearby.

Frazer scooped me off a hard surface, placing me upright on his lap.

I took a wide, rib-stretching breath to calm my budding headache. Big mistake. The strong scents of a damp forest crawled up my nose. That set off a sneezing fit.

Frazer supported my head. "Take shorter inhales and longer exhales."

In—one, two, three.

"Stop."

My lungs obeyed him.

"Now, release it for six beats."

Eyes scrunched up, I pursed my lips and blew out for six counts.

"Good. Keep doing that. It'll help."

"Hurts." I rubbed at my ear. "There's too much noise. I can't block it out."

Frazer made his voice gentle. "Try focusing on a single sound."

"Can't." I rocked my head, biting my lip.

"Yes, you can." He pushed down on pressure points above my eyes, then he pinched the bridge of my nose. "Haven't you ever read a book and had to block out the sound of a ticking clock in the background?"

"I suppose so."

"Then, you can do this," he reassured.

I concentrated on the sound of our measured breathing. Snow, cedar, and citrus filled my nostrils; my brother's scent helped ground me. It was hard at first, but slowly the cacophony in my head quieted; noises separated and became distinct, tolerable. That done, I tried to pry my eyes open again.

Light poured in through fluttering lids. I bore it with gritted teeth. As the brightness cooled to bearable levels, the world swam into crystal-clear focus. My sharper vision made me feel as if I'd worn smudged lenses my entire life only to have finally removed them.

In a few blinks, I absorbed our positioning and our new surroundings.

Frazer and I sat on a sleeping bag, rucksacks and swords at our feet. Through the gaps in the canopy, I glimpsed a windblown sky. The storm had broken, and we weren't within sight of Lake Ewa. We had holed up in a forest; a huge white-blossomed tree stood at our backs.

"Where are the others?"

"They're still at the lake," he said, keeping his voice low for my sake. "After you fainted, Hazel suggested I take you somewhere it would be just you and me. She thought having too many people around would make it more difficult to adjust to your heightened senses."

Good idea.

"How long have we been here?"

"Not long," he said, fussing with the towel I was wrapped in.

"Erm ... Why am I in a towel?"

"You ripped through your top. I had to improvise."

My mind reeled backward. Just before I'd fainted, I'd felt my wings erupt out of my back. That would explain the tattered fabric clinging to my top half, hidden by my makeshift blanket. But it didn't explain why I no longer had wings.

And Frazer? I could've sworn I'd seen wings at his back. There was no evidence of them, though. He'd even changed into a different outfit.

"Did I imagine our wings?"

"No," he said, his voice a cool draft. "It seems they can retract. Mine went under a few seconds after yours, but they're still there—just tucked up against my spine."

I watched him carefully. He seemed neither pleased nor miserable.

"That's not normal, right?" I mumbled, eardrums still tender.

A hollow laugh deflated his chest. "No. It isn't."

I flicked my tongue over my lips, wetting them. "Are you glad you've got wings again?"

"Yes."

His nonplussed tone didn't convince. "You don't sound it."

Frazer's chin went up, and his head relaxed against the silver bark. "I think I'm in shock." I went to say more when he cut me off. "Leave it."

The bond grew hostile. If I went too close, it would growl and arch its back. So I let him stay behind his emotional walls. But to be shut out was a scorpion sting to the heart.

Ugly thoughts surfaced. *Your brother doesn't trust you. He still doesn't open up to you.*

I stuffed those petty demons in a box and hissed at them. He cared for me. He'd shown me that in countless different ways, at countless different times.

Frazer punctured the stuffy silence. "There's something you should see."

With care, he slid me off his lap.

I watched as he rolled up his sleeves. "These tattoos appeared during the spell."

A circle of waxing and waning moons adorned the inner part of his right forearm, and a silvery-blue band was sketched around his left wrist. At some angles, the wavy band appeared to be a bracelet.

I gaped.

"There's another."

Frazer lifted up his ebony shirt, displaying his ribs and another mark.

This one was a spiral of black cursive. The symbols held no meaning for me, but they stunned all the same.

He pushed his top down and said, "Give me your hands."

I drew the edges of the towel aside, faithfully placing my palms in his.

Frazer slid my sleeves up and turned my hands over. My gasp of surprise nearly threw me into another round of sneezing. I wrinkled and tweaked my nose to suppress the reflex. The urge left me, and I focused on examining my new ink.

My right forearm was marked by a delicate star, drawn in black and silver lines, and in the seat of my palm was a golden sun-disk with lace detailing. My left arm bore the same tattoos as Frazer's.

I also checked my side. There, I had a swirl of script patterning my ribs, identical to my brother's.

A chilly breeze blew past, nipping at my rain-dampened hair. Frazer noticed my shivering. He put his arm over my shoulder and pulled me up against him, sharing his warmth.

Once my trembling eased, I murmured, "What do you think the tattoos mean?"

His night-blue eyes glittered. "I think they're our witch markings, although as I understand it, witches choose to tattoo themselves, either with clan sigils or to showcase their magical affinities. But apparently, the gods decided to ink us without permission."

I could tell he wasn't angry. More intrigued.

"We don't have a clan," I said, stating the obvious.

"No, we don't."

I stared at his ink. "Then these must describe what kind of abilities we have."

"Mm."

"I have five tattoos."

I'd stated the obvious again. Frazer still said, "Yes."

From my pack, I'd learned there were four light magic disciplines. Did that mean ...

Frazer listed them. "Sunlight, moonlight, waterlight, and starlight." He laid it out for me as I struggled to accept the conclusion reason had led me to. "You've been gifted all four."

Nerves caused a drought in my mouth. "Wh—what about the fifth mark? What does that represent?"

"I'm not sure." He frowned. "I've only got moonlight and waterlight. There wasn't a third ability."

"How do you know that?"

"Balor told me what I'd inherited when your spirit was rushing toward the gate like a chicken without its head." His stark features darkened.

"Oh." I reached for my courage and put to him, "Do you resent being made a witch?"

"No."

I swallowed anxiety. "What about the twining being made permanent?"

Gaze leaving me, he removed his arm from my shoulder. "I could never resent anything that keeps you breathing."

He stared straight ahead, his jaw squared with suppressed emotion.

"But?"

Frazer sighed. "Listen to our pulses."

He grasped my palm, bringing our hands wrist-to-wrist. Through our fragile, almost translucent skin, I felt the song of our fae hearts. The sound carried and reverberated underneath my breastbone. It was there I realized our heartbeats were synced. Our notes connected.

"You hear that?" He released my hand. "How our hearts beat as one?"

I nodded.

"I'm not afraid to die with you, siska. Quite the opposite. I'm more afraid of living without you." Frazer finger-combed his raven locks. "But we're headed for foreign waters and uncertain times. Conflict will trail us like ticks seeking blood. And if I get you killed—"

"I'm far more likely to be the one who gets us hurt."

Frazer's arrow-straight brows slashed together. "I sensed your power during that spell. A part of it lives inside of me. And from what I can tell, your magic would rival that of even the strongest of witches."

My stomach dropped; my insides disappeared.

His jaw tightened with some unknown tension. "I've become your weak spot. That's what I can't stand."

"How could you be my weak spot?" I asked. "Even if you *did* die before me, that's still more time than I would've gotten without you. Gods, if it weren't for you, I'd probably already be rotting in the ground."

His growl singed the air. Yeah, he really didn't like that. I struggled for the right words—for words big enough, good enough.

"Look," I began. "This new life barely makes sense to me as it is, and without you in it, immortality would be a curse. It's bad enough when I imagine Cai and Liora getting older and weaker while I stay young and healthy." I leaned against the smooth bark of the tree, needing to feel its strength at my back. "I'm trying to say that I feel the same way you do. I hate the idea that I might cause your death someday. But I don't want to be separated from you either ... I want our stories to end on the same page."

His face was dead. As motionless as a funeral shroud. "I suppose we're stuck with each other, then."

Before I could take offense, Frazer dazzled me with a rare smile. It softened the harsh planes of his face, like glass melting in a forge.

Scoffing, I shoved him lightly.

A voice, light with humor, said, *I like him.*

I started at that mental intrusion. *Hello?*

Yes, hello. We've met. Sort of.

Frazer stiffened. "What's wrong?"

I explained.

He got his thinking face on. "Dain mentioned that Zola and Thea would be contacting you. That was probably one of them speaking to you."

I'm Zola, said the stronger, bolder voice.

And I'm Thea, sounded the softer, quieter one. *We'll be with you from now on.*

That's right. And if you don't follow our orders, we'll make a soup of your brains.

My eyes bulged at Zola's threat.

Ignore her, Thea said. *My sister has an awful sense of humor. I promise we're not here to spy on you or to hurt you. We only want to keep you safe.*

Frazer was watching me with a funny expression. "Somebody's talking to you again, aren't they?"

"It's both of the goddesses. Can't you hear them?"

He shook his head, then shifted topics. "Are you ready to return to the lake?"

Was I? The pain in my ears had dulled to a blunt blade, and my eyes had stopped tearing some time ago.

"Yes."

Frazer stood up and offered me his hand. I secured the blanket to my front, and with my other hand I met his grip. He hauled me up easily.

A little part of me had expected to topple over like a newborn fawn. But when my feet met the earth, I was rooted. Not clumsy.

"You should release your wings. The sooner you get used to them, the less of a hindrance they'll be in a fight," Frazer said, pulling his hand from mine.

Free them, how?

Frazer's eyes were wise, seeing through me. "Try willing them to surface."

The tips of my ears heated. Annoyed I hadn't thought of that, I brought my focus to bear upon releasing them.

The skin and muscle of my back grew taut. I was a bowstring ready to fire. A slight twinge. A reverberation. Then my two wings released outward.

The action of lifting and lowering them wasn't dissimilar to moving my arms. Relieved at that discovery, I glanced over my shoulder and viewed them, this time with a clear head. They extended from the crown of my head to my tailbone and were cast in the likeness of bird wings. My feathers were as white as lamb's wool and edged in a glittering gold.

The sight of them made me feel peculiar, contented. I took up so much more space now, but it felt natural. A relief. It was as if I'd always worn clothes that were two sizes too small only to have found an outfit that finally fit me.

Transfixed, I jumped a bit when my brother said, "I should measure your joints so I can put slits into whatever top you're wearing."

"Okay."

"I'll check your wing health while I'm at it." Before I could ask why, he gave me an answer. "I want to see what the gods gave you to work with."

He padded around behind me. I tensed.

Frazer's cold hands pressed against my spine, right beside my left wing. His touch was whisker-soft. Yet my skin crawled, and I shied away.

"It's just me." His voice was honey soothing a sting.

Calmer, I replied, "Sorry. I don't know why I flinched."

"Don't apologize," he said bracingly. "I've told you before, fae don't like people at their backs."

I sucked my bottom lip under my front teeth, nodding. I knew that.

He started measuring my joints with the length of his hands. My discomfort built and built until I was white-knuckling it. "Can you talk to me? Hearing your voice helps."

A pause was followed by, "Have you ever heard tales of where the fae came from?"

My mind stumbled, wondering where he was going with this. "People in the Gauntlet used to say they were created by the gods."

"That's one theory," he said evenly. "But others believe our kind was born out of chaos. Others claim our ancestors were fallen stars. Who knows what the truth is. But what all our stories share is the belief we possess wild souls. The best of us try to control the beast within, but it always emerges, usually when we bite, fight, or fuck."

"I don't think we should talk about fucking. I might actually imagine you doing it, and that wouldn't end well for me."

He snorted. "A lot of people have sex. It's nothing to be embarrassed about."

"Please, stop."

He sighed, massaging and manipulating the muscles along my spine. "What I'm trying to say is that protecting your wings, showing dominance, shielding our kin from threats, being possessive over lovers—it's all normal for us. I don't want you to feel ashamed of these things in the future or overthink them too much."

"How do I control myself?"

"I'll let you know when I find out how."

I sent my eyes rolling. "Great. Thanks."

He chuffed in that catty way of his. "Different things work for different people. Walking under the stars. Meditating. Getting into fights ... but don't do that unless you can win."

The ever-protective brother.

Frazer brushed a finger along my wingtips.

I shuddered. "That tickles."

"Just checking your responses." He moved around to my front. "Everything looks good."

I rotated my wing joints, loosening them of the lingering tension. "You know, they're nowhere near as heavy as I imagined they'd be. They weigh less than a bag of flour."

Frazer grunted. "Fae have a different bone and muscle composition to humans. It's what allows us to fly." He frowned. "Though I must admit, when my wings sprung free, they felt uncommonly light—more air and magic than flesh. Perhaps that's what enables us to retract them without any pain."

I would take his word for it.

"Choose something to change into," he said, lining his chin up with my rucksack.

Holding my towel against my front, I crouched and rifled through my bag. I had little enough to select from. I'd entered Aldar with only the clothes on my back. Our pack had disposed of the uniforms we'd worn as soldiers in training out of fear we would draw attention in matching garments. I'd been left with the few clothes that I'd managed to secure from a cast-off bin in Kasi.

I handed Frazer a linen shirt. He kneeled, laying it on the ground. Using his hands, he noted what length the openings had to be for my wings. Then, with the deft movement of a skilled swordsperson, he sliced two holes into the back of the top.

"It's not exactly pretty." He held the brown shirt up, eyeing his handiwork. "But I can get some proper fae clothes for you once we're in Nasiri."

A potential problem presented itself. "I can live with ugly clothes. I'd prefer to spend the money on, you know, support?"

He looked up at me, confused. I signaled toward my chest.

I received a blank look in return. Gods above.

My cheeks spotted with heat. "I can't wear a human bra anymore."

Frazer blinked. "Oh." He stood and handed me the shirt. "Can you go without wearing one until I get some from Nasiri?"

His serious tone made me want to laugh. I smothered that urge and said, "Yes."

"I'll give you some privacy so you can change," he said, sheathing his sword.

I dared a thorny question. "Aren't you going to put slits in your shirt too?"

He gripped his hilt. "Yes."

The reluctance in his tone unsettled me, but I couldn't think what to say.

Frazer stuffed his bedroll in his rucksack and rounded the wagon-wheel-sized tree trunk, moving out of my sight.

I undressed, discarding my ruined top and bra.

Ignoring the ongoing influx of sounds and smells, I toweled away the last of the rain's dampness from my limbs.

In my nakedness, I cataloged several changes to my body. There was a hint of biceps in my upper arms, which I'd never managed to build, even after months of physical exertion. My shoulders appeared wider, while my ass and breasts were a little rounder, more proportional and a perfect counterweight to my wings.

I wasn't as curvy as Liora or as toned as Adrianna, but instead of scrawniness, I saw and felt strength in my body for the first time. I could work with this, I thought. My body wasn't a fragile twig anymore. It was a willow branch that could bend, sway, and survive a storm.

I moved on from my observations, slipping on stretched-out leggings. Next came the altered top. I was a flailing mess trying to slip my wings through the slits. Several failed attempts later, I succeeded.

Then I stopped. I felt torn between the temptation to check whether my face had changed and the desire not to keep the others waiting for us.

How long does it take to look in a mirror? Zola wheedled.

Good point.

I dropped down, pulling a pocket mirror from my bag. With a flick of my finger, I opened it and found myself staring into the eyes of a stranger.

My dark blue irises were gone, replaced by amethyst ones. I wouldn't be mistaken for a human now, not with that glint in my gaze. It held the intensity of a predator. My skin also glowed with life, and the shadows under my lids had vanished.

I checked out the rest of my oval face—upturned eyes, long

eyebrows, angular cheekbones, and a narrow nose. All the same as before. Curious, I poked at the bony ridges under my gums. That failed to pop my fangs down.

Finished with my vain moment, I stowed the mirror in my rucksack. Luckily, it had additional fastenings that could be used by fae. I'd witnessed Adrianna position the cross-straps countless times, and it was easy enough to replicate. Once I'd strapped my sword to my side, I called out to Frazer, "I'm done."

He circled around the tree, his rucksack secured and his falcon-shaped wings out. A smile broke over my face at the sight. I admired the color of his feathers, like polished tin and a steely, weather-beaten sky. They were my opposite, the dark side of my moon. Overcome, I launched myself at him.

Frazer flinched. His arms rose as if undecided whether to catch me or stop me. He let me pull him into a hug but only tolerated the contact for a few seconds. Then his muscles locked up and pain blasted through our bond. "Siska." An urgent command.

I took a step back. "What's wrong?"

Frazer dipped his head so that his hair fell and veiled his eyes. A refusal to speak. I retreated to our inner world—into our bond. Through that, I felt the rawness of him as he hid his vulnerability under what may as well have been a single leaf. I wished only for something bigger to throw over him and shelter him with. "Is this about your wings?"

That triggered his explosion. He pivoted and punched the tree.

I hopped back as splinters flew. On tenterhooks, I waited for another outburst of emotion.

Frazer braced his palms against the trunk. He stared long at the damage he'd caused, his wings rising and falling with his uneven breath.

"Brata ..."

He heaved in a deep inhale and pushed out, "When they took my wings as punishment, they tore muscle and almost broke my spine. They didn't get a witch to attend me, and without magic to intervene in the early stages of my injury, the damage to my back became permanent. I've lived in pain for years because of it."

My heart twisted terribly. "You never said."

"There wasn't anything to be said or done about it." On the end of another unsteady exhale, he continued. "But now, magic's given me new wings and it's erased my old injury, and for the first time in eighteen years, I'm not suffering."

I was treading in uncertain waters. "Isn't that a good thing?"

Frazer pushed off the silver-barked tree. "It's more than good. But all I can think about is how they could be taken from me again. Because the damage wasn't just to my body." He faced me and pressed two fingers against his temple. "It was up here. My pain might be gone, but the scars are still there."

I knew he didn't mean physical scars. The memory had knotted in his soul, becoming a wound that his body couldn't heal. He turned his cheek.

My spirit took up arms against his despair. I wanted to battle his demons for him. To defeat them and lay them to rest.

Only time and courage can remove the poison from such wounds, Thea said, sounding like tranquil waters.

Zola, the fire and brimstone one, added, *And alcohol. Lots of it.*

Thea was likely right, but I wouldn't leave my brother alone with his demons. I would confront them with him. "But you can retract your wings now. No one can take them from you if they're hidden."

Frazer ran a wretched hand through his raven hair. He looked like a wayward planet searching for its orbit. "They could be forced out of me. Trust me, I've counted the ways."

The heart dropped out of me. Because I knew how his mind worked. He'd likely played out every nightmarish scenario in minute detail.

"Maybe if you fly again, you could find the joy in it?" I suggested. "You could show me how it's done. I want you to teach me."

His face slackened, turning sheet-white. "I can't. I haven't tasted clouds in years. I have to relearn everything I forgot and build strength in the right muscles again. Even when I take to the wing, Adrianna would still be a better choice of teacher for you. I learned to fly by being forced off a cliff, and I refuse to do that to you."

Burning hell. "Who did that to you?"

Feigning indifference, he looked away as if he could create distance between us—between himself and that question. "My sire. He was a soldier through and through. A good male, but tough."

I wanted to argue that. Words to condemn his father were already written upon my tongue, but I swallowed them. They went down like globs of paper.

Frazer's gaze went over my head. "We should get going. Adrianna will be plucking our feathers out if we leave her waiting any longer."

My wings instinctively bristled at the suggestion.

"Ready?" he asked.

I agreed and fell into step beside him.

Our loping strides relaxed me. I tunneled inward and set to untangling what Frazer had revealed. I wasn't arrogant enough to think I could erase his trauma, but I had to do something. He'd freed me from death's noose. Now I had to try to free him, even if his cage was more complex and more difficult to spring open.

I unearthed an idea and burnished it. "Since we can't fly together yet, how about we run back to the lake with our wings out instead?"

His head angled toward me. "Do you think if we run fast enough we'll lift off?"

I poked my tongue out at him.

His night-blue eyes glowed. "All right, siska. You want to run, let's run."

Adrenaline fired into my untried veins. We bolted forward in the same breath. In a click, Frazer had rushed ahead, becoming a silver streak navigating leafy pillars with enviable feline skill.

He pushed me to go, go, go.

But the faster I went, the more air I sipped into powerful lungs. Troubled by the smells of a fragrant forest and wetted earth, I sneezed again and again. That wasn't my only problem. My mind couldn't keep up with my newfound strength and vitality. Soon, I stumbled.

I splayed my wings to save myself. The disturbed air currents flung me on my ass. Frazer doubled back to haul me up. *Don't think. Just move. Listen to your body, and it'll tell you what to do.*

He broke away. I followed him, shifting awareness from mind to body. Just meditating in motion. It wasn't a foreign sensation. I'd done it before when walking or running in nature.

In that mindset, I found myself flooded out with the primal instincts of an ancient species. I embraced them—embraced the nature written in blood and bone and wing. The wisdom there was infinite. It whispered what I might be capable of. To run alongside wild horses. To climb higher than any bird.

I was no longer a broken song with missing notes. I was a fae, free and whole. My body had at last aligned.

The urge to test my limits surged. The female, the beast in me, demanded more. I almost opened my wings, wanting to unshackle myself from the earth's ties. But if Frazer wasn't going to fly, it felt wrong to do it at this moment.

I easily leaped over lonely boulders and fallen logs. I swerved this way, that way, my long legs devouring the distance to the lake.

We arrived at Ewa's stony beach exhilarated.

Lungs and heart barely stressed, I absorbed the scene with sharp eyes.

The island with its gate to the light court had vanished. Now the lake was a smooth, undisturbed expanse, reflecting the iron-fire sky above.

Every undine had disappeared except for my aunt, who was speaking with Hazel farther down the shore, their voices too low for my fae ears to catch.

I shifted my attentions to Adrianna, Cai, and Liora who stood opposite me, idling near their bags and weapons.

My mouth popped open. "What in the starry hell happened to you?"

CHAPTER 6
ON THE SUBJECT OF MAGIC

I stared and stared at Cai and Adrianna. "I don't understand."
"I'm guessing you weren't forewarned," Adrianna remarked.
I glanced at Frazer.
"This is their tale to tell."
Fine. I turned toward Adrianna. She had removed her cropped jacket; underneath was a halter top sectioned with leather and a lightweight fabric. This sleeveless style was perfect for viewing the fresh ink that embroidered three-quarters of her arms in a latticework reminiscent of a beautiful pair of evening gloves.

"This happened during the spell, didn't it?" I said, recalling how at one point the light emanating from the tree-gate had touched all five of us.

"That's right," Adrianna said briskly. "While you and Frazer were on the island, each of us"—she gestured to Cai and Liora—"heard a god in our heads. For me, it was The Smith, Hercule. He said my ancestors were metallurgy witches—which I already knew—and that their gift had been reawakened in me."

"What's metallurgy?"
"I can control metal," she clarified.
Adrianna picked her sword up from where she'd rested it against a log. She held her hand over the steel hilt without touching it. The blade

slowly inched up out of its sheath. A few seconds later, it slammed back down with an adder's hiss. She glared down at her blade disapprovingly. "I suppose I'll need practice before I can gut Morgan with her own sword."

"You'll tell us before you start practicing, won't you?" Cai said, fighting a smile.

Adrianna arched a shapely brow at him. "Scared?"

"Fucking terrified," Cai quipped.

My curiosity got louder. "D'you know why your new markings match your old tattoos?"

"I'm guessing it's because these"—Adrianna motioned to the silver patterning on her brow and collarbone—"are also witch markings. I got them to honor my isä's memory. They belonged to his ancestor's clan back before the metallurgy magic died out of our line."

Our pack took a somber, reflective pause. I broke the silence by rounding on Cai and saying, "Your turn."

Cai's eyes tapered in jest. "Should I get my shirt off?" He tugged on the hem of his short-sleeved V-neck. "Then you can appreciate the full effect."

Eyebrows climbing, I indulged him. "Go on, then."

"All right." He winked at me. "Just for you."

Cai took a handful of shirt between his shoulder blades and pulled it over his head in one clean move.

"What do you think of my sexy new look?" He spread his arms wide.

Liora groaned in mock despair while I perused Cai. The tattoo on his right hand had stretched up and over to his pectoral muscle. The swirling lines showed air in its weakest and strongest forms. From gust to gale to whirlwind.

My eyes dipped lower. That was when I spotted it—a spiral of script on his ribs. Shock charged in. "You've got the same marking as me and Frazer."

He followed the center of my gaze. "Oh. Yeah. We all do."

Adrianna and Liora confirmed that by tugging their own shirts up their bodies.

"We were hoping the gods might've told you what it means," Cai said, pulling his shirt back on.

"They didn't, but I can ask them now."

Three confused expressions met that remark.

"I'll explain about Thea and Zola," Frazer told me. "You do what you need to do."

Gratified, I nodded.

Thea? Zola? Can you tell us what our shared marks mean?

A blunt *Ask Sandrine,* from Zola.

Thea was more generous. *It would be better if you heard this from her. That way your pack can listen and ask questions together.*

I switched my attentions outward. There, Frazer was telling the others about our experience on the island. Once he'd explained that the twining was permanent and that the goddesses were my teachers, I chimed in. "I just asked them about the marks, and they said to talk to Sandrine."

Each of us glanced at my aunt, who was still conversing with Hazel. I decided not to disturb her, not while there was more to be asked and answered among the five of us.

I centered on Cai. "So, your arm tattoo—did you get an explanation for that?"

He huffed. "Yeah. Aeryn, the Sky God, decided to pop into my head for a visit. We didn't have a particularly long conversation, and to be quite honest, he was kind of a dick." Zola's laughter rang out in my mind as Cai continued. "But the short of it is, I've become an air elemental."

"Okay." I drew out that word. "And what's an elemental?"

"It's just a more powerful version of being air-blessed. The only thorn in the rose is that my healing gift's gone." His mouth turned down at a corner, but there was no sadness tinging his voice.

"Aeryn took your healing gift?" I said, indignant.

"No." Cai rocked his head, moving what, in the last month, had become a longer mop of frizzy curls around his face. "Aeryn said that what was happening to me wasn't his doing. It was—and I quote—the magical forces governing the universe." Cai wiggled his fingers, recreating that dramatically. "Then he told me that to be an elemental, my affinity needed to be undiluted. Being earth-blessed was an obstacle to that, so it had to go bye-bye. It's no great loss, to be honest. I was never much of a natural healer. I've always preferred to rely on remedies to treat people."

Adrianna scowled at Cai. "You never said whether becoming an elemental gave you other air-blessed affinities—mind-reading, for instance."

Cai gave her a long look. "Are you worried I'll read your mind?"

"Can you?" she demanded, her eyes talon-sharp.

"No." Cai stuffed his hands in his pockets. "I can't tell what you're thinking."

His gaze left her. It felt dismissive. Totally unlike him. I had a sense it was to hide hurt, disappointment, or some other emotion he didn't want to show.

My heart ached for his unrequited affections. But there was nothing I could do for him, so I turned to Liora. I wanted to know what she had gone through during the spell. She appeared unchanged, apart from the mark on her ribs.

"Li, which god spoke to you? What did they say?"

"Before we get into that, can I hug you?"

I smiled, and we moved for each other.

Meeting in the middle, we embraced. Errant red curls and her floral scent itched my nose. I stopped breathing in an effort to fend off the sneezes.

"I was so scared for you," she whispered in my ear.

I squeezed her tighter. Liora squeaked, releasing a bit of squished air. Alarmed, I let her go. "Did I hurt you?"

Her laughter put me in mind of a singing wind chime. "No. You just took me by surprise."

Unconvinced, I gave her a searching look.

"I'm fine. Really," she insisted, her smile reassuring.

I still swore not to underestimate my strength again.

"Your eyes are amazing by the way," Liora remarked.

I deflected that compliment. "I'm not sure why they changed color. Maybe they'll go back to being blue one day."

When did you find out about them?

Briefly, I met Frazer's stare. *I looked in a mirror while I was changing.*

He nodded.

I turned back to Liora, who was looking at my feathers.

"And your wings," she said. "They're beautiful."

I felt an urge to fan my wings. I labeled that as some strange fae instinct and left it at that.

"It's true. You look almost as good as me," Cai teased. "But what about your baby fangs? Are you going to give us a peek at those?"

"No." I raised a hand over my mouth.

"Come, come, don't be shy." Cai strode over and tussled with me, trying to wrench my hand down.

"Mean." I playfully pushed at him only for him to stumble back onto his ass. Startled, a laugh popped out of me.

I reached out an arm. He batted it away and jumped back up, grinning.

"Sorry," I mumbled, failing to keep a straight face.

"Don't worry." He dusted off the back of his trousers, adding, "I can handle it a bit rough—plenty of practice."

My nose scrunched up. "I don't want to know."

"I don't know what you're implying." Cai assumed an innocent expression, widening his eyes for effect.

I hummed a teasing sound.

"So, Liora, what did the gods tell you?" Frazer asked, nudging us back to where we were in the conversation before the distractions.

"I heard Briar, the Goddess of Healing." Liora's gaze shifted between Frazer and me. "She said I'd become a more powerful witch, but only once the binding is removed."

I could tell she was disappointed. That made me bleed sadness. "At least Hazel can work on removing your bindings now."

"Actually," Liora started, her voice pitching higher than usual, "Briar told me that you were the only witch I should trust to set me free."

Panic swept in. I willed my voice to remain steady. "I'd do anything to help you, Li. But I don't know anything about magic or spells. I could end up hurting you."

Strong, but quiet, she came back with, "You won't."

Her faith slayed and terrified me. Surely a skilled witch like Hazel would be a better option for her?

Thea spoke to the doubts in my head. *Briar is right to place her trust in you.*

Before I could argue that, I saw Liora encircled by angry-red ribbons. They tightened like the pulled strings of a corset. Her head got a touch heavier, that stoop in her shoulders more pronounced.

The vision faded from view as quickly as it had arrived. *What was that? What did I just see?*

Liora's bindings, Thea explained. *Your waterlight enabled you to see that which was hidden, and it is with waterlight that you'll remove her bindings.*

From there, Thea and Zola started talking rapidly, one after the other. Somewhere in the midst of their explanation, Cai and Adrianna asked me what was wrong.

I vaguely registered Frazer telling them to be quiet. He had guessed what was happening, and that my focus had to remain with Zola and Thea.

The goddesses chatter done, I breathed to steady my mind and shake off the sensation of being overwhelmed.

Once I'd composed myself, I faced Liora. "I have the ability to erode other forms of magic with waterlight, so yes, in theory, I can break your bindings."

Liora's spring-green eyes brightened. Before she could respond, Adrianna spoke up. "It's waterlight then? That's the form your light magic took?"

"That. Plus sun, moon, and star," Frazer said, his pride plain in the curve of his lip.

Three faces shone with shock and awe. I wanted to add that we hadn't confirmed I had all four light disciplines. Then Zola snorted in my head. *Really?*

There's no doubt you possess all four, Thea added gently.

Rutting hell. I blew out a tense bit of air.

"Out with it, then." Cai rubbed his palms together in apparent glee. "I want to see this." He gestured to my palms as if awaiting an impressive light show.

"I haven't learned anything yet," I told them.

His features didn't lose their eagerness. "Did the goddesses give you any idea when you can remove Li's bindings?"

I wilted like a flower with too much sun. "I can't say for sure."

Cai kept on. "It's just ... Are we talking days, weeks, or months?"

Pressure constricted my chest.

"Didn't you hear her?" Frazer viewed Cai through glacial eyes. "She doesn't know."

I suppressed a shiver as my brother's demeanor shifted into something entirely lethal. Even the air surrounding him changed. I felt as though a cold wind had just brushed my cheeks, signaling a turning in the weather, a storm beginning.

Hoping to stop the brewing argument, I said, "Zola and Thea said they were going to train me through my dreams. They think I'll retain more information when I'm asleep, which means I should learn my abilities faster than other witches. I know it's not enough—"

"Yes, it is," Liora cut in, raising her voice. "You can't be expected to know this stuff yet. Whatever happens to me is my fault. I'm the one who agreed to the stupid binding in the first place."

My chest splintered.

I peeked at Cai for his reaction. He stared at nothing, his jaw tight, his expression frozen in frustration and concern. I didn't blame him for being impatient with me. How could I? He had a right to ask and a right to be worried.

The heaviest silence I'd ever known followed.

Adrianna pointed her chin at Frazer's hand. "You haven't told us what your ink means yet."

Frazer held up his left hand, showing off the silvery-blue band encircling his wrist. "Waterlight." Then he pushed up the sleeve on his right arm, displaying the circle of moons. "Moonlight."

Adrianna punched out a crabby exhale. "Such a detailed retelling."

That erased the lingering tension. Cai, Liora, and I chuckled under our breath.

Frazer jerked his shoulder up. "What do you want me to say? I've had magic in my veins for about an hour. I've no notion of what I can do yet."

He wasn't the only one. We'd never had a detailed list of abilities—light magic was too rare.

Zola proved eager to fill in the gaps, at least in regards to waterlight and moonlight.

Tiny pulses of shock traveled through me during her explanation. When she was done, I grinned at Frazer. "Zola says moonlight wielders can create shields against magical or physical attacks."

Frazer remained unmoved. "That'll be useful."

"Actually, *I* got that part. You inherited another variation. You can use its properties to bend light." I silently *he-heed*. "You can become invisible."

His eyebrow flicked up. Likely the only shock he'd show.

Cai whistled appreciatively. "I've got to admit, I'm jealous of that one."

"I doubt you'd want to become invisible, brother," Liora said, her grin impish.

Cai rubbed his scruffy chin in mock contemplation. "Mm. You might be right."

Zola's laughter got distracting. I might end up on fire for tuning out a god, but I thought it worth the risk.

"And what of the waterlight?" Frazer asked. "Can I break Liora's chains?"

If only he could.

"No. You don't have that ability. But we both attained a type of second sight." The question mark written on his brow had me continuing. "They think I'll see through illusions and spellwork. And you'll be able to see the future."

Everyone processed.

My attention locked on Frazer. His feathers fluttered in the late afternoon breeze and his dark gaze was dipped and distant, shining with the unknown. He looked like a mystery embodied.

"What is it?" I asked him.

His body shook as if casting off an unwanted thought. "Nothing much—just seeing the future never appealed to me. I'll make it work, though."

That niggled at me; I was certain there was more to his reservations. But that wasn't new. I usually only got half the story with him.

A scrunch of stone nagged at my ear. Frazer, Adrianna, and I swiveled around.

Hazel and Sandrine were moving to join us. Finally. Our pack knitted into a jagged line, awaiting them.

My petite aunt approached. She embraced me—her grip proved stronger than expected. "Sorry for not coming over sooner, but I had a lot to discuss with Hazel."

I nodded and released her.

Hazel's bloodshot eyes flitted over me and Frazer. "I'm so relieved to see you both looking well."

"Thank you," I said, and I meant it. "You saved my and my brother's life."

"I will always help you as best as I can. You're Dain and Sati's tilä—their daughter," Hazel said solemnly. "I consider you kin."

My heart lodged itself in my throat. "I don't know what to say."

"You needn't say anything." She extended her wings. "I'm going to retire to my campsite now. I'll be back before you all leave."

Hazel bobbed her head in farewell. She ascended, striking out for the surrounding woodland.

"I can't tell you how happy it makes me to see you like this, Serena," said Sandrine.

"Being a fae?"

She denied that with a rock of her head. "Healthy."

"Is Serena still the name you wish to go by?" That abrupt change of subject came from Frazer.

I looked at him. Had he lost his mind? "What are you talking about?"

"When your parents spoke to us, they used the name Ena, and it made you happy. Do you want us to call you that instead?"

"I don't know." I got stuck in the cobwebs of my past. "As a child, I loved being called Ena by my mother. I actually hated Serena, because the people in my village would tell us that with a name like that, I was sure to be obedient."

Adrianna loosed a disgusted growl.

"Why didn't you say?" Cai asked, confused. "We wouldn't have called you Serena had we known."

"Because my mother died, and then I only got called Ena when Halvard was angry with me. I wasn't so keen on it after that."

Sandrine muttered a word that sounded suspiciously like, "Ass." She continued in a normal voice. "Sati would've hated that your name, even a shortened version, had been turned into something that pained you. If you can reclaim it for yourself, do."

"You know, Ena's actually a phrase in old Kaeli?" Adrianna told me.

"It is?"

My focus shifted toward Frazer, more out of habit than anything.

He shook his head. "I didn't know. I've only picked up a few words here and there over the years. I'm not up to learning the entire language."

Cai scoffed at his droll tone. "Don't shovel dung on our doorsteps. You're the smartest one here, and you know it."

Not one for compliments, Frazer grew silent and motionless. A crane in water.

"So what does Ena mean?" I prompted Adrianna.

"Light of Life."

Frazer nodded. "That fits."

Emotion swelled, closing my throat and flushing my cheeks.

"Well remembered," Sandrine told Adrianna. "Sati and I were taught the old language. But I must confess, I'd completely forgotten what Ena meant."

"Yes, but you were probably taught eons ago," Adrianna said.

Sandrine raised her eyebrows at that throwaway comment. "Are you saying I look old?"

Adrianna's scowl was equal parts confusion and defensiveness. "No. You look younger than me. I simply meant ... Well, call it fae instinct, but you feel old."

Amusement sparked in my aunt's jade-green eyes. "I see." Sandrine turned to me. "Is it to be Ena, then?"

"Yes," I said without too long of a pause.

"Now that's out of the way, perhaps we can discuss the marks," Frazer said.

He raised his top to show my aunt the rib tattoo. The rest of us did the same. Sandrine stared and stared. "I haven't seen that mark in a very long time."

"You don't seem surprised to see it, though," Liora observed.

"I'm not." Sandrine's voice was soft, but it traveled. "The firstborn reached out to me when the gate was open. They warned me that this would happen."

The five of us traded foreboding glances.

Sandrine walked over to where Cai, Liora, and Adrianna's rucksacks and weapons were still piled alongside my kaskan and quiver. There, she perched on a log and gestured to the ground before her. "Please sit, all of you. This will take some time to explain."

CHAPTER 7
THE KNIGHTS RISE AGAIN

Sandrine waited patiently as the rest of us got comfortable. Cai and Liora were quick to settle opposite her. Adrianna and Frazer moved slower, and with a wildcat's tension coiled in their muscles.

I was the last one standing as I struggled to cross my wings properly. Once I'd succeeded in tucking them under-and-over, I placed my weapons on the ground and used my rucksack as a butt cushion.

With the five of us a willing audience, Sandrine began.

"The tattoo you all bear was once used to identify members of an extinct coven of witches referred to as the knights. I do not know who or what force chose its members, but the coven existed to keep the peace between the peoples of this world and the firstborn. This was back when the gods traveled freely around Aldar and the continent, and every group was expected to obey a set of rules to prevent conflict. If this covenant was broken by anyone—human, fae, sprite, or god—the knights would decide on and mete out the punishment."

"How in a witch's tit could they punish gods?" Cai exclaimed.

That was what I wanted to know.

Sandrine rested her clasped hands on her lap. "Well, the mark could appear at any age, but when it did, it was often succeeded by an expansion or a triggering of new magical abilities, as you've just experienced. This made the knights stronger than the average witch."

"Moons, I haven't blushed this much in ages." Cai pretended to fan his face.

"Don't misunderstand me," Sandrine said, her notes edged with warning. "The coven couldn't have stood against all the gods on their own. But the coven had the support of the people. That was what made it a legitimate threat."

"Then, how did the coven die out?" Frazer asked from my left side.

Sandrine's shoulders inched up. I had a mad urge to clap my hands over my ears when she continued. "Their decline was set in motion when the Dark King, Archon, decided to seize this world for himself."

That was a sharp turn for my mind to corner. The Dark King was the villain of countless tales. He was the devil that humans warded off with charms and rhymes. The idea that such an evil god had walked these lands filled my belly with ice and uneasiness.

"Are you saying that Archon killed the knights?" Adrianna said grimly.

Sandrine grimaced. "A great many of them, yes. Archon started what became known as the War of the Courts. Balor, the Light King, led the Allied Forces against Archon's horde for twenty long years. In the end, the dark court lost, and they were locked away in their world." A bracing breath. "Unfortunately, closing up the dark court while the light court remained open would've been in violation of the covenant. Balor was left with no choice but to leave with his people and shut their gate. As a consequence, the gods from both courts have remained sealed away for almost a thousand years."

Gods' tooth, I cursed silently.

Sandrine let that sink in. "The war doesn't explain why a new generation of knights failed to appear, though. I believe that to be because the magic fueling the coven's existence was tied to need, and with the firstborn no longer interacting with our world, your kind were no longer required and the line dwindled. As far as I'm aware, the knights of that age are all gone." Sadness seemed to drip from her.

"So our marks appeared because a portal to the light court was opened?" Frazer asked Sandrine, his eyes shining, reflecting the early evening sky.

"That, and for the first time in a very long time, our world has witnessed and felt the power of the firstborn again," she said.

"But the gods and the portal are gone again—so will our marks disappear?" I heard Adrianna say on my far left.

"The mark is permanent." Sandrine's pensive gaze drifted over the placid lake. She wasn't looking at me—at any of us. "And it wouldn't have appeared to begin with if the coven weren't needed again."

"Auntie." I called her back from wherever her mind had wandered to. "Why does a world without the firstborn need the knights?"

Sandrine turned to face me. The movement seemed heavy, reluctant. "Because the seals over the gates were set to break after a thousand years, and the courts were closed nine hundred and ninety-nine years ago today."

I felt like a gutted pumpkin; I was being made hollow.

"Fuck me with a broom," Cai uttered.

I would've laughed if I'd had the capacity.

Frazer was short and sharp. "Why were the locks built to fail?"

"Because they couldn't be closed forever," Sandrine explained, her voice rising and falling with a lullaby cadence, as if she could somehow soften the blow. "The firstborn are pure incarnations of nature and magic, and this world needs that energy. Without it, everything declines, generation by generation. Witches aren't born with as much power. Fae experience dwindling birth rates, and humans become more susceptible to disease."

"How is it possible I've never heard about any of this?" Adrianna asked, a scowl in her voice. "I've never read anything about this so-called Courts War."

On the back of a small sigh, Sandrine said, "That's because Balor had all physical records recounting that era destroyed. After that, people could only remember the firstborn's names and their powers, enough to write stories about them, but the war faded from people's minds. The surviving knights and creatures like me were the only ones who could recall the details. It's likely Balor spelled our world to forget."

"Why, though?" Liora voiced from beside Frazer. "What purpose would that serve?"

Sandrine shook her head. "I wish I knew."

If anyone could answer this riddle, it was Thea and Zola. *Do you know why your father did it?*

No answer.

"Where is the dark gate?" Frazer asked.

Sandrine's focus landed on him. "The undines were only entrusted with the location of the light gate."

Liora added, "What about the moon court? Was that locked too?"

"No, it wasn't." Sandrine laid her hands out flat, showing us her palms. "The reason for the light and the dark court's existence is to bring balance to the greater cosmic scale. You close one, and the other gains more influence in this realm, and that never turns out well for anybody. But the moon court was always neutral. It was also needed to act as a bridge into the other worlds. Without it, the dead wouldn't have a way of moving on into the light and dark courts. And we'd have had a great many unhappy spirits trapped here, like a cork in a bottle."

Cosmic scale? Bridge between worlds? My head hurt.

A troubled kind of quiet fell and gnawed at us.

"Just to be clear, you're saying that in a year the Dark King will walk free, and we're the ones throwing his welcome party?" Adrianna said, her notes clipped.

I knew the look on Sandrine's face—pity. "Yes."

That confirmation passed through our pack and connected us in a shared fate; shoulder to shoulder, we tensed, fidgeted, and exchanged grim looks.

"Why in the seven seas didn't they kill Archon back then?" Adrianna demanded, her purring accent deepening into a chesty growl. "Why pass on the responsibility to us?"

Sandrine answered that with a challenge and a question. "Do you think killing a god is easy?"

"So we're stuck with a god we can't kill or lock away—is that correct?" Frazer leveled that question at Sandrine.

Cai stretched his legs. "It definitely sounds like a challenge."

His sarcasm made me and Liora huff.

"Things aren't quite that bad," Sandrine said. "Persephone, Goddess of Fate, discovered how to destroy Archon toward the end of the Court War."

I did not like her expression. It was that of someone readying to deliver unpleasant news.

"Persephone had Balor forge four stones, each of which possessed a branch of light magic. One of those stones is around your neck." Sandrine nodded to me.

Recoiling slightly, I grasped the blue gem. This tiny thing had the power to kill a god? I suddenly felt a shadow at my back, a great wave of change that threatened to flood me out.

Sandrine's voice was tight, almost breathless. "The stones' power can be tapped into by any magical being who possesses the same magic as the stones. So, as a creature of waterlight, I could use the waterstone, but the sunstone would be useless in my hands. However, if a witch could command each stone ... well, with that much magic at their disposal, they'd have the strength to kill the Dark King."

My aunt stared at me, her expression shouting *I'm sorry.*

Don't say it, I begged her with my eyes.

"That person didn't exist a millennia ago. But Persephone foretold of the day when she would. It's you, Ena."

A lurching sensation jolted my middle. Like I'd missed a step and fallen down a never-ending staircase.

Heart in mouth, I fought the hysteria buzzing around my chest. How had my life become Slayer of the Dark King? I tried to picture myself as a mighty warrior blasting that evil bastard into a million pieces and failed disastrously. My imaginary self kept tripping over her feet and screaming in horror.

I couldn't steady my breathing. The air was thinning, my vision shrinking to spots and wheels. I pressed my eyes shut, fighting the dizziness.

Sounds of movement disturbed my right ear. I smelled grass and spring roses. Liora was there, taking the empty spot on my right. "You're not in this alone. We've been marked as knights too. That means our whole pack is responsible for stopping Archon."

My lashes swept up. "I don't want any of you near the Dark King."

Adrianna expelled a sharp, croaky noise. A crow's laugh. "As if you could stop us."

Thoughts of how I could do exactly that marched through my head.

"Besides, En, don't you remember what Maggie I-Can't-Keep-A-

Secret OneEye told us?" Cai looked around Frazer to meet my eye. "She said our pack was brought together for a reason. Well, now we know why. It's so we can fight together, like the knights of old did."

"Only we'll be better than them," Adrianna said sternly. "For a start, we won't all die."

"Yeah, fuck dying," Cai added in an offhand way.

Ancestors help us.

My brother's hand clamped down on my left shoulder. *If one of us was destined to destroy that monster, would you step aside and let us handle it alone?*

I gave my brother a sideways gaze.

Canny bastard.

He made no reply. He was waiting for my confession.

No, I wouldn't.

His face was a blank canvas that any painter would fear to mark. But I sensed what was under the surface. And there was no doubt in him. He believed and trusted that we could do this.

I thought to warn him anyway. *You realize that if I go up against Archon, there's more than a good chance I'll be killing both of us?*

He released my shoulder. *Then, we die doing something important. I'm no hero, but even I can admit that's a good end—a good death.*

I pushed panic away with the force of my iron will. *I guess it's us against Archon, then.*

"There is more to say, but evening is drawing in," Sandrine remarked. "And if we're not to be talking in the dark, we'll need a fire to warm ourselves by." Her head lowered; her eyes showed me sympathy and kindness. "And I think we could all use a breather."

Adrianna's scathing chuff wordlessly said *You think?*

Cai hopped up like his feet contained springs. "Adi and I can scavenge kindling. Frazer, En—will you clear some space for a pit?"

Frazer offered a curt nod, and I said, "Sure."

Cai offered Adrianna a hand to get up. "Coming?"

She stood without his help. "Let's go," she said, flexing her legs to wake them up.

As Cai and Adrianna set off toward the forest, I crouched beside Frazer. There, we dug out a cauldron-sized indent in the soil. Liora pitched in, despite looking feverish. Meanwhile, my aunt closed her eyes; her forehead creased in concentration, she swayed side to side in the cooling air. I fancied she looked like a shaman communing with the dead.

Cai and Adrianna returned with armfuls of twigs. After they laid the foundations for the fire, Frazer chucked them a piece of flint from his bag. From a single spark, Cai birthed a blaze of ruby and citrine. Those tongues of flame scattered embers up into a sky that had lost summer's warmth, only to gain a smudge of indigo and a sprinkling of distant stars.

One by one, we unrolled our sleeping bags and placed ourselves next to the fire. We stayed close enough that we could see one another's faces. Frazer and Liora sat on either side of me, and the others book-ended us.

"You said there was more to say—now would be the time, yes?" Frazer said to Sandrine.

"Yes." Her eyes fluttered open. "We should discuss the other stones you'll need to defeat Archon. They must be found and recovered before he walks among us again."

Adrianna interrupted. "For something to be found, it has to be lost."

"That's right," Sandrine said, her tone rueful. "Before he left, Balor entrusted the stones to his allies. Each person was tasked with passing their stone on to the witch with four light disciplines, either directly or through a descendant. But over the years, these people have disappeared or died, and their stone was lost with them. The undines have tried to see where they are, but our Sight has been blocked."

Disappointment swooped into my gut.

Sandrine watched me. "I do, however, have some information on the sunstone because my father—your grandfather, Atlas—was chosen to be its bearer. The last time I saw him, I was still young and living in Asitar, and my father was preparing to fight a warlord going by the name of Abraxus."

That name provoked reactions from all sides. Adrianna and Cai cursed loudly. Frazer and Liora froze like startled rabbits.

"Goldwyn warned us about him." My stomach clenched into a nervous ball. "She said he planned on invading Aldar—is that true?"

"I heard what she said when I was in the waterstone," Sandrine reminded me. "And much of what she believed was flawed. Abraxus's motives for invading Aldar are a lot bigger than she supposed."

Sandrine grew rigid in the shoulders. "Abraxus was around during the War of the Courts. He lost everything to Archon. So when the gates closed and denied him a chance at revenge, he dedicated himself to building an army that could one day match Archon's. He hunted down strong witches, particularly light-casters, and compelled them into serving him." Shadows entered her eyes. "He also became obsessed with possessing the stones since he didn't think they were safe with anybody else … At least that was what my father believed."

Frazer followed up with, "Do you think Abraxus took the stone off Atlas?"

"No." Sandrine continued, sounding as bleak as the dawning moon. "My mother told me that Atlas hid the sunstone somewhere in Asitar before he died in battle. Unfortunately, he didn't tell me or her where he put it."

Her mood lowered mine. "I'm sorry about Atlas."

She managed a ghost of a smile. "It was centuries ago now, but thank you."

"What would Abraxus do if he found a stone?" Frazer questioned Sandrine. "Would he give it to Ena?"

"Honestly, I'm not sure," Sandrine admitted, her forehead crinkling. "He couldn't use its magic. But as long as he had it, he could use it as leverage over Ena."

Frazer's growl transformed into a cloud of smoke in the twilit air. "How did Abraxus do it? If he had no magic, how could he bring such powerful witches to heel? How do we stop him from doing it to Ena?"

"Oh, he has magic," Sandrine said tensely. "But we can't sense or scent it on him because he's not a witch or a fae, despite having the appearance of the latter."

My aunt paused. I didn't have the heart to hurry her.

"Who or what is he, then?" Adrianna asked as she fed the greedy fire more wood.

"He is a firstborn—the only one to remain here after the gates' closure," Sandrine said, sounding too calm. "His true name is Abel, otherwise known as Archon's son and a prince of the dark court."

My friends' responses grew distant. I'd mentally tumbled down a rabbit hole, and it wasn't until a small hand grasped mine that I landed back on solid earth. I looked at Liora. Her fire-washed features showed horror and resolve.

I wanted to smile at her, but my face had frozen.

"This is crazy." Cai rubbed at his face. As if he thought he might be asleep and wanted to wake up from the nightmare he'd found himself in.

"I know a bit more in regards to the sunstone." Sandrine focused on me, a softness cornering her eyes. "There's someone who's already hunting for it. Sefra."

Wait. "Why is my sister after it?"

"Before his death, your father had a vision of you and the stones. He saw what you'd have to do with them and who you would need to fight. That knowledge was entrusted to your mother, who then told me and your sister. That's why your mother wanted you to go east. To find Sefra, and the sunstone." Her face was suddenly struck with loss.

My mind filtered most of that out, but one thing stuck at the bottom like rocks in a sieve: Sandrine was Sefra's aunt too. That hadn't really sunk in until now. It became an effort not to ask about my sister—about what she was like.

"Hang on." Adrianna waved a confused hand about. "I thought Sefra went to the continent to search for ways to overthrow Morgan?"

"That was one of the things she hoped to accomplish. She thought she might find allies there." Sandrine ran her hands along her thighs, smoothing out her dress. "But her main reason for leaving these shores was to find the sunstone."

"What about the other stones?" Frazer asked, his nails punching into his crossed legs. "Do you have any information on them?"

"The starstone was lost long ago." She stopped for a second—a long second. The light of memory shone in her eyes when she continued. "But the moonstone's bearer was the first High Witch of the Crescent. Upon her death, she passed it on to Dain, her successor."

My mind groaned under the weight of another revelation. "If my father had it and he knew what I would become, why didn't he give it to you or Mama?"

Sandrine looked as if she was holding in a sigh. "He said the moonstone was needed where it was, and that to disturb it would destabilize the land. I think he felt that the longer it was left alone, the better. He wouldn't even tell me of its whereabouts. I think he feared entrusting the information to anyone in case it got out somehow."

I wrung my sticky hands.

"However, there might be a way to find the moonstone and the starstone ... There is a very old, very powerful mirror in Mysaya." Sandrine focused on Frazer. "Have you heard of it?"

No expression. "There are a lot of mirrors."

"None like this." Sandrine's attention dove to the fire. "This one lies in the caverns beneath the castle. It can amplify a seer's power to divine the past, the present, and the future. However, it is incredibly volatile. The only person to have escaped staring into its depths unscathed is Dain. His gift for moonlight protected his mind from corruption, and his waterlight guided the visions he received."

I thought I could see where she was going with this. She wanted us to break into Mysaya, a city that had been captured by Morgan. I'd reached my limit for fear and shock. Now, I just felt the mad desire to laugh.

"And with only a year before Archon rises, we must act upon multiple fronts if we're to survive," Sandrine said, her stressed gaze settling on Frazer again. "That is why I believe if we're to find the stones before Archon is freed, you must head to Mysaya while the others leave for the continent."

The breath went right out of my lungs. Apparently, I could still feel shock.

Frazer's verdict was swift. "You want me to watch my sister sail off to a dangerous land where an unhinged god hunts for light-wielders. Are you fucking mad?"

Sandrine's expression held sympathy, but not agreement. "Frazer, you are one of only two people who can wrestle truth from that mirror, and unlike Ena, you can get inside Mysaya undetected." She concentrated on a spot above his head. "I can already see glimpses of you using your new ability. You have a gift for invisibility—"

"I know," he said, sharp and cutting.

She continued as if he hadn't spoken. "So moving through enemy territory should be a lot less risky for you. Don't you agree?"

No one answered her.

Sandrine addressed Frazer. "I swear, sendrié, I wouldn't suggest this unless I believed it was the best way to protect everyone."

"Do not presume to call me your nephew," Frazer said, the tiny pulse in his neck flickering angrily.

Blankness washed over Sandrine's face. "Very well. Let me put it to you this way. Ena doesn't need you acting as her shadow on the continent. And I think you know that. But if those stones aren't found in time, Archon will enslave the world, starting with her."

That little speech had me livid. How could she ask this of him? To walk across Aurora, hunted and alone, to sneak into a city occupied by our enemies, to enter a castle that haunted his worst nightmares. For that was where Linus, the long-since-dead Aurorian King, had ordered Frazer's wings to be cleaved as a punishment for warning the Sami—the court's elite warriors—that they were to be traded to Morgan. The Sami had fled rather than serve her.

The thought of Frazer facing those memories upset my stomach.

My blood roared. "You're guilting him into risking everything because he might see something worthwhile?" I lifted my chin. "That's not good enough. He could be captured or killed. Then we'd both die, and Archon destroys the world anyway."

"It's unfair and it's dangerous, but it remains the best option." Sandrine's regretful gaze traveled from me to Frazer. "Back when you were deciding whether to kin bond with my niece, I spoke to you through the waterstone. Do you remember what I said?"

No answer.

Sandrine paid no heed to that. "I told you to trust your instincts when it came to Ena. Now with a clear head, ask yourself—which path protects your siska more?"

That manipulation made me want to throw things at her. To bite her. Because I felt Frazer through the walls of my pained heart. He was quietening his emotions, pushing them aside. I sensed his mind running like lightning. He was thinking this through, looking at every angle of every plan.

I couldn't bear it. *Brata?*

I hate it, but I think she might be right.

Emotion choked me viciously. *Just please tell me you're choosing this because you think it's what's best for the world and not to protect me?*

I can't do that. His honest gaze pinned me. *I'm not like you or the others. I'm not a true knight. Yes, there was a time when I would've died for a stranger or a king, but I've seen too much cruelty and too little kindness since then. I will do this. I'll go to Mysaya but it's for you and our pack. Not the world.*

An awful heaviness lined my bones and made them ache. *You don't need to do this for me. We can figure something else out.*

He gave me a slanted smile. *I'm your brata. No matter how powerful you get, I'll always want to protect you.*

Heart twisting, I couldn't get my throat, tongue, or lips to work. So I nodded. Because deep down in parts of myself I wanted to rebel against, I saw the logic in Sandrine's plan. And if going our separate ways led to Frazer locating the other stones, what I wanted paled in comparison to that.

Frazer faced Sandrine. "I'll go to Mysaya."

"Shit." Cai placed his elbows on his knees, his head in his hands.

Liora leaned against me, arm to arm. It was a cold comfort.

An apology in her eyes, Sandrine nodded at Frazer. "Then we'll leave this conversation here." She met each of our stares, some less friendly than others. "Tomorrow I'll take you along the old fae road that leads out of Lake Ewa. It's long been forgotten by everyone other than the undines. The shortcut should help keep the spiders off your tails."

"We're headed to Nasiri. Did you know that?" I asked, unsure of how much she'd witnessed this last month.

A nod. "I've been awake for everything. I was just too weak to contact you."

"How long will it take us to get to Nasiri using this road?" Frazer asked.

"The old roads are faster. It should take less than a day this way."

"Good."

Sandrine frowned at Frazer. "Are you still headed to Nasiri?"

Frazer's voice became a morning frost. "I'm not leaving her tomorrow. I'll go after she's boarded a boat and not a second sooner."

Sandrine fell into a wise silence.

From there, a stilted mood permeated the air. What did you do after such a life-altering conversation? The answer, it turned out, was to go on as before. We had empty bellies that needed to be filled. We focused on that.

As I rationed out a portion of cheese, crackers, and fruit for myself, I observed my aunt walking to the water's edge. She tilted her face up to where the pale clouds attended a freshly minted moon. In that moment of statuesque stillness and distant expression, I saw more of her true self. Of the unearthly undine.

"Is there anything I can do to help you with all this?" Liora asked, disturbing me from my reverie.

I met her troubled features. "Thanks, but no. I'm ... I'm fine."

She raised a dark red eyebrow. "You're fine?"

I admitted that was a lie with a close-lipped laugh. "Okay, no, I'm not. But I'm also not falling apart. I think I'm so overwhelmed that I can't process any of it. I'm not sure I want to."

A weak, knowing smile was my reply.

I turned to sating my hunger with measly, stale food. I felt sure I'd commit any number of sins to taste something delicious again. This conversation—this whole day—had left me in dire need of comfort food.

Pitiful meal done, I removed my boots and climbed into my bedroll. After testing different positions, I gathered my wings in and settled on my side.

I closed my eyes, yet my mind refused to calm. Too much adrenaline.

Without conversation, my new senses opened up. Everything rushed in. The hoot of an owl as it hunted, the shrill bark of a fox as it contacted its brethren, the chatter of bats as they flew under the slender moon. This went on and on. I gave up on sleeping.

Opening my eyes, I watched the stars and counted the outcasts—the ones tinted pink, yellow, and blue. I connected them up in my mind. For it must be a lonely business being a star, I thought. To hang around in the dark, forever separated from others of your kind. I'd been like that once, I realized. But no longer.

I was surrounded by four bodies. By the four stars in my constellation. Their breathing became a lullaby.

On the edge of much-needed sleep, voices pulled me back. I squinted across the low fire. Hazel and Sandrine stood near the tree line. Thank the stars for fae-hearing. I caught every word.

"You didn't have to leave," Sandrine said.

"I thought it might be a case of too many witches around a cauldron.

Besides, I had nothing to add to such a conversation." Hazel's accent had shifted subtly, hinting at a highborn status. "How could I? I was Sati's friend for centuries. Moons above, I was married to Dain. But they never told me about the stones or the gates or the locked-up gods. I've only learned about such things this past week. Sati even kept the fact that you were inside the necklace a secret."

My heart made room for Hazel. I'd known she'd once been married to my sire, and she'd cared enough about Sati to keep a portrait of her. To be kept in the dark about such things must've cut a deep wound.

Sandrine's soft words traveled over the crack and hiss of firewood. "They loved you, Hazel. But they feared what would happen when Morgan came for you—"

"Yes." Hazel crossed her arms and leaned in toward Sandrine. "And when Morgan tried to break into my mind, I let her. I let her have everything except the knowledge that I'd helped Sati and her unborn child. Then I begged and crawled so Morgan wouldn't dig through more of my memories. So don't you dare imply that I couldn't keep secrets."

Gods. I'd had no idea she'd done so much for me—for my kin.

Sandrine's shoulders drooped. "I know. You deserved more. You've done a lot for this family. For our family." A small offer of inclusion.

She got nothing in return.

"I hope you can forgive us one day," Sandrine added.

Hazel's gaze cut over to me and my pack. "I'm upset, but it doesn't change anything. I'll still do whatever I can to help their child. And her brother." Angling her head, she stared long at Frazer. "It's strange, but he reminds me of Dain."

Sandrine hummed her agreement. "He *is* like him. Just as clever, and as loyal as the tide is to the moon. When I first saw him through Serena's"—she shook her head—"I mean Ena's eyes, I suspected Fate's hand at work. Then they spoke to each other with just their minds, and I knew it to be so."

"Do you know how they did it?"

Sandrine glanced over at our recumbent forms. I met my aunt's gaze and realized that she'd figured out I was listening. "People blessed with waterlight can sometimes reflect and share thoughts if they've a will to. Though, it shouldn't have been possible for them to do what they did back then. For one, Frazer's power was latent and sleeping in his bloodline when they first talked, and Ena couldn't access her abilities."

Frazer had waterlight in his bloodline? I wondered at that, confused.

"Something tells me their pack will have accomplished all manner of impossible things before they're done," Hazel said, watching us.

"I think you're right," my aunt replied softly.

"Anyway"—Hazel looked at Sandrine—"I really only came to ask you when they'll be leaving."

Sandrine outlined our plan.

"Would it be all right if I traveled along the fae road with all of you?" Hazel asked. "I'll disembark for other parts once we reach its end."

"Of course you're welcome to come with us." Sandrine paused as if there was something else she wished to add. She didn't get the chance to continue. Hazel was already spinning on her heel and leaving for her camp in the woods.

Sandrine tried to catch my gaze again. I shut my eyes. I couldn't deal with my aunt right now.

I'm glad I remind them of Dain, Frazer said, whispering his thoughts. *He sounds like a worthy male to be compared to.*

You sneaky ass. You've been awake this whole time?

He didn't answer, but the foreign tug at the corner of my mouth made me think my other heartbeat might be smiling.

From there, I renewed my efforts to fall asleep. I counted both stars and breaths. It wasn't long before I tumbled down into darkness.

I was waking up in a coffin, nose and mouth filled with grave dirt.

That scene melded into another—Dimitri blaming me for his death.

Another switch occurred. Morgan's spiders stormed my old village, looking for Viola and John, the only people I cared about there. The warriors did what killers do best. End lives.

Frazer materialized in the middle of the slaughter. He extended a hand. Waiting for me.

I hesitated, looking around at the battle. Cai, Liora, and Adrianna were here now, fending off the invaders, as valiant as always. I had to help them, didn't I? I had to be strong.

Go to sleep, sweet one, murmured Thea from the recesses of my mind.

Zola, her sister, added, *Be strong in the morning.*

"Siska. Come. This isn't real. It's just a nightmare." Frazer kept secrets, but he wouldn't lie about this.

My fear ebbed, and I saw this for what it was. Smoke and mirrors.

I went to my brother. With a shepherding wing, he steered me away. Peace found me.

CHAPTER 8
A FORK IN THE ROAD

"Ena? Ena. Wake up, lazy wings."

That irritating noise disturbed the eclipse of my mind. I opened one bleary eye.

Azure-blues stared down at me. I went to groan and growled instead.

Adrianna didn't take offense. She tickled me.

I batted her hands away. "Unforgivable!"

"Stop squeaking at me and get up."

Adrianna moved on. She stirred Liora, who rose without a hassle. Then came Cai's turn. He was quick to make a fuss, grumbling, "Why are you always up at dawn? It's not natural."

"I don't know, Caiden. Why are you always sleeping in?"

"Don't call me Caiden."

Ignoring their back and forth, I wiped the sleep from my face and sat up in my bedroll.

Within seconds, my fae eyesight adjusted to the gloom. The lake held reflections of dying stars and of a sky straddling the line between night and day. Streaks of blue, orange, and indigo hung over the forest, etching out the trees, giving them depth and form.

Battling morning-brain, I twisted around and grabbed my makeshift pillow—my rucksack. I reached inside my bag and pulled out food that at this point had either grown stale or lost its flavor. I forced down breakfast, eating just enough to satisfy my hunger pangs.

I packed my rations and bedroll away and stood up, inhaling the aromatic air. "Anybody know where Sandrine is?" I asked our group.

"She's gone to get Hazel," Adrianna said, running a stiff brush through her long hair. "We're leaving when they return, so be ready."

Cai muttered mutinously, plucking at his dried fruit. Yeah, he really wasn't a morning person.

The nearby mountains seemed to exhale. Chilled by their breath, I slipped on my boots and shielded my body as best I could with my wings.

Tingles of energy swept through my extremities. At first I thought the sensation was caused by my movement. Then heat prickled my right palm. I went to scratch it and a spark of marigold-colored light escaped my hand. The glowing ember hopped into our dying campfire, rekindling an orchestra of flames.

I leaped away. We all did.

"Sorry! Sorry." I curled my hands into fists. "That was me. Apparently, sunlight equals fire."

Cai's mouth quivered with silent laughter. "Magic a bit jumpy this morning?"

I threw him a sour look only to get blown a sweet and silly kiss. Ignoring that, I checked my palm. No more light. That was little solace; my magic had acted of its own accord. I'd no more control over it than I would a sneeze. That couldn't end well, given how destructive fire was.

Thea tried to console me. *It takes time to learn control. Be patient.*

I cringed. *Just how many of my thoughts are you listening in on?*

We sensed your magic flare and decided to check in.

You'll have to get past your need for privacy, Zola added. *We're here to watch over you, and in case you haven't noticed, you're in a lot of danger.*

How comforting.

My sarcasm was overlooked.

I waited nervously for another surge of magic.

A minute or two passed. Nothing happened.

I gradually relaxed. True to habit, Cai, Frazer, and Adrianna started the venyetä, a series of poses that prepared the muscles for strenuous exercise, or in our case, the hours of walking we did every day. I hadn't joined them for weeks. I wanted to do so now, but one look at Liora on the ground persuaded me against it. She watched the others with a cheerless expression, listlessly nibbling at her food. Yesterday, I'd shared her struggles. The lack of energy and frustration remained as real to me as the dewy morning air I was inhaling.

I crouched beside her. "Do you want me to brush your hair?"

"Thanks." She gave me a peaky smile, unwinding her messy plait. "Whenever Cai does it, he ends up pulling out clumps of my hair. I might go bald if he keeps it up."

"All lies," Cai said as he popped up out of a squat. "Our nieces used to love me combing their hair."

"I distinctly remember there being tears in their eyes," Liora shot back.

"They were tears of joy," Cai argued.

Our pack shared shaking heads and laughter.

Liora handed me a brush from her bag. "Do yours first."

I dragged bristles through my hair a few times. Done. Short straight hair didn't require much attention. Liora's springy curls were a different matter. I was still untangling the humidity from her locks when Hazel and Sandrine strode out of the woods.

My hand froze mid-brush; my nose went up. "Is that what I think it is?"

Adrianna jumped out of a position that mimicked a stretching cat. "Courts, save us." She drew in a rib-expanding inhale and breathed out. "It's coffee."

"Hello, all." Hazel greeted us in the same outfit she wore yesterday, including the black hat and muddy boots. "I've brought something to wake you up."

Adrianna hurried over to her, hand outstretched. "You're a goddess."

Zola tutted and hissed, *Blasphemy.*

I stiffened.

Thea expressed a small sigh. *Ignore her.*

My body relaxed as laughter sounded in my head.

"Enjoy," Hazel said, handing Adrianna the steaming flask.

She cupped the flask as if it were the most precious thing in the world and blew hard over the liquid surface.

Sandrine and Hazel glanced at the fire. If they wondered why it was blazing hot again, neither of them commented on it.

I wove Liora's hair into a plait, then I went to pry the flask out of Adrianna's reluctant hands. After a few sips, I handed the flask off to Liora. She needed the caffeine more than me.

The others prepared to leave. I followed their example, strapping my rucksack on and donning my weapons—their weight was nothing to me now.

"Everyone good to go?" Sandrine's gaze drifted over each of us.

Agreements came from all sides.

Cai kicked stones over the fire, smothering flame and magic.

Sandrine turned, her pearl diadem glinting with the dawn's first rays. She struck north, whistling as she went, calling in firelights to illuminate the path ahead.

We entered the forest that bordered the lake. Here, the undergrowth was bedded with grass, moss, and wildflowers; the silver-barked trees with their star-shaped blossoms shone brightly, like snowfall under a waxing moon.

These trees are unique to Aurora, Frazer said, reading my interest in them. *They're called loula. In Kaeli, it means the beauty of the heavens.*

That fit, I thought.

Before long, we reached an archway that two loula trees had formed with their entangled limbs. They resembled a pair of lovers embracing. Sandrine touched the right trunk, her mouth moving silently.

We waited, breath baited. Nothing happened.

My aunt walked through without a word. We stepped through after her.

Everybody halted on the other side of the archway. "It's not just me, right?" Cai squinted up at where dawn had turned to day.

Liora and I both chorused, "No."

Sandrine dismissed the firelights. They weren't needed anymore. For we stood under a bright sky, a dirt path winding out in front. By the wayside, the loulas' leaves had turned silver and shone with steely fire wherever shafts of weak sunlight penetrated the canopy's veil. The forest's blossoms were falling a petal at a time, like snowflakes. Even the scents differed here. The green heat of summer was gone, replaced by the sweet hay-tang of autumn.

"Is this because we're on a fae road?" Liora asked Hazel.

As we roved, Hazel said, "That's right. Think of the road as a current that moves at a different pace to the rest of the river, one that allows us to cover great distances in a short amount of time. I can't say who built them—"

"The firstborn created them," Sandrine informed.

Taken aback, Hazel's jaw slackened. She adjusted quickly, pushing out a whispering cackle. "Never try to explain anything around an undine. They'll always know more than you do."

We all laughed at that. Sandrine included.

Liora kept asking questions about the roads. Hazel seemed pleased to teach an eager student. From there, they discovered their joint interest in healing. It'd been a while since I'd seen Liora so animated. And I had to make sure it became the norm again.

But what if I messed up the unbinding? What if Liora died because of me? I felt smaller and smaller until I found the strength to halt those dangerous thoughts. One by one, I pulled my doubts out like weeds.

I would save her, I would save her, I would save her.

~

Later, Sandrine called us to a halt.

We had walked for hours, but I barely felt the strain; I had flushed cheeks, a mild ache in my heels, and some stiffness in my shoulders. I reveled in that—in how well my body was coping. No more life-draining exhaustion. No more being stalked by death.

We took respite by the side of the path where the forest lent a voice to the rising wind. After eating, drinking, and seeing to the necessary ablutions, we set off again. Not long after we'd resumed our trek, Sandrine fell into step beside me. "Would you tarry with me awhile?"

"Why?" I halted and hugged myself with my wings, guarding against the fingers of a whirling breeze that was fresh and full of silver leaves.

"I wish to speak with you alone," she said, her jade-greens intent upon me.

Cai took notice of our idleness. "What's going on?"

"We'll catch up," I reassured, waving him on.

Frowning, his lips parted.

"Come on, nosy." Liora tugged him away.

Hazel and Adrianna marched ahead. Frazer, however, stuck to my side.

Sandrine studied my brother. He adopted an immovable mask that plainly said *I'm not going anywhere.*

Not bothering to argue, my aunt faced me. "I don't want to keep you long, but there's something I felt I had to share with you about our kin. I didn't bring it up yesterday because I wasn't sure you'd want the others knowing ... I also felt you'd suffered enough surprises for the day."

I acknowledged that with a humorless noise.

Sandrine nodded as if she understood my non-response. "If you don't want to listen to this, tell me now. It may prove a shock, even though it's nothing bad."

Frazer inched closer, his shoulder brushing against mine in solidarity. I braced for the blow. "Just tell me."

Worry wrinkled her eyes. "I told you that my father carried the sunstone. But I left out the fact he was chosen to protect it by his parents, Balor and Freyta."

It took a moment for those names to sink in. *No.* That was absurd. Ridiculous.

Sandrine watched my face expectantly.

"You're saying Ena's great-grandparents are the King and Queen of the Light Court," Frazer said, almost comically flat.

A soft, "Yes."

My thoughts broke apart and fled.

Frazer assumed the lead when I couldn't form a coherent sentence. "Why didn't Atlas leave for the light court with the others?"

"Not many are aware that Freyta was once fae," Sandrine revealed. "She met Balor during the Court War. They had Atlas not long after and discovered that he resembled the mother in terms of powers. And nobody but a firstborn or a spirit is permitted to enter the light court."

My eyebrows twitched toward each other. "Why was Freyta allowed to live there, then? Or Zola or Thea?"

"Balor made Freyta a demigoddess. But for whatever reason, that process couldn't be replicated for his son. As for the twins, they were born with enough power to be considered firstborn." Sorrow drew

Sandrine's face taut. "It must've been hard to watch his sisters be all that he could not."

I waited for Zola and Thea to comment on that. They didn't.

Sandrine misinterpreted my silence. "I thought you had a right to know." Her lashes dipped. "I also thought it might bring you comfort knowing your mother is with kin. It helps me."

She didn't wear her grief lightly. It aggravated mine and made me bleed guilt. "I'm sorry."

Sandrine blinked as though she'd looked directly into the sun. "What for?"

"Mama died from a human disease," I said, my throat constricting. "And she only became human to save me."

I was pulled into an embrace. Sandrine's spring rain and lotus scent enveloped me. "That wasn't your fault. If anything, you extended Sati's life." A hand cradled my head. "*See,* alätia."

The image of a large room lined with bookshelves consumed my vision. A room that my mother also inhabited, but not as I remembered her. She was fae, and clothed in a backless dress with her golden wings out on display. "I can't abandon you," she said to a tall male with pale skin. "Please, don't ask me to."

The male cupped her cheek. Before the shift to amethyst, my eyes had been his exact shade of dark blue. It had to be Dain. Seeing him, I felt foolish for having believed that Halvard had sired me. I hadn't inherited my mother's looks, and I hadn't shared Halvard's blond hair or brown eyes.

Dain stared at my mother as though his life began with her, and she looked at him like her world would end with him.

"You're not abandoning me," he told her firmly. "You're protecting our tilä and all those she'll go on to save. You must trust me in this. Morgan can't get her hands on you both. It would be the end for all of us."

His hand splayed over her flat belly.

"I don't doubt you." Mama placed her hands over his. "It's me. I can't do this without you."

"You won't be alone," he said, his voice strong. "Sandrine's promised to help. And the firstborn will be there for our child when the time comes."

I couldn't see Sandrine, but I heard her. "I'll watch over your girl. I swear it."

Dain glanced at me or what must've been Sandrine. "I know, kino yatävä."

Then his gaze returned to my mother, to Sati. They watched each other, having a conversation that only the two of them could understand.

Mama finally nodded, her eyes containing an age of agony. "All right, my love. I'll trust you once again. I'll leave."

The vision faded away. I returned to the present and left my aunt's embrace. "What was that?" My voice sounded small, childlike.

"I shared one of my memories with you. I wanted you to see that your mother would've died with her mate if she hadn't been pregnant. She lived six more years because of you." Sandrine's tone became a hammer over a nail. "The only person to blame for her death is Morgan."

A tear slipped past my hastily built emotional walls. I angrily wiped it away. "Thanks for showing me." I wasn't sure if I meant that.

"It's okay to miss them," she said, our shared grief shining in her bright eyes. "Loss isn't a straight road with a natural end. It's a circular path under an uncertain sky. Sometimes there's a downpour, and then there's a drought. The only sure thing is that it always returns."

It was as if she'd climbed inside of my head and told me exactly what I needed to hear. "How did you know what I was thinking? Are you reading my mind?"

"I can't do that without being inside the necklace. But I *was* in your head for months. I like to think I understand you."

I huffed. "Yeah. You were in my head. Then when you left, I get two other people stuck in there. It's like I'm destined to have no privacy."

"I'm not following," Sandrine said, her brow furrowing.

I told her about Zola and Thea.

Sandrine looked speechless. It took her a few moments to gather her thoughts and say, "I understand your frustrations, but you couldn't ask for better teachers than the firstborn. Be sure to learn all you can from them." Her tone shifted. Less awe. More hopeful. "Could you ask them whether my father's soul is in the light court? If it is, and they can commune with him, we might get answers on where he hid the sunstone."

My heart leaped. If the goddesses knew the sunstone's location, I wouldn't have to spend as much time on the continent away from Frazer.

Zola killed my dream. *We can't ask our brother anything. Because he's not here.*

Where is he?

His soul chose the moon court.

I didn't understand what it meant to choose a court. That didn't mean I couldn't hear the pain in Zola's voice. I stopped asking questions for her sake.

Sandrine accepted the disappointing news with good grace. "I see. Thank you for asking them."

Frazer interceded then. "We should resume walking. We're getting left behind."

The three of us started forward.

"I hope I didn't shock you too much with the news of your ancestry," Sandrine said quietly; so quietly that I almost didn't hear her over the brisk wind. "I just felt you deserved to know."

I nodded, hair whipping around my face. "I'm glad you told me … It's actually nice knowing I'm related to Zola and Thea. It makes them seem less intimidating."

Did you hear that, Thea? We've become less impressive. We're already failing in our job as mentors, Zola said.

I couldn't be certain, but her tone suggested she was joking.

I'm glad she feels that way.

I told Thea, *You're definitely my favorite.*

Light laughter was her response.

Sandrine, Frazer, and I walked for a few minutes without any conversation. Time ticked away inside my chest, counting down to the moment when I would part with Sandrine.

I cast a sideways peek at my petite aunt. I had no idea when or if I'd see her again. I didn't want to spend whatever time we had left together in silence.

I settled on the topic closest to my heart. "What were my parents like?"

Sandrine smiled. "Brave. Compassionate. Loyal." She studied me, her gaze keen. "You're a lot like them."

Thinking back, I said, "I don't know. Mama always seemed so confident. She never cared what others thought about her. That's how I remember her, anyway, and how Viola described her."

"Give it a few years, and I think you might surprise yourself with how confident you've become." Sandrine hooked me by the elbow. I had to shorten my stride so we could walk side by side. "Besides, you must remember that Sati had a completely different upbringing to you. After our parents died, I raised and cared for Sati. But since I'm more undine than fae, I have to live at least some of the time in water. That meant she got left a lot with the other undines who adored her and indulged her every whim. It's little wonder she was confident."

Sandrine went on to tell me about my mother's reckless youth, her first marriage, and lastly, how my parents met. When that tale ended, I had to ask, "I saw how they looked at each other in your memory ... Is it always that way between mates?"

"I can't really answer that. I haven't met many mated couples."

My thoughts tumbled out. "Do you think Mama loved Halvard?"

"Are you asking out of concern for your adoptive father?" Sandrine continued shrewdly. "Or because you know you have a mate?"

I worked hard to get my words out. "Does it have to be one or the other?"

Hesitation. "Sati once told me that what she felt for Dain was the strongest thing she'd ever experienced. But I don't think that meant she couldn't care for other people."

That felt like an onion of a sentence. It had too many layers, and it made my eyes sting.

"You have visions—have you seen whether Wilder is my mate?" I asked, revealing my raw underbelly. "I mean there's a chance, isn't there? It wouldn't have clicked into place when I was a human, right?"

Sandrine adopted an open expression. "Do you think he's your mate?"

A question for a question. Frustrating. "I'm asking your opinion."

"The only thing I can tell you about your mate is that he'll love you fiercely, without condition."

I stopped mid-stride, loosening her arm from mine. "How do you know that?"

Sandrine rounded on me. "Because you're not going to settle for anything less." She poked me in the gut. "Got it?"

Down the bond, I whispered to Frazer, *Help*.

No, he replied, humor singing.

"Ena?" Sandrine said, sharper than before.

"Yes. Fine," I blurted out.

She nodded curtly and resumed walking. Frazer and I followed in her wake.

The other half of our group gradually came into view. They were stood next to another archway. I looked through it, expecting to see an end to the fae road. But I didn't. I only saw more of the same landscape.

Once we'd joined the others, Sandrine touched one of the trees that formed the archway and muttered under her breath. Then she stepped back and ushered us onward. One by one, we passed through to the other side.

Autumn vanished. Summer returned.

The sun now dashed the sky in its best colors and spread warmth over the land, like butter over hot toast. When I glanced over my shoulder, the archway was there but the fae road was hidden, disguised to look like the surrounding forest.

Sandrine addressed me. "This is where I leave you."

"Me too," Hazel added.

"I suppose you'll be glad to get home. Salazar must be missing you." I smiled at Hazel, remembering the strange sprite that haunted her sofa.

Hazel's brown eyes softened. "It's sweet of you to think of him. He does get lonely when he's on his own for too long."

Her expression closed up, and she no longer held my eye.

"Nasiri is about four hours that way." Sandrine signaled straight ahead and to the right. "If you need to orient yourself, go above the canopy and find the ocean, then follow the coastline until you find a port town."

Excitement pushed at my every seam. I'd longed to look upon the ocean my whole life. I'd glimpsed it from a distance when I was with Hunter. But I'd yet to see it up close.

Frazer's eyes snagged on mine. The miles of sadness in them shattered me. The sea was where we would part ways. Dread replaced joy so fast, it made my head spin and my stomach somersault.

Sandrine continued. "Morgan will have released descriptions of your pack to local law enforcers, so try to avoid drawing attention to yourselves when you reach Nasiri."

"We'll be careful." Without warning, Cai hugged Hazel. "Thanks for everything. Our pack owes you big time."

Looking a bit shocked, Hazel pulled away. "Not at all."

Cai turned to Sandrine with a smile. They moved and met in a hug that from the outside looked strange given their height difference. Cai stepped back first and strode off toward Nasiri.

Adrianna went after him straightaway. Liora stuck around for two softly spoken goodbyes, then she left too. Frazer stayed beside me.

Sandrine eyed him. "Take care of yourself."

A short nod.

Hazel just watched him, not saying anything.

My turn. I faced Hazel. "Thank you. I know Cai's already said it—"

She held up a hand. "And it doesn't need to be said again. Just be well."

I nodded. Now Sandrine.

Anticipating me, she opened her arms. I walked into her hug and she held me in a way that only parents knew how to do. It was the embrace that said they would shield you from the world forever if they could. I breathed her scent deep into my lungs. "I'll miss you."

That got me an extra squeeze. "I'll miss you too."

Once we'd released each other, Sandrine reached out and tucked my necklace underneath my oversized shirt. "Keep this safe."

"I will. I won't take it off."

"Good," she said with a wan smile. "We'll see each other again, alätia."

Ironically, I knew that was her farewell. I gave her a parting smile, then I walked away. I didn't have the heart to look back.

CHAPTER 9
A HITCH IN THE PLAN

We arrived on the outskirts of Nasiri with a fair afternoon sky overhead.

Concerned we'd attract looks as a group or even in pairs, Frazer insisted on scouting out the port alone. The rest of us stayed under the cover of the loula forest, and I used the kin bond to relay everything Frazer learned to the rest of my pack.

The news wasn't good. *The Eye of the Wind* wasn't expected until tomorrow morning, and the forest bordering the town—the one we stood in—had become dangerous in recent months. A hive of teekran, nocturnal bat-like sprites who feasted on living flesh, roamed the area.

We were left with no choice but to shelter inside of Nasiri. Frazer and I could rely on our recent physical changes to conceal our identities and confuse anybody hunting for us with outdated descriptions. Cai, Liora, and Adrianna weren't so fortunate.

Frazer brought a temporary hair dye back from the town. Cai and Liora used that to darken their blond and red locks. Adrianna's hair, however, was already black. There were no wigmakers nearby, and the silver ink on her forehead would draw stares. As a result, she decided to stay in the forest until sunset. Once the shops were shut and the streets were quieter, she would join us in our accommodation.

And so, without Adrianna our pack entered Nasiri. It turned out there weren't many options for where to stay. We had to settle on a grubby inn called The Blue Crab. The place only had two guest rooms, both of which we booked, ensuring our privacy.

Frazer went to tell Adrianna our location. He promised her that we'd hang a pillowslip from the window to signal which room she could climb into. Almost as soon as he'd returned from the forest, he set out for the marketplace with Cai. Liora napped in the guys' room while they were out.

As twilight fell, I was left waiting for Adrianna alone, pacing the stained floorboards of my room. Solitude had once been an everyday occurrence. Now it was the exception, and I was uneasy with it.

I stopped at the mullioned window and poked my head out into the night. There, I expelled the scents that stuck to the inn's walls. Freed of woodsmoke, tobacco, and unwashed bodies, I refilled my chest with salt and brine—with the song of the ocean. *The ocean.* I was so close, yet I still hadn't caught a proper glimpse.

I searched over the rooftops for Adrianna. Not a single trace of her could be seen; the slice of moon and the stars above were lonely.

The tuneless noise of drunk people singing in the alleyways below started to hurt my ears, and the alcohol fumes accompanying them stung my throat. I retreated from the window and sat on the double bed. Worry picked and niggled at me.

I started when Frazer's thoughts butted into mine. *We'll decide what to do about Adrianna when we get back.*

I locked onto his location. He was several streets away. *Are you and Cai all right? Are you still shopping for supplies?*

We're fine. And no, we're done with that. He was short, but not sharp.

I abandoned all subtleties. *I can sense you're stressed. What's wrong?*

Frazer's lengthy pause ended with, *Someone recognized me in town. His name's Ryder. He worked for the Aurorian Court around the same time as me. But we only saw each other a handful of times and we never spoke. I'm trying to convince him that I'm someone else.*

My stomach rolled. *Do you need my help?*

No, he said quickly. *You're needed at the inn. Someone has to guard Liora and look out for Adrianna. Now I've got to focus on getting this nosy bastard to leave us alone. I'll talk to you later.*

Frazer withdrew from the bond. Forced into an idle situation only worsened my anxieties. The humid air became a pillow over my face; my clothes stuck to my sweaty body.

A scuffing noise sounded nearby.

I leaped off the bed, sunlight already charging my blood.

Adrianna appeared in the window, her face thrown into sharp relief by the light given off by the two lanterns in the room. She climbed into the room, staring at my outstretched hand. "What are you doing?"

Heart still pounding, I lowered my arm to my side and willed the fire in my blood to cool. I managed to smother it, but it felt like swallowing hot coals. "What happened? You're late."

"It took a while to find you." Adrianna snatched the pillowslip from the windowpane and tossed it onto the bed behind me. Then she closed the window. "And then, I had to wait until I could fly in unseen. You should've chosen a quieter part of town."

"We didn't have much of an option."

Adrianna viewed the bare stone walls, the misshapen beams above, and the ancient-looking fireplace. "Clearly. Where are the others?"

"Liora's sleeping next door."

Adrianna's azure-blues narrowed in a piercing look. "And the guys?"

"They went shopping. Frazer needed things for his journey. Cai's restocking our food rations and his witchy supplies."

Her head cocked like a bird. "Then why do you look ready to run out the door?"

"Someone recognized Frazer," I said quietly.

Adrianna's lips parted in a violent curse. "Exactly what happened?"

I summarized what Frazer had told me.

Marching up and down the boards, shaking her head, Adrianna said, "If Ryder doesn't believe Frazer, he could bring us a lot of trouble." She halted in the middle of the room. Turning on her heel, she confronted me. "Tell me where Cai and Frazer are now."

"Why?"

"If I find them, I find Ryder. Then I can follow him and see what he does."

I hated the idea. So did my brother. *Do not let her leave that room.*

His vehement tone alarmed me. *What do you suggest I do? I can't command her to stay. She'd probably run me through on principle.*

Tell her Ryder used to be one of the Aurorian Sami. That might stop her from doing something reckless.

I stiffened. *Was he one of the people you helped escape Mysaya?*

Ryder was stationed in the outlying provinces when the Sami fled Mysaya. The soldiers who weren't at the capital that day deserted their posts or they chose to serve the Solar Court rather than live as outcasts and outlaws. Ryder could've chosen either fate.

"I'm getting gray hair waiting for you to say something."

I met Adrianna's impatient stare and repeated Frazer's revelations to her.

Sighing, Adrianna craned her neck and stared at the low ceiling. "In that case, I suppose Frazer's right." Her gaze dropped to me. "Trailing a Samite would be too dangerous—their kind can track a butterfly through a butcher's shop."

"Did you really just say that Frazer was right about something?" I teased.

She swatted at me. "I can admit when someone else is right, you know?" My twitching mouth had her adding, "I just don't usually say it."

Adrianna propped her sword against the wall and as she straightened up, she nodded to where my wings hung over my stretched-out camisole. "You need some shirts adapted for wings."

I nodded. "Frazer said he'd bring me some back from the market."

"You trust him to buy your clothes?" Her expression plainly added *Are you mad?*

"It's not like he'd choose anything stupid."

"No, you'll just end up with an entirely black wardrobe."

I snorted a laugh. "Maybe. But I'm more worried about Cai. He promised to buy my bras for me since Frazer didn't know what would work for my wing type."

A ghost of a smile lifted her mouth. "Cai must've had more fae lovers than I'd guessed if he knows about such things."

Rats. I hadn't planned on painting Cai as a rogue, not with his feelings for Adrianna to consider. I tried to steer her in another direction. "I think he's just picked up a lot from having a sister and from his female friends."

"If you say so," she said, making it plain she didn't think much of my excuse and that she didn't care either way. Adrianna stepped nearer and sniffed at me. "You smell clean. Does that mean this place has running water?"

"The washroom is through there." I motioned to the door behind me. "The water's clean but it isn't hot."

She waved that off. "It doesn't matter. I can't stand smelling like this anymore."

Understandable. River washes had only done so much for us in the past month; I'd cleaned up as soon as I'd gotten to the inn. Being able to scrub weeks of grime and sweat away had been the best thing about today.

Rucksack in tow, Adrianna cut across the room and opened the slanted doorway. Her feet stopped. Eyebrows perched high, she looked back at me.

"Yeah." I elongated that word. "We had to use the washroom to clean and hang our underthings. There wasn't anywhere else to put them."

"Fair enough."

I got a quick view of the chipped sink, grimy toilet, and the copper basin used for standing baths. Then Adrianna snapped the door shut with her heel.

What now?

I twisted my hands, thinking over my options. Liora would want to hear about Ryder and that Adrianna was safe. But if I disturbed her much-needed sleep, there was no chance she'd return to it. I chose to leave her be.

I withdrew to the bed.

Tedious moments passed. I started fidgeting, chewing nails.

We're back. We're downstairs in the taproom.

I jumped at Frazer's sudden intrusion. *Is Ryder still bothering you?*

Hesitation. *We took our leave of him, but I suspect he's followed us here.*

Nerves fluttered in my belly, like moths around a lamp. *Do you think he knows you're an outlaw?*

I couldn't say ... But if he'd planned on betraying me, it wouldn't have been in his interests to approach us and put us on our guard. I'm still going to linger down here awhile. I want to see if he follows me into the taproom.

My heart was in my shoes. *If you're in danger here, maybe you should just run. Leave Nasiri and head for Mysaya tonight.*

The backlash of emotion coming from him was so intense, it possessed my body. Sorrow rested heavily in my chest. Bitterness swelled in my throat.

Fleeing in the night would only make him more suspicious, Frazer said, his mental voice made of steel and sharp ends. *And if I'm not in the air, he'd just track me down.*

Gods. *Is Cai staying with you in the taproom?*

For now. He wants to be close in case Ryder comes in.

That was that. There was nothing left to say. This cruel twist in Fate's threads had a Samite likely stalking my brother. An elite warrior who might sell my brother out at any time.

Fear billowed into anger. A peculiar feeling snaked through me, as if the chaos beating under my breast had turned into its own creature. That beast raised its head and howled. It needed to protect my brother —to strike out at this Ryder.

My hands curled into angry balls. I fisted the bed sheets.

The washroom door creaked open and Adrianna strode in wearing wide-legged pants and an emerald wraparound top that valleyed her breasts. Towel-drying her hair one-handed, she dropped her bag. Then she froze, her nostrils widened, and her gaze darted to where my hand was burning the bedsheet.

Adrianna lunged to stamp out my embers with her bare hands. That snapped me out of my daze. I vaulted up, blocking her with my wings. "No!"

She stumbled back. "This whole place is made of wood! We'll go up like matchsticks if—"

"You're not hurting yourself because of me! I'll do it."

I spun around and stamped out the sparks with my palms. The tendrils of smoke dissipated, but it didn't feel as if we were out of danger. Not while the sunlight pushed me to use it again and again.

Stop. Stop. Stop. I stifled the instinct. Barely.

What's going on? Frazer was quick, pointed.

My sunlight burned the bed. But it's under control.

Frazer's presence was a moonlit shadow bordering my mind. He encompassed me, offering shelter and silent reassurance.

I made no reply. I just stared down at the damage. I'd burned through the threadbare sheet and blackened the mattress's wool. Sick with anxiety, the sight made me taste bile.

Siska—

I'll be fine. Just let me know if you need me.

I heard a halting, *Same.*

He drifted away, taking refuge in his own mind.

"You good?" Adrianna asked from behind me.

Ashamed over her cautious tone, I said, "I think so."

Adrianna grew wing-close. "Are your hands okay?"

"I guess my own magic can't hurt me," I said, showing her unmarred palms.

"Do you know what triggered this?" Adrianna asked as she flipped the mattress over, hiding the evidence from my loss of control.

I recounted what Frazer had said, adding, "When I thought Ryder might be a threat, my sunlight did that." I gestured to the singed sheet she'd thrown back on the bed. "I didn't even realize what I was doing ... I could've hurt you."

Adrianna met my gaze and sighed. "Quit staring at me with those sad doe eyes. You caused some mild damage to a bed. That's all."

"I almost attacked you when you climbed in the window," I confessed, shoulders knotted. "And that was just because I got startled."

"You didn't attack me, though," she said steadily. "You controlled it."

My fear wouldn't shut up. "But reigning it in felt like stopping a horse from bolting. What if I'm not fast enough next time?"

Adrianna looked at me as if I'd grown an extra head. That reaction made me shrivel up inside. "What is it?"

"I'm just surprised." Frowning, she went on. "It's not like that for me. I haven't really practiced my abilities, but I can sense the metal surrounding us if I concentrate hard enough. And it feels docile. Subservient by nature." Her features set into a sudden and fierce disapproval. "What about Zola and Thea? Weren't they supposed to be training you?"

Her confrontational tone made me smile a little. "Are you expecting them to respond to you?"

A sharp, "Yes."

It's taken us time to prepare your mind for how we'll be training you, Thea answered. *Your lessons will begin tonight.*

I repeated those words aloud for Adrianna's sake.

"But how much can you progress in dreams?" she said, her cushy mouth pursing. "Shouldn't you also be practicing magic while you're awake?"

Side-eyeing the sheet, I said, "I don't think it's safe for me to do that yet."

"You can't avoid using magic because you're scared." Adrianna paused, and her stern expression gentled. "My isä used to say that completing any difficult task was like learning to fly. If all you do is contemplate the fall, then that's what'll happen. So don't look down."

I tiptoed through my words. "Adi ... what happened to your father?"

Her expression shifted into thorny grief. "He died."

For a few painful heartbeats, I thought that was the end of our conversation. It wasn't.

"Diana said he drowned in a shipwreck," she added quietly. "But who knows? Maybe she lied about that, too."

"Why would she do that?" I asked, eyes widening.

"Because she doesn't think I can handle the truth or keep secrets." Bitterness hardened Adrianna's face. She went on citrus-sour, wings bristling. "When I was alone with her, I asked her why she didn't tell me she was working against Morgan. She said that if I'd known, I would've gotten defensive whenever our court were called traitors. She thought I might've revealed our secret to save my pride."

That struck a chord with me. Sandrine had also kept secrets because she hadn't trusted my reactions; no matter her reasoning, it hurt to be kept ignorant by somebody you cared for. With those thoughts circling my mind, I said to Adrianna, "Then she's misjudged you." Her inscrutable, armored look made me want to convince her. "Adi—"

She grasped my hand. "I don't want to talk about Diana."

A firm warning. I had to respect that.

"But I do want you to know that I have faith in you." Her blue gaze blazed as if she wished to brand those words into my skull. "You'll figure this magic thing out."

Her chin lifted an inch. As though daring me to disagree.

"I'll try," I eked out, chest tight.

Long, elegant fingers linked with mine. She squeezed hard.

"Oww," I moaned, scowling at her.

"You deserved it," Adrianna argued nonsensically.

A quick, quiet knock sounded. Our doorknob rattled and turned. Adrianna and I spun around to face the door, our hands separating.

Liora entered the room. She was dressed in cream trousers, nude-colored shoes, and an off-the-shoulder blouse with sleeves that flared out at her wrists. Her ailing features brightened when she saw Adrianna. "You're back."

That was met with a furrowed brow. "You look tired. Shouldn't you rest some more?"

"Don't fuss. I'm fine." Liora not-so-subtly changed the subject by sniffing at the air. "Why does it smell like something's burning in here?"

I cringed. "Because of me. I accidentally set the bed on fire."

Liora pulled the details out of me. When I was done, she was quick to offer reassurance. "I understand why you're worried, but it's normal for a fledgling witch to lose control. Even masters will make mistakes sometimes. That's why witches tend to stick to the Crescent, so that we can watch out for one another."

"We're not in the Crescent."

"You don't need the Witch Court," Liora said stoutly. "You've got us."

"That's what I'm worried about," I murmured. "That I might hurt one of you."

Adrianna drew in a short, frustrated inhale. Before she could go on a rant, Liora cut in. "Cai and I grew up around witches. We know what to expect. And all of us have been trained as soldiers. We can protect ourselves."

I'd no argument for that. No comeback.

Liora glanced at Adrianna. "So, when did you arrive?"

"Not long ago. Ten minutes, maybe."

"Are the guys still shopping?" Liora asked.

Adrianna and I traded looks.

"What is it?" Liora's sleepy face tightened. "What's happened?"

"Cai and Frazer are downstairs. They're all right. It's just …"

"They've attracted the interest of a Samite," Adrianna tacked on.

Liora blinked like a sun-startled owl. "What? How?"

I caught her up on everything Ryder related. Liora was frowning, obviously thinking over her response, when alarm shocked my kin bond. *Siska?*

Is it Ryder?

Yes. He just walked in.

"Crap," I said to myself.

"What's wrong now?" Adrianna demanded.

Liora answered, "Frazer's talking to her."

"How can you tell?"

"Her eyes go out of focus ..."

Tuning them out, I concentrated on Frazer. *What is he doing?*

A crack appeared in his mental-shield. *I'll show you.*

I projected myself up to his mental borders. Frazer reached out and yanked me into his present.

I became immersed, suspended inside my brother's mind. It felt like being underwater. Only peaceful. I could breathe down here.

As Frazer, I was perched on a stool behind the long bar.

Through the tavern's murky light, I watched Ryder. He moved toward me, skirting around the knit of tables.

I cast my gaze toward a table positioned next to the taproom's entrance. Cai sat there, dealing cards, laughing uproariously, and talking with his fellow gamblers. It was a performance. A way to gather local rumor.

I urged Cai to look up. To take notice. To be on guard.

But Ryder reached me first. "We meet again." He gestured to the stool beside me. "Mind if I join you?"

Irritation ran over my skin. I shrugged, feigning disinterest.

Ryder squatted on the seat and signaled to the innkeeper behind the bar.

"What will you have?" she asked, giving off an indifferent air.

He motioned to the mug of ale I nursed in my hands. "The same as my friend here."

My teeth gritted at his familiarity. We were not friends of any sort.

The heavily perfumed innkeeper slid him a foamy pint, then she hurried away to serve another customer.

Swiveling around on his stool, Ryder concentrated on me. He was a handsome male with a slim build and chest-length black hair which he'd tied back. His thin, tanned face supported high cheekbones and single-lidded eyes. The rest of his appearance implied an unassuming air: he wore drab woodland colors, and his clothes were tattered in several places.

Ryder eyeballed me. "I confess, I came here hoping to see you again."

I heaved an exaggerated sigh. "I've tried to be patient, but how many times must I say it—I'm not who you think I am."

He smiled. He did that entirely too much. "I only meant that I wanted to meet you again so I could apologize for pestering you with so many questions."

Bullshit.

I sipped at the watery bitterness of my ale. It was disgusting, but it kept my mouth occupied. It stopped me from telling him to piss off.

"You see, the male that I mistook you for was somebody I've thought of a lot over the years," Ryder said, leaning in. "And I forgot myself in my excitement. To tell you the truth, he really was the most fuckable male I'd ever seen."

I choked. Ale streamed out of my nose.

"Ah. Sorry." Ryder clapped me on the back. "I'm not the most subtle person, I know. I hope I didn't make you uncomfortable."

That was definitely laughter in his voice. Prick.

"You didn't. I was just surprised," I said, dabbing at my streaming nose with my black sleeve.

Nose cleared, I could smell desire on him.

Interesting. I had assumed he'd only said those things to unbalance me.

Ryder reclined, lounging on the stool in a relaxed fashion. "I'm also here in the hopes you'll take pity on a lonely stranger and share a tale or two from your travels. It's not every day you meet a fae working with a human, and as fur-traders, no less."

I groaned inwardly at the story Cai had spun him.

"Although I suppose witches have always had their own ways of doing things," Ryder said as if that were nothing but a flippant comment.

"Why would you assume we're witches?" I asked, peering into my mug.

"Your friend's scent."

I wasn't surprised. Just annoyed. We'd taken one of the concealment charms out with us, but it only worked up to a point. It functioned the same way traveling through water would throw a hound off a trail. In short, it wasn't strong enough to hide our scents from anybody in our immediate vicinity. I presumed that the only reason I hadn't been marked as a witch was because I hadn't used magic yet.

"I hope we haven't misunderstood each other," remarked Ryder. "I'm not interested in the fact he's a witch. I know they sometimes get hassled by people looking for magical solutions to their problems, especially in remote areas such as these. But like I said, I just want to hear your stories."

The amused glint in his eye made his intentions clear. Ryder was baiting me, pushing my commitment to the lies hastily invented at our first meeting.

I calculated my options. I couldn't force him to leave. If I walked out, he'd likely follow and make it awkward for me to return to the inn. Or the nosy bastard would stay here, in the same building as my sister. Unacceptable. That left me with entertaining a fae with made-up stories. Intolerable.

I wanted to slink away, disappear. On the back of that thought, a chill skittered over my skin like an icy breath. I felt as if I'd stepped into a shadow. Something told me that if I leaned into that feeling, I would *become* that shadow. I ignored the impulse, ignored what I suspected was the first stirring of magic within my blood. The last thing I needed was to vanish in the midst of a tavern full of people.

Ryder had taken that moment to sip from his mug. Grimacing, head retreating into his shoulders, he placed it down with a thud. "Gods save me, that tastes like horse piss."

"Is that so?" the innkeeper half-shouted from up the bar.

Ryder had been too loud, and she'd been standing too close.

Heads swiveled in our direction.

Ryder started to apologize. He didn't get to finish. Our innkeeper erupted. "Well, if you don't like the drink here, you're free to leave!"

He exposed his palms in instant surrender.

The crowd of onlookers started mocking him and cheering on Octavia—the innkeeper, I presumed.

With Ryder distracted, I glanced over my shoulder.

My eyes met Cai's. He gave me a sly nod. A signal that he'd follow my lead. I turned my thoughts toward stirring up chaos so that I could slip out from underneath it.

I lurched off my seat and swung around. Picking the closest heckler, I shouted, "That's my friend you're insulting, you rutting worm."

I kicked the bald male off his stool.

Slow from drink, he didn't tuck in his wings before he hit the flagstone floor.

A heavy *crack*. A broken wail.

Octavia's hollering ceased. A hush swept over the room.

Four males shared a table with my victim. These fae stood now, their attention centered on me, their bodies poised for violence.

Good, I was ready for a fight.

Across the room, Cai jumped up from his seat. "You bastard!" He threw his cards down on the table, confronting the blond male who sat on his right. "I knew your cards were too good. You've been cheating us this whole time!"

"You dare accuse me, human," the male growled, his hackles rising.

Cai slammed the blond's face into the table. With the fae reeling, Cai tugged the male's sleeve up to expose hidden cards. Several of the other players stood in a towering rage, pointing and shouting curses at the blond.

My focus darted to my would-be attackers. One of them was dragging the male whose wing I'd broken out of the inn. The other three, now bored with Cai's show, raised their fists and their daggers.

With a silent tread, Ryder appeared at my side. "Need some help?"

"No." I primed my body for an onslaught.

"Tough. I'm not leaving your side until you're honest with me."

"I'm not telling you shit."

Our three aggressors advanced, spitting savagery and throwing sloppy blows. I didn't reach for my sword. I'd no wish to drop bodies.

Block hit. Kick shin. Palm-strike.

More fights broke out, the violence spreading like fire through a water-starved forest. All were spurred on by alcohol and injured pride. Even when my initial targets lay unconscious, I didn't run out of people to punch. More fae surged forward. But Ryder refused to leave my side. It was in vain that I had tried to escape him.

Cai's cry rose above the din. "A little help over here."

My gaze went wide. Two fae were closing in on him. Attacking.

Disengaging from my current target, I made for Cai.

I wove around the wreckage and mayhem. Meanwhile, the tender nerve above my eye throbbed. My siska's worry had escalated. It was spilling over the mental wall I'd built between us. I had to concentrate. So I pushed her out.

I—Ena—returned to the sanctuary of my own mind and body.

Adrianna had her ear flat against the door leading to the hallway. I wasn't sure why. Even for a human, the brawling downstairs would've sounded loud.

Liora was watching me. Seeing that I was "back," she asked, "Are Cai and Frazer okay? Adrianna heard them shouting earlier."

Adrianna spun around. "There was some nonsense about insulting a friend and card cheating." She gestured to the door. "But since the fighting started, I can't pick out their voices. What's happening down there?"

"Ryder's downstairs," I told her. "The guys started the fight as a distraction so they could get away from him. But it's not working."

Liora breathed, "Cai," and marched for the exit.

She got two paces before Adrianna grasped her forearm. "You're not going anywhere."

The air bloated with heat and static energy. Something *else* inhabited Liora. Her voice deepened into a monstrous growl that would make cowards out of heroes. "Let go."

Adrianna looked as disturbed as I was, but she held on, as stubborn as a donkey in a snit. "No, not until you listen to sense. You can't run into a fae fight with no magic, no weapons, and no strength."

"Get your hand off me," Liora snarled, trying to break Adrianna's hold.

In a merciless move, she locked Liora's wrist. "How will you face fae in a brawl if you can't shift me?"

Collapsing to her knees, Liora's face twisted with rage and pain. I winced, remembering that wrist-hold from training. It didn't leave any lasting damage, but it rutting hurt.

Liora's irises changed from green to a golden color. I blinked, unsure if the shift was a trick of the light.

I looked again. Nope. Not a trick. That made my decision for me. "I'll go down there." I peered into Liora's strange eyes and promised her, "I'll help Cai."

That assurance killed the struggle in her. Diminished, sweat shining on her brow, Liora croaked, "Thank you."

Quick on my feet, I ran to Adrianna's bag. I felt exposed in my camisole, so I picked out a long-sleeved tunic with a cut-out section designed for wings. It concealed all my ink except for the sun mark on my palm.

"I thought you were worried about the sunlight acting out?" Adrianna said as I slipped my boots on. "And now you're throwing yourself into a bar fight?"

Ignoring her, I glanced at my bow and sword propped against the wall. The kaskan ensured an injured target but the sword would be better in close-quarter combat. The Utemä it was, then. I belted the narrow blade to my hips.

Then I faced Adrianna. "I won't use magic. Not unless there's no other option."

I started forward.

Movement caught my eye. As quick as a snake's bite, I caught Adrianna's hand as it reached for me. "Don't do that."

Adrianna's head jerked back an inch, but her shock didn't last long. Her sodalite-colored wings flared in dominance.

Without thinking, I splayed my own wings. I brought to bear all my will and set it against hers. I commanded her to *back off*.

She flinched as if I'd hit her.

"I'm going down there." I released her hand.

Adrianna rotated her wrist. Had I hurt her?

"It seems I can't stop you." Jaw clenched, she looked away.

Liora stepped up to my side. "Go," she urged me.

Not delaying another moment, I hurried out of the room.

CHAPTER 10
ALARM BELLS

I ran the short length of the corridor and hurried down the warped steps. Halting on the taproom's threshold, I absorbed the scene before me.

Twenty or so people fought savagely around the wounded and the splintered wreckage of old furniture. From behind the bar, Octavia hurled bottles with deadly accuracy at anyone still standing. "Stop breaking my stuff!"

I wondered if Octavia had heard of irony.

Across the amber-lit room, I spotted Cai, Frazer, and Ryder. They were in the top left corner, hemmed in and brawling with seven fae.

The sight of friend and kin in danger awoke the beast within.

My fangs finally descended. They cut my lip and coated my tongue in something warm and wet. It had to be blood, but it tasted different. Not metallic. Alive.

Adrenaline kicked my pulse into a faster rhythm. The ancient drumbeat squeezed out the ambient noise until my heartbeat was all I could hear. It echoed in my bones and conjured up primal instincts honed throughout the generations. I was a fae. I would protect my pack.

The savage creature within slipped her leash. I dashed forward only to skid on slick stone. My wings flared, saving me from landing in puddled blood and beer.

Carnage clinging to my shoes, I wove across the room.

Even engaged with an attacker, Frazer noted my approach. *Don't use light magic. Not unless there's no alternative.*

I won't. I wouldn't know where to begin.

Two fae blocked my path, striking and spitting at each other. To avoid being caught in the middle, I dove under a nearby table, one of the few left undamaged, and crawled out the other side.

I found myself closest to one of Cai's aggressors, a bullish-looking male who jeered and made wild stabs in the air with a tiny blade.

"Are you actually trying to stick me with that thing?" Cai goaded him. "Your knife's a damned letter opener. Hasn't anyone told you that bigger is better?"

The male roared with unbridled fury and jabbed outward.

Cai stopped a knife to the kidney.

I lunged and punched the bullish male in the wing joint. He wheeled around to face me, screaming, knife swinging.

I struck his nose with the heel of my palm.

Crunch. Blood spurted.

Holy shit. I hadn't just broken the bone, I'd smashed his nose beyond repair.

He covered his mangled face. "You fucking kurpä!"

Cai punch-slammed his other wing joint, and the male let out another scream of agony.

Too bad. I kicked him in the balls with my newfound strength.

The would-be murderer wailed. He grabbed his pummeled plums and toppled over onto his side.

One among our enemies—a brunette female—abandoned her attack on my brother. She dropped to the bull-male's side. "Bo? Talk to me."

His unintelligible groans were drowned out by the *clang, clang, clang* of a bell.

"You've done it now, you louts!" Octavia bellowed. "You've summoned the Bastards!"

The violence slowed to a stop.

Two seconds of silence. Then, "MOVE!"

Our attackers led the charge toward the exit. The taproom's patrons lost their senses, shoving one another and trampling over whomever remained unconscious. Even those nursing serious injuries hobbled and crawled out the door, determined to flee.

Cai was nearby. I grabbed him and shielded him with my wings. My brother—where was he? I glanced left just in time to see Frazer punch Ryder over the ear.

The force of my brother's blow sent the Samite staggering sideways. Before he could fall, Frazer wrapped a muscled forearm around his neck.

I watched Ryder struggle against being choked out, unsure what to do. Then came the sudden screech of, "Bitch!"

The brunette and her wounded "Bo" hadn't left. The female lunged for me.

I countered her incoming knife with a wrist hold. Quick as a cat's paw, I wrapped my free hand around her throat.

"You're dead," she said, her spittle hitting me.

Mercy fled from my heart. I pulled her in and bit her neck, asserting dominance.

The brunette grasped my hair and tugged viciously. Releasing my stranglehold, I knocked her hand away and pushed her back onto her ass, sprawling her over her ball-cupping male.

Her blood tasted foul; I spat it out.

"Leave or die." I slid my sword free and leveled it at my two enemies.

Their eyes narrowed with revenge fantasies.

My sunlight suddenly surged. It burned hot in my veins, promising violence and death. I could tell it wanted *out*. I rammed it down with all my might.

Cai moved to my shoulder, pointing his longsword at the two idiots. "Refusing to make a decision will still lead to your deaths."

My brother appeared on my other side. "Five. Four ..."

I took a step forward.

"We're going," the male hissed, spattering the floor with blood.

Our two attackers limped out into the night.

Temporarily sated by our enemy's defeat, my sunlight mellowed and slumbered once again.

I sheathed my sword. Cai did the same.

Frazer scooped a sleeping Ryder off the floor. Then, without a word, we crossed the destroyed taproom. I considered stopping to check the people on the floor weren't dead, but that ringing bell hadn't escaped my mind.

The Bastards were coming, and whoever they were, they'd cleared out an entire room in under a minute. It wouldn't be wise to linger.

We were almost at the stairs when Octavia blocked our path. Her painted face made a terrifying picture, despite having the texture of boiled cabbage.

"You two started this." She jabbed an accusing finger at Frazer and Cai. "You've destroyed my place and brought the Bastards to my door. And now you think you can sneak upstairs and hide? I don't think so." She growled the last few words, her breath soured with drink.

"Who are the Bastards?" Cai asked.

Octavia's nostrils flared. "They're a gang operating on the outskirts of town. They provide protection for local businesses. Only the 'protection' isn't optional, and neither is the coin they demand for their services."

Frazer spoke low and quick. "We'll compensate you for your damages and for whatever the gang takes in protection costs. And if you keep quiet about us being here, you'll get a bonus. A generous one."

Eyes narrowing, her shoulders dropped down from around her ears.

"We're leaving in the morning," Cai added. "You'll never see us again."

A canny glint sparked in her pouchy eyes. "Going by your fancy steel, I'm inclined to believe you've got the money. But I have to blame someone for this." She motioned to the shattered glass, broken earthenware, and splintered tables. "The gang must make an example out of someone. It's how they keep their reputation as enforcers."

Frazer frowned. "What does making an example out of someone include?"

"A beating, most likely."

"Then blame that couple that just left."

Octavia's reply was swift. She didn't even need to think about it. "Fine. But when the gang is gone, you'll pay me immediately, and you'll clean this place up. Try to cheat me, and you won't live to see morning."

"You'll get your money," Frazer promised. "But we're not cleaning this up for you."

Octavia's ample chest swelled in indignation.

"Do you want our money or not?" Frazer punched out.

"Fine," Octavia huffed, deflating. "Get out of my sight."

She stepped aside and waved at the staircase. I went first, hurtling up the creaking steps.

Adrianna flung open the door to our room and beckoned us in. Cai followed me through and dropped his rucksack to the floor. Liora opened her arms to her brother.

Cai gave his sister a quick, reassuring hug. Frazer came in last with Ryder.

"What happened there?" Adrianna asked, inclining her chin toward the Samite.

"I choked him out." A matter-of-fact statement.

Ryder ended up on the washroom floor, divested of the lockpicks and blades hidden in the lining of his ragged coat. Frazer secreted the collection into his own rucksack and exited the washroom. "If he wakes up, I don't want him hearing us," he said to Cai.

Cai waved his hand. The air in the room grew thicker, denser. A sign that he'd erected a soundproof bubble, keeping us safe from prying ears.

"Shouldn't we interrogate him?" Adrianna said.

That suggestion made it difficult to look one another in the eye.

Cai kneaded the back of his neck. "What if he won't tell us anything?"

With a closed-off expression, Adrianna replied, "Generally, that's where the interrogating bit would come in."

"You mean to torture him?" Cai said bluntly, his hand falling from his neck.

A chill traveled through my blood.

Adrianna's voice dropped below freezing. "You don't have to watch if it makes you uncomfortable."

His face went slack. "This isn't about me being squeamish. I just don't believe we should be torturing people."

A muscle twitched under Adrianna's eye.

"It would be nice if we never had to do anything that compromised our morals," Frazer said. "We'd sleep more soundly. But the harsh truth is if we want to keep the world safe and not get murdered in our beds, we have to think like leaders, not act with the delusions of being heroes."

A painful silence fell. As bad as hearing nails scrape over pottery.

Cai's humiliation showed in the flush of red spreading up his neck and into his cheeks. "I'm not trying to be a hero. He's defenseless."

Frazer corrected him, his tone neutral. "A male with his training is never defenseless. He could snap someone's spine with both hands behind his back. However ... I will agree that in this particular case, torture isn't the best tactic."

Thank fuck.

"Ryder's trained to resist interrogation," Frazer continued. "He'd also be a threat from the moment he woke up."

"What's the alternative? Keep him in our washroom and hope he doesn't wake up?" There was no scorn in Adrianna's tone, only uncertainty.

An idea formed bubble-like in my mind. I addressed Cai. "What if you dosed Ryder with a sleeping powder? Like the one you made for Maggie OneEye?"

Cai's clouded features cleared. "That could work. Although, I don't have any valerian ..."

"You could add more chamomile," Liora contributed.

"It's not as strong."

Back and forth they went. More often than not they preempted each other's meaning before it had been fully voiced—their knowledge of the craft was as daunting as it was impressive. Once they were done conversing, Cai announced, "I can keep Ryder down for about eleven hours with the supplies I've got."

Frazer was the one to respond. "Good enough."

"That only gets us until nine tomorrow morning," Adrianna said, glancing at the wheezy clock on the wax-splattered mantelpiece. "Our ship might not have docked by then." She rounded on Frazer. "I could fly Ryder out to the forest and leave him there. That would give us a head start if he's intent on betraying your location, supposing that he hasn't already."

Frazer snipped that budding idea at the root. "If he'd reported me, the authorities would have already been here and he wouldn't have walked into that taproom."

"Sure about that, are you?" she asked.

Frazer pretended not to hear her question. "As for you flying Ryder somewhere, it's not worth the risk. You could be delayed or attacked. If he wakes up before your ship arrives, I'll knock him out again. That gives us the same head start." He turned toward Cai. "How long will the powder take to make?"

"Five minutes or so."

Cai crouched on the squeaky floor with his bag. There, he gathered ingredients and pressed herbs into a fine powder with his pocket-sized mortar and pestle.

The lull in action brought my exhaustion to the forefront of my mind. I could feel my energy draining away, but I couldn't tell if it was caused by spent adrenaline or if repressing the sunlight had done this to me.

Legs as weak as tissue paper, I sat-collapsed down on the bed. At the same time, I heard a group of fae enter the taproom like a thunderclap.

"Ocy, as radiant as ever! Who are we maiming tonight?"

"It was that idiot Bo and his lover. But they've already gone."

"Shame," replied the masculine voice. "Since we came to your rescue anyhow, you won't mind us taking a few provisions away with us."

"Of course not," Octavia said, sounding as though she could happily stab him.

The gang weren't quiet in their efforts to loot the place. There was a lot of crashing, banging, huffing, and puffing.

Frazer laid his rucksack at my feet. "Your new clothes are inside. I also bought you some shoes so you won't have to wear boots anymore."

A relief. I'd gotten one too many blisters from wearing leather boots in the height of summer. "Have I ever told you what an amazing brother you are?"

"No. And I don't wish for you to start now."

I snorted a laugh.

He coughed. "Also, Cai has the other items."

"You mean my bras?"

"Mm."

I searched his rucksack, taking out the parcels. There were several garments—everything had slits or sections cut out of the back. None of my new clothes would've been considered appropriate for a woman in the Gauntlet. I imagined walking through Tunnock in a cropped top and trousers, wings and fangs out, and I smiled at the thought of my old neighbors' shock.

As the sounds of looting continued, Frazer watched over Ryder, Adrianna stared out of the window, and Liora presented me with her hairbrush.

"Would you mind?" she asked, settling beside me on the bed. "I get too hot with it down."

I took the brush. "Sure."

Liora's scent—the scent of growing things—surrounded me as I started taming the butterfly bush that was her hair. By the time I'd wrangled her dyed curls into a crown plait, Cai had finished the sleeping powder. He took a cautious sniff of the substance. His eyelids shuttered and he swayed a touch.

Alarmed, I moved to steady him.

Cai waved me off and sneezed twice in rapid succession. After dabbing at his nose, he stood with the mortar in hand and walked into the washroom. There, with the aid of a lullaby wind, the powder drifted up Ryder's nose.

No response.

Cai slapped Ryder across the face.

Nothing.

"I guess that means it worked," Adrianna remarked.

Before any of us could reply, Octavia's voice reached us. "You've picked the kitchen and my pockets clean, isn't it time you were on your way?"

A few of the marauders protested.

"Now, now, lads, we've had our fill," one among their number shouted. "Let's get gone."

There weren't any more objections.

The Bastards left with as much noise as they'd made coming in. When their wingbeats faded from fae-hearing, I freed a sigh. "Finally."

"You better still be up there," Octavia called up to us. "Because I want my money *now*."

Cai made a circular motion with his hand. The sound barrier dropped. "We'll be down in a moment."

"Hurry up." Her footsteps echoed and faded away.

"How much d'you think we'll need?" Cai whispered to Frazer.

"Fifty florén should cover it," Frazer estimated.

Adrianna grew spiky. "Diana's money should've been earmarked for essentials—"

"I'll use my portion to repay Octavia," Frazer assured.

Adrianna made a face. She was obviously regretting her decision to share the money out between us.

"I can help out," Cai offered Frazer. "I won some money at the card tables. Might as well use it for this."

Frazer nodded in gratitude. "We should head down before we're dragged out by our ankles."

The guys hastened to where Octavia waited. They weren't gone long, and when they returned they carried with them cutlery, stacked bowls, a bottle of wine, and a clay pot set on a ceramic trivet.

The five of us squatted on the floor, safe in another soundproof bubble.

I pointed my nose at the pot and sniffed at the air delicately. "What's in there?" It didn't seem to smell of anything. Totally bland.

"Yesterday's stew." Cai peeled the potlid off. "I found it hidden in the warming oven. It was the only thing the gang didn't steal."

"That doesn't bode well," Adrianna mused.

Cai shrugged good-naturedly. "It's hot. That's all I care about."

The meal proved too tempting after weeks of cold rations, and everyone ate their fill of the watery concoction. The best that could be said of it was that it only tasted of tough meat and overcooked carrots.

With the pot scraped clean, Cai uncorked the bottle he'd brought.

"Wine?" Adrianna arched a brow. "Is that wise?"

"Wine is always wise," Cai joked. "It's also probably better for us than the water running through these pipes, but you can always abstain. It was meant as more of a gesture anyway."

"A gesture?" I echoed.

"We've been through a lot lately," Cai replied. "We deserve a damned drink."

None of us disagreed.

We passed the wine around, swigging from the bottle. Halvard's weakness for wine gave me enough knowledge to tell it was swill, but the taste of sour fruit on the vine was mildly better than the food.

A few gulps warmed our bellies and relaxed our throats. In the wilds, we'd gone days without sound shields to avoid draining Cai. As a consequence, we hadn't spoken much, not wanting to attract a dangerous sprite or a rogue wanderer. But in this fragile moment we were free to discuss anything, and our chief topic of conversation became our role as knights. We ruminated on what our responsibilities might be beyond stopping Archon, and we found laughter in the madness of our situation. There was one awkward moment, at least for me, when Adrianna mentioned my sunlight struggles. Frazer knew some of it, but he'd no wealth of knowledge to draw upon or help to give, a fact that caused him frustration. Cai could only repeat Liora's sentiments that losing control was natural.

Nearing the bottom of the bottle but far from drunk, our pack's mood shifted. We fell quiet, and the silence stretched thin like butter over too much bread. I felt we were in agreement; all of us knew sleep was necessary, but none of us wished to say goodnight. I certainly didn't. I was desperate to delay the moment where we would go from five people to four.

Frazer broke that tense hush. "Cai, d'you want to divide up the new rations? It'll save us doing it tomorrow."

Cai placed the stewpot and earthenware aside. From out of his rucksack, he pulled parcels of preserved food and we divvied up the rations. Cai laid out two more boxes and nudged the smaller one toward me. "That's for you."

I untied the bow from around the box and lifted the lid. Inside were four bras with cross-straps.

After packing them away beside my new clothes, I asked Cai, "Did you get any odd looks while buying them?"

"Yes." He flashed me a toothy grin. "But then I told the shop assistant they were for my lover."

"I'm flattered," I quipped. "I'd be lucky to have you."

"Feel free to say more things like that," Cai encouraged in a droll way.

"You clean up good," I said. It wasn't my best compliment but I hadn't lied. The guys had washed up earlier, and they both looked better for it.

"I feel so pretty." Cai pretended to preen.

I batted my lashes stupidly. "Aren't you going to return the compliment?"

He tipped the empty wine bottle toward me in a salute. "Your wings are stunning."

Gods above, that actually made me blush. My wings twitched, keen to splay out in some absurd peacock display. I shut that instinct down fast.

"Maybe the wine was a bad idea after all." Adrianna leaned back against the bed's end. "I'll be flirting with Frazer next."

Frazer loosed his typical chuff—a noise that sounded like a cough, a snort, and a growl combined. "Please don't."

I was very clear. "We were just joking, Adi. Cai and I aren't actually flirting."

A relaxed nod was her only reply.

I glanced at Cai. As I suspected, he was sneaking peeks at Adrianna, his expression one of doubt and longing. Liora diverted us, no doubt for her brother's sake. "What's in the last box?"

Frazer slid it toward her. "Open it."

"You can't be embarrassed," Cai said to Frazer, almost gleeful. "How old are you again? A hundred?"

Frazer replied with a scathing look.

Cai leaned in toward him. "Two hundred?"

"Nice try." Frazer pushed him away, but the move had no strength behind it.

On the back of a sigh, Cai said, "Fine. Keep your secrets." His lively gaze skipped to Liora and without a hint of embarrassment, he added, "We bought you liners since we realized you and Ena are due to start your cycles next week." He glanced at me. "Although, Frazer said your bleeds might've changed now you're a fae."

Liora opened the box and peeked inside. "You bought a lot," she said, peering up at the guys, her eyes shining with amusement.

Frazer threw on his best brooding air. "We had to get a selection of sizes since we weren't sure …" He cleared his throat.

Adrianna lost it. Tossing her head back, she erupted into laughter.

"Don't you wear liners?" Frazer asked over this noise, his scowl deepening. "I know some females put a special sponge up there."

Liora pressed a hand over her mouth in a futile attempt to stifle her chuckles. For Frazer's sake, I kept a straight face. "No, you got it right. We use liners." I sounded wheezy from the effort to hold back the laughter rapping at my ribcage.

"Mm." Liora nodded, fighting the smile on her face. "This was really sweet of you both. Thank you."

"It was nothing." Frazer looked perturbed, as if the mention of him being sweet was somehow disturbing.

The liners were packed away. Adrianna dipped inside her bag and fished out a quartz crystal that radiated light waves. "You should take the concealment charm that Diana gave us." She presented it to Frazer.

He hesitated.

"Don't be stupid. The spiders are still out there hunting for us. You need this to confuse any tracking spells they might use. And this one doesn't need charging, remember?" Adrianna gestured for him to take it again. "Cai can keep the other one topped with energy for us."

Frazer nodded softly, acknowledging that logic.

Liora rushed out, "Actually, I don't think he should take that charm."

"What are you talking about?" Adrianna lowered her arm, keeping the crystal in her hand.

Liora looked like she was about to jump into shark-infested waters. "I ... I think we should keep Diana's stone, and Cai should stay in Aldar with Frazer."

I wasn't surprised. I was shocked stupid.

Her face the color of her ruddy curls, Liora braved her brother's gaze. Cai had paled to a grisly white, his mouth agape.

"Someone should be here to watch Frazer's back," Liora told him. "And you're the only one—apart from me—who can teach him how to channel his magic. If he doesn't learn to control it, he won't be able to sneak into Mysaya."

Cai's cheek muscle ticked. "I know why you're doing this. If the binding can't be removed, you don't want me to see you die."

I broke twice. Once for Liora, once for Cai.

She went on, her notes steeled with resolve. "I'm saying this because it's the right thing to do. Frazer has a better chance of success with you by his side."

"I've already considered staying with Frazer," Cai said, his voice strained. "But if I don't go with you, I won't be able to help you when you're unbound. How are you going to deal with that alone?" He shot her a meaningful look.

Liora couldn't hold his gaze. "I'll tell Ena what to expect before she breaks my binding. I'll prepare her."

That straightened my back. Prepare me for what?

Liora had worked as a healer in the Crescent. However, I'd long suspected there was more to her power—something that made her dangerous and it so clearly terrified her, I hadn't resented that she had kept it secret.

Cai finally turned to where Frazer sat beside him. "Do you mind if I come with you?"

My brother's doubt and irritation sang through our bond, but when he faced Cai, he hid it well. "I'm fine with whatever you decide."

Breath bated, our pack waited for his answer. Without looking at any of us, Cai said, "Then I'll stay." He dug out four sheets of parchment from his bag. "And we'll split the last of the spelled paper between us. At least that way we can contact each other if something goes wrong."

Excitement leaped up my throat. Frazer and I couldn't hear each other's thoughts if we were too far away from each other. But spelled paper made long-distance contact possible. Unfortunately, Cai and Liora's supply was limited. They had already used some of it to write a letter to their father, warning him that his children had become outlaws.

"Wasn't the paper only designed to contact father?" Liora asked, staring at Cai from under dark red lashes.

"The paper's made for our clan. Anybody with Verona blood can use it. I just have to rework the spell." To do that, Cai blew over the leaves of parchment and uttered, "Forget."

A glittering dust drifted off the pages. That done, Cai looked at Liora, his face carefully arranged in a neutral mask. "I need a drop of your blood."

No questions. No hesitation. Liora held her hand up to Adrianna. "Can you use your fangs? It'll be easier than using a sword."

Adrianna looked reluctant, but she bared a fang and pricked Liora's finger with it anyway. Cai asked Frazer to do the same thing to him. When both Veronas were bleeding, they stamped each page with their bloody fingerprints. The red stains vanished, somehow absorbed by the spelled paper.

Cai handed two of the leaves over to Liora and kept two for himself. He didn't wait around; he grabbed his things and straightened up. "I'm going to bed. I'll see you in the morning."

He walked out, and the sound barrier imploded with a faint *whoosh*.

That was unpleasant, Frazer voiced through the bond.

I flashed him a *you-don't-say* look.

"I'll take Ryder next door." Frazer stood up, shouldered his bag, and stared down at me. "Rest well."

I wouldn't. "You too."

Frazer nodded. Once he'd left with Ryder, and it was just the three of us, Liora covered her face with her hands. She bowed over her knees, sobbing. That noise quickly became my least favorite sound in the world. Worse, I couldn't think of a damned thing to say.

I rubbed Liora's back. She kept wiping her cheeks with the backs of her hands, but her tears wouldn't stop falling. "I'm sorry." *Hiccup*. "I didn't mean to spring that on everybody. But I knew he wouldn't want to stay. I've been trying to think of how to convince him, and …" *Hiccup*. "I'm sorry," she said again.

"Don't be sorry," I said, pulling her against me in a side-hug. "I should be thanking you. I don't want to leave Frazer behind, but I'm happier knowing Cai will be with him. Frazer wouldn't admit it, but he could use the help."

I heard that, Frazer muttered.

I meant you to.

Liora's tears dried after a couple of minutes. That was when Adrianna stood up and said, "Both of you should get to bed."

My head lifted to meet her gaze. "What are you going to do?"

"Keep watch."

"I can take over from you in a couple of hours—"

"No, you can't," she argued. "I can always sleep on the ship, but if you're going to learn more about your magic, you need to dream. The quicker you do that, the quicker you can gain control."

She had me there.

I undressed and crawled under my pathetic singed sheet in my underthings. Liora shed a few outer clothes and got into the bed beside me.

The firelight lanterns dimmed when Adrianna tapped them one by one. Darkness enveloped us.

Fae-eyes adjusting, I saw Adrianna peer out of the window and scan the street below. Her silver ink glowed under the apple-peel moon.

Time moved as slow as a slug crossing a garden. The stuffy air was my enemy, my pillow was a nightmare. I plumped, fluffed, and nestled into it, but it remained as sad and dejected as ever.

"You can't sleep either, huh?" Liora mumbled on my left.

I sighed. "Nope."

"I've never been to the continent," Adrianna said, "but Diana was born in Mokara. She's taught me a lot about the eastern kingdoms—I could tell you about them. It might send you to sleep."

"I'd like that," Liora said.

"Me too," I added.

Adrianna began. "In my makena's language, the continent is called Teā Orā, the Land of Eternal Sun."

She went on, painting a picture of a continent divided into three kingdoms. Wuyon lay the farthest from us and had closed its borders. Mokara sat in the center, rich in rainforests, waterfalls, and pink sand beaches. Asitar was the nearest to Aldar, a week away by boat. There, deserts baked under a harsh sun, and by night the dunes cooled under stars so bright they hurt the eye.

Liora was soon curled up into a ball, sleeping.

Not far behind her, I left the world and entered a dream. There, I faced eyes, golden and proud, that resembled those of a lioness. The details of the face, however, wouldn't settle. Focusing on the image was like trying to catch a cloud with my mind.

Frustrated, I shifted my focus to my surroundings.

In a blink, a white canvas was filled in and I arrived on a hilltop. Below me, people marched with the tenacity and single-mindedness of ants, but they destroyed one another as only humans and fae could— with steel and magic.

That predator's gaze never left me. I glanced back at golden eyes to see the person's outline had now solidified, enough to determine it was a female with white-blond hair that stood before me.

We've got a lot to show you tonight. So pay attention. The confident tone betrayed her identity. Zola was with me.

Another person joined us on my left.

Sapphire eyes met mine. Again, the face and body were blurred. *Are you Thea?*

Yes. I could've sworn I heard a smile in her voice.

Why can't I see you properly?

It won't be long before we can project better images of ourselves to you. But for now, we'd rather focus our energies on making that which is relevant to your training clear.

Zola announced, *Let's begin.*

CHAPTER 11

TWO PEOPLE IN ONE HEART

Birds punctured my sleep with their morning rhymes. Shoved out of a well of dreams, I was forced into the waking world where other sounds awaited me. The creak of barrels rolled across wooden floors, the gush of tapped beer, the clink of glasses being shelved. By Octavia's shouted orders, I knew she was restocking the taproom.

I pulled my thin pillow out from under my head and pressed it over my ear.

"It's past seven." Adrianna was softly spoken. Odd for her.

I loosed a groan.

"You've slept long enough," she added, a little firmer this time.

She was right, of course. I threw the pillow aside, rolled over onto my wings, and cranked my eyes open.

The ribs of the arched roof came into focus. I waited for the weight of this day to crash into me, but I was numb.

Liora slept on beside me, untroubled by the noise downstairs.

I angled my chin to rest near my right shoulder. With a clear view of Adrianna, I said, "Is this why you're always up so early? Rutting fae-hearing?"

"No." Adrianna pushed off the wall and shook out her wings. "I started getting up at dawn every day because it was the only time I could train in combat without my entire court watching me and reporting back to my makena. Then I just never stopped."

"Oh," I said around a yawn. "That actually makes sense."

An ill-humored snort. "I'm glad you think so." She crossed her arms and changed tack. "So, what happened last night? Did Zola and Thea start your lessons?"

That question scattered images across my mind like a broken string of pearls. Each bead contained a memory. I picked up a few and looked them over.

I saw sun-spears hurled at armies, moon-shields that turned away the sharpest of blades, waterlight being used to cure a curse, and the brightest of all light—starlight—blinding an enemy.

"Yeah," I said, nodding. "They did."

"What did they teach you?" Adrianna asked.

I reared up into a cross-legged position and scrubbed my face. "They showed me how light-wielders use their magic. They wanted me to see what I was capable of."

She made a face. "Is that it? They didn't give you any one-on-one training?"

"What do you mean?" I squinted at her, confused.

"On account of them being light-wielders," she told me plainly. "Although given Balor erased a huge chunk of our history, I wouldn't be surprised if the legends were wrong."

"They aren't wrong," I said under my breath.

She crooked her eyebrow at me. A call for more information.

"I asked them last night if the book I'd read had been right about their powers—"

"What book?"

"*The Darkest Song.* You've seen it before. Wilder lent it to me." I paused, sadness threatening to bury me. Quieter than before, I continued. "It was filled with stories about the gods and their courts. I didn't take them seriously, but it turns out they were mostly true. At least the ones about Zola and Thea. Thea's blessed with waterlight and can dreamwalk. And Zola's gift is sunlight. She only seems to use it to fight people—"

"That's because she's the ultimate warrior."

My eyebrows rose in surprise.

"What?" Adrianna shrugged a shoulder. "She is. They call her the Goddess of Courage. That's why I want her to take a hands-on approach with you. Not everybody gets the chance to learn magical combat from a master."

I detected a hint of awe in her. My knowing smile solicited a scowl and a shift in the conversation. "But if she won't do it, you should ask Sefra to train with you once we find her."

"Why would I ask her?"

"Because Sefra's blessed with sunlight. Like your mother was."

My surprise wasn't subtle. The seam of my mouth ripped open, and I pushed out a depleted sound. "Oh."

"Can you wake Liora?" Adrianna asked. "I need to splash some cold water on my face."

I nodded, distracted.

Adrianna entered the washroom. But I didn't wake Liora up. I was too busy thinking about how my half sister shared my magic. What if I proved to be a slow learner? Would she be ashamed of me?

Zola interrupted that descent into self-doubt. *Don't be ridiculous. You've had access to your abilities for two days, and sunlight is the most volatile of all magical disciplines. It takes most witches decades to master it.*

I'm doomed, I thought dryly.

No, you're not. Half of the battle is not being afraid of it.

What's the other half?

Long, arduous hours of practice, she said, her tone clipped. *If you want to talk about this more, we'll have to do so later. I'm busy at the moment.*

Curiosity struck me. *Really? What are you doing?*

Nothing.

Hello?

No answer.

I shouldn't have been surprised. The sisters were only using the necklace to communicate with me. They were still in the light court, presumably living as they always had. I wondered, then, what a god did all day.

Did they lounge around on divans, being fed grapes and having servants massage them? That didn't seem quite right somehow. From the little I'd gleaned of their personalities, I expected Zola might spend her time drinking and punching people who disagreed with her. Thea, on the other hand, I could see playing a harp beside a stream surrounded by woodland creatures.

I snorted at such stupid visualizations.

Adrianna called out to us from inside the washroom. "I don't hear anybody getting up."

I let my feelings out in a quick roll of my eyes. Then I dutifully shook Liora awake. "It's time to get up."

A puff of air escaped her. A not-quite-there moan.

"It's no use," I said, smiling. "Adrianna will just take our pillows if we don't get up."

"You bet your left tit I will," she called to us.

Liora uncurled like a grumpy cat. "Fine." Her blurry gaze greeted mine. "Just give me a second to remember how to function."

I balked at the sight of her paper-pale face. The image stuck in my throat like lumpy porridge and frightened me more than her once cherry-red cheeks. A fever meant that you were fighting—that you were still here. Liora looked closer to death than life. A soon-to-be ghost. I didn't have the heart to disturb her any more than I already had.

I stood up, stretching my limbs and wings.

The fae bra proved awkward to put on. I had to fiddle with it until I figured out which strap went where. That done, I slipped on canvas-shoes, high-waisted trousers, and a crop top with enough length to conceal the ink on my ribs.

Adrianna walked out of the washroom carrying the clothes we'd left drying in there. She took one look at how slowly Liora was moving around and pursed her lips. I thought she might hurry her. But she just packed away our garments silently.

I took my turn in the bathroom. When I was done in there, I set my sights on attending to my groaning belly.

The new rations were as woefully unimaginative as the first lot. Resigned, I picked a cereal bar out of my rucksack and started in on it.

Frazer's voice flitted into my head. *Are you ready?*

Just eating. You?

Same. Nearly done.

With our separation hanging over our heads like an executioner's sword, my stomach swiftly became a hostile environment for food. I declared breakfast over at a single oat-raisin bar.

Adrianna was refilling our canteens and Liora was cleaning her teeth when we heard movement in the corridor outside. I stalked across the floor and stuck my head out the door.

Cai was hauling an unconscious Ryder downstairs. Frazer moved toward me. I backed up, allowing him to walk into the room and shut the door.

Frazer looked prepared to leave, his bag strapped between his silver wings, his Utemä belted to his side. This was really happening.

My morning stupor vanished. Emotion hit me hard. It was a blow that made me feel as if I stood atop a thin film of ice, unable to do anything but watch as it cracked around me.

I distracted myself. "Where's Cai taking Ryder?"

"He's dumping Ryder downstairs and guarding him until we leave."

"Are you both coming down to the docks with us?" Liora piped up from behind me, her voice reedy and thin. "Or are we saying goodbye here?"

"We're walking with you," he confirmed. "It's the least we can do."

We had more time together then. Just a little more.

Adrianna pointed out what no one else would. "If you do that, our whole pack will be seen together."

Frazer addressed Adrianna, straight-backed. "We'll take the side streets, and Cai and I will leave town as soon as you're gone."

The pause that followed rang with Adrianna's disapproval.

"Fine," she conceded. "Let's get a move on, then."

That call to action made me hurry over to my things. I strapped on the belt that held my sword and secured my bag to my back.

That left my kaskan and quiver. I picked them up from where they rested against the wall.

The sound of crashing water reached me and I froze. For a moment I was back in my old room in Tunnock, pressing a shell to my ear—a shell that my mother had gifted me. The noise faded when a blue thread unraveled, linking my bow to Frazer's hand.

Waterlight can be a guide in uncertain moments, Thea explained. *Follow your instincts.*

My instincts ... The bow's wood seemed to vibrate in my hand, and a strange yearning gripped me. It wanted to be with Frazer. I was sure of it.

I held the bow and quiver up to Frazer. "Take them."

His eyes challenged me. *Why?*

"I thought the kaskan's power only worked for its owner," said Adrianna.

I answered that while holding Frazer's gaze. "I don't think it can tell the difference between us anymore. Either way, its allegiance has changed. It's meant to be with you now. I can tell."

He regarded the bow with a sideways glance. A silent refusal. "If I take that, I'll be denying you a powerful weapon."

"You're not denying me anything if it doesn't work for me properly. Like I said, its allegiance has shifted." I pushed the bow and quiver toward him again. "Take it. Use it to keep you and Cai safe."

No more doubt. He shouldered the kaskan and quiver at once.

Our business finished, we made our way downstairs.

Miraculously, last night's wreckage had already been cleared away. The tavern floor was mostly empty, but the bar was groaning under boxes of supplies. Octavia was there, sorting through everything. But there was no Ryder, and no Cai.

"Where is he?" Liora asked, her tone strung with worry.

Adrianna cocked her head. Frazer's nostrils flared. I tried to emulate them, to listen for Cai and to track his scent. My efforts sent me into a sneezing fit. I didn't make another attempt.

Frazer broke rank and stalked over to Octavia. "Two men came down here—"

"They went into the kitchen." She gestured irritably at the door behind the bar.

"I'll get him." Frazer disappeared into the back room.

He left an anxious air in his wake.

I jolted as a stocky male walked in off the street, shouting, "Delivery."

He stooped, dumping a crate of produce that had seen better days. That explained the quality of last night's stew. Ugh.

Octavia rounded the bar with a surly remark. "You're late."

The male rubbed his chin-whiskers. "Apologies. A ship docked this morning, and the orders to restock their holds came in thick and fast. I've barely been able to catch up."

"What was the ship's name?" Adrianna blurted out.

"I don't rightly recall." Frazer and Cai walked in as the stocky male added, "But if it helps, the captain who signed for the deliveries was called Armstrong."

Without a word spoken, our pack moved for the exit.

"Good riddance," Octavia muttered at our backs.

None of us bothered to respond.

We stepped out into the crisp air. The sky was washed in shades of periwinkle, bluebell, and goldenrod. A beautiful summer morning.

Frazer led us away at a swift pace. We traveled along narrow back-streets lined with weather-speckled cottages. Some were painted in cheerful colors and had window boxes running over with flowers. Others were in need of a lick of paint and had refuse collecting up outside of their doors. Prettiness and disrepair sat side by side, and they looked uncomfortable with each other.

The streets were blessedly quiet. A man towed a handcart past us, his head bent, his mood introspective. Two fae left their abodes to take flight to parts unknown. Barring that, we walked on undisturbed.

Adrianna dared a quiet question. "What did you do with Ryder?"

Striding beside Frazer, Cai replied, "It occurred to me that an innkeeper who's in constant fear of raids would have a place to stash things she didn't want found. I convinced her—or my coin did—to let me borrow it." He grinned at Adrianna. "Dear old Ryder's currently locked away inside the inn's pantry. Octavia said she'd let him out tomorrow."

Adrianna returned his smile. "That's actually kind of brilliant."

"You don't have to sound so surprised."

His tone had been flippant, untroubled. Adrianna still took him seriously. "I'm not in the habit of giving praise, so if I come across as insincere, I can promise you that I'm not."

Always honesty with her. Cai's step and posture seemed lighter for it.

The wind picked up, bringing with it the pungent smell of salt and fish. We had to be nearing the sea. That fact wasn't enough to make me want to reach the docks quicker, but my low mood lifted just a bit.

We took an alleyway overshadowed by the surrounding buildings. As such, our view was narrow and limited. It wasn't until our feet carried us to the end of the road that the port opened up around us and the sea showed herself. The morning light bled into its watery depths, making the above and the below almost indistinguishable.

For a second, all I could do was watch as the ocean drew breath, its surface retreating and swelling only to exhale and wash over the rocky shore. To me, its waves were a pulse—a heartbeat—an echo of the life hidden inside.

It was then a memory glinted at me. I swept back the cobwebs of time and visited with the past.

"*Ena? Are you out there?*" *came a weak voice from inside my parents' bedroom.*

"*Yes, Mama.*"

I pushed open the door.

Mama stared back at me from the bed. "*I've been waiting for you to come visit.*"

"*Papa says you're ill, and I shouldn't bother you unless you need something,*" *I said softly.*

"*How long have you been sitting outside my bedroom?*"

"*Since Papa left for work.*"

I got a pale-lipped smile in return. "*Come sit with me.*" *She beckoned me over with a limp wave.* "*I've got something to give you.*"

A present? I inched inside and closed the door gently.

As I climbed up onto her bed, Mama reached for something on her bedside table. She turned back to me and opened her palm to show me a spiky white object. "*This is a shell. The ocean brought it to me.*" *She placed the shell over my ear.* "*Can you hear that shush-shush-shush sound?*"

I nodded.

Mama laid the shell in my hand. "*That's the ocean's song. If you ever feel lonely or like you don't belong here, I want you to listen to it and remember that this tiny village is just a dot on a very big map. There's a whole world out there waiting for you, and it's made up of oceans, and sunrises, and countries, and things that most people around here could only dream of.*"

I peered at the small shell in awe. "*How does it sing, though? Is it enchanted?*"

"*Not exactly,*" *she said as she swept the hair out of my face.* "*They say that once upon a time, the ocean's spirit took on the form of a woman. It was in this form that she met and fell in love with a man. They were together for many years when tragedy struck. The man ... died, and his soul got trapped among the stars. The ocean's heart broke to be parted from him, so she sang to her lost love for a* year and a day. Her voice was so loud and her grief so strong that every shell in the world was haunted by her melody ever after."

I scowled, wanting the story to get to the good part. "But there's a happy ending, right, Mama? The ocean and the man found each other?"

"They will one day." Her eyes lifted to the rafters. "As of now, he's still waiting for her to join him among the stars."

"How can the sea meet the stars?"

"They meet every night," she whispered. "They just can't touch."

I pouted crossly. "I don't like this story."

"That's because you've got a tender heart." Mama's hand splayed over my chest. "And you must guard it well until you find someone worthy of it."

"How will I know if they're worthy?"

She smiled faintly. "Because they'd fall from the stars just to be with you."

"I don't want them to fall. They could get hurt." I flapped my arms and said, "What if I turn into a bird? Then I could go and find them."

A light laugh sprung from her. "Even better."

I blinked, and the past retreated behind a veil.

"That's it," Adrianna breathed out. *"The Eye of the Wind."*

Her neck was craned left, her stare fixed upon a three-masted ship.

"How do you know it's the right one?" Cai asked.

"Because the name's written on the side of the ship." Adrianna started forward, leading us toward the largest vessel in the port.

Frazer's wing brushed against mine. I glanced sidelong and caught his eye. From one look, I knew he'd witnessed me reliving my childhood. *I haven't thought about that story in a long time. Do you think ... Was she talking about Dain?*

His night-blues were thoughtful. *I couldn't really say.*

She must've missed him so much—and Sefra.

He read the thoughts I left unspoken. *Your mother had you. She wasn't alone.*

I nodded, swallowing past the tightness in my throat.

We passed smaller boats tied to the moorings. They bobbed up and down pleasantly, their bodies creaking, their sails snapping in the wind.

Our pack veered onto a path that jutted out into the water and ran adjacent to our ship. The murmuration of sailors and the rhythmic percussion of lapping waves surrounded us.

The needle of time had wound down to our departure, and *The Eye of the Wind* loomed large. I'd never seen a ship that wasn't in a painting or illustration. The real thing was bigger than I'd imagined. Crafted from loula wood, it had a stunning dove-gray body.

We arrived at the foot of the gangplank. Above us, the crew scurried like bees around a hive, participating in a well-rehearsed work dance. But our pack ignored them, closing in on ourselves. Adrianna, Liora, and I stood on one side. The guys lined up opposite, facing us.

"I'll arrange everything with Armstrong," Adrianna volunteered. "Take your time saying goodbye to one another."

Sorrow laid me low. I was unable to form a response.

Cai's wrist flick brought a sound barrier to life.

"Do you think the captain will know who you are?" he asked Adrianna.

"I'd be surprised if my makena gave him our names," she said. "But if this Armstrong's met her, he might figure out we're related."

Too true. The resemblance was strong.

With an almost formal air, Adrianna addressed Cai. "Be good. Be safe."

His usually lively features fell flat. "I know you're not a hugger. But just this once?"

The corner of her lip hooked up. "Just this once."

They embraced. Cai angled his head so that his lips were over her ear. I didn't hear anything until his voice broke over a single syllable. *Love*.

Adrianna took a very deliberate step back. "Goodbye, Cai."

Her voice had a kindness in it, but Cai's face still drained of hope. I recognized the pain in his eyes, the wound that had been inflicted. It mirrored what I'd been through with Wilder.

Cai was fast to erase the melancholy etched in his expression. It put me in mind of a breeze softening meadow grass, leaving behind an illusion that all was calm. All was well. From behind an unfeeling mask, he uttered, "Goodbye."

Adrianna faced Frazer and placed her fist over her heart. "Hyvästäd nyta."

Frazer mirrored the movement and the Kaeli phrase.

"I'll shout when I've secured our passage," Adrianna told me and Liora.

My nod had her whirling around and marching up the gangplank. Her departure coincided with a tremor in the air and our sound-bubble breaking.

I glanced up at Cai. I assumed he would be staring at Adrianna's retreating back, but he was concentrated on his sister. Liora moved toward him as if in a daze. "I'm sorry."

A month of walking under the sun seemed to fade from his complexion as he paled to the hue of dull ash. "Don't be sorry." He held her in his arms, resting his chin upon her head. "Just stay alive."

She clung to him as though he were a tree in a flood. And I ached all over as if I'd come down with an ague.

Frazer was there, gripping my arm, keeping me upright with a single touch. I wasn't sure who leaned into who, but when his forehead touched mine, tears wetted my cheeks.

To me, my brother was a compass needle pointing north—a fixed point that I could guide myself by. He was also the mirror that told me I wasn't alone. Except now I would be.

The river pouring out of me blocked my airways. I was struggling to breathe, and my grief was getting loud. Before I lost hold completely, Frazer's hands grasped either side of my nape. *Breathe.*

I sucked in reluctant air, thinking, *How long will it take you to get to Mysaya?*

Three weeks or thereabouts.

Promise me that you'll be all right. A stupid ask. An impossible one.

His smile was soft, sad, and lopsided. *I won't be a hero.*

There was no promise. How could there be?

With time running short, I let down every barrier. I embraced our bond with stitch, feather, and fiber. With all of me.

Frazer was more reserved, but he shared as much of himself as he was comfortable.

I couldn't have said how long we stood there, our brows glued together, sharing wave after wave of emotion. From both sides it came, meeting in the middle, the current so strong that it carried me under and I wasn't sure where one person ended and the other began.

A much-dreaded call came from Adrianna. "It's done. The captain's ordered for us to cast off."

Without a fuss, Frazer gathered his sleeves and dried my tears. Embarrassed, I wiped my soggy nose before he could.

Frazer and I retreated from each other's minds. We stepped apart.

To my right, Cai kissed the top of his sister's head. This had her disentangling from him and drawing away. Her expression was wandering—lost, like a flower plucked by a breeze.

Cai's eyes were dry but sunken with sadness. He turned to me and beckoned me in. I embraced him fiercely, whispering in his ear, "Do you have everything? Your concealment charm?"

"Frazer has it," he said, his stubble nettling my cheek.

"Stay out of trouble."

He forced out a laugh. "You too." In a tiny voice, he added, "When you break Li's chains, remember that it's still her."

My mind tripped over that cryptic request. I nodded anyway.

We released each other.

"Don't die," Cai said with a wink.

A serious comment dressed up as a joke. I attempted to follow his example with a smile and said, "Same to you."

"Take care of yourself, yatävä," Frazer told Liora.

Those words tickled my memory. I had an inkling it meant friend.

Liora looked inclined to hug him, but she lost her nerve when Frazer crossed his arms. He tolerated touch from me. He didn't want anybody else getting close, though.

"You too," Liora said, softer than a spider's footstep.

Our farewells done, this had to be the end. So why wasn't I moving?

All around us, sailors leaped over the ship's side, letting their wings soften their landing. They untied mooring ropes as thick as my forearm, and a voice of rusty iron shouted orders from the top deck.

"Time to go," Adrianna said to us.

That command unfroze me, but not Liora. For her, I found the will to move. Interlocking our fingers, I maneuvered her up the gangplank to where Adrianna waited.

We joined her at the railing of the mid deck, and the sails lowered to reveal sigils stitched into the canvas. These markings shimmered like powdered glass caught in the sun, and I assumed magic was at play somehow.

"We can stay on deck for now," Adrianna informed us. "But once we reach Morgan's sea border, Armstrong wants us in our cabin."

"Okay," I said, my eyes stuck on my brother.

Frazer had stayed on the dock while Cai walked away. I suspected that he'd reached his limit. I didn't blame him.

Liora leaned against me. I held onto her as the ship's inanimate bulk came to life. The deck groaned; the shining sails billowed as they filled with an invisible wind.

I clasped the railing so hard it hurt. But I could not stop the inevitable. The cruel current snatched us in its grip, and we crept forward.

Nasiri grew smaller. Frazer's outline blurred, fading.

I leaned over the railing to try to keep him in my sights for as long as possible. To suspend the moment of separation.

Frazer's voice came in, distant but still there. *Two halves of a heart can't be separated, siska. Remember that.*

I was sure I was being torn in two. A sob crawled up from the back of my throat. I clamped my jaw shut, not daring to let it go for fear it would come out in a scream.

My thoughts turned the shade of nightmares. He could be captured, tortured, killed. And I wouldn't be with him. I wouldn't be able to protect him.

Just then, I wanted to dive off the ship and trust my wings to do the rest. He might've sensed that, because he added, *When I'm done in Mysaya, I'll come find you, even if I have to fly across the ocean and desert to do it.*

That staved off the teetering panic. We would always find each other. I clung to that fact and sent him three last words. *I love you.*

Our mind link stretched to breaking, he left me with, *I know.*

Amidst the misery, that made me smile.

∼

- FRAZER -

My wings twitched. To be chained to the land and watch half of my heart sail away was intolerable. Everything inside of me wanted to fly after my blood. To protect her from the dangers she would inevitably face.

I summoned my willpower, beating those instincts into submission and adopting a cold line of reasoning.

My wings weren't ready.

I wouldn't catch up to the ship.

Ena was doing her part. I must do mine.

Tearing my eyes from the empty horizon, I set a determined pace toward the shoreline. I hadn't gone six feet before I felt a sharp tugging underneath my ribs. Ena pulled at me. The bond wanted me to turn back.

I loosed a breathless huff. Times like these I didn't recognize myself. I'd become dependent on another person, something I'd sworn to never do.

From the moment I met Ena at Kasi, I'd seen in her the same loneliness of spirit and weariness of heart that afflicted me. The only difference was that she had all the warmth that I lacked. I'd tried to ignore her, to not care about her, and I'd failed. But I couldn't regret our meeting, even if our twining resulted in my destruction. For I'd lived more with half a heart than I ever had when it was whole.

I growled ruefully at the sentimental hue of my thoughts, and a passerby gave me an odd look and a wide berth. Excellent. Just how I liked it.

Cai's scent led me to the end of the dock. Still no sign of him.

What was he doing? Did he think I had time to trail after him?

I abandoned the town and let my nose guide me out into the surrounding forest. The trees' long silhouettes were capable of hiding a great many enemies. I listened harder and planted my feet more deliberately here. I hadn't detected anyone, but that was no guarantee. A Samite like Ryder had the skill to tail me unnoticed.

Would the sedative have worn off by now? Estimating the time we'd spent at the dock and supposing the drug had worked as intended, I calculated we wouldn't have long before he woke up. The innkeeper's pantry might hold him a little longer, but I couldn't rely on that.

Concerned, I picked my feet up into a jog.

After several minutes, the witchy scent that reminded me of a storm in springtime got stronger. Then I heard a laughing wind and screaming trees.

Breaking into a run, I raced past branches that hung on by their splinters, and a scattering of pearl-hued leaves already dead on the floor.

I halted when I came upon Cai.

He palm-struck thin air. The force of his air-blast knocked him on his ass and the target, a loula sapling, split and crashed to the ground. Losing one of the trees of my homeland had me hissing in displeasure.

Cai stayed flat on his back, arms spread out at his sides.

I prowled over and glared down at him. "Was that necessary?"

"Yes," he pushed out, red-faced and panting.

My eyes slimmed. I was tempted to bite him, but his fit of berserker rage had seemingly passed. He'd needed to hit something, and he had, repeatedly. It was done. So I let it be done.

Cai rolled up in one sudden movement. He seemed unlikely to seek my touch out of comfort, but human reactions were unpredictable. I backed up and gave him space.

"Fuck." Cai grimaced at the felled sapling.

"Why did you do it?"

A wayward hand ran through his hair. "Why d'you think? Because this is fucking brutal. I might never see her again. She's my sister and she could die and I won't be there." He tugged at his dyed locks. "How are you so calm? I thought you'd be worse than me."

"I'm not calm," I admitted. "It feels like my chest is imploding. But I won't deny you may have it worse in this instance. If my siska dies, at least I won't have the hard job of living on after her."

Bemusement marked his wrecked eyes. "You're a dark son of a bitch, aren't you? You know that's not a healthy way to think, right?"

I shrugged my gray wings. "What do I care?"

He blew out a shaky laugh. That died when his gaze traveled around the immediate vicinity. "I didn't think I'd cause this much damage ... I've felled a tree and I'm not even tired. If I'd tried that before becoming an elemental, I'd have fainted."

All I had to say was, "That's good, then."

"I guess it is." He faced me with a frown. "And what about you? What of your magic?"

"What about it?" I said, nonplussed.

He shot me an irreverent look. Not playing that game, I remained silent and watchful.

Cai sighed. "Have you tapped into your power—used it at all?"

"I might've tapped into something when I was talking with Ryder at the inn." Recalling the iciness in my veins, I repressed a shiver. "But nothing before or after."

I didn't tell him that I'd no desire to use my seer abilities. Cai would ask why, and I wasn't about to tell anyone about my rotten bloodline.

"We'll need to start your training straight away," Cai said, retrieving his rucksack from the ground. "Disappearing for long enough to sneak into a castle, find the seer mirror, and get out again isn't going to be easy. How long do we have for you to get it right? How long until we get to Mysaya?"

I turned into a living statue just at the thought of that place. My wings instinctively flexed to loosen the tension knotting my back, and something that had once been as natural as breathing had my stomach rolling. It was an effort to keep my breakfast down.

Losing my wings had almost ended me. And on the same day that I'd been gifted new ones, I'd agreed to revisit the spot where my first set had been cleaved. That memory—that scar on my mind—nagged at me to retract them. Having my wings out was a distraction. Better to keep them safe and hidden from further harm. The only thing that stopped me was Cai. He would wonder why I'd tucked them away, and I hadn't the stomach to admit my weakness.

"Frazer? How long do we have?" Cai repeated as he shouldered his bag.

I swallowed my rising sickness. "I can't fly us there yet, so we'll have to go on foot. At a good pace, we'll reach Mysaya within three weeks. That's if we don't run into trouble in the mountains standing between us and the city."

"What's in the mountains?"

"Deva sprites. Big predators. Rogue fae," I listed grimly. "If you can help me get past them without being disemboweled, I'd be grateful. But once we near Mysaya proper, I'll travel on alone."

He scowled. "I'm here to help, not hide behind your wings."

I adopted my best elder tone. "Mysaya's watched closely. You'd be seen on approach, and you'd only succeed in getting me caught with you."

"All right," he said in a resigned tone. "This is your mission." Cai glanced over my head. "Do you know the way to Mysaya from here?"

"I'd know the way blindfolded."

He grasped the straps of his rucksack. "I'm ready when you are, then."

Orienting myself, I turned to the west and squared my shoulders. With the green sun at my back, I took the first step of a journey that would demand thousands more.

The kin bond strained again, objecting to how my sister and I were moving in opposite directions—that we weren't rectifying the distance between us. I kept moving though, one foot in front of the other.

An hour or two flitted by meaninglessly; my mind stayed blank and my heart kept grieving.

The world snapped back into focus when a group of fae dropped from the treetops. Despite our shock, Cai and I didn't waver. He drew his sword. I nocked an arrow and raised my kaskan, ready to shoot.

Ten fae lined up in front of us, their bows strung tight, their arrows centered on us. Ryder stood at the apex of the group.

"Damn," Cai said, pointing his longsword at Ryder. "The pantry didn't hold you, huh?"

He had the audacity to laugh. "If you lock someone up, you should check the jailor can't be bought off. Octavia betrayed you the second I offered her what little coin I had in my pockets. She even told me that she thought your group were headed to the docks."

And he'd tracked us from there, no doubt.

"I should demand a refund." That would've sounded like a joke if not for the humorless edge to Cai's voice.

"What do you want, Ryder?" I asked, opting for a bored tone.

"You."

"I don't do relationships."

"But you'll do males?"

"None of your business."

He snorted lightly. "Tease."

"Enough games. This is a kaskan bow," I said, raising my voice. "Leave now, and I won't start dropping bodies."

The enemy fae shifted their weight, clearly nervous at being on the receiving end of a kaskan's faultless aim. Ryder, however, was calm, and without a drawn weapon. "You can't kill us all."

"Woohoo." Cai waved.

Ryder glanced his way.

"Hi," Cai crooned. "Remember me?"

Before Ryder could reply, Cai threw his arm out.

I felt the breath of the forest at the back of my neck. It wasn't so gentle when it slammed into the fae. Nine out of the ten got blasted back.

Ryder still stood, one of his palms flat out as if he'd stopped the wind with a gesture. He didn't appear concerned by the loss of his allies.

I scanned him keenly. How had he done that? He wasn't a witch. It was then I noticed a faint glow coming from one of his rings.

Ryder crossed his arms, concealing what I guessed was some kind of protection charm.

"Walk away, Ryder."

"No."

My palm twitched, readying to free the silver string of my bow. "Then we have nothing more to say to each other."

"How about we try to resolve this stalemate before you kill me?"

I hesitated. "What do you propose?"

"We talk," he said simply.

CHAPTER 12
THE BEAST AWAKENS

Time is a slave to emotion. Fear and grief prolong it. Happiness shortens it. That became clear to me as I stood on the deck and a lifetime crawled by.

Aldar vanished from view. Yet I remained as motionless as the ship's figurehead, stuck in the dark web of my mind, an aching emptiness inside my heart.

The wind grew spirited around me. It whipped the spray over the ship's side and splattered my cheeks. I barely felt the sting or the chill of the saltwater. There was a permafrost in my veins that no earthly thing could touch.

I recognized this inner landscape. After my parents died, the world had turned cold, colorless, and hostile. I didn't know how to move through it without them, so I stopped living in it. I shut down. Frazer wasn't dead. But I felt just as numb as I had back then. Just as lost. What had I done in the past? How had I returned?

Memories streamed in, providing answers. I'd willed myself out of that hole for the people around me. I must do the same thing now. For Liora and Adrianna.

The thought of them was enough. Warmth sparked in my chest, slowly melting the frost that coated my bones. Life returning to unfeeling limbs, I released the railing and dislodged Liora from my side. She glanced up at me. Sadness marked her face, but her eyes were clear. We traded a look and reached a silent agreement. It was time to move.

Liora's gaze traveled past me and over the ship. "Where's Adrianna?"

"I saw her walk off a few minutes ago. I didn't see where she went," I said, scanning the twenty or so sailors nearby. They skipped about like seagulls, adjusting the rigging and climbing the masts.

At length, I found her. Adrianna was on the upper deck. Beside her, a male with a sun-and-sea-ravaged face peered through a brass telescope. "The crossing's coming up! Prepare yourselves!"

The grizzled male stuffed the telescope inside a slick-looking coat. This had to be Armstrong: authority emanated from his dauntless shoulders and albatross-shaped wings.

"Get below," he barked at Adrianna. "Take them with you."

The captain jerked his bearded chin at me and Liora.

Adrianna jumped down from the top deck and gestured for us to follow her.

Liora and I started forward, dodging fae sailors as we went. After I stopped Liora from stumbling for the second time, she freed a nervous laugh. "I wish I had your wings right about now."

I didn't shrug that off. I was grateful for them. They shifted my weight better than my arms and kept me balanced, aligned to the rhythm of the ship's rocking. My stepmother had often ridiculed me for having the grace of an ox. She wouldn't have recognized me now.

Up ahead, Adrianna disappeared into an opening in the floor. Liora and I followed her down into a dimly lit space with nailed-down tables and benches. On the other side of the room was a corridor with numerous doors. Adrianna led us through there and into the cabin allocated for us. It was compact, with a closet-sized bathroom and a single bunk bed fixed to the left wall.

Adrianna moved for the wall-rack that hung opposite the bed. There, she stored her bag and the thin, double-edged blade she'd carried since Kasi. I stowed my rucksack and my sword next to hers. Liora was the last person to add her possessions to the rack, but she was the first and only one of us to slump onto the lower bunk. She rested her elbows on her thighs and let her head drop into her hands. I didn't ask how she was. I could guess easily enough.

"Can you see anything?" I asked Adrianna as she stared out of the round window that adorned the far wall.

"A little. We're closing in on the crossing."

I walked over to the bunk bed. "What does it look like?"

"It's a line of black flame suspended on the ocean."

"Flame?" I echoed, alarmed.

Her blues centered on me. "It's not a real fire." She glanced out of the curved glass again. "The border's not what we should be worried about. It's what happens afterward that's the problem."

"What d'you mean?" I asked, afraid of the answer.

"Morgan's vessels are outfitted with devices that show if and where the sea border is breached." Adrianna's mouth was grim indeed. "That means if the Meriden have their ships in the area, they'll chase us."

I grasped the bedpost. "Who're the Meriden?"

"They're a unit of soldiers designed for sea warfare," she said, exuding a grave sort of contempt. "They've got an awful reputation. Most crews choose to drown rather than be taken by them."

Stars protect us.

Liora breathed life into our dying conversation. "Adi, did you find out if the captain knows who you are?"

"I can't be sure, but since he hasn't called me anything other than 'kid,' I'm leaning toward him not knowing." Adrianna glanced up at the wooden ceiling. "I think we should keep it that way if we can. Diana might trust Armstrong, but he doesn't owe us anything past what coin can buy. We can't be sure he won't sell us out if he finds out who we are."

I wouldn't argue with that.

Adrianna craned her neck and peered out of the fisheye window. After an extended lull, she whispered, "We're at the border."

Muscles locked, I held my breath. I focused so hard on what was happening outside that my senses went berserk. I picked up on everything.

Scratch, squeak, scratch. Rats.

Creak, groan, creak. The ship.

Click, whistle, click. No idea.

"We're over the line," Adrianna muttered.

I expected an alarm to sound. Something to happen.

The seconds lengthened. Then Armstrong shouted from upstairs. "Storm ahead!"

What the ...

"That can't be a coincidence," Liora said scarcely louder than a whisper. She looked up at me and Adrianna. "Morgan must've done something. Cursed the border or—"

"If she has, it must be a recent thing or Diana would've warned us about it. And Armstrong never mentioned it. Rivers save me, if he knew, I'll rip his damned cock off." Adrianna made a violent gesture that looked like a threat and a promise.

Thunder crashed overhead like a battle cry.

"Maybe Morgan's found out that we were leaving. And all that"—I signaled to the ceiling and the sky above it—"is to stop us."

"This can't be about us." Liora reached up to grip the frame of the top bunk. "Not even Morgan could make a curse like this work with only a few days' notice."

"It might not be a spell, but it could be Lynx's doing." Adrianna's voice thickened with ill omen as she continued. "He's the only witch I know who could conjure a storm like this."

I released the bedpost, my mouth rounding in surprise. Lynx, the Aurorian Prince, was a light-wielder and servant of Morgan. His strength was legendary. Even knowing that, it was hard to believe anybody could be this powerful. "You think he's here—"

The ship lurched. Adrianna and I flew into the opposite wall.

I crumpled to the floor with a hiss of pain, my shoulder and arm aching.

"Are you okay?" Liora asked, her voice pitched with fear.

"Fine." Grimacing a bit, I pushed myself up into a seated position. With my wings braced against the wall, I said, "Adi, are you all right?"

"Yeah," she said, sounding more grumpy than anything.

Adrianna stood up and held out a hand to me. I clasped her warm palm and clambered up. Teeth clenched, I rotated my shoulder and massaged my bicep.

"The pain won't last long now that you're fae," Adrianna said, eyeing me.

Gratitude for my accelerated healing washed through me.

"Why did the ship do that?" Liora wondered, her wide eyes fixed on the beamed ceiling. "Was it the storm, do you think?"

"Shush." Adrianna's eyebrows snapped together. "I have to concentrate."

I cocked my head and listened to the noise above us. It was hard to shift through all the shouts and orders. Then I caught something that caused my heart to sink to the sea floor.

Adrianna's expression fell alongside mine. "Enemy ships are headed this way. I suppose that rules out the possibility of Lynx being here."

"Why do you say that?"

Her attention cut to me. "Because if he was creating this storm, they wouldn't need the Meriden to capture us. He'd do it alone."

Gods ... I prayed that I would never meet him.

Suddenly a loud, whining whistle pitched the air.

"Brace!" Adrianna lunged for the bedpost.

I threw myself onto the lower bunk. Without thinking, I grabbed the frame of the bed and pulled Liora against me.

A heavy splash sounded and then, *boom!*

An explosion assaulted my eardrums. The resulting shock traveled through the ship's frame and into my fingertips.

"Get up! We're leaving." Adrianna rushed to grab our swords. "If this ship is blown out of the water, then the best place for us is up on deck where we can escape, not trapped under the wreckage and sinking to the bottom of the sea."

Liora and I didn't argue.

The three of us quickly belted our weapons to our sides and shouldered our bags. We ran all the way down the corridor, up the stairs, and out onto the deck.

Chaos greeted us. My senses popped, capturing everything.

The air was drenched in salt and heavy with thunder. Above, thick, angry clouds gathered in a sky splashed with the colors of a malevolent storm.

In every direction, sailors scrabbled to control the ship. Armstrong was a whirlwind of motion atop the upper deck, pointing, gesturing, and bellowing orders, navigating the planks with the ease of long experience.

Hands cupped around her mouth, Adrianna shouted up to him. "How can we help?"

His focus latched onto us. "You can't." Armstrong's bark carried over thunder, cloudbursts, and heaving waves. "Not unless you can stop the Meriden from firing on us or undo whatever Morgan's done to the crossing."

Distracted, he wheeled away. He was done with us.

"Come on." Adrianna grabbed my arm.

With no further explanation, she dragged me forward. I reached behind me and snatched Liora's hand. Together, our trio lurched over the planks and reached the rail intact.

My pulse pounding in time with the waves below, I gazed out at the two black-sailed ships that lingered on the cusp of the storm. Both seemed unwilling to venture forth and risk the sea's venom or the wind's vicious claws.

I wasn't comforted by their reluctance, for even through a curtain of rain, I saw the vessels were larger than ours and the match-sized figures aboard far exceeded our crew's numbers.

Another high-pitched whistle sounded. Terror iced my veins.

"Get down!" Armstrong roared.

Liora and I ducked. Adrianna crouched on our left and extended her wing over me. Our trio held tight to the railing and to one another.

I had a second to regret not having my hands free to cover my ears before the explosion hit behind the boat. Saltwater spewed upward in a geyser, drenching the deck and everyone on it. That had been close. Too close.

"You two need to go." Liora looked at us, her expression one of doom, desperation, and determination. "Fly away as fast as you can."

"Not a chance," I snapped out.

"I'd sooner die," Adrianna added.

Liora pinned Adrianna with blazing eyes. "You have to save Ena. The world needs her."

Adrianna looked like she'd swallowed poison. "Even if we left, we'd die anyway. Because Cai would murder us for leaving you."

Hysteria sunk its fangs into me and I almost laughed.

Adrianna focused on me. Her words struck with the force of a hammer against tongs. "Can you set fire to the ships with sunlight?"

Could I?

I examined last night's dream, mining memories. The more I recalled, the more I lost hope.

To attack the ships from over a mile away might drain me. Distance mattered in magic, and using my power like that would eat up my energy. Without more of an understanding of my limitations, I could overextend myself. I could slip into a long sleep or even die.

There's a better way, Thea said. *Zola and I wanted to give you more time to hone your skills, but we've run out of it. Your only option now is to free Liora. She can destroy the ships.*

I paused, stuck in my shock.

"Ena!" Adrianna fastened onto my arm with a strong-fingered grip.

Jolted out of my stupor, I looked at Liora. "Thea and Zola said I should break your bindings. They think you can stop the Meriden."

Surprise parted her lips. Dread gathered in her eyes.

Adrianna pushed Liora for clarity. "Is that true? Can you destroy them?"

Liora's nod was tiny. Reluctant.

A charged whistle went off again. Lightning flickered above, mimicking the adrenaline that fired through my veins.

The device landed. The sea spat and roared in anger.

I winced, clenching my teeth as the noise ricocheted around my skull. A huge swell formed beneath us, one that battered the ship's sides and rained white foam upon us.

My stomach capsized as we went up and down, back and forth. *The Eye of the Wind* creaked ominously.

I closed my eyes, fearing this was the end.

"Hold her steady!" Armstrong hollered from above.

"Tell Armstrong that I'll handle the Meriden as long as he doesn't order anyone to hurt me," Liora half-shouted to Adrianna.

"I don't understand." Adrianna shook out her wings, showering me with rain and saltwater.

"You don't need to," Liora argued. "Just go."

I thought Adrianna would refuse. In the next heartbeat, she proved me wrong and left our sides at a run.

"Are you sure about this?" I checked with Liora. "I might mess up the unbinding. We could always fight the Meriden."

"You can do this." Her damp hand squeezed mine. "And I'm sorry I didn't tell you what I was." Regret emanated from her. "I wanted to, but I got so scared of how you'd look at me."

"We're moving out of the storm." Armstrong saluted the eastern horizon with an outspread arm. "Be ready to meet the Meriden with swords drawn! They won't show you any mercy so strike fast and true!"

Violent cheers erupted from the crew.

The sea suddenly gentled, the rain eased, and the sunlight peeked out from behind the storm clouds.

"Ena, do it." Liora nudged me. "I'm ready."

What do I do? I asked Zola and Thea.

The answer was immediate. *You already have waterlight within you—it's a part of your soul. But to do something this complex, you need more than your spirit naturally possesses. You must pull waterlight in from the world.*

How do I do that?

Silence.

Hello?

Nothing.

My mouth dried out from seawater and anxiety.

A female materialized out of thin air, popping up on my left.

Startled, I reared back a bit.

The youthful-looking female had olive skin, cornflower-blue hair, and transparent wings. I recognized her by her sapphire eyes. It was Thea. A goddess had arrived and nobody else seemed to notice.

"I'm projecting my image into your mind; the others can't see me," Thea explained. "But I can't keep this up for long, so here's what you need to do." She motioned beyond the borders of our boat. "Look at the ocean—at how the light plays over the water. Listen to the waves. Focus on that and nothing else. Once it consumes your thoughts, you'll be able to feel its energy and draw it in."

I cleared my mind and filled it with the sea. The sight and sound and smell of it.

A foreign sensation rolled over me. I felt I'd left the confines of my body only to get swallowed up by the ocean. I was everywhere and nowhere, riding waves of energy, exhilarated and at peace.

It was then a blue thread appeared before me. It looked like a hand extended in welcome, or even a stitch come loose in the fabric of the world.

"Seize it. Take control," Thea said.

I reached out and grasped the thread. It vibrated with energy. I reeled it in and didn't stop until I'd become a chalice brimming with power.

"Now stand up and place Liora in front of you," Thea instructed.

"We have to get up," I told Liora.

She nodded. I pulled her off the soaked floor.

"What now?" Adrianna asked as she rejoined us.

I shoved my rucksack at her. "Hold this, and don't say anything."

She took it from me, thankfully without a word.

Turning back to Thea, I squeezed all other distractions from my mind. She closed in on my left. With a snap of her fingers, she revealed the red ribbons that encircled Liora. "Watch and copy what I do."

Thea gestured with her fingers, alternating between single-handed and double-handed patterns. Her actions were a push and a pull, a cut and a slice. She targeted one of the knots that dotted Liora's binding.

I mimicked my great-aunt. After a few movements, I saw what I should do next in my mind's eye. Soon I wasn't following Thea. I was dancing with her.

"That's it," she said in a smiling tone. "Waterlight has its own voice. Let it be your teacher."

One knot came undone.

Then two.

Three and four.

Five and six.

Just one more. A single ribbon remained. A thread with no knot.

I paused, uncertain.

"The last thread is the lock," Thea said. "To break it, your will has to be stronger than the witch who cast the binding. Demand Liora's release. Tolerate nothing less."

An image of what to do next flashed behind my eyes. I dove recklessly into a power that could reduce trees to splinters and cliffs to rubble. Being caught in that current felt like being torn apart. I was being dragged under.

"Control your power," Thea said tensely. "Give it purpose."

"I can't," I shouted over the sound of another explosion. "It's like trying to stand still in a flood."

"Then don't stand still. Go with the energy."

I did just that. I relaxed, letting the current have me. It tossed me around as if I were a rag doll, but I wasn't pulled apart. I held myself together with a single thought. Free Liora.

I swept my arm up in an arc.

My power formed a giant, cresting wave—

I swung my arm down and unleashed.

My magic crashed into that last red ribbon. It snapped. The binding vanished, turning into smoke and wind and taking my strength with it. Liora doubled over, gagging and gasping.

Adrianna grasped her shoulder.

"Don't." Liora pushed her back. "Stay away."

Black spots blotted my vision. Light-headed, I buckled at the knees.

"Finally," came a growl from above me.

I glanced up and encountered the slit pupils of my friend. Liora's clothes were shredded as her body melted like candle wax.

I fluttered my lashes, trying to clear my sight of the hallucination.

Liora's shifting form jumped into the sea. Adrianna emitted a horrified noise and spread her wings. But before she could go after Liora, something massive erupted out of the swell and burst into the sky.

A mighty roar terrorized every living thing within hearing distance. A dragon ... A fucking dragon flew straight toward the Meriden.

The absurdity and exhaustion were too much.

I straddled an abyss; my vision flashed black.

Thea crouched beside me, her asymmetrical dress pooling on the planks. "Try to stay awake."

I was slumping and slipping out of the world.

"Ena, you must wake," said the sweet voice.

"ENA," came a much blunter tone.

I pried open my heavy eyes. Adrianna's worried face and the smoky sky behind her swam into view.

"What's wrong?" I asked, groggy.

"You fainted." Her blue wings arched over my head, shielding me from the bright sun.

I sat up and the world tipped upside down. Groaning, I palmed my throbbing head. "How long was I out?"

"A minute. Maybe two."

"Ena," Thea called to me softly. She hadn't left my side.

"I overreached," I told her.

A reassuring smile. "A little, but you'll recover quicker now you're fae." Thea's gem-colored eyes skipped to where her hand faded away. "I wish it was otherwise, but I must leave you. Zola will try to help you with Liora."

"Help me how?"

"Who are you talking to?" Adrianna said impatiently.

"Thea," I said as the goddess blinked out of view.

A roar rent the air. That noise bounced around my ribs and punched fear into my heart.

With Adrianna's support, I staggered up and over to the railing on legs that trembled as fiercely as leaves in autumn.

I absorbed every detail before me.

Towers of sparks and smoke billowed upward. The Meriden's sails burned with the intensity of oil-soaked paper; their masts snapped with the brittleness of kindling.

Liora dipped out from behind an ash cloud in dragon form. She looked about fifteen feet tall at the shoulder with a wingspan at least double that length. Her body was covered in scales that glittered as brightly as rubies under a thief's eye. Two small horns protruded from a serpentine-shaped head, and from her huge maw, she bellowed another blood-soaked challenge at the sailors below.

Most of the Meriden were in the ocean, but a few stubborn fae remained aboard. These stragglers aimed both spear and arrow at Liora. I unleashed a pitiful scream as they shot at her.

Their weapons proved useless, shattering against her hindquarters. Before relief could find me, Liora unleashed a tongue of flame thirty feet long. The soldiers still aboard were consumed or defeated. Smart fae jumped into the water. Desperate ones flew for land.

I refused to turn away, even as smoke irritated my eyes and throat.

Adrianna turned her face toward me. "She certainly kept this quiet, didn't she?"

Her bitterness stung me by proxy.

Liora was a shifter. She hadn't told us. Why? Her earlier words surged to the forefront of my thoughts, revealing a truth. "She thought we'd reject her."

I noted the disgust, wariness, and sorrow that crossed Adrianna's face.

"You suggested firing on them with sunlight," I snapped. "How is dragon fire any different?"

Adrianna avoided my glare. "I didn't think ... I've never killed anybody, Ena." She nodded toward the burning ships. "And watching people die screaming is a lot to stomach."

"I hate it too," I admitted. "But if Liora sees that look on your face, it'll destroy her."

Adrianna stood a little taller. "She won't."

As I looked out to Liora, a problem glinted and overturned in my mind. "Why isn't she turning around? The ships are damaged beyond repair."

"I've heard stories of shifters getting stuck inside of their animal form." Adrianna paused, then added, "And Liora's had her creature locked away for months. Maybe it's liking its freedom a bit too much."

Panic shot into my veins. "Then how will we get her back?"

"I don't know," Adrianna admitted.

Get the dragon to follow the ship, Zola said. *Once she's back with you both, the human in her should fight to emerge.*

That sounds more like a prayer than a plan.

For what it's worth, I'm about ninety percent sure she won't incinerate you.

Not a comfort.

"We have to draw her over," I told Adrianna. "Zola thinks seeing me and you will make her fight the shift."

Doubt showed upon Adrianna's face. "How are we going to get her to come over here?"

Shine starlight into her eyes. That should do the trick.

My heart seemed to stutter. *You want me to blind her?*

Dragons have a second eyelid. You won't hurt her.

My pulse evened out a touch.

I tugged on Adrianna's emerald sleeve. "This way."

She grabbed my rucksack from the floor and followed me up the ladder to the top deck. Armstrong and the female at the wheel watched me pass them with an unflappable stoicism.

At the back of the ship, I got an uninterrupted view of Liora. Now I had to summon starlight. How?

Think about the energy, connect to it, and then reel it in, just as Thea showed you. You won't need any specific movements this time. Only, shine the starlight into a mirror if you can—better to let the glass do most of the work for you.

"I need a mirror," I said to Adrianna, close to frantic.

Her astonishment didn't prevent her from saying, "Don't you have one?"

Of course. Stupid.

I dove into the rucksack she still held and pulled out my pocket mirror.

"I need to shine a light into Liora's face." I handed her the glass. "Hold it steady."

Adrianna tensed. "I will."

I shut my eyes and imagined a night sky threaded with light, each star a pure-white pin in the heavens. Bright. Serene. Beautiful.

Magic swirled around me, but whenever I reached for it, it slipped through my fingertips, determined to remain elusive. I grappled with my impatience as we moved farther and farther from Liora.

You're relying on visualization and intent too much, Thea said in a wearied whisper. *You need more than that to connect with such powerful magic.*

That was more riddle than help.

Thea, would you please rest? Zola snapped. *Leave this to me.*

Thea ignored her. *Ena, starlight is the shepherd of lost souls—it wants to save people. Focus on who you're trying to help. That's how you'll connect to your starlight.*

Okay. I could do this. I had to.

I thought about Liora, about her compassion, courage, and devotion. Finally, a white thread shimmered in the recesses of my mind. I reached out and grabbed it.

The starlight's energy was slow to enter my body. It was also so cold, it felt like plunging into a lake in midwinter. Before I could go into shock, the magic cooled to a tepid embrace.

From my right palm shone the power of an evening star. I leveled my hand over the mirror. I'd become a lighthouse.

Adrianna and I maneuvered the mirror until we hit our intended destination. A dragon's eye.

Liora bellowed in irritation. She tipped her wing and turned in midair. The fine hairs along my nape tingled as the dragon raced toward us.

"I hope you both know what you're doing," Armstrong growled from behind us.

Rounding on him, Adrianna snarled something in Kaeli.

I didn't blame Armstrong for questioning us. There was a very real possibility that Liora wouldn't shift back, and that the dragon racing toward us had mistaken my light to be a threat. As if hearing that wayward thought, my magic dimmed until the star I held was extinguished. Exhaustion slammed into me, and I grasped onto a low-hanging rope.

Liora drew level with our ship and circled overhead. We became mice under a hawk's gaze. That was how it felt, anyway.

The crew mostly cowered under her shadow. A few stared up at her, prepared to meet their end. That couldn't happen. These people were my responsibility. I had to protect them.

A moon-shield might stop her. But just the thought of creating one big enough to cover a moving ship caused my whole body to tremble violently.

I did the only thing I could. "Liora, it's Ena," I yelled, desperation tearing at my throat. "Come down. Come back. Please!"

A strange keening escaped Liora. Tucking her wings in, she dove for the rear of the boat. She crashed snout-first into the deep blue sea.

The white spray flowed over her and her ruby scales shone beneath the surf like underwater treasure. That was until her dragon's body blurred.

I seized Adrianna's forearm. "She's shifting."

Liora popped up. Gasping. Thrashing.

Adrianna handed over my bag with the pocket mirror inside. Then she dropped her rucksack to the planks before leaping overboard. Her wings fanned out, and she glided down to pluck a naked Liora out of the water.

"Here," came a rough grumble.

I spun around to find Armstrong throwing me his long coat. I caught the slippery material with one hand and issued a quick, "Thanks."

Adrianna landed nearby, her wings shielding Liora from view.

I shouldered my bag and hurried over.

At the sight of my friend, I halted mid-step. Liora's dyed hair hung in dripping rattails around her face. A nasty crack in her lower lip oozed blood, and her floral hand tattoo had been added to. Black-thorned roses now extended up to her elbow.

Cradled in Adrianna's arms, Liora stared up at me with eyes that held shock and horror.

I wrapped her up in the coat and wiped the bedraggled curls from her cheeks. As I fussed over her, I detected the shift in her scent. Sugar, strawberry, and grass notes were smudged with smoke and embers. The sweetness of spring had fused with the warmth of summer.

"Are you disgusted by me?" Liora whispered hoarsely from under clumped lashes.

In the same beat, Adrianna and I said, "No."

"Maybe you should be." Her head fell back to rest on Adrianna's forearm.

I didn't get a chance to say anything to refute that. The captain drew closer to us, entering my side view. Deprived of his coat, I had a clearer view of his figure. He was all scarred skin stretched over hard-won muscle. I wondered if he'd gained that body through fights with the Meriden.

"You saved me and my crew from a slow death, and I thank you for it," he said to Liora. "However, burning those ships has changed things —no point in denying it."

My heart dropped like a lead ball. At the same time, Adrianna bristled as if she expected him to throw us overboard.

Armstrong frowned, the lines on his brow deepening. "Once Morgan learns what happened from the survivors, the first thing she'll do is tell her spies on the continent to watch the ports and look out for a ship like ours. She'll be desperate to capture us, not just for retribution, but to ensure she has a dragon shifter under her control." The captain's ruthless mouth twisted down. "I can sail you within flying distance of Casatana, but I won't dock there. Not now."

Adrianna didn't keep the sharpness from her voice as she cut in. "What about the return journey?"

Stars. I hadn't thought of that.

The muscles around his gray eyes wrinkled. "Diana wrote that she wanted me to return you to Aldar, but you'll have to make other arrangements."

Adrianna's spine became a steel sword. "I didn't take you for a coward."

I tensed as growls irritated my ears. The crew had overheard us.

Mercifully, Armstrong remained calm. "I never claimed to be anything but a smuggler." He concentrated on Liora. "As I said, I am grateful for what you've done. But Morgan's been stepping up border security for over a year. More and more smugglers are being killed and their ships sent to the sea goddess. And when word gets out that Morgan's cursed the sea border, the only captains who'll dare such a voyage will be mad or desperate."

My stomach pitched as if I'd swung from the gallows. How in the rutting hell would we get home now?

"Diana will pay you whatever you want—just get us back to Aldar when we want to leave," Adrianna declared.

Armstrong's eyebrows crawled up his face like two caterpillars. "What makes you so valuable?"

Her chin jutted up. "I'm her heir."

A clammy silence pressed in around us. Given Adrianna's preference for keeping our identities secret, I guessed she'd grown desperate.

The captain's eyes circled with shock. "You three are just full of surprises, aren't you?"

"Will you take us home or not?" Adrianna snapped.

"No." That was as abrupt as a backhand to the face. "I'm used to taking risks—enjoy them even—but returning would be suicidal. And money doesn't mean much when you're dead."

I couldn't argue with his reasoning, even as my frustration mounted and my wings twitched in an effort to shake it off. I would find a way to get back to my brother. I'd swim the damned ocean if I had to.

Or you could just hitch a ride on Liora? Zola suggested, humor tickling her voice.

This is supposing her dragon form wouldn't eat me for suggesting it?

Zola's laughter was loud and merry. At least someone wasn't wading through misery.

"I'm sorry that I've brought you and your crew to Morgan's attention," Liora said to Armstrong, the guilt breaking her voice. "I wouldn't have done it if I'd felt there was another choice."

His harsh features softened like butter left out in the sun. "Don't be sorry. We owe you our lives, Dragon-Fire."

He raised his hairy-knuckled fist to his chest and bobbed his head. The other sailors on the deck below and in the crow's nest above copied this silent salute.

Liora tugged the coat tighter around her, all defensiveness and shame.

Armstrong lowered his arm to his side. "You should get some rest. All of you."

He pinned me with a very obvious look. I must have looked half-dead.

Armstrong showed us his back, planting himself next to the wheel. That was the signal for the crew to resume their work. As if nothing had happened.

"Adi, let me down," Liora breathed, sounding weak.

Adrianna paused as if thinking better of it. A tick later, she conceded.

Once Liora was on her feet again, she slipped on the coat and shuffled to the rear handrail. There, she stared at where her flames still consumed everything in their path and ash drifted in a dance, orchestrated by the wind. For her sake, I hoped she couldn't see the bodies floating in the water.

I joined Liora hip-close and Adrianna settled next to me.

We'd gone far enough that the screams in the water had ceased. The rest was silence.

"How can I live with myself after this?" Liora mumbled, her spring-greens still glued to the wreckage she'd caused.

Rutting hell. I feared that one wrong word would send her over the edge.

"The Meriden are infamous for their cruelty," Adrianna waded in, sounding resolved. "You protected us from people who would rape and torture us. There is no shame in that."

Relief and gratitude stirred in me. Adrianna had come through for Liora, despite her horror at what had happened.

Liora's eyes screwed up as if she wanted to cry but had forgotten how. "Maybe they are bad people, but it doesn't erase the fact that I've burned people alive ... I'm a monster."

It was instinct to stretch my left wing over her back. "I felt a bit like that after I killed Dimitri. But I realized that whenever I looked at Frazer, the guilt got more bearable. Because I did it to protect him." I folded in my wing and turned her toward me. "Look at me, Li."

Her pained gaze met mine.

"You saved me. You saved everybody on this ship. You protected us."

She attempted a smile but it crashed badly.

"You're not a monster," I said, staring down at her with a fierce love burning inside of my chest. "Not even close."

Liora nodded, but the doubt never left her eyes.

CHAPTER 13
PART TWO: REFLECTIONS

I woke with a start, drenched in sweat.

Breathing labored, I strived to calm the bellows of my lungs and the erratic pulsing in my sticky fingertips. Once I'd reclaimed a fragile equilibrium, I stared up at the canopy of the top bunk and sighed out in frustration.

This marked my seventh consecutive day of broken sleep. Zola and Thea's training sessions were to blame. My great-aunts had gone from showing me light-wielder battles to throwing me into them. Illusion or not, dueling with other witches felt real, so much so that whenever I got hit, the shock drove me from sleep.

I could take one good thing away from tonight, though. Dream-me had survived longer than usual. It wasn't until I'd messed up using sunlight that I'd "died."

You'd do better if you stopped hesitating. Sunlight will only yield for confident masters.

I know, Zola. You've told me this a hundred times already.

And I'll keep saying it until you listen.

Zola's words changed nothing. Sunlight demanded self-assurance; it required a strong stance and bold shaping. But hurling a light that could burn people alive, even imaginary ones, filled me with nothing but dread and wariness.

Annoyingly, sunlight wasn't my only failing. Star magic had proven unreliable, and I hadn't improved a speck.

These reflections circled, haunting me. Tomorrow we'd reach Casatana—Asitar's capital—and I didn't feel remotely prepared. I'd wanted to have a stronger grasp over my powers before we reached foreign shores, if for no other reason than to protect Liora. Her second skin may be a dragon, but she was also a human, and according to Armstrong, men and women were treated even more cruelly in Asitar than they were in Aldar.

Zola offered her unsolicited opinion. A common occurrence these days. *Stop being so hard on yourself. You're progressing nicely with waterlight—you've never failed to break a warding or undo a curse—and you're a natural with moonlight.*

Perhaps she was right. I had dwelled enough.

I rolled up and sat on the edge of the thin mattress. Adrianna's even breathing suggested she was sleeping soundly above me. Liora, on the other hand, was gone again. I'd been sharing the bottom bunk with her—my retractable wings made the cramped conditions easier—but more than once I'd woken and discovered her side of the bed empty. Her recent experiences had brought on night terrors, and she'd taken to wandering on the deck at all hours of the night.

I decided to search for her, hoping to keep her company and to avoid thinking about my failings.

I stood and pushed out my wings. A noise of contentment tripped off my tongue as I spread them wide.

Adrianna grunted behind me. Whoops.

I quietly stuffed my feet into the shoes beside the cabin bed. There was no point in changing; my nightwear was decent enough.

I slunk out into the hallway.

My eyes easily adjusted to the solid dark, and I climbed out of the ship's bowels without a stubbed toe or bumped elbow.

Above deck, an aromatic night with fast-moving clouds and a star-forest awaited me. As I searched for Liora, a stiff breeze slapped my cheeks and flooded my ears with echoes of creaking wood, flapping canvas, and squeaking rigging.

I glimpsed Liora at the bow and covered the distance in a quick step. The few sailors up at this hour took no notice as I passed them. Their business was to keep the ship afloat, not spy on the flotsam occupying it.

Liora's sleepless eyes greeted me as I planted a hand on the rail. From the salt-stained tracks down her cheeks, it was plain she'd been crying. And there was something *off* about her scent. I wasn't sure what, though. Fae could detect extreme emotions through scent changes. But it took skill and experience. None of which I had.

"Did you die again?" The effort she made to joke with me, to keep things light, showed in her voice. It was weak and worn as if all the strength had been squeezed out of it.

I went along with her act, huffing a laugh that was borne away by the sea wind. "Yeah, I did." Softer, I added, "Why are you up? Did you have another nightmare?"

"I needed the air," Liora said, avoiding the question. She grasped the crisscrossing of rope that hung above her. "This constant rocking is making me nauseous."

The seasickness was likely an excuse. She only heaved in the toilet after waking up from a bad dream.

Liora refused to meet my eye. Her discomfort convinced me to drop the topic.

I bent at the waist and rested my forearms on the wooden handrail. There, I slipped into a state of transient peace. I was nowhere and everywhere at once, swimming through color and emotion, lost to the motions of the journey.

In that timeless stretch, my thoughts drifted to Cai and Frazer, as they were wont to do lately. Where were they? Were they safe? Gods, how I missed them. The lack of them, particularly my brother, was a bruise that refused to stop aching.

Liora interrupted my melancholy. "I can't stop thinking about what Armstrong told us. About Asitar being at war."

That switch in subject shoved me into a recent memory. To when the captain had first informed us that the seven kings—the seven warlords who had ruled over Asitar for centuries—had lost territory to Abraxus. He had toppled six kings already. One remained.

"Are you worried that we'll get caught up in the conflict?" I asked.

"Yes," she said, looking as if a giant boot had flattened her. "Because more conflict means there's a greater chance I'll have to shift. And if—

when—I do, I want you to promise me that you won't let me hurt innocents, and that you'll do whatever it takes to stop me."

I straightened. Her rushed way of speaking suggested she'd been thinking about this for a while. "Stop you how?"

A sharp inhale parted her lips. "I'm asking you to kill me if it comes to it."

My heart crumpled like a cardboard box. "No." I stepped back. "No way."

"Just listen." Liora begged me with her eyes. "When I wear the dragon's skin, my head gets shoved underwater. I become a slave to instincts that would make even the most savage fae look tame. And afterward, it feels as if I'm remembering what someone else has done. Like I was a witness in my own body the whole time." That had her voice shattering like glass. She gathered the shards and croaked out, "It's not fair to ask this of you, but I'm terrified, En. I'm scared of what the dragon might do. And I'd rather lose my life than my soul."

Aware of potential eavesdroppers, I lowered my voice. "When I was worried about my sunlight, you said it was natural for witches to lose control sometimes—"

"This is different," Liora hurried out. "I'm not channeling the dragon. I can't choose when to let it in because it's already there—it's a part of me. A part that enjoyed watching the Meriden suffer." Her face became a picture of self-loathing.

"It is the same thing because the sunlight is a part of my soul too. If it weren't, I wouldn't be able to summon it." I peeled my dug-in nails off the rail. "Let me put it this way: if I'd burned those ships to keep us safe, would you agree to kill me?"

She looked conflicted, torn between frustration, anxiety, and dread. Finally, her features settled. "I wouldn't, but your fire can't kill dozens of people—"

"Not yet," I said darkly. "But in the past week, I've gone from conjuring up a moon-shield for a few seconds to holding it for several minutes. Who knows what damage I'll be capable of in a month or two."

Liora's gaze darted around. I had a feeling she was searching for another viable argument. After ten silent ticks, she whispered, "There's something else ... something I'm scared will make me more unstable."

My core clenched in readiness. "Go on."

"I've been having mood swings lately. At first, I assumed it was an aftereffect of the binding being broken." Her top teeth nibbled her lip. "But now, I think becoming a knight made me an empath." She glanced down at the floral tattoo that now spread up her forearm. "I seem to be able to sense other people's emotions."

Holy fire. I turned inward. *Is it true? Is she an empath?*

Zola was short, perfunctory. *Yes.*

My great-aunts and I had reached a point where we could exchange visuals. In my mind, I stared at them, cross-armed and frowning. *Did the firstborn know this would happen to her?*

A tall, tanned female with choppy white-blond hair raised her eyebrow. *You look about as intimidating as a constipated kitten.*

That's an insult. Not an answer, I told Zola.

Thea mediated. *We had our suspicions about Liora. But with her magic being bound, it was impossible to be sure how the mark would change her. She has nothing to worry about though—she'll make a wonderful empath.*

I wasted no time in parroting that information to Liora.

Her hand released the rope above us. "I've only met one empath. She was another healer, but I never got to know her. No one did. She acted like a walking corpse."

"Why?"

"Because she could feel everyone's pain."

Oh shit. "That sounds …"

"Awful," Liora finished as if she had little energy left to care.

"But being an empath might be different for you," I argued. "Thea said you'll be great at it, and I think she's right. You're a natural. You've always been good at reading people."

"I hope so," she murmured, scratching at the wood of the handrail. "Because the more emotional I am, the harder it is to control the shift. The dragon's never reacted well when I've been overwhelmed."

I stopped and thought about that. "How did you cope before your magic was bound?"

"I didn't," she confessed. "I was only nine when the dragon first emerged. My father didn't want to attract Morgan's attention, so he forbade me from shifting. But no matter how hard I tried, I couldn't keep the beast caged for more than a month at a time. So whenever things got too much, I'd head up into the hills and trap myself in one of the caves there. It was big enough inside that I could stretch my wings. I even learned to fly."

My imagination toyed with the visual of an itty-bitty dragon trapped in a giant hole in the ground. The image stirred up affection, sorrow, and pity. "That sounds lonely."

"Cai was always with me," she said, her chin lifting. "He'd wait outside just so I knew I wasn't alone, and then he'd release me after a few hours had passed."

Disparate pieces of information slotted together. "Li, did your father find out that you were shifting? Was that why he banished you? Because he was afraid you'd get caught?"

"Not exactly." Her throat moved, showing a painful gulp. "About a year ago, my then-girlfriend was attacked where we worked. A male, one of our patients, cornered and raped her."

That revelation punched me squarely in the gut. It stole my breath and any words of comfort I might dare to speak.

"She reported him, but he was a fae noble and she was human. Our coven refused to punish him. So I decided to do it." Guilt wept from every syllable as she continued. "When he left the ward, I followed. I waited until he was alone and addled with drink. Then I flirted with him. He took me out into the forest. I tried to get him to talk—I wanted to see if he felt even a moment's regret for what he'd done. But I didn't get two words out before he started roughing me up."

Liora paused, sipping in air like it was a restorative tonic. Her knotted expression suggested she was about to be consumed by dark thoughts that flourished in silence.

I prompted her. "What happened then?"

Eyes flickering, she wet her lips. "He put a knife to my throat. That was when the dragon took control and ripped him to shreds. Once I shifted back, I went into shock. That was how Cai discovered me. We buried the body together."

I struggled to keep the emotion from my voice as I asked, "How did Cai find you?"

"I'd quit my healer's apprenticeship the day before," she said, leaning against the ship's railing. "Cai heard about it and when he couldn't find me, he scried for my location."

"Why did you quit?"

"Because healers hold life as sacred," she explained. "We swear to preserve it without prejudice and to do no harm. I knew if I hurt someone, I'd be breaking that vow."

"Li, if it weren't for you, that piece-of-shit rapist would still be out there, free to hurt other women," I said with all the conviction I possessed, hoping some of it would rub off on her. "The way I see it, you preserved more lives by ending that evil bastard."

"My father didn't see it that way." My puzzled brow had her adding, "When he heard that I'd quit my apprenticeship, he kept on pushing me for an explanation until I told him what had happened." She winced, her face twisting with shame. "He didn't shout or tell me off. He just said I wasn't worthy of his name. Then he ordered me to bind my powers and leave the Crescent."

"Prick," I said, disgusted.

Her shoulders rose with her next inhale. The movement looked labored, as though she carried a great weight on her back. "It could've been worse. He could've turned me over to Morgan. She collects shifters for blood sport and pays well for their capture. The rarer the breed, the higher the reward. And as far as I know, no one's seen a dragon—real or shifter—in several lifetimes. For that alone, she'd have hunted me to the ends of the earth. And after what I did to the Meriden ..." She got lost somewhere.

My hatred of Morgan stoked my inner fire. In a towering temper, sunlight pressed in, boiling my blood and reddening my skin.

Luckily, my wits were not gone. I couldn't let my magic out. I couldn't lose control. I was on a ship made of wood.

This is what I've been talking about. A fearful reaction will only spur on your magic. It thinks you're being threatened.

Zola's reproach had me gritting my teeth. *Really? I hadn't noticed.*

Thea intervened. *Ena, try summoning waterlight. In its rawest form, it should counteract the sunlight's fury.*

I brought to mind the ocean's song and the river's light. This time, I didn't need to grab a blue thread. The magic surged up from within; my waterlight banked the sun's flames. A fever still squatted inside my body, but it was manageable.

"What's wrong?" Liora asked.

I stared at her.

"Empath, remember," she said, smiling weakly.

"The sunlight got a bit murder-y again." I had a go at a smile and failed. "But it's fine. I've calmed it down."

Liora gave me a sideways look. No doubt she saw my response for what it was—humor masking fear. She let me pretend anyway.

A hush descended. We stood long enough to watch the quarter-moon dip below the waves and get swallowed by the sea. Once a tender sliver of lavender and lemon lined the horizon, Liora suggested returning to the cabin.

I agreed, adding, "Are you going back to sleep?"

Liora snorted under her breath. "I doubt I'll be able to. I have to prepare myself for telling Adi that I can read her emotions."

Rutting hell.

"It might not be as bad as we think ..."

She threw me a look that clearly said *I don't believe you*. "It'll probably be worse, and we should fly away now before it gets too ugly."

"You think we could make it to the moon?"

Liora let out a stunted laugh. "Why the moon?"

I retreated into remembered loneliness. "I used to think about it a lot when I was little, about what it'd be like up there, and if it was better than down here. I even dreamed of the day someone from the moon would come and take me away to live with them."

"Do you still dream about that?" A soft ask.

"No." I smiled. "I don't."

CHAPTER 14
THROUGH THE SPYGLASS

Liora and I returned to the cabin to find Adrianna awake. The three of us decided sleep was a lost cause and dined on gritty oats with the other early risers. The crew were a lively bunch prone to singing lewd songs about sea deities I prayed I wasn't related to. Our trio fled to our cabin around the third song.

Once there, Adrianna and Liora sharpened their swords. And Zola continued my lessons on how to block out mind-readers—mentalists.

I was a few minutes into the lesson, lying on the bottom bunk, when my shield collapsed for the second time.

Zola flashed into my mind's eye. Her golden eyes were unforgiving. Her hip jutted out at an angle and her arms were tightly folded. *You need to concentrate.*

I ground my teeth so hard they would surely turn to dust. Jaw throbbing, I swallowed a frustrated scream. We practiced mental defense every day, but I'd made little to no progress.

Look, I wanted to be the fun aunt who taught you how to sun-spear someone from a mile away. I had zero interest in teaching you mental defense. But you must learn if you're to stand any chance against Morgan. Let's go again. Raise your shield.

I stifled a sigh, closed my eyes, and fortified my mind.

My shield was a veil of silver light, and Zola smashed into it with all the might and skill of a goddess trained in mental warfare. The force of her attack rattled my skull, drove the air from my lungs, and coated my limbs in sweat.

The walls of my shield shook and then collapsed. Zola's trap closed around my mind. I became her slave—a marionette. With a single tug at my strings, she restrained my body and silenced my voice.

I struggled to no avail.

Stop flailing about. You are my blood and you will not break. Focus on what I've taught you. Build a counterattack and blast me out.

I forced myself to stop. To think. To remember. Inspired, I imagined a star-white ember sparking to life, burning bright and fierce, and exploding outward in a giant shockwave.

The pressure in my head vanished. I was no longer an animal with its paw caught in a trap.

My eyes opened as Zola said, *You didn't oust me completely, but you stopped me from digging in any further. That'll do for today.*

I rolled up into a seated position, placing my feet on the floor and my head in my hands.

"Has your great-aunt stopped torturing you?" Adrianna asked me from where she sat, legs folded, in the middle of our small cabin.

I'd revealed that Zola and Thea were my relatives a few days ago. Liora and Adrianna had been stunned but quick to accept the fact. Breathing through my nausea, I rubbed at my temples. "Yes, she's just finished with me."

Liora rose from the floor, abandoning the care of her sword. She settled beside me and put her palm over my damp forehead. Her healing magic worked fast on my snare-drum headache. "Better?" she asked, lowering her arm.

I smile-grimaced at her. "Yes. Thanks."

"Then we should begin your flight lessons," Adrianna said, setting aside the blade she'd been sharpening.

Somebody kill me, I thought.

The pain from my headache might be gone, but I was mentally exhausted, and Adrianna's lectures demanded concentration. Yesterday she had spent two hours describing what to do in high winds. The day before that it was how to spot certain weather patterns. The theoretical was all we had since the high winds and choppy seas we'd been experiencing all week prevented us from taking to the wing. I wasn't overly bothered—I wished to fly eventually, but the thought of falling to my death prevented any real sorrow from emerging at the delay.

Liora saved me. "Before you start, there's something I've been meaning to tell you," she said, looking at Adrianna.

"Oh?" Adrianna raised an arched brow.

"I'm an empath."

"You ... what?"

"I'm an empath," Liora repeated.

Adrianna's head and wings inched backward. "When did that happen?"

Liora repeated what she had confessed to me hours ago.

Adrianna regarded her, gaze contemplative. "Diana has an empath in her court," she started slowly. "He usually acts as a judge in trials because he can divine who has bad intentions and who's telling the truth. If you can learn how to do that, it might help us a lot in the future."

I smiled, relieved she hadn't taken it as badly as I suspected she would.

"Just don't read my emotions." Adrianna showed her fangs. "Or I'll bite you hard enough to leave scars."

My smile vanished.

"I won't do it on purpose," Liora said, her tone careful. "But you need to give me time to learn how to control it."

An argument formed behind Adrianna's eyes. It was extinguished by a timely knock at our door. Glad for the distraction, I jumped up and unlocked the door.

Armstrong's first officer, Maravina, walked in holding a parcel. "The captain asked me to find some clothes for you." She set our gift on the bottom bunk bed. "He thought they might help you blend in with the locals. You can't do anything about how you sound or look"—she stared at me—"but the more you seem like you belong in Casatana, the better. Anybody who sticks out will be an easy target for thieves."

And an object of curiosity for Morgan's spies, I added silently to myself.

Liora opened the parcel. She pulled out three wraparound dresses and pressed the lavender one up against her frame.

"You can't wear that one." Maravina jabbed her pointy chin at the darkest dress. "Humans have to wear black clothes in Asitar to show their status as slaves."

The life drained out of Liora's heart-shaped face. "Oh."

I wanted to tell Liora that she didn't have to partake in such a humiliating spectacle, but common sense overruled my anger. "It's not real," I said instead.

Liora's shoulders knotted themselves stiff. "Not for me, but it is for a lot of people."

I felt a sharp pang in my heart. Why was there so much wrong in the world?

Even we don't have the answers to that, Thea said regretfully.

It was with low spirits I listened to Maravina explain how to arrange our dresses correctly. Once finished, she removed a tin from her jacket pocket.

"You should take this." She handed the tin to Adrianna. "This cream will protect you from sunburn. The continent's summers are a lot harsher than Aldar's."

"Land ahead," Armstrong bellowed above us. "Mara, tell our guests to get on deck!"

A bit redundant. Everyone heard his bellow, including Liora.

Maravina winced, rubbing her ear. "I've never known someone who loved shouting so much. Thank the gods he doesn't feel the need to do it when we're in bed together."

Taken aback, I wasn't sure if I should laugh at that or pretend I hadn't heard her. I settled on the latter.

"I'll see you upstairs." Maravina showed herself out.

Our trio tied our hair back off our faces and changed without chatter. The backless dresses had scooped necklines, full-length sleeves, and long panels of material attached to the hips. These panels looped around the body and tied off at the waist to create a shape fitted to the individual wearer.

I ran my hands down my lilac robe, flattening out the creases and marveling at how the fabric moved with my body.

Adrianna rubbed sun cream into her skin, taking care not to mark her sapphire dress as she went. I was waiting for my turn with it when Zola cut in. *You can hold sunlight in the palm of your hand. Do you really think you're going to get sunburned?*

My mind sat with that for a moment. *But I still get hot—*
It's not the same thing.

That said, when Adrianna offered me the cream, I refused and explained why.

"What about you?" Adrianna faced Liora. "Does your dragon side protect you from burning?"

"Sadly, no, and I'm a redhead," she said, a bit peevish. "If I'm not careful in the sun, my skin ends up resembling cooked bacon."

Liora slathered the cream over every inch of exposed skin.

We slipped on our soft-soled shoes, shouldered our rucksacks, and donned our swords. I ended up with two blades. My Utemä and Liora's rapier. According to Armstrong, humans weren't permitted to carry weapons in Asitar. The rapier had to stay with me until Liora could take up the sword again. I hated it. Liora looked somehow smaller now that she was unarmed.

Done with our preparations, we left our cabin.

The daylight dazzled me when we arrived on deck. Seagulls squawked, but the crew was quiet—disturbingly so.

Heavy boots *clack-clunked* across the planks, signaling the captain's approach. "If my calculations are correct, Casatana will come into view on our left in about five minutes."

Armstrong strode past us, motioning for us to follow him. It wasn't until he'd hustled us over to the ship's side that he continued in muted tones. "Are you still planning to fly into Sashkan Market?"

"Yes," Adrianna answered for us.

Over the last week, the three of us had decided not to land at the docks. That was where our pack was due to meet our contact, Zeke. But if Diana had told him of our physical likenesses and the name of our ship—how else would he know who to approach—he would be expecting five people, two of us women, to disembark. Given that he wouldn't recognize us, we'd seen no worth in stopping there. And after our run-in with the Meriden, we wanted to avoid places that Morgan's spies might be watching for newly arrived foreigners. Luckily, Diana had mentioned a place close to the market that we could ask for Zeke. That was our new destination: The Oasis Lounge.

Adrianna went on. "You told us that Casatana is ruled by a warlord king. Do you think he'd be willing to help Morgan capture us?"

Armstrong's frown exaggerated his hard-earned wrinkles. "Morgan's refusal to trade with the continent has liberated a great deal of coin from a good many pockets, the Spice King's included. So no, I can't see Hasan lifting a wing to help her."

His gray eyes fogged over with shadows and bad thoughts. "Morgan would also have to be a fool to trust him with knowledge of you. Hasan is the last king standing against Abraxus, and he must reckon well that his days are numbered. Granted, I rarely step foot inside Casatana, so I don't know how desperate he's gotten. But his greed for power is infamous, and if he learns there's a shifter and a light-wielder in his city, he'll try to force you into his service. Anything to keep that crooked crown on his head. Something to keep in mind."

Rutting fantastic.

Armstrong retrieved his collapsible brass telescope from his frock coat. None of us spoke while he studied the whisper of hazy land emerging on the eastern skyline.

My heart beat quicker and quicker at the sight of foreign soil. It was difficult to believe that only three and a half months ago, I'd never left the confines of my own village. The distance between who I was then and who I had become—fae, witch, warrior, explorer—felt as far as Aldar was from Asitar.

Armstrong tucked his spyglass into a pocket. "It's about time you left us." The captain addressed me. "Maravina has volunteered to fly you to the market."

Embarrassment heated the blood in my cheeks and ears. Adrianna couldn't carry me and Liora into the city, so yesterday we'd asked for the captain's help. I'd had to lie and invent a wing injury when he'd asked why I couldn't fly. His curiosity was understandable; fae usually took to the wing around thirteen. To still be grounded at eighteen was unheard of.

"Connors, take the wheel from Maravina," Armstrong hollered over my head.

Liora peered up at him. "Where will you sail to now?"

His mouth wound up in a clockwork smile. "I believe a long vacation to distant parts unknown may be in order."

Maravina reached us, and my stomach churned with nerves.

"Take care of yourself, little dragon," Armstrong said, planting a scarred hand on Liora's shoulder.

"You too."

At that tame reply, he released her and faced Adrianna. "I'll send word of your arrival to your makena as soon as we land. Is there any message you wish for me to pass on?"

"Tell her that we need a captain to take us back to Aldar and to message us via her contact," Adrianna said, the judgment obvious in her gaze.

The captain addressed her with a cool disregard. "I'll do that."

Not waiting for the grass to grow underfoot, Armstrong marched off, barking instructions left and right.

"We should take off from the rear of the boat," Maravina suggested.

"Why?" I asked.

"There'll be less wind resistance."

Maravina led us up a stair, past the wheel and to the stern. There, she showed me her palms. "Do you consent to being picked up?"

"Yes," I said, surprised she had even asked. Most fae didn't.

She gingerly lifted me against her chest. I thought she must've actually believed the story about my injury.

Once I was secured, Maravina stood on the railing. Adrianna copied her.

We leaped into an unclouded sky and instantly met with wayward sea winds. Tugged in opposing directions, it was a struggle to remain aloft, to keep to our course, and the bumpy motions had my stomach leaving my body.

The open ocean's caprices mellowed as we neared the gentler breathings of land.

Belly settling, I was similarly pleased and apprehensive to make my first proper study of our destination. With an unhurried eye, I browsed a country of rounded bluffs, reddish-brown earth, sandy beaches, and turquoise reefs.

The city was located on a hilltop, its thick walls protecting a sprawl of square structures, each crafted from stone and tile that blushed peach in the lemon rays of the sun. These buildings were built onto tiers. On the lower levels, one-story houses were crammed into untidy rows. The villas with their vast courtyards, fountains, and hanging gardens sat higher up on the hill. The former clearly belonged to the poor, while the latter was the domain of the rich.

I was alert, wide-eyed when we flew over the docks. Dozens of ships were anchored there, attached to the roots of the city. I watched out for anybody suspicious as we continued over crenellated walls and watchtowers. A fool's task. There were fae in every direction, and any good spy would know how to hide in plain sight.

"The market is up ahead," Maravina announced.

Following the bob of her head, my gaze latched onto a warren of narrow streets. The outlying stalls were exposed to the elements. Most were small and rickety, with their wares laid out on a single table. The stalls close to or in the center of the market looked much larger and were partially covered by colorful awnings.

Our descent into that pulsing chaos was marked by countless smells and sounds.

I strived to shorten my breath and mute the hundreds of conversations happening everywhere at once. My efforts didn't stop me from noticing that Kaeli and the common tongue were being spoken side by side here, along with a third language, guttural and flat in tone.

Maravina and Adrianna landed smoothly on the market's outskirts. Liora and I were lowered to the ground.

Legs unsteady after days at sea, I untucked my wings and spread them out. Balance restored, I asked Maravina, "Where will you go now?"

It wasn't on to *The Eye of the Wind*. Armstrong had mentioned that whoever flew me to the capital couldn't immediately rejoin the crew in case they were followed.

"I've a place outside the city," Maravina said. "I'll stay there until it's time to return to the ship."

"Thanks for helping me," I told her.

A small smile. "Good luck on your travels."

We each bid her farewell. I watched her disappear into the heaving crowd; my hope that she and the crew would be safe went with her.

CHAPTER 15
THE FLESH MARKET

I cast my gaze around the marketplace, taking it all in.
We had arrived in a land rich with sun, spice, and color.

I grimaced at the clamor even as I basked in the beauty of the unfamiliar. I'd been raised among a grim and conservative people in a place of harsh winters and short summers. Casatana was a world away from that.

The Sashkan Market bustled with fae clad in bright shades, vibrant headdresses, and lightweight dresses similar to ours. I guessed these choices helped them endure and defend against the heat beating atop our heads.

The warmth seeped into my body, into my very soul. Sunlight tingled in my fingertips, but nothing pushed out into the world. The magic seemed content to stay near the surface, moving lazily through my veins like honey poured out of a pot.

My attention snagged on the blue scales shimmering behind me. I glanced over my shoulder.

Adrianna's flared wings covered mine and Liora's backs. From a deep well of generational memory, I recognized the instincts triggered in her as she herded our trio together. She was in wolf mode, protecting the pack.

I raised my voice over the din, asking, "What's wrong?"

"The crowds make it impossible to tell if we're being followed—that's what's wrong." Her gaze hopped about. "And we've still got to search for the lounge amidst this mob."

"Maybe we could buy a map from a cartographer?" Liora suggested, hunching into her shoulders to keep from being jostled. "We have the money."

Indeed, we did. Before we'd left the ship, we'd decided that using gold to buy everyday items would draw the hungry gazes and grasping fingers of others to us; Armstrong had helped us by exchanging some of our money for Asitarian coins.

"It'll be quicker to ask for directions," Adrianna countered.

"Let's ask a vendor, then." Liora's eyebrows drew together with worry. "Either way, we should move. We don't look right just standing here. Especially me and Ena. We don't blend in, even with the right clothes."

How true. I, alone, had feathered wings, and with the dye in Liora's hair long-since faded, she was as conspicuous as a red rose in a garden of sunflowers. Adrianna was the only one who appeared local with her pitch-black hair and scaled wings.

Adrianna's sweaty hand grasped mine. "Keep ahold of each other. We don't want to get separated in this chaos. And be careful with your bags." She looked around with profound skepticism. "This is a pickpocket's paradise."

"Won't it look odd for a fae to be holding hands with a slave?" Liora said under her breath.

"I could grab your arm? That might make it look more aggressive," I suggested, hating the words coming out of my mouth.

Liora nodded, her face carefully blank. I took her by the forearm.

Adrianna went first, leading us into the crowd. I felt myself shrink amidst the crush. The noise, the stink; it made my head spin. My discomfort grew when I noticed the funny looks we were attracting. Many stares lingered longer than they should.

By dodging carts and throwing elbows, we arrived at our first stall. There, Adrianna initiated a conversation with the male vendor.

I identified the gentle oscillating pitch of Kaeli, and while I didn't understand the words, it was clear things weren't going well for us. The merchant kept shaking his head, making repeated gestures toward his inventory of hard-boiled sweets. The situation devolved, ending with him shouting and shooing us away.

Adrianna dragged us off, muttering, "Hideous old toad."

"What is it?"

All steam and iron, she ranted, "That bloated boob had a thing against Mokarans. That's why he wouldn't help, prejudiced prick."

I scrunched up my brow. "Why would he assume you were Mokaran?"

"Because of my accent."

"Your accent's Mokaran?" I said, feeling like the village idiot.

Adrianna hummed, confirming that. "Diana still has a Mokaran accent. I picked it up when I was a faeling, and I can make it thicker if I try. I thought it'd be better to be taken for a Mokaran here. But if he's anything to go by ..." She huffed out a bit of air.

We approached more vendors. No one was willing to give directions. In the meantime, my ears were battered by countless stallholders competing for custom and haggling with buyers.

Around every corner we discovered something different. There were entire rows dedicated to selling spices, exotic fruit, embroidered rugs, and trinkets that shone in the dusty light. Other alleys specialized in cutting hair, telling stories, and soaking fabric in vats of dye. It was a dream for my eyes and a nightmare for my nose. For the hot air was laced with incense, chili powder, and the dirt kicked up underfoot—a fact that brought on several sneezing fits.

When we came to a street of baked goods, I quickly forgot about my sore ears, gritty eyeballs, and irritated nose; my mouth watered, delighted by the scents of sugar-icing, melting butter, and bitter chocolate.

It was on this pathway that Adrianna accosted the owner of a cake stand. I couldn't understand a word of their conversation, but unlike the others, this merchant didn't ignore us or shoo us away.

Adrianna soon raised a fist over her heart, signing her gratitude and respect. Then she pulled me and Liora forward.

I dragged my hungry gaze away from the cakes to ask her, "Did we get what we needed?"

"Yes. Finally," she said, her quickened step prompting sweat to gather and stick in every one of my nooks and crannies. "We're headed to the Meat Shambles. That's where we need to take the turnoff for The Oasis Lounge."

The stores slowly dropped off, then disappeared. We swapped a fabric sky for a real one. For a wide expanse of cerulean blue.

Adrianna, Liora, and I released one another.

We had reached a public square, an open space. Directly ahead a crowd gathered, staring up at a stone platform that supported six people. Five were human. The sixth person—a male—called out to those on the ground, noting their bids on the human flesh on display. *The Meat Shambles.* A sick joke to call it that.

The male atop the platform, the ringmaster of this revolting business, pointed to a person below. "The lady in white wins the bid! Valkien naillä voita tarjeksen!" he cried out, alternating between the common tongue and Kaeli.

A man with his ribs showing and wearing only a scrap of modesty cloth around his hips was unbound from the other slaves. His chains hit the floor with an unforgiving *clank*.

I watched the man—the slave—limp down a stair located at the side of the platform. Presumably to be handed over to his new owner.

"Mother save us," Liora whispered.

Horror burned my throat as I scanned the four slaves left. I noted their wasted faces, their slumped postures, their dead eyes. Had the bidders missed the misery on display? How could they not see that suffering didn't discriminate? It didn't stick to a single culture, race, or species; the language of emotion was universal. I would know. I'd been human and then fae, and I didn't feel less as either.

Yet, not a single person in the crowd looked troubled when the trader hauled forth another man for consideration. For them, this was the norm. Perfectly natural.

That apathy rubbed salt and lemon into old wounds. I had been sold once, my whole life weighed and exchanged for a bag of gold.

Anger fanned my sunlight into an inferno, one thirsty for revenge. For blood and violence. I wasn't weak anymore. I could stop this.

Zola's authoritative snap sounded in my head. *This isn't the time or the place for fire and fury. You could hurt innocents.*

And if I did nothing? Wouldn't that be hurting innocents too? The humans were being chained like chattel. I could end their suffering. I could turn the slavers to ash and wind.

"Ena? Ena, talk to me."

I couldn't. Liora was just a distant thing playing across the surface of my consciousness. I was locked inside my mind and the walls were burning down.

"What's happened to her?" Adrianna said from the other side of my prison.

"She's hurting."

"Can't you heal her?"

"It's not that kind of pain."

Liora pressed two fingers to my wrist, checking my pulse. A hiss sounded. The contact ceased. "I can barely touch her. She's red hot."

I'd hurt Liora. That thought punctured through the madness. Regaining some sense, I tried to smother my magic. But I'd swallowed the sun. The heat was everywhere. How could I escape it when this land called to the fire in my bones and even the color of its earth seemed brushed with flame?

I managed a whisper. "It wants the slavers dead ... The sunlight."

Adrianna planted herself in my way, blocking my view of the platform with outstretched wings. "I get it, they're pond scum. But we can't win this fight, and we can't find Zeke or Sefra if we're rotting in a dungeon."

The sunlight whined, its pride almost robbing me of my hard-won reason.

"If you lose control now, you'll see your power as the enemy," Liora said quickly, softly. "It'll be reduced to a set of shackles. And trust me, that never ends well."

That cut straight through to the heart of me. It woke me up.

Thea gave me a way out, an answer. *Remember the waterlight. Use it to dampen the sunlight.*

How could I have forgotten that? I turned my sight inward and tunneled deep, listening for the water in my soul. An image of a pool swam into my head. I dove feetfirst into the liquid light and it doused the fever within.

Back in my right mind, I found I had a swollen tongue as dry as chalk and a head full of thorns. Still, I wasn't setting the world alight. That was something.

Adrianna and Liora came into focus.

"I'm better now," I reassured them.

Liora's shoulders relaxed. Adrianna exhaled relief.

"I'm sorry," I said, shamefaced. "I just snapped seeing people sold like that."

"I don't blame you." Liora hugged herself. "This whole place feels rotten and sick."

Gods. "Your empathy?"

She nodded, appearing as pale as a fish belly.

Adrianna's ear cocked. She looked as though someone had stepped in her shadow. On a turn of her heel she spun slowly, her gazed fixed upon the platform.

I followed that peculiar gaze of hers.

The slave trader was dragging a woman to the front of the stage. He spoke rapid Kaeli while holding her there by the neck, like a dog would pin a rat.

The bastard tugged up the hem of her black sack-dress. The woman was naked underneath, her pregnant belly bulging. No tears were shed—her chin stayed high, but her gaze remained elsewhere. I fancied she was taking refuge in some sacred inner space that no person could despoil.

In one blink, the woman was haloed in a glowing blue light. A connection came into existence between us, a thread that traveled out from the center of my chest and rooted in her belly—in her child.

The auctioneer dropped her dress and called out for bids to begin. Fewer hands went up this time. Someone nearby made a callous remark. "He must be mad. I wouldn't take soiled goods if you paid me. That half-breed she's carrying should be drowned at birth."

Rage tore at my throat. "Adi, we have to help her."

Her azure-blues were glued to the pregnant woman. "We can't." Gaze shuttering, she rocked her head as if to clear it of distraction. "It isn't safe for her to be with us. What would we even do with her?"

I grasped her arm. "You don't understand. There's something different about her." I lifted my gaze up to the woman onstage. "My magic, my second sight—whatever it is, it wants us to help her."

Adrianna seemed unmoved by that revelation, intransigent.

"Why don't we buy her? Then we can free her later?" Liora suggested.

I was about to raise my hand, damn the consequences.

Adrianna beat me to it, shouting, "Two."

The revolting auctioneer sneered. "The bid is already at five notes."

"Coins are worth more than paper," Adrianna countered with icy formality.

Her bearing had all the marks of high nobility—somehow she looked down on the auctioneer despite the fact that he stood higher than her. I guessed she had learned that trick from Diana.

An oily smile crawled up the trader's face. "Sold to the beauty in blue. Give the money to my guard."

He was all charm. How predictable.

The auctioneer unchained the pregnant woman. He shoved her sideways, toward the platform's stairs and to the hulking guard waiting there.

"Follow me," Adrianna muttered out of the corner of her mouth.

Liora and I did as instructed.

Adrianna veered left and led us around the crowd, not through: a good idea since we had announced to a lot of people that we carried coin.

Reed screens cornered off a private area to the left of the podium. This was where the guard had disappeared with the woman. We found a gap in the screens and stepped through. Inside, we were shielded from the crowd but not from the steps leading up to the stage, nor from the trader, who was already onto selling another person.

The woman we'd bid on stood a few feet from us. Her toffee-colored hair framed a square, tanned face. Long lashes outlined cocoa-brown eyes that stared back at us, terrified.

A male with a head as naked as a mole rat loomed over her short frame. He kept a possessive grip on the woman while making a *give-me-money* motion to Adrianna.

She eyed the satchel strung over the guard's shoulder. "Where are her papers?"

"Coin first," he grunted.

Adrianna peeled off her rucksack.

"Move slowly," the guard said, palming the hilt of his blade.

Adrianna froze slightly. "I'm getting your money. That's what you want, isn't it?"

He leered at her. "I can't be too careful. People have tried knifing me before."

"I wonder why," I deadpanned.

A very soft snort came from the woman. It sounded more like surprise than anything else.

The guard slapped her so hard she was driven to her knees. My body felt the violence of that hit as it had never felt a strike before.

In tones of lethal calm, Adrianna said, "Enough. Let her go."

The guard's smirk was sly and satisfied. A fox stealing eggs from a chicken coop. "She's not your property yet." He tightened his grip over the woman's thin wrist. "And you'd be fine with me softening this whore up if you knew her child was a shaytak."

"My baby is no demon," the woman said from her knees. Her accent was thick, and her voice was cracked from thirst, yet she remained defiant.

My respect for her grew tenfold.

"Shut it, filth!" The guard slammed his boot into the woman's ribs, and an exhale was forced from her lungs.

She coiled in on herself like a snail, gasping as if she was breathing in through a constricting tube. As she shielded her swollen belly with starved limbs, my own womb throbbed in sympathy. In the same instant, reason and restraint broke within me. Rage of a primal nature had become my master again.

Sunlight fired into the seat of my palm.

Adrianna acted first. She dropped her rucksack and drew her blade. Lunging, she stuck the tip of her sword under the bald male's chin. In a tone as cold as a dead man's dirt, she said, "Release her, or I'll tell your boss you're threatening his sale."

Anyone with a drop of sense would have conceded. Unfortunately, this male had none. He laughed in an ugly manner. "You stupid kurpä." He angled his head ever-so-slightly, not enough to nick his skin with her blade but enough to signal to the platform behind him. "You think I care if that limp dick gets his money? This is just a side-job. My regular one is with The Watch. We're the city's sentries, and nobody threatens one of us and gets away with it." Neck tendons bulged, shit-colored wings tensed. "So unless you want to spend the rest of your life in a cell being raped by guards, I suggest you lower your blade."

My hackles rose.

"Fine. You win," Adrianna said, her voice dropping to a honeyed whisper.

Wait. What?

She lowered her sword from his chin.

The guard released the woman's wrist. His eyes were flint and spark as he charged Adrianna, punching out with a fat fist. An arrogant move. He hadn't even reached for his short sword.

Adrianna blocked his sloppy blow with her free hand. Then, with a practiced flick of her wrist, she brought her sword up and struck him in the middle of the forehead, hilt-first.

All that useless, arrogant muscle crumpled to the ground.

I glanced about, frantically searching for anyone who might've seen the guard felled. But the trader's greedy attentions were consumed by potential customers, and we were hidden from the crowd's view.

Adrianna quickly sheathed her sword and donned her rucksack. Liora hurried to the pregnant woman's side and grasped her wrist. A few seconds later, she whispered, "Your baby's fine. You've just got a fractured rib. I can heal you, but—"

"We have to run," Adrianna said, picking up the woman.

A yell rent the air. "What have you bitches done to Abner?" The auctioneer towered over us, glaring down from the top of the steps.

Adrianna sprinted out of the gap in the screen. Liora and I ran after her.

The auctioneer's shouts pelted our retreating backs. "Someone call The Watch!"

We rushed across the square and hit a crowd. So many bodies acted like quicksand under our feet, slowing our progress. People stared. No one tried to stop us.

I caught ahold of Adrianna's belt. At the same time, Liora clasped my hand. We'd become a chain, a snake, struggling to weave through the masses.

Losing patience, Adrianna shouted, "Get out of the way. She's in labor!"

The crowd parted in a begrudging way. We went faster and soon arrived at the fringes of the market.

Adrianna darted into a side-street. "Where are we going?" I asked as we left the market and swarms of people behind.

"The only place we can go," she puffed out. "The Oasis Lounge."

I prayed she recalled the directions and we weren't following her pride.

My skin pebbled as we hurtled deeper into the cooling shadows of the alley. We angled right, left, and right again. Taking another sharp bend, we turned onto a road stained cobalt blue.

"It should be down here," Adrianna pushed out, breathless.

Imposing structures ran parallel to us as we raced onward. I felt hemmed in, trapped, and made vulnerable. To be ambushed on this road would prove fatal.

"Here," Adrianna panted. "It's here."

We halted before a door with a hatch inset at eye level. The dark wood bore heavy hinges, silver studs, and the words The Oasis Lounge.

Arms full, Adrianna kicked the door. "Hello in there!"

The small hatch opened to reveal a pair of dark eyes. "Mitär hellut?"

Adrianna peered at the male. "We're here to meet someone named Zeke."

The gatekeeper wavered, studying our general disarray.

Adrianna repeated what I assumed were the same words in Kaeli.

The wooden hatch slid closed. A noiseless pause was followed by a welcome click of the lock. The door swung open. Thank the stars.

The male motioned for us to enter. I heaved relief into my lungs when our group walked into a modest-sized courtyard. A cyan-blue mosaic decorated the ground in geometric shapes. A fountain that featured a scene of seduction took center stage, and potted citrus trees stood proudly by the wayside, their scents invigorating, clearing my stunned mind.

The door locked behind us.

"Wait here," instructed the gatekeeper.

Then he was away, striding up the courtyard and through a white door that opened into a two-story building.

"I can heal you now." Liora approached the woman in Adrianna's arms. "I'll have to touch you, though. Is that okay?"

Blood beaded on the woman's cracked lips as wariness thinned them. The sight pried open an aching chasm within my heart.

"Here." She pointed to her side with ragged, dirt-lined fingernails. "It hurts. I worried about baby."

"I can ease the pain, and I'll check on the baby again," Liora said calmly.

A beat of hesitation. Then, "Yes. Please do."

Liora palmed that swollen belly. My witchy senses noted how the world seemed to bend toward her. How the air had become perfumed with spring-fresh things.

I couldn't have explained how or why, but while she worked, the anxiety cantering through me slowed to a trot, and the residual burning in my legs left me. As if Liora was healing the very air around her.

Without losing focus on the task before her, Liora asked her patient, "What's your name?"

"Slavers took name," she uttered, eyes reddening with unshed tears.

Full of frost and fire, Adrianna said, "No, they didn't. Nobody can do that."

The woman's features sharpened with suspicion. As if she suspected Adrianna was a tiger in disguise. A villain dressed up as a friend. Still, she gave an answer. "It's Anya."

"You should know that we only tried to buy you so that we could free you, Anya," I told her. "You're not our slave."

Her thirty-something face regarded me with nothing but distrust. She aimed her shrewd gaze at Liora. "They free you?"

For a handful of seconds, Liora looked lost. Then her color deepened as blood rushed to her cheeks. "Actually, I was never a slave to begin with. I'm pretending to be one."

"You odd to do this," Anya said, frowning.

Liora smiled awkwardly. Then she refocused on her healing work.

"Do you have anywhere you can go in the city that's safe?" Adrianna asked Anya.

Gaze downcast, she shook her head.

Adrianna's eyes met mine for a pulse. I read the meaning in them and nodded.

"Are you happy to stay with us until you can figure something out?" Adrianna followed up.

"Not happy for long time," she said in a broken form of the common tongue. "But I stay with you."

I lapsed into sadness, into pity and affection.

"I've fixed the fracture to your ribs," Liora said, her hands leaving Anya's belly. "But you're dehydrated and malnourished. I can't do anything about that except make sure you get what you need."

Not wasting a second, Liora handed her the water from her rucksack. Whatever doubts Anya had about us, they didn't stop her from taking the canteen. She was already taking sips, her cheeks sagging in relief when Adrianna set her down.

When she was done, Anya handed the canteen back to Liora.

I couldn't ignore my own needs any longer. Throat sticking mid-swallow, I raided my rucksack for my canteen. The water within was lukewarm and leathery tasting. I didn't care; it eased my parched mouth. I swiped my tongue across my lips and teeth, savoring every drop.

As I stowed my canteen, the white door ahead of us creaked open. From out of the two-story building stepped the gatekeeper and with him, a female.

"I am Jada, the mistress here," said the female, stopping in front of us. "Tell me why you have come to The Oasis Lounge."

There was something innately intimidating about Jada. Not only did she loom over us, forcing our heads up and exposing our throats, but she carried off her golden dress with a plunging neckline and matching thigh slits in a manner that screamed unshakable confidence.

Adrianna stood as tall as she could without rising onto her tiptoes. "As we told your sentry, we've come for Zeke."

She regarded us as a horse would a fly. Entirely uninterested. "Why would you look for this person here?"

Adrianna hedged. "A friend of Zeke's mentioned that we might ask for him here."

"I see," she said, eyebrow lifting. "And what do you want with this Zeke?"

My mind paused, acknowledging her affected notes. I suspected she was hiding a strong accent. That didn't detract from the melodic quality of her voice. Paired with how beautiful she was, it was hard not to wilt in her presence. She had dark skin that shone like satin, and her waist-length hair was an untamed mane of tightly coiled curls.

"We need his help," Adrianna said, her tense jaw stiffening her words.

Jada's walnut-colored eyes swept over us. "Yes. Josiah informs me you arrived in quite the panic. That seems to suggest you were fleeing from something. Who or what was chasing you?"

"We'll explain as soon as we've seen Zeke."

"That won't do. Tell me what trouble you've brought with you." Jada motioned behind us. "Or you will be made to leave."

Josiah, the gatekeeper, grasped a dagger tucked away in a sash at his midriff.

Adrianna stalled. I was at a loss too.

Jada would surely throw us out when she learned the truth. We had no claim upon her; we could offer no inducement save coin, and what bribe would be enough to shelter us from The Watch, not to mention Morgan's people?

"We saw Anya at the slaver's market," Liora said, glancing at her. "We bought her because we wanted to free her. But before we could take her away a male working for the trader hurt her." She singled Adrianna out with a nod. "My friend stopped him and we were forced to flee with Anya. Also, before we misunderstand each other, I'm not a slave."

Adrianna and I exchanged looks. Liora had put her trust in this female. Had she sensed something with her empathy, enough to realize it was safe to do so?

"That is obvious," Jada said. "No slave in Asitar would dare speak with such authority." Hand on hip, she confronted Adrianna. "Did you kill this male?"

"I don't know," Adrianna replied archly. "I didn't hang around to check his life-signs."

Jada's cool gaze cut away from Adrianna. In bloodless tones, she said, "I suppose it doesn't matter. Either way, you'll have attracted the attention of The Watch."

"We've no desire to create problems for you," Liora went on, mediating. "If you can just help us contact Zeke, we'll leave."

Jada lapsed into quiet, withholding judgment.

Anya squirmed, joining her hands under her belly. "What is it?" I asked.

She grimaced. "I need washroom."

"You may use our facilities." Jada glanced at Josiah. "Show her where to go."

Anya seemed to withdraw into herself. "I won't go with strange fae."

"I understand." No pity. Just acknowledgment.

Jada's focus snapped to Adrianna. Quite suddenly, she declared, "Zeke isn't here. But he did mention that people might come asking for him. If that were to happen, he had me swear that I would get word to him and assist whoever showed up. So, Watch or not, I am duty-bound to offer you shelter."

"Then why did you interrogate us?" Adrianna demanded.

"Because he described who might come, and you don't match his description." A canny glint in her eye emerged. "However, there was a phrase you were supposedly given. Tell me what it is and I'll help you."

"Aurinka perista itän," Adrianna reeled off.

"Thank you." Jada moved into a side-on stance. "I'll ensure you have a private room inside, one which I urge you to keep to. I can't vouch for all of my patrons' loyalties, and it would be better for everyone given your situation if you showed your faces as little as possible."

"How soon before you can contact Zeke?" Adrianna asked.

"Soon enough." Jada spun on her heel and stalked off.

No longer required, Josiah returned to his post at the gate.

The rest of us walked in Jada's footsteps. She halted at the white door, her hand upon the bronze handle. "My establishment is spelled to prevent fae-hearing from working at full capacity, but I would still advise you not to use Zeke's name until you're inside your own room. There are those who might recognize it and would interrogate anybody asking after him."

That said, Jada went through the entranceway and held the door ajar for us. With a graceful sweep of her hand, she invited us in. "Welcome to The Oasis Lounge."

CHAPTER 16
STRANGERS AMIDST SMOKE

I stepped over the threshold. The sunbaked sky disappeared, replaced by a nightly light. That transition had bright circles peppering my vision.

Dazzled, the smothering of another sense—my fae-hearing—shot panic into my veins. The foreign magic pressed a pillow over my head. I became a bird without wings, grounded and vulnerable to predators.

Blinking rapidly, my sight cleared and my pulse evened out. The first thing I saw was Adrianna wincing and rubbing her ears. "Courts, that's horrible."

"Even I can feel it." Liora touched her earlobe.

"Our dampening spell is a powerful one." Jada viewed the room proudly. "We don't like spies here."

Threat or innocent comment? Her tone made it hard to tell.

"Elijah." Jada beckoned over a man from in front of a small podium—a greeter, perhaps. "Put these ladies in chamber three." She did not forget Anya's needs. "It has an attached washroom. You may take your relief in there."

"Thank you, mistress," Anya said.

"You are most welcome." Jada turned to Elijah. "Take care of them until I return."

He dipped his head. "Of course, mistress."

"Where are you going?" Adrianna asked Jada.

"To send a message to our mutual friend."

Jada marched toward a staircase in the far-right corner. At the same time, Elijah faced our group. "This way, please."

He whirled about on sandaled feet and started forward, leading us down the center of the room. I absorbed the lounge with an interested gaze.

A canopy of wine-red fabric covered up the ceiling. Likewise, gilded rugs concealed the floor. There was nothing cold or rough on display. Everything from the plush furnishings, the partially shielded booths, and the stained glass lanterns created an intimate atmosphere.

Fae were everywhere, getting their hands sticky with dice, cards, and money. Many indulged in hard spirits and a sickly sweet-smelling smoke, which was sucked out through multi-stemmed glass instruments. The incense burners also polluted the air by puffing out heavy sandalwood, clove, and amber scents. The mixture of these aromas and the heat made me want to crack a window, but there were none. We were trapped in a gilded cage—a decadent world of smoke, sin, and shadows—all at once stunning, confusing, and stimulating.

With so many distractions at hand, none of the customers or human servers stared as we passed them. Even though Adrianna and I stood out with our brutal weapons, iron-tense shoulders, and road-dusted clothes. In short, this was the perfect place to hide.

The only people to note our presence were the six armed fae that guarded the outskirts of the room. Their eyes tracked our movements until we stopped beside a paper screen, one of five set into the right wall.

Elijah slid open a screened door. Beyond was a moderate-sized space decorated with a solid wood table, a few rugs, and a dozen cushions.

Elijah stepped in first. We four piled in after him.

A magicked ceiling fan summoned a whirl of stale wind. I exhaled with relief when it hit me in the face, dispersing some of the stuffiness that assailed my nostrils.

"There are refreshment lists on the tables. Can I get you anything to start?"

Adrianna assumed authority. "We'll take four jugs of water. And to save time, perhaps you could just bring us a selection of your best dishes?"

"Of course." Elijah's smile was bland, clearly practiced. "The Medley combines popular foods from all over Asitar."

"Excellent. Thank you."

"I will return shortly." He bowed and left us.

Anya moved toward the rear wall. There, she opened another screened door, this one smaller, and hovered in the entranceway. "It is okay if I use washroom?"

I just stared. Was she really asking to relieve herself?

"You don't need our permission," Adrianna said evenly.

That didn't get a reply. Anya entered the washroom and shut the door.

I dropped my rucksack and laid aside the two swords I carried. Grateful for a chance to rest, I settled atop a gaudy cushion that bordered the low-standing table. Stationary and deprived of fresh air, I struggled to ignore my discomfort—the layer of slimy sweat that stuck to my skin, my ripening smell. Gods, what I wouldn't give for a bath.

Liora lowered herself onto a cushion beside me. But Adrianna—she paced the length of our chamber.

"I know you're anxious," Liora said to her. "But we've got a moment to sit and breathe—"

"I'm not anxious." Adrianna spread her wings and rounded on Liora as though mortally offended. "And what did I say about reading me?"

"You realize those are contradicting statements, right?" I said, unable to keep the amusement out of my voice.

Adrianna shot me a look that promised murder.

"I'm sorry." Liora grimaced, rubbing her temples. "I wasn't trying to pick up on anything. I'm just having a hard time shutting everyone out."

Sympathy gripped my heart.

"Fine. I'll admit to being extremely alert. As I should be—we're in a fucking smoke den." Adrianna pointed a thumb over her shoulder. "Half of those people are cooked on grundä. It doesn't speak well for Zeke that we can ask for him here, does it?"

"What's grundä?" I inquired.

Adrianna resumed pacing. "A drug."

"Like alcohol?"

"Stronger. Like poppy seed tea."

Instant wariness. That drink could relieve pain. It could also cause addiction. I'd seen it growing up, even in my backwoods village.

Anya rejoined us after a short stretch. Forgoing the chubby cushions, she lay flat on the floor, on a rug. Those long lashes of hers drooped heavily.

I worried she hadn't chosen somewhere more comfortable out of fear of some barbaric social custom. "Are you okay down there?"

No response.

"Anya?"

Her eyes flew open. "Oh. Yes. Fine. Floor helps lower back."

Everybody's heads went up at the *tap-tap-tap* on the screened door. "It's Elijah, your server. May I come in?"

"Yes," Adrianna said.

Elijah and two other servers entered. Between them, they carried four jugs of water, a bowl of rose-petaled water, a towel, and a tray laden with dishes that included flatbreads, a bowl of olives, and a chicken dish flavored with sweet oranges. A pot of mint tea was also served to us. A tradition, according to Elijah.

I pointed to the bowl of rosewater now on the table. "What's that for?"

"It is for your hands, my lady. In case you wish to wash them." In a hurry, he added, "It is something we provide for every guest. Please, take no offense."

"No offense taken." I smiled as kindly as I could without leaning into patronizing sentiment.

A marked blink. He seemed unsure how to interpret my friendliness. I noticed his gaze travel over Liora's and Anya's relaxed postures. The masculine line of his shoulders unknotted a bit. Then Elijah *click-hissed* at the other servers. They bowed and retreated from the room.

Alone with us, Elijah said, "The mistress wanted me to convey a message. She has gotten word to your mutual friend, and he will arrive soon."

Liora and I expressed our gratitude.

Elijah bowed his head. "With your leave, I shall go."

"Yes," Adrianna said, distracted. "Thank you."

Eyes on the floor, he backed out of the room.

Adrianna started to pull clothes out of her rucksack.

"What are you doing?" I asked.

She didn't look up as she responded, "If The Watch are on the lookout for us, we should be prepared for running and fighting. I don't want to do either of those things in a dress. Not when it has no use. It certainly didn't help us blend in any."

Guilt crept up on me like low-lying fog. I'd been the agent of our misfortunes. Still, I couldn't regret it. Not with Anya lying beside us.

Without any preamble, Adrianna stripped. Her casualness would've surprised me once. But I'd grown used to it after living in proximity to fae for months; they tended to be freer with their bodies than humans.

"I guess we should change too," I said to Liora, who nodded.

Adrianna focused on Liora. "Have you got black clothes?"

A muted, "Yes," was her answer.

I peeled off my lilac dress. The material was damp and flecked with dirt, but I folded and stowed it neatly anyway. That girl from the Gauntlet hadn't died completely, and while I hadn't grown up as poor as others in my village, I'd never worn anything as beautiful as this dress. It deserved to be treated with care.

I pulled on linen trousers and a wrap top that tied off beneath my wings. Then, reluctantly, I slipped my hot feet back into my shoes. Task finished, I caught Anya sneaking looks up at Adrianna while she buckled her belt.

"Is something wrong?" I asked Anya, who had remained recumbent on the floor.

She licked her lips. "You might put it here." Anya tapped a spot underneath her swollen breasts. "Females wear belts high on waist. It is fashion."

"It's too awkward to draw a sword out from that high up," Adrianna remarked.

Going by Anya's expression, I thought she might've regretted speaking up. "Do you follow fashion?" I prompted her.

"I did," she mumbled. "I was seamstress to great fae lady before I taken."

"What happened?" Liora asked gently.

Anya clasped her belly.

"You got pregnant?" Adrianna guessed. "That ass-fungus back in the market called your baby a shaytak—was that why they took you? Because they believed you carried a demon?"

"What is ass-fungus?" Anya said mildly.

Liora and I spouted laughter.

"A person so repulsive that they grow fungus in odd places," Adrianna replied, as if that were the most normal thing in the world.

"That is good and right." Anya massaged her protruding stomach. "And my baby no demon. They steal me away because I love male very much, enough to keep his child. That why they drag me to market," she bit off, her bottom lip trembling.

Stars. Her child was a demi-fae—offspring of a human and a fae. They were considered abominations in Aldar and the Gauntlet. Asitar was no different, it seemed.

"I not ashamed," Anya said, her features hardening as she stared up at the fabric ceiling.

She must have misinterpreted our silence. I wanted to rectify that. "We're not judging you, if that's what you think. We don't control who we love, and we shouldn't be punished for something we can't prevent."

Anya struggled up into a seated position. "You love someone? Someone you not meant to?"

My mind and heart filled with Wilder. "Yes."

"Your love ... human?" It looked as if she expected to be hit.

"I don't mind you asking me questions, Anya, even if you think they're inappropriate." I tipped my head toward Adrianna. "My friend over there is as blunt as a rusty sword and I'm well used to her."

"You like my honesty. I know you do," Adrianna said, confident.

"She says honesty." I mimed a set of scales with my hands. "I say rudeness."

Adrianna snorted, unconvinced. Anya, meanwhile, seemed lost.

"And no, the person I loved wasn't human. But our relationship was still forbidden."

Anya angled her head, waiting for me to go on. When I didn't, her gaze left me. She stayed silent, accepting that was all I would reveal. In the end, she was a stranger, and confessing to more would be foolhardy. Except, when I stared at her for long enough, I had the oddest sensation. That of a current connecting us. As if we traveled along the same river.

"Do you know where the father of your baby is?" Liora asked Anya as she finished changing into her black outfit. "Perhaps we could help you get back to him somehow."

"He dead." A hopeless croak. "They kill him."

Anya's eyes watered. She refused to blink—refused to let the tears fall.

"Can you go stay with family?" I asked softly.

She sucked in a ropey inhale through her teeth. "I have little family, and none who care for me."

I met Liora's and Adrianna's gazes. We shared our dismay wordlessly. Where would Anya go? Where would she be safe? With answers out of our reach, I sat at the table and scrubbed at my hands until they were clean. Adrianna and Liora joined me in my task.

"Come eat with us, Anya," Liora said, dishing up.

She stared at the food with a rabid hunger. Yet she made no move toward it. "I no way to repay you."

"We don't expect you to pay us," Adrianna corrected as she poured out four glasses of water.

Anya approached the table with the caution of a deer moving out into an open field. All she lacked were the flattened ears. She washed her hands with the rosewater and the cloth first. It took her several dips in the bowl and passes with the steaming towel to shift the filth from her skin. Anger stung my veins like snake venom. I wanted to punch something, namely the slavers.

She reached for the bread. It was clear to me by the small tremor in her hand that she'd been waiting, hoping for this moment ever since the food had arrived.

With a powerful thirst and a need to refill our canteens, the decanters were emptied in minutes. As for the food, I was a queen at a banquet. I ate better than I had in months. Not that they had starved us at Kasi. But we hadn't been allowed as much as we liked. If we had dared ask for more, the answer had always been no, or in one memorable case, a hit to the head with a ladle.

The extra food was even more appreciated now. My appetite had only grown since becoming a fae-witch. It seemed being a channel for primal forces demanded more food—more energy.

We spent ten minutes on our meal and on light conversation. Anya didn't contribute; she was too busy stuffing herself. Liora intervened at one point and explained to Anya that she showed signs of starvation, and it would make her ill to eat too much at once. Anya complied, even while looking crestfallen.

When the last scraps of food were gone, the only thing left to do was wait. And wait we did.

A quarter of an hour went by. I knew this because Adrianna drew her pocket watch out every minute or so to announce the time, always with rising amounts of agitation. Liora dealt with the tension by sitting as still as a cat on a wall. Anya napped on the floor, her head supported by a cushion.

After a while, Adrianna resorted to peering out a crack in the screened door.

My anxiety was peaking, acting like bugs under my skin. I attempted to calm my mind—my magic—by watching the hypnotic light show created by the lanterns.

"I think he's here." Withdrawing from the crack, Adrianna turned to face us. "A new arrival's talking to Jada. Their conversation looks intense."

Liora and I got up.

Adrianna stepped aside, allowing us a look through the gap. Liora stood in front of me, closest to the screened door. I peered over the top of her.

Jada was easy enough to spot. Tall and serious looking, she stood beside the entrance, chatting to our possible "Zeke."

Our contact was of middling height and slight of build. An unobtrusive male with unremarkable features.

Everything grew muffled. As if I were immersed in a lake. I recognized it for the magical nudge that it was. My waterlight enabled me to see things as they really were. To see through spells and disguises. In those moments, my Sight would trigger an image or a disturbance in my hearing.

I looked at the male again. His visage blurred, as if I eyed him through smudged glass. No matter how I squinted or stared, the image stayed fragmented.

My wings tingled when the male glanced in our direction. He

nodded distantly at something Jada had said and uttered a few words in return. Then he was leaving her and hurrying toward us.

I closed the screened door with a snap. "Draw your swords."

Adrianna freed her blade. Then, "Why?"

"Because whoever that is, he's disguising his real appearance," I said, hurrying over to where I'd left my Utemä.

"You think he means to deceive us?"

"I hope not," was all I said.

Liora grabbed her rapier before helping Anya up off the floor. "Stay behind us, okay?"

"I will do so." She backed up to the opposite wall.

I was strapping my sword to my side when a light hand knocked at the door. Azure-blues blazing, Adrianna motioned for me and Liora to flank her. We formed a defensive line out in front of the table. And Anya.

I released my Utemä and channeled moonlight, readying to create a shield.

"Come in," Adrianna said.

The male slipped inside, closing the door behind him.

He froze to the spot. Through the haze around his features, I noticed him staring at our blades. They pointed at him like three accusing fingers. Then his focus cut to my open palm, raised in warning.

"Zeke" put his hands up in surrender. "Aurinka perista itän."

That key phrase blunted my suspicion. I released my magic, lowering my arms and my sword to my side.

"You claim to be Zeke, then?" Adrianna said, not dropping her defensive stance.

"I don't claim anything. I am Zeke." He tugged on the neck of his tunic-robe. There, on his bare shoulder, was a tattoo of a little bird with blue wings.

Releasing his collar, he added, "Jada seems satisfied that your group is the one I've been looking for." His voice was wrong. Too flat. Too neutral. "But why didn't you arrive by boat? And where is the rest of your group? Diana said to expect a male, a man, one female, and two women."

"Why are you disguising yourself?" I asked him.

He went preternaturally still. "What do you mean?"

"You're using magic to conceal what you look like."

"He likely jinn," Anya said from behind us.

My misgivings about him returned. As far as I knew, a jinn was a sprite with a talent for illusionary magic. But the only jinn I'd heard of was Shaytan, the Dark God of Mischief, infamous for his tricks and glamours.

"I thought their kind had gone extinct," Liora said, her voice bright with interest.

"Are you a jinn?" Adrianna asked, colder than a mountain spring.

"We don't have time for this. Jada mentioned your troubles with The Watch. So before I got here, I checked in with an informant of mine. He told me that the two of you"—he motioned to Adrianna and me—"have been accused of stealing a slave. And the male you attacked has accused you of being Abraxus's sympathizers."

That was the last thing I'd expected to hear. How had we acted as sympathizers? Because we stole a slave?

"You were also seen running into the western sector of the city," he continued. "I've managed to feed The Watch a false trail, thanks to a few well-placed friends. But we should leave immediately."

Rutting hell. What had I brought down on us?

"Are you getting anything from him, Li?" Adrianna asked.

It took a few heartbeats before Liora answered. "It's hard to get a read on him. I think he's worried and frustrated, but that could be anybody else in this room."

"You're an empath?" the male guessed.

Liora didn't confirm or deny that.

"Look, we're not going anywhere with you while you're under a disguise," Adrianna argued. "If you can create illusions, how do we know that tattoo on your shoulder isn't fake?" Good point. "So, either lift the concealment or—"

"Or what?" he challenged. "You need me to escape this city and to find the person you seek—she's why you're here, isn't it?"

That ultimatum whipped up my temper. I wouldn't stand for him baiting me with information about my own sister.

"Where is she?" I asked, anger clipping my words.

"I received a message from her about a week ago," he replied, toneless. "It said that if I wished to contact her, she would be checking in regularly with a nomadic community we're both friendly with. If anyone knows where she is, it will be them."

"Where is this community?" Adrianna asked.

He cocked a brow. "Before you get any ideas about going without me, you can't navigate miles of featureless desert without a guide. The dangers are countless."

"Surely you understand why we're reluctant to trust you?" Liora mediated, her notes persuasive, leading. "Can't you just drop the illusion, if only for a moment?"

"Let me get this straight," he said plainly. "You all refuse to admit why you avoided the docks or why your party has changed members. You made off with a slave and made such a mess of it that you've captured The Watch's attention, and yet you demand I prove my trustworthiness?"

We were getting nowhere.

"There was a change in our plans since meeting Diana, and some of our group couldn't come with us," Adrianna explained, sounding downright royal. "We realized that landing at the docks would be pointless since you wouldn't recognize our party, so we thought to ask for you here."

"And we only bought Anya to free her," I added defensively.

"Admirable. And where will you take her so she might be safe?"

A winter blight seemed to seize my entire being. "We're not sure, but we'll protect her until we can find somewhere suitable."

His voice showed emotion for the first time. Strong with scorn, he said, "So you took her without knowing how she might live free? You do know that if you're caught, she'll be executed for your crimes."

Shame burrowed into my heart like a worm through an apple. Was he right? Had I done more harm by insisting we buy her?

Have faith in yourself, Thea said kindly. *You were drawn to her for a reason.*

Either way, I didn't have the heart to respond to Zeke. My silence was infectious, and a painful kind of quiet gripped the room. Each side had drawn their battle lines. Yet he had the higher ground. We had to go with him. We had to take the risk. Before I could concede defeat, he pressed a knuckle to the bridge of his nose. "Vitun tardem."

I got the distinct feeling I'd been cursed at. He clicked his thumb and forefinger together, and a tingle of magic pricked my tailbone and rushed up my spine.

The illusion dropped. And I saw him.

Zeke stood a couple of inches above me. He was athletically built and outfitted in tan trousers, brown boots, and the robe-tunic I'd already glimpsed. Leather armor covered his forearms, and a weapons belt, lined with a dozen knives and a sword, crossed his chest and waist.

The bronze wings at his back puzzled me. I looked for more clues as to his heritage. He appeared fae, and handsome at that. Then I spotted the mangled, almost melted flesh around his olive-brown throat. He looked as if he had lived in a collar. Had he once been a slave?

"Wh—what are you?" The crack in Adrianna's voice got my undivided attention. She might've looked less shocked if she'd found a ghost rifling through her underwear.

Confused, I glanced back at Zeke.

He also seemed surprised. That alarm lasted a very long minute before his features relaxed and his scaled wings spread out, giving us a show. For a brief flash, his hazel eyes glowed blue. "Hello, princess."

His voice—his real voice—was more pleasing to the ears than the monotone from before.

"How do you know I'm a princess?" Adrianna demanded.

"Your makena told me," he said, a tad cool. "Lucky for you that she did. If it weren't for the fact that Diana would string my guts for her stockings, I would've left you here rather than reveal myself." He yanked the collar of his robe down and revealed the bluebird tattoo again. "Just in case you were still in any doubt of who your mate truly is."

Mate. My mouth hung down, suspended in disbelief.

Adrianna stalked up to him and swung at his bearded jaw. Zeke allowed it to happen, taking the hit expertly, relaxing and rolling with the motion.

"How dare you." Adrianna trembled with rage. "How *dare* you try to hide the fact we're mates."

"What are you talking about?" Zeke faced Adrianna, his grimace as bitter as bad ale.

"Your disguise blocked the bond from forming. That's the only explanation for the delay. That's why you were so desperate to keep it up, wasn't it?"

Zeke's black eyebrows beetled together. "I had no idea what you were until after I dropped the illusion. I didn't think I could even have a mate since I'm only part fae." He acknowledged Anya with a glance before returning his focus to Adrianna. "Your friend was right to guess that I'm a jinn—half of one anyway. And jinn magic is illusion made flesh. It distorts other energies. That's likely the reason for the delay."

A mulish look crossed Adrianna's face.

"Do you still believe I wanted to deceive you?" Contempt crept into his features. "Or are you just mad that your mate is a half-breed?"

She stiffened. "I don't care about that."

"If you say so," he said flatly.

"You're an ass," she snapped.

Zeke and Adrianna stared each other down like two predator cats. All pride and aggression.

The screened door *shushed* open. Jada came in, sporting a grim look. "We're about to be raided by The Watch."

CHAPTER 17
TRAPPED

I tightened my grip on my sword-hilt as panic flipped my stomach upside down. The Watch was coming ... How would we escape? Where could we go?

"My informant said Nala's leading the raid." Jada's gaze swept over our group. "She must've found out that they're here."

"How long do we have?" Zeke rushed out.

"Five minutes at most."

"Ahin," Zeke hissed.

"Who's Nala?" Adrianna asked Zeke.

"She's the captain of The Watch."

"And a ruthless bitch." Jada focused on Zeke. "I've already instructed Elijah to lead the staff out through the tunnels. Are you bringing them?" She motioned in our direction.

"We can't go with you," Zeke told Jada. "If we do, we run the risk of Casatana locking down while we're underground. It could take days, maybe weeks, for the king to relax the extra security. We can't afford to be stuck here for weeks." He didn't bother to look at us—at his mate—when he said that.

"Atchi." Jada's nostrils widened with a frustrated sigh. "At least wait here until I've told my patrons about the raid. There'll be a stampede for the doors. If you leave with the crowd, you might manage to sneak past The Watch."

"There's one more thing." Zeke glanced over his shoulder. "Anya, you should go with Jada. It's too dangerous for you to remain with us."

Anya joined us from the rear of the room. "I not want to go with strange fae." She bobbed her head at our trio in a timid way. "They attack fae for me and heal me. I stay with them."

Tenderness and concern bubbled up inside of me.

"You can't come with us." It wasn't Zeke denying her, but Adrianna. "My friend can't fly." She looked at me, outing me as the damned chicken of the fae world. "She'll need me to carry her. Zeke needs to do the same for my other friend. There's nobody left to take you. I'm sorry."

That stark reality deflated Anya.

"Are you headed to Alhara?" Jada asked Zeke in an undertone.

"I hadn't planned on it." The muscles in his bearded jaw flexed. "But with The Watch riled up, we'll have to get out of the skies and out of sight for a bit. And Alhara's the best place to hide out."

"If that's where you're headed, it makes sense to take Anya there too," Jada said. "It's the safest place for someone like her. I can fly her there once we've gotten out of the city."

"How do you plan on getting out?"

"If you give her a disguise, I'll sneak her past the north wall after the sun sets tonight. It should be possible if it's just the two of us." Jada turned to Anya. "Are you willing to come with me?"

A hesitant nod.

"Then we need to move."

"Us too." Zeke turned to glance at our trio. "Get your bags."

I sheathed my Utemä first. In the next breath, I rushed over to the table and shouldered my rucksack.

Liora and Adrianna did the same.

Back at the screened door, Zeke snapped his fingers. Anya's visage shimmered and shifted. She looked like a fae—still pregnant, but taller, with blue wings.

Jada addressed Liora. "You can't carry a weapon if you expect to slip past The Watch."

Her bluntness irritated me like coarse sand. Before I could argue with her, Liora nodded and said, "I know." She held her rapier out to me. I didn't move for it, so she added, "Take it."

The look on her face, her stoic acceptance, killed me. But I did what she said. As I returned her blade to the sheath on my belt, Jada told Zeke, "Don't die, saliq. Your people need you."

"The same to you, sayrai," he said soberly.

They met in a one-armed embrace. I side-glanced at Adrianna for her reaction. She absorbed Zeke and Jada's intimacy with blank composure.

"I see you at Alhara," Anya said, her gaze marking our trio.

Liora forced a smile and nodded. I couldn't bring myself to do the same; I wasn't confident we would see her again.

Jada slid the door open and slipped out into the main room of the lounge. Anya followed her closely.

"What's your name?" Zeke suddenly asked Liora.

"Liora," she answered.

Zeke flicked a brow at me. A silent ask.

"Ena."

His tiger eyes pinned his mate.

In a wooden tone, she said, "Adrianna."

The line of his shoulders rose. His mouth opened—

"The Watch are coming!" Jada shouted. "Leave now! Get out!"

A stunned silence fell.

I frantically searched for Jada in the smoke-filled room. *There,* on the left, by the stairwell. But Anya was nowhere to be seen. *Howwherewhen?*

Jada ducked under the stairs and vanished. The entrance into the tunnels must be there.

Her fleeing triggered an explosive burst of activity. Everyone, even those severely inebriated, stumbled and pushed and sprinted toward the exits. Half of the crowd went left and out the entrance, and the other half moved to my right, seeking the double doors at the rear of the lounge. They streamed out into two courtyards—the one we'd come through, and the second, which was just unadorned stone.

Zeke grasped Adrianna's hand. "What are you doing?" she demanded.

He avoided her eye. "Hold onto one another."

I clasped hands with Adrianna and Liora.

"Don't let go," advised Zeke.

He led Adrianna, Liora, and me out of the chamber. We pushed toward the rear exit, sticking to the outskirts to avoid being crushed in the thick of the crowd.

I felt magic bleed into the world. Then I caught glimpses of fire outside the double doors.

Flames the color of an autumn sunset clipped the fae who had escaped and gotten airborne. They fell from the sky, ablaze, and were lost in the city. Hysterical screams pierced my ears like needles.

The fifty or so fae who hadn't quite left the courtyard turned and surged toward the other exit, seeking to escape the hellfire nipping at their wings.

The fire didn't follow them inside.

Zeke continued toward the back doors. Adrianna yanked on his hand and halted our group. "Why are we still going this way?"

Zeke turned his head and glanced down at her. "Because the fire witch is here to scare everyone out the front door. That's where The Watch will be waiting to ambush them."

I surveyed the mob, crushed together and forced to leave in single file. Sure enough, a cry came from outside the front door. "You are all under arrest. Surrender now, and you won't be harmed."

"Lies!"

"No surrender!"

The clash of steel rang out. Yet all the fae continued to leave out the same door, preferring to face swords rather than witch-fire.

My feathers quivered. It seemed the wolves were baying at our doors, and we were no better than sheep inside of a pen. My trail of thought stopped dead when the tongue of flame whipping around the rear doors ceased.

Seven fae touched down in the courtyard. A female and six males. Fear swelled inside of my chest, and my throat doubled in size. I recognized one of them as the slaver's guard that Adrianna had knocked out.

Zola's yell rattled my brain. *Ena, shield the door.*

I broke from our group and sprinted into the center of the room. Nobody remained on this side of the lounge; my path was clear.

Planting my feet hip-width apart, I raised my hands and *pushed*. A barrier sourced from moonlight blocked the exit. It was almost transparent, made partially visible by a faint opal-like sheen on its surface.

Adrianna and Liora ran to my side.

"A little warning next time," Adrianna snapped.

Before I could reply, the slaver's guard pointed his meaty claw of a hand at us. As if he could strike us dead with a gesture. "That's them! Those are the bitches who attacked me."

"Nice welt, ass-fungus," Adrianna snarled at him.

I saw exactly what she meant. In the middle of his forehead, courtesy of Adrianna's blade, was an ugly bruise as blatant as a blood stain on a white handkerchief.

In a fit of fury, he hurled a knife in our direction. To strengthen my barrier, I crossed my fists over my chest. The blade hit my shield ... It bounced off.

I kept my spine straight even as relief weakened my knees.

The female, with hooded eyes and cropped hair, strode up to our attacker. She seized the bald male by the ear and yanked him down to her eye level. It looked absurd; she was half his size. "I said they were to be taken alive, Abner. Return to The Watch's House. I'll deal with you later."

She shoved him away.

Head bent, Abner backed up. "Sorry, Nala."

Knowing the female's identity, I marked her out as both the main threat and a mystery. She had led The Watch to the lounge—how had she known where we'd fled to?

In a few wingbeats, Abner was gone. But six fae were still left to challenge us. All wore red underclothes, leather armor, and a bandoleer strapped to their chests. The uniform of The Watch, perhaps.

"We need a plan," I whispered to Adrianna and Liora. "My shield won't hold forever. We've got maybe five minutes, two if they start attacking it."

I trailed off as a stranger joined our huddle. The surge of panic prickling my temples eased when the male's visage blurred in a telling way. It was just Zeke; he had adopted another disguise. He looked heavier, taller, with blunt features.

Nala stalked up to my moon-barrier. "What is your name, light-wielder?"

A question for me, one that I ignored. Zeke faced our trio, partially interrupting our view of the courtyard with outstretched wings. That sign of disrespect provoked Nala. "Who are you? How dare you show your back to us."

Zeke whispered to me in his own voice, "Can you shield us all if we run out?"

I wracked my mind, imagining how I could do such a thing. I'd seen other witches conjure bubble-shields in my training, but I hadn't gotten there yet.

"No."

In the background, I overheard one of the males say, "Let's get this done, Nala."

"That's right," another male added. "The sooner we catch them, the sooner we'll get our reward."

A dark chuckle sounded. "The king will blow his nuts when we bring him a light-wielder."

"Ena, you're going to have to drop your shield," Adrianna said under her breath, paying no heed to the chatter outside. "Then we'll fight our way out. It's the only thing we can do."

"Agreed." Zeke's gaze went up and over me. "And we have to take them out before the rest of The Watch joins them."

I glanced back to see what he was looking at. The Oasis Lounge was empty, and the front door hung on by a single hinge. Outside, Jada's customers battled fae in robes, but my perspective was limited. I couldn't make out who was winning, or how many fought.

Nala raised her voice. "I was going to give your group the chance to surrender to us peacefully, but since you're clearly too stupid for that—Calix, attack that shield! I want it down."

From over the top of Zeke's wings, I glimpsed red dust filling the air.

A fireball blasted into my barrier. Then a second, and a third. My palms grew slick as I held off their hammer-like blows.

"Drop your barrier on my signal," Zeke told me.

I struggled to form words, to concentrate on anything except holding the shield. "We'll be burned alive if I do that."

"They'll stop the attack before that happens," Zeke said, sounding certain. "Nala won't risk killing a light-wielder."

"What then?" Adrianna pulled two daggers out of Zeke's bandoleer.

"I'll send an illusion out there to draw their fire." His gaze slid down to where Adrianna casually palmed his knives. "Then I'll run out and fight them. You follow."

Adrianna got a mutinous look in her eye. I wasn't sure if Zeke noticed, but he stepped into her personal space and dipped his mouth to her ear. "If I die, head southeast and seek the Shyani Tribe. They camp in the shadows of the Tazil mountains."

I caught his words only because I strained to hear them.

Another fireball slammed into my shield. I wobbled, and panic rode through my body like a bolting horse. Protect. Protect. I must protect them.

"Let's get out of the way of the initial blast." Zeke waved us over to the wall.

No argument. We ran into the right-hand corner where our enemies couldn't see us.

"What's taking so long, Calix?" Nala demanded.

"She's strong."

"Too strong?" Nala's tone was poison in the ear.

A short, sharp, "No."

Calix doubled down on his attack, unleashing a torrent of flame.

Gritting my teeth, I held. Barely.

Illusions of the four of us shimmered to life. Then Zeke gave me a somber nod. "Now."

I relaxed my arms and stoppered my moonlight. My shield gone, fire streamed into the room and ignited the awning above us. The smell of burning fabric seared my nostrils.

"Stop," Nala shouted from outside. "I want them alive."

The fire-stream died.

With a wave of his hand, Zeke sent our likenesses racing out into the courtyard. Curses and yells sounded.

Nerves surrendering to adrenaline, I drew my sword.

Liora's hand traveled to my hip, to where I carried her rapier. With a steel-lined expression, she freed her blade; it hissed a wicked little sigh. At the same time, Zeke sprinted forward. Adrianna matched him, step for step, refusing to wait a second longer.

Liora and I followed in their wake.

Zeke reached the doors. Faster than I could blink, he hurled knives into the courtyard. At his side, Adrianna flung her borrowed daggers with such unnerving straightness that I suspected she was controlling them with her metallurgy. She'd practiced her skill every spare hour on the ship coming over. It had clearly paid off.

Liora and I reached the courtyard.

Blink.

A blue-winged fae was skewered with steel and moaning his last.

Blink.

Nala tossed Adrianna and Zeke aside with a great gust of wind.

Blink.

A green-winged and a yellow-winged fae descended upon them.

Blink.

I conjured a moon-shield in front of me and Liora.

Blink.

Nala blasted my barrier with air. At that, I clocked her as an air-blessed witch.

Flap-flap-flap. I spotted two fae landing behind me. Liora swung her sword at them. She missed, and the two males seized my arms in pincher-sharp grips. They pushed, pushed, pushed—

I was slammed spine first into a stone wall. My wings screamed out in pain. Disoriented, my magic slipped away.

Two males alike in appearance pinned my hands, my sword too.

The black-winged one muttered in my right ear. "Nala works for Morgan."

My entire body went cold.

The red-winged one whispered in my other ear. "She was the one who marked you flying into Casatana and tracked you here. If she wants you, that must mean Morgan does too."

"But we can take you somewhere that you'll be safe," said Black-Wing.

"Where?" I asked, struggling against their hold.

His breath hot upon my cheek, Red-Wing said, "Abraxus's camp."

Riding high on the thrill of the fight, I masked shock with bravado. "Is anyone in The Watch actually working for Hasan?"

Black-Wing huffed. "Yes, and they deserve death for serving such a male. He's a murderer and a pervert—"

A high scream arrowed through my soul. Liora?

My focus skipped ahead. In the middle of the square, Nala gripped Liora's shoulders. My friend was frozen in place, her expression twisted in anguish.

Adrianna and Zeke fought on the opposite end of the courtyard. They battled Green-Wing and Yellow-Wing with steel, fist, and fang.

I had to reach my friends. Desperation fueled me and brought out my fangs. I attacked Black-Wing's neck with them and warm blood filled my mouth. Hissing, he stumbled back.

I pivoted, head-butting Red-Wing. His nose *cracked* and spurted blood. I seized that moment to shove him back a few steps.

Hands free, I leveled my Utemä at both brothers. "Get out of my way. I won't ask again."

Red-Wing gripped his nose. With a grimace, he *crunched* the bone into the correct position for healing. Black-Wing stanched the bleeding at his nape with a hand and studied me with an odd expression. It was that of somebody who'd baited a kitten and found a snarling mountain lion take its place. "You can trust us."

"I doubt that," I snarled, all fang.

They performed a synchronized head-turn and stared at each other. "Then we'll prove it," said Red-Wing.

The twins whirled around and charged forward. I sprang after them.

Black-Wing reached Nala first, smashing his fist into her ear. Stunned, she released Liora. Red-Wing caught my friend before she collapsed.

Nala recovered quickly. Drawing a long knife from her bandoleer, she twirled and swept her arm out, almost catching Black-Wing's ribs.

Red-Wing left Liora to me and moved to flank his twin. Outnumbered, Nala retreated a few steps. "Filthy traitors."

"Bit hypocritical of you," Red-Wing scoffed.

One of Nala's obsidian eyes twitched. "How so?"

Black-Wing emitted a stark laugh. "We know you work for Morgan. I hope she's paying you well to sell out your own country."

Liora suddenly pushed me away and growled at Nala. That sound, deeper than any fae could make, caught Nala's attention.

Liora's outline shimmered. The shift began, claws first.

Nala jumped into the air, her wings beating madly. Red-Wing and Black-Wing vaulted after her.

I pounced on Liora's vibrating form, wrapping my wings around her. "Don't. Let her go."

The signs of her shift paused. "You don't understand," she croaked. "Nala's a mind-reader. A mentalist."

Oh. Shit. "What did she see?" I said under my breath.

Liora slumped, her body returning to normal.

Slowly, I released her.

She spun around. I was braced for dragon eyes. I got human ones rimmed with shame and anxiety. "She was desperate for details about you. I managed to keep most things from her, except your name."

Trepidation building, I asked, "Which name?"

She understood immediately. "Serena Smith."

That was some consolation. Better that than Raynar or Lytir.

"I'm so sorry." Liora glanced guiltily at the apex of my wings. "If Nala reports this to Morgan, she'll find out about you."

I saw it all there in her face. Morgan would hear that Serena Smith had wings. That I was fae.

Black-Wing landed in front of me. "My brother's going to stay on Nala's trail. Abraxus will want to keep an eye on her."

"Abraxus?" Liora questioned.

I'd think about the twins and their offer later. Adrianna and Zeke needed me. As I turned toward them, Black-Wing pulled a knife out of his bandoleer. He threw it ahead of me, in Adrianna's direction.

The blade skewered Yellow-Wing's neck. He slumped to the ground, already dead.

I halted. A bit stunned.

Free of her opponent, Adrianna looked to where Zeke still fought. With a spin of her hand, she released her sword. It sliced through the air and embedded itself into Green-Wing's skull. He toppled over, the finality of his situation never dawning upon his features.

Adrianna fell to her knees. Her trembling hand still extended toward her blade. She must've guided its providence with magic.

As Adrianna's kill lay bleeding over the ground, Zeke yanked the blade clear of the corpse and wiped it clean upon his trousers. Then he was by Adrianna's side, slipping his hand under her elbow. Batting him away, she stood on her own and took her sword from him.

"Come with me." Black-Wing had his palm flat out toward me.

Before I could refuse, a voice sounded overhead. "Benjamin! What's happened? Where's Nala?"

Black-Wing—Benjamin—muttered under his breath, "Ahin." His eyes lifted to where six red-robed fae hovered above us. They were high enough to avoid the black smoke billowing off the lounge's roof, but they weren't so far as to miss the details of the scene before them. There were three dead members of The Watch on the ground, and Benjamin stood quite casually with us.

"He's a fucking traitor! I knew it!" yelled a female.

"Oh, please, you're just sore I wouldn't bed you," Benjamin shouted up at her.

"You'll pay for this," yelled an older-looking male.

"I'd like to see you try," he goaded. "You idiots are as lead-winged as you are lead-headed."

"Muzzle yourself," Zeke snapped.

"Etri, go for reinforcements," came a shout from above. "The rest of you, attack!"

Five fae dove, their swords pointed at our bodies.

You must act, Zola urged.

I moved away from Liora and clapped my hands together. Unlike the stars, it wasn't hard to summon the sunlight. I drew my palms away from each other, and a ball of flaming light expanded between them. I stepped forward on my right foot and punched upward.

Light and fire slammed into an incoming female. The fireball set her robes alight, eating through fabric and tissue quicker than any wildfire. I didn't watch her fall to her death. I hadn't the stomach for it.

The fae scattered as I conjured a second, third, and fourth fireball. Two of my attacks struck true, hitting a male and a female. They screamed and sought to beat out the flames, but my power wouldn't be denied. The sun's fire only burned brighter and hotter, consuming them. They dropped out of the sky, silenced. One body smashed into the ground before me, and I stared upon the deformed remains. The stench of charred flesh assaulted my nose. Horror soured my stomach.

The other fae sped away, their assault suspended. Just in time. Exhaustion broke over me, and my magic abandoned me. I was spent.

Adrianna lifted me into her arms. I barely noticed. Barely cared.

Benjamin addressed me again. "The entire Watch will be chasing you the second you get airborne. But if you follow me to Abraxus's camp, you'll fall under his protection."

"I can't go with you," I said to him.

Impatience pinched his features. "You can't out-fly The Watch. Not for long, anyway."

"You heard her," Adrianna said, her tone a warning. "The answer is no."

"Don't pick me up," Liora told Zeke.

"Why not?" he asked.

"Because he's right." Liora gestured to Benjamin. "The Watch won't let us leave this city. And we don't have the strength to fight them off. But I can stop them from following." Her burdened gaze found mine. "I'll shift and protect our backs."

The lump in my throat was sudden and painful.

With a shaky hand, Liora picked up her rapier from where she had dropped it during Nala's mental siege. She hurried over and slid it into the second sheath on my belt.

"Don't use magic again for a while. Not even to get my dragon's attention."

I was about to argue; Liora squeezed my hand. "You're drained. It could kill you."

"We can't just leave you," Adrianna said to Liora, her face shining with distress.

"You don't have a choice." Liora shucked off her rucksack and chucked it at Zeke, who was still wearing his disguise. "We'll just have to hope that my other half has enough sense to follow you."

She didn't waste any more time. Her dragon emerged, bursting out of the confines of its human shell. "That's my cue to go," Benjamin said hastily.

Adrianna huffed as he flew off. "Coward."

Transformation complete, Liora placed her front paws up on the stone wall. The dragon hailed the world with mighty wings, casting us and the courtyard into shadow. She crouched and with an unexpected grace, leaped into the sky.

The currents stirred up by her flight were immense, almost knocking Adrianna and Zeke flat. They recovered quickly, and we, too, ascended into the smoke-choked sky.

I stole a last look at the courtyard below, at the bodies we had abandoned. We'd been in Casatana less than a day and we'd brought death to the place. Guilt lashed and struck me underneath my ribs, drawing my heart's blood.

Liora raced ahead of us, clearing the way for Zeke and Adrianna.

I spotted the other members of the raiding party as we passed over the burning rooftop. Thirty or so red-robed fae stood in the front courtyard, presiding over the dead or restrained bodies of the lounge's former patrons.

In the short time it took us to reach the edge of Casatana, we had a cloud of about twenty foolish fae giving chase.

The pealing of bells echoed throughout the city and the sky. A warning, a call to arms, that had sentinels quitting the city walls below. They joined the hunt for us as we left behind buildings of stone for cracked earth.

Liora tipped a wing, gaining momentum in the turning. I watched her fly back the way we had come. She sailed overhead, her chest expanding, her neck scales brightening with brewing flame. Exhaling fire, she torched about a dozen of our pursuers.

Our pursuers fell into disarray. Many retreated. Others shot arrows at her. For a moment, I couldn't breathe. But I needn't have worried. The arrows might as well have been toothpicks for all the good they did against her hardened scales.

Zeke and Adrianna strained to go faster, faster, *faster*.

I kept my gaze locked on Liora. She was air and fire made flesh; she outmaneuvered every fae and unleashed death upon them.

We flew farther and farther away from her. The growing distance broke me. I pictured the stars. I thought about Liora.

Starlight trickled in like an ice cube sliding down my spine. Adrianna spotted my glowing palm. "Rivers drown you. You heard what Liora said —you shouldn't use magic."

"I don't have a choice. We can't lose her."

Leveling my arm over her shoulder, I aimed my white light at Liora's lizard-eye. But my target was constantly moving, and the strong sun weakened my starlight so much that I struggled to see it and focus it into a beam. There was another problem. Without a mirror to reflect the starlight and to focus it, the task of sending it across such a distance had energy pouring out of me like water from a leaky bucket.

"Ena, stop," Adrianna said, ferocious in her anxiety.

No. I had to keep going for Liora. The light just had to be stronger. I had to be stronger. I reached out for more magic. The starlight refused to oblige me.

Abandoning that scheme, I searched within my own well of power—for the starlight that lived inside of me. All I found were cooling embers. Just a hundred dying stars.

The light in my palm flickered.

My vision fuzzed. I'd become a flame soon to be snuffed out.

Stop drawing on your magic. You're hurting yourself, Thea warned.

Zola was more of a yeller. *Let it go, now, or you'll die. And so will Frazer.*

Frazer. That name rang through me. It divorced me from my immediate emotions and pulled me back to my senses.

For him, I threw everything into stoppering my magic. But it was too late. "I'm sorry," I whispered to my brother.

"What for?" came a voice.

A dark chasm opened up before me. I dropped into it.

CHAPTER 18
OUT OF REACH

-ADRIANNA-

Red foothills and flat-topped mountains lined the horizon. I would've enjoyed such beauty if not for the fatigue burning through my wing joints like acid.

For hours we'd flown over a wasteland of clementine-colored salt, and all under a harsh sun. We had landed once to draw water from a hidden ground-well. After fifteen minutes of rest, Zeke had insisted we resume our journey. He'd made it clear that I shouldn't expect another break—we'd only stopped for that long because Liora's dragon-self had returned to us, and she'd needed that time to change forms and examine a still-unconscious Ena.

Now, Asitar was on the cusp of twilight. And with no end to our flight in sight, it wasn't my physical maladies alone that pained me.

I never dreamed I'd find my mate in this lifetime. And there he was, flying beside me with Liora in his arms, never once meeting my eye. At best, he was disinterested. At worst, he hated me for the trouble I'd brought him. I growled at that thought, at the hurt it caused me.

The noise disturbed Ena; a sleepy groan parted her lips.

Breath hitching, I glanced down at the friend in my arms. Her eyes flickered beneath their lids, but she didn't open them. I knew I had nothing to worry about. Liora had diagnosed her with magical exhaustion, and she wouldn't regain consciousness until her body let her. That didn't stop me from wanting to slap her. Anything to get her to wake up and ease the anxiety scratching away at me.

"Start your descent," Zeke cried out from my right. "My home is at the foot of the mountains."

His home?

Zeke went into a controlled dive. I copied his movement.

We soon neared a flat hill that backed onto a taller slope. Zeke landed on the plateau first. He bent down and lowered Liora to the lifeless ground.

I set down beside Zeke and Liora. Everything ached. I suppressed shiver after shiver, the desert's nighttime chill cooling my sweaty skin.

Zeke stepped out in front of us. The disguise he'd adopted during the fight at The Oasis Lounge was gone, and he looked good. Annoyingly so. To keep from staring at his spectacular ass, I said, "Your home is a barren rock."

"Were you expecting a palace?" he asked, his back to me.

I ground my teeth together. *Prejudiced prick.*

Zeke drew invisible circles with his hand. Before I could ask what he was doing, Liora neared me and Ena.

I shifted Ena higher up in my arms. "Is she any better?"

Liora pressed two fingers to Ena's neck. "Her pulse is still slow. But that's normal after being drained."

I exhaled anger and irritation. "I'd say she's lucky not to be dead—stubborn fool. Why did she have to go and use magic when she knew she was tired? She'll be lucky if I don't bite her when she wakes up."

"She was worried I'd fly off as a dragon and leave all of you," Liora said, staring at Ena with sorry eyes.

I opened my mouth to tell her to quit with the guilt, but I was distracted by the air in front of us. By how it shimmered as though disturbed by a heat wave.

Not twenty feet away, a fortress appeared. It spanned the breadth of the hill and stood roughly three levels high. A thick wall with numerous towers guarded the large building; the rear was protected by the mountain's spine.

"For all your talk, it seems only one of us is living in a palace," I said sharply.

Zeke's bronze wings tensed. "I don't live here alone."

My heart failed. "Who do you live with, then?"

He refused to face me. "I founded it for people fleeing the bonds of slavery."

The relief that rushed through me was as unwelcome as it was intense. This had to stop. I couldn't, shouldn't fall this easily. Not for a male who didn't seem interested in me.

The entrance to the fortress—a large wooden gate—inverted noiselessly.

I spied open space, just brown dirt, beyond. An elder female walked out of this courtyard. She wore a plain dress cinched in at the waist with braided rope, and a leather satchel hung over her shoulder.

Zeke's stony reserve cracked. "Did you miss me, Tia?"

Humor glinted in her eye. "Not even a little."

I despised how deep and pleasant his laugh was. Damn this mate bond.

"Tia, these people are my guests. This is Adrianna and Liora." He pointed to us in turn. "The female asleep is named Ena. She's overextended herself magically, and I imagine could do with some time in your infirmary."

"Are you a healer?" I asked Tia.

"That's right." Her eyes ran over me and Ena. "I promise we'll take good care of your friend."

"Thanks, but she already has a healer." I let that hang for a second before adding, "Liora's our healer."

Far from being offended, Tia's apple-shaped cheeks shone with a smile. "Then allow me to offer a fellow healer somewhere more comfortable to tend their patient." Her emerald-green wings covered her arms. "Let us get inside. It's much too cold to be standing about."

"I've got to head out again, Tia," Zeke said.

What?

"I figured you would," Tia said. "You never stand still for more than two minutes. Take this." She handed him her satchel. "As soon as I heard about your approach, I shoved some snacks and a flask of water in there just in case."

With a half-smile, Zeke took the satchel. "What would I do without you?"

"Starve, most likely," she replied dryly.

"I need to speak to Zeke alone for a moment," I said to Tia. "Can you take Ena and Liora to your infirmary?"

Before she could answer, I stepped forward and held out Ena. Tia didn't hesitate; she lifted her weight from my arms. Ena wasn't heavy, but I'd held her long enough that my arms were almost numb. I rubbed my sore muscles to stimulate the blood flow.

Liora moved to stand beside Tia. "Thank you for this," she said in what was obviously an attempt to smooth out the rough edges of my rudeness.

"You're welcome," Tia replied.

They left together, disappearing inside the complex.

I rounded on Zeke. "Where are you going?"

"Somewhere with people."

Irritation spiked my bloodstream. "Are you trying to piss me off with that answer?"

His impassive expression cracked with a huff of laughter. "No. I'm just not used to explaining myself. It doesn't help that I'm exhausted." Zeke's shoulders heaved with a sigh. "I'm leaving because Hasan is going to hunt us. So will Abraxus—if only to stop us from falling into the king's hands. And this landscape isn't as deserted as it appears. The dunes are infested with sand sprites; the mountains are home to numerous tribes. Both of which could be persuaded to give up information about passing travelers. I thought if I conjured a likeness of Liora's dragon somewhere populated, it might throw any pursuers off our trail. It might buy us some time."

"Then I should come with you."

He hoisted his eyebrow up an inch. "Am I growing on you?"

I wanted to punch him in his perfect jaw again. "No, but you shouldn't go alone. What if you're attacked?" Feeling exposed, I added, "We might never find Sefra if you don't come back."

Those cat's eyes flashed at me. "If I don't return tomorrow, ask Tia to point out where the Shyani Tribe reside on a map." His deep, rich voice gentled. "Go inside, Adrianna."

"Do you really hate me so much that you'd shun my help?"

He wavered. "Is that what you think—I hate you?"

"You can barely stand to look at me."

Emotion irritated my eyeballs. If I shed a single tear, I'd scream.

"I don't hate you," he said, squinting into the distance.

I palmed my steel hilt. "But you blame me for what happened today."

"Your actions have caused a lot of trouble," he said, frowning. "Jada's business is likely ash. And her patrons are either dead or imprisoned." As he shouldered Tia's satchel, he added, "But you and your friends aren't solely responsible for today's events. I could've done things differently too."

"What do you mean?"

His green-brown gaze met mine. "I noticed Ena when she flew over the docks. If I'd listened to my instincts and followed your group, I might've gotten to you before things turned to shit."

My insides shriveled up. "You noticed Ena? Why her, specifically?"

Rivers curse me, had I actually said that out loud?

I got a blunt, "Because she stands out."

My mouth grew as dry as the earth beneath my feet. "Meaning?"

"Feathered wings seem to be unique to Aldarians. I don't think they've been seen in these lands since trade stopped with your kingdom."

The iron-grip over my lungs eased. "If you don't hate me, why are you so determined to go alone?"

No answer.

"Fine," I snapped. "Be an ass."

Eyes hot, I turned away. He didn't let me get far.

Strong fingers seized my wrist. "Adrianna."

He pulled me back around to face him. With barely a foot separating us, his scent washed over me. Smoke and sand and musk. I melted inwardly.

"I've had one priority for a very long time," he said, his honeyed baritone gliding over my skin like silk over thighs. "To save as many people as I could from the kings of Asitar."

His head slanted down, sending waves of black hair tumbling forward. I stared boldly into his blown pupils as his lips parted inches from mine.

"But it we get closer—if our bond develops—one of us, at least, is going to have to give up our home."

"I don't expect you to put me before your people," I said, chin high. "I know what it is to have a duty."

"Exactly." An unnamed emotion flickered over his face. "You're a princess of Aldar. That's where your home and duty lie. Mine is here."

I stepped back, but he didn't release my wrist. "So, you want to avoid each other, is that it?"

That question cost me something to say, and his hesitation stung my pride. "Not avoid, exactly. Just not spend more time together than what's necessary. If we must part ways, then it might be best. Do you disagree?"

I swallowed angry words. They burned my throat. In a fit of madness, I blurted out, "If you wanted me to ignore you then you shouldn't have looked like this."

His lip twitched. "What is it about my appearance that offends you?"

"Everything." I glared at him.

He laughed up at the skies.

That smile. Ugh.

His gaze met mine. "If it makes you feel any better, you're not alone in your suffering." In the darkening twilight, his irises glowed a bright fire-blue. "Your scent makes my entire body hard."

That infuriated me. I wrenched my arm from his grip, breaking our intimacy.

He blinked, and his eyes cooled to their normal shade. "I should go."

There was no emotion in his voice. Fine. Just fine. Without a backward glance, I about-turned and marched into the fortress's courtyard. The gate closed behind me.

A static charge traveled through my wings. I guessed that it was his magic—his illusion—concealing and protecting and locking us in.

I looked back and waited, frozen, until his fast wings graced the sky.

Frustration and resentment raged in my blood. I would hold fast to those feelings until I no longer wanted him. The sooner that occurred, the better for both of us.

∽

-ENA-

In the still waters of my unconsciousness, a strong current stirred. I surrendered to the pull. To the unknown.

Darkness gave way to illumination. Candlelight flared in lanterns, and a never-ending corridor stretched out ahead of me. One of smooth timber and black-glass mirrors that were positioned mid-wall.

I walked along, treading the floorboards. There were no windows, but I had the strongest feeling that I was perched on an island in the midst of a rushing river. I was safe, but a foot away from primal forces that could rip me apart.

"Ena?" A rushed whisper.

I halted, turning toward the voice. "Hello?"

"Over here."

I hurried over to an oval, silver-framed mirror. It was not my face in the black glass, but another's.

I twisted around. Nobody stood behind me.

Returning to the mirror, I beheld a male with alabaster skin, strong brows, and raven-wing hair. I had seen those features once before, in Sandrine's vision. Only now he was smiling at me. My bones, my very foundations, recognized that this male had gone into their making. That he had sparked my life. "Dain?"

A sure nod answered me. I was gripped by ice and fire, shock and excitement.

His keen gaze traced my features. "Sati was right. You do look like me."

A wave of emotion dashed me against what felt like rocks. I reached out and touched glass. Just glass.

Disappointment blistered my soul.

"I can talk to you here," Dain said, his eyes saddening. "But our physical selves remain in separate worlds."

Part of me could be called relieved. At least I wasn't dead.

"But where are we—what is this place?" I gestured around the passageway.

"I can't give you a definite answer on the where," he said calmly. "If I were to guess, I'd say we're outside of time and in between worlds. I've often wondered if this might be the source of a witch's second sight.

That those with the right sensitivities could access this place remotely and gain wisdom from being unmoored from the present."

I absorbed that as best my dazed brain would allow. "Why haven't I heard of this place before?"

"Because most witches can't come here," he explained. "They don't even know it exists."

"What makes us so different?"

"I gained the ability to visit this place after looking in a mirror blessed by the gods. The same one that Frazer now seeks."

Surprise clanged through me. "How did you hear about that?"

"Zola and Thea keep us informed."

That made sense. They were my mother's kin, after all—a thought that never stopped being strange.

Dain continued. "As for how you came to be here, you're a dreamwalker."

I felt as if I'd just heard an off-key note played. "Thea didn't tell me that I was like her."

"She didn't know," he told me. "Your magic grows and advances alongside you, which means certain abilities won't show themselves immediately. But your finding this place is proof that you are a dreamwalker."

"Our meeting here wasn't accidental, was it?" I said, taking a guess.

He gave me a lopsided smile. "No. I lost much of my magic when I died. But I'm still occasionally graced with a vision. I foresaw our meeting here tonight, and the words we exchanged. So I decided to break the rules." My confusion was mended by his adding, "The dead shouldn't meddle in the affairs of the living."

Alarm and interest cut through me.

His stare turned as keen as a crow's. "But I had to see you. I had to give you a weapon of sorts, against Abraxus. It's probable that at some point you're going to cross paths with him. And if you do, you must *not* fight him. Instead, tell him that he made me a promise long ago. Tell him that Dain Raynar expects him to keep it."

"I don't understand."

"You will."

That somber promise ruffled my feathers.

Dain angled his head as if he was listening out for something and repressing the urge to glance over his shoulder. "I must leave. But you can stay, and I think if you wish it, you could find another mirror and go for a walk."

"A walk?"

A bright-eyed smile softened his sharp cheekbones. "Dreamwalkers can project their minds almost anywhere. Follow your heart. It'll lead you to who you wish to see most."

He took a step back.

"Wait." I placed a palm on the glass. "Don't."

Longing kept me there. He raised a hand to the mirror, acting as my reflection. Yet we couldn't touch. "Goodbye, tilä."

Then he left. Just like that.

I felt a wrenching under my ribs. In a short time, Dain had become another string to my heart. I missed having a relationship with him. I missed too many people, it seemed. But if my sire was right, I might see my brother again.

I went from mirror to mirror. None of them worked as the first one had. Until I came to a floor-length gilded frame. The dark glass rippled as a sheet would when caught in a breeze. It had a fragility to it that made me think of the skin atop cream, a mere cobweb that could be swept away.

Not thinking, I stepped straight into the frame. The corridor disappeared.

I materialized on a sunlit vantage point—a plateau. Below me, mist hovered over a silver-barked forest that seemed to go on and on, without a beginning or end. This vast and fertile land could only be Aurora.

On the edge of my vision, I spotted movement.

I spun around. Joy burst through me like the sun through the clouds. "I actually found you."

A non-response from my twin. All enthusiasm died.

Tentatively, I tried to grasp his arm. My hand went straight through his body. It seemed that to him, I was mere spirit. Neither flesh nor bone. The knowledge that a reunion would be denied to us choked me.

I watched him, desperate for clues about how he was. I'd violated my limitations in the waking world; I'd gone too far and used too much magic. But by the look of him, I hadn't weakened my brother. He stood up straight, an unmoving pillar. His expression was set in the usual shades of coolness, except for the eyes. They were almost black in their intensity.

I felt for our bond. It remained a loving ember glowing in the distance and was of no help in discerning his feelings.

Frazer's eyes shuttered as he released a long exhale. Jaw tight, he lifted his palm and glared at it in a manner that would've had a lion shrinking from him.

Magic happened. Light arced off his skin. These moonlit bands knitted into an intricate web over his hand. For a second, he appeared to be wearing a silver glove, and then his whole hand disappeared.

I freed a short, delighted laugh. If only I could've cheered him on in person.

"Frazer?" A low shout sounded from down in the forest.

That mellow lilt winded me a bit. I searched for Cai among the tall trees.

"If you keep sneaking off like this, we're going to put a bell on you."

That wasn't Cai. I searched for the owner of that voice to no avail.

"What have you been up to?" I wondered aloud at Frazer.

My twin's focus broke. His hand became visible again.

Sighing out through flared nostrils, he peered at the distant horizon. At a far-off hazing of brown, green, and white. I suspected that I stared at the backbone of a mountain range.

Frazer stepped up to the edge of the raised plateau, his face a gloomy but determined mask. His wings twitched. But he didn't take flight. He didn't move a muscle. Trepidation and trauma marked his features.

Sorrow wreathed me.

Not taking the leap, he backed up a pace. "Soon," he whispered to the wind in a challenge and a promise.

I watched as he made to climb down from the highland. The surrounding scenery suddenly lost color, as did my brother.

"No," I breathed.

I clung to the image of my brother as I would hold to an anchor in a swell. In vain, I struggled. I was wrenched away and thrown into another vision.

I appeared inside a pavilion set atop an arena. Wilder flanked me.

Stars ... I drank in the sight of him—my water in the desert.

All six-foot-more of him was dressed in black leather and red cloth.

He was clean-shaven, and his caramel-gold locks were shorter than when I'd last seen him. These changes only made him more striking, more intimidating, and just as chest-achingly handsome.

I tracked his gaze to the sand pit below.

Mother save us. Fae, animals, and humans battled one another in a circular ring. It was a brutal shedding of blood with no mercy shown. One practice among those with wings seemed to be dropping their victims from different heights to see what injuries could be inflicted. The pained screams and the bangs of metal twisted my guts up.

Wilder's rasp of a voice startled me. "Why do you persist in this madness? You claim we need humans to match the threat from Abraxus's army, and yet you're in an awful hurry to put those precious numbers—most of them untrained children—in the ring to be butchered."

"Don't underestimate children," said a soft, cold voice that had snowflakes frosting my back. "They're often far more resilient and impressionable—"

"You mean they're easier to manipulate," Wilder said, keeping his focus on those fighting and dying in the arena's ring.

"Quite." An amused tone. "They make better soldiers when we've had time to indoctrinate them into the proper and right way of things."

Gathering my courage, I wheeled around. Before me, a golden throne rose up and dominated the pavilion. It was atop this throne that I got my first look at Morgan—the fae who had murdered my birth father. I wasn't sure what I had expected. Glowing eyes? Bloody teeth? Something that really shouted evil.

But she was beautiful, with flawless skin, silky hair, and crimson irises that while spooky, were not unattractive.

She continued. "As for your claims that I'm slaughtering the humans needlessly, my actions are never needless. Quite the contrary. I see a great *need* for this exercise. For starters, it'll prepare the soldiers for the Kula."

"The Kula is a blood sport," Wilder replied flatly. "Its sole purpose is for fae to indulge in their worst impulses and hunt down humans. And as I have said many times, an army divided won't function as well as one that operates as a seamless unit."

"Agreed," she drawled. "But don't forget a weak spot in any shield decreases its effectiveness. That is what this exercise is designed for and what the Kula is for. It separates the strong from the weak."

"It is a waste of life," he argued.

"Nothing will be wasted." Her plump mouth stretched into a smile, revealing her white-*white* teeth. "After all, even the dead have their uses."

Wilder spun on his heel. He glared up at Morgan, not with anger, but with fear and suspicion. "What does that mean? How do the dead have their uses?"

"That is not your concern," she said in polished notes.

"Anything to do with our forces *is* my concern. You made me Prime Sabu, remember?"

Morgan rose from her throne. Her wings unfolded. The membrane seemed as thin as a dragonfly's. The color—a scarlet and ink-black—put me in mind of a creature that beckoned prey in with their vivid coloring only to serve up an ugly death.

"Come." She pointed in front of her with a single elongated fingernail.

Wilder prowled over to the throne. I dogged his steps.

"Closer." A venomous ask.

He stepped up onto the second stair of her throne's podium. There were three in total. On this middle level, he met her eye-to-eye.

I stole a quick glance around. Extravagantly dressed fae sat at a fair distance from the throne, but they retained a direct eyeline to their queen. Yet, not a single one dared to spy on Morgan and Wilder. Their attention was purposely fixed on the savagery below.

"Let me worry about our numbers," she said in a haughty tone. "Your focus must stay on preparing our forces for war."

"As I have been doing for several weeks," Wilder said, his stare holding nothing but disdain. "Eventually you'll have to tell me why, since we're not currently at war with anyone. I can only prepare the soldiers so much—"

"You will lead a legion to the Riverlands border within the week. You'll camp there and wait for my signal to attack."

My breath snagged on shock.

Wilder's eyes tightened at the corners. It was the only shock he allowed himself to show. "You plan to attack our allies?"

There was a devious arch to her eyebrow. "Diana failed to apprehend her daughter in her own lands. Therefore, she is either incompetent or she has betrayed our alliance." That last word was snarled. "I've been leaning toward the latter since I received news that your whore has fled to the continent—Liora and Adrianna, too. Diana is one of the few people with the means to buy them passage out of Aldar. Such treachery can't go unpunished. We must make an example out of her and her limp-winged court."

No, no, no, no, no.

"Do you hear me, Wilder?" Morgan asked in mockingbird tones.

"Yes, unfortunately."

"How does it feel to know Serena has abandoned you?" She stroked his jaw with the back of her finger. "Are you sad, my pet?"

Wilder simply raised an eyebrow. "Quite the opposite. I'm thrilled."

Her finger paused upon his jaw. "Oh? Why is that?"

"She got away from you, didn't she?"

Morgan didn't react to his sneer. She leaned in and pressed her scarlet lips to his ear. "Did you know?" Her poisonous voice dipped. "Did you know she had a way of becoming fae?"

An immortal stillness possessed his body. "What are you talking about?"

"I thought it unlikely too," she whispered to him. "I'm even inclined to believe my informant was tricked, but she seemed quite sure. Whatever the truth is, I will discover it. My people will root them out and once they're back in Aldar, I'll have you perform kuarväc on Diana. That should leave quite an impression on your whore."

For the first time, I wanted to use sunlight. I wanted to play smoke a bitch. But when I reached for my magic, there was nothing there. For whatever reason, I couldn't access it in this state.

"You disgust me," Wilder said, strangling his sword hilt.

Morgan's head jerked back from his ear. She seized his throat with one hand and punched her red nails deep into his skin.

He tipped his throat back, exposing it. "Do it."

I lunged for Morgan. My hands traveled through her.

Another voice intruded. "My Queen?"

"What is it?" she snapped.

"The arena has its champion. They wait for you to acknowledge them."

I looked to my right, to who had interrupted. Hunter.

His face was an empty portrait—a sky missing sun and moon and stars. The sight crippled something in me.

With a hiss, Morgan released Wilder. "You're boring me," she said, malice burning deep in her garnet eyes. "Go to the barracks and wait for instruction."

He wheeled around and walked away. Frustration howled inside of me.

One giant tug later, and I was out of there.

I sat bolt upright in a strange bed.

Thea expressed her relief. *Thank the stars. We couldn't reach you.*

Zola's spirited voice joined in. *You are a pig-headed idiot. And if you ever scare us like that again, I'll spend an entire week torturing you with my singing.*

That threat went in one ear and out the other. My mind ran at full speed, obsessing over the things I'd learned. Frazer and Cai were okay. But Diana and the Riverlands weren't. They were in danger.

"You wake."

I turned my head to see the woman sitting by my bedside. My thoughts slowed. "Anya?"

A nod.

"Where's Adrianna? And Liora, is she here?"

"They watch over you. But they get hungry. I offer to take their place. They not sure at first, so I show them this." Anya pulled a dagger from out of her sleeve. "Jada give it to me before she leave. I tell your friends if someone try to hurt you or me, I stab them quick. They satisfied after that."

Liora was here. I hadn't lost her. I let that thought center me.

"Where are we?"

Anya re-hid her blade, saying, "They call it Alhara. Zeke shelter runaway slaves and other victims of kings' rule here."

Adrianna's mate housed escaped slaves? That definitely made me like him a bit more.

I took a peek around.

We were in a rectangular room. Two rows of beds lined clay-colored walls, and embedded in the ceiling were what appeared to be glowing crystals—they were the sole source of light.

Everything stank of a caustic cleanliness until a temperate breeze drifted in from glassless windows on my right, refreshing my senses, cleansing them of that artificial smell.

Unimpeded by curtains, I viewed a salt-flat landscape stretched out underneath a sea of stars that flickered like candles in a sacred space.

"How long have I been asleep?"

"I not sure." She frowned. "I arrive only few hours ago."

I tried again. "How many days have passed since we parted?"

"That yesterday." Anya indicated a wall clock opposite us. "Time over there."

The clock read 11 AN—After Noon.

With only an hour to midnight, I'd lost a whole day. Almost two.

The *tick-tock* echoed accusingly as it counted down precious seconds and minutes that shouldn't be wasted. Diana had to be warned. Then I had to find Sefra, the sunstone, and avoid being captured by Morgan or Hasan or Abraxus. Gods, it was enough to make me want to hide under the bed.

Anya, who'd sat in a wicker chair with her legs propped up, now lowered her feet to the flagstone floor. "You drink."

I traced a fingertip over cracked lips and winced.

Anya leaned over to my right bedside table. With a tongue drier than day-old toast, I watched her pour water out of a pitcher into a glass.

"Thanks," I said, taking the glass from her.

The water slopped a bit in my eagerness to drink it. "Slow." Anya waved in downward strokes. "Sip."

I steadied my hand and took smaller gulps. Water had never tasted so good.

Footsteps drew my focus to the left. A green-winged female in a robe approached me. "Hello, Ena. My name is Tia. I'm the healer here."

She stopped beside my bed. "You might not be aware of this, but you suffered a burnout from using too much magic. That's why you're here. I'd like to examine you again if that's all right. Just a routine checkup."

I finished my water and set the glass aside. "Okay."

She placed her cool hands on top of mine. Tingles scuttled over my skin. I sensed a not-uncomfortable pressure push at various points of my body. The procedure lasted mere seconds.

Tia drew a notebook out of her robe and plucked a pencil from behind her ear. "All right, Ena, your pulse and energy readings are back to normal." After jotting down a line or two in her journal, she continued. "But you must wait at least a day, if not two, before using magic. Give yourself time to recuperate."

I bobbed my head in silent agreement.

"Good." Tia snapped her notebook closed and pocketed it.

I stood, determined, if a tad light-headed. "I need to find my friends."

"No, you don't," Tia said curtly. "I sent your friends to eat and wash, which is what you need to do. You won't be good to anyone half-starved and stinking of death."

That bladed my gut. I looked down at myself.

My clothes were soot-stained. They also smelled of smoke, toil, and something charred. A flashback to a burned body invaded my memory. I ran from it, saying, "I need to talk to them now."

Tia scowled. Before she could scold me, Anya heaved herself out of her chair. "I search for your people. I tell them to come to infirmary."

Quickly, I said, "You don't have to do that."

"I want to go." Anya gave me a faint smile and instantly looked younger, more in her twenties than her thirties. Although, the fact she'd washed the grime from her face might've contributed to the youthful glow. "I sit too long, and my ass sleeps. Short walk good for me and baby."

Clasping her belly, she exited the room via the opened double doors.

"I overheard Anya talking with your friends," Tia said to me. "She's content to stay in Alhara, at least until after the baby is born. You can rest easy knowing she'll be looked after."

"I'm glad."

Tia regarded me with kind eyes. "Anya told me what you did for her. A loyal and lonely heart like hers won't ever forget it."

I didn't return her smile.

"You regret it?" she guessed.

My head sunk into my shoulders. In that moment, Tia exuded a perceptiveness that reminded me of Liora. Perhaps all healers read people clearly, empath or not.

"Yes and no," I said honestly. "Helping her kicked down a lot of cards. It cost some people their lives and it brought us to the attention of our enemies."

"Did you know what would happen before you helped her?"

"Of course not."

"Then forgive yourself," Tia said as if the matter was simple. "Regretting a good deed won't benefit anyone or anything."

"True." I tried to mute my guilt. "Where can I wash up?"

"Go to the end of the infirmary, and it's the door on your right."

"Thanks."

"You and your friends' things are there." Tia pointed to where our rucksacks and my sword waited a few feet from my bed.

Grabbing my bag from the pile, I walked to the door Tia had indicated. I stepped through it to discover a large washroom.

It had all the basic utilities and a sunken tub set against the back wall. That thing was calling my name. But I didn't have time for a proper bath right now.

I washed up using the sink and picked out clothes that would best cope with what I'd seen of Asitar. A hot, dry-as-sticks, infertile land. I dressed in linen trousers, my now blood-speckled shoes, and a white tunic that would reflect the sun. I looped the attached sky-blue ribbon around my waist and pulled in the loose material.

I abandoned the washroom and entered the infirmary again.

Tia was nowhere to be seen. Returning my bag to the pile, I was considering hunting for my friends when—

"You're awake then. Good. I can finally tell you what an idiot you've been."

I twirled around.

Adrianna was in the entranceway. She stood in vanilla-colored pants that were buttoned up the sides of the calves. Her indigo V-necked shirt had a gold-patterned collar, and her hair was knitted into several braids that were styled like rope.

We met in the middle of the room.

"You used magic knowing it could kill you." Adrianna twisted the knife deeper into my gut by adding, "And Frazer."

"I thought I had it under control," I said, my voice puny and pathetic. "I was wrong."

"Will you do the same thing again?"

I shook my head.

A pulse feathered in her jaw. Then she moved on. "I wasn't sure about leaving you with Anya and Tia, but Liora did her thing"—Adrianna waggled her fingers in a mock spooky way—"and divined they had good intentions. Just, you know, in case you were feeling abandoned by us."

"I wasn't. How are you?"

Her puffy eyes and limp wings weren't a promising sign.

"Tired." No bullshit.

"Were you able to get any sleep?"

"I napped in the bed beside you. A few hours would usually be enough for me to feel rested." In a quieter tone, she confessed, "But not today ... Liora says I'm drained from using the metallurgy."

"You were amazing. You've never used your power under pressure before, but you—"

"Killed someone without blinking?" she said starkly.

That muzzled me.

She broke eye contact. But I didn't miss the armor that had dropped from her features. I came face-to-face with Adrianna's underbelly. Raw. Real. Sad.

Worry blotted my emotional landscape. "You did what you had to do."

"Yes," she said in hollow agreement. "I did."

Conflict tore at me. Given her current mood, it seemed cruel to break the news about her makena. But she had to know. "Where's Liora? I've got something to tell you both."

"She said she wanted to visit the temple down below. We can go search for her if it's urgent."

My brows clashed together. "A temple? Is Zeke very religious?"

"I don't know if he is or isn't," she said, looking as if she'd bitten into a lemon. "But according to our extremely chatty cook, the temple was there before he took over the place. It was actually built by your grandfather."

Surprise struck a cord within me. "Atlas?"

A nod. "The cook said he's famous for having ruled over much of Asitar, mainly the eastern provinces. Apparently, Alhara was one of his court's residences when he was alive." She waved her hand around the room. "I had half a mind to start poking around, in case he hid *it* here. But since it's unlikely to be anywhere obvious, I thought we should hear what Sefra has to say before ransacking the place."

Was it possible the sunstone lay nearby? I scanned the immediate area as if hoping it'd pop up and wave at me. Stupid.

"So, do you want to go to the temple? Liora's probably still down there."

In heavy spirits, I said, "No. I shouldn't wait any longer to tell you this." I took a breath and blurted out, "I found out I'm a dreamwalker. I saw Dain. He said I shouldn't fight Abraxus if I run into him. Instead, I should remind him of some promise he made to my father."

She absorbed that, her expression shifting from shock to skepticism. "Abraxus is known for forcing light-wielders into his army, and his spies just saw you using your magic. But Dain wants you to talk to him? Isn't that a bit ... well, crazy?"

I didn't contradict her. "There's more. I visited Frazer—"

"You did?" she exclaimed. "Is he okay? What about Cai?"

Her passion and concern took me aback. I had assumed she would be less worried about the guys than me and Liora. Feeling a tad ashamed of myself, I said, "They're okay, I think. I couldn't talk to them. But then ... Adi, I saw Wilder. And Morgan."

Adrianna's eyes flared.

I continued, recounting my vision of Morgan—of what she planned to do—as best as my memory allowed. Once I was done, I added, "But I figure Zeke must have a way of communicating with Diana. So if we can get word to her—"

"Let's go." Adrianna bolted for the infirmary's exit.

I ran after her, entering a corridor of clay and sandstone. Veering left, we passed by windows that overlooked a garden filled with spiky beauty. With cacti, agave, and aloes.

Keeping pace with her, I asked, "Where are we going?"

"To find Tia," she said, her breathing disordered. "She was walking this way when I went in to see you."

We raced the length of the hall and halted at a crossroads. Tia was visible down the right path. "Were you looking for me? I was just about to bring this to you." Tia lifted up a tray that held a bowl of soup.

I slowed, but Adrianna didn't stop running until she reached her. "We have to contact someone in Aldar. Can you help us?"

Tia's expression screamed sun-stunned bat. "Well, no. But Zeke might. He's just arrived."

"Arrived?" I queried. "Where did he go?"

"He was worried we'd be tracked, so he went to lay a false trail," Adrianna explained.

Smart plan.

"Where is he now?" Adrianna demanded of Tia.

"He was about to retire to his study. It's—"

Adrianna stopped her with a raised palm. "Is that the one with lots of books and a big desk?"

A suspicious brow. "How did you know that?"

Adrianna was already moving past her.

As I rushed around the healer, she said, "Wait. You need to eat."

"I will," I called back to her. The acoustics of the space amplified the sound, and my own voice echoed in my ears more than once.

Adrianna halted in front of a doorless entranceway a short way down the corridor. "It's up here."

A thigh-burning spiral staircase awaited us. Around and around and around we went. Mid-stair, in between lungsful of air, I asked, "Adi, how *did* you know where his study is?"

"I nosed about a bit," she confessed shamelessly. "I wanted to check he wasn't hiding any nasty surprises."

"And?"

"I didn't find any whips or chains or bodies in the cupboards. So I guess he gets a pass for now."

I held down laughter. "Was that a likely scenario?"

No response.

The staircase ended in a low door. Adrianna wasted no time in bursting through it. I followed, close on her heels, into a circular room lined with bookshelves.

To our immediate right was a sturdy desk that had an empty bird-cage atop its dark wooden surface. A small piano and an armchair rested opposite us, as did a pair of doors that led out onto a large balcony. Zeke was out there, peering up at the white-as-cotton moon. Our invasion, however, caused him to turn and step back indoors.

I swept his visage head to toe. He was barefoot, wearing wide-legged pants. His cream-colored shirt had half the buttons undone, exposing brutal scars and cut muscles.

"Have you come to nosey around my room again, princess?" Zeke placed a glass of what smelled like black tea on the nearest shelf. "Or are you storming my private quarters with the intention of showing your friend your current reading project?" With one finger, he fixed the misaligned spine of a book. "Was this one giving you ideas?"

That had Adrianna snapping, "Nothing of the sort."

I could almost feel the heat radiating off her.

What the rutting hell was in that book?

"No?" His head inclined in a teasing way. "You didn't like what you saw in there? Not even position number four? I've always been a fan of it myself."

Adrianna huffed, feigning boredom. "You mean the one that prioritizes the male's pleasure—why am I not surprised?"

He batted back as playfully as a cat's paw. "That's only true if the female doesn't enjoy giving up control."

"Which I don't."

He flashed her an edged smile. "Sure about that, are you?"

"What do you care?"

He sidestepped that loaded question. "I'm simply trying to draw the truth out of you. But perhaps a straightforward approach is better. I'll come right out with it—your scent is everywhere. You were clearly sneaking around my study—why?"

Tense silence pressed in.

I was forgotten and left wondering about that book.

I'd quite like a look myself, Thea admitted.

I experienced silent amusement that Thea had said that and not Zola.

I doubt there's anything in there I haven't tried three times over.

Too much. I mimed being sick in my head.

Zola went all lofty on me. *Prude.*

My thoughts were disrupted by Adrianna's confession. "I wanted to get a better idea of who you were and see if there was any chance you might double-cross us."

He froze. An icicle would've had more movement. "You think I'd sell out my own mate?"

Adrianna managed to sound both flat and thistle-sharp. "We're not acknowledging the bond, remember?" A defiant chin. "And you said it yourself; your people come first. They might be punished if you're found helping us. Perhaps you decided we're not worth the trouble."

I'd obviously missed a lot.

Zeke perched on the arm of his cushy chair. "You saw how well-concealed Alhara is. Nobody can see past that illusion, not unless I wish it. Therefore, the people here are as safe as I could make them." He propped up a brow. "Have you any other reasons to think I'd betray you?"

"Not specifically," she said, standoffish. "Just a lot of question marks."

"Ask away."

"For starters, how can you glamour away a whole fortress? Surely it'd drain you."

Zeke's reply was succinct. Almost formal. "Alhara was already hidden by ancient jinn magic when I found the place. I still don't know how it worked or how it sustained itself. The illusion only started to wane a few months ago. Sefra was the one who helped me put up a new concealment spell. It uses a crystal that draws on the power of the sun and provides energy for whatever spell is bound to it. Sefra invented it."

My sister had invented *that*. Holy ...

Adrianna wasn't done. "And where does the money come from to run this place? You must earn a fortune to keep up such a stronghold."

"I stole a lot of money."

Gods. That was stark.

Adrianna grimaced. "You're a thief?"

His tiger's gaze was blistering. A fierce fire that couldn't be quenched. "I stole once, and from one person. Is that a problem?"

Emanating high pride and hurt feelings, she said, "I suppose you have to fund your sex book addiction somehow."

Close to laughing at a totally inappropriate moment, I clamped my wobbling lips tight and bottled the laughter wanting to burst free.

Zeke arose in a predatory manner, his chest vibrating with a growl. He looked torn between needing to bite her and wanting to kiss her.

I crab-stepped away from them. Things tended to break around angry fae. Like limbs and teeth.

Zola mused with liveliness. *When mates meet, things tend to get intense. It's just sexual tension. I'm sure the only thing they'll be breaking is the bed as they—*

"Stop talking," I said aloud.

That got Adrianna's and Zeke's attention. I coughed to cover the awkward moment. "Zeke, we actually came here for a reason. And it's got nothing to do with sex or books or being a thief."

I gave Adrianna a pointed gaze.

Horror struck her face. "I didn't mean to get so sidetracked."

"What's wrong?" Zeke said suddenly, intently.

Adrianna's hands tightened into fists. "We need to get a message to my mother as soon as possible."

A hesitant, "Why?"

Adrianna repeated what I'd told her about the Riverlands. Lastly, she added, "How long will it be before we can get word to Diana?"

Zeke rolled a breath in and out of his lungs. "I can contact Diana tonight. She'll be warned, I promise."

"How are you going to get word to her tonight?" I asked, wondering if he had a magical method of contacting someone, like a store of spelled paper.

"Diana and I each own one half of an enchanted mirror. When activated, the shards can be used as a two-way communication device."

"I've never heard of such a thing," Adrianna remarked.

"That's because mirror magic is a lost art, another specialty of the ancient jinn. The few devices that've survived over the centuries are considered priceless. It was a minor miracle that I found the one I did." Zeke peered at Adrianna closely. "Will you be all right?"

"What does that matter?"

"It matters to me," he said without a hint of embarrassment.

"How can I be fine?" she challenged, suddenly loud. "Morgan is about to march on my homeland and sentence my kin to be nailed into a coffin alive." Her voice stuck as if all the air had gotten squeezed from her lungs.

Rutting hell. That's what kuarväc was?

Adrianna was usually always straight-backed. That composure crumbled before my eyes as her spine, the strength that held up her body as a beam would support a house, failed her. She bent over double, hands on thighs, and fought to breathe.

Heart leaving my chest, I reached for her.

Zeke beat me to it. He hauled her in close.

She hugged him back. Their embrace was an oil and fire mix: aggressive, protective, supportive. A fierce affection.

I thought to give them their privacy when Adrianna withdrew from her mate. "I want to be the one to speak to Diana," she said, sounding in control again, if a bit winded.

Zeke bobbed his head. "And after that, sleep. You look exhausted."

"Don't fuss," she grouched.

"Are we leaving tomorrow?" I asked.

Another nod. "We'll leave at first light while it's still cool out. Let's say 6 BN."

"You're still coming with us, then?" That much-too-light question came from Adrianna.

"Of course," Zeke said solidly. "The surrounding terrain can be dangerous for people unaccustomed to it."

Adrianna's face lost emotion. Feeling awkward, I addressed Zeke. "I heard you mention the Shyani Tribe in The Oasis Lounge. Is that where we're headed?"

"Yes."

"How far away are they?"

"Ten hours as the fae flies." Zeke went to his writing desk. There, he unfurled a scroll and used books as paperweights to pin it flat. "You'll get a better sense of the journey from this."

Adrianna and I flanked him.

I gazed down at a drawing of the eastern continent. I'd heard the continent was five times the size of Aldar. But stars, it really was huge. I stored that map in my memory vaults as best I could.

Zeke bent at the hips and braced his palms on the desk. "This is Alhara." He tapped at a spot in the center of Asitar. It seemed that we were right beside a mountain range that dominated the northern sector. "And the Shyani settle here in the height of summer."

He traced a diagonal line down the map. Southeast it was, then.

Something occurred to me while I stared at the distance we had yet to travel. "Since we're being hunted, wouldn't it be better for the Shyani if we stayed away. If we got word to them about our situation, maybe Sefra could come here instead."

Zeke uncurled and stretched his spine. "I considered that. But none of our messenger birds have flown the route before. And a courier is out of the question because the community wouldn't trust a stranger, not even one carrying a handwritten note from me. So I think we must go ourselves."

"Right. I should go tell Liora all of this."

Adrianna faced me, her azure-blues unusually dull. "I'll come find you both after I've spoken to Diana."

"Or you could sleep," Zeke countered.

"Stop nagging." A snap.

I fought a smile. "It wouldn't be a bad idea to get some rest."

Her lip drew a grumpy line. Almost a pout. *Almost.*

"Can you tell me how to get to the temple?" I asked Zeke.

After giving me instructions, he added, "I'll meet you in the infirmary around six. Don't be late."

Setting off alone, I retraced my steps and went down the spiral staircase. From there, I traversed the fortress's long corridors. Now that I no longer ran at full tilt, I could look upon my environment with fresh eyes. The vaulted ceilings carved with sun emblems and tongues of flame in particular drew my attention. Had my grandfather designed these details?

It's possible, Zola said, more reserved than usual. *He shared our gift for sunlight.*

Not a surprise. Who better to protect the sunstone than someone who shared its power?

Such musings were postponed when I caught a whiff of Liora's scent. That sweet smokiness, along with Zeke's instructions, led me to another circular staircase. Blue-fire torches bracketed the passageway and illuminated a path that went underground.

There was no handrail; I flared my wings and touched the dewy stone for balance. I descended into mystery and shadow.

The stair soon ended, opening out into a cavernous space dotted with hanging lamps. Hundreds of candles stood vigil over twenty or so statues guarding the walls. From the offerings strewn at their feet, I suspected the effigies belonged to the light gods.

My gaze centered on the temple's sole occupant. Liora was ahead of me, standing before a statue. She wore leggings, a white undershirt, and a plum-colored shift dress. Her curls were piled high atop her head in a messy bun.

I footed it over to her.

Liora greeted me with relief. "How are you feeling?"

"Not bad." I wavered. "How are you?"

Her mouth folded into a poor smile. "I've been better."

"I've seen Adi. But she didn't tell me what happened after I blacked out." My fears grew dark wings and gained air. "The last I saw of you—"

"I was firing on The Watch."

"Mm." That was all I dared to say.

"I killed many of those chasing us," she said as if afraid the world would hear her sins and judge her for them. "The rest fled back to the city. I remember wanting to go after them. But somewhere in the back of my mind I realized I couldn't lose sight of you all. That was when I left the city and caught up with you."

That was promising. "Maybe you've got more control over the dragon than you thought."

A tiny sigh spilled from her. "I hope so. If I thought I could control it and only act in self-defense, I could make peace with all the violence."

"Even though it goes against your healer's vow?" I said carefully.

"I chose a different path when I set out to punish my ex-girlfriend's attacker," she said, her features haunted but fierce. "I never planned on killing him. But I also don't want to sit back and watch as evil people get away with rape and murder just because the world values them more. And I want to protect the people I love. Those things are more important to me than my vow. That's why I'm down here. To apologize to her."

She motioned to the statue facing us. I spared a moment to study the effigy. It was of a flower-crowned female surrounded by baskets of food. "Who is she?"

"Briar, the Goddess of Healing."

I waited a beat before moving us on. "There are a few things I need to tell you."

Everything spilled out. The dreamwalking. The conversation with Zeke.

Liora's first reaction was to say, "When you saw Frazer, did you get the sense they were nearing Mysaya?"

I thought back. "Not really. Frazer said before we left that their journey would take them about three weeks."

"And how long has it been since we sailed—nine days?"

"Sounds about right."

Liora bit her bottom lip in angst.

My waterlight sounded from somewhere to my left, distracting me. Following the river's song, I walked past Briar's statue and stopped at the next one. It was another female, her hair dropping to her waist, her hands clasped.

Thea whispered to me that this was Juna—Briar's mate.

My fingertips grazed Juna's. I *moved*.

I arrived in a garden under a teardrop moon. The encircling wall was overgrown with the droopy heads of wisteria, the tangled vines of climbing roses, and the star-shaped petals of jasmine.

Whywherehow? Those questions drifted through. I regarded them in an abstract way. Truthfully, I didn't much care. An inscrutable peace had centered me. All objections and curiosities seemed muted.

Come. Find me.

That whisper was the shiver up my spine. The thrill in my blood. The shudder of my feathers.

A large shadow danced in the corner of my eye.

I about-turned to confront it.

The shadow sprang down a path bordered by pink heather, blue anemones, and yellow-throated violets.

Happiness bubbled up like sparkling wine. It came from nowhere, from nothing, and suddenly all I wanted to do was give chase.

The shadow exited the garden through an arched trellis. I went after it, and beyond, giant trees sprouted up. I traveled through the shaded forest, my tread more cautious than before.

The wind breathed, *Why run when you can chase shadows standing still?*

That riddle made me halt, thinking.

It clicked quickly. I conjured starlight within a breath. That elusive magic was easier to reach here—wherever here was.

Not five feet from me, a cloak of shadow fell and revealed the outline of a fae. Their features remained hidden, but their physicality suggested a masculine body. They were taller than most, with a strong build and black-feathered wings at their back.

Save me, elämayen.

Pulse galloping, I closed the distance between us. I reached out to touch his wings—

My mind was thrown backward out of the vision. I was in the temple again, and Liora was waving a hand in my face.

"I'm here. I'm okay," I mumbled.

She sighed, lowering her hand. "What happened? You just stopped responding to me."

I recounted the details, finishing with, "What d'you think it meant?"

Anxious butterflies twirled around my belly.

"Juna's the Goddess of Love. They say she perceives the future of relationships and can even guide certain couples toward each other." Her tone rose suggestively. "Maybe she was showing you to your mate?"

That made my stomach perform a feeble flip-flop. The fog of memory descended. Maggie OneEye's words—her prophecy about my mate—rolled through me. *His heart and soul are dying.*

That would explain why he'd asked me to save him.

A sword of revelation swung through me, cleaving me from self-delusions. My chest ached as a bruise to a bone would. Yet I felt clear-headed. Finally.

I pushed myself to verbalize the realization. "If you're right, then Wilder can't be my mate. He's not as big as the male in the vision, and he doesn't have black feathers. It's not him."

Liora comfort-touched my back. "I guess it's stupid to ask if you're okay?"

"It isn't, and I think I am, actually."

Her head tilted, curious. "Really?"

Conflicting emotions tore at my throat. "I'm disappointed. But I've got my answer. At least I don't have to wonder anymore."

"I suppose so." A doubt-filled pause was followed by, "D'you think maybe deep down you're relieved it's not him?"

Sadness and confusion dusted my soul.

"I'm sorry," she said by my shoulder. "I shouldn't have asked that. I'm acting as nosy as Cai."

I sucked in a shaky trail of air through my teeth. "It's fine. And you're not totally wrong. I am relieved in a way. There were moments when I would look at Wilder and I couldn't breathe for wanting him. Like I was drowning and coming up for air at the same time." My heart creaked like an old thing. "But when I told him about Maggie's mate prophecy, it was the beginning of the end for us. I thought he deserved to know. I thought …"

"That it had to be about him?"

The understanding in her voice killed me.

"I couldn't imagine it not being. But he didn't agree with that, and he pulled away. Even after he swore the guardian bond to me, we weren't the same. And now I don't see how we could ever be what I'd hoped for, not when I'm the reason he's bound to Morgan."

"How is it your fault?" Almost an angry tone.

"Because if I'd listened when he said it was dangerous for us to be together, Morgan might not have dragged him out of Kasi."

"Morgan is the only one culpable for his fate," Liora interrupted. "Besides, it's not as if he took his own advice. He chose to get closer to you."

"True," I admitted softly.

I rubbed my neck and allowed my head to fall back.

There was so much left unsaid between us. We felt unfinished.

"So not including the stuff with Wilder, how do you feel about the vision? About *him*?"

There was a smile somewhere in her voice. It diverted me.

I met her spring-green gaze. "When Mama appeared to me, she said he was meant to help me somehow. But in my vision, he was asking me to save him. I've no idea what to think or how to even go about finding him. How can I with all this craziness going on? And then there's a part of me that doesn't really want to meet him."

"Because of Wilder?"

"Actually, no. It's because the more I think about it, the less keen I am on the idea of the bond just happening. It feels like it's being forced."

"Mm."

"You don't agree?"

Her mouth tightened in at one side. "I was just thinking about when we first met. It felt like I'd known you for years. Maybe that's what it is to find your mate? It's just a magical confirmation of a natural sympathy, and that you fit together."

I couldn't help but smile. "That's a nice way of thinking about it."

Liora's rosebud lip hooked up into a dimpling grin. "I thought so."

"I suppose I could always try ignoring the bond," I said as an afterthought.

"Is that possible?"

I shrugged. "Adi and Zeke seem to be trying to. Although from what I saw upstairs, it won't be long before one of them cracks."

Liora's expression grew as dark as a new moon.

"What is it?"

"I was thinking about Cai." She released a troubled sigh. "This is going to be hard on him. He's never had his heart broken before. It was always him doing the breaking. That sounds bad, I know, but he was always kind and faithful with his partners." My expression had her adding, "Well, for the two days his relationships usually lasted."

I chuffed, and she went on.

"But I think he truly loves Adi."

My heart fell for what seemed like an age.

After a shared quiet, we traded looks.

"Do you need to sleep again before we leave?" she asked.

"I'm wide awake. How about you?"

A pale smile. "I couldn't sleep a wink right now. Do you want to explore the fortress a bit more? It'd be nice to see more of it before we go."

I was about to agree when my magic interrupted us for the second time.

A golden trail appeared. It started at my feet and led me to another statue that was undoubtedly Zola's.

What are you talking about? It's hardly a good likeness—they made my nose far too big.

Ignoring the goddess, I walked around the back of the tall sculpture. The golden thread had formed four patterns on the temple's wall. I recognized them instantly because each pattern was engraved on my skin in forever ink.

"Holy hell."

"What is it?" Liora had patiently stuck by me during my weirdness.

"Magic. I think it guided me here."

A fifth emblem appeared on the rock face. It was a globe overcast by a shining sun. This sigil was much smaller than the others and placed in the bottom right-hand corner, almost as if it was intended to act like a signature in a painting.

That sneaky fuck. Zola's tone was all awe and shock.

Who's sneaky?

Like calls to like, Thea said as if to herself.

I lost my patience. "What are you two on about?"

Liora wisely said nothing.

The last symbol to appear belonged to Atlas. It was his emblem, Zola explained.

Thea added, *You're looking at the workings of a very powerful spell. Think of it as a horn that, when sounded, is only heard by a specific group of people. This one works magic to magic, and only those with the four light signatures could've heard its call.*

So just me.

Everything lined up. *So you're saying that Atlas meant for me to find this? That somewhere beyond this wall is ...*

Betraying her excitement, Zola blurted out, *The sunstone.*

CHAPTER 19
A TWIST OF FATE

Shock and thrill pulsed through me. "I can't believe it."

"Erm, Ena?"

I turned to Liora. "They think the sunstone's in the wall. Or beyond it."

Her face brightened as though touched by the dawn. "Really?"

I repeated Thea's explanation about Atlas's spell. "Now that I've said it out loud, it almost seems too easy, doesn't it? That we've ended up in exactly the right place."

My tongue stilled as the past collided with the present.

Liora's red brows nudged together. "You've figured something out?"

"I was just thinking about how we came to be here." Dazed, I went on. "If I hadn't felt drawn to Anya—if we hadn't tried to help her—Zeke wouldn't have brought us to Alhara."

A short gust of surprised laughter parted her lips. Liora's attention drifted to the rough-hewn wall, curiosity shining through in her gaze. "But how are you going to get the stone?"

If I'm correct, you must place your hands where the symbols are and push all your magic to the surface simultaneously. Don't release it. Just let the spell sense that you're gifted with the four light disciplines. Thea reeled that off in such a succinct way as to give the impression she'd been politely waiting until Liora and I had finished speaking.

In a faltering move, I placed my palms flat against the wall. I reached for the stars' cold light, the moon's glow, the sun's warmth, and the water's shimmer.

The effort to channel felt akin to struggling through a bog. My burnout must be to blame for that. It was then I recalled Tia's advice to abstain from magic. Oh well. This was too important to put off.

Minutes were swallowed up. As soon as I'd latched ahold of one discipline, another would slip away into the background. They seemed to mute one another. Water cooled sunlight. Starlight weakened moonlight.

Sweat and energy were spent. Once I had achieved a tenuous balance, empty silence was my reward. A nonevent.

My spirits plunged. Before they could hit rock bottom, the symbols started to glow. An illusion dropped.

I stumbled back. A thick-set wooden door had appeared in front of me. An almost indiscernible sigh echoed throughout the temple that we stood in. The sound carried a weary weight, as if someone was tired of withholding their secrets.

Leashing my magic, I focused on Liora. "I have to go in there. Alone."

She glanced at the door, wariness narrowing her eyes. "I suppose you must. Atlas might've set magical safeguards to stop anybody except you from entering. But I'll be right outside. If you need me, call out."

I answered with a chin bob.

Tense, I pushed down the metal handle and swung open the door. Even after what was likely centuries, the hinges were silent, still free from corrosion.

High on adrenaline, I stepped into a pocket of darkness.

The door closed of its own accord. That *bang* caused my heart to stumble and made me gather my wings against my spine.

Don't panic. Don't panic. Don't panic.

Shit. I was totally panicking.

Sun-colored crystals flickered to life. I blinked and a room was revealed. The anxiety squeezing my ribcage loosened.

I drew in an expansive breath and peered around.

The space was square-ish, not very big, and absent of decor. No markings. No nothing. Had we been wrong?

Zola tutted. *Of course we're not wrong. Atlas wouldn't have carved out a space in solid rock for no reason.*

Thea contributed, *He would've likely hidden the stone from plain view. But you should be sensitive to such a potent source of sunlight. It is in your soul, after all.*

Right, except I can't sense anything.

She wasn't defeated. *Walk around. Touch, feel, smell—look for anything unusual.*

I started my search, repressing several sneezes as my scuffing feet stirred up whorls of dust, time, and memory.

The right wall was quick to capture my attention. My fingertips picked up a section of stone at eye level that felt warmer and looser to the touch.

Skin rising in miniature bumps, I rubbed and pushed at the surface. The top layer came away easily enough, showing itself to be dried mud—not stone.

Determined, I kept at it until the veneer of red-tinted earth completely crumbled. A small hole was revealed.

I reached in and pulled out a rosewood box. Blowing off the powdered dirt, I uncovered my grandfather's sigil.

This was it. It had to be.

I expected to discover the box locked. But when I unclasped the latch, the lid swung back on undemanding hinges.

Inside I found a knuckle-sized gem—a cut and polished citrine. Breath poised, I plucked it out by the leather lace it was strung on.

I put the box back into the wall and placed the necklace over my head. The crystal fell against my chest, settling next to the waterstone.

My victory was stolen by a flush of wild heat. It rushed through my veins, bringing with it a feeling of heady power. I could breathe fire. I could move mountains.

Flames as yellow as the sun encompassed my hands.

There was no pain, only a sense of being in a runaway carriage and outside the windows a forest was ablaze. The magic in the citrine was unlike that of the waterstone. It was restless and aggressive. It challenged and dominated.

The sunstone's testing you, Ena. You must show it that you are in control.

Zola's advice wouldn't stick. I couldn't think through the dizziness as the fire grew hotter in my hands and the surrounding air burned up. It became unbearable—unbreathable. I'd suffocate.

I tried to channel waterlight, but the second that I reeled in its cooling magic, the sunstone vaporized it. Its magic was too powerful. Its fire too strong.

Thea was all urgency and alarm. *Use the waterstone, Ena. It's the only source powerful enough to counteract these effects.*

"I thought the stones were to be used against Archon?" I rasped. "Won't I weaken it if I draw on its power now?"

The stones are connected to deep wells of power. You can use some of its energy now. It'll have recharged long before the Dark King walks free.

Mouth white-wine dry, I croaked, "How do I do it?"

Draw on your magic like you normally would, but focus on pulling it from the waterstone.

Don't overdo it, though, Zola warned. *If you take in too much of the stones' energy before you're ready, you could die.*

At this precise moment, I didn't care. I'd do anything to escape the inferno that was soaking my back, thighs, and face in sweat.

I called in waterlight. But not from the world: from the stone alone.

A tidal wave crashed through me. I didn't have to direct its wrath. It acted as an angry beast woken from a nap, and its fury was aimed at the thing threatening its slumber. It clashed up against the sunlight. Two predators fought inside of me; a dragon and a kraken warring for dominion.

Neither side won. But they did neutralize each other. The wildfire running rampant through my veins was subdued. Made manageable.

The flames in my hands sputtered out. My relief tasted like chalk on my tongue. Alkaline to the acidic.

As water and fire laid down their weapons, I was left feeling washed out. The air had grown thinner and staler. It went down worse than hot, gelatinous soup.

I staggered toward the door.

A large male blocked my next step.

I went back on my foot and gaped up at him. Despite the almond-hued wings, nobody could've mistaken him for pure fae. He looked half-god and half-lion, with a glorious mane of golden and copper hair.

Exposure to a strong sun had weathered his skin. It had aged him, but it had also lent a ruggedness to features that would've seemed too perfect otherwise. Indeed, his face and body looked carved from marble. Then there were his jade-green eyes.

It can't be ...

Fuck.

My great-aunts' inarticulate comments confirmed my suspicions. "You're Atlas."

"More or less."

He stared at me, his eyes flashing with cold fire. Even in death, he had the visage of an undefeated warrior. It was in the strength of his build and the proud wearing of his armor, which consisted of a bronze breastplate, bracers, and greaves. I had a feeling that if I wanted to avoid being flattened verbally or physically by him, I had to act as a wolf, not a frightened hedgehog.

"How are you here?" I asked, voice clear, shoulders back.

"I'm not." He palmed his sword. "I am in the moon court."

"Then, how am I speaking to you?"

I dared to near him, to push a hand through his torso.

Atlas raised an imperious brow. He obviously thought I was an idiot. "Some spirits can move between the moon court and this realm. But only if there is an object or person powerful enough to anchor them here. Given my connection to the stone, I was able to bind my spirit to it before I died. Enough that when I sensed it being disturbed, I could come back for a short time."

"Okay. But why would you bind yourself to it?"

"First, do you possess any of the other stones?"

"Why do you need to know?"

"Answer me, faeling."

It was the absolute command of a fae not used to being denied. And he seemed wholly unaffected by my stubborn jaw.

Just tell him. He won't give in first. Trust me.

Zola's wisdom upended my rebellious mood. "I have the waterstone," I admitted.

"But not the others."

That didn't require a response. I held my tongue.

Atlas folded his muscled arms. "Have you heard rumors of the starstone's location?"

"Your daughter, Sandrine. She told me it was lost."

The muscles in his face smoothed out in surprise. "Is she well?"

"She is."

"That's good," he said gruffly, his features thawing.

"Don't you want to hear more about her?"

I dreaded any subsequent questions about Sati. But I couldn't deny him information about his daughters.

"A year and a day would not be enough time to hear all I would like about my daughters, and we should not get sidetracked. Even now, my spirit begs me to return to my rightful place. So I must discharge my duty and help the light-wielder. That is you, I presume?"

His *tone* was made tolerable by the hint of humor underlining it.

"Yes. That's me."

A speculative look. "Indeed. Then hear this—Abel has the starstone. Are you familiar with the name?"

The bottom dropped out of my stomach. "Yes. I mean, he goes by Abraxus now. But how did he get it?"

"I imagine he killed its bearer and stole it," he said roughly.

Gods-damn it. I'd started to hope there was more to Abraxus than his ugly reputation. After all, Dain believed he had enough honor to uphold a promise. But if Abraxus murdered to possess the starstone, that didn't bode well for me.

Another thought struck, horrifying in nature. This news would delay our return to Aldar; we couldn't sail until the starstone was in my possession.

"Is there any way you could be mistaken?"

"No." Firm. Harsh. "In my last battle against Abel, I injured him. And for a brief second, the cloaking spell he used to conceal his power slipped. It was then I caught sight of the starlight collaring his neck. There can be no doubt. It is the whole reason I bound myself to the sunstone: so I could pass on the information to the wielder."

Curiosity urged me to ask, "What happened after you wounded Abraxus, or Abel?"

"I became surrounded by his soldiers." He continued as if reading from a boring book. No emotion. "My magic was almost spent, and I'd sustained too much damage to fight my way free. So I ran myself through with a sword."

Rutting hell.

Thea sighed. *Oh, Atlas.*

"Was there no chance of surrender?"

His expression turned positively leonine. "Fuck surrender. I wouldn't have given Abel the satisfaction."

A pained laugh came from Zola. *As obstinate as ever, I see.*

I hurt for her. I couldn't help it. "There's something I should tell you." Deep breaths. "I'm your granddaughter. My great-aunts—your sisters—are communicating with me via the waterstone. They can hear everything we're saying." I pushed on. "I'm telling you this in case there's anything you want to say to them, anything I can pass on to them."

Atlas looked as if his opinion of me couldn't get any lower. "Are you mad? Or do you simply possess an awful sense of humor?"

"I'm not lying to you. Anyway, I just thought I'd offer. I mean, if you're in the moon court, you're not with your family, right?" I ended awkwardly.

My great-aunts gave me the right words to say.

I lined my chin up to those suspicious eyes. "You and Zola used to set each other's toys on fire. And Thea said *Cherry tree*, and that you'd know what that meant."

Atlas blinked twice. I gave him a moment.

When the shock faded from his face, his reaction proved unexpected. His eyes hardened into ice-chips. "You are wrong to say that I am not with my family. I chose the moon court because my wife is an undine and all of their kind settle there. She is my world. My family. I had no reason or desire to be parted from her." All emotion was buried as he added, "Besides, I never really belonged in the light court. I wasn't worthy of it."

The sisters were as silent as snowfall in the forest. But I wanted answers. "Why weren't you worthy of it?"

His jaw muscles bunched together. "I'll answer that by giving you some advice—be careful with the stones. Only use their power when there is no other option. And if you survive your encounter with Archon, rid yourself of them. Throw them into the ocean and never look back. They're not worth the cost."

My wings fidgeted. "What cost?"

A dark look; a warning. "The stones *are* power. There is little that cannot be achieved with their magic at your disposal. The only limitations are those of your imagination and spirit."

"Not my body?"

"Of course not," he said, staring at me, nonplussed. "There is no difference between your flesh and that of a less powerful witch. It is the level of understanding you have of your magic and your talent for channeling it that determines your potential."

I tucked that away for later examination.

"But to wield such power comes with countless temptations. Surely you can see how in the wrong hands the stones could do great evil?"

I paused, worried about where this was going. "Yes, but I wouldn't—"

He waved a flippant hand. "I do not mean to imply you are evil. I am simply saying that even the purest of souls might feel tempted by the sunstone's power."

"Did you?"

Atlas's gaze drifted to the crystal in question. "Yes. At first I only used it to protect others. But the more I saw of the world, the more dissatisfied I became." Self-loathing contorted his features. "I wished to shape it in my image. To end the pain and the suffering. So I created my own court. I led people to their deaths in order to defend my vanity project." He cleared his throat. "It'll be different for you, of course. But every person has a tendency toward some evil, and power has a way of bringing out the worst in us. Remember that, faeling. Don't make my mistakes. Don't play at being a firstborn just because you can."

I detected regret, guilt, and sorrow. Atlas was bleeding internally.

All this time, he felt unworthy, Thea whispered.

We thought he must hate us for leaving him in your world, Zola told me, sounding as if she had a head cold.

The next question I asked Atlas was for me. "Is that why you hid the sunstone? Because you'd grown worried about using it?"

"It was at my wife's bidding that I hid it. She foresaw that Abraxus would come for us. That was when I decided to give it up for good." With a grave look, he told me, "Now that I've said what I needed to, I must go. My energy is almost spent."

Tell him that we love him.

I repeated Thea's words.

A stiff nod. "I'm pleased they are watching over you." His eyes turned friendlier, and that unhappy mouth moved up into its first smile. "I shall be sure to tell my wife about you. She'll be thrilled to know our love and our kin lives on through you. I wish you well against Archon, materie. May you do better in this life than I did."

He vanished. I stood, feeling unglued for a second.

Then the door opened as if the room knew its task was completed.

I moved for the exit in a stupor, leaving that stuffy space behind. On the threshold to the temple, I drew in a super sweet inhale. Gods, it was like coming up for air after being underwater for too long.

"Ena," Liora exclaimed, almost pouncing on me. "Oh, thank the mother and the maiden." She pulled me forward a few steps. "We couldn't get to you—"

"I'm all right. Just tired and sweaty."

Adrianna appeared at Liora's shoulder. "I could bite you."

"What for?"

She threw an angry arm out at the door behind us. "For not coming to get me before you went in there, obviously."

I glanced at Liora with a question in my eyes. She returned my gaze rather sheepishly. "Sorry. I got worried when you weren't answering my calls, and the door was stuck fast. I thought we might need fae strength to open it."

"Is that it?" Adrianna gestured to my new necklace.

I plucked at the leather cord the gem was threaded onto. "Yes."

In brief detail, I recited my discovery and the time spent with Atlas. The only thing I concealed was his fear I would become corrupted. That would only worry them.

Adrianna and Liora withdrew into their own thoughts for a lengthy moment.

Busying myself, I massaged the stressed muscles of my nape and rested my wings against the temple wall. I felt as if I'd been pushing boulders up a hill.

Liora began. "I feel like we should be celebrating—"

"But Abraxus carries the starstone," Adrianna finished.

One step forward. Two steps back.

"How in all the moons are we going to get it from him?" Liora wondered aloud.

A nervous exhale puffed out my cheeks. "Confront him? Steal it? Who knows?"

"Maybe we don't think about that yet," Adrianna suggested.

I straightened on shaky legs. "What are you saying?"

"We've got a win." Her eyes landed on the citrine. "The rest of it can wait. At least until we find Sefra, and then with her help we can tackle our Abraxus problem."

"Sounds good to me," Liora said.

Talk of the future brought to mind a question too important to delay asking. "Adi, were you able to warn your makena?"

Her gaze skated away. "Yes, but my news wasn't a surprise to her. She already suspected that Morgan was planning an attack soon. And Diana's as prepared as she can be." Her features were taut, as if she was afraid to give an inch and reveal her emotions. "But Morgan's forces greatly outnumber our own, and our court is vulnerable on all sides. Our border with the Solar Court is too vast to defend for long, and the Meriden will block any exodus by sea. I'm not sure what's left to my people except to flee into the countryside, or to settle in for a siege."

"I'm so sorry, Adi."

"My makena's smart. She'll figure something out." Her lips pressed together in a way that said *It'll be okay because it has to be.* "There's one more thing," she added. "I told Diana about Armstrong refusing to take us back to Aldar. She said she'll try to think of something, but that he was the only captain she knew of who was trustworthy."

Gloom burrowed in. How in the rutting hell would we get home?

"Should we head upstairs?" Liora's terribly bright tone suggested she wanted to distract and rouse Adrianna.

I played along. "I'm all for that." I rotated my shoulders and wings. "The sunstone's worn me out. I want a lie down in the infirmary, even if it's only for an hour."

"I'll join you," Adrianna said to me. "I didn't get much sleep before Liora shook me awake, yelling about sunstones and what a reckless idiot you were."

Unlikely.

Liora hit her arm. "I did not say that."

Knew it.

Deciding to push this light mood, I asked Adrianna, "Wouldn't you rather have a private room than stay with me in the infirmary?"

"What are you implying?"

Feigning innocence, I raised both brows. "I thought you wouldn't want our company."

"Whose company am I meant to want?" Adrianna asked, her eyes tapering.

I simper-smiled at her. "I can't answer that without being bitten."

A growl snagged in the back of her throat.

I flashed my teeth.

"Okay," Liora said, elongating the word. "Let's go."

Adrianna and I were silent but agreeable.

The three of us moved for the spiral staircase—the only way in or out.

Midway across the room, my eyes snagged on a statue of a female holding a pair of scales. I guessed the stern but beautiful likeness belonged to Persephone, Goddess of Fate, Queen of the Moon Court.

She was the goddess who'd foreseen me. She had predicted I would wield the stones against Archon. How much more had she seen? Was my fate already written? And if so, what did it say?

I could've sworn the statue's eyes followed me. As I left the temple, I couldn't shake the feeling of being observed. Even while I slept, I dreamed of timeless eyes staring out from the darkness. Fate, it seemed, was watching me.

CHAPTER 20
A MEETING WITH A STORYWEAVER

Time slipped away like sand through relaxed fingers. It turned my hours in the infirmary into minutes, and soon our trio was up, readying ourselves for the flight south. I had a quick bath, dressed, ate breakfast, and refilled my canteen.

The cook, who Adrianna had labeled as chatty, appeared in the infirmary at Zeke's request. She brought a great deal of unwanted conversation and several packets of fresh food, which we added to our store of rations. The cook finally left us at five minutes before 6 BN—Before Noon.

We had not long to wait before Zeke joined us. Anya, too.

"I thought Anya may wish to say goodbye. Luckily, I was right and hadn't disturbed her sleep for nothing." Zeke pulled his rucksack off his shoulders and drew out swathes of white material. "These will help protect your scalp from the sun. Cover your head with them as I have done."

Zeke handed out the scarves. Liora frowned down at hers. "Shouldn't this be black?"

His reply proved to be welcome news. "No. The Shyani don't hold with slavery."

As I took my own scarf, I studied his head-wrap for tips on what to do. I couldn't burn, but at the very least the covering would keep the wind out of my hair.

Once our trio had secured the material around our scalps, Zeke told us, "You should get your water containers out so you can hold onto them. We've got ten hours up in the air, and we can't stop to rest, not when we're flying over the Sickle Dunes."

"Why? What's so bad about them?" Adrianna asked.

"It home to the sidir," Anya said grimly.

"And they are?"

"Sand sprites. They'll attack anything that threatens their territory," Zeke answered. "Then there are the scorpions and snakes and, well, you get the idea. You can't take a squat in the dunes without something sinking its teeth or stinger into your balls."

"Then I feel sorry for the animals," Adrianna deadpanned.

Laughter snaked out of me and Liora. Zeke's amusement didn't leave his eyes.

Adrianna snatched up her bag and pulled out a tin. She shared the sun cream inside with Liora, and together they started to apply it. It was then Anya sidled up to me.

"Is something wrong?"

"No." She captured her lip in a nervous bite. "But I thinking after baby is born, I work for you. As lady's maid."

Stunned, I struggled to iron out the knots in my tongue. "Anya, I'm not in any position to keep a lady's maid. Why would you want to serve me anyway? You're trained as a seamstress."

She raised her chin, determined. "If you give protection, I not mind what I do. I good at scavenging, and I can hunt with slingshot."

Adrianna's laugh was stark. "I like you, Anya."

Anya addressed me again. "And someone in kitchen said feather-winged fae come from Aldar. If you returning there, I not mind moving. Outside Alhara, there only death waiting." She placed her hands protectively on her belly. "And the healer, Liora, she speak to you as equal—as friend. If that possible in Aldar, it somewhere I wish to go."

Ah, rats.

I decided on honesty. "It's true that we're from Aldar. And we will be going back. But I can't say when. We might have to leave before you give birth."

"Then I make journey on my own." She pursed her lips. "I not afraid."

My guts twisted up with awkwardness. "It's really dangerous for ships to make the journey to Aldar. I don't know if you'll find anybody willing to take you. We're also not safe people to be around. There are people in Aldar who want to hurt us. I don't want you getting caught up in that."

Her face fell.

A sense of obligation to her grew within me, and an idea bloomed. "I want to give you something."

I retrieved my bag from our trio's pile of possessions. Delving inside, I detected the cold metal at the bottom—the two coins that Hunter had given me after selling me at Kasi.

I presented the money to Anya. "Take these."

She stared at the metal in my hand. "Gold?"

"Yes."

Her brow furrowed. "You not need it?"

"No, and I don't want it, either." I pressed the gold into her palm. "Trust me, the only thing this money is good for is helping you."

She nodded, and her fingers closed over the coins.

"I hope you and the baby will be safe," I told her.

"Thank you." Her gaze glided over the others. "I go back to sleep now. Goodbye."

Liora's was the most heartfelt farewell. Adrianna and Zeke offered a word or two, then they went back to discussing the upcoming flight in murmurs.

Anya left the infirmary. For her sake, I hoped I never saw her again.

Following Zeke's suggestion, I extracted my canteen from my bag and slung its short leather strap over my shoulder. I donned my rucksack and strapped on my weapons belt next.

Zeke broke from Adrianna, announcing, "If you've got everything, then we should head to the roof. That's where we'll be taking off."

Adrianna, Liora, and I trailed after Zeke. We climbed three sets of stairs before arriving on the rooftop garden.

I drank in the landscape before me. On my right, the rising sun crested over weathered mountaintops that looked like the humps of giants. Alhara's rocky bones were warmed by the dawn's vibrant orange and butter-yellow hues. The very stone glittered and glowed at the light's attention. Stunning.

Out in front of me, in the middle of the roof terrace, stood a fountain depicting birds in flight. Their delicate beaks sprayed water into the air. These jets fell into a silvery pool—a reservoir—that two humans used to soak the surrounding soil plots with. I recognized a few of the sun-loving plants living in these beds: there were date palms, pomegranate bushes, and fig trees. My nose told me that orange blossom, lavender, and rosemary were also grown here. The humming in my ears suggested many a crafty bee was gathering nectar from this vegetation, spinning it into honey in their combs.

My interested stare moved on to study those tending the garden. Out of the six people present, all of them carried the signs of past hurts: crippled wings, missing fingers, scarred faces. Yet they greeted Zeke with smiles. They looked content, happy in one another's company. It didn't seem to matter who was fae or human. These wayward wanderers had found a home together.

Zeke extended a palm out to me. "May I?"

Politeness. A surprise. I took his outstretched hand. "Thanks for doing this."

He scooped me up. I was made marginally more comfortable by the fact he'd wrapped his weapons belt around his hips instead of wearing it across his chest.

I reacted instinctively, coiling my arms around his neck.

An aggressive growl sounded, causing my feathers to puff up like a cat's tail when startled. Primed for an attack, I turned my head toward the noise. It had come from Adrianna.

Her gaze swiftly darted away. She couldn't honestly think …

Zeke expelled a strange purring chuff. Adrianna's bones seemed to soften at that.

"I'll go first, shall I?" he asked her.

As sharp as a hatpin, she said, "Fine," and hoisted Liora up into a hold.

With a flap, Zeke filled the scaled membrane of his wings with morning air. As we soared upward, I stole one last glance at Alhara and thanked every star in the heavens that we'd visited.

I absentmindedly touched the neckline of my tunic. Realizing what I was doing, I stayed my hand from seeking the sunstone that was tucked beneath the cotton. Its magic was currently dormant, but I feared disturbing it and provoking another test of wills.

Zeke and Adrianna ascended to where the land opened up, horizon to horizon. The grand vista, the sheer vastness of it all, made me feel small, inconsequential—a speck of dust on a page.

We swam through that bright blue expanse for an unknown pinch of time. As the budding sun warmed sky and earth, I occupied my mind by focusing on what we flew over.

The splinter in the heart of Asitar—the mountain range that sliced down the northern sector—ended. We veered left and flew deeper inland. There we found endless desert. For the most part, the coppery sands were as calm as a dried-out seabed, life long since extinguished. Then strong winds blew and that stillness transformed into a thing of shape and motion; dunes rippled, becoming an undulating sea. Nothing existed except sand and sky and wind. And us.

At my first glance of colorful freckles smattering the desert, I nodded down to them, asking Zeke, "What are those?"

"Settlements. But most of them double as mass graves."

"Was it the sidir?" I whispered, bug-eyed.

The muscle under his eye appeared to twitch. "No. The settlements were raided by the kings' warriors."

"Why?" I asked, my throat tight.

"To demand tribute from them, either in coin, food, sex, or slaves," Zeke said, his face harder than a bronze statue. "Any resistance would bring death to all, and the tribes that didn't fight were left decimated. I've known plenty that starved outright."

Words fled. Anger remained.

I gathered myself. "But six of the kings are gone. Has that not made things any better?"

Hatred brutalized his mouth. "It should have. But the fall of the others has only made Hasan turn to more brutal methods of control. Then, there's the next generation of warlords who are looking to fill the power void left by the kings. Abraxus has kept the majority of them in check, but he can't squash every wannabe tyrant. His forces are stretched too thin as it is."

This only added to my bewilderment. I'd heard such different accounts of Abraxus that I couldn't riddle out his true nature at all. He was a dark god obsessed with revenge. A hunter of light-casters. And the warrior who had driven my grandfather to take his own life. On the other hand, Abraxus hated Archon, and my father expected him to keep a promise.

"What's your opinion of Abraxus?"

The downturn of Zeke's chin had the sun catching the flecks of brown-gold in his irises, outshining the green tints; his gaze locked with mine. "Bear in mind I've never met him, but from what I've heard, he's smart. Ruthless. And he inspires loyalty in people."

"Is he good? I mean, is there good in him?"

Zeke considered this for so long that I assumed he'd decided to ignore me.

Suddenly, "I do not think he is wholly good or bad. His war-band has outlawed slavery and offers protections for any human who joins his company. He has done the same for demi-fae and sprite hybrids, who make up a large portion of his forces." He continued, his notes growing low and rough. "Anywhere else on the continent, they would be chained and abused."

My thoughts scattered this way and that. Abraxus respected human freedom? And Zeke was a hybrid. Did he like Abraxus? I couldn't tell. His face was an impassive mask as he went on. "But Abraxus doesn't strike me as a male of peace or mercy. He exists in a constant state of warfare. And war makes widows and orphans out of all of us."

I pored over my knowledge of Abraxus and the continent. It wasn't enough. To figure out the best method of retrieving the starstone, I needed more information on his character.

"I have a question," I voiced. "Aldarians think they originated from the continent, and some of them blame Abraxus for forcing them from their homeland. But I heard something called the Eastern Alliance was also responsible. Do you know if and how the alliance connects to Abraxus?"

Zeke took my inarticulate attempt to satisfy my curiosity in stride. "I am not yet four hundred. The events you're speaking of happened almost seven centuries ago."

"Oh."

"I'll tell you about what I've read, though. It will certainly pass the time," he said dryly. "Back when the seven kings were just warlords, they formed the Eastern Alliance to combat Abraxus's and Atlas Lytir's forces. Then after centuries of fighting, Atlas convinced them to take his side and join his forces."

My worldview upended. "Atlas allied with those monsters—why?"

Zeke gave me a funny look, as if he couldn't fathom why it would mean so much to me. "Because of Abraxus. He was the greater threat, with huge numbers at his command, many of them human. Atlas agreed to order his people out of Asitar and to give the dragon's share of his fortune to the kings on the condition they fought Abraxus with him. In the end, Atlas and the kings stood victorious—barely. After that, Atlas's court left for Aldar. The seven warlords declared themselves kings, and Abraxus went missing. Most thought that he had died during their last battle."

I soaked that in and connected the puzzle pieces. "So Atlas ruled what became known as the Aldarian fae? He's the one responsible for them leaving the continent?"

A simple nod, and I was reeling.

"When did Abraxus return to Asitar?" I asked.

"He popped up again a few hundred years ago. Since then, he's been building his forces and fighting with the kings."

I had a lot of answers, but there were still blank spaces. Gaps that made me feel uneasy. "Out of interest, what was Atlas's reign like?"

"That era's known for its prosperity, its heroes, and its hedonism," he ended with a smirk.

Hedonism? That painted a picture of great feasts and sweaty orgies. The thought of my grandfather encouraging that made me want to scrub my mind out with soap.

"Atlas also had a reputation for being fair to the humans in his court," Zeke added. "But he never supported their right to be equal. That was one of the reasons so many humans sided with Abraxus."

Disappointment trickled in. I was a coward; I didn't ask more questions.

Hours passed. By noon, I was baking in an oven-heat and suspended in misery. The dry air stirred up by Zeke's wings stole every drop of moisture in my mouth. I sipped from my canteen to soothe my tongue, but the relief lasted mere seconds, then it felt like I was swallowing sawdust again. My acute discomfort had one upside. I hadn't the energy to worry about our enemies or about meeting my sister.

As the day wore away, the dunes slowly disappeared and an unbroken trail of mountains popped up in the distance. From my recollection of Zeke's map, I knew them to be the Tazil—the shark-toothed slopes that separated Asitar and Mokara.

The farther south we went, the more life appeared; determined succulents, tough grasses, and palm trees adorned the wide sweeping of dusty earth.

I glimpsed the Shyani Tribe's site in the light of late afternoon. Thousands of domed shelters were wedged between the Tazil slopes and a wide river that flowed lazily down the land. On the non-occupied side of the water, a herd of camels grazed on the stunted grasses. I'd only ever read about such creatures. Their strangeness fascinated me.

Zeke whistled to Adrianna. They met eye-to-eye on the same heading. Nods were exchanged.

Adjusting their wings, they tilted into controlled dives and descended fast.

Zeke and Adrianna landed on a riverbank, a fair way from the settlement. I noticed the relief on their faces when they set me and Liora down: I imagined they were glad to be free of our weight. My feet had barely touched sand when a female strode out to meet us. She carried a spear.

I stepped out in front of Liora. She moved to my side and gripped my wrist. "You don't need to protect me."

Her actions had me checking myself. I'd felt driven to guard Liora, the weakest physically, and I'd done it without thinking. An instinct that couldn't be ignored. Frazer's past behavior suddenly looked very different. I'd resented him for guarding me so intensely when I was human. Now I realized it was simply his fae nature playing out.

The female halted not far from us. Her cloud-white tunic had a light blue sash tied about the waist. The beige trousers were tucked into ankle boots, and a turquoise shawl covered her head.

I had a brief moment to note that her lips were inked with tiny words before she said, "I am Efrie. Mother Yuma waits to receive you. Please follow me."

The accent had a pleasing rhythm; the pitch oscillated up, down, up, down.

Our guide spun around and moved toward the settlement.

Zeke went first. Our trio stalked in their wake.

As we journeyed toward the community, I noticed it was encircled by a high-hanging rope held aloft by poles fixed into the earth. Attached to this borderline were dozens of dancing but soundless wind chimes.

Ever observant, Liora asked about this oddity before I could.

Zeke had the answer. "They've been spelled so only the sidir can hear them. The sprites can't stand the sounds they make. It keeps them away and stops them from attacking."

As we walked into the encampment proper, Efrie yelled out in a language of clicks and rolling vowels.

From out of large decorated tents and lean-tos came the Shyani people. They formed a kind of honor guard as we passed, holding their fists over their hearts.

Full of disquiet, I concentrated on studying their living arrangements.

The shelters were spaced out well, giving room for each unit to hang clothes, host an outdoor fire, and nurture future food in several lightweight plant boxes. Quite a few predatory birds loitered atop randomly placed perches, and I couldn't tell if they belonged to anyone.

After a few minutes, we arrived at the biggest structure yet. Like many of the others, it was crafted from a material whiter than vulture-picked bone and painted over top with pictographs. The skill of the artists lent the images a reality and intelligibility that allowed me to understand them as stories. Stories that traveled with the Shyani. That were revered. Beloved.

Efrie blocked our group from going any further. "Wait here." She drew a gauze curtain aside and dipped her head inside the shelter. "They've arrived, Mother Yuma."

"Excellent. Send them in," came a voice from inside the tent.

Turning back to us, Efrie said, "Please remove your weapons before entering the wikan."

Wikan? That was new.

Next to me, Adrianna stilled. "Our weapons?"

"You can't expect to meet their leader with swords in hand," Zeke said under his breath.

Adrianna's nostrils flared. I thought an argument might be imminent, but surprisingly, she gave her blade up to Efrie. The rest of us followed that example.

The four of us patted down our clothes, shaking them free from dust. I also took a moment to gulp down the last of the water. The tepid liquid flecked with sand almost choked me. I packed the canteen away, nose wrinkled in disgust.

Suitably prepared, our group went inside.

The tent's frame consisted of a latticework of wood held together by dyed rope. Four straight columns supported the crown of the shelter. A small hole in the roof provided a spot for light to flood in and smoke to escape. At present, the central wood-burning stove was cold, nothing but ash. But incense rose from lanterns dangling from the ribs of the ceiling. These fragranced the parched air with vanilla, sandalwood, and a spicy scent I couldn't label.

Taking shorter breaths to avoid sensory shock, I stopped before a low table. Next to this centerpiece stood a striking female. A leader, for sure.

Zeke swung his arm out toward us. "Mother Yuma, let me present Ena, Liora, and Adrianna."

Yuma's upturned eyes ran over us one by one.

I, in turn, studied her. Strong, dignified bones defined her face, and golden ink adorned her lip. Similarly, her earrings, septum ring, and the bands clipped into her neatly stitched, multicolored braids were gilded. The dress she wore draped to her feet in wine-red and copper folds. Yuma was a color wheel.

"I'm glad to see you've all arrived safely," she said, clasping her hands.

"You make it sound as if you were expecting us," Adrianna remarked.

"I was."

"Are you a seer?" Liora guessed.

Yuma's eyebrows knitted together. "Ezekiel, didn't you tell them what the Shyani are known for?"

"Apologies." He bowed his head. "It didn't seem important at the time."

"The Shyani are storyweavers," Yuma began, her voice sweeter than molasses. "A handful of us here receive visions of the past, and our community chronicle them in our embroideries and paintings. We also have bards and performers among us who take the stories out into the world and perform them so that others might learn about them." A polite smile. "Now that's out of the way with, please come—sit with me."

She gestured to the knee-height table with her ocher hued wing.

Zeke settled on my far left next to Adrianna. I placed myself in between my two friends. Yuma chose a spot opposite me, where she could face us.

We sat among sun-bleached cushions, tapestries, and blankets. They were crafted from wool, both in its fluffy form, and in its dyed, woven one.

"Efrie." Yuma's chin pointed to something beyond my wings, lining up with the wikan's opening. "Please bring food and strong coffee, emphasis on the strong."

"Yes, Mother."

I looked over my shoulder. Efrie was already striding away, leaving her post outside the tent.

"You know, I prefer a nice wine," Zeke said in such an easy way that I assumed a friendship must exist between them.

"No wine." Yuma smiled in his direction. "You must be sober if you are to join tonight's festivities."

"We're not here for festivities," Adrianna said, a bit spiky. I expected her patience had been worn thin by stress and exhaustion.

Zeke interceded, using a respectful tone. "We're here for Sefra, Yuma. We need to know where she is."

A nod, as if she'd expected that. "Sefra is several leagues north of here." Yuma focused on me. "I sent her a message via falcon a few hours ago. In it, I told her that I'd seen you flying across the Sickle Dunes. And given who you were with"—she motioned to Zeke—"I thought you might be coming here to find her. I've no doubt that once your sister receives my letter, she'll fly here as fast as her wings can carry her. If I'm correct, she should arrive in camp tomorrow."

My stomach catapulted out of my body. "You know she's my sister?"

"Sister," Zeke repeated, quietly questioning that.

I didn't respond.

"Sefra told me about you," Yuma continued, her topaz gaze centered on me. "And since I don't wish for there to be lies and half-truths between us, I must tell you—I know Archon is due to return. And I know you're the witch who can stop him."

I mentally stopped in my tracks.

"I've had visions of you for a long time," she added gently. "Not many. Just bits and pieces of what you've been through to get here."

Zeke made an incredulous noise. "This explains why so many people welcomed us when we walked through the camp." He eyed me. "I've been traveling with a future legend."

My neck stiffened. I hadn't earned such respect.

"Has your tribe been spreading stories about Ena?" Adrianna scowled at Yuma. "Because—"

Yuma held up a hand to stop her mid-flow. "We don't tell stories about Ena outside of our camp. We don't even use her name. If we refer to her, it is only as Light-Wielder or Alia Akaran in our tongue." She gestured around. "My tent is also protected from magical interference, so you can be reassured that our words will remain between us. The only tales my tribe spread about this business are those forewarning people about Archon's return." A sigh. "As it is, very few people believe us."

"We've heard Balor, the Light King, might've erased the memories from when Archon was around," Liora said. "Is that also true for everyone on the continent?"

"Yes," Yuma replied. "That is why it's so hard to convince anybody of the truth. Luckily, whatever Balor did, it couldn't stop the storyweavers from seeing the past."

"Mother Yuma, may we come in?"

"Yes, please do."

Twisting around, I watched Efrie and a shorter female enter the wikan. They each held a platter with pitchers of water, bowls of dates, and a steaming pot of coffee.

They placed the trays down on the table. Yuma's mahogany-bright cheeks shone as she smiled up at them. "You are dismissed for the day. Go, start tonight's celebrations a little early."

Their eyes lit up like firelights in a dark wood. Such glee. They thanked her and hurried out.

Yuma insisted on serving us herself.

At the request of my greedy belly, I started popping dates into my mouth. Once the corners of my gnawing hunger had eased, I sipped gratefully at a cup of coal-black coffee.

"You may want to withdraw your invitation to the festivities after you hear what I have to say." Zeke eyeballed Yuma, his gaze taking on a straight, serious quality. "Both Hasan's and Abraxus's people witnessed Ena using light magic. They'll be hunting for us."

Yuma threw me a look. A soft, "I see."

I lost my appetite for both food and drink.

"We're putting you in danger by being here," Zeke stated. "If you wish us gone—"

"You have long been a friend to this tribe. As has Sefra. The Shyani don't take such things lightly, and we certainly don't abandon our friends." Yuma was a lioness in that moment, fierce and proud. "We also wouldn't dare to refuse the Light-Wielder shelter from her foes. Our whole tribe would be damned to the darkest pits of hell for such a sin."

I was about to deny that, to reassure her when—

Too right, Zola said rather savagely.

You can't be serious?

Silence answered.

Yuma added, "That being said, I can't afford to underestimate Hasan and Abraxus. I'll send out extra scouts to watch the surrounding area, and I'll keep our warriors on high alert."

Zeke inclined his head out of respect.

"I need to leave soon," Yuma announced, cradling her cup of coffee. "I've still got to oversee the preparations for tonight. But before we part, I have an offer for you three." Her crooked smile was for me, Adrianna, and Liora. "Many moons ago, the Shyani rediscovered a spell to summon one's familiar. If you're interested in such a thing, I would cast the magic myself. There's no rush to make a decision, of course. You'll want some time to think it over."

Zola harked a laugh. *Things just get more and more interesting.*

Meaning? I prodded.

No response.

Adrianna led with, "I can't think it over when I don't know what familiars are."

"Same," I added.

Liora said to us, "They're animals that act as sort of companions or attendants for witches." Her gaze flitted to Yuma. "But they're not supposed to be real. I always thought they were just a children's story." In those last few words, her tone became a question mark.

Yuma set her tin cup down with a clink. "Forgive me, but aren't you a shifter?"

Loud silence.

"I saw a dragon when your group fled Casatana," Yuma told Liora. "I presumed you were the shifter, since the others in your party were visible to me—was I wrong?"

Her spring-greens turned stormy. "No, that was me."

"Then you aren't aware that your dragon is your familiar?" Yuma asked, her brow puckered.

Liora's face was shock personified.

Yuma shook her head and clicked her tongue. "Witches have an infuriating habit of hoarding knowledge, and this is the result of such greed." She gestured at Liora. "A youngling terrified of her own gifts."

Liora's mouth moved soundlessly. A few tries later, she found her voice. "Are you saying that I can turn into a familiar?"

"Not at all. Familiars aren't human or fae. They're powerful sprites that adopt the form of an animal. A demonstration, perhaps." Her head swiveled toward Zeke. She dipped her chin in a slight nod. A prompt.

He stuck two fingers into the corner of his mouth and whistled. It was a soft, warbling tune with short notes. A *tu-tu-twee.*

I gaped, slack-jawed, as a tiny creature appeared atop Zeke's shoulder.

"This is Kat."

His introduction had the bluebird fluffing up her wings and singing a sweet tune. "Stop showing off," Zeke scolded, but his tone wasn't firm. In fact, his voice was as soft as churned butter.

The bird hopped from his shoulder onto Adrianna's.

"Traitor." Zeke narrowed his eyes at Kat playfully.

Adrianna stared at the bird, her features bemused. Liora, however, was a shade below white at this point. "I don't understand. My dragon isn't separate from me. Are you sure it's a familiar?"

"Yes." Yuma's voice was low and kind, honey to the ears. "In the case of shifters, the witch's and the familiar's souls are like magnets, bringing them so close together that they fuse into a single body. They don't need the summoning spell. The rest of us, however, do. And our call often goes unanswered. As an example, only thirty pairings exist in our community, even though the entire camp—over three thousand—have attempted to bring forth a familiar."

"I thought being a shifter was an ability," Liora said, breathless, almost trembling. "I thought I was a monster because of how violent I could get. I ... my familiar killed somebody. I bound my magic because of it." Stiff-necked, she dug her nails into her palms, stretching the skin tight over the white bones of her knuckles. "I caged an animal for months."

She looked close to going over a cliff edge. I grabbed her knee, wanting to keep her grounded.

"The dragons of old were certainly fierce, but they were not mindless monsters," Yuma told her. "Was the person killed a danger to you or your loved ones?"

I said, "Yes," when Liora hesitated.

Yuma gave a sage nod. "Dragons are even more protective than fae. Without the ability to communicate with each other, your familiar would've sensed your fear and reacted to it in the only way it knew how, which for a powerful predator would be to eliminate the threat. The spell will give you the ability to talk to each other. That should help stop these misunderstandings between you." She eyed me and Adrianna. "Familiars summoned by a spell can also communicate with their witches, and others if they wish it."

I grappled with that information, wondering what it could mean for us in the future.

"But what is it that they do, exactly?" Adrianna glanced at the familiar on her shoulder. "I understand how a dragon could help a witch, but what can a tiny bird do for me?"

Kat chirped shrilly and vanished.

"You upset her," Zeke remarked in a droll tone.

"It's a fair question," she argued. "And what if I ended up with something even more useless, like a toad—how would that be helpful to me?"

A rib-tickling picture pushed to the forefront of my mind. That of a grumpy-faced Adrianna totting around a warty toad. I mashed my lips and forced down laughter. "It could be worse."

She fired back. "Could it? Could it, really?"

I faked an innocent tone. "You could get a flea. Or a dung beetle. Maybe a nice newt."

Adrianna rolled her eyes, smiling despite herself.

Yuma and Zeke laughed.

Liora remained mute, occupied by thoughts she didn't want to share. My heart twinged.

"I can't guarantee anything, Adrianna, but I've never known a familiar to be useless." Yuma went on. "Even now, my familiar is off delivering my message to Sefra."

Zeke added, "They also make amazing companions."

I mulled that over.

Yuma held up a hand. "But as I said, don't feel any pressure to decide now. I can give you until tomorrow—"

Liora blurted out, "I'll do it."

I blinked at her.

Yuma dipped her chin and studied Liora from under raised brows. "You don't want to think it over?"

"No." A show of resolve. "I can't ignore it when we're connected like this. And I won't keep trying to leash it when it's an independent being. The only thing left to do is develop some kind of relationship with the dragon. This might be my only chance to do that and understand it ... to understand my familiar." A conscious correction.

Yuma smiled, teeth gleaming in the smoke-and-dust light. "I can't pretend I'm not relieved. Over the years I've met too many unbonded shifters who misunderstand their power and live in fear of transformation. Some learn to suppress and control their familiar over time, but it only leads to exhaustion for the witch and resentment for the sprite."

Liora looked completely spent. Every notion I had for comforting her fell short of what I wished I could do, which was erase the pain and shock.

"Before I show you where you'll be sleeping tonight, I should mention that it's possible for somebody to share a familiar." Yuma concentrated on me and my brooding brow. "It would be very unusual. But there've been instances where a familiar chose two people because they shared close spiritual ties. Just something to keep in mind."

Ah.

Yuma stood. "If you'll follow me."

Our group rose from the soft floor. We collected our weapons from the rack positioned outside the entrance. Then we stepped in behind Yuma, who led us to two nearby shelters.

"This one is for you, Ezekiel." Yuma gestured to the smaller tent. "Ladies, you'll be in the larger wikan."

Zeke palmed his chest. Faking offense, he said, "You're keeping me separate? Don't you trust me, Yuma?"

Her lip curved up on one side. "I do. But your friends won't get a wink of sleep if they have to listen to your vicious snoring all night long."

That drew a good-natured laugh out of him.

Yuma pushed her shoulders back. "I hope you four will honor us by attending our summer festival. Our celebrations usually go on for three days, but tonight is when we share our stories. It is a special time for us, and if Ezekiel hasn't forgotten all of our traditions, perhaps he can show you how we do things here."

"It's only been two years since I last visited," he said, a touch exasperated. "My memory isn't that bad."

A challenging look. "It has been almost three, which you well know. Still, I shall forgive it." She patted his arm affectionately and then addressed all of us. "If you need to see to your bladders, there are covered pits set up on the outskirts of camp."

"Just follow the smell." Zeke smirked.

Yuma smacked him with the back of her hand. "They do not smell." She continued on. "I'll have my sons and daughters fetch water from the river before the sun sets. That way you might wash before the nighttime celebrations. Enjoy yourselves this evening. I shall join you at some point. I've a tale to share with you."

At that, she departed.

Adrianna marched straight into our wikan without a word to Zeke. Liora and I were left standing there with him, as awkward as hermits at a party.

"The festival officially starts at sundown. I'll see you then." He entered his shelter.

Liora met my eyes with a look that said *What is going on with those two?*

I shrugged my shoulders and wings.

We made for our wikan's canvas door.

Inside, the domed space had sparse furnishings: a firelight lantern, blankets stacked on top of a wooden trunk, and a low bed large enough for us to share.

As our feet trod over rugs adorned with pictures of animals and spoked wheels, we kicked up the scents of weary thread and miles of sandy roads.

I quickly covered my mouth and nose. *Achoo!*

Adrianna had already divested herself of sword, bag, headdress, and shoes.

Liora and I followed her example.

We relaxed on the bed. Sitting. Lying. Processing.

When the stale air seemed to suffocate, I fanned my face. "Gods, I miss Cai. Think about what an amazing breeze he'd conjure for us?"

Liora smiled, but it was tainted with sadness and worry.

I was loath to load their minds with more weight. But I had to relay what I'd learned earlier, or the details might scatter like autumn leaves, escaping me.

"Zeke told me something while we were flying here."

"Was it a warning about these storyweavers? About Yuma? About his damned bird? Because that might've been nice. Ass." Adrianna hit the pillow beneath her. Fluffing it. Viciously.

"No—nothing like that."

Adrianna freed a sulky huff.

I went all in. "Atlas was the one who exiled the Aldarians from Asitar. He planned it."

Their confusion prompted me to repeat Zeke's words as faithfully as I could.

Once done, Adrianna scowled. "I'd no clue that Atlas was involved in the exile. But then, hardly any records survived that period. I guess they were too busy with the fleeing to put much down on paper." Almost a scoff.

Liora's expression caught my attention. "What is it?"

Dragged from her reverie, she glanced up, startled. She sucked her bottom lip between her teeth. "I was thinking about Abraxus. About whether we could use the fact he wants Archon dead—"

A blast of arid air blew into our tent, making the doorway flutter.

The three of us froze like rabbits spotting a dog.

"What the hell was that?" I breathed, gripping the covers underneath me.

Had Archon somehow heard? That wasn't possible—was it?

Zola snorted a bit too loudly. *The gateway is closed and unless I'm mistaken, he can't see into your world. It was a breeze, nothing more.*

Liora wet her lips nervously. "Anyway, it was just an idea."

"What idea? You didn't even finish your thought?" Adrianna pointed out.

Liora avoided our gazes as she tucked her feet under her ass.

"You want to try talking to him?" I guessed, a strange feeling spreading through me. It was caution mixed with resignation. As if I'd reached a point of predestination. I wasn't surprised to find myself there, but I also wasn't keen on where I stood.

Her shoulders rose in an uncertain bump. "Maybe." Pitching her voice lower, she continued. "We need the starstone, right? And since Dain doesn't want us to fight, we're left with two options—we try to steal the stone from Abraxus, or we ask him for it."

Adrianna gawked at her. "You want to meet a dark god and ask him to give up something he killed to get his hands on?"

"Allegedly," Liora corrected. "We don't know if he actually killed—"

"Are you serious right now?" Adrianna asked, her brows snapping together.

Liora was unruffled, undeterred. "I'm aware it's a risk meeting with him. But if he wants Archon gone, then he's going to have to hand over the stone at some point."

"Yes," Adrianna interrupted, "but in the meantime he could kidnap Ena and force her to serve in his army."

"I know he's hunted light-wielders in the past, but Zeke said his warband has outlawed slavery. Perhaps he's changed," I said without much conviction.

Adrianna gave me a *don't-be-naive* look. "You'll find a lot of leaders only follow their own rules when it suits them."

"What if we could get him on his own?" Liora took a thinking pause before continuing. "He might listen to reason if we had Sefra with us and presented enough of a threat to him. And then Ena could repeat what Dain said."

"Like an ambush," I said.

A tilt of her head. "More like a negotiation ... with weapons."

Adrianna and I laughed lightly.

Zola growled out, *I know what Dain told you. But Abraxus is relentless in his pursuit of revenge. If you ask him for the stone, he'll realize who you are. And once he learns you're his way to end Archon, there's no telling what he'll do—*

Enough, Thea said.

I didn't think it was smart to ignore Zola. For speaking with Abraxus felt about as dangerous as tugging on a tiger's tail and trusting it wouldn't bite my hand off. Still, what other options were left to me? To steal from a dark god? I was no master thief.

Realizing I needed advice on what to do, I said, "I don't want to decide on anything until we meet Sefra and hear what she has to say. She's lived here so long, she might know something that could help us figure out what to do next."

Adrianna answered with a tiny nod.

Liora simply said, "Agreed."

Feeling burdened by the choices before us and heavy headed from baking in the sun all day, I lay down and slipped into slumber, Adrianna and Liora alongside me.

CHAPTER 21
A SLAVE'S REVENGE

Wilder bent over a sink and threw his guts up. I wanted to comfort him, to rub the spot between his wings. Impossible. I wasn't really here. My body remained in Asitar. Only my spirit, set free by dreamwalking, was with him.

He spit out the remainder of his bile and set the faucet running. Wilder straightened up to stare into the mirror overhanging the sink. His complexion was washed out, almost gray, and the skin underneath his eyes was dark and pinched.

I wanted to stay with him and figure out what was wrong. That wasn't to be. I woke to the sound of the settlement bustling with activity, the celebration imminent.

The dying sun created a patchwork of light upon our floor, and the lengthening shadows were as good as clock hands, urging me to wake the others and relay what I'd seen.

We talked in circles for a while. Adrianna ended that. "The simple fact is we don't know what's wrong with him. And we won't figure it out by sitting here, going over and over it."

That was what she said. Her expression told a different story. I suspected she was terrified that Wilder's out-of-character behavior had to do with his orders to invade the Riverlands. I prayed that wasn't the case.

From there, our trio ate in a rush, then set out to relieve our bladders.

Mission completed, we returned to our wikan to find someone had left stacked buckets, a canister of river water, olive-scented soap, and several thin towels.

Adrianna poured the river water into our makeshift standing baths, and when the three of us were undressed, we stepped into our individual buckets. As I scrubbed away the desert's harsh touch, Zeke called to us from outside our wikan. "Are you three ready?"

Adrianna refused to reply. Liora answered for us. "Almost done."

"Does that mean I'll be waiting minutes or hours?"

Adrianna glowered at the closed tent flap. "Why would it be hours?"

"I've noticed people say 'almost done' when they are nowhere near being so. And I can hear splashing. If you're in the middle of bathing, I should return to my wikan."

Bristling, Adrianna whipped out, "Do as you please. I'm in no rush to put my clothes on."

A half-groan, half-growl escaped Zeke. He sounded as if he'd been kicked in the nuts.

Cheeks hurting, I tried to contain my laughter.

Liora and I swapped a look. Big mistake.

Her shoulders shook. My wings trembled. Noises escaped both of us.

In the midst of this, the sound of Zeke's footsteps reached me. It seemed he was retreating.

Adrianna looked pleased, smug even.

I didn't understand their back and forth. They seemed to be circling each other's orbits, pushing each other's boundaries. To what end?

The rapidly cooling air pushed me to abandon the standing bath. I toweled myself off alongside Adrianna and Liora. Chilly, I pulled on the first fresh clothes I found in my rucksack. Those were cozy leggings and a high-necked shirt patterned with stars.

Thinking ahead, I dumped my old water out into Liora's tub.

"Err, Ena?"

I gestured to my empty bucket. "Throw your dirty clothes in there. Both of you. We may as well clean them while we've got the water."

Adrianna and Liora dumped their things in. I added mine.

I refreshed my tub with water from the canister.

Liora kneeled on my left. "What should I do?"

"I don't mind doing it. I've always found the action kind of soothing." I rubbed at the garments with soap and a firm hand. "Well, unless you're doing it for hours, then it stops being relaxing real quick."

"You've scrubbed clothes for hours?" Liora said, tone searching.

A double shrug. "My stepmother liked giving me piles of soiled clothes and the harshest soap she could find. She'd inspect my hands afterward and laugh at my 'washerwoman's hands.' The day one of my fingernails fell off, she said she'd put a salve on it and rubbed salt on it instead." Harsh laughter hiccuped out of me. "She really was crazy."

Thick silence reigned. I didn't dare look over at Liora as she plunged her hands into the tub. She massaged the garments in a tame, distracted fashion.

"You never said it was that bad," Adrianna remarked.

I peeked up on my right. Adrianna stood over me, a frown upon her brow.

"Well, it's over now." I wrung the suds out from my top. "Elain can't hurt me anymore."

Adrianna and Liora didn't push the conversation further. Without fuel, the topic died. Lather. Rinse. Repeat. That was what I did. And I ignored the knots of emotion in my body.

A few minutes later, our garments were hung up over the rafters to dry.

I donned dusty shoes and strapped on my sword belt. At this point, carrying a weapon was an ingrained response. Besides, our enemies wouldn't care that tonight was a celebration.

Readied, we ducked outside. A veil of lavender twilight greeted us.

Suspense and magic suffused the air. It was a feeling—a mood. As if the world was holding its breath. As if anything could happen.

"Zeke," Adrianna barked.

He stepped out of the neighboring shelter in a brown leather jacket, hardy trousers, and his weapons belt looped around his hips.

I saw Adrianna sneaking an appreciative look at him.

"This way," Zeke said as he stalked past us.

Our trio followed him. Fledglings after a mother goose.

Zeke stuck to a dirt path that wove between the shelters. The Shyani had gathered in groups, in whatever free space there was available. They sat or stood around elevated fire pits, taking turns telling stories. Some simply orated their tales while others acted them out, using magic, song, or puppets.

I caught more than a few individuals staring at me as we walked. Prickling with embarrassment, I resisted the urge to hide behind my wings.

Farther along, stalls sprung up on either side of the path.

Zeke slowed to a stop. "If you want food or drink, here's your chance."

I breathed in deeply, expanding my ribcage in all directions. Eyelids fluttering in bliss, I sighed out, "Is that hot chocolate?"

Zeke chuckled softly. "Refreshments are on me."

He dipped his hand into his trouser pocket.

Neck rigid, Adrianna said, "You don't have to do that."

"But we'd like you to," I blurted out.

Adrianna shot me a reproachful look. I pouted, rubbing my belly.

That got a roll of the eyes and a laugh out of her.

"What would you like?" Zeke asked, smiling.

Liora and I requested cups of chocolate heaven. Adrianna, coffee—no milk.

Zeke got our drinks and wine for himself. He bought almond pastries and date-filled cookies for snacks.

Loaded up, we traveled to the fringes of the encampment and arrived at the sandy riverbank.

I gazed up at the lopsided moon, loving the way it cast a silvery light over the landscape, making it gleam as brightly as newly polished cutlery.

Zeke forged ahead, guiding us to a free brazier not ten feet from the rushing river. "This'll do."

He dropped down onto one of several tattered cushions.

Angling my sword away from my body, I settled on Zeke's left. Liora quickly took the space available next to me.

Adrianna hesitated for a moment before sitting down on Zeke's right.

Our shared focal point was the smoldering fire. It kept the cool arms of evening at a distance and sweetened the air with the earthy tang of hay.

There, I engaged in the eating of cookies and the sipping of melted chocolate. Adrianna and Liora joined me in my indulgence.

Zeke fed our hungry fire scrub-grass from the basket provided. That caused the flames to complain. The hissing sounded like rain dashing against a window. That and the gurgling river noises were a massage to my ears.

"You might've already noticed, but the tradition here is to sit with friends and offer up a story. Who wants to go first?" Zeke's tiger eyes sparked. "How about you, princess?"

Adrianna let her feelings out in a growl.

Liora lazily batted away the curious moths hovering over her, possibly mistaking her strawberry, cherry, and copper strands of hair for tongues of flame. "I think you should, Zeke. You can show us how it's done."

"Good idea," I chimed in.

"All right," he said. "Let me think."

Adrianna pounced on his hesitation. "I want to hear how you became a thief and who you stole so much money from."

Liora and I swapped apprehensive looks.

"That's not a bad idea." Zeke raised his wine goblet to his lips. "I suppose you of all people deserve to hear it, since it involves your makena."

Adrianna slowly lifted her wings. That movement was akin to hearing a high-pitch blast in my ears. My wings snapped in closer to my spine as my fae-blood whispered that she might be about to attack him.

Zeke, meanwhile, sipped at his wine, playing at being nonchalant. Then he pretended to be distracted by an almond pastry. He was reaching for it when Adrianna smacked his hand away. "Stop being a dick."

A benign smirk. "You're far too easy to rile up, princess."

Adrianna's gaze cut away. "Get on with it."

That sobered Zeke.

"Fair warning. My story is grim." He placed his goblet on the copper-tinted sands. "There was a time when I was enslaved to Ba'zac, the Jewel King."

With a subtle twist of his fingers, an illusion flickered into being a few inches above the brazier. It appeared to be a pregnant female in silhouette. Her features weren't drawn in, but she stood tall with hair flowing down to her waist.

"When it became known my makena carried the child of a jinn, Ba'zac raided her village and took her as a prize."

Flaming chains grew out of the earth and latched onto the female's wrists. The shackles dragged her along behind a horse, still pregnant.

Zeke arranged his features into a wooden look. "He killed my makena after she gave birth to me. I was put in chains before I could speak and was used in every way you can imagine not soon after. Then, in the summer of my fiftieth year with him, Ba'zac took me to Mokara."

Fifty years? Horror flowed in, making a stone out of my heart.

Adrianna looked sick to her stomach. Her gaze glued itself to the ropey scar on his neck, the one I had guessed was made from being forced to wear a collar.

"There, we toured the nobles' houses," he said. "They indulged Ba'zac's every whim, and in return he gave them access to the best jewels in the world."

Dozens of fae appeared over the brazier. They feasted, smoked, and compared gems in a palace built among a sea of clouds. Half-naked dancers slunk around, performing but not respected; humans and wild animals stared at the bars of their cages; fire-eaters ate danger for a pittance.

"At one of these parties, I walked in on Diana being assaulted by a pus-bag calling himself a suitor."

I peered at Adrianna and soaked in her reaction. Her fingers were curled around her tin cup, her grip looking tight enough to snap a fae's neck.

"I pulled the male off her and we ran for it." Zeke stopped to nibble at a pastry. He continued, chewing as he spoke. "It wasn't long after that she sought me out and asked me to join her scheme to steal from the Jewel King."

Skepticism edged into Adrianna's voice. "*Her* scheme? Why would she rob Ba'zac?"

"Her kin had promised her hand in marriage to a wealthy Mokaran prince," Zeke said. "But she'd already fallen in love with the king of an Aldarian court."

"Isiah?" Adrianna eyed the spot where his illusions had appeared.

There was such a need in her expression. I thought she might be desperately hoping to see her father.

Zeke's wavy hair bounced as he nodded. "Diana wanted to elope with Isiah, but she needed money—a lot of it—to compensate her parents and stop a blood feud. And the Jewel King was rich enough to secure freedom for all of us."

"How did you do it, then? How did you steal from him?" Adrianna breathed, engrossed in the tale.

"I knew which port Ba'zac would sail out of to get back to Asitar," Zeke recollected. "At that point, I could've predicted his damned bowel movements."

He conjured a silly image of a male straining over a toilet.

None of us laughed.

Zeke stopped picking at his food and stared into the fire instead. He seemed lost inside his own story—his own head. "Isiah waited at the port with a ship luxurious and cheap enough to tempt Ba'zac into hiring it for his passage home. But for the rest of our plan to work, I needed to access my jinn abilities, which were controlled by Ba'zac through a spelled collar. Diana found and bribed a Mokaran witch to remove it."

His hand raised an inch, only for him to ball it up into a fist. I suspected he'd been about to touch his scarred neck.

"From there, I boarded Isiah's ship and acted as if nothing had changed." Zeke kept on, the words flowing out of him now. A river that couldn't be stopped. "Diana went too, stowing away below decks. On the first night of our voyage, I disguised myself as Ba'zac's personal servant. I slipped a sedative into his and his entourage's food. Once he'd fallen asleep, we imprisoned Ba'zac in the ship's hold. The guards were thrown overboard. And trust me, their deaths were kind given their crimes."

Zeke threw more fuel into the flames. Our communal fire leaped, casting him in an angry light. In a bloody darkness.

"We sailed to Ba'zac's palace." Zeke projected another illusion over the brazier. It looked like a jade-green castle built on a cliff. "I disguised myself to look like him. Then I met with his general and told him I'd discovered where Abraxus stored his wealth. I sent Ba'zac's entire army north with orders to seize it."

That was bold. Reckless, even.

"What happened to the army?" Adrianna's normally rich voice was reed-thin as she focused on the white heart of the fire.

"I sent their location to Abraxus's camp." Zeke stopped to drink deeply from his wine goblet. After wetting his throat, he continued. "I heard later that Ba'zac's soldiers surrendered and swore to fight for him instead."

"And Ba'zac?" Liora followed up.

"We chained him to his own dock and fed him poison." No regret. No mercy. Just a matter-of-fact tone. "My message to Abraxus included where the Jewel King would be if he wanted to take his head for himself." He created another illusion. This one was of a tall shadow bringing a sword down executioner-style upon a shackled male's head. "Abraxus claimed the victory and shouldered all the other kings' displeasure for it."

"As you'd planned," Liora guessed.

"As I'd hoped," he corrected. "Anyway, after the army left we looted what vaults we could open. We split the wealth amongst ourselves and with the palace slaves. Then I gave Diana and Isiah one half of the jinn mirror that Ba'zac had stashed away."

"Why?" Adrianna asked.

"They wanted a way to contact me in the future. And given what they'd done for me, I didn't mind being their eyes and ears on the continent. I funded Alhara with the money I'd stolen. And that was how I became a thief." *The end,* his abrupt silence implied.

I ate my fourth cookie and studied Adrianna from under lowered lashes. She fidgeted, crossed her legs into a different position, and did anything but look at Zeke.

"Someone else has to take a turn," Zeke said, leaning back on his hand and pulling his knee up to his chest.

Liora seized the proverbial sword. "I'll go next."

Her tale was about a young woman who could enter the bodies of woodland creatures. Within their skins she lived a carefree existence, until the day she met a young noble. For him, she gave up her power only to be betrayed and abandoned.

Liora's story didn't have a happy ending. It was a cautionary tale.

Adrianna still didn't seem keen to speak. Fine.

I drew in an inhale that shook around the edges. Then I spun them a tale that my mother, and later Viola, had told me. It was about a fisherman who discovered a mermaid washed up on the beach, injured and nearly dead. He nursed her in secret; the two fell for each other. They were separated by misfortunes and misunderstandings, but unlike Liora's story, mine ended happily when a sea goddess reunited the couple and revealed their union was fated.

Liora smiled when I was done. Zeke and Adrianna were silent, reflective. I had a feeling it was too romantic for their tastes, either that or they were distracted.

"Your turn, princess," Zeke said to Adrianna.

A sigh. "I'm not much of a storyteller."

"Then tell us something true," Zeke stated.

Adrianna frowned, considering.

The wait had my attention drifting. I stared up at the fire-kissed wings of insects and the smoke-blurred stars, tuning my fae-hearing into the other voices traveling along the scalp-tingling breeze: monsters, sword fights, and sky races were my companions.

"Before Morgan ruled in Aldar," Adrianna began, "there was a king who wanted to match me with his heir. Diana refused to agree to an arranged marriage since I was still too young, but she sent me to their court on occasion to keep the peace. I hated the idea that I might one day be made to marry somebody, so I acted out, anything to get the heir to hate me. But he just shrugged it off. I'd be a brat. He'd pull faces and tell awful jokes."

"That sounds like Cai growing up," Liora remarked.

"Growing up?" I quipped. "That's Cai now."

Liora's lively eyes darted to mine.

Our mouths quivered with close-lipped laughter. When we recovered, Liora said to Adrianna, "Sorry, I interrupted."

"It's fine." Adrianna went on in flat notes. "Anyway, one day the heir and I attended a ball. There was a group of young nobles who made some comments about my court. I came close to losing my temper, which wouldn't have reflected well on me. But then the heir showed up and chased the worthless worms off with a glare. He suggested we leave the party, and I was in such a foul mood that I went with him. We ended up spending hours racing up and down corridors, bashing each other with wooden swords. He became my friend that day. My only friend, truth be told."

"Was that the beginning of your love story?" Zeke remained expressionless, although I fancied his voice had gotten sharper. More clipped.

She huffed under her breath. "He was like my big brother. And I was only eleven at the time. He was seventeen."

"Who was the heir?" Liora asked, her tone making me think that she already suspected his identity.

I had in no way anticipated the answer to be, "Lynx Johana."

My jaw dropped. "You knew him? Why did you never say anything?"

"Because I was ashamed." Adrianna continued, her voice a noose growing tighter with every word. "A year after that ball he joined Morgan. When I heard what had happened, I wouldn't listen to a word against him. I defended him." A sneer bracketed her mouth. "Then when Morgan visited my court and brought Lynx with her, I snuck into his room. I told him that I was his friend. And that I knew he wouldn't serve Morgan willingly."

"What did Lynx say?" I asked.

Wings tight, she said, "He looked me dead in the eye, as I am with you, and he said he didn't need an annoying brat for a friend. That he'd been nice to me because his father had pressured him into it, and that I was never to speak to him again. And I didn't."

My heart ached for that younger version of Adrianna.

"Why did you choose to tell that story, Adi?" Liora said, her gaze keen.

"I've just been thinking about Lynx a lot lately. About what will happen if he's involved in the attack on the Riverlands. Mostly, I've been trying to figure out how to kill him before he hurts my people," she ended darkly.

Her violent thoughts unsettled me, although I couldn't have said why.

In the corner of my eye, I spotted movement. I glanced right to where Yuma strode toward us. Her cape-dress was dyed a marine blue and printed with golden words. The long sleeves had slits so she could move her arms free of them. Her head-wrap was a match for the dress.

"Enjoying the festival so far?" Yuma unfolded the collapsible chair she had brought with her.

We muttered assurances and exchanged pleasantries. But when Yuma sat upon her stool and peered down upon us, an expectant quiet fell.

By our toasty hub-fire, under the cold veil of night, she began. "I walk amongst you tonight to tell the Great Sorrow of Abraxus, or Abel as he was known in the beginning."

My pulse kicked up a notch hearing his name.

"Our story starts millennia ago, right here in Asitar, with the House of Lytir, famous for their light-wielders and warriors. That House had ruled over this land for generations. But at the time of the Court War, when the light and dark gods fought one another, Freyta Lytir was the reigning monarch."

The tiny hairs on my neck spiked. My great-grandmother had ruled over Asitar ... I suppose I understood why her son, Atlas, had established his own court here.

I directed my question inward. *Why didn't you tell me Freyta was once Queen of Asitar?*

Our mother doesn't have time to talk about when she ruled over some dusty mortal kingdom. She barely has time to eat breakfast. I mostly forgot about it.

Rutting Zola.

I quickly tuned back into Yuma's story.

"Freyta had two close friends: Desmi and Nyx who were, in their own right, powerful witches," Yuma said, using her whole body in her storytelling. "The three females were brave and fierce, and when they heard that Archon had marched his army into our world, they sailed to Aldar to fight against him. It was during this time that Desmi and Abel met each other."

The way she had said that ...

"They fell in love, didn't they? Abel and Desmi?" Liora guessed, her voice soft and curious.

A dark god in love with a fae? My mind buckled at that.

A dignified nod. "It took a while for them to admit their feelings. Years, actually. But eventually, Abel became a spy for the light court and their allies. When Archon discovered his son's deceit, it was said his anger shook the very earth. Archon cursed his son mid-battle and stripped him of much of his power. That was the first wound that father would deal to son."

The tale stilled on her lips. I couldn't tell if her pause was genuine or used for dramatic effect.

"That terrible war went on for twenty years. There was, however, some joy amidst the horror. Abel and Desmi had a daughter named Amara. Freyta and Balor married and had their own children."

Of which I was the best, Zola joked.

I stifled a groan.

"What about Nyx—what happened to her?" Liora asked.

"She went missing," Yuma said, and a cloud of gloom dropped over her features. "Freyta and Desmi searched and searched but could never find her. They feared she had died. The truth was far worse. Archon had captured Nyx, seduced and twisted her until she became his most loyal puppet—his Dark Queen."

Adrianna interrupted with a wave of her hand. "Wait. The Nyx in your story is *the* Nyx?"

My mind's eye received an image from one of my great-aunts. I saw a beautiful woman, her hair as black as nightshade berries and her eyes as cold as the space between stars. She seemed as lethal as a wolf with an empty belly.

"Indeed," Yuma answered ruefully. "Nyx turned up at the light court camp when Archon was weeks away from declaring defeat. She explained away her absence with lies and trickery. Then, when everyone was off their guard, Nyx slew Desmi in her own house."

The hitch in my intake of breath was shared by Liora.

Yuma pressed on. "But Abel's torment was not over. For after the death of his wife, he discovered his daughter had been taken into the dark court by Nyx on Archon's orders. Abel begged the light gods to help him go after her. But they refused."

Cracks spider-webbed across my heart. "Why?"

Yuma's hand went wide. "I can't say. I do not speak for the gods."

Thea answered me instead. *That would've been suicide for our family and for our allies. The dark court is a world of fire and ash, and home to countless evil creatures. Even the air is toxic. The only beings capable of surviving in such a place are those unfortunate enough to live there and know its horrors well.*

I was prevented from thinking up a response when Yuma finished with, "And that was my story. That was Abel's greatest sorrow."

Zeke shifted, stretching his spine and wings. "That certainly fills in a few gaps."

"How much of that had you heard before?" Adrianna asked.

"Not enough." A lacking response.

"I should move onto other groups and other stories." Yuma focused her attention on me. "Abraxus has a part to play in the war to come. And whether he sides with you or opposes you, it's to your benefit to know his history so that you might truly understand his motivations. That is why I told you about his past."

I fastened onto a strand of thought: had I learned anything that would make retrieving the starstone easier? And what about the moonstone?

"Do you know how I'm supposed to defeat Archon? D'you know about the stones? Have you seen where they are?" I asked, phrasing the question to conceal my knowledge of the sunstone and the waterstone.

"I know of them, but not of their locations." Yuma's forehead clustered with wrinkles. "I've tried for a long time to see where they ended up, for Sefra's sake as much as yours."

My tongue felt woolly. "Because she was looking for one of them?"

A nod. "Yes. A task that's put her in a great many dangerous situations. Many of which were made worse by the fact she was trying to hide her magic along the way, for fear of being hunted as a light-wielder. By the kings and by Abraxus."

He wasn't Abel anymore. Understandable. That person must've been a very different creature to the one that walked the earth today. A male without love or kin. A male consumed with revenge. I pitied him, I realized.

He's the reason Atlas is dead. He's—

Zola, be quiet.

I grimaced at the sisters' responses. I wasn't sure what I thought about Abraxus anymore, except for the fact he was complicated and confusing.

Yuma stood up and folded her chair. "I must move on. I'll perform the familiars' summoning in my wikan tomorrow morning for whomever wants it. Enjoy the rest of your evening, for it is young and so are you." A wink.

In a graceful gait, she moved on to another group up the riverbank.

"I'm not that young," Adrianna uttered under her breath.

"Don't take it personally. She calls anyone under five hundred young." Zeke picked up his goblet and rocked up onto his feet. "I'm exhausted. Are you three staying out?" He did a sort of hand shrug toward the honeycomb of shelters. "Or do you want to walk back together?"

"We're staying," Adrianna answered for us.

Zeke stuck a hand in his pocket. "All right, then. Night."

Off he went.

Adrianna eyeballed his retreating wings, longing slipping past her guarded expression.

"Adi, why don't you go walk with him?" Liora suggested. "You clearly want to."

"Don't read me," Adrianna warned, turning toward her.

"I wasn't," she replied, exasperated. "But it's obvious—"

"Keep your observations to yourself," Adrianna said, her eyes blazing like match flames.

Anger and irritation closed in on me. "Seriously? When have you ever kept your observations about us to yourself? We care about you, Adi. Let us care."

Adrianna's wide mouth compressed slightly. I braced myself for an argument. All I got was a frustrated sigh. "He's confusing me."

"Is he?" Liora questioned. "Or are you confused about how you feel about him?"

Adrianna held our gazes reluctantly. "Both."

Feet tingling from lack of movement, I said, "Could we walk and talk? My legs are falling asleep."

"Let's just head back to the tent," Adrianna groused. "There's nothing else to say except maybe that males suck and if I didn't like dick, I'd marry one of you and have done with it."

A cawing laugh broke from me. "No thanks."

Her eyes took on a tapered shape, as if she was contemplating taking a bite out of me. "What—aren't I pretty enough for you?"

"It's not you. It's me." I palmed my chest. "I'm not worthy of such beauty."

A snort. "Bitch."

Liora popped up. "As much as I'm flattered to be considered, you should probably stick to dick. Women can be just as confusing and frustrating as men."

I stood up. "We're doomed, then?"

A sober nod. "Yep."

We shared a morbid laugh.

Our trio gathered what we'd brought and returned our tableware to the food stalls. Luckily, Adrianna picked up Zeke's scent even among so many people, and we made it to the wikan without getting lost.

None of us felt compelled to stay up. The day was done, and we with it.

We changed into our nightwear, tucked ourselves in, and waited for oblivion. Adrianna and Liora found their slumber, if their deepening inhales were anything to go by. But with the ongoing festivities, I had to work on ignoring the voices coming from neighboring shelters.

I focused on Frazer. On Cai. On Wilder. I prayed that I could dreamwalk again. That I could see the people I missed most. Finally, I entered my dreamscape.

Time ended. Space expanded. I flew through a heron-blue sky, searching, searching, searching for loved ones.

A shadow flashed in my periphery. I turned to catch it, but it was already gone. An urgent whisper rode the wind. *Find me, elämayen.*

I couldn't make out the tone of voice at all. I tried, but it was like attempting to hold fast to running water.

"Where are you?" I asked my mate.

The rest was hollow silence.

CHAPTER 22

THREE SISTERS

I straddled the earthly plain. Not asleep. Not awake. Somewhere in between. But the early stirrings of life in the camp soon proved as effective as a crowing rooster in my ear.

Sleep shattered, a dim light collected behind my eyelids. I pried back that thin veil and our tent took shape. Everything was cast in the gray cloak of early dawn. But outside, an everyday rhythm was already humming away. I grounded myself in cook-fire smoke, hot onions sizzling in pan-oil, black coffee, yeast, and voices hoarse from overuse.

Beyond that, I sensed color returning to the land. The warming of sand and rock, a freshness brought on by a dewy moisture in the air, an anticipation that couldn't be defined.

I reflected on last night's successes and failures. Thanks to Zola and Thea's teachings, I'd mastered a bubble shield that protected me and others from all sides. But I hadn't dreamwalked. I hadn't seen my brother. And so today would be another day spent wondering if he was safe, wondering if he was mastering his moonlight. I had heard my mate, though—hadn't I? He'd asked me to find him. How could I even go about doing that?

Zola suddenly attacked my mind, testing my defenses.

Claws. Claws inside my mind.

The respite that I'd gotten at Alhara was well and truly over with.

She shredded through my defenses as if my mental walls were made of wet paper.

I endured her brutal blows as best I could.

Eventually, her mind-daggers withdrew.

I turned over onto my side. Head hanging off the bed, I sucked in deep breaths and tried to control my gag reflex.

When the dizziness abated, I rolled over onto my wings. Staying in that position, I watched the morning spread over our canopy like frosting over a steaming cake.

A need for an anchor, for something familiar, niggled at me. I reached for my waterstone, clutching it in my damp palm. Its smooth roundness and gentle coolness comforted me enough that I could sink into my body's sentience. I unclenched, muscle by muscle, relaxing my weight into the mattress.

Breathing back to normal, I sat up and glanced left.

Liora was curled up in the middle of the bed like a shrimp. The apple-red halo of her hair had somehow escaped her plait and spilled over her pillow onto mine.

Adrianna was on the far side of the bed, frowning in her sleep. An idea nudged my lips up.

I stood up on the coarse rug, skirted the bed, and toe-walked over to Adrianna. The plan was to pounce on her, to rock her awake as she had so often done to me.

I leaned over and reached—

Adrianna's hand snapped out and caught my wrist midair. "Don't even think about it."

"Come on, lazy slug." I jostled her hip with my other hand. "Get up."

Eyes shut, Adrianna stuck her tongue out.

"You're the least princess-y princess I've ever known."

"I'm the only one you know," she grumbled, releasing my wrist.

"I've read books."

She snorted. Then I knee-climbed over Adrianna, causing her to curse me out. As I edged myself in between my two friends, I adopted a singsong pitch. "Liora?"

One eye opened. "Have you been possessed?"

"Not that I know of."

One eye closed.

"Fine." I heaved a dramatic sigh and crawled off the bed.

Set on changing, I dug through my rucksack.

I wasn't satisfied with a single garment. I chose one thing only to toss it aside and restart the whole process. Engrossed in that, I didn't notice Liora watching me until she said, "Do you need some help?"

I turned sheepish. "Maybe. I'm not sure what's gotten into me."

"Could it be that you're excited to meet your sister?"

A waterfall of emotion crashed over my head. Amidst discussions of familiars, gods, and storyweavers, such thoughts had tarried at the corners of my mind. Until now.

Swaying, I dropped down onto the mattress. "Yeah. I guess I am."

"Then why do you sound as if you're attending a death ceremony?" Adrianna remarked.

"I don't know anything about Sefra, other than she used to be a queen and is apparently a genius witch-inventor," I said with a flat stare.

"And?" Adrianna queried. Simultaneously, Liora said, "Ah."

My focus glued to Liora. "It's not just that she's intimidating—what if she blames me for our mother's death?"

That was hard to get out.

Adrianna went the dismissive route. "Why would she? You didn't kill her. Some awful disease did."

"I know that."

"Do you?"

"Yes." And I did. "Sandrine showed me one of her memories of Dain and Mama. And after seeing the way she looked at him ... I know she would've stayed and died with him if she hadn't been pregnant. I couldn't have saved her by not being born. And if she hadn't put my safety first, I never would've gotten to know her." Thick-tongued, I added, "Sefra might not see it that way, though."

"If your sister blames you, that says more about her than it does about you," Liora declared.

Adrianna grunted her agreement. Their support bolstered me; I managed to pick out something to wear.

After that, Adrianna, Liora, and I started breakfast. I had my cheeks stuffed with candied fruit like a squirrel mid-autumn when Liora brought up *the* question. "Have you two decided if you'll try summoning a familiar?"

"I'm going to," Adrianna declared, brushing biscuit crumbs off her lap.

I swallowed the fruity pulp with a gulp of water from my canteen. "I'll come to the summoning because I want to talk to Yuma about it. But I'm leaning toward not doing it."

"Why?" Adrianna asked, beginning her venyetä practice.

"Because of Frazer. If there's a chance he'd share my familiar, it feels wrong to do the spell without talking to him first."

Adrianna bent at the hips and laid her palms on the ground. In her forward fold, she said, "He would agree to anything that helped you."

"That doesn't make it right."

Her lack of a response didn't feel like agreement. More like acceptance.

My attention snagged on Liora, on her frown and anxious eyes. "What is it?"

"Nothing," she said, her voice muffled, her hand hovering over her mouthful of peanuts.

The look on her face ... "Really?"

Quieter than a field mouse, Liora admitted, "I'm just worried what my familiar's going to say to me. What if it hates me? I did shove it into a cage."

"You didn't know what you were doing." I scrambled for the right words. "And once you can speak to your dragon, you can explain everything."

That fell woefully short of comfort. Liora still conjured up a grateful smile.

A minute or two later Liora and I finished breakfast. Adrianna, meanwhile, segued into another routine she'd set herself—a magical practice that involved levitating swords around the room.

Liora and I gave her a wide berth while performing our own venyetä practice. We persevered to the end of our routine, enduring the wikan's rise in temperature.

Adrianna was the last of us to quit. When she did, she copied us and wiped the dampness from her limbs with a towel. Then, after chugging water, she propped a fist on her hip and said, "So, should we go find Yuma?"

"Isn't it a bit early to ask for an audience with her?" Liora voiced.

Adrianna quick-marched up to the canvas door. "Yuma said to come in the morning"—she pulled back the scrap of material—"and it's morning."

I viewed a sky streaked in shades of peach—the pit and the flesh.

"Let's go," Adrianna said, making it sound like a command.

Leaving the shelter, we walked the short distance to Yuma's tent. Efrie, the guard from yesterday, met us with a head bow. "Is Mother Yuma available?" Liora asked.

"Come in," Yuma called out from the depths of her wikan.

Efrie moved aside and our trio ducked inside the domed shelter. The furniture had been rearranged, clearing the way for an unlit fire pit and a pile of blankets to take center stage.

"Has anything been seen of Abraxus's or Hasan's forces?" Adrianna asked Yuma.

I tensed in anticipation of the answer.

"If they had, I'd have called for an evacuation." Yuma spread her arms out in a welcoming gesture. "Sit with me."

Kneeling, she adjusted the gauzy folds of her white dress: a simple garment that had a cinched-in waist and sleeves that fell to the floor.

Adrianna, Liora, and I settled around the fire pit like points on a compass. Yuma was our north, our guiding star. I sat in the south. Adrianna east. Liora west.

"Liora, I have your answer." Yuma looked to me and then to Adrianna. "What about you two? Will you try the spell?"

Adrianna relayed her choice, her agreement.

Yuma faced me. Waiting.

I collected my thoughts. "Are familiars with us for life?"

"They are," she replied. "But if they get injured, they enter a dormant state until they've regained their strength. A kind of hibernation, if you will."

Hearing that decided me. "Then, I don't want to do it. I think there's a decent chance I might share a familiar, and I don't feel comfortable making that choice for him. I've no idea how he'd feel about living with one for the rest of our lives."

Yuma lifted a cushion. From underneath, she drew out a palm-sized notebook and tore out a page. "These are the instructions for the spell. That way, you can perform the summoning later if you wish." She handed the sheet of parchment to Liora. "You might also find an opportunity to help other shifters with it."

Liora passed the spell on to me for safekeeping. I tucked the page into the pocket of my high-waisted trousers.

Yuma picked up the box from beside her. Unhinging it, she plucked a match out of its depths and flicked it against the box's strike-paper. The resulting flame was lowered into the pit. There, it caught the herbs stacked amongst the kindling and a fragrant blaze was born.

When the fire burned strong, Yuma spoke again. "Before we start, I should tell you that the spell will create a likeness of your familiar." She dragged the hem of her dress up, showing us the black outline of a falcon on her thigh. "Is that a problem for either of you?"

Adrianna and Liora chorused, "No."

Yuma sat back on her heels. "Any more questions before we start?"

"Will it hurt?" Liora asked.

"It stings a little when the mark is formed, but the pain soon goes."

Open silence. No one disturbed it.

"Lie down and relax," Yuma told them in a dulcet timbre. "Ena, you may do as you choose, only don't interrupt."

I settled in to watch.

Liora and Adrianna reclined on the animal print blankets.

Amidst drowsy-making perfumes, Yuma clapped and chanted. The language she used was foreign to me, but her rhythmic way of speaking spun a spell. Mesmerizing. Soporific. Unearthly.

Adrianna and Liora dozed off.

Untethered, I slipped in-out, in-out, in-out.

Darkness and light.

Knowing and nothing.

Reality and fantasy.

Animal calls of every kind sounded inside of my head. One among them sent a shiver bolting up my spine, although I couldn't pinpoint which call had caused it.

All other noises fled before a tremendous *roar*! That snapped me out of my reverie. Adrianna and Liora twitched in their reposed states.

Yuma's chanting quieted. Then stopped. She raised her hands toward my friends, spreading her fingers out like a ring of mushrooms. "Awaken."

She clapped loudly.

Liora sat bolt upright, gasping as if she were air-starved.

I dashed to her side.

Grimacing, Liora pulled off her mint-green top and sat in only her bra. Before our eyes, the image of a poppy-red dragon materialized on her right side. The wavy lines of its lithe body extended from her ribs to the top of her hip; the color looked flat but when the light hit, the ink glinted as brightly as her dragon's scales.

Anxious, I scanned the flush that mottled her cheeks. "Does it hurt?"

"Yes. It's passing though."

She looked up at me. I inched back, my head sinking into my shoulders. "Li ... you've got a golden ring around your pupils."

Liora blinked several times. That was her only response.

I'd no notion of Adrianna awakening until she said, "I don't feel any different."

"It would seem you don't have a familiar, Adrianna," Yuma informed kindly.

"Oh." A nondescript tone.

I turned my head sideways, glancing at her. "Are you disappointed?"

Her heavy frown lightened. "No. Not really. It's probably for the best. I've never been very good at taking care of things."

That was that. She really didn't seem bothered.

Yuma killed the fire with the bucket of sand she had on hand. She bustled around wafting a hand fan, clearing the air of lazy smoke.

Looking rattled, Liora attempted to put her top on the wrong way and ended up with her head in an arm hole. I readjusted the shirt until she could pull it on herself.

"Can you hear your familiar?" Adrianna asked Liora.

"No. Maybe it doesn't want to talk to me—"

My name is Isolde, not "it."

My mouth popped open upon hearing that haughty rebuke. Stricken-faced, Liora said, "Isolde ... Her name—"

"I know," I said. "I heard her."

"Me too." Adrianna tucked her toned legs underneath her.

"Isolde is a beautiful name," Yuma remarked as she drew aside the wikan's flap, hooking it onto the canvas.

I twisted, glancing outside. Ten feet or so away stood Zeke. His back was to us, and his wings were pointed toward the sky. The golden sunlight glinted off his bronze scales, making them look like coins in a fountain.

He turned to face us. "Is the ritual done? May I enter?"

Yuma swept her hand out, inviting him inside. Kat, Zeke's familiar, swooped into the shelter first.

Chirping happily, the bluebird landed on Adrianna's head.

I pressed my fingers to my lip, hiding a smile.

"Remove yourself," Adrianna told Kat sternly.

Zeke bared his teeth in a grin. "She just wants to say hello."

Adrianna said, "Hello, Kat," even as she tried to shoo the bluebird off. When that proved a failure, she added, "Why in the seven seas would she call herself Kat, anyway? She does know she's a bird, right?"

"She chose it to mock the predators that hunt her." His mouth hooked up into a tiny half-smile, giving him a sly air. "So, what happened during the summoning? Do you and Ena have familiars?"

"I don't have one. And Ena decided not to do the spell. But if you want to meet a dragon, you can say hello to Isolde over there." She extended an open hand in Liora's direction.

Expression serious, Zeke faced Liora. "It's nice to meet you properly, Isolde. Thank you for what you did for us in Casatana. Without you, we'd never have escaped."

Liora's forehead puckered, but not in anger. In bemusement. "That made her very smug."

Zeke chuffed.

"I'm afraid I need my wikan for other business," Yuma said pointedly.

Our trio got off the floor.

"Do you know when Sefra might be arriving?" I asked Yuma, stomach hopping.

A maternal smile. "In the evening, I imagine. In the meantime, I hope you can enjoy the second night of our festival. Tonight is when we dance and sing." Her smile expanded into a youthful beam.

Zeke led the three of us out. We halted outside the wikan, and the air grew leaden with unspoken words. Adrianna and Zeke couldn't seem to look at each other, but they weren't thinking of excuses to part either.

Liora broke the standoff. "Zeke, do you want to come back to our tent?"

"Sure," he said, stuffing his hands in his pockets.

Adrianna glared daggers at Liora. That scowl was at odds with the cute bluebird on her head. I buried my laughter and tucked the memory away to show Frazer one day. Our group walked to our wikan.

We spent the morning and the better part of the afternoon sprawled out on rugs beside the bed, talking about this and that. It was awkward with Zeke until it wasn't. The food and wine we'd procured from a door-to-door seller certainly helped the conversation flow better. Although, Adrianna and Zeke shied from ever mentioning the past or the future. Too painful, perhaps.

As the almost unbearable heat of midafternoon steamed our wikan, a stranger's voice sounded outside. "Hello in there? May I come in?"

"Yes, come in," Liora said by way of a greeting.

A female with wiry silver hair swept aside our wikan's door. She hovered in the frame of the entranceway. "Forgive the intrusion. I've come to invite you to one of our communal wikans. It's a tradition for our people to gather before the official celebrations begin. I thought you might want to join us."

Adrianna was all caution. "Can we take our weapons?"

The elder's eyebrows climbed up to the rafters. "Of course. Most of our people walk around armed. We also have racks in the wikans if you want to leave them in there when the dancing begins."

"I definitely want to go." Liora glanced at me. "What do you think?"

"Sure." I stood and extended a hand down to Liora. "We could use some fun."

She took my hand and I pulled her up.

"I'll walk over and check it out with you," Adrianna said, standing. "But then I want to come back here and train some more."

I felt a twinge of sadness at that.

"Lead the way," Zeke said to the elder.

Adrianna, Liora, and I grabbed our swords on the way out.

It wasn't long before we arrived at a large area of open space, in the center of which was a stack of wood taller than me. A bonfire waiting for a match. Several pavilions had been erected on the fringes of this clearing. Tracks in the auburn earth suggested this layout was only recently assembled.

The elder guided us toward the wooden pavilion on the left. Stepping up onto a patio, she pulled aside a gossamer curtain and walked under an awning.

The four of us followed her. Inside, hanging fans whipped up a spelled breeze, lessening the heat considerably. Thank the gods.

Hundreds of females and dozens of males relaxed on the floor. Refreshments, books, and grooming implements circulated among them.

"What do you think?" the elder asked.

"I've never seen anything like it," I said honestly.

The elder smiled widely at me, assuming that was a compliment. I'm not sure if it was or wasn't.

"I'm going to explore. I could do with stretching my legs." Zeke not-so-covertly checked out Adrianna's reaction. "I'll see you later, then," he said, as if offering her something.

"Bye," she said without looking at him.

He walked out, disappearing behind the curtain.

When his footsteps faded, Adrianna released a shuddering exhale. I suspected she'd been holding her breath. "I came. I saw. Now I'm leaving."

"You're sure?" I said, wondering if I could coax her.

"Yes." A resolute tilt of the chin. "I want to practice my magic when I don't have to worry about impaling one of you."

A thin line formed between Liora's brows. "Were you worried about that?"

"You're a healer." Adrianna lifted her shoulder. "You could've fixed any damage."

"I can't heal severed limbs," she argued.

"All the more reason for me to train when you're not with me." Adrianna sucked in a shaky breath. "The Riverlands is about to be invaded. I tried to forget that for a while. To think of anything else. But I can't ... I need to *do* something. I'll find you later on."

She turned on her heel and left without a backward glance.

Liora and I exchanged heavy looks.

"Please sit wherever you'd like," said the elder guide.

We thanked her and moved off. I led the way over to an unoccupied patch of cushioned floor. There was a weapons rack nearby. We hung our swords there and settled in amidst the knots of people.

For the next few hours, the groups surrounding us shared aromatic tea, cardamom coffee, and a wide variety of snacks with us. A few people who spoke the common tongue entertained me and Liora with the odd story, but for the most part, the Shyani gave us privacy and maintained a respectful distance.

By early evening, many of the Shyani had taken to napping or sunning their wings on the patio outside. Others were beautifying themselves and their companions. There was even a piercer who had set up in a corner of the pavilion.

"D'you want to get a piercing?" Liora asked, tracking my gaze.

Temptation tickled me. "Maybe one day. Just not today."

Not when the piercer might not understand the common tongue; a language barrier wasn't ideal when asking somebody to jab needles through your skin.

I looked at Liora. "What about you? Do you want to get something done?"

She shook her head. "Isolde isn't keen on the idea."

"Why not?"

Her eyes unfocused, tuning into that inner voice, perhaps. "Because she doesn't know what would happen when I shifted."

Isolde's husky voice reached me. *I'm loath to say it because gold suits our coloring, but the jewelry would likely fall off during every transformation. Or worse, I'd swallow it and Liora would have to pass the metal. From what I know of human behinds, that would be rather painful for her.*

A startled laugh escaped me. "She's nothing like I thought she'd be."

"No, she's not." Liora's heart-shaped face fell. Guilt and relief were written over the same page—the same expression.

Noticing my searching gaze, Liora avoided my eyes. She didn't want to talk about it. And I wouldn't push her.

I looked through one of the baskets of cosmetics shared among the different groups in the pavilion. I'd never applied makeup before, and so many options stuffed my head full of fog and feathers. "I wonder why they've got so much makeup?" I said more to myself than anybody else.

"We've got our own company of actors," said a brunette sitting nearby. "We create the cosmetics for use on the stage, and there's always more than enough to go around."

Liora asked a follow-up question about the acting group.

It was at that point Adrianna appeared in the pavilion, sword in hand. She set her sheathed weapon on the same rack as ours.

Adrianna sat beside me, one leg on top of the other. She smelled of soap, and her coal-black hair tumbled to her waist like textured seaweed oscillating under the sea.

"Are you okay?" I asked her softly.

Liora watched her, also interested in her answer.

Adrianna's lips thinned. "You're both looking at me as if I'm about to die. Stop it. It's annoying. I'm fine. The Riverlands will be fine." Such a determined tone as though she thought her will alone could make it so.

For her, I changed the subject and faked casualness. "Are you done with your training?"

She nodded while rifling through a basket of cosmetics. "I didn't want to stop, but I'm not stupid enough to keep using magic when I'm close to being drained."

A pointed jab at me.

"Have you made any progress?" I asked, keeping things light.

Adrianna picked up a kohl pencil and faced me. "Look up."

My eyes widened. "Why?"

Adrianna held the pencil up threateningly. "Because I'm going to stick this up your nose."

"What?" I recoiled.

Adrianna loosed a faint laugh. "I'm joking, thick head." She rose onto her knees and leaned in. "Be quiet and hold still."

"Are you really going to do my makeup?"

"Obviously," she said, gripping my chin.

I narrowed my gaze, eyeing her suspiciously. "You're just doing this to shut me up, aren't you?"

"Shush," was the answer.

Wanting to leave this place with my eyeballs intact, I stilled.

The minutes skipped by, and my tailbone started to ache from inactivity.

"You're done." Adrianna sat back, giving me an appraising look.

Liora handed me the pocket mirror she had used to apply the shimmer to her eyes and the deep-pink tint to her lip.

I stared into the looking glass. That sneaky fox. Adrianna had turned out to be a deft hand at cosmetics. I had a groomed brow. A smoky eye. A dash of color on my lips.

"Thank you," I murmured, feeling oddly emotional.

Adrianna didn't acknowledge that. She focused on eating bits of this and that, mostly dates which she popped into her mouth two at a time.

I went on to manipulate my hair into tidy twin braids. Liora had just finished sweeping her curls into a tight bun, tying it up with a green tie that she'd found, when two faelings practically skipped into the pavilion, chattering away in their native tongue.

"What's going on?" I said to nobody in particular.

A grinning female in the next group over answered me. "The bonfire's about to be lit."

Everyone stood and ambled outside. Nobody grabbed their weapons upon exiting. So we didn't either.

We followed the herd out into the open-spaced square. People streamed out of the surrounding pavilions, stepping out under a sky that reminded me of summer lilacs and a string of bluebells in a meadow. Faint stars were already glittering, courting the early-rising moon as the evening darkness gathered around.

"Should we try to find Zeke?" Liora's suggestion halted our steps.

"No need." Adrianna pointed her chin straight ahead. "He's there."

Her eye line helped me locate Zeke. He was across the square, strolling toward the unlit bonfire.

"Why don't we get closer to the fire?" I suggested.

"Good idea," Liora added.

I moved through the mass of people. Liora trod in my footsteps. Adrianna, too.

The Shyani cleared a path for us. I mumbled my thanks as I walked past.

We arrived at the front of the crowd. Zeke stood opposite us on the other side of the ring we'd created around the pyre. His eyes landed on Adrianna. They lingered for a moment before his gaze moved on, sweeping the crowd.

I side-peeked at Adrianna. She stared at the tower of wood, her face fixed, blank with apparent disinterest. I suspected this was forced by the tension gripping her neck, wings, and shoulders.

Movement stirred to our right. The Shyani were giving way to someone, as they had to us. From out of the throng, Yuma appeared in a sapphire-blue dress with a plunging V-neckline and a belt of braided silver thread.

She stopped in front of the pyre. "This is our midsummer," she cried out, splaying wings and arms.

Cheers erupted. I stuffed my fingers in my ear holes.

Yuma waved, wordlessly calling for silence.

Quiet pressed in.

Yuma surveyed the sea of faces in a stoic manner. "Our tribe have always been wanderers. We take root wherever we settle and scatter our tales as the desert dandelion dusts its seeds." She paused for a moment. "When our task is done, we move on to wherever the four winds take us. We claim no country—no land—as our own. The world is our home, and when it suffers, so do we. In the coming months, when the darkness threatens, I hope that we, as a tribe, can remember that."

Surveying the crowd, I saw nods, tears, and frowns.

Yuma's gaze pinned me. "To the one we've named Alia Akaran, I would ask that you do me the honor of igniting our hearth-fire and renewing the life's blood of our tribe."

Shock rippled outward. I heard it in the tiny gasps. I saw it in the open mouths and wide-eyed glances.

Lighting their hearth was obviously a big honor. Rutting hell. Why, *oh why* hadn't I inherited my brother's ability to become invisible?

Liora's elbow nudged me discreetly.

Right. I strode forward and planted myself before the tower of kindling. Countless eyes were on me, but nobody offered me matches or a lit torch.

Zola squawked a laugh. *Don't be dense. Light it with sunlight.*

A hot flush of nerves rankled me. The sunstone might trigger. What then?

Hold fast to the waterstone. Let it anchor you.

Thea's advice steadied me.

I loosened my wrists, shaking my hands out. I'd performed under pressure before. As a human, I'd fought fae in front of an audience. As a fae, I'd broken Liora's bonds while pursued by the Meriden. If I'd done that, I could do this.

With barely a thought or a plea, sunlight fired through my veins.

I drew a circle in the air. Steady. *Steady.*

Aiming for the seven-foot cone of ironwood, I struck outward. The bonfire blazed up something fierce. Pure-white embers escaped the crown, spiraling up, up, up. As if those sparks were off to make new constellations in the smoke-smudged sky above.

I heard crickets ...

The Shyani erupted in claps and cheers.

I had a moment to feel relief before the sunstone woke up.

Stress walloped my heart as its magic pushed to be let out, to be used. Palms sweating, I reeled in the waterstone's cooling essence.

I heard a *hiss* in my head. Then my sunlight went off to sulk in some remote corner of my soul.

Wings sagging, I released a weighted exhale.

Yuma clapped her hands once for quiet, then she raised her palms. "Go! Enjoy yourselves!"

The crowd dispersed. Some wandered off to parts unknown, but many moved downwind of the bonfire, assembling in front of a pavilion that was being set up as a stage.

Yuma and I were joined by Adrianna, Liora, and Zeke.

"Interesting speech, Yuma," Zeke murmured.

Fine lines branched over her face. "Indeed. But tonight is not for fearing the future. It is for embracing the present."

Smiling, she left us to walk among her people.

Prolonged silence. That was shattered when Adrianna confronted Zeke. "What are you staring at me for?"

He opened his mouth, then closed it. "You look nice," was all he said.

"Oh." Adrianna broke eye contact first.

"Shall we move away from the fire?" Liora suggested.

The heat was getting a bit much. Our small group moved to follow the crowd. We ended up with our backs to the bonfire and our attentions fixed on the musicians. A foot-tapping song started up.

"Want to dance?" Liora's bright gaze skipped between me and Adrianna.

I was thrown into the past, to when Elain mocked me and the other children shunned me during the festival dances. I wished such moments had died alongside my human body. Yet they haunted me still.

Our ghosts only hold as much power as we give them, Thea whispered.

I sucked in a strengthening inhale. "I'm in. Adi?"

A curt nod. "Let's go."

"Really?"

"I want to forget that everything's falling apart. At least for a few hours."

She marched off. My heart fell a few inches.

Zeke watched her leave with an intensity that could've rivaled my brother's. Was this what it was to be mated? An emotional mess?

Liora grabbed my hand. Linked up, we sliced through the heaving crowd of merrymakers. We joined Adrianna near the front of the stage.

"I wish Cai was here," Liora half-shouted.

I refrained from rubbing my ears at the noise levels.

"He'd love this," Liora added, leaning in. "You've never seen him dance, but he tends to lose control of his limbs when he does. People have to stand back ten feet just to avoid getting injured."

I burst out laughing at the visual. That swiftly segued into a vicious tug on my heartstrings as I thought about the guys. I imagined that Frazer was with me for a moment. I knew exactly what he would be doing. He'd be standing on the outskirts of the crowd, refusing to dance, silently taking it all in.

The musicians transitioned into a faster, more up-tempo song.

Adrianna moved, flowing from one pose to another, interpreting the melody with her arms and shimmying hips.

Liora threw herself into the music and the movement.

The feral beats got inside of me. Under their influence, I let my body take me where it wanted to go. I became a sensual and wild thing. And unlike in the Gauntlet, I didn't feel like a chicken among birds. Here, I rode the same emotional tide—the same wave as everyone else.

My tired old insecurities were shelved and left to gather dust. And right alongside the two sisters of my soul, I lost myself to a sky full of song.

-ZEKE-

Taller than most, I could see her dancing near the stage.

My gaze locked onto her. Mate. Mate. Mate.

That word pulsed through me as her movements chased a rhythm that my body longed to match. Pangs of longing started in my chest, cascaded down my spine, and ended in my groin.

Jaw fastened shut, I punched out an aggravated breath. This thing—this connection—was getting stronger. It made the ever-present hole in my heart ache worse than ever. As if my body sensed a remedy nearby and was punishing me for not taking it.

I flexed my hands into stressed balls. This passion threatened to topple all reason. All duty. It would not do.

Yuma flanked me. "Why are you doing this to yourself?"

"How d'you do that?"

"What?"

I peered down at her. "Pop up when you're least wanted and most needed?"

Not a hint of a smile. "Resisting the bond will only bring heartache."

A statement that didn't require much from me. I could ignore it. I didn't. "How did you know? A vision?"

"I am *old*, Ezekiel." She shot me a chiding look best suited to a teacher lecturing their student. "I've seen and scented mated couples before. They have their own orbit. Their own language. It wasn't hard to figure out. I am, however, finding it difficult to understand why you're pushing her away."

"I spent all morning with her." A pathetic defense.

Yuma loosed a throaty noise. "You forget how well I know you. You're hot-blooded, and as hard-headed as a goat."

"Thanks," I said, dripping sarcasm.

Yuma went on as if she hadn't heard. "If there is something you want, you go after it. You devote everything to it. The fact that you're hanging back and not snarling at every person currently coveting your mate tells me everything I need to know."

People? What fucking people? I scanned the crowd, chest puffing out, violence brewing in my veins.

When it struck me what I was doing, I smothered those instincts. It took every drop of self-control I had.

I squeezed my eyes shut, pinching the bridge of my nose. "People rely on me, Yuma. I can't let anybody distract me from that."

"People rely on me, too," she countered. "But some things are bigger than our little corner of the world."

I frowned. "What are you saying?"

Her mouth parted in a sigh. "I'm saying it might be worth trusting the magic that brought you two together. It could turn out to have a greater purpose behind it."

I freed a joyless laugh. "Yuma, so help me, if you say everything happens for a reason, I'll bite you."

"You're throwing away a chance to be happy, even if it's only for a day or a week," she said, devastating me. "Whatever time you have with her is time you'll never get back. Why aren't you making the most of it?"

"Because." The next words barely made it past my lips. "She's going back to Aldar, and neither of us knows if we'll see each other again. If I let myself get close to her, I'm not sure what I'll do when she leaves."

"You think you'll follow her?" she guessed.

"Maybe ... Eventually."

"Perhaps you're meant to."

I sent a low growl rumbling up my throat.

Her grimace was pitying. "Why don't you try to get out of your own head for a bit? You could join the singers? You know how I love your singing."

With a soothing smile, she slipped away. No doubt to give unwanted advice to another unfortunate soul.

I palmed my chest, at where that longing lived. I had to find a distraction, a respite, anything that didn't involve pulling my mate into my arms and compromising myself.

~

-ENA-

The song ended.

Liora grasped my wrist and motioned toward the stage. Zeke was up there, joining the other performers.

I tapped Adrianna's arm.

"What?"

I pointed to where Zeke stood with a violin at the ready.

Adrianna's gaze lifted to the stage. She froze at the sight of him.

The music started up again, decorating and marking time with its rhythms. Zeke disappeared inside the music, his fingers strong and sure upon strings and bow, his expressions as alive as every note wrung from his instrument.

Adrianna turned her back on him. She tugged Liora and I into the thick of things. I went willingly, pounding my feet to the beat—to the floor of the song. I painted my emotions with the long lines of my body.

Weightless in spirit. Grounded in body. Meditative in mind. That was what dance did for me. I'd never known that until this moment.

Linking arms with strangers, I twirled and weaved among them. And I laughed—I laughed so much my cheeks hurt.

A few people jostled for my attention. I danced with them, but as soon as they got too friendly, I moved onto the next person. Tonight I would be untethered, unclaimed. Not fixated on a confused and repressed love, nor bound to an unknowable mate that flitted around the edges of my life, never materializing.

Our trio reunited during a song break.

Onstage, a fellow musician passed Zeke what looked to be a gemstone. He mouthed something over said object. I felt a thrill surge through my nerve endings. It was magic—magic was in the air.

Zeke pocketed what I now suspected was a charm and rolled up his sleeves, exposing arms corded with hard muscle and scars.

Putting bow to violin, he led the musicians into a slower tempo that stretched notes to sustain the passion. The music dropped in a natural pause, and that was when he lowered his instrument and sang. And holy fire, he could sing.

A smooth baritone, the volume of which was magically magnified, shifted the mood from rowdy to relaxed. Everybody watched him, swayed in place, or pulled their partners close. The words to his song weren't in the common tongue, but somehow I understood him anyway. This was a confession. A story of longing.

Zeke focused on Adrianna. She was all he saw.

This time, she didn't turn away. Adrianna was glued to the spot, her chin high, blood flaming her cheeks.

They stared at each other, bound in a strange embrace. That continued until the music crescendoed.

There was a huge applause; Zeke cared nothing for it. Handing the violin off to another musician, he jumped off the stage and closed the short distance to Adrianna.

They stood before each other. Not blinking. Not breathing.

I wasn't sure who moved first. In an eye-blink, they collided into a fevered kiss that looked as if it could make the world stand still.

My heart grew three sizes bigger, expanding in joy.

Eyeballing Liora, I said, "Should we take a break?"

She nodded her agreement.

We walked to the right, leaving the couple and the dancers behind. On the outskirts of the square, Liora faced me, smiling warmly. "Thank the moons those two acted on their attraction. I was going crazy channeling their emotions."

I frowned. "You couldn't block them out? At all?"

That snuffed out her smile. "Isolde thinks I've struggled so badly because they're mates, and their connection operates on a higher level than most. But the truth is I've nobody to teach me how to be an empath. Until I do, this sort of stuff will keep happening."

I nibbled my lip. Where would we find a teacher amidst this madness?

Wincing, Liora rubbed her temple. "I need to find something to eat. Isolde won't shut up about it."

"Is she hungry?"

I do not need to eat. But I'd like to share my human's experience of food. I was thinking we could start with a lovely cow leg. That will do quite nicely.

An uneven laugh floated out of me. "That was a joke, right?"

Liora groan-chuckled. "I don't think it was, actually."

My reply never formed. A desert wind tickled my damp nape, cooling the sweat there. A blue ribbon—my very own trail of breadcrumbs—materialized.

I stared and stared at it.

"What is it?" Liora asked, alarm tightening her melodic voice.

"My magic wants me to take a walk."

A slow nod. "Then we should listen."

I guided us away from the celebrations, walking in step with Liora along a well-trod path. The ribbon ended once we reached the settlement's outskirts and the riverbank.

"The trail stops here."

"Perhaps your magic wants us to wait for something," she replied.

I searched the great expanse, anticipation gurgling inside my belly. It wasn't long before my gaze snagged on something moving in the north. I waited for it to come into focus. When it did, I murmured, "There's a fae coming this way. And two birds."

"Do you reckon it's her? Your sister?"

"I don't know," I whispered.

"D'you want me to leave?" she asked softly.

Mind skip-skip-skipping, I couldn't find my voice. It was buried under nerves.

Liora made the decision for me. "I'm gonna go back and join the dancing. But I'll walk slowly. If anything happens, shout out."

A faltering nod was all I managed.

Liora left.

I stood alone, struggling to calm my moth-wing pulse and staring at the female who winged her way toward me on the back of a black wind.

CHAPTER 23
THE SHIELD AND THE SWORD

***

The female landed about thirty feet upstream from me. The eagle and falcon accompanying her flew overhead, toward the settlement.

The stranger marched toward me at a quick gait.

My pulse erratic, I made a study of her oval face, searching for a resemblance. The narrow nose, modest pout, and angular jaw were similar. But there were stark differences: so many that a wellspring of doubt interrupted my assumption about who she was. Her eyebrows were blond and arched, not dark and straight; her cheekbones were flat and broad, not high and sharp; her hair was a lion's mane, not a raven's wing.

She stopped before me. I met her jade-green eyes. The same color as Mama's. And Sandrine's. Even Atlas's.

My insides did a funny flop.

Her head tilted. Appraising. Questioning.

I nodded. Answering. Confirming.

She pulled me down into a fierce embrace.

The idea that she might hate me evaporated. In its place was relief and a wide-open door to affection that came from nowhere and nothing. It defied logic and reason, but my blood recognized hers. This was my sister.

I had to stoop to return her hug. In her embrace, intricate plaits of yellow hair tickled my cheeks. She stretched her wings to the four corners of the sky, and I had to appreciate the marbled blue and golden freckles staining them before she wrapped me up in their leathery membrane.

I breathed my kin in. Her scent belonged to the free winds, to the desert, and the hot sun. To a lotion made of olives and shea butter. To the leather and fur of her overcoat, and the cold metal of her sword.

Her chest expanded against mine. I sensed she was taking my scent in, as I had with hers.

We released each other.

Sefra gently brushed the baby hairs away from my face. "Yuma told me your name is Serena."

"It is. But I go by Ena."

She nodded distantly, tracing my features almost reverently.

Throat sticking, I forced out, "You have Mama's eyes."

My remark wiped the emotion off her face. A flat expression was left behind. "She's not with you, is she?"

A painful whisper stumbled over my lips. "No."

"Tell me," she breathed, her lips bloodless.

Heartache bludgeoned me. "She died in the Gauntlet."

In a sharp move she turned her head to the side, chin trembling. "Yuma saw you in Aldar months ago. She mentioned that Mama didn't seem to be with you." Voice breaking up, she added, "I knew then something had gone wrong. She never would've left you."

Tears stung my eyes as they met the bitter chill of the desert night. My body was finally recognizing the frigid temperature away from the crush of bodies. I covered my arms with my wings, conserving heat and fighting off the shivers.

"What about the waterstone?" Red-eyed, she faced me. "Mama was carrying it before she left Aldar—"

I pulled my blouse's neckline down. "I've got it. And I found the sunstone. It was at Alhara, Zeke's place."

She ogled the citrine. "I ..."

My sister seemed suspended in shock. "Sefra?"

She startled as if I'd screamed in her ear. "We have a lot to catch up on. And we will. But we've got to move—"

"What is it? What's wrong?"

Stress creased her brow. "On the journey here, Yuma's familiar spotted The Watch and an armed unit of mercenaries traveling in this direction. If Hasan's forces keep to their current course, they'll be here within the hour."

Horror sluiced through me. "They've come for me and my friends."

Sefra's eyes flared. "They're hunting you?"

A nod. "So is Morgan. And possibly Abraxus."

After several shocked blinks, she drew in a reviving breath. "All right. One crisis at a time. Yuma's familiar has already warned her about the attack. But I should speak with her in person, and you need to get ready to leave."

"I'm not doing anything before I find my friends."

"Well, where are they?"

I glanced over my shoulder. The tall flames were clearly visible against the dark sky. "They shouldn't be too far from the bonfire."

"Good." Sefra's hand slipped under my elbow. "That's where Yuma is."

"How do you know?"

"My familiar is with her," she said, and she pulled me into the maze of wikans.

As we ran, a horn blasted from somewhere up ahead.

"That's Yuma." Sefra picked up the pace. "She's gathering the Shyani."

The clamor of an agitated crowd grew louder. Nearer.

Adrianna dropped down in front of us, my sheathed sword in hand.

I skidded to a halt.

Sefra was guarding me before I could blink. "Who are you?" she demanded, wings splaying in a threat.

"That's Adrianna Lakeshie." I stepped out from behind Sefra. "She's my friend."

Sefra's wings collapsed. *"Adrianna?"* She freed a short laugh. "Gods, I'm sorry. I didn't recognize you."

Neck and shoulders tense, Adrianna said, "I'm not surprised. I was eleven the last time we saw each other." Her attention cut to me. "Yuma said The Watch is coming."

"I know. Where's Liora?"

"With Zeke," she rushed out. "They've gone to grab our bags."

Adrianna handed over my Utemä.

"Does Li have her weapon?"

A nod. "The swords are the first thing we went for."

I looped my Utemä onto my belt.

Sefra shepherded me with an extended wing. "Come on. Yuma's not far. My familiar says she's about to make a speech."

Adrianna didn't even question that.

The three of us raced to the square. The bonfire still burned brightly, but nobody was dancing anymore. The area was packed, shoulder to shoulder, wing to wing. There were even fae hovering midair.

Yuma addressed the crowd from the musician's stage. "Anybody who can't fight, who is infirm or underage, you will leave for the meet-up spot at once," she called out in a magically magnified voice. "To those of you who can do battle, outfit yourselves appropriately and meet me at the riverbank. That is where we will make our stand."

"How many oppose us, Mother Yuma?" a concerned voice cried out.

"Zephyr puts the count at about five thousand." A falcon dropped out of the sky to perch upon Yuma's shoulder. Her familiar, no doubt.

Alarmed conversations sprang up everywhere at once.

Yuma waved for silence. "We're outnumbered. That is true. But if we break their ranks, we can slow them down and give those who can't fight a head start. When our task is done, I'll lead the retreat into the Tazils." She gestured toward the mountains that towered over the camp. "Make for the hideouts. Stay there until it's safe to show yourselves. That is all." She clapped her hands. "Go. Prepare yourselves."

Yuma exited the stage.

The crowd scattered, rushing away on legs or via wings. Over shouts and panicked voices, I heard, "Adrianna!"

"Zeke!" Adrianna rose onto her tiptoes. "Where are you?"

Sefra flicked out her hands. A cloud of embers floated upward and spelled out "Zeke."

Stars ... Her control over sunlight had seemed effortless.

"Zeke, can you see that?" Adrianna yelled. "Do you see your name? Move toward it."

It didn't take long for Zeke to find us. He had strapped his bracers to his forearms and his bandoleer of knives across his chest. Liora, red-cheeked and worry-wrinkled, was running alongside him. They each carried an extra bag.

Adrianna and I relieved them of our rucksacks.

Sefra snuffed out her hanging sign. "Zeke, you have my thanks for getting my siska here safely."

"Don't mention it. It's good to have you with us, Sefra."

They clasped forearms. A warrior's greeting.

I introduced Liora and Sefra while shouldering my rucksack.

Nods were exchanged.

"So, what now?" Liora aired.

"We speak to Yuma." Sefra strode off.

I stalked after her. The others followed.

Guilt pressed in at seeing so many terrified faces in the crowd, at seeing how people gripped their loved ones tight for fear of losing them.

We arrived at the side of the musician's stage. Yuma was there, discussing tactics for the coming battle with three fae already in armor. When she spotted our group lingering, waiting, she told the warriors, "Give me a moment."

Yuma broke away to join us. "Sefra, thank you for your early warning. You might very well have saved us."

They grasped wrists.

"Say nothing of that."

"Now, you must go." Yuma's eyes cut to me. "Before they get here."

"I'm not leaving your people to fight while I run for it. We brought The Watch here." I motioned to Adrianna, Liora, and Zeke. "It's our fault."

"How, though? How did Hasan's army discover where we were?" Adrianna glanced around as if she suspected a master spy to emerge from the sea of frightened people.

The falcon on Yuma's shoulder clicked its beak. I sensed it wasn't objecting to her suspicions, it was merely asking her to be silent. That this wasn't the time to question how we'd gotten here. That would come later. If we survived.

"I wish I knew," Yuma said, her heavy gaze never leaving me. "And I understand that you feel responsible for this situation. But it was my choice to shelter you because I wished to keep you safe. Because you're important to my tribe. To the world. And if Hasan's soldiers capture you, it could be disastrous for everybody. So, please go—and go quickly."

My mind and heart went to war. I didn't want to be stubborn for the sake of my pride—to play at being a hero when it might make things worse. But to leave the tribe now felt *wrong*. For reasons deeper than the obvious. That wrongness resonated in my bones. In my gut.

Sefra addressed Yuma. "How about a compromise? I'll join the fight. My power will be an asset, and I'm not known to The Watch. As for the others." Her focus skipped to me. "There are some decent caves in the mountains behind us. They can hide out there until you sound the retreat. Then we'll leave with your people through the Tazils."

"If you use sunlight, you'll make yourself a target," Yuma warned.

Sefra's jade-greens flitted to me. "I can't afford to conceal my power anymore. Besides, my task in Asitar is done. I'll return to Aldar as soon as my siska is ready."

I lightly nipped my lower lip. I wanted to tell her that we weren't done in Asitar, not while Abraxus possessed the starstone, but with battle imminent, it could wait.

"I'll fight too," Zeke chimed in.

Adrianna opened her mouth and drew a sharp breath.

Anticipating her, Zeke said, "It makes sense for me to go. The Watch never saw my real face, only an illusion."

"Then make me look like somebody else, and I'll fight by your side," Adrianna insisted.

His eyes softened. "I can't do that. Any illusion I place on you might not hold, not with my energy and focus being used up in the fight. And if you're recognized, you'll be swarmed."

"I swear if you're trying to put me off because of some overprotective male nonsense—"

"That isn't it." He gently clasped her neck. "I'm quite happy for you to come save me if things go to shit."

Adrianna's eyes became itty-bitty triangles. "You can bet on it."

He pressed his lips to hers in the softest kiss imaginable.

Yuma palmed her brow, sighing. "None of you are under my charge, and therefore I can't send you away. If you're resigned to do this, then don't delay getting into position. Now I must go and see to my people."

Yuma hurried off into the crowd.

Sefra rounded on me. "I'll show you to a cave where you can take shelter."

"You take Li. I'll take Ena," Adrianna told Zeke as she plaited her hair in swift, nimble movements.

"Why d'you need to take Ena?" Sefra asked.

A blush crept up my neck. "I can't fly. Not yet."

Sefra's pale blond brows snapped together. I wasn't sure if she was disappointed in me or just surprised. Either way, Adrianna was quick to defend me. "I've taught her the basics. We just haven't had a chance to put the theory into action yet."

But we had. Today. Shame coursed through my blood. So much had been running through my head, I hadn't made it a priority.

"Then that's something we'll have to rectify," Sefra said firmly. "But for now, I will carry you to the cave."

Not wasting a second, Sefra scooped me up. Her blue-gold wings took us up into the skies faster than any fae I'd ever flown with.

We raced over the settlement toward the mountain peaks, and all the while a dozen thorny fears gnawed at me. The worst one being how many would die tonight?

∽

For forty minutes Adrianna, Liora, and I endured a heart-pounding wait in a mountain cave located above and behind the settlement. The high vantage point provided a clear view of the camp, the half-mile-wide river, and the stubbled plains beyond. From there, we witnessed the Shyani's struggle to prepare for our enemies' arrival. The wikans were abandoned, the camels chased away, the bonfire snuffed out. Those being evacuated left.

A swarm of fae could be spotted on the horizon. Nerves stretched thin, I watched them draw closer to us and to the three thousand Shyani that stood with the river between themselves and the enemy. The tribespeople lined the bank, ten rows deep, dressed in armor of all kinds: leather, mail, and steel plates. The only uniformity in their ranks were the strange words painted over their bodies and garb.

"I hate this." Adrianna backed away from the cave's mouth and paced the length of it. Not that she had much room for movement; the cave wasn't large, and all our rucksacks were piled up at the rear.

"We all do," Liora breathed, her expression pained.

I wondered if she was channeling Adrianna's emotions again. Still, better for Liora to be up here than down on the ground. I imagined being among anxious soldiers would be hell for an empath.

Fear drummed at my ribs when from within the enemy ranks, a horn sounded. Thousands of Hasan's soldiers halted in midair. They had stopped just short of crossing the river, staying out of range of our arrows.

A section of their forces wore brown leather armor and red cloth—the uniform of The Watch. The rest of the soldiers had donned blackened steel.

Two fae left the main unit. These representatives descended, waving a banner.

From our ranks, three people went to meet them. One of them was Yuma.

The two groups conversed on our side of the sandy shore.

I yearned to do something. Anything had to be better than this—than the waiting.

The exchange between the groups didn't last long. Hasan's people retreated behind their lines.

"That's that, then," Liora said, her grim expression reflecting my own mood.

Adrianna squeezed in between me and Liora.

Another horn blast. With that, it began.

Shouts sounded. Shields were raised. Bows were strung.

My breath stalled as countless arrowheads glinted in the moonlight and bowstrings were released from both sides.

Twang. Hiss. Thwack.

Arrows struck hundreds of targets, killing enemy and ally alike. I flinched; my held inhale shook loose.

The enemy's front line shifted. Archers were replaced by spear-carrying soldiers. This unit dove down from their position on high, aiming for the Shyani.

Before they could crash into our ranks, sun-yellow embers shot upward into their faces, exploding on impact and proving as lethal as glass shards to the eyes.

Screams pitched the night air. The Shyani dragged the blinded warriors down from the sky and staked them to the ground. Ruthless, but effective.

Hasan's army switched tactics again. A hundred black-armored fae—mercenaries, I presumed—surged to their front line and hit our people with air gusts, fireballs, and jets of water drawn from the river below. From where I stood, the attacks looked weak. At least in comparison to the witch battles I'd seen in my dreamscape.

Our side beat the mercenaries back with arrows, sunlight, and a flock of attack birds.

"Those birds are illusions," I said for Adrianna's benefit.

She looked at me, her expression stripped of armor. As raw as rusted iron. "Zeke must be alive then."

I nodded, throat tight.

A sand tornado spiraled into being, appearing suddenly on the Shyani's flank. On an ill-fated wind it tilted toward our ranks.

"That has to be a sidir," Adrianna rasped.

I found the panic and fear in her voice more terrifying than the ungodly howls of the sidir. I was so used to Adrianna being the steadfast one.

"Shouldn't the camp's protections be repelling it?" Liora said.

Silence answered her.

As the sidir stormed through the Shyani's ranks in a swirl of deadly sand, our warriors scrambled to escape the twister's destructive path. The unstoppable sprite moved this way and that, causing as much death and disruption as possible.

Hasan's army seized that moment—that opportunity. Thousands flew across the river, swooped down from above, and crashed into the Shyani.

Sefra's embers were nowhere to be seen. Was she hurt? Was she dead?

Our enemy pushed their advantage; our defenses started to fray. Weak-kneed with panic and horror, I grasped onto the lip of the cave mouth.

Howling sand. Spilling blood. Clanging steel. That was all I saw, smelled, and heard on the wind.

"I can't stand this," Adrianna breathed, shaking her head, her complexion turning waxen as all the blood seemed to drain from her face. "I have to do something."

That was all the warning we got. She sprinted over the ledge in front of us and leaped off the mountain into black sky.

"Adi, wait," I shouted at her retreating form.

She didn't look back.

"Gods-damn it," I cursed. "We can't let her go alone."

A grim-faced Liora replied, "No, we can't."

I exchanged a dark look with her. "I guess I'm about to take my first flight during a rutting battle."

"I've got a better idea. Or at least Isolde does." The burnt gold circling her pupils expanded while the spring-green shrunk. "You'll have to jump on."

"Jump on?" I echoed.

Not answering, Liora quickly stripped bare. As she straightened, her bones reshaped, her skin hardened, and an extra limb grew out of her tailbone.

"Oh gods," I whispered, backing up a bit.

Liora raced forward before she'd finished shifting.

"Shit. Fuck. Wait!"

She dove off the ledge and my heart plummeted with her.

I rushed over to where the mountain dropped away and glanced down. Below, Liora completed her transformation. Isolde's thirty-foot-long body banked and circled around to me, supported by ruby wings. She stopped, hovering several feet out from the mountain. *Let's show them how strong and wild our fire burns, light-wielder.*

Instinct born from years as a human stuck my feet to the ground.

Don't think. Just jump.

I expelled a nervous bit of air. "Right. I can do that. I can do this."

For my friends. For my sister. I backed up and took a short run at it.

The edge came upon me—

I leaped. I fell.

A mad, dangerous thrill rushed through me. My flight lessons flitted out of my head. I acted on impulse, stretching my limbs and wings out like the fletching of an arrow. Gaining a little control, I managed to belly-land onto rock-hard muscle.

A pained groan punched out of me.

Hold on, Isolde ordered.

I shuffled up to sit in between her shoulders and grabbed the nearest golden ridge that lined her elongated neck.

With a single flap, we darted over the settlement.

My stomach lurched. I adjusted my movements to hers as best I could. But as it turned out, riding a dragon was no easy thing. Holding on for dear life, I yelled, "We need to destroy the sidir."

I shall rain hell down upon it.

But we didn't have to go to the sprite. It arrowed straight toward us in a barreling, groaning whirl of sand.

Isolde sucked in a long inhale, her scales heating the insides of my thighs.

Grit irritated my eyes. The sand demon was close. Too close.

Isolde showed the world a dragon's strength. She blasted the sprite with a mighty column of flame and fury.

A wave of heat more brutal than that found in a forge ricocheted into me. I threw an arm over my face as the sidir blazed up in a column of bright white light. It unleashed a ghastly screech and disintegrated within seconds, pelting the ground with a hail of cherry-red sparks and liquid fire.

Isolde pitched left. I pinched my knees in and leaned with her. She put on a burst of speed. We were fleeing. "What are you doing?" I shouted over the din of fighting, dragon wings, and a cold wind.

I need a moment to rekindle my fire.

Oh.

The *whoosh-whoosh* of fae in flight registered with me.

An awful spark of dread jumped from my tailbone up my spine. Feathers bristling, I twisted my neck to the right. Behind us, about a dozen black-armored fae pursued. Worse still, they were led by Nala, Morgan's spy from The Oasis Lounge.

I was surprised there weren't more of them. Logic suggested that we weren't being swarmed because Nala didn't want us taken by Hasan's army. She wanted to sneak us away from the fight for Morgan.

"Nala's coming after us," I yelled down to Isolde. "And a few others."

Isolde unleashed her aggression with the swish of a barbed tail and a growl that held the power and threat of an avalanche.

"Now!" Nala's shout carried over the wind.

They didn't draw bows or swords. No magic was called upon. Instead, they pulled spherical objects out from bags secured at their waists.

Isolde turned to face our enemy. Her scales warmed beneath me, but she was too late to stop Nala and the mercenaries from throwing metal balls at us. As the spheres spun through space, they shed their exoskeletons and expanded into shining silver nets.

My body reacted before my thoughts could assemble. I brought my palm up and out, summoning a shield that shone with the silver-spoon color of the moon. The barrier formed in front of me and Isolde.

The chainmail-like nets slammed into my shield, which died as static ran through it. Those nets were infused with lightning. They had to be. Lightning was moonlight's only weakness.

My entire left arm trembled as the shock from the lightning entered my bones. The pain was dull, like a toothache. Still, it had been enough. The giant nets fell to the earth, useless.

Isolde unleashed a boiling river upon our would-be captors. They performed a series of aerial gymnastics to avoid being cooked alive.

Attempting to catch a few in her fire-blast, Isolde canted left. That staccato movement was my undoing.

Dislodged, I slid off the dragon. I reached out, desperately trying to grab ahold of something—anything. All to no avail. I fell toward a quick death.

Shock froze my brain.

Fucking FLY!

Ena, use your wings! Use your wings!

My great-aunts' commands were a bucket of ice water dumped over my head. Tucking my elbows in, I flipped over. Through strands of wild hair, I beheld thousands of wikans and a hard ground rising up to meet me.

Terror blistering my insides, I snapped my wings out. The wind's fists slammed into them; the drag tore at unused muscles and wing joints as they fought the earthly forces seeking to reclaim me.

I beat my wings once, twice, and gritted my teeth against the pain.

"Ena!"

From the corner of my eye I saw my sister swooping down. "Tilt your body back. Arms out for balance. Keep the muscles in your legs relaxed."

The brain fog kept me from replying. I just followed her instructions.

I was going to crash. I was going to crash. I was going to crash.

Somehow, I overshot the shelters and ended up over the square we'd danced in.

I executed a messy landing, skidding in the dirt, missing the lifeless bonfire by a few hairs. My legs and wings throbbed and my knees were scraped raw. But I was alive.

Sefra landed and yanked me up by my bicep. "I saw you falling. Are you all right?"

I shook my arm loose of her grip. "I'll be fine."

Sefra looked unharmed. Thank the ancestors.

A dragon roared above me.

I craned my neck. Isolde baited our pursuers into following her to the riverbank, away from us.

"Let's get you out of here," Sefra said.

I showed her my palms. "Isolde needs you more than I do."

Her brow furrowed. "Isolde?"

"The dragon. It's Liora's familiar. She's a shifter."

A pause. "I won't leave you."

"They were throwing nets charged with lightning at us," I argued. "I don't know if that can bring down a dragon, but we can't risk it. You have to help her. *Please*, Sefra."

A conflicted pause.

"Boiling hell," she exclaimed, grabbing my wrist. "I'll go, but only if you hide."

Another earth-splitting bellow made my gut spasm. Had Isolde—Liora—been injured?

Sefra pulled me into an empty pavilion. "Stay here. They'll be looking for you. I'll be back when I can."

The second she was up and away, I freed my Utemä. I'd no intention of hiding, not when my friends were out there.

I peeked out from behind the pavilion's curtain. There was nobody flying directly overhead. Darting out into the square, I went left and picked a direction that ran toward the clashing of swords and the sight of fae fighting in the distance.

Almost at my chosen path, I heard fast footfalls somewhere ahead of me. I raised my sword and readied a moon-shield.

Two fae appeared from behind a bend in the track. Relief bloomed in a breath. I lowered my sword and muzzled my magic.

Adrianna and Zeke, sans any disguise, raced over.

"They're looking for you." Adrianna lifted me, sword drawn and all.

Still running, she gained air with a few flaps of her dark blue wings. The wind suddenly grew claws, and I was torn apart from Adrianna.

A crazed tempest threw me backward. I corkscrewed through empty space, and my faithful Utemä was ripped from my hand.

Bubble shield, Zola ordered.

I crossed my arms in an X-shape over my chest. A moon-shield ballooned outward, insulating my body and cutting off the whirlwind's power. I tumbled down and landed in a crouched position.

Stomach rebelling, I straightened up and spread my wings for balance. My dizziness settled; my vision cleared. Nala and fewer mercenaries than before—nine, maybe—descended into the square, landing not far in front of me. How had they evaded Isolde? Had they hurt her? What about Sefra?

Such thoughts were driven from my head when Adrianna and Zeke charged our enemies from behind.

The mercenaries split off into smaller units. Four fae engaged Adrianna and Zeke, working on separating the mated pair. The remaining five fae, including Nala, used their bodies as a barrier, an obstacle between me and my friends. Such movements seemed pre-planned, rehearsed, and seamless enough to stem from a hive mind.

Nala waved her hand at me, and the tempest that buffeted my shield died. Eyes alive with malice, she unsheathed a sword from between her wings. "I suppose we'll have to do this the old-fashioned way."

The mercenaries facing me also drew their swords. One of them called out a strange-sounding word. I tasted magic on my tongue right before a line of interlocked metal shields materialized. This barrier fanned out in front of their group, protecting them from me.

All right then. I kept my left hand raised, my moon-shield with it.

But my right hand stabbed outward like a righteous sword. With that movement, I hurled a sun-bolt at their unit. It passed through my moon-shield harmlessly, hitting their metal shields and obliterating them.

The blue-winged male on the far right collapsed. Drained or dead.

A female mercenary flicked her wrist and cried out, "Siaf!" Phantom blades popped up over her head, their pointy tips aimed at me.

I struck first. The gray-winged female ducked just in time, and my bolt of fire passed over her head, fizzling out.

The sunstone pressed at me. It wanted me to use *more, more, more*. It was so aggressive, so volatile, I feared it would burn through me until there was nothing left. Until I was ash and ember.

Concentration wobbling, my moon-shield vanished.

Nala pounced on that vulnerability. She slammed me with a gust of wind, but it was weaker than before. I only stumbled back. "Take her! Take her now," Nala barked, retreating a bit.

Coward.

I channeled the stars. Their cold and subtle touch frosted my veins as three mercenaries charged me. Fifteen steps out. Ten.

I blasted starlight directly into their faces.

Dazzled, they reared back, squinting and blinking.

I worked hard to hold onto the elusive starlight, but it felt like trying to keep water in a leaky bucket. There wasn't time to fight that or to panic. I ran directly at the closest blinded fae, the gray-winged female.

At the sound of my approach, she swung her scimitar outward. Before she could gut me, I blocked her attack with a moon-shield. I reached outside my barrier and grabbed her hand. With a twist, I snapped her wrist back. Her bone gave way with a *crack*. She cried out, releasing her sword into my grip.

Stepping back, I aimed for her throat. My body led, the sword followed. I overextended and my blade passed clean through her neck. The female's head toppled right off her shoulders.

Holy shit. I couldn't have done that as a human. The strength of my fae bones repulsed and excited me equally.

My moon-shield flickered out. To preserve my energy, I didn't summon it again. Instead, I about-turned to face the males who hung back, blinking rapidly to clear their vision. The nearest mercenary still rubbed at his streaming eyes. He was my next target.

I advanced.

Our steel crossed, and we came into a sword-bind. I hadn't fought blade-to-blade since Kasi. But my muscles remembered what to do.

I used the momentum of my sword to push his away. I lifted off the sword-bind and snapped my blade's edge in toward his torso. He proved too slow to stop it; armor kept his intestines in his belly, but I'd bludgeoned his ribs. As he tried to stumble away, I lunged and stabbed him through the neck.

My third opponent was a hawk-nosed male.

He parried my overhand strike. I covered his blade with my own, pinning it against his chest, messing with his balance.

I kicked his heels out from under him. As he went down, I hit him on the jaw with my hilt. I ended his life at the jugular.

"Aren't we fancy?" Nala jeered.

My fangs nicked my gum-line as the coward finally approached, twirling her blade effortlessly. A performance meant to intimidate.

I noticed she kept her head angled down. She had learned from watching the others. Not that it mattered. Starlight didn't want to answer my call.

Nala rushed me. The crossing of our swords rang out.

Thighs burning, I moved through the steps. I'd had excellent tutors in the art of the sword. Nala was still better than me.

Time passed, weighed by my missed blows and her near hits. Her technique made it clear she was trying to injure me, not kill me. I suspected that was the only reason I wasn't already dead.

Nala delighted in goading me about how sloppy I was getting.

"You're tiring, aren't you? Morgan's going to love breaking you. If you surrender, I'll call off the attack."

Enough. Burn the bitch, Zola growled.

Fine. I'd have to risk the sunstone's eagerness.

I managed to land a kick to Nala's midriff. It didn't floor her, but I pushed her back a few steps. I seized that moment to retreat, to drop my borrowed sword, and to draw upon my sunlight. Its violent heat bloomed in my heart center and flushed my blood in seconds. I mimed the action of drawing a bow.

Nala snapped out a claw-hand. Her power slammed against my skull, against a hastily raised mental-shield. If I hadn't practiced guarding against such attacks, I might've buckled. Instead, I bared my fangs. "You lose, bitch."

Nala kicked off from the ground. I freed my sun-arrow.

She cartwheeled through the air, avoiding the flight of my arrow.

Shit. Fatigue sapped the strength from my limbs. I didn't know how many attacks like that I had left in me.

"No!" Adrianna's scream shook the sky, the noise lost to the ceiling of the world.

I couldn't help it. I glanced sideways.

A mercenary lay dead at Zeke's feet. But there was another attacker, a female, closing in on him. Zeke swung wildly at her, blood blooming along his collarbone, staining his white undershirt and the leather chest armor he must've borrowed.

Adrianna descended into a blood rage. Fangs drawn, she dipped her chin and charged the two males who opposed her. They matched her aggression with a reckless fighting style.

Movement flashed in my periphery. I twisted around.

With wicked triumph, Nala raised a metal sphere from her belt-bag. She had obviously kept one of the lightning nets, waiting for the perfect moment.

A white-hot fire-whip suddenly wrapped around Nala's neck.

I glanced up. Sefra had returned.

My sister's power burned through skin and muscle like it was nothing. The whip vanished into smoke. Nala collapsed, dead, the dormant metal ball clutched in her hand.

Sefra landed near Adrianna. My sister swung her sword and wielded her magic in tandem. To my eyes, she was a whirlwind of steel and a living torch combined. It took a handful of moves for her to destroy two well-trained fae.

Adrianna, freed from her opponents, levitated her sword through the air and impaled the last mercenary—the female who had hurt her mate. Not missing a beat, Adrianna lurched toward Zeke like a failing heartbeat.

I hurried over to them as an ashen-faced Zeke collapsed to his knees. Adrianna was beside him in a second, supporting his back and ripping his hand away from his clavicle. The cut was above his armor, almost at his neck. It was shallow, wide, and it had an evil look to it. Black veins branched out from the main site of the wound.

"You stupid male." Adrianna's voice cracked at the end.

My heart broke for her.

"Sorry, princess," Zeke pushed out. "I fucked up."

Adrianna's hard gaze snapped to me. "We need Liora."

I glanced over the wikans to check on Isolde. She was diving down, crashing into the enemy's ranks from on high.

"Liora can't help him," Sefra said heavily.

My gaze dropped; my stomach disappeared. "What do you mean?"

"Liora's a healer. Of course she can help him," Adrianna argued.

"I've been poisoned," Zeke rasped, sweat on his brow. "I can feel it—it's ice in my veins."

Sefra picked up the blade responsible for injuring Zeke. She sniffed the steel only to toss it aside with a rattling hiss of disgust. "They bloodied the blade."

"What does that mean?" Adrianna demanded.

"It means his cut can be healed, but the poison in his veins can't be cured by a healer." Sefra focused on Zeke. "We have to get you to a shaman."

"There should be one among Hasan's forces," Zeke said, his brow creasing in pain. "They're the only practitioners I know that can control the sidir."

"And if we can't find this shaman—then what?" Adrianna asked, voice strained.

Zeke palmed his collarbone again, applying pressure there. "The poison proves fatal within a day or two."

"That's not going to happen," she said, almost snarling at that.

The howls of more sidir sent cold tremors into my wings. Ten sand sprites appeared on the edge of the battle. Rutting hell.

Isolde raced toward this new threat with flames licking the side of her mouth. The sidir twisted and turned to avoid her fire-stream.

I couldn't see above the wikans from this spot, but I heard the shouts of pain and panic as the sidir attacked fae fighting in the air and on the ground.

My heart collapsed into horror. Yuma had to sound the retreat soon, didn't she? How much more could the Shyani take?

Isolde broke off her attack and rushed toward us on fast wings. She came in for a swift landing and, with a surprising amount of grace, set her four clawed feet upon the earth. There, Isolde shrunk and shifted into Liora's naked body.

"Give her this." Sefra slipped off her tan-brown overcoat, revealing a sleeveless leather tunic ringed with mail.

I reached Liora as her legs went out from under her. Throwing the coat over her shoulders, I asked, "Are you okay?"

"Yes," she wheezed, sliding her arms into the sleeves.

With my help, she stood. I met her frazzled gaze and blinked. "The golden rings around your pupils are gone."

Looking troubled, she said, "It must be because Isolde's dormant. She had to recoup her strength. But my energies aren't exhausted. I can still heal."

With that, she hurried over to Zeke. As she tended to him, Sefra filled her in on why we still needed a shaman.

Zeke's cut soon closed, but the black veins remained. It was only when Liora had finished healing that she spoke, her face bleak. "There might not be a shaman once the sidir are done."

Adrianna marked her with a sharp gaze. "What do you mean?"

"The sidir that have just arrived, they're not attacking us." Liora straightened up and peered over the wikans to where the fighting raged on. "They're killing Hasan's people."

"Why would the sidir suddenly be on our side?" I asked our group.

A loud screech sounded above us. I peered up and saw a giant eagle, its feathers gleaming a reddish gold under the starscape.

I thought I recognized it from earlier. "Is that ..."

"It's Cora, my familiar," Sefra said, anticipating my question. "She says there's another army approaching—"

She was cut off by a horn that rent the air, as ominous as the first crack of thunder.

A mile-long line of people riding winged beasts appeared over the mountain peaks behind the settlement.

"It's Abraxus's army," Sefra said with an awful kind of finality.

Fear dried my mouth out.

"Has he come for Hasan's forces? Or for you?" Liora said, eyeing me anxiously.

Sefra turned to me. "You said Abraxus might be after you before—why?"

"His spies saw me using light magic."

Dread and worry collided in her expression. I died a bit at that.

"All of you go," Zeke ground out. "Leave me. I'll only slow you down."

"So, that's it? You're giving up?" Adrianna gripped his bearded jawline. "What of your duty to those in Alhara—would you abandon them too?"

He pulled her hand from his face and held it tight. "I'm not giving up. But if the sidir are being controlled by a shaman, then Abraxus must have one in his army. I can appeal to his forces to cure me of the poison. They will. I'm half jinn. I'm valuable."

"We're not going anywhere, Zeke," Sefra chimed in soberly. "If we flee, we'll only succeed in getting them to chase us, and we can't out-fly a herd of furies. I doubt any fae could for long."

"What are furies?" Liora asked.

"They're distant kin to the dragons." Sefra's attentions settled on Liora's alarmed expression. "Only furies are smaller, and they spit acid instead of fire."

That was it. I had to find my Utemä. I felt naked without it.

I scanned the general area, and my fae-eyes found it fast in open space. Metal sharp enough to shave the hairs off a spider glinted at me in the moonlight, its silver shine a stark contrast to the reddish earth beneath it.

I raced over and picked up my sword. "We could hide in the wikans," Liora suggested from behind me.

I spun around, sliding my sword into its sheath.

"Furies have an excellent sense of smell. They'd find us." Sefra's gaze traveled up to where Abraxus's army hovered over the mountains. "Our best bet is to join the Shyani. We're vulnerable out here—"

"Hasan's army lies below," a male shouted from atop the mountains, his voice impossibly loud. "This is your chance for revenge, for justice, for blood!"

Thousands of Abraxus's soldiers cheered. I felt a smidge of relief that they were in fact after Hasan's soldiers. Not me. Not yet.

"We make for the riverbank." For the first time, a queenly authority entered Sefra's demeanor.

Adrianna tugged her sword free of the female she'd killed. Then she slung Zeke's arm over her shoulders.

"I can walk," he grouched as she stood and pulled him up with her.

"Your legs are wobbling," she pointed out bluntly.

He didn't have a comeback for that.

"Forgive me"—Sefra hauled Liora into her arms—"but you're not wearing any shoes."

A tad awkward, Liora said, "It's fine. Thank you."

"Stay close," Sefra ordered, eyeballing me.

Her eagle familiar darted ahead of us. Our group raced after her; we went down a dirt path, twisting left and right.

"Hökkan! Charge!" yelled that male from the mountain.

I prayed it wasn't Abraxus himself.

The *flap* and *whoosh* of wings told me the furies weren't stationary anymore. They were on the move. I didn't dare look back lest I stumble.

Two males sprinted around a corner and into our path. They halted fifteen feet out from us. I had a second to absorb their uniforms. The Watch.

They pointed their swords at us. In the same breath, I flicked my wrists out and shot two fireballs at them. I ran past the screaming males as they dropped to the ground attempting to quench my flames by rolling on the dusty earth.

But that was not the end. Four mercenaries appeared up ahead, fleeing from the battle and the sand sprites.

Hesitation gripped me. With the sunstone burning my chest and my energy waning, I feared indulging the sunlight. Feared that I might lose control.

Before I could decide what to do, red-hot sparks exploded in the mercenaries' faces. The four fae stumbled about, yelling out in pain.

I looked to my right. Sefra had done that with a snap of her fingers. She hadn't even put Liora down.

My sister led us into another run. We raced onward, and the sound of countless beating wings got closer and closer. The furies were gaining on us.

We ran into more fae—more enemies. I went for my sword, but I didn't get to draw it. This group darted out of our path and into a nearby wikan.

I stumbled mentally. "What—"

"They don't want to fight," Sefra interrupted. "They want to hide. Let them. They won't escape, whatever they do."

On we went. I didn't see the end of the settlement coming; we rounded a bend and came upon it suddenly.

We slowed to a stop on the edge of the sandy riverbank.

My brain struggled to accept the images flooding in. The chaos and death and violence. I didn't have time to think or feel anything; the furies bolted overhead like a cauldron of bats.

The five of us huddled together. I brought a hand up, ready to shield us if the situation demanded it. But the ferocious beasts didn't bother with us.

Bile rose up my throat as the furies crashed into the airborne fae. They bit and tore at anybody wearing the garb of Hasan's forces. The riders on their backs struck out at our enemies with magic and arrows, their aim deadly.

With the furies in closer proximity, I saw they were covered in black scales. They had a frill of skin around their necks that flared whenever they spat venom or performed a flight maneuver.

A horn was blown somewhere above us.

Dozens of furies dove toward the riverbank. The Shyani dropped down low, arms and wings thrown over their heads. Sefra lowered Liora and guarded her. Adrianna did the same with Zeke, only she pushed him to the ground.

Fearing that the furies were about to target us, I drew a shield over our small group. The drain on my energy made me tremble.

I watched, heart in my mouth, as the dexterous furies snatched up people in red or black uniforms. Their lethal claws ripped fae to shreds in seconds. Our enemies stopped running into the settlement to hide when the furies sniffed them out like cornered rabbits.

The truth sunk in then. The furies were still targeting Hasan's people.

I dropped to my knees. From relief or exhaustion, I couldn't tell. Unable to hold it, I released my moon-shield.

Hasan's army broke apart before my eyes. Those that weren't killed outright turned around and flew back across the river and over the flat plains. But their wings weren't fast enough to out-fly the furies or the sidir, who forced sand down their victims' throats, causing fae to fall to the earth like puppets with severed strings.

Bit by bit, the violence on the riverbank ebbed.

The aftermath was what remained.

Blood, shit, and smoke stung my nostrils. The dead were everywhere, lying amidst shattered shields, broken spears, and splintered arrows. Their blood had intermingled with the sand. The earth was red.

A mental fog descended. I disconnected, watching passively as what I assumed were healers started to move around and work in the thick of things, tending to the injured, even when their patients screamed at them to stop the pain, to not do this or that.

Liora stepped away from our group.

"Where are you going?" I asked Liora as she walked off.

"To help," she said in a quiet tone lined with steel.

To me, she looked absurdly small and vulnerable as she stepped carefully over the battlefield in bare feet, aiming for the nearest person in need of a healer.

I wasn't sure what to do—where to go.

"There's Yuma," Sefra announced.

My sister's gaze pointed me downstream, where Yuma wandered among the survivors, consoling and organizing. Her long braids were swept up into a large bun, and she'd changed into tough leathers overlaid in places with painted mail. Zephyr, her falcon, was gliding on a dark wind overhead.

"We should talk to her." Sefra held a hand out to me.

I grabbed it and let her pull me up. Flaring my wings to steady myself, I glanced down at where Adrianna crouched beside Zeke. He was sat up, but he looked nauseous, and his wings hung listlessly from his back.

"Are you staying here?" I asked Adrianna.

She nodded, as if that was all she was capable of. My heart knotted up in concern for her. For Zeke.

Sefra set off. That pushed me to go after her.

We met Yuma farther downstream. "I'm sorry for your losses, Yuma," Sefra said by way of a greeting.

"Me too," I added, hating how worthless my words felt.

"Thank you." Yuma looked as if she'd aged a hundred years in a day. "There will be time to honor the dead. But right now we need to decide what we're going to do, and quickly."

Her attention skipped to the fighting over the plains, and then onto me. "Abraxus likely tracked Hasan's army here. If he knew they were looking for you and your companions, then he's already guessed you're here. If he asks after you, I can say you've already fled."

"Two of his people already saw me in The Oasis Lounge," I said, stress churning up my guts. "If they've given him a physical description of me, I won't be able to hide. Not with these." I flared my feathered wings.

For a second I considered retracting them. But ultimately, it seemed pointless. His people would recognize my face, not to mention Adrianna's and Liora's.

"Then, I'll grant you sanctuary." My puzzled look had Yuma adding, "I'll claim you as part of my tribe. That way if Abraxus takes you against your will, I can demand that you're returned to me. To refuse such a request would be a declaration of war. My people are well-liked in Asitar, enough for him to think twice about raising arms against us. It's the only protection I can offer you."

Sefra used my silence to say, "We can still try to make an escape."

One look at her, and I could tell she didn't think we'd succeed. Yet she had offered anyway. She had given me the choice. And if we ran or flew away, what then? Would the furies and their riders give chase? Quite possibly.

I thought back to my conversation with Adrianna and Liora. We had discussed then what to do about Abraxus. Circumstances might not allow for us to get him on his own. But with any luck, he still carried the starstone on his person.

I felt the weight of that moment. I was at a crossroads, and if I made the wrong choice ... Well, I didn't want to think about what could happen.

Looking out on the destruction, I made my decision.

I focused on Yuma. "I don't want you putting yourself or your people in any more danger, not for me. Besides, it might benefit everyone if I meet Abraxus." I pretended not to see my sister opening her mouth, and I forged ahead. "He's got the starstone."

"He … What?" Sefra gaped at me. "Are you sure?"

Even Yuma seemed surprised.

"As sure as I can be." I crossed my arms. "Dain also said that if Abraxus found me, I shouldn't try to fight him. I should talk to him instead."

Sefra's head inched back into her shoulders. "*Dain* told you that? But he's …"

"Dead. I know," I said, chest twinging. "It was his spirit."

After a few beats of thoughtful silence, she added, "Did he tell you … Do you know who Abraxus is—who he really is?"

I nodded. "And I know I'm the key to his revenge against Archon. That's why I think he might give me the stone if I ask for it. I have to try anyway."

Her pause was uncertain, skeptical, and worried. I saw the words *This is a bad idea* cross her face as clearly as if she'd shouted them.

Yuma ended the silence. "I'll be expected to enter Abraxus's camp to thank him for his assistance to my people. If you're resolved to meet him, then you should accompany me. It might help you to be with someone who's met him before."

I frowned. "You've met him? Why didn't you say?"

She shrug-ruffled her wings. "The meetings were short and only about my gaining approval to travel through his territories."

"I'll go with you too," Sefra declared in a stubborn way.

"Are you mad? You're a light-wielder," I whisper-hissed at her.

A pale eyebrow arched. "Am I? How extraordinary."

"Sefra, if he realizes—"

"So it's okay for you to meet with him but not for me?"

That shut me up.

"I'm coming with you, and you won't convince me otherwise," Sefra finished, countenance resolved.

I know I'd feel easier if she went with you, Thea needled me.

"Fine," I sighed out. "I need to tell Adi and Li."

I spun about and walked up the riverbank. Sefra and Yuma trailed after me.

We reached Zeke first. He still sat, his head slumped in his hands, Adrianna a statue beside him.

Yuma fussed over Zeke when she discovered what was wrong with him. I pulled Adrianna aside and outlined what I planned on doing. "Do you want me to go with you?" was all she said once I'd finished.

I looked down at Zeke. "You should stay with him."

Adrianna's gaze slanted toward her mate.

"He'll be okay," I said softly. "We'll ask for a shaman the second Abraxus's forces make contact."

That only got a tiny nod. Then she asked, "What about Liora? Will you take her?"

"The Shyani need her more, don't you think?"

She must've agreed because she changed tack. "And the stones you already have? Shouldn't you give them to me or Liora? You don't want him getting his hands on them," she ended under her breath.

The stones stay with you, Zola ordered. *If your plan to talk to Abraxus goes badly, you'll need to use their power to defend yourself.*

Thea added, *And Zola and I should be with you when you meet him.*

An odd choice of words, I thought.

"My great-aunts want me to keep them with me," I explained.

Adrianna pursed her lips. "If Sefra's going, I won't fight you on this. But if you need us, send up a beacon with your magic. If he tries anything—"

"I got it," I said, holding her piercing gaze.

She finally nodded, accepting my decision.

I set my sights on Liora, who had continued tending to people in the not-so-far-off distance. As soon as I'd reached her and caught her up, she nodded nervously. "I'll come with you."

It didn't take long to persuade her against that. I suspected it had nothing to do with my protests and everything to do with the injured surrounding her. Their pleas for help weren't something she could ignore. She returned to her healing work, and I turned toward the river, toward where Abraxus's army destroyed the last remnants of Hasan's forces. I waited there for the dark god to show his face.

CHAPTER 24
A PAINFUL REVELATION

Under a gibbous moon, I watched as the sidir vanished into the west, unneeded, their job done, and the furies and their riders settled on the plains across the river.

The minutes crawled by on all fours, and every second that passed was another moment spent dwelling on what might happen next. On whether I would soon meet with a god, a prince of the dark court.

When the opportunity to divert my mind presented itself, I seized it. Yuma had organized a group to move the bodies peppering the riverbank. To separate the dead from the injured.

It was the stuff of nightmares: the smell of fresh arterial blood, the ugly wounds on their bodies, the tears of grieving mourners. But I couldn't stand about doing nothing, ignoring the pain around me. That would've been so much worse.

Sefra stuck by my side, helping me in my grim task. Liora continued seeing to patients upstream from me. Adrianna guarded a clammy-browed Zeke.

"Mother Yuma, people are coming."

That warning was shouted out again by a few other Shyani.

Sefra and I halted on our way to pick up another body. I cast my gaze a short distance away, to where Yuma held her growing list of the dead. Her strong chin was pointed up at the sky. I followed her line of sight.

Three fae had left the encampment being established on the other side of the cat-tailed river. These emissaries flew over the water toward us. Before they landed, I recognized two of them from The Oasis Lounge in Casatana: Red-Wing and Black-Wing. The twin spies were accompanied by a third male with hair braided along his scalp.

Yuma strode down to meet them.

Should I join her now or wait? Before I could decide whether to walk straight into the wolf den, I was spotted by one of the wolves. Black-Wing nudged his brother and nodded in my direction.

Red-Wing's focus skipped to me.

The twin's jaws wagged. There were too many sound disturbances for me to hear them, but whatever transpired led the strange male in the group to stare at me. He beckoned me over with a curl of his fingers. My stomach flipped.

"Still want to come with me?" I whispered to Sefra.

"If you're going, so am I."

All right then.

Palms sticky, I paced down to the river's edge.

Black-Wing greeted me in a tone too cheerful given where we were—what we'd just lived through. "I thought you'd be off hiding somewhere."

What was his name again? Benjamin?

Red-Wing grinned. "Thanks for making our job so easy."

"You're welcome," I said, notes smothered in sarcasm.

A raven of all things swooped down and perched on the unknown male's shoulder.

"I'm Azmodayus," said the unfamiliar fae. "This is Benjamin and Rafi. We've been sent with a message from Abraxus, Commander of the Free Companies. He wishes for you and Yuma Najiri to join him in his tent."

"I'll also be joining them," Sefra announced.

"The invitation did not ..." Azmodayus's eyes unfocused. A few scant seconds later, he said, "Never mind. You can come."

Wait. What?

"Have you been empowered to take requests?" Yuma asked Azmodayus.

"What is it that you want?"

"My people are in urgent need of healers and supplies," Yuma said, her voice strong and clear. "I don't want to wait to ask for Abraxus's help in this matter—not with so many people in pain."

The raven on Azmodayus's shoulder croaked. I could've sworn Azmodayus paused, as if to listen to it. Suspicion turned wheels in my mind. Was the raven a familiar? It didn't act like any normal bird I knew.

"Abraxus has already ordered our healers to assist your people," Azmodayus said. "They'll be dispatched shortly."

Movement stirred in my field of vision. Adrianna was marching over, determined. She didn't bother with the niceties. "Do you travel with a shaman?"

Azmodayus tipped his head. "Why?"

Sefra spoke first. "We have a friend who's been poisoned with a bloodied blade."

That didn't stir Azmodayus. His expression remained set in unfeeling rock. "The shaman's energies are currently depleted—"

"I don't care." Nostrils flaring, Adrianna looked ready to breathe fire. "Your shaman has to help him."

"Please," I said, adding a grain of politeness.

Azmodayus addressed Adrianna. "As I was about to say before you interrupted, I can place your friend in the shaman's tent. That will allow him to be worked on as and when Tefór's strength allows."

"My mate isn't going anywhere alone, and why do we have to go to the shaman's tent?" Adrianna asked, suspicion underpinning her words.

"Because that's where he and all his supplies are." No sarcasm. Just plain fact. "Benjamin will show you and your mate where to go."

Adrianna's jaw tensed. But she didn't dig her heels in for long. "Fine."

I shared a fleeting look with Adrianna. A silent goodbye and a *be careful*. She glanced away first and turned to Benjamin. "This way."

Wheeling about, she walked off. He fell into step behind her.

"You three"—Azmodayus's inky gaze traveled over me, Yuma, and Sefra—"follow me."

I didn't have to ask Sefra to carry me. She lifted me into her arms without a second's pause.

"Are your wings injured?" Azmodayus asked me. "Do you need healing?"

The raven's head jutted forward. It seemed very interested in my response.

"No. I'm fine."

"Then, why are you being carried?"

Heat singed my cheeks.

"She's tired," Sefra lied. "Drained."

Azmodayus nodded. "Very well. This way."

The raven on his shoulder was the first to take off. Azmodayus went second. Rafi third. Yuma fourth.

Sefra ascended, and my throat thickened up as if I'd gulped mud. This suddenly seemed like the worst idea in the entire history of ideas.

You're committed now. You'll just have to make it work.

Zola sounded sour enough to curdle milk. I didn't react to her being short with me. Not when she'd lain her brother's death at Abraxus's door.

We touched down on the opposite riverbank. Sefra set me down on stunted grass.

Azmodayus led us along a wide path through the encampment. The raven flew ahead of us, croaking loudly, announcing our arrival to all.

Groups of people flew into this new camp from every direction. These arrivals weren't clad in war paint, armor, or blood. I suspected they were reserve soldiers or part of a non-warrior contingent of Abraxus's Free Companies.

These newcomers joined the bloodstained fighters in building up a settlement from nothing. All around me, fae and human worked side by side. A rare sight. But stranger still were the other beings that helped them: those that appeared human but sported curly horns atop their heads, those that looked fae but had moss for hair, scales for skin, or fire for wings. Together these people assembled tents and cots, fed and stabled furies, and prepared fires and cookware.

Azmodayus stopped at a finished tent the color of desert earth, of honey and apricot. A large ring of space surrounded it, separating and marking it out as important.

At the curtain door, Azmodayus gestured to an empty rack. "Weapons go here."

Yuma conceded at once. Sefra and I were more reluctant.

Azmodayus and Rafi weren't done. They patted the three of us down, searching for concealed steel. Once satisfied we weren't hiding anything, Azmodayus said, "Wait for me to announce you."

He faced the fabric curtain of the tent. Before he could go inside, two people popped out. Alarm knotted up my already sore muscles. Sefra inched nearer, sticking closer than a high-noon shadow.

The new arrivals were as different as could be. One was a short male with a bald scalp inked in spirals, skin the color and texture of tanned hide, and a silver beard that he'd thrown casually over his shoulder like a scarf.

The second male, however, was a tower of lean muscle. He stood a few inches above me in overlapping pieces of dark leather studded with metal and stitched with silver thread. I didn't see any weapons on him, but he was intimidating enough without them. His blood-speckled brow, prominent nose, and scarred mouth weren't pretty or friendly, and the bony spikes fixed to the mantle of his bat-colored wings looked lethal. But his eyes were the thing. They looked ancient, hollowed out by experiences I suspected were painful or regretful. For there was a cynical cast to his gaze, a hard edge that hinted he'd seen much of the world and found it wanting.

"Well met, Yuma." His gaze shifted to me and Sefra. "I am Abraxus, leader of the Free Companies."

His baritone sounded pleasant enough, not cold or cruel like I'd expected. The accent was neutral, precise.

"This is Tefór, my shaman." Abraxus signaled to the male beside him. "I was about to send him to attend to your poisoned friend."

Sefra was quick to challenge that. "How did you hear about that so fast?"

The raven flew down and perched on Abraxus's wing-claw. "My familiar, Danu, relayed the words from your meeting."

I gave the bird a wary glance. That explained a few things. The raven eyed me back, its dark stare unsettling. I looked away first.

"Have you ever cured somebody struck with a bloodied blade?" Sefra asked Tefór.

The shaman's bushy eyebrows slashed together. "Are you questioning my abilities, faeling?"

Sefra punched out a disbelieving laugh that was almost a cough. "I'm hundreds of years old. Hardly a faeling."

A contemptuous snort was followed by, "If you're not over a thousand, then you're a faeling to me."

"This is why you don't have more friends," Abraxus remarked. "You're much too annoying."

His voice was flat, but his eyes held a glint of dark humor.

"Friends. *Pah*," Tefór barked. "Who needs 'em? Burdensome creatures, always expecting you to remember things, attend things, and listen to their drivel. No thank you."

Turning a cold shoulder to the shaman, Abraxus faced Sefra. "Contrary to how it may appear, Tefór is more than capable of curing the male. But your friend will have to remain here for a day or so while he heals."

The shaman mashed his lips in a gummy manner. "He won't be worm-food. Let him be grateful for that."

I gritted my teeth. What an ass.

Abraxus sighed in a long-suffering way, rubbing the spot under his eyebrow. "Go away, Tefór. See to your new patient."

"Fine. But I'm leaving because I wish it, not because you told me."

With that, the shaman hobbled off, a great deal of huffing and puffing accompanying his movements. I had a perverse desire to laugh. This meeting wasn't what I'd expected.

Abraxus looked at Azmodayus and Rafi. "You have an hour. Then you're to take first shift as my guard."

"Yes, Commander," they said in a double act.

"Go." Abraxus pointed his chin up and away.

Rafi and Azmodayus left.

Yuma addressed Abraxus. "Thank you for coming to our aid. You saved a great many of my people today."

"And you helped me weaken an evil king."

Yuma's eyes narrowed a touch. "How did you know where his forces would be?"

My pulse skipped.

"I have a spy inside Hasan's camp. They told me that a sidir enslaved to the king had spotted people flying toward your settlement." Abraxus's cheerless eyes skipped to me. "Those people resembled a group of witches that Hasan has become determined to hunt down. So much so that the idiot risked sending his forces into the open and into a territory that wasn't his in order to retrieve them. And here we all are."

I shook internally. I'd brought disaster to the Shyani simply by being in their vicinity. Was that my future? Had I become a curse to anybody who dared help me?

"If you knew Hasan's forces were coming here, why didn't you warn us?" Yuma asked Abraxus, toeing the line between accusatory and diplomatic.

"I only heard from my contact a few hours ago," he said, as bland as potatoes. "And my entire company raced here as fast as our wings could carry us. Even if I'd sent a bird with a warning, it wouldn't have reached you before us."

Did I believe him? No. Not really.

"But I'm also not sorry it turned out like this," Abraxus added. "The Shyani have spent years traveling through areas my warriors have liberated. You've long enjoyed the freedoms that my people have fought for, without bearing any of the cost. I think it's about time your tribe picked up their swords instead of sitting back and letting others die for you."

Yuma's chin remained up, but her eyes flicked down. She wasn't speaking up or defending herself. And although it pained me, I couldn't bring myself to argue his point.

Abraxus went on. "You and I have never been friends, Yuma. But we haven't been enemies either. I do not wish for that to change. Therefore, to prevent any bad will forming between us, I'll put my camp at your disposal. Your warriors will be fed, healed, clothed, and offered shelter for as long as they want it."

"Thank you." Yuma's gratitude sounded hollow.

"I won't keep you any longer. I know you must be eager to return to your people," Abraxus said, making his desire to be rid of her plain. Then he confronted me. "I wish to speak with you alone, light-wielder. Oblige me."

Not a question. A demand.

"She's not going anywhere without me," Sefra insisted, wings twitching.

He shot her a look that would've made grown males shit themselves. "Isn't that up to her, Sefra?"

I felt a nasty lurch in my midriff.

"You know who I am?" Sefra's finger hooked around my thumb. From the tension in her grip, I thought she might be about to push me behind her.

"Obviously," he replied, expressionless.

The agitation and hostility rolling off my sister tasted like chili flakes on my tongue. Fearing what would happen if she lost control, I told her, "It's okay. I'll go with him."

"No." That was almost a plea. "You shouldn't be alone with him."

Sefra hadn't said that quietly. I peeked up at Abraxus, worried about his reaction. He didn't seem bothered by her blatant distrust of him. His attention was fixed on me.

I *really* didn't want to be alone with this male. I'd only spent a couple of minutes with him, and I felt off-balance. He veered between menacing and disarming. A combination that threatened to be persuasive and manipulative.

But if I went with him, I wouldn't have to worry about Sefra. I could focus on getting the starstone. Courage rising, I pulled my hand from hers and said, "I'll be all right."

The conflict was clear upon her face. She didn't hide or conceal much, it seemed.

Yuma directed her next words at Abraxus. "I want it understood that this girl is a friend to my people. Should harm come to her—"

"Do not threaten me, Yuma," Abraxus said, his voice deepening and hardening so much it gave me the shivers. "Besides, we're only going inside my tent. I'm not taking her to the fucking moon." He drew aside the curtain to his shelter. "After you, light-wielder."

Sefra was fearless and bold in her address to him. "If you lay a single wing on her, I'll kill you."

He flashed his teeth in a lethal chuckle. "Is that so?"

Flesh studded with goosebumps, I stepped out in front of Sefra. Since I was taller than her, Abraxus had to stare at me instead.

A shadow left Abraxus's face. As if it was retreating from daylight.

I glanced back at Sefra and Yuma. "I'll see you both later."

Facing forward, I walked straight into his lair: the tent's innards turned inside out, and I was torn across space.

I appeared in the middle of a lonely landscape. Underfoot were rolling hills carpeted in spires of grass that danced in a temperate breeze beneath a dreamy moon. A fury, one of the largest I'd seen, raced across the cloudless night sky.

Abraxus flanked me. "Speak."

"Where are we? How did we get here?"

"It's somewhere in southern Asitar, miles from where we're currently encamped."

And miles from my sister. From Liora and Adrianna.

Danu, who'd stayed on his wing during our relocation, now flew off.

Abraxus slowly walked on ahead of me, running his hand through the foxtails. "As for how we got here. I created a bridge in between two locations."

He made that sound so simple. Quite normal. I struggled to form a response to that, so I pointed up at the beast above. "Is that your fury?"

"Yes. I sent her here earlier. As a reward."

"A reward?"

"She did well in the battle. And she likes the hunting grounds in these parts."

"What's her name?"

Abraxus stopped and whirled, facing me. "How about you give me your name first? Then I'll tell you what hers is."

I held his stare. Here stood a wild animal, and I couldn't show him my throat.

"It's Ena." A gnat might've sounded louder than me.

Blink. "Well, Ena, my fury is called Tula. Now, shall we get to it?"

"Get to what?"

"My people said that you've used sunlight and moonlight." He started circling me. "That's a particularly rare combination in a witch. I have seen it once before, however, and their magical signature was nothing like yours. There's more to you, which leads me to think you've been gifted with other disciplines. Care to share?"

His casual act was like a dog licking a hand only to sink its teeth into palmy flesh.

I sucked in a breath. No going back after this. "I can use waterlight ... And starlight."

Abraxus halted about fifteen feet in front of me. His dark, mutable eyes bore into me. "So here you are at last."

His unimpressed tone hit me hard. A spiked mace to my breastbone.

In an abrupt motion, he strode closer. "How old are you?"

Refusing to be intimidated, I lifted my chin an inch. "What does that matter?"

"Must I repeat myself?"

I pulled my wings in closer to my spine. "Eighteen."

A barking laugh. "Eighteen? The future of this world is in the hands of a faeling barely out of swaddling." He gestured aggressively to the sky, yelling, "Great fucking plan."

A blush scolded my cheeks. Prick.

"Show me your magic," he demanded.

I bristled. "Why?"

"I want to see that Balor and Persephone weren't mad to put their faith in a damned prophecy, and that you can actually take on the Dark King—one of the most powerful gods in the whole constellation—and win."

Pride dented, I fired back. "And help you get revenge against Archon?"

He stilled. "Pick your next words carefully."

"I'm not trying to piss you off," I said, balling up my hands. "I'm trying to show you that I'm not as clueless as you think I am."

"What is it that you think you know?" he asked, his voice dipping below freezing.

"I know Archon's your father. And that Nyx killed Desmi and stole your daughter."

Abraxus's outline seemed to expand as menace rippled off him. It stuck in the back of my mouth like hair and made me want to heave my stomach contents onto the ground.

I showed my neck in a submissive move that my inner fae demanded. She—my female—understood the dangers better than a mind that still clung to a human way of thinking could.

His wrathful gaze held me. "I would ask where you'd heard about my history with Archon. But since you've been staying with the story-weavers, I won't bother."

"I didn't hear it from them," I said quickly.

"Liar."

His snarl plucked at my nerves worse than tweezing hair.

Don't outright lie to him, Thea warned. *He was a member of the dark court for eons. All of their inhabitants are excellent at discerning truth from lie. They must be, in order to survive.*

Well, crap.

"Okay, I didn't learn it *all* from the storyweavers." Thinking it was best to change tack and get to the point, I said, "Look, if you want Archon dead, you can't rip my head off no matter how much you might want to—agreed?"

No answer. Fine.

"Wouldn't it be better if we worked together?"

A painful silence shouldered in between us.

Finally, he said, "What are you proposing?"

The tightness gripping my lungs loosened. "To start, I want the starstone. I know you have it or had it."

As smooth as silk, he asked, "How would you know that?"

"That's not important. It belongs with me."

His disdain was exhibited in a raised eyebrow. "Maybe it does. But as I said, I need to see your powers first. Then we'll discuss the starstone."

Frustration simmered beneath my skin. "So, what? You want me to perform? Attack you?"

A humorless laugh. "If you can make a dent in me, go right ahead. In fact, I'd thank you for it."

I recognized the look on his face: a bottomless despair and a numb acceptance that the emptiness inside was all there ever would be. That if he saw a light in the void, it would be a mirage.

Abraxus made a *go on* gesture. "Well?"

Danu settled on Abraxus's shoulder. The raven eyed me expectantly.

Great, I thought gloomily. More people to watch and judge me.

I channeled sunlight, shaping a sword in my mind. That visualization led to a golden blade manifesting in my hand.

Abraxus snapped his fingers and cloaked my sun-sword in shadow. His magic smothered mine in seconds. The blade vanished.

I drowned the sunlight in my veins and sent out an invisible wave of waterlight toward Abraxus.

He raised an irreverent brow as my magic rolled over him. The waterlight and bright moon above revealed a dark halo emanating from his body.

You're seeing a glimpse of what firstborn energy remains to him, Thea informed.

Interesting. But it didn't help me in this moment.

I dammed up my waterlight and pushed out a moon-shield.

Danu flew off. He must've known what Abraxus would do next. The dark god blurred toward me and punched through my moon-barrier.

It collapsed. Instantly.

Winded, my knees went out from under me. I fell to the soft ground with a nosebleed.

He backed up a few steps. "Show me the starlight."

"Fuck you," I spat at him.

A derisive huff. "I've heard every profanity in every tongue you can imagine. If you're going to curse me, at least come up with something original. Now get up."

Not wanting to fuel his doubts about me, I wiped the blood from my nose and clambered up on weak legs.

I concentrated on pulling in starlight. A faint palm-light was the result.

Abraxus waved a hand. "Enough." His chest expanded in a bracing inhale. "All right. This is the plan. You'll stay with me and I'll train you to fight Archon. It'll take a lot of work and it might already be too late, but all we can do is try."

That stopped me cold. I collected my thoughts enough to blurt out, "I'm already being trained."

His eyebrows snapped together. "By whom?"

"That's not important."

"Of course it is. Because if this is all you can manage in eighteen years, you need a new teacher."

The color of my thoughts turned an angry red. "I've had my abilities less than a month."

"A month?" he said, sharper than a freshly whetted blade. "Has that got anything to do with the fact you used to be human?"

My stomach turned like the sails of a windmill. "How did you know about that?"

"Because one of Morgan's spies—one Nala Tran—sent a message to the Solar Court after she failed to capture your group in Casatana. I was made aware of the contents of this letter. In it, she described how she'd read your friend's mind. She said she'd found Serena Smith. The lightwielder and former human."

I groaned internally. "Couldn't you have intercepted her message?"

"That wasn't possible." Refusing to elaborate, he added, "I'll admit that if you've only had a short time to hone your abilities, then your lack of skill isn't as discouraging."

He cupped his chin in a thoughtful way.

"Then why not give me the starstone?" I urged him.

"If I gave it to you now, you couldn't handle it."

"What are you talking about?"

"Do you possess any of the other stones?"

"No." That answer tripped off my tongue before I could think twice.

"Lying again," he said, his eyes flashing.

Abraxus raised his palm. Everything vanished.

No more earthly smells and cool breezes. No more stars and moon. The total absence of light stole my sense of time and space. I felt the walls of my own existence bend around me, suffocating me.

I reached for my magic and found dead silence. The loss was a crack in my soul. I hadn't realized how much I'd come to rely on it.

I wanted to scream and rage, but there was no strength in my voice. No fire in my belly. No hope in my heart.

A disembodied voice sounded. "The dark can be as revealing as the light. It shows the magic of the two stones you already bear. Their power's already close to overwhelming you. *See*."

A blue shimmer and a sunset glow appeared at my chest. These colors expanded out from my body by a few inches and vibrated there, like an enraged pulse.

"Yet, you seek to carry another one?" A pause. "Take it, then. See what happens."

The world returned. Light. Life. Time.

I sucked a shaky breath deep into my lungs.

Abraxus stood before me. I had half a mind to punch the bastard, but what he held up distracted me. A thin black chain held a sugar-white diamond. A speck of black lived in the middle of the stone; it looked like a drop of ink.

"What is that?" I pointed at the dot. The flaw in the gem.

He made a rough noise in his throat. "I'll explain later. Are you going to take this or not?"

Abraxus held out the starstone.

I took it without thinking.

My vision flashed white and black. Then I knew no more.

∼

I woke up as abruptly as I'd passed out.

Rearing up on my elbows, I glanced around.

The world seemed to be standing up on its tiptoes, quiet and expectant, waiting for the golden promise of dawn to become more than just a flash upon the plain. For the sun to ascend to its lofty throne.

Abraxus was sitting past my feet, his fury curled up around him. Tula raised her triangular head to look at me.

Wary, I returned her intelligent gaze.

She made a *chit-chit-chit* noise. A call of sorts.

"Hello?"

A mewl-yip answered.

Abraxus stroked the glossy hide of her stocky neck. Tula closed her liquid-black eyes with a rumbly purr. Adorable.

Without eye contact, Abraxus asked, "Are you still determined to take on the starstone?"

At that, I realized the starstone wasn't in my hand anymore. Panic hitched underneath my ribs. He'd taken one stone—what about the others?

I peered down the front of my blood-spattered shirt. A relieved sigh escaped me upon finding the two stones untouched.

"Why did the starstone do that to me?"

Abraxus twisted his upper body toward me. "I told you. Because you aren't strong enough to take possession of it yet. I don't think it helps that your starlight's so weak. Although, I won't blame you for that lapse. It's Zola and Thea's fault."

Zola's growl was so loud it resonated in my chest.

"How did you know ..."

"About Zola and Thea?"

A stunned nod.

"I sensed their energy in the waterstone when I used my power on you." He nodded at my chest—at where the waterstone sat beneath my shirt. "Balor's daughters are communicating with you, aren't they? I presume to train you in everything but darkling magic."

"Why would they teach me darkling magic?" A knee-jerk response.

His face looked like an incoming storm. "They didn't tell you?"

My chest constricted. "Tell me what?"

"You have darkling magic."

"I don't." I shook my head. "I can't. They would've said something."

The goddesses were eerily silent.

Abraxus looked at me with pity and contempt. "You're going to have to lose that naivety, and fast, if you want to survive what's coming. You also need to accept the fact you have darkling magic." Another order. "If you don't, your starlight won't develop and you won't be able to use the stone."

"I don't understand," I forced out a bit breathless.

He sighed. "Starlight and darkling magic are two sides of the same coin. They illuminate and strengthen each other. Meaning, you can only grow stronger in one if you practice both. That is, unless you're a god—which you are not."

I struggled to order my thoughts. "Practice what? What exactly does darkling magic do?"

"It can manifest in various different forms," he told me. "Yours is chaos. That's what resides in the stone."

Doubt drew my brows down. "I've never heard of chaos magic."

"That's because the only other person in the world who can claim to possess it is sitting in front of you."

My heart damn near stopped. "You use it?"

A sarcastic look. "Yes. Do you have a problem with that?"

I'd no energy to sweeten my words. "I've got the same magic as a dark god. I'd call that a problem."

"Former dark god," he corrected. "And magic does not have a morality. It simply is. It is what the wielder uses it for. Now, will you try channeling chaos, or will you hide behind prejudice and stay weak?"

That challenge stiffened my backbone. I had to become stronger to defeat Archon. That's all there was to it. "What would I have to do?"

Abraxus turned to Tula. "Stay."

The fury offered him a slow blink. As if she understood.

In one fluid move, Abraxus unfolded his legs and stood. "Take a walk with me."

He strode forward, his gait putting me in mind of a big cat stalking through long grass. I jumped up and joined his side.

"You start by finding the chaos within yourself," he said.

"Bit vague."

"Then let me be clear." Abraxus rounded on me, bringing us both to a halt. "You're your own worst enemy."

I resisted the urge to back up and put distance between us. "Meaning?"

"You've known what it is to exist inside a cage." He stated that like an irrefutable fact. "To be without voice or wings. To be reduced to the smallest parts of yourself and to live that as your truth."

The past became a sea monster. It prowled the hostile depths of my mind while I grabbed an imaginary oar and paddled as far away as I could.

"That's over now." He tapped my temple twice. "But this is still holding you back. Your mind has become your prison."

I batted his hand away. "Stop it."

He didn't. "I read souls. And I see yours. The little bird has grown up to become powerful, but she'll only leave her cage when the situation demands it or when someone's there to hold her hand."

Anger and shame gutted me.

Abraxus showed no mercy. He kept pushing me. "Tell me, is your only wish to kill the Dark King? Have the two firstborn in your head convinced you that your only worth is as a weapon?" He went back to walking around me in a circle. Back to being a wolf—a predator. "What else could you do? Have you thought about that? Have you experimented with your magic outside of the confines of your lessons?"

My shoulders bunched up. "How is this helping me channel chaos magic?"

"Chaos lives and breathes when we're uninhibited. At its best, it's freedom. And at its worst, it's destruction. Is it any wonder it hasn't manifested in you? You're keeping yourself small, Ena. That's why the chaos hasn't presented in you before now, not even by accident."

My spirits plummeted, crushed beneath those words.

"To channel it, you must relive a moment when you've experienced true freedom—when you've let go. And if that doesn't work, think about when you've wanted to destroy someone. Not just kill. Destroy," he ended as if that were an everyday occurrence.

I didn't want to think about the latter option, so I turned my sight inward and searched for times when I had felt free. I decided on a recent memory of dancing with Adrianna and Liora. Hard to believe that had only been a few hours ago.

Abraxus continued. "It might be easier if you close your eyes. It's in the shadows that we feel safest—that we feel able to fully be ourselves."

Close my eyes? With him prowling around me? Not a chance.

I tried to dredge up that sense of being unburdened. All I got for my troubles was a headache. "It's not working."

"You're stiffer than a corpse," he observed dispassionately. "The key is surrender. Stop trying to force it. Just let it be."

"No offense, but it's difficult to relax with you nearby," I said, close to snapping.

He stopped circling me and stared at me straight-on. "I want Archon gone. You know that much at least. What could I gain from harming you?"

Fair point.

I focused on my chosen memory and unclenched, muscle by muscle.

My imagination or my magic brought me to a standstill on a bridge over a limitless void. I had to jump. I felt it in my bones. I had to trust something unknowable. To let the world take me where it wanted.

I had no choice. I leaped.

As I fell, the magic found me. It rushed in as if it had been waiting, and it claimed me as its own.

The sensation of falling ended with a jolt to my stomach.

My palms itched. I glanced down at my hands. There, several tendrils of darkness wove around my fingers. The shadows acted shyly, evaporating under my gaze like fog under a hot sun.

"Not bad for a first try," Abraxus said coolly.

I had chaos magic. I hadn't really believed it before. Hadn't wanted to.

And Thea and Zola had kept this from me.

I splayed a palm over my chest where my necklaces rested. *Why didn't either of you tell me about this? You must've known I had darkling magic.*

Thea projected her likeness to my left. Her presence increased my wariness. Why show up now?

Thea's sapphire gaze darted to Abraxus.

He was looking directly at her.

"Can you see her?" I asked.

"No, but I can sense her," he replied, his tone glacial.

Thea's face was a conflict in motion. There was intense dislike, but also something softer, sadder, as she peered up at him.

My great-aunt quickly shifted her attention to me. "Our father thought you might be different to other witches. That you might manifest starlight without the need for darkling magic. That's how it's always been for him. And since you share Balor's blood, he hoped you'd take after him."

"You could've mentioned it was a possibility—why didn't you?"

"Because we couldn't have instructed you in the use of chaos magic. The only person who can is Abraxus. And Balor didn't want you seeking him out, at least not unnecessarily." She freed a soft sigh that shuttered her eyes. "He feared you'd learn things that would unsettle you."

I felt cold all of a sudden. "I don't understand."

"You will," she replied, subdued. As if she carried the weight of a hundred suns on her back. "Tell Abraxus what Dain said to you."

"What's that got to do with chaos magic?"

"Just tell him, Ena." Her round eyes bled sympathy; regret, even. "Zola and I haven't told our court that Dain broke the rules to speak with you. We've tried to help you in our own way. But as for the rest of it ... we didn't think it was our place to say anything. Forgive us."

She faded away, leaving me with more questions than answers.

"What's wrong?" Abraxus demanded.

My thoughts went this way, then that way. I wanted to exit this conversation, but my ignorance would needle at me incessantly if I did.

Fighting past the lump in my throat, I said, "There's something you need to know. My father told me that if we were to meet, I should remind you about a promise that you made to him. And he wanted you to know that he expects you to keep it."

His gaze tapered. "Who was your father?"

"Dain Raynar."

A loaded pause.

"Not possible." His notes were sharp enough to flay skin. "Dain is dead. He's been dead for your entire lifetime. He can't have told you anything."

My gaze dropped to Abraxus's stress-clenched fists. Worried that he was about to strangle me, I explained. "I was able to talk to him while he was on the other side. I'm a dreamwalker."

His jawline squared off in disbelief. "Who was your mother?"

"Sati Lytir."

Abraxus's eyes flared, a dark fire sparking there. He moved for me.

Fear compelled me to call up a moon-shield.

His fingertips halted inches from my barrier. "I'm not going to hurt you." In harsh tones speaking of salted wounds, he added, "Just let me look at you."

"You are looking at me," I said, totally confused.

"Ena. Please."

A dark god was actually pleading with me. Alarm spread through me, disturbing my bowels, making them watery.

I released my moonlight to the ether.

Stepping into my space, he gripped and lifted my chin. As he stared into my eyes, his pupils dilated; black consumed indigo blue.

I was pinned beneath his gaze, feeling like a butterfly under the collector's needle, and the sting—the pain—was the same. I was five seconds from biting him when something shifted in Abraxus's expression. His sun-touched cheeks drained of color, becoming a shade of ash and ruin.

His mouth opened and some voice deep inside of me screamed *Don't say it!*

"I wish you were lying for both of our sakes." Releasing my chin, he murmured, "Your eyes are different, but I see him in you now. I see my son."

I froze, my mind static, my heart a block of ice. "What are you saying?"

He gave me a straight look. "I'm your grandfather."

CHAPTER 25
THE TRUTH AND LIE OF THE FIRSTBORN

Horror drained the life out of me. "You can't be."
"I assure you, I can," he said calmly.
I couldn't stop shaking my head. "No."
"Yes."
"Stop it!" My voice fractured.
"I know this must be a shock—"
"A shock," I screamed in his face. "This is more than a shock!"
Turning my back to him, I searched for a way out. I had to get out. Get away. Leave this body. Leave this life.
It can't be. It can't be. It can't be.
Zola? Thea? Tell me this isn't true.
I'm sorry, but it is, Thea said in a small way.
The truth didn't set me free. It tossed me into the worst hell imaginable.
Abraxus was my grandfather. Worse than that, the Dark King was my great-grandfather. I had been chosen to end my own kin.
That, there, ended me. I'd blocked out too much for too long. I'd tried to hold it together through the revelations, the changes, and the expectations. This was the lightning bolt that shattered my inner fortress. It tore down my protective walls and shook my foundations.
My legs went out from under me. "I can't do this. I can't do it."

"What can't you do?" Abraxus crouched beside me. Perfectly calm.

Dismantled, tears made rivers of my cheeks. "Any of it."

"But you will."

"No," I groaned. "No, I can't. It's too much."

Half out of my mind, I reached for the root of my kin bond—for my anchor. What would Frazer think of this? What if he looked at me differently? What if all my pack did?

Those thoughts inflicted a pain akin to having my organs scooped out with a blunt spoon. I unleashed a scream that wasn't fae or human. It was agony incarnate.

"Try to breathe," Abraxus murmured on my right.

Not wanting him to watch my implosion, I sobbed, "Go away."

Dry stalks snapped. A soft snout nuzzled me. I reared back as that simple touch shocked me.

It was just Tula. She placed her head in my lap and whined.

A surprised hiccup escaped me. Hand shaking, I petted her warm, smooth hide.

The comfort and acceptance that only an animal could provide stanched the inner bleeding that the sharp knife of truth had dealt me.

Tula went on to curl her fifteen-foot-long body around me in a crescent moon shape. I lay down next to her. There, I cried out the shock, horror, and fear. I drifted away on it. The only thing I could've compared it to was the sensation of being stuck in a tiny boat while violent swells battered it, trying to capsize it.

Eventually, the emotion that had tossed me about in a violent surf calmed. It turned into ripples against a lakeshore. Then even the ripples stopped.

I washed up on land; I could think straight again. The problem was that the world had restarted, and the business of living had to be gotten on with. For me, that meant satisfying a need to know more. To understand.

With limp arms, I pressed myself up into a seated position.

The sun had climbed a few rungs of the sky ladder. Other than shifting about a bit, Tula had remained where she was. Abraxus stood a little way off, surveying the gilded light that made the flaxen grasslands gleam.

I went to wipe my cheeks free of salt and misery with my shirt, but the blood spatter on it stopped me. I used the back of my hand instead.

Not trusting my legs to support my weight, I asked Abraxus from the ground, "Who's my grandmother?"

He turned toward me, a frown upon his brow. "Desmi, of course." He said that as if there could be no other option. No other possibility.

I grasped at a memory, saying, "Yuma never mentioned a son when she told me about Desmi and Amara."

"Storyweavers aren't infallible," he said, beating his clawed wings in irritation. "Quite the opposite. In fact, I once asked Yuma what she'd seen of me and my family. It was very little and none of it included Dain."

Curiosity niggled at me. "What were Desmi and Amara like? And my father—what was he like when you knew him?"

Abraxus's eyes emptied out, his face turned gaunt. "I won't talk about them."

A part of me wanted to argue against that. But how could I when his entire family had been taken from him? Of course he couldn't talk about it.

I stowed my disappointment. "And the promise? What was the promise you made to my father?"

Abraxus looked off to his side. Apparently addressing thin air was preferable to staring at me. "A long time ago, Dain had a vision that I'd meet somebody important to him. He asked that I do everything in my power to help her—you—survive." His facial muscles pulled tight against harsh bones. "Our relationship was nonexistent by that point. And I knew if he was contacting me, he had to be desperate. I wanted his forgiveness. I wanted my son back. So I agreed."

"Will you keep your promise?" I asked, fearing the answer.

He beheld me as if the very sight pained him. "I would not break such an oath. Nor should I wish to. You are the only kin I have left in this world."

Conflicting emotions and uncertain words lodged in my throat.

Abraxus approached me, his hand outstretched.

It was then I noticed his silver wedding band. He wore it even after all these centuries. That steadied me. I wasn't sure why.

I straightened up with his help. "If you're serious, then why don't you give the starstone to Sefra? It won't affect her, and she can pass it on to me when I'm ready."

"I won't entrust it to anyone less powerful than myself."

"You don't know that you're more powerful—"

"Yes, I do."

I cursed him silently. "You promised to help me."

He came back with, "That doesn't mean doing everything you say."

"Maybe you just want to keep the stone for yourself?" I said coldly.

A bemused look. "Why would I bother? I can't use starlight. The stone is no better than a pebble to me."

I flashed back to what Atlas had said about the starstone, about how he thought Abraxus had acquired it. "Then why did you take it from its original bearer—the one Balor entrusted to carry it and hand down to me?"

"Teren, you mean?" An ugly look marred his face. "Do you know what happened to him?"

"Did you kill him?" I asked, not bothering with guile.

"Yes," he admitted without a hint of hesitation. "And you would have done the same."

A blink. "Why?"

"Let's walk." He made a restless motion to the horizon. "I hate to be standing about."

I obliged, ambling alongside him.

"Balor entrusted the starstone to Teren because he was the only witch still alive who could use starlight. But the stone's power proved too tempting for him." His features formed unforgiving lines. "He was always weak-minded. It wasn't long before he went mad and started killing everything and anything that got in his way. The day he murdered a faeling was the day I ripped his heart out of his chest."

Horror sliced through me. "A faeling ..." I stopped and whirled toward him. "You don't think that I'll turn out like him."

"No."

His reassurance didn't oust the uneasy feeling in my heart.

We traveled side by side. I could almost hear the cogs of his mind turning. Before he could ensnare me in whatever he was plotting, I said,

"I know of another way you could fulfill your promise to my father—you could help me and my friends return to Aldar. Most captains won't risk the crossing, but perhaps with your contacts ..."

"I'm not convinced you should be returning to Aldar."

And there it was.

"You won't stop me from leaving," I told him.

"Did I say I'd try?"

I shot him an evil look.

"I won't force you," he said, cool as could be. "But I will make a case for you staying with me."

"I don't want you to."

"Afraid I'll succeed?"

Irritation flared my nostrils.

"Just hear me out." He didn't wait for me to agree. "Thea and Zola were too young to face Archon in the Court War, which means you're learning to fight your enemy from people who know nothing about him other than what they've learned from second-hand accounts." This time, Abraxus halted. "Ena, doesn't it seem odd that Balor picked them to train you?"

Disquiet rattled me.

Don't listen to him, Zola snarled. *He's a manipulative shit.*

Venom seeped into my mental voice. *You've got no right to talk about being manipulative. You tried to keep me from my own grandfather just because you were worried about what he'd tell me. So keep your opinions to yourself.*

Silence answered. Good, I thought savagely.

"To be honest, I hadn't really thought about it," I told Abraxus. "But I'm guessing you think it's odd?"

"To answer that properly, I'd have to tell you what happened after Nyx butchered Desmi and dragged Amara into the dark court." Cold sorrow and hot anger infused his notes. "I begged Balor and Freyta to help me retrieve my daughter. They refused and insisted that marching into Archon's territory would be suicide. They had to lock me up to stop me from trying to kill them all."

Does that sound like someone you should be listening to? Zola snapped.

Zola, stop. You're not helping.

I ignored both of them.

Abraxus went on, spinning his tale. "By the time they released me,

Persephone had already made the prophecy about you. And d'you know something? Balor was *angry*. He was angry that one day there would be someone powerful enough to destroy Archon, and to do what he'd failed to do for so long."

My dead laugh rang out. "You think the Light King was jealous of me?"

"Yes."

My amusement died. Fuck. He was serious.

"Not only that, but he was scared of you, Ena," Abraxus persisted softly, intensely. "Because you're a prophesied god-killer—an extremely powerful one at that. You also have to be trusted with the stones, which will only make you stronger. Taking that into account, don't you think it's in his best interests to mold you in a way that serves him and the light court by having his daughters watch over your every move?"

Doubt morphed into a snake that twisted around my heart and squeezed. "But if Balor wanted to spy on me, why didn't he become my guide?"

A scornful huff. "Because he wouldn't want to grow attached to you."

"You know Balor's my kin? He was my mother's grandfather—"

"All the more reason for him to keep his distance from you."

I bridled my suspicions and challenged him. "You say Balor's trying to control me, but how are you any different? You only told me this story so I'd lose faith in Zola and Thea and train with you instead."

He crossed his arms. "That's partially true. I do want you to stay. But that doesn't make what I've said untrue. I've been upfront and honest with you from the start. Can Zola and Thea say the same?"

My lips pinched together. "No, but I'm still not staying. Can you accept that? Or are you going to treat me like all the other light-wielders you've forced into your army?"

"I don't do that anymore," he said, his brows drawing down, becoming as brooding as my brother's.

I failed to mask my disbelief. Abraxus read my expression, adding, "I left your sister alone, didn't I? Or should I say half sister." He frowned. "She's Sati's girl, correct? I can't recall who her father is."

"Lycon. He ruled the Solar Court before Sefra," I said distractedly.

He nodded as if I'd made him recall some distant memory.

Deciding to be direct, I asked him, "So why don't you hunt light-wielders anymore?"

His chest expanded in a shallow sigh. "There was a time when all I could think about was the dark court's return. I set about gathering the most powerful allies I could, but thanks to dick-for-brains Balor, they'd lost their memories of the war," he said bitterly. "Most thought I was mad. The surviving knights remembered, of course, but they followed Atlas's lead like the mindless sheep they were."

"What did Atlas want them to do?"

"Atlas thought his father must've had a good reason to erase people's memories. So instead of preparing for a future war, he set about rebuilding the Lytir legacy." In a temper, he gritted his teeth and a pulse went in his jaw. "Such vanity and stupidity made me lose whatever restraint I had left. That was when I started pressing witches into my service."

Disgust coated my tongue. "And then?"

Abraxus resumed his walk across the prairie. We stretched our legs together and he continued. "I realized my methods were making me into my father. That was when I made a vow to do things differently so that when I face Archon again, I won't be looking into a mirror."

My thoughts knotted up like the roots of an aged tree. I couldn't even begin picking it all apart to decide what was right or wrong—who was good or bad.

Abraxus sighed up at a windblown sky. "I understand you don't trust me, but is there another reason you're so eager to return to Aldar? If you stayed, we could sail to Aldar as soon as I've dealt with Hasan. We could meet Morgan on the battlefield together, with the full might of my army behind us." His wings flared in a thirst for violence, creating a malignant shadow on the fertile ground.

A long pause.

My hesitation to share made him scowl. "I've given you my truth. Aren't you going to return the favor?"

I conceded with half a truth. "Morgan's preparing to attack the Riverlands. I want to go back because I want to help protect their court."

"A noble goal, but your being there would only motivate Morgan to attack them harder and faster."

Oh crap.

I took a deep lateral breath. "Look, I have people back in Aldar. I won't be apart from them for a day longer than I have to. Not when Morgan's after them." I chose a different tack. "What if Desmi were in Aldar? Wouldn't you do anything to be with her?"

He struck, tongue sharp. "Is that it, then? This is all about getting back to your mate?"

That unbalanced me. "No ... I haven't met him yet."

"But you know he's out there?"

I offered a tiny nod.

Abraxus's misery devastated his expression. "When you find him, protect him. Morgan and Archon specialize in aiming for the hearts of those important to us. It's how they control people. And death is preferable to losing a mate." His gaze narrowed on me. "But if it isn't your mate, who is it? Who is so important to you?"

He really wasn't going to let this go. And despite his promises, I doubted that I'd be allowed to leave his camp if I didn't give him a satisfactory answer.

I licked my lips nervously. "My friend, and my brother. That's who's so important." His obvious shock had me adding, "He's not that kind of sibling. We were kin bonded. And when I was dying, he twined his life with mine."

"Dying?" He sounded furious.

"I was. I'm not now," I babbled. "But when I became fae, the gods made the twining permanent. So can you understand why it's not a good idea for us to be separated? We protect each other."

"What reason did they give for making it permanent?"

The sharpness in his voice had me faltering.

"Because my magic was too much for one person to handle."

Disbelief darkened his face. "How powerful is your brother? Is he as strong as you, magically?"

I hedged. "He's been gifted with moon and waterlight."

A growl moved his chest. "The more passive side of light, then. You want to be careful. Don't ever leave him alone with a firstborn. That includes anybody from the light court—do you understand?"

I stopped in my tracks. "What are you saying?"

He faced me, eye-to-eye. "I'm worried Balor made the twining permanent as a way of insuring that if you went rogue, he'd be able to end you through your brother."

My stomach dipped sickeningly.

That is not *true.*

Our father would never—

I palmed my forehead. *Shut up.*

"I may be wrong," Abraxus said in a tone that made it clear he didn't believe that.

A baleful violence surged through my veins. "Let's hope so, otherwise, I'll have the death of two gods on my hands."

He gave me a sideways look. "You'd do that? You'd kill Balor?"

Not caring if Zola and Thea heard, I said, "To protect my brother? Yes."

Abraxus's eyebrows flicked upward, seeming surprised and impressed at the same time. That expression turned into a frown. "But why is your brother in Aldar? Why isn't he traveling with you?"

I led us into movement, roaming down a small hill, saying, "He stayed to look for the other stones, or at least find out where they were hidden. This was before we knew you carried one."

Abraxus's gaze snapped toward me. I certainly had his attention with that.

I added, "And it's dangerous what he's doing."

"So you fear for his life, and by extension, yours?"

"That's right."

His rugged face developed more creases than crumpled paper. "I see."

That was it. That was all he said for many minutes.

Then, "I suppose you must go back. But stay in my camp until tomorrow. That should give us time to prepare for your departure."

"Prepare?"

"We need to arrange your transport. That's what you wanted, isn't it? I've a ship that can sneak you past Morgan's sea border without alerting the Meriden, so you can relax on that front."

That sounded perfect. "You're really going to help me leave?"

He swiveled around, confronting me. "I don't like it. But it sounds like your brother needs your strength, and so long as he's vulnerable, so are you."

Abraxus whistled.

Tula burst up out of the grass and into view.

A raven's squawk sounded above us.

When the animals were within touching distance, Abraxus snapped his fingers.

We *moved*.

The four of us materialized in Abraxus's tent. The interior was sparse: lanterns, storage trunks, and a large table with chairs.

Danu was already on Abraxus's shoulder. Tula was by my side.

"I'm going to speak with your sister." Amusement made his mouth crooked. "My guess is that she's the one pacing outside the door."

Tuning into my senses, I noticed the set of agitated footsteps. "She can't hear us, can she?"

"My tent's warded against eavesdropping from the outside."

"Why d'you want to speak to Sefra?"

A canny glint entered his eye. "I find myself inspired to come to terms with her."

"What does that mean?"

"It means I'd like her as an ally."

Avoiding further questions, Abraxus strode out ahead of me. I followed him outside.

Sefra was walking up and down in front of the tent about twenty feet away. The trail of footprints scuffed into the arid earth suggested she'd been doing it for a while.

To my right, Azmodayus and Rafi flanked the entrance. Upon seeing their commander, their muscles locked and their spines lengthened. It was the stance of soldiers respecting their superior.

Sefra noticed us then. She rushed over to me, asking, "Are you okay?"

"Yes." A lie.

"You look as if you've been crying," she said, grasping the tops of my arms, her shrewd eyes traveling over my face.

"I'm fine." That sounded hollow, even to my ears.

She rounded on Abraxus. "You. What did you do? Where did you take her? Because it wasn't just into that damned tent."

At her aggressive posturing, Azmodayus and Rafi reached for their weapons. Tula popped her snout out of the tent.

I grasped my sister's wrist, ready to form a shield around her.

"Enough." Abraxus's command was loud, absolute. "Sefra is my guest. There will be no need for violence."

My spine almost bowed as his authority owned my very bones. Azmodayus and Rafi bobbed their heads in a parrot-nod.

"Tula," Abraxus said, gazing back at her. "Go to the stables."

Tula slunk past me. A safe distance away, she spread her wings and vaulted up into the morning sky.

I slowly released Sefra's wrist.

Affection softened her eyes. "I should be the one protecting you."

"We can take care of each other."

A faint and guilty smile was her reply.

"And you don't need to protect me from Abraxus," I added.

Her brows crossed. "I don't?"

I opened my mouth. Nothing came out. I couldn't explain everything when my soul was still reeling, still dealing with the aftershocks of revelation. I didn't want to witness her reaction when she discovered certain truths.

"I'm sorry," I muttered. "I can't explain."

"It's okay. Whatever he said—"

"Abraxus wants to speak with you," I said, putting distance between us with a backward step. "He'll tell you what we've spoken about."

Confusion and doubt plastered over her features.

"You want me to tell her everything?" Abraxus said in an undertone.

What was the point of keeping the unhappy truth from her? "Yes."

But I couldn't stay and listen to everything again. I couldn't watch my sister learn the truth. Unless she already knew ...

I turned to Abraxus. "I want to check on my friends. Can you have someone take me to them?"

"You mean the injured male and his mate?"

I nodded.

"Consider it done. But before you go, I want you to agree to have dinner with me tonight. I fear the male's injury will prevent him from attending, but at Casatana I heard you had two other people with you. A shifter and a female. They'd be welcome too. As is Sefra." That last bit was said reluctantly.

I couldn't bear to be the object of their stares for longer than I had to. "Okay. I'll have dinner with you."

"I'll send someone for you around 7 AN." He glanced at Rafi. "Take her to Tefór's tent. Then organize another shelter for her so she can rest up near her friends."

"Yes, Commander." Rafi's brown eyes settled on me. "It's this way." He made a little gesture sideways.

I didn't dare catch Sefra's eye as I retrieved my Utemä from the rack beside the entrance. I walked off and stuck close to Rafi, but I didn't interact with him. Trying not to dwell too much, I glanced at the passing scenery.

The tents and interweaving roads were designed in straight, ordered lines, unlike that of the Shyani settlement. Rafi seemed to know exactly where he was going, a fact that suggested their encampment was set out according to a prearranged plan. Everything I saw reinforced the notion that Abraxus's company was regimented, organized, and familiar with a nomadic lifestyle.

We circled a large area that had been cleared of spiky grass, the dirt raked over and smoothed out. People of all kinds were utilizing this as a training area, sparring and grappling with one another.

A minute or so later, we arrived at our destination. Tefór's tent was different from the others surrounding it. The triangular entrance was crowned by the antlered skull of a stag, and the canvas was white with the iconography of large cat paws, bear claws, and bird talons painted on the outside.

"This is where I leave you," Rafi said, sounding hesitant.

"Bye."

"... Bye."

He walked away as I lingered outside the tent, idly scanning the standing shelves of herbs that wrapped around its exterior. My cowardly desire to avoid everybody was interrupted when Liora pulled aside the curtain door.

A book in hand, she stepped out. The makeup from hours ago was gone, and so was my sister's overcoat. Liora now stood in a pattern-and-bead-embellished dress crafted from tawny animal hide. It had wide-cut sleeves, long frills, and no shape to it. Her feet were clad in leather slippers two sizes too big. I didn't recognize any of her garments.

"Thank the mother," she said, relief shining on her face. "Tefór told us that he'd left you at Abraxus's tent, but that was hours ago. We were just talking about coming to find you."

"Sorry. I hadn't planned on being gone that long."

Liora stared into my eyes, her brow wrinkling. "What's wrong?"

I stiffened. "Shall we go inside?"

A pause. "Sure."

She held the tent's flap back for me.

I walked inside. In two blinks, I'd captured the space.

Wind chimes made out of bleached bones hung from the ceiling. The floor was littered with rugs marked in arcane symbols, a portable fire pit that hadn't been lit, and several runic-carved trunks that had been thrown open, revealing drums, books, crystals, feathers, bells, shells, and charred wood.

The shaman had obviously been in the middle of unpacking.

On my left, a gossamer screen acting as a room divider was yanked aside. Adrianna appeared. "About time. Liora and I were about to mount a rescue mission."

I gazed into the adjoining room behind her. Zeke was splayed out on a double bed in there, asleep by the looks of it.

"How's Zeke?"

"Tefór's helped him through the worst of it." Scowling, Adrianna scanned my features. "In fact, he looks better than you do."

That comment washed through, not disturbing or bothering me.

"Where's Tefór?" I glanced around absently.

"He didn't want to move Zeke, so he moved into one of the neighboring tents to sleep." Her lip tugged down. "Did you get the starstone?"

I blinked at her. "Should we be talking about this here?"

"The tents are warded against eavesdroppers," Adrianna countered. "So? The starstone?"

"I wasn't strong enough to take it."

"What does that mean?"

"Exactly what I just said. I couldn't hold it without blacking out."

Liora and Adrianna exchanged a concerned look.

"And what was Abraxus like?" Liora asked in what I felt was a forced light tone.

The first word that sprang to mind was intense—an intensity that seemed to stem from restlessness, internalized rage, and a vulnerability that he resented. I simplified it. "Complicated. He's agreed to help us, though."

"Help us how?" Adrianna folded her arms.

"He's got a ship that can get us home. Past that, I don't know. We're supposed to meet him later for dinner. We'll probably talk about it more then."

"*Dinner?* We're having dinner with him?" Adrianna echoed incredulously.

Her tone made me add, "You don't have to come. I'm sure you'd prefer to stay with Zeke."

"Ena." Liora's eyes added what she had left out—*What is it? How can we help?*

The thought of confessing sent imaginary bugs crawling over my skin. But I couldn't keep this from them. And a part of me just wanted it over with.

My mouth smoke and ash, I said, "Abraxus is my grandfather."

A hush fell.

"Sorry. What?" Adrianna said blankly.

"He's Dain's father."

"Holy shit," Liora whispered.

A mirthless laugh spilled from me. "Yeah."

The quiet kept going, pulling at my teeth and grating every nerve. I couldn't stand it anymore. "I'm going for a walk."

"Don't you want to talk about it?" Liora said, her eyes worried.

"No," was all I could manage.

"It doesn't matter," Adrianna blurted out almost defiantly. "Abraxus might share your blood, but that doesn't make you family."

"We're your pack," Liora said stoutly. "We're your family."

That hit me hard. I nodded, vision blurring. "It's not so much him that I'm upset about. It's the other ... It's Archon. And all the lies." I felt sick. "Sorry. I need some air."

I left the tent, my mind spinning like a waterwheel in a flood.

Anxiety winding me up, my ears stopped working properly. Noises were either too loud, too quiet, or totally garbled.

I started running, anything to get away from this feeling. People stared at me as I sprinted past. I suddenly longed to fly. To leave everything behind.

My wings instinctively arced; unveiling. With a few powerful strokes, I got up into the air. I wasn't graceful about it. In fact, I must have looked like a fledgling struggling to leave the nest. It wasn't in me to care.

I failed to gain any real altitude and almost grazed a few tents. It was a minor miracle I didn't crash.

Somehow I made it to the outer limits of the army camp. Then I kept going until I couldn't hear the soldiers anymore.

Joints screaming, back wrenching, I crash-landed onto dirt, sand, and stubby grass. My body went limp.

I'm sorry, Ena. Really.

Thea's softness hardened my heart. I rolled over onto my wings and said to the sky, "Don't bother."

In brisk notes, Zola said, *Look, we didn't want to add to your burdens. Our first responsibility was always to train you. Not to reveal painful family secrets.*

In that moment, I hated her. I wanted to channel sunlight out through my eyes and burn a hole in her head. I wanted to fling the waterstone into the deepest fires of hell. I wanted to break it. To break everything.

Nobody had warned me. Not Zola or Thea. Dain could've told me when we met in the dreamscape, only he didn't. And Sandrine? Sefra—had she known?

I sat up into a hunched position. My entire body clenched as if it could contain the fear, frustration, and fury choking me.

Useless. I couldn't keep it in anymore. I scream-howled, unleashing my rage upon the world. The empty land trembled as a magical shockwave blasted out across it. It seared away the betrayal, the pain, the self-doubt. I simply became.

The sunstone nudged at me. But all of my magic was thrown into those shapeless strikes, and the other disciplines prevented sunlight from dominating.

I struck out again and again until the bursts were significantly smaller and dominated by a graying light. I was dimming. Draining.

Overextended, I spooled my magic back in and collapsed.

Splaying out a wing, I made it into my pillow. There, on the flat plains, I drifted in and out of consciousness.

Apathy had me in its jaws as the earth warmed under the morning sun. I was motionless for who knows how long.

The sound of wingbeats motivated me to look upward. My heart dropped when I spotted Sefra.

As she executed a perfect landing, I sat up.

Sefra reached down and clasped my hand. She hauled me up with laughable ease and started to dust me off. Her facial muscles were tense, controlled. But her eyes? She looked close to tears.

"Did you know I was related to him?" I whispered.

That had her pausing her dusting of me. "Gods, no. If I had, I would've told you the second I realized you wanted to meet with him."

I trusted that. Perhaps I shouldn't.

Sefra enveloped me in a hug. All I saw were soft blond braids. It made it easier to blurt out what was torturing me—what was weighing on me more than anything else. "Did Abraxus explain what happened to the original carrier of the starstone?"

Sefra released me and inched back. "He did." Her lips whitened as she pressed them together. "I'm not sure if I believe him or not."

A feeble shrug. "I do. When I retrieved the sunstone, Atlas's spirit came to me. He warned me about using the stones. He said that carrying it had made him into someone he didn't like."

She frowned, understanding dawning in her eyes. "You think that'll happen to you?"

"I have to wield all four of them—who knows what that'll do to me?" I glanced off to the side, showing her my cheek. "What if Balor suspects I'll become like Archon? Maybe that's why he didn't want his daughters to say anything." I felt faint when another horrifying thought struck. "What if Dain believes that too? He had a chance to tell me, but he didn't."

She cupped my cheeks and pulled my eyes back to her. "You are not Teren or Atlas." Her hands lowered to her sides. "As for the rest, we don't know what Balor or Dain think. But even if they suspect you'll take after Archon, that would be an ignorant assumption. Our ancestors do not determine our destiny, neither do they define who we are. Our choices are the only worthwhile measure of a person."

I tried to get her words to stick. I wanted them to drown my self-doubt. But I still felt as if I was treading water, trying not to sink to the bottom of a cold ocean.

Sefra nudged my chin up. "You will get through this."

I breathed into my shredded chest and nodded. "I know."

What other choice did I have?

CHAPTER 26
DINNER WITH A GOD

Sefra and I returned to camp to find Rafi had secured us a shelter next door to Adrianna, Zeke, and Liora. Our tent was stocked with a water dispenser and a standing copper bath. I made quick use of them and scrubbed off the post-battle blood spatter. Sefra flew off to retrieve our rucksacks from the cave we had taken them to before the battle.

When Sefra returned, she went next door to hand my friends their bags. She came back with Liora, who had decided to give the mated couple their privacy and sleep in our tent. I was worried Liora would ask me how I was again or at the very least shoot me furtive looks. It didn't turn out that way.

Given we'd all lost a night of sleep, none of us were interested in conversation. I quickly fell into oblivion. All too soon, I was thrown back out.

I woke up before the sun had set on this awful day and found my emotional landscape to be a wide vista of nothingness. The shock, fury, and self-doubt were forgotten. I'd lost them in the void, it seemed.

For what felt like a long while, I stared up at the canvas canopy, thinking, drumming my fingers on my belly.

Somewhere along the way, I stumbled on a tenuous peace that bloomed out of a single thought: being related to Archon and Abraxus didn't change what I chose to stand against. It didn't change who I loved or who I wanted to protect.

I looked to my right and smiled at Liora. She had burrowed so far under our thin sheets that the only part of her left visible were a few stray strawberry curls.

Then I turned my head left. Sefra was lying on the floor, asleep on a rolled-up coat and a lioness's fur.

My sister twitched in her sleep. Yet she never switched positions. She remained on her back, wings carefully folded against her spine, her hand latched onto the hilt of her sword.

Sadness crept into my chest at the sight. How long had she lived on the edge? Had she known a moment's peace in Asitar?

"Get up, sleepy bums!"

I startled, arching up into a sitting position.

"Awaken, you filthy fiends!"

I located the noise near Sefra and relaxed. She'd warned me about her sprite-possessed timepiece and how it enjoyed yelling obscenities when acting as an alarm call. The fact it was waking us meant we had fifteen minutes before dinner with Abraxus. Gulp.

Cora screeched indignantly from atop the bottom bedpost where she'd decided to keep watch over us. *Dreadful thing! I tried dropping it off a cliff once, but Sefra stopped me. She finds the stupid sprite amusing.*

That was the first I'd heard from Cora. I was about to reply when—

"Don't make me sing! You know I will," shouted the muffled timepiece.

"Oh, do shut up," Sefra groaned.

Liora expelled a huffing moan in agreement.

"Ah! The mistress awakens. My noble deed is done."

The timepiece made a *clunk-clunk* sound, then, blissful silence.

I changed into three-quarter-length trousers and a white shirt with a cut-out section in the back that accommodated my wings.

As I waited for the others to get ready, I showed my hand to Cora. She bowed her head in silent permission.

I stroked her auburn plumage, keeping a watchful eye on her talons that were the length of my fingers and sharp enough to create deep grooves in the bedpost.

Not a minute later, I picked up on the soft tread of approaching footsteps. "The Commander awaits," came a high-pitched voice from outside.

My hand closed on empty air as Cora vanished in a blink. I reared back, surprised. Sefra's chuckle was short and sweet. "Don't worry. She just needed a rest."

"Are we ready?" Liora's gaze skipped between me and Sefra.

She got two nods.

We exited the tent to find our escort waiting patiently. A little stunned by her appearance, I halted.

Doll eyes, tapered ears, and rosy cheeks looked back at me. She was shorter than me by about a foot, had small pink wings, and her thumbs were hooked into a wicked belt of meat-cleavers.

"Are we waiting for anyone else?" she asked us.

"No." Adrianna had chosen to stay with Zeke.

"Follow me, then."

She turned and walked off, her two-toned pigtails a-swinging. We pursued her, sipping in the fresh and restful air of the evening.

"What's your name?" Liora asked our guide.

"They call me Cleaver."

Liora wasn't intimidated. She went on. "Is that your weapon of choice?"

"Yes. I was forced to be a knife-thrower in a circus before Abraxus found me. Now, I hack my enemies to pieces with them." So matter-of-fact.

Liora stopped asking questions after that.

As we traversed the camp, I noticed passing soldiers watching me. Oven-hot blood coursed into my cheeks. Perhaps the story of my inept flying had spread.

Sick of the stares, I was actually relieved to reach Abraxus's shelter. Two unknown soldiers guarded the entrance. They performed a quick weapons check. At the end of which Cleaver started to announce our arrival. Before she'd finished, Abraxus yanked aside the curtain door and stepped out of his tent.

Liora did a little mouse-jump.

"Thank you, Cleaver. Dismissed."

She beat her chest with a closed hand and left.

"Did you manage to get some rest?" Abraxus asked me.

I said, "Yes," but I didn't want to talk about me. "How are the Shyani doing?"

"Settling in. Most of the wounded have been saved."

"I don't want to get in the way of your people." Liora looked guarded as she addressed Abraxus. "But I'd like to help out. I'm a healer."

He marked her with a stare that wasn't cold or friendly. It looked calculating, as if he wished to take the measure of her. "We haven't been introduced. I am Abraxus. And you are Liora—yes?"

The line of her shoulders tensed. "How did you—"

"My people tailed Nala—the witch who invaded your mind in Casatana—and they found out that she'd sent Morgan a message. In it, she spoke of how she'd seen Serena Smith and two of her known associates. The princess, Adrianna, and the red-haired witch, Liora."

"Oh. Well, yes, that's me," she stuttered. Just a little.

"As to your offer, it's kind," he said, his tone polite. "But we've plenty of volunteers and more than enough healers to go around."

Liora's face fell, but she didn't argue. Judging by her rigid posture, I thought she might've been afraid to.

Abraxus drew the curtain door aside. "Come in."

His deep-set eyes tracked me as I moved into the transformed tent. A table dressed in crisp white linen had taken center stage. It was laden with crystal goblets, stoneware plates, and a silver candelabra. "You went to a lot of effort," I noted.

"You say that like it's a bad thing." His smile was crooked.

"It isn't, as long as you're not snake-oiling us," Sefra said mildly.

"No snake oil here." Letting the curtain flutter closed, he gestured to the chairs. "Please sit."

Abraxus strode to the head of the table. Sefra settled on his immediate left.

Three spots remained. I chose to sit on Abraxus's right. Liora lowered herself into the chair next to me.

"Help yourself," Abraxus told us.

"What kind of animal is that?" I stared at the haunch of meat in the middle of the table. "I don't think I've seen it before."

"It's an ibex. Tula caught this one herself." He pointed to it proudly with a knife. "But there are plenty of other dishes if that's not to your taste. Help yourself to whatever you'd like."

The dinner began. The conversation did not.

I was halfway through my meal when Abraxus broke the uncomfortable silence. "So Ena, did Sefra tell you about my proposal?"

Eyes agog, I said, "Proposal? As in marriage?"

Abraxus cleared his throat of shocked laughter. Sefra smiled at me, showing an affectionate kind of amusement.

"I'll take that as a no, then?" I muttered, embarrassed.

"I was referring to a business proposal," Abraxus corrected me.

"And I said I needed time to think about it," Sefra interjected, dabbing at her mouth with a napkin. That delicate gesture didn't hide her flexing jaw.

"Think about what?" I said, echoing her.

Sefra tossed a glare in Abraxus's direction. "He wants our money."

"We have money?"

Abraxus caught my eye. "Sefra's the wealthiest person in Asitar, not counting Hasan."

"Is that from when you were queen?" I asked Sefra.

She shifted in her chair, her wings rustling against the wooden frame. "No. It's money I've made whilst I've been here. I decided to make it a priority because I knew we'd need a mountain of coin to fund a war against Morgan. Not to mention enduring whatever difficulties we might face when Archon returns." She fiddled with the cutlery on her plate. "I succeeded in that, at least."

"Where did all the money come from?" I realized that it might be rude to ask only after I'd said it.

"I made a few investments, which've paid out well for us. I also invented something—a type of spelled stone."

I cut in. "The self-energizing one?"

"That's right." A flickering smile. "And when I started to sell them—"

"She made a fortune," Abraxus finished. "During our talk this morning, I suggested a trade. If she loaned me enough money to purchase a fleet of ships, I'll use what I find in Hasan's banks to pay her back with interest. I also promised to destroy the Meriden with said ships."

Frowning at him, I asked, "Don't you have any money of your own?"

"I claim no personal wealth." He rested his elbows on the table and steepled his hands together. "Everything we take from the kings is sold.

I use the coin to sustain everybody in my camp and finance our campaigns against Hasan and the local warlords."

I looked across the table at Sefra, who seemed far from convinced. "Would buying a fleet of ships ruin you?"

"No, it wouldn't."

Damn. She *was* rich.

I sipped at my wine, needing a moment to process. Lips puckering, I savored the honey, marmalade, and citrus notes that tingled on my tongue.

Liora joined the conversation. "How long are you planning to stay in Asitar?"

Abraxus's thick brows lowered. "That depends on how fast I can remove Hasan from power. I've dismantled his regular army, and our victory last night eradicated his best soldiers. But he's got deep pockets, enough to buy more mercenaries. And unfortunately, it's not as simple as storming Casatana." A flash of dark hatred ravaged his face. "I learned long ago that the kings will do anything to keep their crowns. Even if it means starving their own people or hanging children from their castle walls to discourage me from laying siege to it."

That shriveled my stomach, souring my appetite. "Then how are you going to defeat him?"

"You don't have to worry about that." He straightened in his seat and looked dead ahead. "I've been working on a strategy to destroy him for some time, and we're almost ready to implement it. No matter what, Hasan will be gone by winter."

"Is your army aware that you expect them to leave their homeland to wage war on another continent?" Sefra challenged him.

Abraxus picked his goblet up. "They've always known about my plans to overthrow Morgan, and they don't question my motives because of the number of assassins she's sent to try to kill me over the years. But I've given them my word that I won't order them to leave until after we've freed Asitar and established it as a people's republic."

People's republic? I'd never heard of such a thing.

Sefra kept on at him. "What about Archon—do they know about him? Or are you lying to your own people?"

That comment was alcohol thrown onto the fire. "You have no right to lecture me on lying. Last I checked, your people think you fled from Morgan to save your own skin."

Sparks leaped from Sefra's fingertips. Rutting hell.

Abraxus viewed her hands, unafraid—unimpressed. "I will tell them about Archon. And they'll be given the choice to fight or flee. But I won't say anything until we've dealt with Hasan. It would affect morale."

Sefra clenched her hands, snuffing out her angry embers. "What if most of your people refuse to sail to Aldar? You'll be without an army."

He shrugged. "Some will stay. But most will follow me."

"That's a bit arrogant, don't you think?" she said in clipped notes.

He swirled his wine in a thoughtful manner. "Just confident. For many people, this was their first real home. The first place they felt accepted. We're as much of an extended family as the Shyani."

Sefra's lips turned white as she pursed them.

A sip of wine later, he went on. "We don't have to like each other, Sefra. The fact is, we've both chosen to oppose Archon and Morgan, and the surest way of defeating them is if we band together. If you doubt that, then consider this. Even now, Archon is gaining influence in this world through Morgan."

"What do you—"

"Morgan and Archon are communicating."

That had me in free fall.

"That can't be." Sefra turned a ghastly shade of beige. "The gates are closed."

"But the moon court remained open." He slid his thumb over the rim of his glass. "That place has ... let's call them back doors into the other two courts. It's how souls are still moving onto where they belong. However, there are certain spirits—very strong ones—who can use these doors to sneak back out of their respective courts. I believe Morgan and Archon have been taking advantage of this loophole by having the dead relay messages between them."

I was upended, questioning everything. How many of Morgan's evil actions had been orchestrated or influenced by Archon?

"You're not sure, though? How can you be?" Sefra said, her tone carrying an uncertain air.

He destroyed that assumption with a firm rebuttal. "I'm not wholly sure about the method, no. But they are communicating. For years she's been claiming that I'll sail to Aldar—why? Why is she so terrified of me? It's because she knows who I am. Her practice of death and blood magic has also grown to the point that she's doing things only those in the dark court have knowledge of. She positively reeks of my father's influence."

I felt as if I'd crashed through ice and into breath-stealing waters. "Magic like creating a guardian without consent?"

He nodded.

Sefra looked so stunned that I asked her, "You hadn't heard about that?"

"No," she said, rather absently.

Liora captured my hand under the table. I supposed she might've sensed the emotional blow I'd taken when thinking about Wilder.

Sefra snapped out of her blank shock, adding, "If she can create slaves like that—"

"It doesn't bode well," Abraxus finished.

A painful pause.

Like a bloodhound with a scent, Abraxus pressed Sefra. "Has hearing our enemies are collaborating convinced you that you're better off with a demon who's on your side than no demon at all? Or do you still wish to cling to your mistrust of me?"

Sefra hesitated at that proverbial fork in the road.

Abraxus's focus darted to Liora when she loosed a huff under her breath. "Something to say, little dragon?"

"Not really," she said, side-eyeing him. "Just that you're very good at getting people to do what you want."

"Have I lied, empath?"

I wasn't surprised that Abraxus knew what she was.

"I don't know. I can't get anything from you," she replied coolly.

"Do you want to feel what I feel?"

I felt the threat behind those words.

Blank-faced, Liora said, "All right."

Something dropped from behind his eyes. "I want to stop my father from laying waste to this world. I want him dead for killing my wife and stealing my daughter. I want to make Morgan bleed for murdering my son. And I also want to stop them from hurting Ena. She is all I have left of them."

Liora's fingers trembled in mine as she held his searing gaze. I confronted Abraxus. "Stop it. Leave her alone."

"Of course, materie." He broke eye contact with Liora.

A sudden gasp escaped her as if she'd been holding her breath.

"Are you okay?" I asked.

She pulled her hand from mine. "Yes."

But she wasn't. That was obvious in the way she avoided my gaze. In the way she reached for her cup of sparkling cordial and gulped it as if she thought that could steady her.

The prolonged silence ended when she set her goblet down and gathered her nerve to meet Abraxus's gaze. "I can sense how much you want to protect Ena. But your hatred ... your desire to destroy your enemies is stronger."

"Thankfully, those two goals are one and the same." In that moment, his expression made me think of a fox slinking out of a chicken coop with feathers stuck around his mouth. He looked as if he'd already won.

Sefra sighed. "I want full access to your financial accounts. If I'm satisfied with what I see in them, we can start to discuss a loan." She finished on a weary note.

"Excellent. We've got something to celebrate, then."

Abraxus clicked his fingers. The table was cleared of wine and savory dishes. In their place, sweet delicacies and pots of steaming coffee appeared.

I barely blinked at his tricks. I'd already witnessed what he was capable of. Liora, on the other hand, stared openly. Sefra strived to look unimpressed and failed.

At the sight of such deliciousness, my hunger came screaming back. I hadn't finished my main meal, and I'd burned through a lot of energy recently. I loaded up on everything and had at it.

Nobody spoke. A relief.

I was slumped in my chair, nursing a swollen stomach and sipping on bittersweet coffee when Abraxus restarted the conversation. "So, materie, what do you plan on doing once you return to Aldar? Apart from looking for the moonstone, of course."

"Trying to stay alive?" I deadpanned.

Abraxus's dark eyes glittered with irritation. "Aren't you interested in defeating Morgan?"

I readjusted, lengthening my spine. "I'm aware she has to go. And I'm prepared to end her myself. But short of allowing myself to be captured, I've no idea how to get a shot at her without your forces to draw her out."

He smirked. "I'm glad to see you've got brains and backbone. I had my doubts about the latter when you fell to pieces at the thought of being my granddaughter."

Sefra hissed in displeasure. It didn't bother me much, though.

Humor vanished from Abraxus's features. "You're right to think that without a large army at your back, infiltrating her court would be nigh impossible. But you can begin to gather her enemies against her." He leaned in, propping his elbows on the table. "And I know where you should start."

"I'll bet you do," Sefra muttered over her coffee cup.

He made no sign of having heard that. "I realized after our talk earlier that we might solve two problems with one solution. In other words, we can get you home and save the Riverlands Court at the same time."

Sefra's face could've turned mortal flesh to stone. "What do you mean *save* the Riverlands?"

Oh, rats. My mouth went dry at the prospect of telling her. I did it anyway, recounting Morgan's plan to conquer Diana's court.

Sefra's horror and shock lasted only seconds. She rounded on Abraxus, radiating the intensity of the sun itself. "How can you save them?"

Abraxus's reply was aimed at me. "Every Meriden vessel has now been charged with guarding the eastern sea border. No normal ship or crew is getting past that."

That turned my bones to sand and my bowels to water.

He drew his thumb down the corner of his scarred mouth. "Thankfully, I've access to a ship captained by a siren—the last of her kind. With Indy's talents, you can sneak past the blockade and reach Kastella without being boarded. And once Indy has cleared a path for you via the sea, Diana and whoever else is holed up in the capital can sail away in their own ships."

A memory of a map interrupted my thought path. By my recollection, the Riverlands capital was next to the sea, right on the eastern coastline, near to countless Meriden.

"How is one siren going to do all that?" Liora asked.

"You'll see for yourself soon enough." He set his palm down flat on the table before me. "The point is, if Diana can get her people somewhere more defensible, she can regroup and strike out from a place of strength. At the very least, she'll gain the opportunity to choose when and where to meet the enemy in battle. With the Riverlands army behind you, you might actually make a dent in Morgan's forces—unless Diana's too cowardly to fight."

Sefra looked dangerously close to killing him as she said, "Diana isn't a coward."

Abraxus talked over her, addressing me. "You'll also need the witches on your side if you're going to break Morgan's grip over Aldar. The quickest way to gain their loyalty is to challenge her for the right to rule the Crescent as High Witch."

Liora choked on her coffee.

It took a moment for my brain to catch up. "What does that mean? Would I have to fight Morgan?"

He stopped me with a raised palm. "You don't have to duel her to win. The covens don't follow normal lines of succession. They follow power. If you can prove you're stronger than she is magically, the crown is yours."

"That's how it used to be." Liora's face reflected deep thought, as if she was actually considering this as a possibility. "I don't know if the coven leaders would still honor that tradition. The older ones have survived this long by staying loyal to Morgan. And the newer ones got their positions because of their fealty to her."

"If they won't honor their own laws, get rid of them," Abraxus said dispassionately. "You don't need them anyway. You need to convince the people under them—those that have been most hurt by Morgan's tyranny."

"How do you propose I do that?" I asked, feeling as if I were balancing on a shoestring, about to fall a thousand feet or more.

"You'll have to figure out the details." He rested back in his chair. "But essentially, you need to make people believe you can stand up against

Morgan and win. Right now, there aren't any witches who would dare challenge her because even if they seized the Crescent, they'd be flattened when she goes to claim it back. The only way to really beat her is to overthrow her in Alexandria as well. But to do that, you need support from within the Solar Court. Luckily, you have a claim to the Solar crown and a right to declare war against Morgan." He ended that speech with a little smile.

Shock and denial ran through me. "Sefra is the Solar Queen. Not me."

"Your sister can't be queen again," he stated coldly. "She forfeited that right when she fled Aldar."

"That isn't fair," I argued. "She did it to find the sunstone and to find a way to defeat Morgan."

"It's all right, Ena." Sefra threw Abraxus a dirty look before she turned back to me. "He isn't wrong. No matter my reasons or excuses, the Solar Court wouldn't want me to rule again. I'll always be the person who abandoned them. And honestly, I don't want the crown. I wasn't well-suited to it."

I was verging on desperate. "But your father was the king—how can I be entitled to anything when I wasn't related to him?"

"He made our mother joint regent," Sefra explained. "In fae law, that gives her and any of her faelings a right to the throne. It's not as strong a claim as mine. But as we've already discussed, that's not going to happen, and since I don't have any other heirs, you're the next in the line of succession."

Wilder had mentioned I might be in line for the throne. I hadn't really believed him. Until now.

Panic overrode my next breath. "This is crazy. I'm eighteen. I don't know anything about ruling a fae kingdom. Nobody would want me as their queen."

"You'll learn," Abraxus said gruffly. "As for the rest, you might be surprised. If you let it be known that you're the daughter of Dain and Sati, those who supported them in life would likely offer their support to you."

I was overwhelmed, head underwater. "Do you have any idea what you're asking of me? Isn't finding the moonstone and destroying the Dark King enough rutting responsibility?"

"Ena." That word was so firm it stilled my tongue. "Once we've ripped Morgan's grasping fingers off the Solar crown, every scheming politician and greedy noble will be trying to take over. You can't risk handing that responsibility off to them when Archon is still in the picture. What if the new ruler refuses to believe he's real? I'd have to kill them, and that wouldn't go down too well at the Solar Court. So, unless you want me to be torn apart by an angry mob—"

"You really are a manipulative bastard," I seethed at him.

His eyes sparked with dark humor. "I'm a bastard for the right reasons, though."

"Give it a rest," Sefra said, an octave away from growling.

His chest moved in a small sigh. "Ena, I'm simply trying to get you to see that you're more than the weapon we point at Archon."

"I'm not just a weapon. I'm a knight," I declared.

Neither Sefra nor Abraxus looked surprised by that.

"You knew?" I asked both of them.

"Yuma told me," Sefra replied with a sheepish smile.

Abraxus simply said, "Firstborn can sense you." His eyes darted to Liora before he went on, pushing me. "But knights fulfilled their roles in different ways. Some forged weapons, others were spies, and a chosen few became leaders—as you should be."

"You have an answer for everything, don't you?"

He mimed buttoning his lip. Quiet shoved its way into the tent.

I drank my coffee, dismissing the idea over and over. In less than a month, I'd gone from human to fae to knight. Now, heir apparent? At this point, I was just a piece of driftwood getting tossed about in an unfeeling sea, subject to the current's caprices.

I know you don't want to hear from us right now. But I agree with Abraxus. At this point in time, it would be incredibly risky to let an unknown take over from Morgan. I, personally, wouldn't wish to trust the lives of my loved ones to a stranger.

Thea, in her own gentler way, was as cunning as Abraxus. She'd said the one thing I couldn't argue with. The one thing I'd shove doubt aside and take on any burden for. My family. I glanced sideways at Liora.

She nodded. "We'll help you."

I blew out a weak laugh. "Crap."

Abraxus eyeballed me. "You got there, then?"

"Did I miss something?" Sefra said shortly.

His mouth twitched. "She's accepted her royal responsibilities."

"Go to hell," I snapped at him.

"Already been," he quipped with a wicked smile. "It didn't agree with me."

Ha. Ha. My eyes rolled in their sockets.

"There's one more thing before I think we should call it a night." He poured himself his fourth cup of coffee. "I'd like Danu to accompany you to Aldar."

At that, his familiar appeared on his wing's claw.

Abraxus ignored the raven, adding, "He knows everything that I do about chaos magic. And if I can't be with you, my familiar is the next best thing to a teacher. Danu can also relay messages between us."

"What's chaos magic?" Liora asked.

"I'll explain later," I promised.

A simple nod of acceptance.

Sefra looked straight at Abraxus. "How's he going to relay messages to you from Aldar? The mind-to-mind connection with familiars doesn't last past a few miles."

Abraxus held out his forearm. Danu hopped down onto it. "Well, our connection does." He stroked the raven's silky black wing with the back of his finger. "He's a lot stronger than other familiars."

I wondered then if he'd always had a familiar. Or if Abraxus had only summoned Danu after he'd lost everyone else.

The second one. He was lonely.

That husky voice made me stiffen. I peered at the raven. *Did you just read my thoughts?*

He clacked his beak. *I only skim surface thoughts. Nothing too intrusive.*

"Are you kidding?" I snapped.

"What is it?" Sefra asked.

Once I'd explained, my sister glared at Abraxus. "Were you going to mention that? Or is your bird a spy?"

Danu emitted a squawk of indignation.

"I wish for him to help keep my granddaughter alive. That is all." Abraxus's response was respectful, if a touch icy.

I leveled a look at Danu. "If I get the sense you're spying on me, I will pluck out every one of your feathers. Do we understand each other?"

The raven cocked his head in a staccato move. *You'll do.*

"Then it's decided," Abraxus said.

As if to solidify that statement, Danu flew over and perched upon my wing mantle.

Thank the stars, my feathers cushioned the sharpness of his talons. I still didn't like him near such a vulnerable area. I was severely tempted to flick him off.

"I think it's time we had a look at my financials, don't you?" Abraxus said to Sefra.

Her nod was stiff.

He rose to his feet, dominating the surrounding space. "Ladies, please stay and eat as much as you want."

"When will we be able to sail for Aldar?" I asked quickly.

"I'm in the process of contacting Indy. It shouldn't be long before you get a departure date," he said in a heavy way.

Sefra vacated her seat. "You'll let us know as soon as you hear from her."

"Naturally."

My sister stared him down even though she barely came up to his chest.

He motioned toward the exit. "After you."

"No. After you," Sefra countered.

Abraxus clucked his tongue. "Fine."

He strode out without so much as a goodbye. I supposed it shouldn't be a shock that a dark god wasn't sentimental.

Danu made a coughing noise. *You've got him wrong. The only books he reads are tragedies and romantic poetry. It's all sentimental nonsense and horrifically maudlin.* His wattle plumage fluffed as he emitted a soft, *ha ha ha*.

"That's creepy," Liora said, eyeing Danu.

The raven didn't comment on that. He flew off after Abraxus.

"We should go speak to Adi," Liora said. "She should know about Abraxus's plan to help the Riverlands."

I rose from my chair. "Agreed."

We headed out to where a star-strewn nightfall awaited us.

The guards who'd manned the entrance were gone. But the lanterns strung up tent-to-tent illuminated Benjamin, Rafi, Azmodayus, and Cleaver about thirty feet out in front of us.

Cleaver and the twins were lounging on barrels, drinking from scarred tin mugs. Only Azmodayus faced us, feet together, hands behind his back. "We will be your guards during your stay here. The Commander ordered it."

Rafi hopped off the barrel when he saw me.

"All of you?" I asked.

Cleaver loosed a cawing laugh from atop her barrel, swinging her legs up and down. "Yes, but Az is the only one watching over you tonight. Much to Rafi's disappointment."

Rafi pushed Cleaver off the barrels with a single shove. She popped up straight away. First, she chucked her mug at him. Rafi dodged that. Then she threw and landed a knife in his shoulder faster than I could blink.

"Gods-damn you, Cleaver!" Rafi staggered back a step.

Benjamin guided his grumbling twin away, saying, "We're going to the healer's tent."

"Be grateful I avoided the major arteries," Cleaver shouted after the retreating twins.

Protective instincts flaring, I inched closer to Liora. In the same breath, Azmodayus released a weary sigh. "You shouldn't have done that, Cleaver. I'll have to write you up again. What is this, your tenth time this month?"

"Twelfth," she said proudly.

"Go to the field kitchen." Azmodayus gestured right. "You're on disciplinary."

Cleaver shrugged and left.

Azmodayus turned to me. "Where to?"

"Tefór's tent," I said.

He led the way, hand on sword. The camp was surprisingly quiet as we walked along. I supposed that made sense if the shelters were warded against eavesdroppers.

Once we arrived at the shaman's tent, Azmodayus stepped off to the side. "I'll be out here if you need anything."

Liora and I entered.

Adrianna relaxed on the floor, her head bent over a map of some kind. Zeke was propped up next to her, his back against a vertical storage trunk. A plenitude of pillows and blankets supported and comforted him. His shirt was loose, and white enough that I spotted the bandages wrapped around his clavicle.

"You both look in one piece." Adrianna scanned me and Liora.

I blew out a wobbly laugh. "All the damage is internal."

"How are you?" Liora asked, sitting down beside Zeke.

He gave her a pale-lipped smile. "I'm feeling good. Better, anyway. Tefór finished another healing session a couple of hours ago."

I settled in between Adrianna and Liora.

"So, how was it—your dinner with the dark god?" Adrianna asked.

I pulled a pillow into my lap. "About as strange as you'd expect."

"Is that it? Just strange?"

Liora and I glanced at each other. From there, we took turns telling them about Abraxus's plan to aid those in Kastella. Once we'd finished, Adrianna strode into the adjoining room and rifled through Zeke's rucksack. "Haven't you heard of privacy, princess?" he drawled. "Or do you just choose to ignore it?"

Adrianna hushed him. She returned to our floor-circle with one half of a double-sided mirror. She held the glass up and spoke into it in Kaeli. "Natä min, Diana."

A flat quiet reigned.

Adrianna repeated the same phrase five times. On the sixth try, Zeke intervened. "She's probably busy."

Adrianna glowered down at the palm-sized mirror as if she could make her mother appear within its depths through sheer will. "But this could save them. She has to respond."

"We'll keep trying," he assured her, his voice softer than usual.

Keeping ahold of the mirror, Adrianna lowered her hands to her lap and looked up at me. "Anything else happen at this meeting that we should know about?"

With a leaden heart, I relayed what Abraxus wanted me to do. To be High Witch. To be Queen. Lastly, I mentioned that Danu was coming with us to Aldar.

To all that, Adrianna said, "He's got this all figured out, hasn't he?"

"You've got to give it to him though—he's an intelligent son of a bitch," Zeke said appreciatively.

Adrianna shot him a lemon-sour look.

"What?" His mouth curved into a lopsided smile. "He is."

She clucked her tongue before turning to me. "I know how much you want to reunite with Frazer." Her gaze skipped to Liora. "And you with Cai. I won't blame you both if you leave for Mysaya after we reach land. I have to stay with my people and see they get somewhere safe. But you two don't."

Being separated from my brother was a wound that wouldn't close. I still said, "I'll only leave once your people have escaped the Meriden."

The decision was a stone in my gut. But it was the right one.

"Same," said Liora. "Cai will understand."

Our conversation went on for the better part of an hour. Liora and I detailed the rest of the dinner's events. Then I carefully filled in the blanks from my first meeting with Abraxus—mostly those related to my possessing chaos magic. By the end, it felt like we'd talked everything to death. Zeke was the first to surrender to exhaustion. "I'm going to have to go to bed."

That was my opening. "Me too."

I rolled up off the floor. Liora rose beside me. But Adrianna stayed seated and eyed the mirror. It was obvious she wasn't sleeping any time soon. "Adi, do you want me to stay up with you?"

"No."

I wasn't surprised at that reaction.

"See you in the morning, then."

Zeke nodded. Adrianna ignored us.

Liora and I went outside. Azmodayus was waiting where we left him. He walked us the short distance to our tent.

One look inside our shelter confirmed that Sefra hadn't returned yet. I thought about waiting up for her, but my brain felt water-logged. I needed sleep.

Too much time later, I decided my brain must hate me. Beside me, Liora's breathing had deepened and evened out. But me? I lay in bed exhausted, my mind determined to torture me. Thoughts, thoughts, thoughts. They pecked at me like seagulls at a feast.

The violence of the battle.

Meeting my sister.

Being related to Abraxus and Archon.

Having chaos magic.

Failing to take the starstone.

Choosing a crown.

Sailing to the Riverlands.

I went around and around until I found a kernel of hope in the missing part of my heart. *Frazer.* I'd no idea when I'd be free to seek him out, but I had a way back to him now. That thought wasn't my enemy. It was a stepping-stone into much-needed sleep.

CHAPTER 27
GOODBYE

※

Awaken.
I came gently into being.
Opening sleep-heavy eyes, I glanced around a dimly lit tent. Sefra was stirring. Liora was not.
Abraxus wishes to speak to you and your sister.
Having recognized Danu's mental voice, I pushed myself out of bed, shed my nightwear, and dressed in yesterday's clothes.
Sefra changed next to me. Unlike me, she chose to strap her weapons—a sword emblazoned with a sun emblem and a dagger topped with an eagle pommel—to her sides.
We walked outside together. I could smell the approaching dawn, even though its light hadn't brightened the sky. Still, Abraxus was visible to me. He lingered a few steps from the entrance with Danu on his shoulder. I had to squint to see the raven, even with fae-eyes. His feathers melted so well into the background that only the faintest trace of him could be seen.
"I thought you should know that Indy's contacted me," Abraxus said quietly. "She's agreed to meet us at Mykkanos Bay at 5 AN. I'll open a portal for us close to the bay," he added. "That'll save you the flight to the coast."
Surprise claimed me first. Excitement swiftly followed.

"Can you portal anywhere?" Sefra asked.

He grumbled low in his throat. "There was a time when that was the case. But no longer. Nowadays, my abilities are limited by a number of factors, one being distance."

I wrapped my wings around me, guarding against the pre-dawn chill. "I suppose it was too much to hope you could portal into Alexandria and take out Morgan."

A soft, *Ha*. "That would certainly have made things easier. Unfortunately, those places are warded against unauthorized magical entry." His shadowed gaze flickered to Sefra. "Are you ready to go?"

"Where are you going?" I asked.

Sefra turned toward me. "I meant to tell you last night, but you were asleep when I got to the tent—I'm going to visit Inacia with Abraxus." My nonplussed expression had her adding, "It's an island to the south of Asitar that operates as an independent country and a bank. That's where our money's stored. I have to go there to transfer funds to Abraxus, and to withdraw everything in my vault so we can use it in Aldar."

"Do you want me to go with you?"

"You can't," Abraxus said, absolute. "Hasan's put a huge bounty out on you. And disguises won't work in Inacia. Not even magical ones."

"Hasan wants you dead," I argued. "That isn't stopping you from going."

"Yes, but I'm me."

Insufferable ass.

"Be outside my tent ten minutes before 5," Abraxus told me as Danu flew over and landed on the mantle of my wing.

Not bothering to wait for my reply, Abraxus soared upward as if will alone propelled him. Sefra tutted up at his retreating form. "How anyone mistook him for fae I'll never know." Her eyes met mine and she smiled reassuringly. "I'll return in a few hours."

"And if you don't?"

Her smile dropped into a serious line. "I will."

She dipped inside our shelter for a handful of seconds. She came out wearing her overcoat. Her rucksack was strapped between her leathery wings and a pair of eye-goggles hung around her neck.

Sefra kissed me on the cheek before leaving in a flurry of wingbeats.

Since you're already up, we should take advantage of an empty training field.

I looked up at Danu. "To do what?"

Isn't it obvious? We need to start your lessons in chaos as soon as possible. You're so far behind, you might as well be flying backward. To the training field!

He lifted a black wing. His version of pointing, I supposed.

I'd already spent the entire night in a lesson with Thea. But I didn't care. I wanted to learn. I had to if I was to wield the starstone one day.

"I should tell Liora where I'm going."

Very well.

A raven still clinging to me, I entered our shelter. I walked up to the camp bed and disturbed a Liora-sized lump under the covers. She groaned, "By the sisters, what's happened now?"

I recounted what had transpired outside, adding, "Anyway, I only woke you because Danu wants to teach me chaos magic, and I didn't want to leave without saying something … I'm actually not sure I should leave you here alone. There weren't any guards—"

Benjamin and Rafi are standing watch outside. You just didn't see them.

Oh. "Never mind. Benjamin—"

"I know. I heard Danu too." Liora kicked the sheets down and blew a curl out of her face. "It's okay. I'm up. I want to come with you."

"I'll be outside while you get changed."

"'Kay," she said around a yawn.

I stepped out into the darkness. "Danu, where are they?"

The raven performed another wing-point that took my eyes to a stunted-looking tree. Its gnarled limbs quivered at my attentions.

"Are you going to come down?" I said, not bothering to raise my voice.

Two males dropped from on high into a crouched position.

"Why were you up a tree?" I asked, bemused.

The twins drew near. Red-Wing—Rafi—raised his hands in a gesture of surrender. "We're not stalkers."

I crossed my arms and narrowed my eyes at him.

Benjamin smirked at his brother. "Ignore him. He gets awkward around females he finds attractive."

Rafi didn't scold his twin, but he did shoot me a shy smile.

Oh dear.

"We're here on guard duty," Rafi blurted out. "But we thought we'd stay hidden to give you a sense of privacy, and to ambush any would-be assassins."

"Thanks, I guess." I signaled to Rafi. "It looks like the healers fixed up your knife wound."

He puffed his chest out. "It was nothing. Just a scratch."

My eyebrow arched. "Right. Well, you don't have to lurk up trees anymore. I was about to go to the training field."

Liora abandoned the tent, appearing in black leggings and a short white dress patterned with roses. She held a pillow and a woolen blanket.

I faced the twins. "I suppose you have to come with us."

"Sorry, feathers. There's no getting away from us," Benjamin quipped.

Danu croaked atop my wing. *Are we waiting for the grass to grow? Start walking.*

I thought he might've projected that to everybody present because Benjamin said, "This way."

He led us forward. Rafi stayed by my side and talked my ear off. I caught Liora sneaking us looks, her mouth hidden behind her pillow. I suspected she was concealing a smile.

Rafi seems sweet.

I didn't respond to Thea's soft remark. Last night, she had appeared in my dreamscape as normal. We'd ignored Zola's absence and everything else that had happened. I was good with that. I refused to neglect my magical studies out of stubbornness or hurt feelings. But the trust I'd placed in her and Zola had been broken, and I didn't have it in me to pretend otherwise.

After a short walk, we arrived at the training field, an area of flattened earth stripped of grass. The targets and weapons had stayed out overnight.

Danu quit my wing to perch atop the nearest sword rack.

"Need a sparring partner?" Rafi aimed his bright smile at me.

Danu squawked. *She's here to practice magic, boy. Not your silly sword tricks.*

Rafi's smile vanished.

Grinning, Benjamin slapped Rafi on the shoulder. "I'll spar with you, little brother. You could use the practice."

Rafi glanced at me sideways. "We're on duty. We shouldn't let ourselves get distracted."

"I'd actually prefer it if you trained," I rushed out. "I don't want an audience for this next bit."

"What about her?" Rafi frowned at Liora, who stood by my right wing.

"She's my best friend," I said smoothly. "It's different."

His brow puzzled. "Well, I don't want to make you uncomfortable. So, if you're sure ..."

"She's sure." Benjamin steered him away.

They stalked over to the other side of the earthen field.

Liora spread her blanket out on the ground. "Are you sure you don't want to head back to bed?" I asked her.

She nodded, bleary-eyed. "Definitely. I haven't trained with weapons or practiced hand-to-hand in ages. I'll get rusty if I don't keep it up." She yawned again. "It just might take a while for me to get started."

Danu snapped his beak. *Enough chitter-chatter.*

I faced him, giving him my undivided attention.

The familiar began strutting along the weapons rack. Much as a leader would before their troops. *Abraxus gave you a basic idea of how to conjure chaos. But you've yet to learn of its many properties. It can influence emotions. Mutate species. Manipulate other people's magic. Block out light. Warp reality.*

I interrupted. "How the hell can it warp reality?"

He went on as if I hadn't spoken, using his wings and talons to animate his words. *And that's the beauty of chaos magic, it's highly versatile and can be handier than a lock-pick in a prison. I will have you perform a series of tests to see what abilities it has gifted you. You will not complain or whine.* Danu stopped pacing and confronted me, beak-on. *Ready to discover what you're capable of, fledgling?*

I crossed my wings and planted my feet hip-width apart. "I'm ready."

∽

-LIORA-

A groan escaped me. "I'm going to be sick."

Having been thrown off-balance by Benjamin, I lay on my back like an upturned tortoise with the midday sun blazing overhead. My chest moved rapidly as I sucked in air; the scent of cool steel, damp sweat, and baked earth caught in my throat.

"Don't be so dramatic." Benjamin hauled me up.

"I'm not." I marked him with a firm look. "And I'm done."

"We've only been sparring for an hour." Benjamin pouted.

I stowed my mounting impatience. Fae really didn't understand the concept of human endurance.

"I'm just not used to training in such hot conditions."

He cocked his head. "Are you seriously blaming the weather?"

"It happens to be true," I argued. "And I'm not getting heat stroke so you can have someone to beat on."

Tolerance at an end, I strode away, my limbs like jelly.

"Quitter," he yelled at my back.

"Bully," I shouted into the hot air.

Benjamin freed an easygoing laugh behind me. The sound pierced my heart. Such light teasing reminded me of Cai. Love and fear mixed in my blood.

I offered up a prayer for my brother, the same one I'd said to myself a dozen times while in Asitar. Maiden, Mother, Crone, please take my brother into your care and keep him safe.

I wove around the other fighters until I arrived at the edge of the training field. There, I propped my practice sword on a rack and removed my sparring gloves, returning them to one of the many storage boxes lined up on the ground.

Turning my attentions inward, I began a body check.

Red blotches marked my dominant hand. Just a basic friction rash. I shook my hands out, loosening my wrists.

An aching back compelled me to send magic to the area, where it created a tingling sensation. Repressing a shiver, I focused on the information I received from my healing senses. The muscles were fatigued, close to straining. Since it would cost more energy to ease the soreness magically, I chose to let them heal naturally.

Body scan completed, I turned toward my real source of concern. Ena.

She hadn't stopped moving since before the dawn. First she had experimented with chaos magic. Then she sparred with Azmodayus. Now she was practicing hand-to-hand with Rafi.

I'd persuaded her to rest twice, but her breaks hadn't lasted for more than fifteen minutes. Her white shirt was wet with perspiration, her hair was stuck to her nape, and her wings drooped a few inches lower than they should.

Exhausted or not, she wasn't stopping. All I sensed from her was a determination to improve in every way. It was the stuff of rock and iron and diamond.

A deep hum resonated through me. I recognized it immediately.

Isolde? You're back?

I was surprised to feel relief sweep through me.

Sweet human. I am perfectly well. You, however, are in pain. What is it that ails you?

I picked up on her concern. *I was sparring. It's nothing to worry about.*

If you say so, kitsä.

What does kitsä mean?

I might tell you one day.

I held in an annoyed huff. She loved mysteries and riddles. Another thing I was getting used to.

In my periphery, I spotted a familiar blond female striding out of the maze of throughways and shelters. My belly flip-flopped.

I turned my head and took in Sefra's appearance. She still wore the knee-high boots, studded bracers, and sleeveless chest armor from the battle. But the sapphire-blue undershirt and eye-goggles around her neck were different. Her daffodil-yellow hair was also braided in a different way, pulled tight against the sides of her head and sprayed out into a ponytail.

A flush of want rushed through me. Ena's sister. Fae. Former queen. Terrible idea. That was the chant I'd perfected at dinner last night.

Isolde emitted a rattling chuff. A dragon's laugh.

Sefra stopped on the outskirts of the training area, her brown leather and cream fur coat hung over her arm.

I saw the keen interest on her face as she watched Ena spar. There was something else—something more subtle, something buried deep. Grief. Guilt. Loss.

When Ena noticed her, Sefra plastered on a smile and waved.

Ena exchanged a few words with Rafi before walking over to meet her sister. Their physical differences put them as the sun and stars colliding. At least to me it did.

I was about to find a task to occupy myself when Sefra spotted me. With an insistent hand, she gestured for me to join them.

I willed my pulse to calm as I closed the gap between us. Ena's amethyst eyes cut to me. "I was just asking her how it went with Abraxus."

The worry agitating my best friend hit me. I tried to block it out, to visualize a shield of protection, but like all the other times, nothing worked.

"It went according to plan, which, given our circumstances, is the best we could hope for," Sefra said, her eyes haunted by tired shadows.

"Where's the money we're taking to Aldar?" Ena asked under her breath.

"There were too many money chests to fly back without taking multiple trips, so Abraxus portaled everything—us, included—into his tent. I left the chests in there."

Ena's anxiety surged again. "Is it safe to leave the money in there?"

"Tula's guarding the tent, so I'm not concerned about thieves. And I doubt Abraxus will seize the money we're to take to Aldar with us." Sefra's wings flared and fluttered irritably. "Not when we need it to fight Morgan."

Her wings calmed, settling against her spine. I couldn't help admiring the color of them. They were cast in the likeness of my favorite gemstone: lapis lazuli.

We should be guarding their money. A fury is nothing compared to a dragon.

Isolde's interest in treasure slipped through in still images. Trunks of silver coins. Rubies as big as chicken eggs. Gold bars to match her eye color.

You picked the wrong person to bond with if you love treasure. I don't have a coin to my name.

A grumpy, *I have a healthy appreciation for it. That is all.*

I wasn't confident enough in our relationship to tease her about that yet.

"Are Adrianna and Zeke still in their tent?" Sefra asked, surveying the practice field.

Avoiding direct eye contact with her, I said, "I visited them a while ago to tell them about our ship arriving this afternoon. Zeke said he's going to Mykkanos Bay with us and saying goodbye there. Then Adi told me not to disturb them again. They're planning to spend their last few hours together alone, without interruptions."

Sefra's lip twitched up at that. "I see." Turning to Ena, she added, "I saw you fighting out there. You looked great."

A rosiness bloomed in Ena's porcelain face. "Thanks. I actually only came out here because Danu wanted me to practice chaos magic."

Sefra eyed her sister's blush. "And how did that go?"

I felt like a sponge, soaking up Ena's embarrassment. I finally understood what Frazer had meant about Ena being expressive. She was all heart.

"Danu tested me for a bunch of different abilities," Ena hedged. "But I only tested positive for one so far."

"Which was?" Sefra prompted.

"I can interfere with other people's magic."

Sefra's pale brows drew together. "How did you figure that out?"

Ena looked away, her wings drawing closer against her spine. "Danu came up with this idea that I should nick my hand with a blade and Liora would heal the cut while I tried to meddle with her magic. But Rafi said it'd be better for my concentration if he cut his hand. And well, it was a stupid thing to do in hindsight."

"Why? He seems fine." Sefra peered over at Rafi, who was chatting with his twin on the opposite end of the field.

"Well, I did manage to stop Liora healing his wound. But then I panicked seeing how much he was bleeding. I accelerated her power, and somehow Rafi grew an extra finger."

Sefra blinked.

Ena blurted out, "Then it fell off. I stopped experimenting with chaos magic after that."

"Rafi's hand is fine, though," I added. "Benjamin actually thought it was hysterical. He swears he's going to keep the finger as a memento."

Sefra burst out laughing. The noon sun hit her eyes, making them glitter like rain clouds backlit with unexpected sunshine.

Isolde planted an image in my mind. In it, she batted her eyelashes and pursed her nonexistent lips into a kissing face. Cheeks stinging, I ignored her.

Sefra pressed a hand over her mouth as if she could shove the rest of her laughter back inside. After winning the battle over her features, she removed her tanned hand from her wind-chapped lips.

"How would you feel about sparring together for a bit?" Sefra asked Ena lightly.

"I would, but Rafi made me promise him another round. He thinks he can win the next one." Ena's smirk was small but mischievous. "But if you want a challenge, you could ask Azmodayus or Cleaver. They're incredible."

Ena indicated where the pair in question currently fought each other. They were fast, skilled, and completely without mercy.

Sefra loosed a thin laugh. "I don't want to get in the middle of whatever that is."

"So, what are you going to do?"

She hitched her rucksack a bit higher. "I might go wash up. Then I'll visit Yuma. I want to check in on her before we leave."

Grim reality paused the conversation. In the quiet, Ena's guilt swelled, clawing its way into my belly and heart.

"I'm sure she'd want the chance to say goodbye to you both." Sefra's gaze went between me and Ena. "I'll ask her to come to Abraxus's tent to see us all off."

"I'd like that," Ena said, her voice lacking strength. "I want to know how she is."

"Me too," I chimed in.

"I'm going to get back to training." Ena motioned to the practice area.

Sefra put on a smile. "All right, well, if I don't see you before, I'll meet you outside Abraxus's tent."

A nod. "Okay." Ena eyeballed me. "Are you partnering Benjamin again?"

"Definitely not."

A short laugh. "See you in a bit, then."

Ena spun away, and as she walked up to Rafi, he said loudly, "Ready for another round, gorgeous?"

"My name's Ena," she said firmly.

"Ena Gorgeous."

I held in an eye-roll.

Isolde weighed in on that. *Is that what passes for courtship among the two-legged? How peculiar.*

My curiosity about dragon courtship was shelved when Sefra grinned at me. "He likes her."

"I know," I said. "He's going to be disappointed, though."

"He isn't her type?" Sefra tried to phrase that casually. I still detected the keen interest underpinning her question.

"To be honest, I'm not sure. I've only known her to be interested in one person."

"Who was that?"

"You should probably ask her that."

Sefra seemed to remember herself. "Of course. Sorry."

That beautiful, heart-filled gaze branded me. I read and cataloged her expression; she had the look of a person lost. Yet I didn't sense anything past the odd flicker of emotion. She must keep them on a tight leash. Or she could block my power.

"It's just ... I wasn't there for her growing up. I can't help wanting to catch up on everything I've missed. I'm ashamed that almost everything I know about her I've learned from Yuma."

Her openness disarmed me. From Aldarian history, I knew Sefra had reigned for a long time. She had to be centuries old. But she wasn't like the other elder fae I'd met. Reserved. Cold. Unreachable.

Relief seeped in. For Ena.

Only Ena?

Oh, shut up.

Isolde's chuckle moved through me like swirls of smoke. I overlooked that and refocused on Sefra. "Ena knows you came to Asitar because you wanted to help her. To help everyone."

"And what do I have to show for it?" Her expression turned flinty. "I've flown from one end of this country to the other, searching for the sunstone and for allies to fight with us against Morgan and Archon. And

I failed, spectacularly. All the while, my people suffered at Morgan's hands, and Ena had to manage alone."

My heart strained. It ached for her. "You didn't find the stone because Atlas spelled it to hide from anybody who wasn't light-blessed four times over. Nobody but Ena was ever going to find it."

Her mouth popped open and stayed that way.

I went on. "You've also made enough money to mount a war with. That doesn't sound like you failed to me."

Hot blood scorched my face as she stared and stared at me. With my red hair, it likely looked as if my whole head was on fire.

"I can't tell you what a weight you've lifted off my mind. I've long been haunted by the idea that I'd failed her." Sefra's gaze slid to her sister.

I followed her line of sight.

Ena was sneaking looks over at us. Had she heard our conversation? I occasionally forgot Ena was fae, with all that entailed. Despite her big-ass bird wings.

"I suppose I'd better get on if I want to visit Yuma," Sefra said, her eyes fixing on me. "What will you do now? Back to sparring?"

"I should. I need the practice."

"You don't enjoy it." An observation. Not a question.

"I don't mind it, but I've no natural ability." I freed a self-deprecating huff. "Maybe that's why Isolde—my dragon—chose me." Sefra's confusion had me adding, "Because she knew my being a healer wouldn't be enough. That I'd need her to protect me and do things that a human couldn't."

Isolde clucked at me. *Silly kitsä.*

"Or she chose you because she cared for you."

A frown marred my brow.

Sefra continued. "I once asked myself the same question—why me? Why would Cora choose me? She told me it was because her soul matched mine. That we belonged together. Sometimes you just know, you know?"

Her smile warmed me to my backbone and had my innards hopping about like an overexcited rabbit. She seemed oblivious to her effect on me. "Until later, then."

"Yeah ... Later."

Moons, why did I have to be so awkward?

I watched her leave, unable to turn away.

∼

-ENA-

The last few hours in Abraxus's camp went by on fast wings. After sparring, I cleaned the sweat from my limbs, changed outfits, ate to replenish lost energy, and that was it. We were due to leave.

Our trio, along with Zeke, Yuma, Sefra, and Danu met Abraxus outside of his tent.

Rafi and Benjamin lingered in the background, continuing to take their guard duties seriously.

"Say your goodbyes," Abraxus told me.

Facing Yuma, I said, "I'm sorry for all the trouble we've caused you."

"I knew the risks in sheltering you, and I would do it again." She caught my hand between her flattened palms. "May your story live long, Alia Akaran."

Unsure what to do with that, I merely said, "And I hope your story never ends."

A faint smile tugged at the golden lettering on her lips. "You are sweet. I hope we will meet again."

"Thank you, Yuma. For everything."

She released my hand and lowered her head into a respectful bow. I returned the favor with a clumsy bob of my head. Adrianna, Liora, and Sefra shared their own goodbyes with her. Zeke did not, since he would see her again soon.

Yuma left us to go her own way.

"Ready?" Abraxus asked only me.

Glancing over my shoulder, I waved to Rafi and Benjamin.

Rafi beamed at me and raised a hand in farewell. Benjamin only nodded.

I turned back to discover Abraxus was glaring at the two males. "Have they made advances toward you?"

"What? No."

When he wouldn't stop staring at them, I slapped his upper arm and hissed, "Stop it. You're being ridiculous."

His gaze snapped to me, eyes wide. "Did you just hit me?"

"Erm. Yes?" I stared at my hand, shocked at my own boldness.

Danu freed his creepy *ha, ha, ha* laugh from atop Abraxus's wing.

Sefra's shoulder bumped mine as she angled in front of me like a lioness protecting her cub. Abraxus scowled at my sister. "Your fear is unnecessary. I would not hurt her."

He spun around and ducked into his tent. I followed him first. The others trailed after me.

Inside, Tula sat on her haunches guarding the twenty or more shoulder bags that cluttered the space. All the other furniture had been removed.

Abraxus patted Tula on her cat-shaped head. "Go rest. You did well."

Tula nudged my hip.

"Bye, Tula," I murmured, stroking her neck frill.

Not bothering with anybody else, the fury walked out of the tent with a waddling gait.

Abraxus snapped his fingers. Our group was dragged through space. We came to an abrupt stop on a treeless hilltop dotted with stumpy grass, sandy earth, and rocks eroded by time and wind.

Half a mile ahead was a settlement sheltered by a natural bay. Every structure was crafted from bleach-white stone, topped with vibrant blue tile, and positioned to make the most of the view and the sea breeze. The only things that marred the beauty of the place were the all-too-frequent signs of fire damage.

Abraxus stepped closer to my left side.

"What happened here?"

"Mykkanos used to be under the control of the Slaver King." Abraxus seemed to disappear inside of himself—into a haunted house of memory—as he gazed down at the settlement, the wind disturbing his ear-length hair. "When the Slaver scum heard I was on my way, he set fire to the place before I could free the people caged here. It took me years to dismantle his operation and dig him out of the rat-holes he'd hide in to avoid me."

"But you got him eventually?"

"I did. And I made him pay for every life he'd destroyed." He met my eye, his expression guarded. As if he waited for judgment.

I viewed Mykkanos Bay again. The smoke that stained the structures and the caved-in roofs became scars and screams in my mind. "Good."

"I've done my best to rebuild," he added. "And to protect the people who wished to return and make this place home again. But there are so many towns like this, and so many local warlords who love to raid them."

I didn't miss the weariness hanging off every note. He was exhausted by the endlessness of it all. I felt that truth in my bones.

Sefra neared. "Has our ship docked?"

"It has."

"Which one is it?" she asked.

Not looking at her, he replied, "The biggest one."

There weren't many ships to choose from—a mere handful. Our vessel was quite obviously the largest in the bay, with a sleek body that was stained chestnut brown. Three proud masts carried vibrant turquoise sails emblazoned with silver harps.

"I'll transport the bags into their hold. Then we'll walk down together."

Another click of his fingers. The bags vanished.

"Why don't you portal us onto the ship too?" Sefra asked him.

"I prefer not to advertise my abilities."

Danu flew toward the coastal town. Abraxus walked in the same direction, and I kept pace alongside him.

With her shorter legs, Sefra had to jog to keep up. Adrianna and Liora fell behind, choosing to stick close to Zeke who, despite walking fine, didn't look up to hurrying.

To pass the time, I decided to satisfy my curiosity where Abraxus was concerned. "You know Aldarians don't think you can use magic. How have you managed to hide it all these years?"

"For a long time, that wasn't far from the truth," he replied. "Archon stripped me of everything but the dregs of my power, and if I used magic at all, it would weaken me for days. Ironically, that was the only reason the other firstborn and the remaining knights allowed me to stay in this realm."

"What do you mean?"

"Have you heard of the covenant?"

I raked through my memory. "Wasn't it a set of rules the knights enforced to keep the peace?"

"That's right. And without going into the specifics, let's just say I wouldn't have been allowed to stay in your world if I'd been at my normal level of power. Essentially, I was so weak, I didn't register as a firstborn anymore." His indigo gaze flitted over to me. "But as the centuries went by, my power started to regenerate."

"How did it do that?" I was made a little breathless by his pace.

Abraxus continued, his head angled down toward me. "The firstborn aren't like witches. Our very beings are woven into the fabric of the universe." He placed his palms on his chest. "I do not reside solely in this body. I exist in multiple places at multiple different times." That went completely over my head. "This interconnectivity ensures we've access to unlimited power. Archon couldn't cut me off from that, not without killing me, which he failed to do. But he did damage the channels that allowed me to draw in my magic."

"And these channels, they've healed?"

"For the most part," he said with a curt nod. "And when I realized they were repairing themselves, I decided to conceal the fact; as much as I could, anyway."

"Why?"

He gave me an intense look. "If our enemies aren't aware of what we're capable of, they find it harder to defeat us."

I nodded, recognizing the wisdom in that.

Ten minutes or so later, we reached the border wall protecting the town. Abraxus waited for the others to catch up before guiding us toward a rough stone archway that bore the marks of having once been a gate. Two sentries flanked this entrance to Mykkanos. They lowered their heads as Abraxus passed them by. He gave no sign of having seen them.

Beyond the archway, a set of dazzling white steps awaited us. I went down them after Abraxus.

It wasn't long before I realized we were traveling down a street. Eggshell-blue doors with bronze knockers stood on either side of us while bright pink azaleas spilled over from walled gardens. Indeed, nature appeared to have overtaken the entire town, at least in the case of the abandoned buildings. They were overcome—overgrown—with moss and mold and trees.

I noticed several people relaxing outside a tearoom that backed into the street. The second they saw Abraxus, they raised their fists to their chests in a salute. But for the most part, the place was quiet.

The steps ended at a circular port. From there, we walked the short distance to our vessel. As we arrived, a woman strode down the gangplank to meet us.

She had catlike eyes, a gap in her front teeth, and her rose-gold hair was bound up into two buns atop her head. There were no wings, and yet her skin had a pearly sheen to it, which meant she could never have been mistaken for a human.

My eyes widened a little when I checked out her bow-frilled blouse, thigh-high boots, and a hitched-up skirt attached to a waisted corset via leather straps.

"Hola there!"

She stepped down onto the stone dock, an inch taller than me in those boots. Hands on hips, she grinned at us in a slightly maniacal kind of way. "Is this my cargo, Brax? They're a good-looking group. What a relief! I was fed up with staring at my sailors day in and day out. Most of them look like wrinkled walnuts."

"How many times must we go through this, Indy? Do not call me Brax," Abraxus snapped. "And your cargo only involves the ladies." He motioned to Zeke. "Not the male."

"Do they have names? Wait!" Closing her eyes, she placed two fingers on her forehead. "I'm a natural intuitive. Let me see if I can guess them."

Exasperated, Abraxus raised his eyes to the sky. He quickly reeled off our names.

In a good-natured tone, Indy said, "Those are excellent names. I wouldn't have guessed any of them."

My ribs ached from holding in bewildered laughter.

"Indy," Abraxus barked, clearly out of patience. "Can you check if twenty-three bags have arrived in your cargo hold?"

"Sure thing, Boss." She performed a two-fingered salute.

Indy walked up the gangplank and disappeared below deck, where it sounded like most of her crew were holed up.

"You definitely attract some interesting characters," Sefra said, staring up at Abraxus.

"Much to my dismay," he deadpanned. "Now perhaps you'd like to spend time with those interesting people while I speak with Ena?"

Sefra lifted her chin. "Eager to be rid of me?"

"Yes." No hesitation. Just stark truth.

She blew irritated air out through her lips, then shifted her focus to me. "Do you want me to stay?"

Standing between my sister and my grandfather, at the center of both of their attentions, I wished I could've been anywhere else. I decided it was better to avoid an argument. "No, it's okay. You can go. I'll be along in a minute."

Her expression showed reluctance, but she nodded anyway and moved off to hug Zeke goodbye. Then my sister boarded the vessel, which by the name painted on the side was called *The Dragonfly*.

Cora materialized, flying over to perch on the ship's figurehead—a beautiful woman blowing into a conch shell.

"Bags are aboard," Indy shouted from the ship's rail. "All twenty-three accounted for."

Abraxus loosed a disgruntled grumble. "Good. Now go away."

"You got it, Brax." She saluted him again and wandered off.

Liora took that moment to embrace Zeke. "Be well," she said to him.

He released her with a kind smile. "Hyvästäd nyta, Liora. That means farewell but only until we meet again in Kaeli. Rough translation."

"It's beautiful."

Liora stepped onto the gangplank and stopped. She spun around on her heel and addressed Abraxus. "Thank you for helping us." The golden ring around her pupils bled into her green irises. "But if you betray my family, Isolde will roast you alive and eat you. God or not."

Abraxus's spiked wings spread wide, becoming wrath and ruin. Two rows of shark teeth pierced his gum-line. "Not if I eat you first, little dragon."

I prepared to jump between them.

Liora freed a hoarse chuckle that did not wholly belong to her. It seemed Isolde could surge to the surface without a full shift.

Liora-Isolde strode onto the ship. At the same time, Zeke and Adrianna put some distance between me and Abraxus. The couple talked in low voices. Their fingers interlocked as they held tight to each other.

Giving them their privacy, I turned to my grandfather. He was retracting his multiple fangs when Danu swooped down and landed on my shoulder.

"Take care, old friend," Abraxus said to his familiar.

I winced as the raven squawked. "What if he needs to rest?" I asked, rubbing my ear. "Will Danu reappear with me? Or will he snap back to wherever you are?"

The raven ruffled his feathers as if in protest.

"I doubt that will be a concern," Abraxus said wryly. "Danu hasn't needed to recoup his energies in over two centuries."

Show-off.

Danu must've heard that thought because he dug his talons into my shoulder. I hissed at him, fangs drawing down. He clicked his beak at me in return.

"How lovely to see you both bonding," Abraxus drawled.

I turned my scowl on him.

Abraxus grew somber. "Be smart. Be strong. Listen to Danu."

I held his gaze. "I'll listen if he has good advice. But I won't be a dog on his or your leash. And that includes any other gods. Light or dark."

His eyebrows rose up like soldiers on a battlefield.

"Do we understand each other?" I challenged.

"Good girl." His smile extended ear to ear.

Gods, he was a riddle and a headache.

"I expect I won't be able to set sail until the start of next year, but if I can come earlier, I will."

"Earlier would be better," I said.

"I know." His response was grim.

"Keep the starstone safe." I stole a glance, but there was no sign of the necklace's chain. "I'll be taking it from you the second I can handle its magic."

A nod. "As it should be. Until we meet again, materie."

With that, he turned about and marched off.

"I need your help to return to Tefór," Zeke yelled at Abraxus's retreating form. "I've still got a couple more healing sessions left."

"Why do you think I'm walking? I'll wait for you at the top of the steps," he replied, not looking back.

Hand in hand, Adrianna and Zeke neared me.

"I should go." Zeke frowned at Abraxus stalking up the street we'd walked down. "I don't trust him to not disappear on me."

I watched Adrianna for her reaction. But she wouldn't meet my eye: her entire body was locked and tight with tension. I noticed a familiar mirror in her hand. I pointed to it and asked, "Is that the jinn glass?"

"Mm," was her only reply.

Eyes rough and grieving, Zeke explained, "I gave it to her so she can contact Diana."

I stepped toward him, arms spreading wide.

He responded with a one-armed hug, never letting go of his mate.

"Thank you," I breathed. "If it weren't for you, we'd be sitting in Hasan's jail right about now."

His amused huff disturbed my hair.

I disentangled and drew back. "Be safe."

"You too."

I walked up onto the lemon-wax-scented ship alone.

By the muffled timbre of Sefra's voice, I guessed she was below decks. Liora, however, was standing at the railing opposite, staring out at the sea. I joined her.

"It doesn't feel real," she said.

"I know," I murmured. "We're really going back."

Moments later, Adrianna arrived on deck. Without a word to us, she marched over to the front of the ship and stayed there, her spine as straight as her sword's steel. She stared at the waves and the port in a way that made me think she wasn't seeing anything but her own pain. Kat, Zeke's familiar, appeared on Adrianna's shoulder, keeping her company.

My heart hurt for her, and for Zeke.

"She'll need us," Liora whispered sadly. "Even if she doesn't admit it. She's hurting. It's ... I can barely breathe. I am trying to block her emotions out, I swear. But ..."

I rubbed her back. "Hey. It's okay. I know."

Her throat bobbed.

"We'll figure this out," I said more resolutely than I felt.

I wasn't even sure what I was referring to: Adrianna's heartbreak, Liora's lack of control over her empathy, or everything we were responsible for.

Over the next few minutes, Indy called out several orders in preparation for our departure. The sailors from below joined us on deck and answered every one of her instructions. Yet, by and by, I realized Indy's commands weren't only for the crew. They were for the ship itself. *The Dragonfly* was conscious. Or it acted like it. The rigging moved, the anchor rose, and the sails dropped on their own.

Indy settled behind a wheel that sported tentacles for spokes. In her high voice, she shouted, "Time to fly, my love."

The Dragonfly lurched away from the port.

My wings splayed. Liora latched onto the rail.

Kat sang out, her tune soft and warbling. That was her final goodbye to Adrianna.

The bluebird leaped onto the back of the wind and flitted away. I followed her flight path up to where Zeke and Abraxus lingered above Mykkanos. They stood still, watching as we left Asitar.

Inside a handful of heartbeats, we were speeding over a white-capped sea, leaving a land of blazing sun and burning sand behind. And as the turquoise sails above me strained for Aldar, I tuned into my kin bond. Not caring that he couldn't hear me, I whispered, *I'll be with you soon, brata. I'm coming home.*

CHAPTER 28
PART THREE: A WATERY GRAVE

I spent my first evening on *The Dragonfly* deep in conversation with Sefra. In the beginning, we shared need-to-know information about our enemies and the stones, amongst other things. Then, bit by bit, we filled in the details of our lives. Of who we both were. Of what we had in common.

However, by night's end, Sefra wanted to discuss only one thing—that I hadn't flown at high altitude. She offered to act as mentor and persuaded me to take a flying lesson with her the following morning, weather permitting.

The next day, I couldn't stomach breakfast, so I went to stand in the middle of the deck ahead of schedule. The sky was cloudless, the sea was calm—all in all, the conditions were perfect.

Before long, Sefra strode up to me wearing leaf-buckle ankle boots, a ruffled blouse, and a ruby jacket with turned-up sleeves. "You're early," she remarked brightly. "Eager to get started."

The word "no" crossed my mind. Not wanting to dampen her mood, I locked that answer up inside and decided on a half-truth. "Actually, Liora's sort of taken over our cabin. She's started those empath exercises you recommended, but she was finding it difficult to meditate with somebody else in the room. So I figured I'd leave her to it and come up here for some fresh air."

Sefra frowned. "I hope the exercises work. I only had second-hand accounts of what's helped other empaths to control their gift."

"It's better than nothing."

She hummed her agreement.

"How's Adrianna?"

Stress thinned her bowed mouth. "Quiet. Tired. I don't think she slept."

My top teeth nibbled my bottom lip. I hadn't seen Adrianna since last night when we'd managed to contact her mother through the jinn glass. Diana had reluctantly agreed to our plan to abandon the capital alongside her army and Kastella's citizens. After that, Adrianna had retreated to the cabin she shared with Sefra. I had a feeling she would stay there until tomorrow—until we reached the Riverlands.

The thought of tomorrow lifted my spirits a little. Our return journey was shorter than we'd dared hope and was only possible because of *The Dragonfly*. According to Indy, it was inhabited by an air sprite that propelled the ship to unparalleled speeds.

"Ready to begin your lesson?" Sefra asked.

I sipped in a bit of nervous air. "Not just yet. I should tell you something first, something I forgot to tell you last night."

Her head tilted to one side. "What is it?"

I hip-leaned against the vessel's railing. "I told you that Mama was the one who said I should come find you."

A slow nod.

I went on. "There was another part to her message. She asked me to tell you that she was sorry for lying to you."

A stunned blink was succeeded by several rapid ones, as if she needed to clear her eyes of dust, or more likely, of memory and emotion.

"Are you okay?" I asked.

A croaky huff. "No, not really."

"What's wrong?"

Sorrow touched her eyes. "I wasn't there when our mother became human. But we'd planned to meet up after her transformation. When I saw her, I couldn't bear the thought of her going to the Gauntlet alone. The grief from losing Dain and the spell to turn her human had made her look so fragile. I begged her to sail east with me. I told her that I'd protect her and the baby, but she insisted on following the plan she and Dain had agreed upon. We argued."

Sefra's lips pinched together. "It was then she said that Dain had foreseen us reuniting. That it wouldn't be our last goodbye. That she would be fine. She lied to me, and then she left."

Oh. *Oh*. "I'm sorry. That ... She shouldn't have lied."

"I wish I could hate her for it. But I can't. I don't." To the wide-open horizon, she whispered, "Anan sinuelle anesi, mi makena."

A long and mournful minute passed. Then she rounded on me and buried her misery beneath a calm veneer. "I think it's time we take to the skies. What do you think?"

"What if I can't keep pace with the ship?" I said, my skin pebbling with a shiver.

"If we lag behind, I can give you a lift back." She shot me a grin bordering on arrogant. "That's the upside of being five hundred and twenty-nine. I've had centuries to develop my skills and mature my wings. I won't have any trouble keeping up."

I gaped. "Five hundred ..."

A sunny laugh parted her lips. "I know. I look good for my age."

She really did. If she'd been human, I would've put her in her mid-thirties.

Sefra extended a hand. I didn't take it. Her head cocked questioningly. "Don't you want to fly?"

I couldn't cage my worry anymore. It spilled out of me. "I don't want to fall."

Her gaze turned shrewd. "Why would you fall? Have you ever seen a fish forget how to swim? It'll take practice and commitment to build up your stamina, but the actual exercise of flying will come naturally to you. It does to all fae. One day you'll find that you trust your wings more than you do the earth beneath your feet."

I struggled past the tightness laying siege to my throat to say, "I fell during the battle with Hasan's forces."

"That was different. You came off a dragon's back. You weren't prepared—"

"What if I don't have the same instincts as a fae because I grew up human?" I blurted out. There it was. My fear.

Shocked silence festered.

She began in a careful way. "I can't imagine how hard all of this must be for you. To go from being human to fae, it must feel as if you're scrambling to catch up."

Yes. Yes, it did.

Sefra clasped the side of my wrist. "But let me just say this: magic may have changed your body, but it couldn't transform your soul. And your soul has wings. Once you believe that—once you allow yourself to be who and what you truly are—I know you'll find those instincts that you aren't sure exist."

I thought that over. "You think I've always had the soul of a fae?"

Her countenance radiated pride. "Yes. And whatever form you were given, you've always had my blood. You've always been my sister." Her warm fingers slid through mine. "We might not look alike, and we have centuries standing between us, but we are rooted. Here." She lightly tapped my chest. "I see through to the heart of you, alätia, and you burn too brightly to stay chained to the earth." Her chin lifted and she stared up at a cerulean sky. "The currents of the world can be found up there. It's where your spirit can break free and you can forget the worries you have down here."

That speech made me weepy and summoned my courage all at once. "All right. Let's do this."

Sefra's gaze dropped to me. I flashed my wings, expressing my willingness.

Her even mouth creased into a beautiful smile.

Gait assured, she led me up onto the top deck, avoiding the thirty or so sailors playing instruments, singing jaunty sea-songs, and partaking of strong spirits.

Once we reached the rear of the ship, Sefra scooped me up. We ascended with a powerful *swoop-swoop* of her leathery wings. She hadn't lied. She raced the wind quicker than any other fae I'd come across.

Sefra leveled off when we'd achieved a great enough height that *The Dragonfly* resembled a toy boat.

After giving me a few initial pointers on how to glide, she added, "Remember to listen to your body. Find your own rhythm. And don't fight the currents."

"Got it," I said, anxiety making me sound breathless.

"I'll be right beside you."

"Mm," was all I was capable of.

Sefra adjusted me in her arms. I ended up face-down with my feathers pressed against her front and her arms crossed over my chest. I snapped my legs together, engaged my core, and tucked my elbows in.

"Tell me when," she said softly.

Stomach whirring, I braced internally. "Now."

She released me.

I dropped several feet before splaying my wings. The air pressure caught me. I was buoyed; I was gliding.

Sefra slipped into a flanking position. "Don't tighten up. Stay loose and take measured breaths."

I did as I was told.

"Nice. Now beat your wings."

I dared a single flap. Panic popped in my gut when I bobbed up and down. It set my limbs a-wobbling and dried out my mouth.

Sefra continued to call out instructions from my right side. Listening to her advice smoothed out my movements. It gave me the confidence to relax.

I fully dropped into my body, settling into the landscape. My senses opened up to the whine of the winds, the vast horizon, and the endless ocean. I enjoyed the moment and found a few seconds of peace. Then it happened.

My kin bond burned like a brand beneath my ribs. I screamed and screamed. Pain—there was so much rutting pain.

Moonlight blasted outward in a giant shockwave, seeking to protect me from my invisible enemy. Out of the corner of my eye, I saw Sefra blown back by my magic.

I crumpled and fell through space like a broken-winged bird.

My waterlight tugged at my mind, gifting me a vision of a forested valley that ran between steep mountains. Frazer was in front of me, struggling to stand up. His features were crumpled in agony, his wings retracted, his hands shaking.

A deep voice sounded from behind me. "I'm sorry."

I couldn't turn to see who it was. I was stuck, a cork in a bottle.

Lightning flashed, passing me and hitting my brother in the chest. I unleashed a wordless scream and my vision snuffed out. Reality pressed in.

I was still falling through space toward an uncaring ocean. I couldn't move. My body didn't seem to belong to me.

Urgent shouts rattled around my skull.

Snap out of it!

Open your wings!

That jolted my frozen brain into action. I beat my wings. Once. Twice. Thrice.

All in vain. I was going to hit the water.

Shield!

Do it now! Do it, or the shock will kill you.

At the last moment, my training snapped into place. I encased myself in a moon-shield with half a thought. The barrier took the initial impact. Then it burst like a bubble.

I crashed feetfirst into a brutally cold underworld. The impact bludgeoned me, plunging me into shock and driving the air from my lungs.

Kick for the surface, you idiot!

I reached for the tender light above, thrashing my aching, numbing limbs. Not fast enough. Not strong enough.

My vision spotted.

Your brother needs you, Ena.

I kept swimming. I wanted the warmth back. I wanted life.

A blinding agony. A stabbing light. Then, nothing.

CHAPTER 29
ALÄTIA

Fate, it seemed, wasn't done with me. I was saved from a cold ocean grave by my sister, who mercifully hadn't been hurt by my rogue magic.

Not long after my near-drowning, Cai contacted Liora using their spelled paper. On it, he wrote that Lynx had captured Frazer and taken him to Mysaya.

I refused to feel that. If I did, I would break into a million pieces. I cauterized my bleeding heart and made it into a stone instead.

In his note, Cai also mentioned that he'd teamed up with Ryder, the Samite we met in Nasiri. The magicked paper was limited, so we didn't get an explanation for how and why this had happened. Cai only said that they were attempting to persuade Ryder's friends to help them free Frazer.

Armed with this information, Liora and I chose to go straight to Aurora. There, we would join Cai and figure out how to save my brother.

Adrianna took longer to decide what to do. Only after speaking with Diana again was she convinced to accompany us rather than aid in the liberation of Kastella, the seat of the Riverlands Court.

Day bled into a sleepless night and back into day again.

Underneath a morning sun, I waited at the front of the ship alongside Adrianna, Liora, and Sefra. Danu clung stoically to my shoulder.

Together, we looked out on Morgan's cursed border, a thread of black fire that ran north to south in an uninterrupted line.

"Time to plug up your holes, my beauties," Indy cried out.

I pushed the fabric plugs provided by the crew into my ears. Then I glanced back over my wing.

Indy was easy to spot up on the top deck, thanks to her outfit. She dazzled in a top hat, frilly corset, velvet shrug, and stripy trousers. Her brass goggles had interchangeable color lenses fitted on one side and an adjustable magnifying glass on the other.

I watched on as the siren started to sing.

The earplugs muffled sound, but they couldn't block out everything. The melody evoked a feeling of desolate moors and fog-laced woodlands. Of secrets and disguises.

Indy had explained her siren's blood gave her an affinity for enchantments. The one she currently wove would force the cursed sea border to ignore her. For the spell that alerted the Meriden when and where a ship crossed it to look the other way.

Her voice summoned a thick mist from the chilly sea and the warm air. This magical fog gathered around, cloaking us.

I couldn't see ten feet in front of me. It wasn't until we were right on top of the border that I noticed the soundless onyx flames fluttering beneath us.

The fire remained idle as we sailed over it. All was quiet.

Hamstrung with nerves, the seconds ticked away inside my chest. Every beat of my heart was so loud, I half-fancied my innards had been swapped out with clockwork. I didn't mind it, though. It reminded me that I was still here. That my brother lived.

Indy stopped singing. The mist parted little by little to reveal an untroubled sea and a cloud-dappled sky. It was done. We were past the barrier. The storm hadn't triggered.

I released a tightly strung sigh. A few cheers went up.

But our relief and elation proved to be short-lived. For as *The Dragonfly* accelerated, skipping over the sea like its namesake, the dreaded sails of a Meriden warship became visible in the distance.

I didn't know if meeting them was bad luck or if Indy had failed to fool the spell placed on the border. It was all the same whatever the reason.

The ship approached at a rapid pace and drew close enough for me to see the crew aboard. They hurried about the planks, fiddling with a large device that latched onto the side of their warship. I wondered what it could be. A few seconds later, I got my answer.

The Meriden pulled a lever. This caused the device to spin around on an axis and slingshot a metal ball at us. A bony fist ensnared my racing heart.

"Hold on to your hats," Indy shouted.

Danu left me. Likely in search of a safer perch. I yanked Liora down to the planks and moored us to the handrail. Adrianna and Sefra grasped overhanging ropes.

The Dragonfly tipped sideways in a sickening motion. Gritting my teeth, I clutched Liora and the rail with all the strength in my fae bones.

Boom!

To the left of us, a geyser-like jet erupted from the ocean. The explosion wasn't close enough that the water sprayed us, but it still caused my eardrums to ring with a vengeance.

The ship popped back up, correcting itself. Thank the gods.

Disoriented, my hearing went in and out. I only got every other word of Adrianna's shouts. "If that crazy ... doesn't sing ... so help me, I will ... to death with ... hat of hers."

An instant later, the sweetest of lullabies breached the air. Even with the plugs in, I was lulled into a stupor that melted my very bones.

I released Liora with a yawn wide enough to click my jaw. In a daze, I watched through the gaps in the railing as we approached the Meriden. One by one, those aboard lost their battle with the enchantment and slipped into slumber.

We sped by the warship like a dagger in the dark.

Indy quieted once we'd left it far behind. I focused on a single fixed point, pushing my brain to adjust. Others slapped their cheeks and rubbed their eyes.

Feeling somewhat revived, I stood up. Liora scrambled up beside me.

My gaze went out ahead of me. A slip of land was visible.

"We're home," Liora croaked.

I concentrated with a desperate eye on the farthest possible point. I wanted to be there already. To become that distance. Frazer was out there, dead ahead. I could sense him, like the summer bird feels winter's approach.

The cage that contained my emotions rattled inside my chest. I held the door closed. I could not let out that which I'd buried. It would consume me. And Frazer needed me sane. Not screaming into pillows.

As we entered shallower shores, the gentle breathings of a fair kingdom brushed my cheeks, disturbed my nape-length hair, and kissed my wings.

Our pace slowed. Crawled. Stopped.

I turned about at the sound of the anchor dropping.

My attention latched onto Indy. She tramped across the upper deck and slid down the banister on her ass. Then she skipped over to us.

"How much time have we got before the Meriden wake?" Sefra asked Indy.

"Thirty minutes or so."

Brow furrowed, Adrianna confronted Indy. "What about the warships off the coast of Kastella? There's eighty of them. Is your enchantment going to last that long on them?"

"I can't say for sure. As I mentioned yesterday, I cannot enchant every member of such a fleet. Some, but not all. But that Riverlands Queen seemed ready to fight her way out when I spoke to her through your little mirror thing." Her eyes held a demonic glint as she added, "I'm certainly confident that we'll be victorious in the end. This ship might not look very fierce, but you should see her in a sea battle."

Her praise set the ship's deck vibrating, purring like a cat whisker-deep in cream. Adrianna failed to look reassured.

"I'm going with them to the coast," Sefra told Indy. "Just to say goodbye."

"It's good to say goodbye," Indy said, nodding.

I supposed she was being serious, although it was hard to tell with her.

Danu swooped down from wherever he'd taken refuge and flew off toward the shoreline. *Let's go.*

Cora popped up over the ocean. Her sharp eagle gaze sticking to the raven, she followed him toward land.

"Do you mind carrying me?" I said, facing Sefra. "I don't think I could take off from a ship yet, not without getting wet."

A soft, "Of course."

She picked me up, rucksack, sword, and all.

As Liora was lifted into Adrianna's arms, she said, "Thanks, Indy."

She bent at the hips, sweeping her top hat off in a final farewell.

The four of us took to the skies. We traveled over gray-blue waters dotted with boulder-sized islands. All the while, Aurora grew nearer.

Adrianna and Sefra landed on a rocky beach awash in sparkling foam and driftwood. There were no settlements in sight, only the pearl and white-jasmine shades of a loula forest.

Sefra lowered me to the ground. I spread my wings, using them as counterweights until my legs adjusted to the solidness underfoot. The second I felt grounded, I shifted my focus to my sister, who was staring off into the bump of trees, an odd expression on her face. "Are you all right?"

Her gaze darted to me, a faint smile already forming on her lips. "I'm fine. It's just strange to be back."

"Good strange, or bad strange?" I asked.

"Good," Sefra answered in a middling tone. "It just doesn't feel real." After a tiny head shake, she faced the three of us. "Are you sure you've got everything? Your money? The map?"

Sefra had pushed a pouch of florén into each of our hands earlier on. Just in case, she had said. As for the map, Indy had provided that. It turned out she had stacks of them from all over the world. And we would need one to guide us to Cai's location.

"I've got everything," I told Sefra.

"Me too," Liora said.

Sefra turned to Adrianna. "I'm going to need your half of the jinn glass now."

Adrianna burst out with, "This isn't right. I should be headed to Kastella. Not you. They're my people."

"We've gone through this," Sefra said firmly. "Ena can't carry Liora yet. It'll be difficult enough for her to fly such long distances. They need one of us to go with them."

"Yes, and it should be you," Adrianna argued.

A manic urgency tore through my paper-thin patience. "Adi, you heard Diana last night. She's got a plan, and she wanted Sefra to help her with it. Not you."

I spotted a tiny flinch. Then her features became a wall of polished marble to hide the hurt. "I'm aware."

I hated upsetting her. But I couldn't afford to spare her the truth. And Diana had been resolute. She planned to flee Kastella and sail north, escaping the watchful eye of the Meriden. From there, she would disembark in Aurora, leave those who couldn't fight on the ships, and march her soldiers to the land border that the Riverlands and Solar shared. Diana would then order the attack on the legion set to invade her court. And she had wanted Sefra to aid her in that task.

"You should trust your makena's judgment in this," Sefra said to Adrianna. "If I show up in support of the Riverlands Court, think about what that'll do for Diana's image. It proves the rumors about her betraying me are lies, and it suggests we've been conspiring together for years. It makes her seem like a brave rebel. Meanwhile, Morgan will look the fool."

Adrianna set her lips in an angry line. I was about to snap again when Liora discreetly clasped my wrist. Her gaze caught mine. She shook her head once, then released my hand.

Sefra went on, her blue and gold wings flaring. "Look, you're wasting time we don't have. Any minute now, Frazer could be transported to Alexandria. If that happens, your chances of rescuing him become nonexistent."

Those notes were as cold and hard as frozen roots. They made me want to bow my head. To bend to the will of an elder fae.

Jaw clenched, Adrianna retrieved the jinn glass from her rucksack. For a few moments, she stared down at it, unwilling to part with a device that enabled us to contact her mother. I understood her reluctance. Without the mirror, we wouldn't know what happened to Diana and her people. But Sefra needed it more than us. With it, she could talk to Diana and they could execute a coordinated attack on the Meriden.

Adrianna shoved the glass at Sefra. "Here."

That surrender was made of sharp thorns and bitter grapefruits. Sefra pocketed the jinn glass.

To end the tricky pause in the conversation, I addressed Sefra. "Before you go, I need to ask you a favor. If you meet Wilder on the battlefield, please don't kill him. I know he's fighting for Morgan, but he's not doing it willingly. And he's my guardian ..."

I opened and closed my mouth twice. No good. The rest of the sentence wouldn't come out.

Her expression emanating sincerity, she said, "Wilder served in my army for many years, and while we weren't close, I considered him a good male. I would never hurt him unless there was no alternative."

My heart plummeted. That wasn't a promise.

Sefra hauled me into a hug. I squeezed her back, my inner defenses wobbling.

"I'll join you as soon as I can," she said, drawing away from me.

I forced myself to nod.

She looked over my shoulder. "You better not have been lying about being able to locate me."

I followed her sightline to where Danu and Cora perched on low-hanging branches.

The raven's answer sounded in my head. *Why would I lie?*

"There are many reasons you might. It would depend upon your motives."

My goal is to keep Ena alive. That is it. If she has need of you, I'll come find you.

A frown colored Sefra's tone. "But you won't tell me how you can track me?"

I'm me.

Sefra emitted an annoyed noise.

I glared at the infuriating bird. He'd said that he couldn't contact anyone mind-to-mind when they were more than a few miles away, the exception being Abraxus. Yet he'd sworn that he could locate Sefra if I needed her help or when the time came for us to reunite. He was so obnoxious and obtuse that my trust in him was minimal.

"I should go," Sefra announced.

I jerked around at that.

Jade-greens paused on Liora and then Adrianna. "Safe travels."

Liora offered a faint, "You too." Adrianna said and did nothing.

Cora abandoned her high perch. As she passed by me, she chirruped. *Trust yourself. Trust in your strength.*

As her familiar headed back to the ship, Sefra backed up a few paces.

"Take care of yourself," I told her.

She raised her chin. "I'll see you soon, alätia."

I forced a small smile that died fast.

Her wings uncrossed, then she was up and away. Despite her assurances otherwise, I was left wondering if I'd ever see her again.

CHAPTER 30
FAMILIAR FACES

I watched Sefra right up until the moment she boarded *The Dragonfly*. Then I drew the bracing sea air into my lungs and wrenched my gaze away. As I turned around, Adrianna said, "Li, get the map out. I want to have a look at it before we take off."

Liora retrieved a sheet of parchment from her bag. The three of us crowded in to stare at the spot that marked Cai and Ryder's location. They were waiting for us in a forest that fringed the Metori—the mountain range that encircled Mysaya.

From previous conversations, I knew it would take about a day and a half to reach Cai. The thought of flying for that long had bees buzzing about my belly.

Adrianna's gaze dropped to Liora. "Keep the map out in case we need to check our trajectory. I'll be back soon."

A careful nod.

In an abrupt move, Adrianna hauled me into her arms. Her dark blue wings raised us up, up, up. Danu exited the forest and ascended alongside us.

Adrianna's wooden expression soon grated against me.

"I'm sorry. I know you're angry that I took Diana and Sefra's side."

"You're not sorry," she said, nostrils ballooning. "We both know you'd say the same thing again to stop me from delaying our rescue mission."

Those sharp words were arrows of truth, silencing me.

"This will do." Adrianna leveled out. "If we go any higher, we'll be visible from a long way off."

I glanced below and above. We'd come a fair distance from the loula woods, but we weren't even close to touching the cotton-clouds.

"Are you worried about us being hunted again? Do you think Morgan knows we're back from Asitar?"

My concerns were met with a cool non-answer. "It doesn't hurt to be cautious."

Agreed.

Her expression inscrutable, she asked, "What now? Should I drop you?"

"Can you get me into a face-down position?"

It wasn't a smooth transition. When I stared at the ground, I wobbled internally. The last time I'd flown, I'd ended up in the rutting ocean. Before I could lose my nerve, I said, "All right. I'm—"

She released me.

The sudden drop stole the breath from my lungs.

My wings snapped out into their full glory. As my joints absorbed the shock, I fought the urge to lock up.

"Just go straight," came Adrianna's voice.

"'Kay," I called out weakly.

Adrianna dove, backtracking toward the coast.

I was left alone with Danu, who flanked my left. He was quiet for a change, shelving his usual wry comments and indignant criticisms. Strangely, his lack of mocking made me more nervous.

I beat my wings and jumped ahead.

Anxiety spiked my nervous system.

I was hot; I was cold. My skin nettled and flushed.

Adrianna and Liora joined me inside of a minute. It soon became painfully obvious that despite carrying a heavier load, Adrianna could have flown circles around me and still ended up ahead.

I cautiously flapped my wings. Once. Twice.

An irregular wave of air pitched me upward. Gut rolling, I scrambled through what I'd learned on updrafts. The answer flashed across my mind. I performed the wing-tuck technique until the turbulence ended.

You're too tense, Danu croaked. *Inhale as you bring your wings up. Exhale as you send them down.*

Freeing a held breath, I obeyed. In. Up. Out. Down.

The world got smaller and less scary when I settled into that rhythm.

My mind slowly relaxed, sliding into every stitch of my body. I'd experienced the same feeling when training in combat and weapons. It grounded me in the moment and made me aware of how every movement impacted my muscles and joints.

I couldn't have beaten Adrianna in a sky race, but I cut the gap between us in half. That was enough for a light pride to fill me up like water in a sun-soaked glass. I wouldn't be left behind.

The sun climbed higher and higher, inch by inch, but the loula forest below remained unchanging, apparently endless.

Around midday, I neared my breaking point. Exertion sanded my mouth. Fatigue burned my muscles. I counted breaths. I visualized my brother. I fixated on the horizon. All useless.

Ena, you have to get to ground.

Thea's warning came too late. Fear flash-boiled through me as cramp claimed my core. That was the end for me.

I faltered and slipped into a messy dive. Danu followed me in a flurry of frenzied wingbeats, pitching the air with his alarm call, a *kraa-kraa-kraa*.

From somewhere up above me, I heard Adrianna shout. "Stabilize your core!"

I was already trying to do that and failing. My stomach muscles refused to listen to me as spasms tormented them. The pain of those wicked cramps caused me to lose all control over my limbs.

Tuck your wings in before you crash through the canopy, Danu rushed out.

The onrush of wind had blown my hair into my face. Sight impaired, I'd trouble gauging how close I was to the crown of the forest. But the second that the snow-white blossoms of the loulas filled my vision, I retracted my wings rather than tucking them. The fae in me would rather risk breaking both legs than a wing.

I went down, down, down, branches whacking and twigs scratching me.

The trees released me from their embrace; the world opened around me, and I pushed my wings out. They slowed my descent, but I still hit the ground hard.

Rattled and in shock, my first thought was gratitude. I wasn't dead. And I'd missed the moss-freckled boulder that squatted ten paces away.

Then came the mind-ripping abdominal pain. I couldn't get away from it. Whimpering, I curled up into a protective ball.

Through streaming eyes, I watched Danu land beside me. He hopped up to my face and took a vicious peck at my cheek.

"Leave me alone, you crazy bird," I groaned, batting him away and clamping a hand over my aching cheek.

I was checking to see you weren't dead.

"Bullshit," I pushed out, winded.

A string of colorful curses and rapid wingbeats sounded overhead. My nose picked up cloves, clementines, bonfires, and sweet grass.

"It's okay." Liora's heart-shaped face swam into view. "I've got you."

Her small, strong hand grasped my wrist. She must've discovered the roots of my injury, because she laid her hands on my belly. As her earth-scented magic rolled over me, the cramping in my gut quickly abated. With the pain gone, I could think clearly and move freely again.

Liora removed her hands from my stomach and rocked back onto her heels. "How are you feeling?"

"Better," I said hoarsely, pushing myself up into a seated position. "Thank you."

"What made you fall?" Adrianna glared at me like a bull ready to charge.

"Stomach cramp."

"You're a rutting idiot." Her scaled wings hitched up in agitation. "I should throw you into a shit-stained sea."

I blinked. "That's a new one."

Liora flashed me an off-center smile. "At least she didn't call you ass-fungus."

"Not yet, anyway."

Adrianna's face tightened in anger. "This isn't a joke. What were you trying to prove? If you need a break, then speak up."

"I thought I could handle it," I replied, shamefaced.

She disregarded that and blurted out, "You won't save Frazer if you're dead, you know."

Temper stoked, a growl resonated silently in my chest. I was half a second from unsheathing my tongue.

"That's enough," Liora said to Adrianna in a tone that shouted *Back off*.

Heated silence fell.

Adrianna was the first to shift her furious gaze away from me. "You should start doing sit-ups." That abrupt instruction, obviously meant for me, was followed by her warily scanning our surroundings. "We might as well take a break since we're already grounded."

We took thirty minutes to slake our thirsts, appease our appetites, and stretch out the kinks in our bodies. Refreshed, we resumed our journey.

Two additional breaks punctuated the afternoon. The latter was spent by Lake Ewa. I felt strangely homesick standing beside its mysterious waters. The truth was, I missed my aunt's wisdom and support. I longed to tell Sandrine about my adventures in Asitar, and that I'd found Sefra. But we couldn't even search for the area where we'd last met the undines, since it was hidden by magic.

By day's end, we left Lake Ewa behind. It wasn't until we sailed over a sea of trees in the waning light that Adrianna slowed her wings. She waited for me to catch up and called out, "Do you think you can land in the same tree as me? I don't think we should camp on the ground, not when we don't know what kind of sprites and animals roam these parts at night."

"I'll try," I said, doubting myself.

Adrianna didn't wait for a more confident response. She canted into a smooth dive. Body half-broken, I trailed in her wake.

She picked the biggest loula in the vicinity. Still in flight, she pierced the canopy and disappeared from my sight.

I was amazed when I succeeded in landing on top of the same loula. It helped that the tree's leafy crown was broad and thick. Not trusting my wings to maneuver me onto a particular perch, I retracted my feathers and climbed down the loula's silver skeleton. Danu glued himself to my side.

I didn't have far to travel before I spotted Adrianna and Liora resting on their own perches. I chose a bough near theirs. Together, we shared a dreary meal in the gathering dark. The only external noises came from the hungry beasts drifting through the woodland below, and our only conversation revolved around Diana, Sefra, and the people from Kastella. Had they escaped the capital?

That last question provoked Adrianna to ask Danu, "You said you could track Sefra—where is she now?"

Somewhere east of here.

Adrianna's eyes flashed in the darkness. "Are you joking? She was sailing to Kastella; of course she'd be east of here."

Danu headed her off before her anger picked up speed. *I never said I could give you her exact location every time you asked. I can track her, but it's like following a compass. I'd have to set out in search of her to actually find her ... I will say she feels north of where Kastella should be.*

"That sounds like they escaped, then. They must be sailing for the Aurorian coastline already," Liora said, and somehow it sounded more like a prayer than a reasonable assumption.

After that, we didn't bring up the Riverlands. I had a feeling we were too exhausted to continue to speculate, dwell, and worry aloud. That was true for me, anyway.

Adrianna was the first to figure out our sleeping arrangements and how we should secure ourselves to the trunks. Following her example, Liora and I freed the cross-straps from our rucksacks and tied them together. We used the makeshift rope to secure our bodies to the trees, and we stuffed our bags between our thighs.

Beyond exhausted, I checked in with my kin bond. I sent my awareness outward, traveling along the pure-white thread that connected me to Frazer. I felt it end somewhere ahead of me, somewhere in the west. That meant Frazer hadn't yet been taken to Alexandria.

Thank the stars.

Last night I had attempted to catch a glimpse of him with my dreamwalking ability. I had failed, even after Thea had instructed me on how to access my gift. Entering a meditative state and concentrating on where I wanted to go or who I wished to be with was the key. Now I repeated those steps.

Time crawled by and I still couldn't get to him. All the while, the last image I'd had of Frazer struggling to stand up, his face riven in agony, tormented me worse than splinters under my fingernails.

I wanted to scream and unleash my frustration and fear. With the force of an iron will, I pushed the violent emotions away and watched as twilight surrendered its nightly secrets. I spied a smattering of pink, blue, and white stars wink into being through the gaps in the dancing leaves. The moon's chubby face wasn't in view, and yet its brightness made the loula trees luminous.

At some point, I slipped into a quiet place.

Thea pulled me to her to continue our lessons. In this dreaming state, my body and mind could still find rest. Today, though, my spirit proved weary beyond measure. I couldn't concentrate. I wasn't committed. Thea conceded defeat and cut our practice session short.

I woke up to discover the sun had not yet risen to say hello. Eyes adjusting to the gloomy hour, I made out Danu's inky outline. He stood farther along my perch, motionless, acting as our vigilant sentry. "Anything happen?"

It's been unutterably boring.

"You're up, then."

My head swiveled left. There, I met Adrianna's gaze.

"Did you sleep?" she asked in a stilted tone.

"A little. You?"

"A bit."

Our staggered conversation felt unnatural. Exhausting. I turned my attention to untethering my rope anchor. As I stretched my wings out and reattached the cross-straps to my backpack, Adrianna murmured, "I want Frazer back too."

Her soft confession had me freezing.

She sighed. "I just can't seem to think straight about anything at the moment. Everything feels upside down."

That chipped at my heart. "Same."

Her response was, "You can stop pretending to be asleep now, Liora."

"I wasn't pretending. I was waiting for an opportunity to say something," she replied, her voice light with innocence.

"Uh-huh," Adrianna deadpanned.

"Ena," Liora said quietly. "Has Frazer been moved?"

Pulse accelerating hard, I tuned into the bond. As soon as I'd confirmed his location, I went on living and breathing again. "He hasn't been moved south. It feels like he's still in the same place as he was yesterday."

Her exhale shook. "That's good."

Indeed.

I readied myself for another grueling day. When our bodies' needs were met, we got airborne. The dawn appeared like a lit torch in the east, announcing itself in a burst of blue-gold flame.

I'd healed somewhat from yesterday's pace. Nonetheless, my body was as stiff as a plank when I sailed through open sky once again. That rigidity worsened when faced with a wind still clinging to its nocturnal chill.

Not long after we had ascended, the unchanging scenery was interrupted by razorback lines that etched out the horizon. Mountains, almost certainly.

The hours edged by in an uncomfortable haze. During this time, the Metori transformed from a smudge into a mountain range that knitted unknown parts of the world together. That view kept me going, reeled me in. Cai was there. I had to hold on.

Just when I thought our journey would never end, Danu barged into my dejected thoughts uninvited. *Your dragon friend's signing to you.*

My gaze skipped to where my friends flew out in front of me. Liora was currently waving at me from over the mantle of Adrianna's wing.

I gave her a limp wave back.

Liora pointed to where the forest bumped against the mountains that stood across our flight path. Snow covered the sky-stabbing peaks of this mighty range, clouds cloaked its steep slopes, and mist haunted the valleys that broke up its roots.

I waved again to show I'd understood her.

Adrianna began her descent. I tilted into a dive, the early afternoon sunshine glancing off my white-gold feathers.

It wasn't long before I landed roughly on the ground. Nursing a stitch, I doubled over and breathed deep into my diaphragm. My face stung from windburn, and everything ached. But I hadn't sustained any real injuries. That was the important thing.

Liora was there in a moment, palming my shoulder. "Let me."

I straightened up and studied her freckled features. "Are you sure you've got the energy to spare?"

"Yes."

Her magic permeated my skin, soothing raw muscles, rusted joints, and the crick in my neck. "Thanks," I said, exhaling relief.

"You need to drink something. You're dehydrated."

I nodded.

Liora left my side and moved for Adrianna. "You next."

"I'm fine," she argued in bratty tones.

"No you're not," Liora countered.

She really wasn't. Her flagging wings and wind-dried lips said it all.

Adrianna flashed her teeth. The action had no real menace to it, though. Dismissing that non-threat, Liora grabbed Adrianna's wrist.

I surveyed the terrain. The lofty peaks loomed up ahead. They were hard and rough unlike the ground underfoot that had been softened by fuzzy lichens, spongy mosses, and several flowers: sorrel, fireweed, and rock-jasmine.

Danu flew down onto my wing. I hissed, "Do you have to perch there?"

He was an unfeeling gargoyle, devoid of response.

Ass.

I unslung my rucksack and retrieved my canteen. I didn't bother to steady my movements for the unwelcome guest on my shoulder.

As I drank, I witnessed the fatigue lifting from Adrianna's body. She straightened as if she'd cast aside a huge weight. Her healing finished, Liora stepped back.

Adrianna offered up a reluctant, "Thanks."

I centered my bag between my wings. "Where to now?"

Before Liora could check the map, Adrianna spoke. "Cai said he was about fifteen miles out from where the Ivôr valley cuts through the Metori. I saw the valley on approach." She inclined her chin upward. "It's straight ahead."

Holding onto the straps of my rucksack, I said, "Let's go, then."

Liora assumed the lead. A rare sight, since her shorter stature meant she had to take two steps for every one of ours.

The minutes sliding by, we marched over flinty stones, fragrant plants, and gnarly roots that twisted through the earth like white snakes.

That monotony ended when magic brushed over my skin, the sensation reminiscent of fingernails tracing a palm. Not exactly unpleasant. But it caught my attention. As did the sudden itching in my ears.

I froze mid-step. "Can you feel that?"

"It's a spell." Liora halted beside me. "I don't know what kind."

"It's as if somebody's stuffed cloth in my ears," I added.

"My ears do tickle a bit," Liora said, frowning as if she barely detected it.

"It's magic designed to limit hearing and smell." Adrianna joined me wing to wing, her head cocking in the way a deer does when searching for predators. "Humans won't be affected as much. But fae ..." She trailed off, shaking her head.

There's a male above you.

Judging by Adrianna and Liora's stiffened postures, I knew Danu must've extended his warning to them.

Adrianna and Liora went back-to-back with me, their weapons raised. I also freed my Utemä. Its steel would have to be enough. Our journey here had taken its toll. I had little energy left for light magic.

Pearl-white leaves quivered in a telling way. A few quickened heartbeats later, a fae dropped from a tree into a crouched position. He landed in front of me with barely a bounce upon loamy soil.

The male studied us as he rolled up. "Well met." His unnerving gaze flitted up to where Danu perched on me. "Nice bird."

"Hello Ryder," I said, my tone guarded.

Adrianna and Liora flanked me. The three of us relaxed our swords to our sides.

"We've seen each other before, haven't we?" Ryder asked me with a smirk.

A tiny nod. "I was in a bar fight in Nasiri. You were there."

His smile grew teeth. "That's right. It was before Frazer knocked me out. I'd remember your feathers anywhere."

"Where's Cai?" Liora asked, her melodic notes coming out sharp.

"I'll take you to him. But I should retrieve something first." Ryder craned his neck toward the forest's mantle and whistled.

A rope dropped from somewhere above. Ready for anything, I assumed a fighting stance and raised my steel again.

A boy awkwardly slid into view. My sword-arm slackened.

Once grounded, he joined Ryder's side.

I gaped. "Gods above."

"There are no gods," said the very serious boy.

"Billy?" His blank gaze had me adding, "Do you remember me? We met when we were taken as slaves from the Gauntlet."

The boy from almost four months ago had changed. He was no longer quite so thin. His brunette hair was longer and tied up at his nape; his square face was free of dirt—free from the neglect he'd suffered in the Gauntlet. The clothes that hung from him were also no longer rags. They were well cared-for, as were the two knives strapped to his belt.

"I remember." His scowl deepened. "But you were human back then."

That piqued Ryder's interest. With a sly smile, he said, "Well, isn't that something."

Avoiding his gaze, I went on. "Why are you here, Billy? How did you end up with Ryder?"

"I didn't. He's here visiting my pack."

I put two and two together. "Pack? As in the Winged Fiends?"

A nod.

I faced Ryder. "Those are the friends you're trying to get to help Frazer?"

His chocolate-brown irises pinned me. "Cai warned me that you'd recognize the pack's name. I take it that you've run into the Fiends before?"

Mood darkening, I replied, "You could say that."

"Aren't they the wingless worms who left you to be recaptured by the Wild Hunt?" Adrianna's lip curled in disgust.

I emitted a throaty noise of agreement. "They chased off Hunter and Kesha. But they only granted Billy and another boy called Brandon refuge in their pack. I got picked up again and sold at Kasi."

"Great," Adrianna said scathingly. "They really sound like people we should be turning to in a crisis."

I peered down at Billy. "How is Brandon, by the way?"

He shot me a dark look that boded ill tidings. "The Wild Hunt set fire to the forest we were living in. Brandon didn't make it. Neither did Hawk."

Sadness caved in on me for a boy whose chance at life had been stolen from him. I wouldn't weep over Hawk's death, though. He'd been the Fiends' leader, the one who'd abandoned me to the Wild Hunt.

Billy lifted a stout chin. "I got the female who murdered Bran, though. I shoved an iron-tipped arrow straight through her eye."

Rutting hell. I spotted Liora clenching her fists beside me. She looked nauseous, likely from channeling Billy's emotions. She needed a distraction. She needed her brother. "Can you take us to see Cai now?" I asked.

"He's up at the Fiends' camp." Ryder gestured behind me. "This way."

Ryder strode off, his shabby boots moving silently across the earth. Billy kept stride with him as if it were a point of pride.

Adrianna snatched at my sleeve before I could follow them. "Are we sure about this? What if Ryder forced Cai to write those messages? This could be a trap."

"I couldn't sense anything from Ryder," Liora said under her breath. "He's got his emotions locked up. But he didn't ask for our weapons. That's got to count for something."

Danu chose that moment to fly off and disappear into the maze of trees. "Where's he sneaking off to?" Adrianna scowled after him.

An uncertain pause.

Liora rolled her weight from foot to foot. "Trap or no trap, we can't stand here forever."

"I think we should risk following them. What else are we going to do?"

Adrianna sighed. Then she nodded.

I set off, sword in hand. Adrianna and Liora walked alongside me.

When our trio closed in on Ryder and Billy, two masked people jumped down from the treetops and landed before our group. The strangers carried unstrung bows, but their unfriendly eyes suggested they might fire on us at any given moment.

I halted and gripped my sword tighter.

Adrianna and Liora moved shoulder-close to me.

"Ryder, who are these people?" asked the slim-built fae on the right.

"Fox, these are Cai's friends." Ryder sounded unconcerned, and yet his mouth had set into seriousness.

I had a faint recollection of the blazing red hair and the striking fox mask that concealed the upper part of his face. Fox had been there when I'd encountered the Winged Fiends months ago. I couldn't tell if he recognized me or not.

"Hound, go and tell Bear about our new arrivals. And you can bring Cai here while you're at it," Fox ordered.

A short man with prominent jowls raced off at a loping gait. That movement kicked up the low-hanging mists swirling around our feet.

After a couple of minutes of awkward silence, a voice called out, "Li!"

Hearing that lilting accent pitched in excitement sparked joy in me. It lightened some of the heaviness in my heart.

Adrianna, Liora, and I searched among the loulas for a glimpse of him.

Hound reappeared first. Then, *there*. Cai was running, his long legs eating up the earth.

He was here. He was safe.

Liora gasped out, "Thank the light."

She sprinted over to meet her brother. I hung back with the others, giving the siblings a moment.

"Now that's sorted, we should return to our posts. Billy"—Fox angled his head, indicating a spot next to him—"you're with me."

"What about Ryder?" Billy demanded.

That drew a lopsided smile out of the Samite. "I patrolled the border as a favor to Owl. But my place is with Cai."

Billy let out a grumpy, "Fine."

Once Hound had rejoined them, Fox said, "Move out."

The three sentries returned to the canopy by flight or ladder. Without a word, Adrianna, Ryder, and I started forward.

Cai was spinning Liora around in a hug, yet his carefree grin was nowhere to be seen. He looked rougher: his hair was a mess, as if he'd been scraping his hand through it too often, his hazel eyes were bloodshot, and a fresh scar marred his cheek.

"Thank the moons you're okay," Cai said, releasing her.

Liora's neck angled so she could look up at her taller brother. Sadness and concern were written into every corner of her face. "You're hurting."

She placed her palm over his cut cheek. The skin knitted together as good as new. Cai caught her wrist as she lowered her arm. "You got your magic back?"

She nodded. "And I'm not just a healer now," she said, her accent strengthening in her brother's presence.

"You were never just a healer." Cai's brow crinkled. "Although, I'd really like to know what the gold in your eyes is about."

"I'll tell you later."

Liora moved off to his side. That gave me a direct line of sight to Cai.

His gaze went up and rooted to me.

Looking uncertain, he extended a hand. I walked straight into his arms. As they closed about me, I got a quick hit of vanilla and peppermint. "I missed you," he murmured next to my ear.

I exhaled softly against his nape. "I missed you more."

An arrogant huff. "Obviously."

I clucked my tongue and pinched his bicep. He freed a faint chuckle as I stepped away.

"It's good to see you," Adrianna said as she initiated a one-armed hug with Cai.

Face slack in surprise, he wrapped his arms around her. Adrianna only allowed the contact for a few heartbeats. As she pulled back, Cai said, "I've convinced Bear and Owl to meet with all of you. I'm hoping we'll be able to persuade them to help us with Frazer if we tackle them as a unit."

"Are Bear and Owl the leaders here?" Adrianna asked.

"That's right," Cai replied.

I decided not to mention that I'd met Bear before. It wasn't important. "Why would us being here change their minds?"

"Because we're witches," Liora chimed in. "Powerful ones. If we can show this mission has a chance of success, they might be more inclined to support us."

My insides felt like wrung-out rags. Like I was being squeezed and twisted. "Can we see them now?"

A nod. "They're expecting us."

Cai went first, acting as our guide. As we moved quietly over root, leaf, and twig, I searched for the absent Danu. I'd no luck in finding him. Sneaky bird.

The muffled sounds of a settlement soon reached me.

"Who's responsible for the sensory distortion?" Adrianna asked, looking around. "They must be powerful to protect an area this big."

"That's Owl. He's an elemental like me," Cai explained. "But he's learned to merge air magic with spells in ways I've never seen before." That was envy creeping into his voice.

"Owl is also my connection to this pack," Ryder informed us. "He used to serve with me as an Aurorian Samite. Owl owes Frazer the same debt I do."

"Is that why you want to help rescue him?" I said, flanking Ryder. "You feel like you owe him?"

"Yes."

"Was your meeting Frazer in Nasiri a coincidence?" I asked.

"No," he admitted. "I heard about the price on his head through a network of outlaws that I've become friendly with over the years. After that, I trailed after the spiders rumored to be hunting your pack. Doing that got me to Aurora's southern border. From there, I decided to visit the port towns. I thought you might try to escape east or head over to one of the smaller islands surrounding Aldar. I got lucky in Nasiri."

My eyebrows pinched together. "What happened between then and now? How did you end up here?"

He let out a bark of a laugh. "I ambushed Frazer and Cai after they left Nasiri, and I tried to convince them to let me travel with them. They refused. I could see I wasn't going to get anywhere with them—not like that. So I let them leave. Then I snuck into their camp that same night and was rudely ousted by a nasty wind."

Cai landed a bruising hit to Ryder's bicep. "You deserved it. You crept up on me while I was pissing."

That punch didn't break his stride. "I didn't creep. I maintained a respectful distance, and I kept my eyes closed."

Cai shook his head in mock despair, causing his soft blond curls to sweep over his forehead.

"Anyway, after that, I kept showing up at their camp uninvited," Ryder said, a cheeky grin dimpling his slim cheeks. "When they realized they weren't getting rid of me, Cai had me swear some hideous spell-oath that ensured my silence on their movements. I traveled with them openly after that." His smile faded as he added, "Although, Frazer never told me what he was doing or where we were going."

That didn't rouse any pity in me. "It's safer if you don't know the details."

No comment.

Freed from conversation, I worked on constructing an argument that could convince Bear and Owl to help us rescue Frazer. The problem was, there were too many unknowns. Like why had Lynx taken Frazer to Mysaya when Morgan ruled from Alexandria?

The first signs of habitation appeared, distracting me from troubled thoughts.

I scanned the area, eyeballing the randomly plotted tents. Their exteriors were crafted from muddied canvas and tattered hide. The small groups of people in sight manned outdoor fires on which they cooked and boiled water. Nobody was masked. Yet the thirty or so people out in the open had an edge to their gazes. The second they spotted us—strangers walking in their midst—they laid hands on their weapons. There was no laughter. Little talk.

This atmosphere stood in stark contrast with the Shyani whose settlement had been a moving city of light and color, home to thousands … And we'd brought a battle and destruction to their tribe.

What if we brought the same horrors to these people? This camp looked like a temporary refuge, and not a very comfortable one. It didn't seem capable of surviving a minor blizzard, let alone the wrath of a powerful enemy. I'd no time to mull over that thorny issue because Cai was motioning ahead to the biggest tent in the vicinity. "We're here. That's Bear and Owl's place."

CHAPTER 31
A DISCOVERY MADE IN DARKNESS

Cai led us over to a four-sided shelter with a smoke-flap on the roof. He drew aside the canvas door and we filed in one by one.

I observed a modest-sized space that smelled of wood, spirits, damp moss, and dried grass. The floor was covered in woven rush rugs and tracked-in pine needles. The dug-out fire on the far right was smokeless and encompassed in a stone ring.

A roughly built table was the central focus of the room. Parchment stacks, ink bottles, quill shavings, and half-drunk glasses of whiskey littered the unpolished surface.

Cai motioned to one of two fae who were seated at the table. "That's Owl."

The male indicated was slender, brown-haired, and yellow-eyed.

Cai gestured to the next chair over. "And this is Bear."

I cast a sharp eye over the second male. His stocky build and shaggy black hair matched my vague memories. Only now Bear's mask was gone, revealing his rugged looks and wiry beard. His brown eyes swept over us, showing no signs of recognition when it came to me.

"These are my friends Adrianna and Ena." Cai signaled to us in turn. "And this is my sister, Liora."

"Merry meet," Liora greeted them politely.

"They're here to help me rescue Frazer," Cai added.

"Are they also wanted by Morgan?" Bear asked.

"Yes."

"Is that a problem?" Adrianna pitched her voice in a challenge.

A grumble rippled through Bear's barrel chest. "It would only be a problem if you weren't. I don't trust law-abiding citizens."

His black beard twitched. I couldn't tell if he was smiling or frowning.

Owl grew animated, signing to Bear. I could guess the meaning of his simpler gestures, but much of his silent language was too complex for me to follow.

Once Owl finished, Bear turned to face us. "My mate asks that you make yourselves comfortable." He beckoned us over with a large hairy hand. "Sit with us. I've a feeling we'll be here for a while."

I chose a seat directly across from Bear and Owl. Liora placed herself on my right. Ryder took the spot on my left. Cai and Adrianna sat at a right-angle to me.

"Before we go any further," I started, "I want to hear how Frazer got captured."

Cai winced, and I noticed light lines on his forehead. Those wrinkles hadn't been there a few weeks ago.

"Ryder, Frazer, and I were ambushed by a mountain tribe. They didn't put up much of a fight, and they fled when we started dropping bodies. We interrogated one of the wounded fae who'd gotten left behind. He told us that his tribe had been paid to report any strangers traveling through the Metori to Mysaya." He skipped over what happened to the injured fae, adding, "A few hours later, Ryder spotted Lynx in the sky. We took cover, but he started circling the area. Frazer shot at him with the kaskan." Cai faltered, his voice cracking.

Ryder picked up the story. "Lynx destroyed the arrow and flew straight for us. Frazer said he'd draw him away so we could attack him from behind. The crazy bastard somehow retracted his wings, then he ran out into the open. Lynx hit him with lightning and grabbed him before we could reach them. I tracked them for about an hour before I lost sight of them. Then I flew back and brought Cai here."

Bear added, "Ryder told us that Lynx looked bound for Mysaya. I sent a few people to scout the place out, and they spotted Lynx right enough. They also glimpsed somebody chained in a tower who matched

Frazer's description. I can't guarantee that it's him, though. Like I said, it was only a glimpse, and by people unfamiliar with him."

Keep it in. Don't let it out. I gulped down the emotional hellfire clawing at my vocal chords. Throat aching, I said, "It has to be him. Frazer's somewhere west of here. So is Mysaya. Lynx is there. It all fits ..."

Bear frowned at me. "How would you know where Frazer is?"

"They're kin bonded," Ryder answered for me.

My head pivoted left. "Frazer would never tell you that."

"He carried the traces of another person's scent when I traveled with him." A calm reply. "You seem to know his location, and I've seen your face when you talk about him. You'd die for him. If you add it all up, it's hard to come to any other conclusion."

That nicked the frost I'd encased my heart in. Feeling as vulnerable as a kitten without claws, I slid my hands into my lap to hide the tremor in them.

Bear leaned forward in his chair. "If you're set on rescuing him, you should know what you're up against. The city of Mysaya might be abandoned, but Morgan still has about two hundred soldiers guarding the castle. Even if the Fiends were to provide backup, with Lynx standing guard there's little hope of retrieving Frazer."

Owl's features were conflict-ridden. His free hand still gripped Bear's in support of that judgment, though.

An ungenerous frustration burned through me. Then I remembered what I'd seen of the camp so far. The people outside didn't deserve to be dragged into this mess. Neither did my friends.

"I came here hoping you'd help." I met Bear's and Owl's forceful stares. "But I understand that you need to protect your people. I won't think less of anyone for not coming with me. I can go alone."

"No, you can't." Liora angled toward me. "Because this is about more than just rescuing our friend. This is our job. And we should do it together."

I read what she couldn't add in the depths of her wiser-than-her-age eyes. That first and foremost, our pack were knights. Frazer's task to look into the seers' mirror and find clues to the moonstone's location belonged to all of us. For good or ill, we were bound together and destined for Mysaya.

"Agreed." Adrianna's striking gaze met mine. "I'm with you."

That show of support erased any lingering tension between us.

"En, you've got to know this could be a trap," Cai said, marking me with a gloomy look. "Morgan might be using Frazer to get to you. She must've heard how close you were at Kasi by now."

"If you are who I think you are, then Cai might be right." Ryder studied me as if waiting for me to confirm or deny something. When I said nothing, he continued. "There was only meant to be one female in your pack—that's what the wanted lists said. But after hearing Billy's revelation about your past ... nature, I'll take the leap in assuming your identity. And if I'm right, then you should know the price on your head is double that of your friends."

"How insulting," Adrianna said in mock dry notes.

Ryder smirked before turning to me again. "Mysaya doesn't have a standing army. Just a personal guard to repel any groups stupid enough to try to raid it. From the outside, it looks like an easy mark. Morgan might be hoping you make that mistake and rush in without thinking."

I retreated into logic, using that to cool the flames of panic. "Why would Morgan do that when she thinks I'm in Asitar?"

"Wait." Cai held up a splayed hand. "When did Morgan discover you were in Asitar?"

"We ran into someone who worked for Morgan. She managed to break into my mind." Liora's countenance clouded with the shadow of bitter recollection. "She didn't get much. But it was enough to confirm who and where we were."

Cai stared, wide-eyed and horrified, at his sister.

I fiddled with my necklace strings. "Trap or not, I'm going to Mysaya."

"Then we should prepare as if their goal is to capture you," Ryder suggested. "If we can anticipate their actions, we can outmaneuver them."

I guessed that meant Ryder was also coming with us.

"There's something I need to say first." Straightening in her chair, Liora's attentions fixed on Bear and Owl. "Morgan has allowed the Wild Hunt to kill your people and burn a forest down around your ears. Even if you don't help us, your pack will still suffer under her rule. If you want to be free of her, then rescuing Frazer would be the first step toward achieving that goal."

Owl concealed his thoughts behind a veil of restraint. Bear, on the other hand, wore his wariness and suspicion openly.

She hesitated, her brow furrowing in a way that made me think she was weighing what to say and what to conceal. "You see ... there's something in Mysaya that will help in the fight against Morgan and her allies. And Frazer's the only one who can get it."

It made me uneasy to reveal so much to strangers. Still, Liora had the empathic power to navigate this situation. I had to give her my trust.

"But I know words aren't going to convince you," Liora said to Owl and Bear. "So in return for your assistance with Frazer, I'll give you something your pack needs."

Bear's gaze narrowed on her. "What is it that you think we need?"

"Over half of the people in this camp are shifters." Fearlessly, Liora went on. "I can sense it. Or at least my animal can."

My jaw dropped.

Bear's dark brown wings stiffened. Owl cocked his head half an inch, the movement more bird-like than anything. I detected a dagger-sharpness emanating from him that wasn't there before.

"For most of my life, I thought being a shifter was a curse." Clasping her hands on the tabletop, she explained what familiars were. Then she added, "Basically, it comes down to this. I've found a way to talk to my animal. Because of that, I've developed a relationship with her. It wasn't always like that, but it is now. And I'll show your pack how I did it—if you help us."

Bear was the more visibly shocked of the two. His gaze lowered to the table in what looked like an attempt to block us out and reflect on everything he'd heard. Owl pulled his mate out of his troubled reverie by signing to him.

Meanwhile, Cai gaped at Liora as if he'd never seen his sister before. Adrianna looked tense, watchful. I was a wayward muddle of conflicting emotions.

Bear suddenly rounded on Liora. "What is your animal?"

Liora's sprightly voice lowered and deepened. "I am the incarnation of the great dragons. But you may call me Isolde."

"What will you do if we don't help you?"

The golden rings around her pupils became wheels of fire. "My human and I will leave without sharing our information."

"Our kind are being hunted down and sold for blood sports," Bear growled out. "We're dying out because our young can't control their animals. Because they draw attention to themselves and that's how trackers find them. But if our cubs could speak to these familiars, as you call them, they could teach them to be cautious. We could save our kind from extinction. And yet you're using this information to bargain with us?"

His nails slowly lengthened, turning into five-inch-long claws.

Liora-Isolde's features darkened. "Are you challenging me, Bear?"

Magic pulsed through the space in a heatwave. It reeked of dominance and power and was designed to subjugate those who were weaker.

Everyone averted their eyes. Except me.

Liora-Isolde noticed my resistance. When that green and golden gaze turned on me, my fae instincts combined with my magical strength surged to the surface. My female would not bow, not even to a dragon. "That won't work on me."

She gave me a feral smile. "I should hope not."

Before I could riddle out that remark, her attentions had moved on to Bear. "You won't guilt me into giving you the information. My offer is what it is. I'm not asking for your pack to engage every last soldier. We just need to create enough chaos in Mysaya to distract the sentries, then we can sneak in and retreat once we have Frazer."

"Save your breath," Bear grumbled. "There's no prettying up a steaming pile of shit."

Liora-Isolde bumped her chin up. "Do we have a deal or not?"

"I'm getting too old for this," Bear said, rubbing his forehead.

The mated couple then shared a series of micro-expressions. That silent interplay ended when Owl glanced at me and nodded.

I guessed his meaning. "Thank you."

Bear crossed his muscled forearms causing the veins to bulge there. "Very well. I shall pick our best warriors to assist you in this insanity. That is if we can come up with a solid plan and then two more for when the first one goes wrong. And you"—he almost stabbed that word at

Liora-Isolde—"will teach us everything you know about communicating with our animals."

"Of course." A short, almost peevish reply. "But I won't give you the specifics of how it's done until after you've followed through on your word."

Cai fidgeted. He seemed irked at this change in his sister.

"So be it." Anger pulled Bear's eyebrows down into a V-shape. "But I won't allow my people to get into it with Lynx. If you can't handle him, I'll order a retreat. No exceptions. I refuse to become a mouse under that demon's paw."

Owl slapped two irritated fingers to the middle of his palm. That erased Bear's scowl. "I know you cared for him once, but whoever he was when you were at court, he isn't that person anymore."

I waded in on that. "Leave Lynx to me."

Six bodies tensed.

"You shouldn't face him alone," Adrianna warned. "It's not hyperbole when they call him the most powerful male in Aldar."

The moisture evacuated my mouth. I tried to swallow and couldn't. "Just tell me what his abilities are. I'll figure out the rest. You said he could summon lightning ..."

"That's right," Ryder said. "He can also control shadows and hide in them. Past that, I don't know much about him or his limits. The Sami never spent much time among the nobles."

Adrianna threw more horrifying facts at me. "I've seen him use his shadows to transport himself, too. When we were young, he could get from one side of the castle to the other in the time it would take for me to drop a stone to the floor."

"Hold on." Cai held up his hand. "Are you saying you knew Lynx?"

Adrianna hit him with an impatient look. "Yes, but let's not get into the how and when now." She refocused on me. "I'll go with you. We can fight him together."

I licked my lips. "No—"

"Don't play the martyr," Adrianna snapped. "It's annoying and stupid."

There was more in her expression than irritation. Fear and concern lurked there as well.

I held my temper and argued calmly. "I'm not. But I'll have to attack

Lynx with everything I've got. I don't want you anywhere near that, not when my sun-strikes could kill you." Ignoring her scowl, I continued. "Frazer and I also need to figure out how to complete his mission once he's freed. You'll be more useful buying time for us with the sentries. You'd be wasted acting as my bodyguard."

Adrianna looked off to the side and sighed. For her, that signaled acceptance.

Bear stood, picking up different maps of the area. "Well then, if we're doing this, we should get a start on how to go about it."

Hours of conversation later, Bear waved his weary hands, a signal that he was done. "We'll have to resume this in the morning," he said, scrubbing his face with his palms. "I can barely keep my eyes open."

My insides swelled with relief. After the exhausting flight here and the little sleep the night previous, I could've lain down on a rock and found an adequate pillow.

Everyone except Bear and Owl exited the tent.

Out in the open, I was greeted with an evening light that knifed through the breaks in the canopy and puddled across a well-trodden ground.

Ryder said goodbye and went to seek out his own shelter. That left Cai to show us to his tent that housed his rucksack and bedroll. I removed my shoes before entering the cramped space and unslung both weapon and rucksack.

Still clothed, I laid out my bedroll and slipped into it. I placed my bag underneath my head to act as a pillow. It was better than a rock, anyway.

I'd set myself up for sleep. I hadn't anticipated that Cai would start asking questions within the privacy of a soundproof bubble. First, he wanted to hear about Sefra and the sunstone. From there, he and Liora fell down a rabbit hole. I didn't participate in their rapid discourse except to mention that Abraxus was our ally. And my rutting grandfather. I gave short answers to the questions that followed. Cai quickly got the hint and stopped asking me about him. Adrianna only spoke to grumble about Danu disappearing on us and to voice her desire to know Sefra's location.

I only realized I'd fallen asleep when I heard, *Wake up!*

That jolted me up into a seated position. I glanced around the tent in a mental fog. Everything was cast in a midnight gloom. My friends appeared to be asleep. There were no signs of intruders. "What ..."

Finally. I thought I was going to have to peck your cheek again.

Recognizing Danu's voice, I caged a sleep-starved growl. *What d'you want?*

I need to show you something. Come with me.

Why? Where have you been all this time?

I've been doing what I do best—watching and listening. Now, if you wish to save Frazer, come outside and follow me.

Damn him. *This better not be a joke.*

Don't be a simpleton. I've better things to do than play childish pranks.

I punched out an irritated sigh. *Fine.*

Instincts attuned to potential dangers, I strapped my Utemä to my hip and left the tent.

As I slipped on my shoes, I clocked soft wingbeats. Danu appeared from out of the veil of darkness and landed atop my bright feathers. In a staccato move, he jabbed his beak toward the back of our tent. *Go that way.*

Grumbling internally, I walked to where he directed me.

I wandered bleary-eyed through the forest for a few minutes. All the while, Danu refused to give an answer as to what we were doing or how it could benefit my brother.

I was about to give up when we traveled past the camp's sensory warding. My world expanded, doubling. I hadn't realized what a relief it would be to hear and smell as a fae did again. It oriented me in an unfamiliar environment.

Not far now.

"Until what?" I muttered at Danu.

Wait for it.

The forest thinned out, and a sound of water rushing over rock reached me. Then I saw it. Through the gaps in the trees, a swarm of firelights danced over a river.

I soon left the forest and stepped onto the riverbank.

Ferns and flowers sprouted out of rocks and tree stumps. The surrounding trees were crooked, seemingly drunk on water with many of their roots pressed deep into the riverbed. Their branches shaded the slower-moving pockets of the river where reeds popped up to be tickled by a cool breeze.

Danu launched himself off my wing and settled down on a small boulder beside the riverbed. My feet carried me over to him. I tucked in my wings and squatted on the pebbled ground. "Want to tell me what we're doing here?"

There is an ancient fae road that spans the breadth of the Metori. Abraxus used it many times when he lived in Aldar. Its entrance has always been hidden, but if you can find it, it will take you to Mysaya in a matter of hours. It's certainly a safer option than your current plan to fly over a mountain range prone to extreme weather shifts and teeming with any number of tribes who might attack you.

Excitement beat beneath my breastbone until my mind caught upon a snag. "What do you mean if I can find it? Can't you just take us to this road?"

Come, come. Think, child! His feathers puffed out. *Abraxus hasn't set foot in these lands in centuries. Even if he could recall where the entrance is and pass the knowledge on to me, landscapes change.*

"Point taken," I said tartly. "But how do you expect me to find the pathway?"

Is that magic in your veins, or mud? Are you not a witch?

I crossed my brows. "You get more condescending with every comment. Are you in some sort of competition with yourself?"

Answer the question.

I stifled an exaggerated sigh. "I'm a witch."

That's right. I've been watching you over the past few days—

"How delightfully creepy," I deadpanned.

He raised the volume of his mental voice. *And I've observed that while you work hard to improve upon your skills, you don't experiment beyond the confines of what you're being taught, which is a mistake, since you can't assume any teacher could guide you into realizing your full potential. How could they when nobody has possessed chaos and all four light disciplines before?*

"You want me to experiment with magic ... That will help me find the path?"

The raven bobbed his head. *Yes. And if you thought more like a witch, you might've figured that out for yourself. Now, waterlight is known for its ability to divine truth.*

"I've already tried dreamwalking."

Danu rattled his beak, interrupting me. *Quiet!* He waited to see if I would argue. When I didn't, he continued. *You probably failed in your endeavors because places like Mysaya are warded against forms of magical infiltration. The same can be said for the palace in Alexandria.*

I groaned inwardly. Of course Mysaya would be warded.

Danu went on. *But the old fae road won't be warded. So you must search for Frazer through the bond while also commanding your magic to find the best route toward him. That should be enough to lead you to it.* He pointed a wing at the wide river that mirrored a button-shaped moon, a hundred firelights, and a million stars. *It's easier to work with waterlight when you're physically close to a source. Get to it.*

I called for the energy of the water to join with my soul, and a blue thread presented itself to me.

Inspiration struck. I imagined the thread winding around my kin bond. I held the braided fibers in my mind and sent my will lancing through them. *Show me the quickest route to my brother.*

The silvery voice of a woodland river answered back. *Follow me.*

My spirit was wrenched from my body. I flew over forested land, following the river upstream, all the way to the feet of the mountains. Beneath those majestic peaks, I traveled straight through a waterfall. I had a second to acknowledge the presence of a hidden ledge before being plunged into darkness.

In this phantom state, I'd only to think of starlight for three bright sparks to appear and illuminate the tunnel ahead. I sped through it for what seemed like forever and a day. When it did end, I was hauled straight toward a slim fissure in the stone.

I arrived on a plateau, halting at the very edge of it. Below, the mountains encircled a valley dotted with three lakes. To the right of these pristine waters was a walled-in city, complete with a castle. I recognized the scenery from one of Frazer's memories. This was Mysaya.

That sight was torn from me as the world was thrown in reverse. I landed inside my body with a jolt and a gasp.

It worked, I take it? Danu asked.

I stood and turned on my heel. My feet were swift in returning me to the forest. Danu trailed after me, fastening his dreaded talons upon my wing.

I'd been walking for less than a minute when I heard a *crunch* of leaves. Halting, I reached for my shield and my sword: my moonlight and my Utemä.

Nose in the air, I inhaled a whiff of musk and fur. A red and white fox trotted out from behind a loula. The sleek creature shifted into a very naked male. I released my magic to the ether and averted my gaze. "Were you following me?"

"Yes and no. I noticed your leaving, but I couldn't leave my posting. So I sent for someone who could track your nightly wanderings."

"Who was that?"

The *swoosh* of beating wings reached my ears.

A fae touched down on mossy earth ten feet in front of me. His hood concealed his face, but I'd seen his outerwear before. The brown leathers. The hardy boots. The dark green cloak. "Hello, Owl."

He pushed his hood back and those startling eyes settled on me. The male gestured to his mouth with one hand and then motioned toward me, encouraging me to explain myself.

"We have to wake the others." A splinter of regret pierced my solar plexus. I hated robbing my friends of much-needed sleep. It couldn't be helped, though. "I know how we can get to Mysaya without being spotted."

Owl's inscrutable face transformed with a smile. He nodded to me, silently saying, "*Well done.*"

CHAPTER 32
BOTH SIDES NOW

-FRAZER-

I was outside of my body, linked to life by a single thread. Below, I sensed only pain. I didn't want to return there.

A feminine voice echoed through dark space. *You must. Remember your siska.*

My frayed thoughts realigned around a name. Ena. She was the string fastening me to the earth. I could not cut it, and for a fleeting moment, I wished that I could. Without my siska's strength, I might've escaped. I could've left behind my grief and met those I mourned for in the afterlife.

The stranger's voice returned. *You won't meet Layla again, Frazer. Let the dead rest. Be brave. Live.*

Those words were a knife piercing my chest cavity. To stay sane, I kept memories of that old loss locked up in their appropriate place and focused on the only person still living that I loved. I followed that unbreakable bond back into a prison of meat and bone.

Awareness accumulating, I sensed the cold metal around my wrists and the hard bed underneath me. My bladder was full; my muscles ached.

Eyes shut, I backtracked through my recollections.

Ryder, Cai, and I were traveling through one of the forested valleys of the Metori. Lynx appeared in the distance. I shot at him. When that failed, I ran out to draw his attention from Ryder and Cai. Lightning slammed into me. Pain followed.

I plunged into a thick fog that only vague images interrupted. Rough hands shook me awake, forced me to drink, and changed my sheets whenever I lost control of my bodily functions.

Tuning into the present, I prepared to confront my imprisonment.

I pried my eyelids apart. My sticky gaze traveled over an empty room adorned with silver floorboards, a beamed ceiling, and a chandelier that dripped grape-sized diamonds.

Countless memories stirred, making my retracted wings itch under my shoulder blades. The grand decor was familiar. It belonged to the Mysayan castle, to the place I had worked in as a royal guard for years.

This wasn't the room where my last set of wings were cleaved, but that trauma lived in the deepest parts of me. It haunted my very bones. Even to be inside the same building again was enough to pump dread through my circulatory system.

Sweaty palms. Dry mouth. Rapid pulse.

Disgusted by my body's weakness, I fought to master my uneven breathing and to conquer the dizziness threatening my equilibrium. I only succeeded in dragging in the scents of night jasmine, loula sap, and ever-sweet roses. Another nauseating reminder of where I was.

Fuck. I had to get a grip. I'd planned to infiltrate Mysaya all along. I should be making the most of this situation.

Despite my best efforts, it took a very long minute to subdue the anxiety gnawing at my insides and to think of what to do next. I started with my most immediate concern: my bulging bladder.

My shackles clanked loudly when I planted my feet on the cold floor.

I stilled. There were no guards in the room, but they would be lurking nearby. I certainly wouldn't have been forgotten about.

Careful not to disturb the noisy chains, I stood and relieved myself in the bucket beside the mattress. Once I'd finished, I stared longingly at the jug of water on offer. It was on the floor, within reach. I ran my tongue over my teeth, failing to summon enough saliva to soothe my parched throat.

I clenched my jaw and my hands. No. To drink would be a mistake. The water might've been drugged. It wasn't worth the risk.

Turning my thoughts to escape, I sat on the bed and tested the manacles' grip over my wrists. There was no give in them. Even if I broke a thumb, I wouldn't slip a hand free.

I searched for a tool to pick the lock. My efforts were proving fruitless when a mountain-chilled breeze brushed my cheek. I glanced to the right, to the back wall. Glass doors led out onto a balcony and to the night sky beyond. One of these doors was ajar.

My heart sunk, inch by inch. The guards were either incompetent, overly confident, or this lapse in security was a trick—an invitation for somebody to attempt a rescue. Had I become bait? Cai and Ryder weren't with me. Was this for their benefit?

The sound of a running river reached me. A noise that had no visible origin, and yet it whispered a name: Ena.

Fear flushed my bloodstream. Within a tick of our shared heartbeat I'd located my siska. Ena was in Aldar.

That meant she would be coming for me. I knew that as surely as I knew the sun would rise. And I'd become the cheese to lure her into this giant rat trap.

My wings suddenly nudged my shoulder blades. They wanted *out*. That desire to flee, to take to the skies, could only mean one thing; there was a powerful predator nearby. I pushed my instincts down, down, down, and kept my wings caged. "I know you're there. Show yourself."

Movement caught my left eye. I turned my head in that direction. A shroud of shadows parted to reveal Lynx, standing tall in black and red armor.

He padded over and halted a few feet from me. Inky-black irises, so unlike the color I remembered, stared down at me.

I searched for signs of my old friend in his gaze. But at some point he must've learned the art of concealment. His face was impassive. Detached.

I cast off the silence first. "How long have I been out?"

"Three days."

No wonder I was so hungry. I hadn't eaten in three days.

"Why are you here?" I asked heavily.

"To interrogate you," he said in that deep rumble of his.

I retreated into a passionless place. "What about? My sleeping habits?"

"Queen Morgan wants information on Serena Smith. If you refuse to cooperate, I'll have to shock you."

I put on a casual tone. "I'm surprised Morgan isn't here. I thought she'd want to tear me into strips personally."

His giant wings twitched, betraying troubled spirits. "The Queen is currently away from court and unreachable. Until she returns, I'm the only one who knows where you are."

I raised a skeptical eyebrow. "Are you saying we're alone? You haven't got any other prisoners chained up nearby?"

Lynx shot me a knowing look at that shameless dig for information. I didn't care. I had to try. If there was the slightest chance he'd tell me whether Cai and Ryder were here too, I had to take it.

"The only other people on the castle grounds are the soldiers based here," Lynx said. "But they won't come into this part of the castle. These are my lodgings."

A tenuous relief filled me. I couldn't trust what he'd said, but it felt good to hear the words. To have hope that the others were safe. "Why am I not in Alexandria?"

He squared his shoulders. "The Queen never stipulated where your interrogation was to take place."

"Why bring me here, though?"

"My lightning strikes have triggered heart failure in the past. Mysaya was closer than Alexandria and has a healer in residence."

Suspicion tapered my eyes. "Is that really the reason, or are you punishing me?"

"What are you talking about?" he asked, frowning.

The image of a curved blade flashed into my mind's eye. The feeling of cold steel slicing through feathers, muscles, and bones gripped my body. The overwhelming scent of fear and blood invaded my nostrils once again. I pushed—*shoved*—those nightmares away, rearranging my features into a mask devoid of emotion. "The last time I was under this roof, my wings were cleaved for defying your father. Then he forbade me from ever returning to his court. I thought you might've brought me here to taunt me with old memories. To punish me for the same reason your isä did."

He grimaced. "I don't want to punish you, Frazer."

"Why not?" My limbs were almost vibrating with tension as I added, "I helped the Sami escape. If they'd been here when Morgan arrived, she wouldn't have taken offense over their refusal to serve her. She might've been more lenient toward your court."

"That's crazy. She—" A strangled noise escaped him. Features spasming, he clasped his throat and clenched his jaw. When that fit had subsided, he continued. "You aren't to blame for what happened that day."

My thoughts ran to skeptical places. Was this a ploy for me to lower my guard? Or was he hinting that he wasn't the traitor everyone believed him to be?

I couldn't hold the question in anymore. I'd been desperate to ask him for years. "Why do you serve Morgan?"

The life seemed to drain out of him. "Because it was the only decision that I could live with. That's all I can say."

"Are you her guardian?" I asked sharply. "Did you swear yourself to her?"

A muscle jumped under his eye.

I cursed.

"Frazer, I have to start the interrogation."

The pulsing veins in his neck and the tremor in his fists showed a battle was taking place inside of him, and a loss of control was near.

"What can you tell me about Serena?" Lynx demanded.

My jaw turned stubborn.

"Just give me something—anything," he said, softer than before. "I've been ordered to get answers out of you, and I won't be able to stop torturing you until you concede. The Queen might want you alive, but that's the extent of her concern. She won't care if you end up as a drooling mess."

He wasn't wrong. An intransigent attitude might result in my passing out again. Then escape would become impossible.

An idea took shape. "You want to know about Serena? What would you say if I told you that she can't sing?"

A weighted silence nudged between us.

"There are specific questions the Queen wanted answered," he said hesitantly. "But for now at least, I think whatever you're willing to say about Serena will be considered valuable. Understand?"

I dipped my chin in a nod.

"Just how bad is her singing?" he asked.

"Diabolical," I said. "She sounds like a cat being stepped on."

"Have you ever told her that?" Lynx dropped to the floor, crossing his legs and wings.

"Why would I?" I shrugged a shoulder. "It makes her happy."

A slow nod. "Keep going."

Picking over my words, I replied, "She smells like sugar. At least she did when she was at Kasi because she'd steal sugar cubes from the food hall."

His head cocked, bemused. "She ate sugar cubes raw?"

I shuffled up the mattress to rest my sore body against the smoothed-out wall. "If she'd been doing that, I would've seized them so her teeth didn't fall out."

"What was she doing with them, then?"

"She fed them to the horses that lived in Kasi. For some reason, she enjoyed being around the beasts."

I hadn't understood why. They were flighty, stubborn animals at the best of times.

Lynx's fingers tapped out a rhythm on his knee. "What else?"

"She's mad about books. I caught her sniffing the pages of one once."

Genuine curiosity seemed to spark his next question. "She likes the smell of them?"

"I'm not sure. But it was disturbing," I deadpanned.

A short puff of air escaped him. It was a miserable male's laugh.

Then, "Do you love her?"

Irritated at his abrupt question, I picked and cleaned my nails. "I don't love anybody."

He nodded once, then cut his gaze loose from mine. "The Queen was led to believe you became Serena's lover while at Kasi. But I think your connection's of a different nature."

My heart banged up against my ribs.

Lynx went on, unrelenting. "There's a witch's scent mixed up in yours. I can smell their magic on you." His chest rose with a deep inhale.

"The entire time you've been here, that secondary scent hasn't faded, even though you haven't seen anybody but me for days."

A shameful pit opened up in my stomach. I hadn't predicted our merged scents being a problem when I'd asked Ena to kin bond with me. I'd assumed we would live as soldiers in separate camps, wherein my "lover's" identity could remain a secret. Even if we'd been posted to the same location, we could've hidden our bond by letting it circulate that we were involved.

Still, I didn't despair. Lynx couldn't be sure Ena was my bonded. He also hadn't guessed I was a witch in my own right. I had an advantage there.

"It sounds as if you're suggesting I've made a bond with Serena." I slipped on a scornful mask. "In which case, you must've lost your wits. Fae can't bond with humans."

A convincing lie. To my knowledge, nobody had kin bonded to a human before.

He eyeballed me. "It might not have been possible when she was human. But before the Queen left the court, she told me that Serena had become a fae."

Brutal bands of terror constricted my lungs. How and when had that been discovered? I pushed out a mocking laugh that sounded off. "Then she's as crazy as people say she is."

"I'm telling you this so you don't suffer needlessly for denying what the Queen already knows to be a fact," he said, his face collapsing into weariness. "I'm well aware you'd rather chew your own arm off than betray someone you care for. All I'm saying is, save yourself whatever pain you can."

My cheeks and ears heated. "Tell me, if you're so concerned about my welfare, why don't you fight your orders?"

It was difficult for a guardian to refuse to follow the orders of their charge, but there were ways to do it. I'd seen people in this very court "misinterpret" Linus's orders. It just required a subtlety of mind.

Lynx regarded me with a grim look. "Have you forgotten what she's capable of? If one of her subjects finds out how to work around her commands, she doesn't just punish them—she finds their weak spot and eviscerates them."

He was defeat personified.

"You've given up."

"Yes, I have," he admitted. "Living this way has eaten away at my soul like rot devouring fruit. I can't even end things myself because my Queen has forbidden it. My only hope is that someone stronger comes along to take me out."

"Death isn't something to hope for. It is the end of hope."

Tonelessly, he replied, "I thought that once too. But I find I'm becoming more like my makena every day. There are gaps in my memory. I barely sleep most nights. And if I lose my wits, it won't be me that suffers."

I stiffened at that reminder of his makena, of Grace Tsári who had seen and heard spirits—those that clung to the earth, lacking the will or ability to move on. Eventually, their trauma broke down her mental defenses, driving her to insanity. She had drifted into another world, unable to recognize reality or her own son.

"It took a long time for Grace's power to overcome her. I doubt—"

"Being a prisoner in your own body has a tendency to accelerate madness." His words weren't pretty, but they cleansed a festering soul-wound. Lynx wasn't serving the mad witch happily. He hated what she'd made him into. That was plain at least.

"For what it's worth, I never believed you wanted to be Morgan's pet. I don't know what happened all those years ago to make you swear to her, but I'm sorry I couldn't protect you from it."

A sad smile that wasn't really a smile stretched his mouth. "You couldn't have stopped it." His head pivoted in the direction of the open doors. There, he peered out at that sweet-smelling night. "I'm ready to die, Frazer."

My insides iced over as a theory formed. Lynx had imprisoned me in the almost deserted Mysaya instead of the dungeons of Alexandria. He also seemed to suspect I was kin bonded. Therefore, he'd know Ena could locate me, and he'd left the balcony doors open. Was this his attempt to subvert his orders? Did he think Ena was powerful enough to kill him? More importantly, was she? If she couldn't, he'd surely take her to Morgan.

Lynx rose up in a violent motion, his muscles flexing, his wings trembling. "I can't hold off from asking her questions anymore. You should prepare yourself."

I held out a shackled hand. "Give me your belt. I don't want to bite out my tongue if I seize."

Throat bobbing, he extracted his sword from his belt and propped the blade up against the wall, out of my reach. He handed the leather strap over to me.

I took it, saying, "There is a future where you can be free."

"Release won't come until she's dead, and I'll lose my mind before that happens."

All I gave him was, "We'll see."

Tension gripped his wings. "How did Serena Smith become fae?"

"I don't know," I lied.

"How was she able to use light magic when she was still a human?"

I repeated the same line.

Lynx's expression shuttered. "Lie down."

I reclined on the mattress and stuck the belt between my teeth.

Lynx raised a hand. Lightning lanced out, striking me. The pain was monstrous, a burning, piercing, twisting kind of hell. Every nerve screeched like nails against pottery. I stayed conscious, though, which meant he'd lowered the strength of his shocks.

"What are Serena's secrets?"

Breathing heavily, I shook my head. His power jolted me again, setting fire to my flesh.

Lynx repeated another question that I refused to answer. More agony. Again and again, on and on it went.

I endured it. I had to. My siska needed me sane. I held onto that thought, using it as a lifebuoy in the violent sea that threatened to rip apart every seam that made me who I was.

CHAPTER 33
THE OTHER GATE

The night after I met with the Winged Fiends, I led sixty of their best fighters through a dark forest toward the hidden fae road. It wasn't a hard task. I just had to follow the river that Danu had guided me to yesterday. That would take us where we needed to go.

For over two hours, the pleasant ruffling of water, the singing of nocturnal birds, and the chirping of crickets were our constant companions, as were the countless woodland sprites interested in our rescue party. I thought the beasts might attack, but they maintained their distance, preferring to watch us from creepy shadows.

Gradually the riverbank steepened and we had to move inland to avoid the slippery slope. Sweat dampened my skin from the soup-thick humidity, and my leg muscles burned from the climb.

I craned my neck, hoping to glimpse the mountain range that housed our shortcut. But I failed. The canopy's branches were tightly knitted, and the sky was marbled with silver-lined clouds that hid both stars and moon.

I put my head down, refusing to be discouraged. This lack of light would work in our favor later on, if the same weather conditions existed in Mysaya. The harder our group was to see, the easier it would be for our surprise attack to succeed. As I looked behind me at the figures that melted into the scenery, I knew we had managed to minimize our visibility. Our group wore black clothing; the rucksacks, weapons, and fireless torches we carried were inconspicuous.

"How much longer is this going to take?" said one of the Fiends.

You're nearly there.

Short on breath, I said, "Danu says it won't be long."

"Is he really a familiar?" someone asked eagerly.

"Yes," I replied.

"I wonder if he'd answer some of our questions," a soft voice muttered.

"It's the least they can do for us," answered a grumpy-sounding fae.

I cringed at the tense air. At the resentment in it.

Many of the Fiends had struggled to adjust to the knowledge that their shifting abilities came from sprites. They had nearly mutinied after learning the secret of contacting their familiars was being withheld from them—that it was being traded for their support in our mission. Liora had prevented an outbreak of violence by shifting. Faced with a dragon, the greatest of predators, the Fiends had submitted.

"Cai, that's the tenth time you've almost walked into a tree," Ryder remarked from my left.

I glanced in their direction. There, Cai tugged his elbow out of Ryder's grip. "That's because I can barely see three feet in front of me," he grumbled. "Just be grateful for your fancy fae-eyes and don't let me break my nose."

"I am, and I will," he replied cheerfully. "But why don't you let me carry you? Your face is too pretty to get messed up."

Bear chuffed. "Stop flirting."

"What can I say?" I could hear the smile in Ryder's voice. "I don't believe in being serious during grim times. It makes for too much misery."

That struck me as wise.

On the back of the wind's breath, I detected the sound of crashing water. I sped up, paying no mind to my aching feet.

The trees parted. I stepped out into a glade.

Danu was quick to fly down and land on my shoulder. I stifled my agitation at those sharp talons biting into my muscles.

The rest of the company joined me. Together, we gazed up at the thinly forested slopes of the Metori—at the mountain range that stretched in an unending line north to south.

The next stage in our journey was located on our right and came in the form of a sugar-white waterfall cascading into a deep plunge pool. The water hit the ground with such force, it produced a cloud of what looked like powdered glass. This mist curled through heavy air in glittering whorls and coated my eyelashes in a glistening dew. It would have been a beautiful spot, almost peaceful, if not for the stunted tree that loomed before us. The trunk looked diseased, twisted, and rotten, with toadstools decorating it like warts, and bony fingers grasping for any intruder who dared pass by. Its scent infused the space with dead things—with wood-damp and leaf-rot.

"Is this it, then?" asked one of the Fiends.

"This looks like an evil place," added a nervous-sounding fae. "We should turn back."

"Get ahold of yourself, Rabbit," someone barked.

"Shut it, Dog."

"Why don't you hop on home if you're so scared?"

"Enough," Bear said in a low-to-the-ground rumble. "Ena, I await your lead."

He handed me an unlit torch. I cleared my throat of nerves and spoke to the group. "The tunnel inside is narrow, so don't crowd the entrance. Move in single file."

I secured the torch under my armpit and retrieved a matchbox from my trouser pocket. Not wanting to waste energy on magic so early on, I drew out a tiny stick and struck it against the touch paper.

A witch's cackle of a wind sprung up from nowhere. It blew out the match and sent the spooky tree's branches smacking together like the toothless gums of an old woman.

Danu squawked, and I could've sworn that killed the wind. *Get on with it,* he urged me.

Right.

Ignoring the faint tremor in my hands, I lit another match and set the fragile flame against the torch's special wax coating, which would ensure a water-resilient flame.

Holding the ablaze torch aloft, I strode over to the side of the waterfall. There, I found the concealed ledge.

Danu clung onto me in readiness. I carefully stepped up onto the narrow shelf and pressed my wings against the rock face. The rough surface would scrape my wings, but I chose to endure the discomfort. Because even with spray stinging my face, I could see the forty-foot drop waiting for me should I stumble. And if I fell, I didn't want to go over backwards.

Torch lifted, I crab-walked along the shelf. If I hadn't been searching for the entrance, I doubted that I would've found it. The jagged gap blended into the surrounding granite so well that the eye wanted to travel past it.

Glad I didn't have to stoop, I slipped inside the tunnel.

I spun around and peered outside, raising my torch to illuminate the ledge. Fear spiked my pulse as Liora and Adrianna moved up onto the lip of rock. I was more concerned watching them move along the shelf than I had been doing the exact same thing.

Liora reached me first. I extended a hand to her.

Without a torch to burden her, it was a simple thing for her to grasp hold of me. I helped her through into the tunnel.

She expelled a wobbly exhale. "Thanks."

Breaking our handhold, she wiped her palms down the front of her trousers.

I detected the *tap-clunk* of boots over the deafening roar of the falls. Bathed in my torch's firelight, Adrianna's face appeared in the entryway. "Start walking." She waved me on. "The others are coming through."

I turned and stared into the gloom. It was a narrow space, which would prevent anybody from overtaking me. I would have to set the pace here.

On the back of that thought, I started a swift march through the roots of the mountain. A minute or so later, a soft shout sounded behind me. "I'm the last one through."

That was that then. We were all committed.

Our group traversed the steadily rising path as quiet as sleeping mice. Using her timepiece, Adrianna announced when our first hour in the tunnel had passed. She marked the second hour, which coincided with the strike of midnight, in the same way.

It didn't take much—an unvarying landscape and a confined space—for my chest to swell with anxiety. I managed to bottle my panic by tuning into the kin bond. Through that, I sensed the other half of my heart getting closer and closer. That kept the angst from overwhelming me.

Eventually, the gradient leveled out. It was then I spotted an end to our cramped conditions and hurried through that last stretch of tunnel.

I moved into a cavern and was slammed with a wave of muggy heat that smelled faintly of sulfur. That familiar buzz of magic traveled through me. Only this wasn't a friendly kind. It was an oppressive force that battered my skull and overturned my stomach.

Liora appeared at my side. I could tell by the way she glanced around with anxious-wide eyes that she sensed the hostile energy squatting in this space.

Adrianna joined us, her nose crinkling. "What is that?"

"We don't know." I raised my torch a little higher, illuminating as much of the area as I could. It looked like a perfectly normal cave.

Cai was the next one through. "Fuck me."

"What's wrong?" Ryder emerged out of the passage.

Shut up all of you, Danu said from my shoulder. *Not many people can sense the power in this room, and your bringing it up will only make the Fiends more on edge than they already are.*

Liora was the fastest to adjust and cover for us with Ryder. "We were just wondering why it smells strange in here."

He sniffed the air once. "I don't think it's anything to worry about. There's probably a hot spring nearby. The Metori are known for having them."

When every member of our party was crowded inside the cave, it became clear that nobody sensed the menacing magic besides our pack. There were a few remarks made about the peculiar smell. Ryder's assumption about the underground hot spring was repeated. That closed down the chatter.

Bear and Owl approached me.

"Is this it, then? The end of the road?" Bear asked.

I gestured to the seven-foot-tall fissure on the far wall. "The mountain plateau's outside. We'll have a view of the castle from there."

Danu butted in. *Send the Fiends on ahead. There's something we should discuss. It won't take long.*

I was about to refuse when he added, *It's important.*

Gods-damn him. I had a suspicion that if I ignored him, he'd dig those horrid talons of his into my collarbone until I conceded.

"Cai, can you take the lead?" I asked, trying to be subtle.

Bear's thick brows stood up. Owl motioned to me as if to say *Don't you want to do it?*

Liora, genius that she was, answered for me. "I'm using this cave to undress before my shift. Ena's going to stay with me. Cai and Adi can lead you out."

Adrianna scowled. Cai cocked a brow. But if Bear found my reluctance to leave at all strange, he didn't show it. "As you wish." He faced his people and raised his voice. "Listen up, everyone. Once we're outside, speak only when you have to. Stick to the plan. And don't be stupid."

What an inspiring speech.

Shut up, I told the raven.

"After you," Ryder said, his eyes fixed on Cai.

Without delay, Cai marched toward the exit, hand on his pommel, and slipped out the narrow gap sideways. The night swallowed him up. Adrianna went after him.

A muted queue for the doorway formed.

My feet stayed glued to the floor, as did Liora's. When it was only us left, Liora whispered, "What's going on?"

I gazed up at the bird expectantly. "Ask Danu."

The reason you feel so uncomfortable in this place is that the gateway to the dark court is hidden atop this mountain.

We stared at him, speechless.

I didn't mention it before because I thought your pack might reject this route out of fear, and this was by far the safest route to Mysaya. It was also important to know if you were like the last generation of knights who could sense whenever the dark court's energy was present. Among other things, it helped them detect and track creatures from that world.

"So this was a test?" My gaze narrowed upon the bird.

Yes.

Totally unapologetic.

Anger bit, and fear bayed. "Fine. We'll deal with this later. I want to get out of here."

"Me too," Liora whispered. "I should change first, though. Otherwise they'll be wondering what we were doing in here."

There's no need to lower your voice, Danu said. *This is a fae road, remember? It exists outside of our space and time. Nobody outside can hear you.*

It struck me then that I couldn't hear our group. That made me want to leave even more.

Liora began removing her clothes. To give her some privacy, I walked up to the entrance and stopped there, waiting to go through.

My gaze drifted to the cave wall. An odd compulsion to touch the pitted rock seized me. I didn't think about it. I just did it.

My consciousness ripped from my body. I was thrown forward, winging over foggy seas and giant plains pocked with holes that vomited noxious gases. Hundreds of lava-caked mountains spat out fire and ash. These expulsions blanketed the black earth below, choking the little vegetation that grew and struggled for life.

The first scream sounded. Then another and another. Screams so broken and desperate they stole my breath and pushed my heart to pound like the hooves of a spooked horse. That gallop became a drumbeat. A prelude to death and war.

I blinked and materialized in a giant hall. My vision blurred, keeping me from focusing on the details of the space.

A hand gripped my bicep and whirled me around.

I was confronted with a void in the shape of a man. It—he—leaned in and sniffed me. I felt the breath of his power upon my cheek. A rank evil. A devourer of worlds.

In that abyss there appeared eyes of silver fire. They bored into me, and it was as if a cage fell down around my mind. Caught in his net, I sensed him all around me. Here was a master of all that was rotten and twisted, capricious in judgment, vicious in strength, tyrannical in control, whose domain was torment and naked aggression.

That entity, as old or older than the stars, started to laugh. The noise echoed, growing louder and louder as if a madman were running at me. Gaining on me.

I couldn't speak. I couldn't move.

Thea's and Zola's voices sounded from far away.

Get out of there, Ena.

Move, you fool!

I jumped back into my body.

Liora released her hold on my arm. "What happened? Danu said I had to stop you from touching the cave wall."

Dizzy and disoriented, I was slow to note the alarm in her voice and how the stones burned my skin. I'd dropped my torch; it was on the ground with its flame sputtering out. And Danu had several of my feathers sticking out of the corner of his beak. *Don't look at me like that. I was trying to snap you out of it.*

"Ena?" Liora prompted me, a cloak wrapped around her nude body.

I gave her a reluctant summary.

Liora paled. "Who do you think it was?"

Was it him? I directed that question inward.

Yes, Zola said, her voice hard.

My blood iced over.

You dreamwalked into the dark court, Thea sounded out in worried notes. *Nobody should be able to do that.*

I thought she might add something—something reassuring. She didn't.

"It was Archon," I whispered to a patiently waiting Liora.

Her cheeks hollowed as her mouth swung open.

Danu's talons pressed into my nape, but it didn't hurt. If I hadn't been acquainted with his cantankerous nature, I might've interpreted that as an effort to comfort me. *This isn't the time to dwell upon such things. You have a job to do, remember?*

Intended or not, he had helped me. He jerked me into action. "We have to go," I said, chin rising. "Today is about saving Frazer." Archon could wait.

Liora nodded and proceeded to gather her garments off the floor. That done, she pointed to the fissure with her sheathed rapier. "You first."

That scraped against every instinct. "Hold my hand."

She pursed her lips.

"Yeah, I know," I said, guessing the source of her disapproval. "I've become an overprotective, overbearing fae. Just humor me."

With a tiny smile, she slipped her fingers through mine.

Careful not to touch the cave walls, I sidled through the threshold.

CHAPTER 34
THE SOUND OF THUNDER

I pulled Liora out onto a plateau two hundred feet off the ground. The night air pressed in, hot, sticky, and charged with danger.

"Are you okay?"

"What's going on?"

Adrianna and Cai gathered in close.

Ignoring them, I studied the bare mountain shelf. "Where are the others?"

"Gone," Cai answered. "Owl will signal us when everyone's in position."

"Why did you want to stay in the cave?" Adrianna eyed me and Liora fiercely. "And don't give me that shit about wanting to undress."

Belly flip-flopping, I summarized events for them. Liora pulled her cloak tighter about her. Cai and Adrianna shared an uneasy expression.

"Do you think Archon knew who you were?" Cai asked.

My eyes went down. "I don't know."

Danu ruffled his wings. *Archon couldn't have read your mind, but he would've sensed you were a light-wielder.*

Adrianna glared at Danu. "Why didn't you tell us where the dark gate was beforehand? What else are you hiding from us?"

Hiding? Nothing. Refusing to tell you for your own good? A great many things.

Adrianna's lips parted to give what I expected was a sharp reply. Before she could continue, I said, "Let's just focus on Frazer."

"Can you sense where he is?" Cai said. "His exact location?"

Taking in a deep breath, I gazed out at the landscape.

The plateau was bookmarked by granite rock faces. As a consequence, I had to walk to the edge of the shelf for an uninterrupted view. Adrianna, Cai, and Liora joined me there.

Together, we stared at where the shoulders of snow-dusted mountains sloped down into the valley below us. In this basin three lakes dwelled, their silvery waters acting as a willing canvas, reflecting the night sky above. The surrounding undergrowth consisted of purple heather, yellow gorse, and brown rushes.

My gaze cut right and landed on a wall that spanned the valley and bridged two mountains. Those battlements protected a castle and a small city with ornate spires, dainty turrets, cylindrical towers, and crystal lanterns that from afar twinkled like constellations.

To the rear of the city, a plain populated by mutilated tree stumps and the ruins of old buildings nestled between the mountains and stretched out to the northern horizon. The only things living in that graveyard were nettles, brambles, and other spiky plants.

I thought of my brother amidst that scene of death and beauty. Instantly, his faint heartbeat tickled my ears. I went from root to root, to where our link ended in him, and found his general location. *Frazer?*

I nudged his mind only to discover his mental-shield had shattered. The usual maze of sharp edges, dark corners, and locked doors in his head were gone, replaced by a graying fog. I couldn't get at him. Frazer just haunted the place. A mere ghost.

Fear punched me in the gut. But I decided not to mention my concerns about my brother. "He's in a room somewhere beneath the topmost tower."

"Were you able to speak with him?" Cai said.

"No. But he's definitely there."

Cai frowned. Adrianna was certainly about to ask more questions. Liora distracted them by pointing to the valley floor. "It's Owl."

The spotted owl flew up and over our heads, hooting softly. That was our agreed-upon signal. The Fiends were in place. On a turn of his tawny wings, Owl left us and sped toward the city.

The four of us shared a look of solidarity but no farewells.

"You'll need to back up and give me more space," Liora said as she slipped off her shoes and gave them to Cai, along with her clothes and sword.

Cai, Adrianna, and I backed up. Liora went to the far side of the plateau, and that was where she shifted. I'd seen the transformation before, but it never got old. Liora's short frame and flaming hair disappeared. A fifteen-foot tall, ruby-scaled dragon took her place.

The familiar lowered her serpentine head and met us eye-to-eye. Her nonexistent lips parted to reveal extremely pointy teeth.

"Are you smiling or planning on eating us?" Cai joked.

Isolde's chest vibrated with what I assumed was laughter. *If I was going to eat you, I wouldn't tell you beforehand. Meat always tastes so much sweeter when it doesn't die in fear.*

Cai pushed out a tiny laugh, a sound that was accompanied by a wince.

There's no need to fear me, little one. Hop on.

"One second." He shoved his sister's things into his bag, all except for her sword. Cai looped that onto his belt.

Isolde stuck her front leg out. Using that as a mounting block, Cai hoisted himself up and settled between her shoulders. "I'll see you both soon," he said firmly.

Adrianna gave him a nod.

My palms grew clammy. "Yes, you will."

Cai gripped a ridge on Isolde's neck. "Giddy up." He clicked his tongue.

Isolde released an amused puff of air. *Put your fingers in your ears.*

Oh gods. I clapped my palms over the sides of my head. Isolde roared, signaling the Fiends to start the attack. She crouched, spread her wings wide, and launched herself into the sky.

I held my ground as the downdraft battered me.

"Balor's balls!" Cai's voice pitched so high it would've made dogs howl.

"Cai doesn't appear to be a natural dragon-rider," Adrianna said dryly. She rounded on me. "Ready?"

Before I could respond, Danu soared up and away.

"What are you doing?" I asked, watching him pursue Isolde.

Abraxus wants you to be queen. A queen can handle her own affairs.

Ass.

Adrianna eyed the raven. "I don't trust that wretched bird."

"I never would've guessed." My mock surprise wasn't subtle.

She snorted. "Come on. Let's do this."

Adrianna lifted me. Last night, we had settled on her carrying me. Given my previous experiences, I didn't trust that I'd land smoothly or stealthily. I also had little confidence I could avoid the fighting and reach my destination safely.

Without delay, Adrianna ran off the lip of the ledge. We flew straight toward a stirring of chaos.

By the time we reached Mysaya proper, our attack was well underway. Isolde was painting the outer wall in garnet, amber, and sapphire flames. Cai used his power to direct her fire-stream toward the dodging soldiers. His aim was flawless. Lethal.

Along the outer wall, the shifters who had control over their counterparts changed into their human forms, taking out soldiers at key watch posts. The rest of our group abandoned their hiding spots in the valley's underbrush. Our masked warriors flew up onto the battlements to provide support.

Adrianna's wings strained to gain as much height as possible. The fighting below was enough of a diversion that we got over the outer wall without being targeted.

Bells pealed from within Mysaya. That alarm call coincided with about seventy fae flying out of the castle with bows, spears, and shields.

I drew down the light of the moon, but my protection wasn't needed. Isolde passed underneath me and arrowed straight for the newly airborne soldiers, cutting through space like an eel through water. From atop her back, Cai conjured a whirlwind and blew scarlet powder over the enemy.

Isolde followed that up by expelling a river of fire at the soldiers.

Agonized screams punctured the world. Those dusted from head to toe exploded, their limbs clubbing those around them. The fae smattered with less powder still went up like oil-soaked paper.

"Rivers save us," Adrianna whispered.

Guilt and horror were twin blades slipping between my ribs. Ryder had handed Cai magicked powders he'd acquired from the black market.

All he'd said was that they would amplify the damage that Isolde could do. I'd never imagined the effects being that horrific.

Despite that loss of life, more people left the castle. These fae learned from the deaths of their predecessors and stayed out of range of dragon fire. Instead, they shot arrows at Isolde from a safe distance.

"They're not retreating," I observed.

"That's because they've got Lynx. They don't think they can be beaten," Adrianna said over the din of swords, shouts, and wingbeats.

Yes. Where was Lynx? With my brother? Agitation mounted inside of me. I became a wolf with her haunches up.

"Which room is Frazer in, Ena?" Adrianna said, her tone edged with stress.

I fixed on the topmost tower. It took half a second to sense his location at this short distance. I pointed to the doors that opened out onto a moonstone-colored balcony.

Adrianna landed on the ivy and rose covered railing. I was lowered to the floor while she remained perched above me. A protective gargoyle.

I mouthed, "Go."

Her shrewd gaze skipped to the double doors, which were set ajar, their glass panes tinted with the light that bloomed from within.

Concern scrunched up Adrianna's brow. "That has trap written all over it." She whispered so low and the fighting was so loud, I barely heard her.

I mouthed again, "I know."

Her shoulders slumped. "Watch yourself."

I nodded.

In a graceful move, she twisted about and leaped into thin air. A few flaps of her scaled wings and she was joining in the violence at Isolde's side.

I crept along the balcony, my pulse thrashing in my ears. When I neared the doors, I crouched and peeked through a glass pane.

Beyond, I spied a room floored with silver wood. The chandelier was spitting out seeds of star-fire and illuminating where my brother lay on a low bed, his wrists in chains. His skin looked paler than milk under moonlight except for the purple smudges under his eyes, which stood out as angry bruises.

Frazer? Talk to me. Frazer!

Nothing.

Nobody could sleep through this noise. Had he been drugged?

I slipped off my rucksack and scanned the room. Once. Twice. Three times.

If Lynx was in there, he was cloaked in darkness. Refusing to wait any longer, I dipped inside my bag and plucked out another of Ryder's acquisitions—a vial of corrosive powder that only reacted to and dissolved metal.

I shouldered my rucksack and slipped inside the rectangular room.

My feet hesitated.

Nostrils ballooning, I drew in a deep inhale. Flowers. Dust. Frazer. A hint of someone else's scent lingered. It wasn't strong, though.

I went left, dashing across the room. Once I reached the bed, I quietly set my rucksack and the vial of acid on the silver floorboards.

Frazer was so still. I touched his mind and found it fuzzy at the edges.

"What happened to you?" I sat up on the bed and with trembling fingers, I brushed oily strands of hair off his clammy brow. "How do I help you?"

My desperate pleas were answered by Thea. *His brain's shut down in an effort to escape the pain and to heal the damage that's been done to it. But you can illuminate the darkest of spaces with starlight, even those ruled by the mind.*

She sent me a series of images that showed me what to do next. Following her instructions, I projected myself up to the borders of Frazer's mental landscape. He had no lantern to guide his way. He was indeed lost.

I pulled in the cold power of starlight. It was surprisingly easy to channel. Maybe because this place belonged to the mind, to imagination. Then I released wave after wave of dazzling magic.

The graying fog receded. Gloomy moorland was uncovered.

I spotted him in the distance, atop a small hill. I stoppered my magic and screamed, *Frazer!*

He spun toward me.

Within a beat of our shared heart, he'd tugged me into his mind.

I stumbled and ran and flew at him. He exploded forward, sprinting for me.

Before we could embrace, our eyes opened at the same time. Back in the outer world, we looked into each other—into our mirrors.

His pupils flared in recognition. "You shouldn't have come," he croaked out through chapped lips.

"But I did." I sat back and gave him space.

Grimacing, he tried to push himself up. I supported his wingless back and helped him into a seated position.

Eyes on me, he said, *We can't leave yet. I haven't looked into the mirror.*

I had expected that. *We'll worry about the mirror after you're free.* I handed him the vial off the floor. After explaining its purpose, I added, *It won't hurt you, so don't waste time being careful. It'll take a few minutes to eat through the metal.*

Before he could unscrew the lid of the bottle, his head cocked sharply in the way of the bird hearing the cat approach.

A clap of thunder rolled overhead, shocking me.

Eyes wide, teeth clenched, Frazer clasped my hand. *That's Lynx. The second he shows up, you need to attack him. Don't hesitate or we'll both end up in chains.*

I could kill him. Are you all right with that?

Yes.

Frazer swiftly poured out the powder from the vial over his manacles. The steel *hissed* in protest. It bubbled and melted in spots.

Adopting an untroubled mask, I stood up. All the while, I reeled in more sunlight than I ever had before. It was my only option—my only chance at defeating someone so powerful.

My magic cackled in wicked delight. The sunstone warmed at my throat, seizing the chance to feed me its energy. I resisted it. I was already a pot dangerously close to over-boil.

A slip of darkness disturbed the gossamer curtains. The balcony door whispered shut. *Skip-skip.* My heart thumped.

The air infused with static energy. It forced the hairs on my arms to rise up on to their tiptoes.

I flinched as lightning struck the ground outside. The resulting flash etched out the dark silhouette of a male standing in front of the double doors.

To protect Frazer from wayward magic, I darted into the center of the room. There, I stopped and drew my arm back. I struck out with my palm and hurled a sun-spear at Lynx's shadow. In the same tick, he shot a lightning bolt at me.

I threw up a hasty moon-shield.

Our magic-streams crossed each other—

The shock destroyed my shield, slammed into me, and knocked me backward. My wings splayed, preventing me from cracking my skull against hard wood.

"No!" Frazer's scream was unholy.

I palmed my chest where warmth bloomed.

"You're not taking her." Frazer was raging, a male possessed. "I won't let you take her!"

Get up. Zola again.

I wasn't in pain. I just felt strange. Relaxed and enlivened.

With effort, I sat up. Lynx was opposite me, lying on the floor. His leather chest armor was cracked and blackened. But apart from seeming a bit stunned, he looked fine. My magic had failed.

Rutting hell. I'd have to use the stone.

"You're okay?" Frazer rasped. "How are you okay?"

"I don't know," I said under my breath.

Lynx rolled onto his front. He was pushing himself up.

Grasping for the citrine beneath my collarbone, I struggled up and faced off against a very tall, broad-shouldered male clad in black and red armor. Refusing to be intimidated, I raised my chin and confronted his cauldron-dark stare.

In that one look, we were trapped in a second—in an eclipse. Two strangers collided, and everything realigned so that we fell into the same orbit.

My gaze traced his features. The strong chin, sharp jaw, and poker-straight nose put me in mind of chiseled marble. But for every harsh line on his face, there was a softer one. The mouth was wide, gentle, and made for smiling. His eyebrows were expressive, mischievous, and his thick lashes framed lonely eyes.

The last of his shadows skulked away, unveiling his large wings.

I forgot to breathe.

He was a secret unlocked. A question answered. A vision remembered.

Lynx spread his onyx wings out; the silky feathers stroked the beams above. Lightning arced off his body, forking from wingtip to wingtip.

The female in me recognized this as a performance. An invitation. My body understood what to do. Like the tide to the moon, I went to him.

Thunder-browed, he watched me carefully—disbelievingly.

I raised my hand, daring to disturb the wisp of hair escaping from where he'd tied it up. In the diamond light, the color ranged from an inky black to a mink brunette. I let my tingling fingertips travel to touch his golden-brown cheek. As skin touched skin, lightning passed through me. I felt like I was gulping whiskey.

"It doesn't hurt," I said softly.

Lynx sucked in a surprised inhale. I matched that unsteady breath, and the scents of leather, bergamot, stormy skies, and jasmine soothed and intoxicated.

His rough fingers grazed a pulse point in my neck. That single touch pushed my heart to whine like a violin bow, frantic and wild against the strings.

Lips inches apart, he whispered, "Elämayen."

That flipped some hidden lever. It made me glow, radiating out light and heat.

Lynx's forehead touched mine. Eyelids fluttering, he basked in my power as if he were a rock under a burning sun.

Our magic had found its equal in each other. The stitches of our souls began to unravel, yearning for each other. They met in the middle and tangled in an eternal embrace. We were mates. Forever.

On the back of that realization, time started again.

Lynx's forehead wrinkled against mine. I pulled away and looked up at him. His expression was a bitter reflection of our reality. We were a tragedy waiting to happen.

Frazer pulled me out of my own thoughts with a sharp, "Ena."

I turned to him. Frazer was rigid. His constraints hadn't left his wrists. "He's your mate?"

A tiny nod was my answer.

Horror clawed down his face.

Lynx folded his wings and stepped back from me. "I'm sorry," he said, as if to both of us.

My heart hurt.

Adapting quickly, Frazer confronted Lynx. "If she's your mate, you can fight Morgan's orders. *Protect* your mate, Lynx. That instinct is stronger than any guardian bond."

He was Morgan's guardian? Disappointment swooped in.

"The Queen's order to capture her was absolute." Lynx's eyes shuttered. "I can't misinterpret or ignore that. There are no loopholes."

I avoided his gaze. "Do you wish you could let us go?"

My weak murmur got an immediate, "Yes."

Somehow, that made our situation worse. More pitiable.

Lynx kneeled down. "I've captured you."

Wait. What?

He presented me with his throat. That sign of submission had nausea souring my gullet. Was this him working around the bond? Was he allowing me to kill him?

I couldn't sense his emotions or thoughts, but there was a thread—a feeling—linking us. Hurting him and severing that filled me with mortal dread. It would've been an easier task to saw off my own leg.

Lynx's palms grasped my outer thighs. "Hurry."

No, no, no, no, no, NO.

His forehead beaded with sweat. "I have her. Serena ... Ena's not fighting."

He repeated that again and again.

Zola's notes were clipped, frustrated. *Just knock him out.*

I latched onto that suggestion. "Don't look," I said to Lynx.

"I wish I could've known you." He squeezed my thigh gently. Then he shut his eyes.

My vision burned at that goodbye.

Frazer tugged at my thoughts. *I know what I said before, but you can't kill him.*

I'm not going to.

He fell into a trustful silence.

Conversation over, the noises of disorder and violence rekindled my attentions. I had to act. To be quick. Hand trembling, I struck under his chin with all the strength I could muster.

He teetered. But he didn't go down.

"Sorry." I hit him again in the same spot, wincing at the impact.

Lynx tipped backward, his wings splaying.

I crouched and stuck my fingers under his nose. As soon as I felt the air disturbed by his breath, relief leveled my racing heartbeat.

Frazer growled and cursed. "Help me get these damned things off."

I sprang up and ran over to where he struggled with the manacles. Adrenaline strengthening our muscles, we pulled apart the corroded metal in under a minute.

Frazer tossed the shackles onto the mattress. "I'm guessing that craziness outside is for my benefit?"

"They've been distracting the guards so I could get to you."

He massaged his chafed wrists. "Do you think they can hold out while we find the mirror?"

"Our pack won't leave without us, you know that. But Ryder is here with his friends, and they'll retreat if things go badly for them. They might stay if they know Lynx isn't a threat."

I glanced over my shoulder at Lynx.

"We have to leave him," Frazer said, reading my thoughts.

It would be pointless to stay. Stupid, even. And yet.

"Remember what Maggie OneEye said about him?" I didn't wait for a response. "His heart and soul are dying. And I had a vision of him, Fraze. He asked me to save him."

"Lynx admitted to me that he's living a nightmare." Frazer had ruthlessly cut out all emotion from his voice. "I don't know why he swore to Morgan, but it wasn't out of any love or respect for her. Still, what's done is done. We can only save him by ending her."

The rational part of me agreed. But I couldn't lift my foot to leave him. I didn't fully understand why, nor did I feel entitled to my emotions. All I knew was that my soul was imprinted with this male's.

"My mother said I'd need him if we wanted to save Aldar."

"Siska." That tone—it was almost a sigh.

Danu materialized overhead with a piercing squawk that made me jump. In protective mode, Frazer hauled me into his side. He emitted a breathless grunt, and the echo of his pain ran through my body as if it were my own.

"What's wrong?"

"It's nothing that won't heal." He nodded up at the raven. "What is that thing?"

"Long story." I eyeballed Danu. "What are you doing here?"

He settled on his favorite perch, my wing. *To warn you that there are enemy soldiers searching the castle for Lynx so he can help them end the battle and kill all of us. I'm here to ensure that doesn't happen.*

"Meaning?"

You're going to have to stay and sever Lynx's connection to Morgan.

Frazer bared his teeth at the raven. "That's not possible."

The raven clacked his beak at Frazer. *Are you all-knowing? Do you have thousands of years of experience rattling about that head of yours?*

Frazer replied with his darkest glower.

I thought not. Now, shut up! Danu cast a raisin eye upon me. *Bonds are made from the stuff of creation. To unmake such a thing requires an opposing force of equal strength, which in this case means chaos magic. In this moment, I'm sure you're pleased to be Abraxus's granddaughter.*

Frazer's gaze ensnared mine like a butterfly in a net. "Is this talking bird as mad as it seems, or does it speak the truth?"

My stomach plummeted. "He's not mad."

For once it was Frazer who lacked mental discipline. I sensed his currently weak mental-shield fluttering, disturbed as if by a violent breeze. Questions mired in confusion ran through his head. But there was no disgust or horror directed my way. Thank the gods.

He flashed me an irritated look. "As if I'd care who your relatives are. But this is a conversation best left for later." He addressed Danu. "How long would it take her to break the bond?"

I've seen it take under a minute or up to twenty. But that disgusting leash— he arced a wing in Lynx's direction—*is an affront to the very magic that created it. I think as long as you don't pass out from the effort, it won't take long.*

My inner scales tipped into a decision. *What would I have to do?*

I had to give it to him, his instructions were precise without being overly complicated. He even refrained from insulting me the entire time. When Danu was finished, I said, *Will you go find the others? Tell them to retreat and that they've done their job. We'll meet up with them later.* A lie? Maybe.

I won't tell them that. But I will check that they're not dead for you.

Before I could argue with him about that he disappeared, leaving behind a single black feather atop my lily-white wing.

A groggy moan sounded.

"Ena." Frazer grasped my wrist in a warning. "He's waking up."

I turned around. Lynx was sitting up, pinching his nasal bridge.

Was Fate laughing at me? Just as I was about to act, the thick-headed male had to wake up.

Frazer sensed my resolve. *If you're doing this, then I'm staying too. I can draw his attention away from you.*

I won't have you being a shield for me.

The stubborn male didn't bat an eyelash or move a muscle. *Are we doing this or not?*

I could feel his resolve solidify in the bond. And I knew once he'd decided something, I wouldn't stand a chance of changing his mind. It would be like arguing with the rocks and the wind. I marched over to where Lynx cradled his head in his hands. Frazer went with me.

Lynx squinted up on our approach. "No. What are you doing? Why are you still here?"

"Focus on me." Frazer crouched beside Lynx. "We're not going anywhere, so don't fight us. Do you remember the last time we sparred together?"

"I'm not worth whatever you're trying to do." Lynx was so hoarse, it sounded as if he'd been screaming for a night and a day.

Frazer went on, perfectly calm. "Remember how I beat you, little lion?"

Tuning their conversation out, I drew upon waterlight so I could see what I had to destroy. As magic filled my vessel up, my perspective changed. Lynx became eclipsed by a shadow bearing his likeness. In this darkness, I saw the evil bond tethered to his solar plexus. It was a wine-red thorn that dripped poison and hissed vile commands. *Capture. Interrogate.*

The next step required me to hate, to want to ruin, wreck, and devastate—that was the only way to sever the bond.

I dwelled on the hurts that Morgan had caused me.

Killing Dain. Enslaving me. Taking Wilder.

Stealing the life that I could've lived. The one where my mother taught me to fly over the ocean, and Dain raised me to be a witch.

Resentment grew within me. I sucked in that vengeful poison. It became fuel on the fire. Lye in the wound. With my soul full of demons, a howling void of chaos yawned wide in my mind's eye.

I paused. If I messed this up, I could make things worse.

Do it, Zola pushed. *Rip that bitch's leash from his neck.*

You must try, Thea encouraged.

I concentrated on what was before me. Frazer was still acting as a distraction, but the muscles in Lynx's neck, shoulders, and night-black wings were coiling tighter and tighter. He'd lose control soon.

On the tail end of that thought, I spooled chaos in and funneled it out into the world where it escaped like smoke billowing up a chimney. With two fingers, I pointed toward Lynx and willed that dark mist straight into his chest.

A tremor shook him, root to stem.

I curled my fingers up to mimic claws; the movement guided my magic to loop around the root of the guardian bond like a snake constricting its prey.

Morgan's bond suddenly woke up and struck at me.

I endured, absorbing what felt like a physical blow to my gut.

Lynx clawed at his breastbone. "Go," he croaked.

That simple warning made him hunch over and cough up blood.

A chill ran through my veins. I moved toward Lynx. Frazer stood and stopped me with a look. *There's nothing you can do. This is the guardian bond punishing him for disobeying orders.*

Lynx leaked shadows and tiny pulses of lightning.

Fear pinched me. *Brata, get behind me.*

Frazer vanished from view. *I'm borrowing your sword.*

Panic fired into my gut. *Why?*

His outline flickered back into view. Just for a second. Then he wrangled his magic and disappeared again. *Trust me.*

I felt my Utemä disturbed; unsheathed.

Terrified that in this state one of them might accidentally kill the other, I bore down on the guardian bond so hard that my head pounded, my nails punched into my palms, and my pulse sped faster than a falcon could fly. The twisted thorn started to wither and rot. Not fast enough, though. Lynx surged upward. He showed me his palm—

Frazer reappeared, swinging the flat side of my sword at Lynx's knee.

Lynx collapsed with a grunt, sending weak bolts of lightning throughout the room. They caused Frazer to stagger, but the offshoots weren't strong enough to level him.

I had to end this. A sliver of Morgan remained in Lynx. I snarled at it, "I feel you, bitch. But he doesn't belong to you. He never did."

I stepped back and yanked on the rope tying him to his slaver. It strained. It struggled. Then it gave.

I ripped that disgusting thing out by its roots. It used its dying breath to blow me off my feet. I landed on my back, my wings bent awkwardly beneath me.

Something *cracked*.

My vision spotted as a white-hot fire exploded in my right wing. I glanced up and saw bloody bone. My beautiful wing, broken. Ruined.

Kill me. Let me die, please.

"I'm here." Frazer kneeled beside me. "It's okay. We can fix it."

He reached out to touch my feathers.

"No!" I held up my hands. "Stop. Don't touch me."

"I can feel your pain. I know how badly it hurts." His fingers steepled through mine. "But I have to realign your bone before it starts to heal."

I had to get away from him. From his cruel, cruel hands. I tried to roll onto my side and crawl away. The effort sent agony firing through my wing, shoulder, and spine. I gagged and almost blacked out.

Frazer firmly clasped the scruff of my neck. He wanted to pin me, to hold me in place.

I snarled and clawed at his face. He seized my raging hands. "Vit helvat! Yrït, autan, siska!"

"Don't touch me," I roared.

I tried to draw my wings in. And the bastard flicked my nose.

That tiny sting stunned me.

Frazer seized upon my stupefied state and forced my arms down. "We don't know what will happen if you retract them without my setting the bone. If it doesn't heal right, you might never fly again."

My brain realigned around that knowledge. Until that moment, I hadn't realized how much I wanted to keep flying.

"Ena?"

Lynx's rumbling voice forced my head up.

Frazer growled protectively.

"I'm not ... Whatever she did to me, I can't feel the compulsions anymore."

Lynx crouched on my left, his bulk taking up the whole of my sight.

Then I saw his eyes. They were framed in shock, exhaustion, and concern. But the irises ... they were no longer cauldron-black. Their amber hue was flecked with a darker whiskey-brown.

My waterlight trickled in unexpectedly, revealing a tiny scar where the thorn had existed. The only bond left in him was ours. "I destroyed it." I loosed a short, fractured laugh. "Morgan can't control you."

"Can you hold her down?" Frazer asked Lynx.

I glared at Lynx. "Don't even think about it."

"I won't." Calm. So calm. "But I need you to look at me. Focus on me."

Shock made me stupid. I stared straight into bright amber.

"Stay still, Ena," Frazer said.

I went to turn my head, to look at what he was about to do.

Lynx stopped me by gripping my chin, dragging my gaze back to his. Then he gently chanted in a language I'd never heard before. I might not have understood the words, but I felt them easing my mind and body.

Frazer seized my wing in a merciless grip. Stars save me.

A grating noise scraped the air. Back arching, I howled so loudly that my ears popped. I sobbed and sobbed.

Lynx's song accompanied me. It went on and on. His notes were soft and the melody rich in earthly power. The pain grew distant. I drifted, dazed, sedated.

Frazer steered me into awareness with a mental nudge. "It's done. You'll have to be careful not to jostle it, though. I don't have a splint handy."

His voice faded as Thea said, *Retract them. It'll help keep the wing in stasis until Liora can heal you.*

Swaying internally, I met my brother's midnight-blues. "Thea said I should retract them. Help me up?"

My brother growled in disapproval. That didn't stop him from maneuvering me into a seated position. With half a thought, I pulled my feathers underneath my skin.

"How did she do that?" Lynx's gravely purr melted me in the middle.

"I like your voice."

A short surprised laugh left him. "I like your voice too."

"Oops." I hadn't meant to say that out loud.

Frazer lightly growled at Lynx. "This is your fault."

"Better to be sedated than in blinding pain," Lynx countered.

"I need your help with something. Are you willing?" Frazer asked him.

Lynx blinked at that abrupt change in topic. "What is it?"

Frazer propped me against his front. "I need to find a mirror. It'll be somewhere below the castle. Seers might've come to use it in the past. Do you know where we could find such a thing?"

"Yes ... but what you're looking for isn't a mirror. It's a pool of water housed in our vaults. Anybody who's ever looked into it came out witless. Except—"

"Dain Raynar," Frazer cut across him. "We know."

"What could you hope to gain from the pool, though? You're not a seer." Lynx's handsome face developed lines.

I didn't like that. I leaned over to where he knelt and hooked his mouth up with my finger. "That's better."

Frazer coaxed me back against his chest. "Don't move around so much." He focused on Lynx again. "Actually, I am a seer. We can talk about how later on."

Hesitation. "Fine. But the pool can only be accessed from this wing of the castle—you'll need me to open the door to the vault stair."

"Get me into the vaults, then take Ena and find her pack," Frazer said curtly. "They're the ones tearing apart your castle. Get them to safety if you can."

Alarm cut through my mental haze. "I'm not leaving you behind."

"The pack's in danger for every second they spend here."

"They're not alone. Danu said he'd watch over them. And they've got the Fiends."

"The Fiends?"

I didn't elaborate. Instead, I babbled, "But you might be weakened after you look into the mirror. If that happens, you'll need us. So there. Lynx and I will guard the vault door. It's settled."

My focus darted to Lynx. He seemed to be struggling. I made it easier for him. "Isn't it, *mate*?"

His features smoothed out. Lynx's gaze went behind me to Frazer. "She wins."

Frazer freed an exasperated sigh. "Can you stand, Ena?"

"I'll carry her." Lynx scooped me up in one fluid motion.

I didn't mind. His arms were big. And he smelled ... My heartbeat took off at a gallop. *Ba-boom, ba-boom, ba-boom.*

A grunt off to my right stole my attention. I glanced sideways at Frazer and my insides ached to see his movements labored and slow.

I cupped my hands around my mouth and whispered, "Lynx?"

"Mm?" He lowered his head as if we were about to share a secret.

"Can you carry Frazer around too? He's in pain."

Lynx's small smile slipped. "That's my fault."

"It's Morgan's," Frazer corrected.

He shouldered my rucksack and picked up my sword from where he'd dropped it. Without another word, he stalked off. Lynx strode after him, easily keeping pace.

We reached the exit, a door positioned across the room from the balcony. Lynx dipped his head closer to me. "We have to be quiet."

I nodded primly and pursed my lips tightly.

Lynx winked at me.

We passed through the threshold and out into a corridor. It was empty. Yay.

Lynx and Frazer forked left.

They speed-walked along corridors, around corners, and down a flight of stairs. It was around then the soporific effects of Lynx's song waned, and the ache in my back returned. It wasn't as bad as before. But it upset my stomach and made me sweat pain.

I bit my lip, trying not to cry out. A whimper still escaped.

"It'll pass," Lynx said, his voice lowered. "Just try to relax. I've got you."

Those last words somehow released the tension that locked me up. As each muscle relaxed, the throbbing eased a bit. I settled my head against his shoulder and for a while at least, I let him carry me.

CHAPTER 35
THE SILENCE OF THE DEAD

Lynx, Frazer, and I arrived on the first floor. From there, we turned into a stately corridor brightened solely by crystal lamps and rowed with quartz pillars. In between these stalagmite-like columns hung paintings depicting white mountains, green valleys, and silver forests.

Lynx stopped before a door. Dull, dark, unremarkable.

"Let me down," I told him quietly.

My feet touched dusty floorboards. I willed my face to remain blank—to not show the cheek-biting pain wrenching my back.

Lynx pressed a flat palm against the door. A final-sounding *click, clunk* rang out. The lock was sprung.

Frazer handed over my rucksack first, then my Utemä. "If anybody tries to hurt you, poke them with this. Got it?"

"I remember how to use a sword," I said tartly.

"Glad to see you've sobered up."

I glowered at him to mask my embarrassment.

He started to spin around. I stopped him by dropping my bag and grasping him by the elbow. *Are you sure about this? Your mind's only just recovered. I can look into the mirror—*

Frazer pulled his arm from my grip. *You've already freed me and broken Lynx's bond. You've done your bit. Let me do mine.*

But you're in pain.

So are you.

Stalemate.

The pale crescents of his nostrils flared into full moons. *Siska, I'll be fine.*

What if you're not? I should come with you.

A very abrupt, *No. I know how you think, and if you see me struggling even for a second, you'll try to take my place. I need to do this without distractions.*

My chest caved in a silent sigh. *Maybe this will help, then—you don't need to search for the starstone's location. I already know where it is.*

His moody eyebrows lifted a little. *Where?*

Abraxus has it.

That drew his brow down. *I see we've a lot to talk about.*

I only nodded.

Frazer faced Lynx. "Can I open the vault from the other side?"

He shook his head, stirring that rebellious lock of hair that had escaped his pinned-back style. "It wouldn't recognize you unless you were added to the door's spell, and there's no time for that. We'll have to keep it open."

That settled, Frazer slipped through the vault door without closing it.

My feet itched to follow. Shelving that instinct, I sheathed my sword and stowed my rucksack against the wall where it would be out of the way.

"How's the wing?" Lynx asked softly.

I didn't have it in me to lie. The blinding agony was gone, replaced by a constant irritating ache located next to my spine.

"It hurts, but I'm not disturbing the break while my wings are retracted."

Lynx hip-leaned against a pillar. "How does the retraction work?"

"I think about pulling them in, and it happens," I said, meeting his amber gaze. "I'm not sure how it works. They were sort of given to us. I used to be human ..."

No surprise registered.

"You knew?"

He dipped his chin. "Morgan."

No more Queen. It was simply Morgan.

"What did you mean by us?" he asked.

I frowned, confused.

"You said they were given to *us*?"

Shit. My eyes darted to the vault door. Should I tell Lynx?

"Frazer?" Lynx straightened up from the column. "He got his wings back?"

I avoided his stare.

Lynx didn't seem upset that I wasn't answering him. "That's ... Gods. I'm happy for him."

The conversation dropped off. In the quiet, I listened out for how close and how vicious the ongoing fighting sounded. Until Lynx asked, "Is there anything you want to ask me?"

"What do you mean?" I said, focusing on him.

His expression was expectant if a bit uncertain. "I thought you might have questions for me."

I understood then. "No. Well ... Yes. I will have. But right now, I can't think of anything except for the fact that my friends are in danger." Throat raw with emotion, I continued. "I should be fighting with them."

"But you can't leave your brother," he finished.

My eyes narrowed. "How do you know he's my brother?"

"I heard him call you siska," he said plainly. "Your scent also used to be mixed up with his."

"Used to be? Are you saying I don't smell like him anymore?"

"No, you don't," he said. "Our bond changed that."

My brain stopped working as we kept looking at each other. That daze ceased when Lynx glanced up sharply. "Someone's coming this way," he said, hearing things that were beyond my new fae senses.

Lynx stood in front of me, guarding me with a warrior's body and a blackbird's wings. Pride nipping at me, I joined his side. "I'm not hiding behind you like a lost child."

"I'm not asking you to be less than you are." That hit a nerve. "But if soldiers see you standing here, their guard will go up."

I glanced ahead at where the corridor forked off. "Then pretend you've caught me."

"If that's what you want." Almost a whisper.

He lightly clutched my elbow. I braced, refusing to react to his nearness, even when his feathers kissed my upper arm.

Several shaky breaths passed my lips before I heard boots running over hard stone, their echo strong in the acoustic space.

Danu's voice invaded my head. *I'm headed your way with Adrianna and Owl. I've told them that Lynx is your mate, but your mule-headed friend won't listen to reason. She plans to attack him.*

I darted in front of Lynx before Owl and Adrianna could round the corner. "Adi, I broke the bond between Lynx and Morgan. There's no reason to hurt him."

The approaching footsteps slowed and stopped.

Determined to guard Lynx as best I could, I backed up until his broad chest bumped against my back and the top of my head rested in the valley of his collarbones. I felt as though I was glued up against a volcanic stone that was getting hotter and hotter, the contact nearly burning me. I tried not to think about how and what that made me feel.

"How do I know he's not forcing you to say this?" came Adrianna's suspicious response.

"Because he's not."

It wasn't lost on me how lame that was.

"And he really is my mate. Danu was telling the truth."

The raven popped out from behind the corner. Lynx tensed against me and gripped my shoulder as the raven flew toward us.

"It's okay. He's a friend. Sort of."

As obnoxious as ever, Danu landed atop Lynx's wing. The similar shade of their feathers made the raven look like a mere extension of Lynx.

Adrianna slowly rounded the bend and walked out into the corridor. Owl appeared beside her, palming the knives holstered in his belt.

They eyeballed the way I guarded Lynx. A scowl darkened Adrianna's brow.

"He's not under Morgan's control anymore," I told her.

I assumed she would declare that to be impossible. Instead, she said, "That doesn't mean he's on our side."

Lynx released my shoulder and moved to my side. "Hello, Adrianna."

Her azure-blues frosted over. "Remember me, do you?"

"Of course," he said clearly.

With a silent tread, Owl was the first to walk toward us. Lynx signed to him, using complex hand and finger movements.

Breaking her rigid stance, Adrianna strode up to me. "Where's Frazer? Danu said you'd found him."

"He went to look in the mirror," I said, chin-pointing to the vault door. "We're standing guard while he's down there. Have you seen Cai and Liora?"

"No," she punched out. "Owl and I were fighting together when we spotted soldiers sneaking into the castle. Then Danu showed up." She scowled up at the stoic raven. "He said they were looking for Lynx, but that you were with him. I had to come make sure he hadn't murdered you."

That aggravated me like a nettle rash. "You weren't with us, Adi. He tried to work around Morgan's orders to capture me."

"I'm sorry," Lynx interrupted, eyeballing Adrianna. "I'm sorry for what I said to you the last time we met. But you needed to hate me, otherwise you would've tried to help me and Morgan would've punished you for it."

Adrianna's features twisted up. "You can't just decide to play the good guy. You've killed and tortured for Morgan—"

"I've never killed for Morgan."

That was said so quietly, I thought I'd imagined it.

"You ..." Red-faced, her rage rendered her momentarily incoherent. "Only you would be shameless enough to lie about that."

Unease lodged in my chest.

"I'm not lying," he said coolly. "When I swore to be Morgan's guardian, I altered the vows. I promised to do whatever she asked of me except to kill for her. And she agreed." Grim-mouthed, he admitted, "Of course, my caveat meant little in the end. She's still used me to hurt countless people."

"You must've known that would happen, and you vowed to be her guardian anyway." Adrianna continued, her voice loaded with accusation. "So, *Dark Prince*, why bind yourself to her if you're not an evil piece of shit?"

"I did it to protect what remained of my court," he said, as if that were an obvious fact.

Strangely, I felt it was.

"When Morgan was visiting Mysaya," Lynx started, "she attended a banquet thrown by our court. I never found out who, but someone or several someones working for her dosed our feast with odorless poison. I was the only one who was given a paralyzing agent. Our entire household died painfully, my father was beheaded, and I couldn't do anything to stop it." Lynx didn't blink, lost in bad memories. "Morgan sent her people to butcher the royal guard and our strongest fighters. Then she paraded the elders and the faelings in front of me. She swore they'd be the next to die unless I became her guardian. So ... I agreed if she guaranteed the survivors' safety."

Horror and sadness wrung out my heart. "And did she?"

"She sent them to live in camps," he said, his body clenching like a fist.

Owl signed, his gestures sharp, violent. That left me in no doubt about what he thought of such places.

Adrianna challenged Lynx. "You've had years to concoct this story. Why should we believe you?"

I winced at the grating friction in her voice. At that forced harshness.

Lynx released a tired sigh and the stiffness left his frame. "I suppose there are those in the camps who could corroborate my story, but they're not here right now. At this moment, I've got nothing except for my word, which is worthless at this point. My future actions will have to serve as your proof."

Her expression remained forged from unforgiving lines.

This is all very touching. But we have a castle to conquer.

Danu's remark made him the center of attention.

"He can talk?" Lynx curved his wing around his body so that he could stare at the familiar face-to-face.

"Unfortunately, yes." I confronted Danu. "Why are you talking about conquering a castle? We came for Frazer."

I'm aware, he replied dryly. *But with a witch as powerful as Lynx by your side, you could defeat what soldiers are still standing and take back Mysaya. That would be a huge blow against Morgan. That is what you want, isn't it? To end her rule?* That blacker than blackberry gaze swept over us.

I turned that possibility over in my mind.

"Even if we win here today, Morgan won't let us keep Mysaya," Adrianna commented. "And we don't have the numbers to stand against thousands of soldiers."

His tail feathers wagged dismissively. *You should at least fight to stay the night. It would be better if you don't move those in your group who've been injured. You've also the opportunity to raid Mysaya's supplies while you're here. Better you take advantage of them than let Morgan have them.*

Lynx broke the thoughtful silence. "That's not a terrible idea."

I reached a decision. "You should go with them," I said to Lynx, nodding to Adrianna and Owl. "Danu's right. You have the power to end the fighting, and as long as the soldiers think you're on their side, they might not surrender."

"I'll go once Frazer's returned—"

"There's no need. I'll wait for him."

His brows clashed together. "I can't leave you with a broken wing."

"A broken *what?*" Adrianna's gaze cut to me and turned into a glare. "Why didn't you tell me?"

"I'm fine." I wasn't.

"We should get you to Liora."

"Stop fussing."

Her nostrils went like bellows as she strained to rein in her temper. To hold back the argument she wanted to have with me.

Danu jump-flew onto my nape. *I'll stay with her.*

"Apologies if that doesn't fill me with confidence," Adrianna said tartly.

It would if you'd seen me in a battle. I'm an expert at plucking out eyeballs.

My nose wrinkled. Disgusting.

Craning my neck, I peered at Lynx. "As long as this fighting goes on, the group that accompanied me here are in danger. Help them … Please."

His features crumpled a bit. "All right. I'll go."

"If anybody on our side sees him, they'll attack," Adrianna argued. "Even if Owl and I are with him."

"I can take care of myself," Lynx said, marking her with a steady gaze.

"Fine." Adrianna's tone made it obvious that nothing was fine by her. "But if you do anything suspicious, I'm blasting your wings full of metal."

"You can try." He walked a tightrope between teasing her and challenging her.

Owl signed for Lynx to take the lead. Before he took a step, Lynx stared at me for what felt like a very long second. I glanced away first.

He prowled off, retracing our steps from earlier. Owl tracked after him. Adrianna surprised the stars out of me by initiating a hug. "Stay safe."

"Don't hurt him," I whispered into her ear.

She freed an oddly pitched growl. I must've grown fluent in fae noises because I understood that as her reluctantly agreeing.

Adrianna marched off. The three of them took a turn and disappeared, leaving me alone with Danu. Too many days consumed by stress, fear, and fatigue consumed me. I couldn't put on a brave face anymore.

I slow-collapsed onto a dusty floor and braced my back against the wall. Danu moved over to perch on my kneecap. *This isn't the time for a nap.*

I didn't listen. Exhaustion became a thief, sneaking up and stealing time.

Danu kept digging his talons into my thigh, but he couldn't stop me from slipping in and out of the present. Finally, I blacked out.

Wake up!

I came to curled up on my side with a raven viciously pecking at my sore earlobe.

Get up. Someone's coming.

My nap, while unplanned and foolish, had alleviated my injury. When I scrambled up, I suffered only a slight twinge in my back.

"I can't hear anybody," I whispered.

All I detected were the faint sounds of violence.

Wingbeats agitated, Danu flew up onto my shoulder. *Fool. Haven't you realized I can sense the minds of those nearby? Now, hurry up and hide in the room opposite. With any luck, you won't have to fight. But if whoever that is takes an interest in the vault door being opened, you'll need to take them by surprise.*

I dashed into the room across from me, rucksack in tow.

The space was illuminated by moonbeams streaming in through tall windows and balcony doors. Those ghostly shafts highlighted several instruments that were cloaked in sheets yellowed with age. The fingers of a piano, the veins of cellos, the mouths of flutes lay silent. Forgotten and abandoned.

Danu settled his talons upon the statue of a violinist. I stored my rucksack in a corner and waited a few feet in front of the door, my hand on my hilt.

It didn't take long before the *tap-clack* of speedy steps traveled through stone and mortar. I begged my pulse to calm and made my breaths shallow, fearing the dust in the air would send me into a loud sneezing fit.

I heard the fast footsteps grind to a halt.

In preparation to rush out, I liberated my sword from its sheath. The soft sigh of my steel reminded me of a breeze cutting through the blades of grass.

Boom!

The door was blown off its hinges.

Leaping aside, I narrowly avoided being hit. I rolled up as the door catapulted into a grand piano. The screeching and splintering was ungodly.

A female strode in wearing spiked armor. Hunter had once sported a similar outfit. My heart sunk at the knowledge that this warrior was in fact a spider—a favorite of Morgan's—which meant she likely possessed elite skills.

The warrior slapped her hands together, causing piano fragments to rise into the air. She punched outward.

I performed a sideways tumble, somehow keeping hold of my Utemä.

The wreckage slammed into the giant gilded mirror behind me.

I was showered in splinters and flecks of glass.

Zola began. *She's a—*

I know.

I popped up to face the earth elemental. They were preternaturally strong and had unparalleled endurance. A moon-shield wouldn't last long against their hits.

She twirled her wrist. Instruments trembled under their funeral shrouds, creating discordant songs. Wood cracked. Keys chattered. Strings whined.

Magic kindled. I launched a sun-spear at her. Faster than I could blink, she blocked my attack with a floating drum.

Crap.

Blind, Zola shot out. *Strike.*

Zola's commands were so familiar by now that I instantly understood.

I raised a shining palm. It was weak, hastily conjured, but it caught my attacker unawares. Eyes shuttering, she threw up a palm to protect her face. I didn't get the second I needed to shape another sun attack.

Even with her vision impaired, she managed to levitate a guqin—a seven-stringed instrument—and fling it at me. I dodged that. Barely.

Danu darted at the witch's face, squawking, clawing, and pecking. The elemental didn't scream, but she did lose control of her magic. Other objects flew around the room. None of them came close to hitting me.

I didn't give myself time to think. I sprinted at the spider, sword raised.

To avoid her flapping arms and the raven, I ducked and aimed for the lower part of her torso. My master-forged sword impaled her abdomen, piercing both leather and flesh.

Danu fled the scene. I yanked my sword out and straightened up.

Falling to her knees, the female applied pressure over her wound. She stared down at the blood trickling through her fingers, and a wry smile pulled the corner of her mouth up.

I blinked to clear my vision, but the image stayed the same. I hadn't been seeing things. She really was smiling.

"You're the light-wielder, aren't you? The one the Queen wants?" She peered up at me. "They said you had wings now. I guess the rumors were wrong."

"Why do you care who I am?" I asked, but what I really wanted to know was why she was spending her dying breaths on me.

"Because if you are her—if you're the light-wielder—you'll want to hear what I've got to say."

She stopped to wheeze, to suck in strangled breaths. I was about to tell her not to speak when she continued, her tone labored. "I saw Lynx Johana fighting with the rebels. He was killing the Queen's soldiers. Maybe it's an act to gain the rebels' trust, but if it isn't and he's escaped the Queen's control, find out how he did it. Use that to free the others from their bonds. Start with Wilder Thorn. I heard you two were close."

The ground beneath me disappeared.

I edged closer to her. "Is Wilder a friend of yours?"

Gods, had I killed somebody important to him?

Gaze turning glassy, she confessed, "You can't afford to be friends with anybody in the Solar Court. But he was kind to me when nobody else was."

I couldn't think of a single thing to say to that.

The witch collapsed back onto limp green wings and stopped putting pressure on her wound. Blood gushed. Her life seeped away, becoming red paint on a cold floor. The sight made me feel ill.

"What are you doing?" I asked her.

"Ending it." That croak was exhausted, determined. "This is mercy for me, light-wielder. For that, I promise I won't haunt you from the other side."

I crouched cautiously. "What's your name?"

Tears and sweat intermingled, dampening her cheeks. "Eleanor."

"Thank you, Eleanor," I said, low and emotional. "I'll do that. I'll free Wilder."

"Good luck," she whispered.

Danu settled on my shoulder. "Goodbye."

I flinched. I'd heard ravens could mimic speech, but I hadn't thought it would sound so real.

Eleanor mustered a rueful smile. Then she slipped away, passing out of my sight. Empty silence remained.

I rose with a heavy heart. Dazed, I went through a series of unthinking motions. I wiped my sword clean with one of the sheets that had covered the instruments. Then I sheathed the blade and strapped my bag onto my back. Danu remained fixed to me all the while.

Before exiting the room, I draped a blanket over Eleanor. With that done, I couldn't bear to stand there for another second.

Out in the corridor, the vault door didn't appear to have moved. I breathed a little easier knowing I hadn't missed Frazer.

"Morgan forced Wilder into their bond." I glanced sideways at Danu and added, "Do you think that makes their connection different? Stronger?"

The raven clacked his beak. *Morgan is toying with creation magic every time she forces and abuses bonds. For anybody, even a firstborn, that's like lighting yourself on fire and hoping you don't get burned. If anything, her link to Wilder will be weaker because of the unstable magic that crafted it.*

My heart grew wings. Then Danu cut them from me. *However, when Morgan learns that Lynx is no longer under her control, she'll take steps to prevent you from doing the same to her other guardians. So if you truly wish to free Wilder, you must act fast. You'll need Lynx's help.*

I gaped at him. "What? Why?"

Because I've sensed his abilities, and he's your best bet at sneaking into enemy territory.

"I don't like the idea of dragging him into this," I countered.

His second eyelid flashed at me. *Isn't that his choice to make?*

"I'm surprised you're not trying to talk me out of this," I remarked.

The plumage on Danu's head developed a windblown look. *The name Wilder Thorn is not unknown to me. Abraxus heard of his promotion to Morgan's Prime Sabu. Therefore, if you* can *pull this off, the strategical merits will be numerous.*

Indecision plagued me until I heard, *Siska?*

Thank the stars. *Are you okay?*

I'm nearly at the door.

I waited, picking at my nails, too scared to touch the vault door in case it triggered it to close.

A few anxious heartbeats later, Frazer appeared. He looked haggard, his face pinched as if he was suffering from a headache. I quickly put my hand under his elbow. He leaned against me, letting me support him. That alone told me how much he had to be hurting.

"We need to find the others. We should start preparing," he said through lips as white as desert-weathered bone.

"Preparing for what?"

"For the attack."

Goosebumps rose along my arms. "What attack?"

Breathing unevenly, he replied, "It doesn't happen tonight. We might have to flee. The future's in motion."

"Brata, you're not making much sense."

"Sorry." He rocked his head as if he wanted to shake something loose. "It's just a lot. I saw dozens of possible futures. It's hard to keep them all straight. Can you wait for me to explain? The others need to know parts of what I've seen too, and I don't want to repeat myself."

Can you at least tell me if you found the moonstone?

His eyelids drooped.

"It doesn't matter," I said, regretting my question. "Tell me when you're ready."

Frazer forced open his eyes and looked at me. *Dain ... he buried it in the Crescent. But we can't take it. Not yet.*

Confusion crinkled my brow. Seeing that, he continued. *Dain created the barrier between Aldar and the Gauntlet using the moonstone's power. If we remove it, we'll be taking away the only thing that's preventing Morgan from staging a full-scale invasion of the Gauntlet.*

I was stunned, bursting with questions. But he looked as if a single breeze would knock him flat, so I tucked them away for another time and asked, "Where should we go? Lynx, Adrianna, and Owl went that way." I gestured to where the corridor took a turn.

Frazer's clammy forehead furrowed. "Why were they together?"

After I had explained, he said, "Let's head in the same direction."

We stumbled toward the turn in the corridor and rounded it. Up ahead, a heavy oak door waited. I got us through that and out into another hallway. This one was lined with statues of fae posed as fierce warriors and several mullioned windows. As it was dark outside, the view was obscured; the grimy glass acted as a mirror showing me and my brother walking past.

As we crossed another threshold, Frazer said, "The army used to be housed in this section of the castle, so stay alert. There might be soldiers holing up in here, hiding from Lynx."

I gripped my pommel with my free hand as we traversed silent hallways. Every closed door became suspicious. Every shadow, an enemy.

Frazer was the first to hear a familiar voice. He directed me toward it, and quite quickly we arrived at a viewing gallery that overlooked a huge entrance hall. The ceiling was bridged by sculpted loula beams, the chandelier dripped webbing and extinguished crystal stars, and the obsidian flagstones were marred by muddy feet and streaks of blood.

Frazer and I veered left, taking one of the two winding staircases that led to the foyer. That attracted the attention of the people below: Bear, Fox, and Hound.

Fox and Hound hurried off. Bear met us as we stepped off the staircase. He was battered, bruised, and bloodied. But alive. Thank the light.

"What happened to your wings?" Horror permeated his every syllable.

"I can retract them."

Bear frowned at the space above me, at where my wings would normally be visible. "Interesting talent."

"Is the fighting over?" I asked.

A joyless nod. "When the soldiers realized the Dark Prince was fighting with us, most of them panicked and fled."

"Where's Lynx now?"

Bear's feathered wings flexed and shifted restlessly. "He's sweeping the lower town, hunting for any soldiers who might be hiding out there. Owl, Ryder, and Adrianna went with him. Before they left, they mentioned you had liberated your brother. Congratulations."

Sincere but gloomy, I noted.

"That's right." I made a tiny gesture to my left. "This is Frazer."

Bear nodded a greeting.

Frazer tugged his arm away from me, silently insisting on standing on his own.

I surveyed the area again. Archways crafted from pure-white marble bordered the square space. These framed several side-passages branching off the main hall. Out in front of me, a pair of open doors towered twenty feet high. A courtyard of quartz and moonstone lay beyond.

"Where are Cai and Liora?" I asked Bear.

Brown irises slid to me. "They're with our wounded. Fox and Hound have gone to tell them that you're here."

Wounded. Guilt burned like a hot rock in my core. "How many injured?"

"Thirty-two," he responded gruffly.

I forced myself to ask the question. "And how many dead?"

"Two confirmed dead. Three missing," Bear growled out. "As for Morgan's soldiers, we've counted eighty-five bodies so far. But dragon-fire destroyed more than a fair few of them. Made it difficult to tell ..." He stopped, sighed, and rubbed his eyes. "Point is, we might never know exactly how many of them died tonight."

I pushed my heart down, sealing my emotions in my throat.

"It should be eighty-six," I murmured. "I met a spider earlier. We fought. Her body's upstairs."

Frazer's surprise trickled in through the bond.

"Better her than you, light-wielder," Bear said in a hard way.

I was quiet, entrenched in morbid thoughts.

Hurried footsteps brought me out of it. Cai and Liora raced out of a side-passage. They looked as if they'd been dragged backward through prickly bushes. Scratched and bruised. Hair everywhere.

They joined us, smelling of sweat, smoke, and strangers.

"Adi mentioned your wing." Liora anxiously studied me. "Can you bring it out? I'd prefer to see what I'm healing."

I cringed at the idea. Liora's concern tipped over into sympathy. "It's okay. I can heal it like this."

She gently clasped my wrist. The pang in my back melted away as healing energy flowed into me. "Better?" she asked me, releasing my wrist.

I shrugged and stretched my back. "Much. Thank you."

A smile. "Good."

Cai faced Frazer, looking more serious than I'd ever seen him. "I failed you."

"You did not."

He set his shoulders into a firm line, as if accommodating for the weight of responsibility he was taking on. "I couldn't stop Lynx from taking you."

"Enough." Frazer was stern but not cruel.

Bear interrupted, addressing me. "Speaking of your mate, Owl said you'd broken his bond to Morgan, is that correct?"

All eyes cut to me. My brain failed to connect to my mouth.

"It is," Frazer answered for me.

"Your mate?" Cai echoed, his eyes rounding. "Who ..." He stopped himself as the pieces connected in his mind. "Wait. *Lynx?* Lynx is your—"

"Yes."

Liora's expression cleared. Cai, on the other hand, gaped at me. "Holy shit."

An awkward laugh knocked against my teeth. "I know."

"I've ordered my people to leave Lynx alone since Owl has vouched for him," Bear told me. "But I can only do so much. Lynx is almost as hated as Morgan, and their fear of him may get the best of them. Just a friendly warning."

That chafed, irritated. "Lynx only became Morgan's guardian to protect his people."

Intense curiosity surged in my kin bond. Frazer wanted to hear that tale. Bear, however, remained unaffected. "Perhaps he did. But hate and fear are hard stains to shift."

Frustration skulked in my heart.

The *swoosh-swoosh* of wingbeats pulled my focus. I peered out into the courtyard that was centered around a large flawless statue.

Lynx landed there. Adrianna, Owl, and Ryder touched down behind him. The four of them headed toward us.

Gaze intense, Ryder walked straight up to my brother. Frazer raised his hand, delivering a firm warning. "No hugs."

Ryder swapped earnestness for mischievousness, an expression that made his brown eyes glitter. "How about a kiss, then?"

I hid a smile as a growl rattled Frazer's breastbone.

"Did you find anybody in the lower town?" Bear questioned our new arrivals.

Owl, Ryder, and Lynx each contributed to the answer. In short, no, they had not.

"This is *very* upsetting," Cai whispered to me.

My brow became a question mark.

"Your mate is taller than me." He pouted. "We'll have to exchange him for somebody shorter."

I couldn't help but smile and jostle him with my elbow.

"Did you get to the mirror?" Adrianna asked Frazer in an undertone.

Frazer didn't bother lowering his voice. "Yes."

Adrianna's lips parted, then she wavered. I sensed she wished to ask about the moonstone.

"The answer to your next question is yes, and it's safe where it is," Frazer said with a silencing glance. "Right now, we've got more immediate concerns. And since we're all here, we should discuss them."

That grabbed everybody's attention.

"The choices we make in the next few days will be crucial in determining what our chances are at defeating Morgan." He went on in a flat pitch as if he were commenting on nothing more exciting than today's weather. "If we stay and reclaim Mysaya, we'll be taking the first steps toward ending her. If we leave, things get a lot harder for us down the road."

Stress gripped all of our bodies.

Arms crossing, Adrianna asked, "How do you expect us to hold Mysaya with so few people?"

"We get more," Frazer retorted.

An image skipped down our kin bond. "Diana?"

He nodded. "And her army."

Adrianna scowled. "Diana already has a plan."

"I know, and it won't work." Frazer stared straight ahead, submerged in thoughts too deep for me to penetrate. "Diana intends to meet Morgan's forces on the border between the Riverlands and Solar. But therein lies a legion of ten thousand waiting to meet them."

"What happens?" Adrianna asked, her eyes widening.

"The Riverlands army will be forced to retreat, but not before they lose a great many soldiers," Frazer said, focusing on Adrianna. "But if they come to Mysaya, we can help them fight and they won't have to meet the legion out in the open. They'll be somewhere defensible."

"Are you a seer?" Bear asked Frazer.

"I ... Yes."

"You're just full of surprises, aren't you," Ryder remarked, gazing at him with open admiration.

"What happens if my court comes here? Do we win?" Adrianna demanded.

Frazer squinted as if something was hurting him. "I saw a legion arriving to take Mysaya back from us three days from now, at dawn. The outcome of the battle seems to depend on our individual actions. All I know is that there's at least a chance of success if we're all together. That chance goes away if Diana continues along her current path."

"Why would Morgan wait that long to reclaim Mysaya?" Bear voiced.

Lynx chimed in. "Probably because she's not in Alexandria."

"Where is she?" Adrianna made that sound like a threat.

"I'm not sure." His expressive eyebrows clashed. "There've been periods over the years where she disappears from court. Nobody seems to know where she goes."

Cai dragged a hand through his unruly hair. "Let's say we defeat this legion. Won't Morgan just send more warriors?"

"I don't think so." Frazer pinched his nasal bridge. "I can't see another battle at Mysaya."

That wasn't much of an answer. Troubled looks were exchanged.

Danu made his presence known. *Given how much Morgan fears Abraxus invading, I doubt she'll commit huge numbers to another direct attack straight away. My guess is that if you win, she'll turn to her preferred mode of warfare to take you down.*

"Which is?" I asked.

Threats. Manipulation. Blackmail.

Great. Rutting fantastic.

"Such a cheering thought," Ryder quipped.

Cai huffed.

"If you're certain about this, then you've got my support," Adrianna told Frazer.

I looked at her, shocked by that show of faith.

"Seers are notoriously unreliable," Bear stated.

"True." Adrianna watched a stoic Frazer. "I've never been a fan of them for that reason. But Frazer wouldn't risk our lives if he wasn't sure about this."

Owl signed at Bear. I thought he might've said something like, *Agreed. I trust Frazer.*

"What do you think?" Cai eyeballed Bear. "Want to be part of the rebellion?"

"The Fiends will spend the night under Mysaya's roof," Bear said in a grumbly tone. "And I want the spell that'll allow us to contact our familiars. After that, we'll see."

The silence he left in his wake seemed to say, no promises.

"If this plan is going to work, we need to contact Diana as soon as possible so that she'll have enough time to get here before the legion." Adrianna concentrated on Danu. "Where's Sefra?"

Many miles northeast of here. But don't waste your breath voicing some simple-minded notion of flying off in search of her and Diana. Even if I could get an exact location, they'd be long gone by the time you arrived. I'm your best chance of reaching them quickly and getting them here before the legion arrives.

Adrianna refused to conceal her doubts about Danu. They showed up clearly on her face.

Lynx drew attention with a wave of his hand. "Wait. Are we talking about *the* Sefra? As in the former Queen of the Solar Court—that Sefra?"

"Yes," Adrianna said shortly. "The last we saw of her, she was headed to help Diana. Unless something's gone wrong, she should be with her now."

"And Danu can locate Sefra." I bumped my shoulder up to indicate the raven atop it. "He won't tell us how, though."

Lynx didn't question any of that. He just glanced at Danu and cocked a curious eyebrow.

Our group went on to debate what message to give to Diana. Once the wording had been settled, Adrianna insisted that Danu repeat it several times before trusting him to get it right.

If you've decided to help Wilder, don't delay, Danu warned me. *Go tonight if you can ... I'm trusting you not to die. If you do, Abraxus will skin me.* That was his farewell. He flew out the double doors, melting into the velvety darkness.

Nerves sloshed around my guts. Had I decided to help Wilder?

A voice traveled up from the depths of my mind. *Yes.*

Then you must take Lynx, Zola intruded on my thoughts. *This is one of the few things I actually agree with that feathered prick on.*

I checked my mental-shield wouldn't betray any runaway thoughts before starting to plot. Luckily, Frazer was busy conversing with the others on what kind of patrols and nightly protections they should set up throughout the city, and he didn't notice anything unusual in my inner landscape. Liora, on the other hand, kept shooting me searching looks.

My plans hit a snag when Lynx offered, "I don't mind taking the first watch over the city walls."

I raced to think of how to dissuade him. "But you must've used up a lot of magic. Aren't you exhausted?"

His features gentled. "I'm not drained."

"Show-off," Cai said flippantly.

Everybody except for me, Cai, Liora, and Frazer stiffened. It took me a second before I realized they feared Lynx's reaction. But my mate just smiled. "Jealous?"

Cai gave him a mock flat look. "You go too far."

Lynx's laugh brought me out in goosebumps.

"No offense intended," Bear told Lynx. "But I'd prefer it if you didn't take on the watch. My pack will be more comfortable with their own looking out for them."

Lynx was polite. "Of course. I understand."

I was cheering on the inside.

Frazer's eyes fixed on me, his gaze sharper than usual. Rats. I reinforced my mental-shield.

From there, Ryder, Bear, and Owl departed for the city wall. Liora chose to sleep on a cot in the healers' ward. Cai went with her, determined to help out where he could.

I hinted that the rest of us should retire to our beds. The only way I'd get out of Mysaya without my brother knowing was if he was asleep. Luckily, Lynx, Adrianna, and Frazer also voted for sleep.

Lynx guided us upstairs into the soldiers' quarters. I'd already passed by these rooms with Frazer. They were plain to the point of depressing, with little to no furnishings. Only a bed, a lamp, and a storage chest.

"I'll take this one." Adrianna pointed to a random bedroom.

Frazer faced me. "Want to share a room?"

I could tell his intention was to talk. To share what had happened during our separation. Guilt seeped in and rotted my insides. "Sure, but I want to speak to Lynx first."

I found myself at the mercy of three stares. My facial muscles worked hard to conceal the stress and embarrassment running through me.

Adrianna didn't attempt to dissuade me as I'd thought she would. Instead, she aimed a stabby glare at Lynx. "Hurt her, and you'll wake up with your wings on fire."

Her threat discharged, her duty done, she marched into her room.

Frazer's little finger touched mine. *What's going on?*

I forced myself to look at him, otherwise he'd never believe me. *Don't you think I should talk to him? He's my mate and we've hardly spoken.*

My brother hesitated.

I hated it. I was lying to him and making him doubt his instincts.

But if I'd confessed, he would've insisted on going with me. And just this once, I wanted to protect him.

Frazer eyed Lynx. They seemed to enter into a wordless conversation. Threats and wariness were woven amongst something gentler, more familiar.

Be careful if you're moving around the castle, was Frazer's parting advice. *The Fiends don't have the discipline or training of soldiers—we can't rely on them for our safety.*

Okay.

"Can you take my bag?" I said, shrugging it off.

Frazer took it without a word. He picked a room adjacent to Adrianna's and disappeared inside. I'd actually gotten away with it. I couldn't believe it.

"Where do you want to go?" Lynx murmured.

"Is there anywhere that we can talk without being overheard?"

Realizing how that had sounded, my cheeks became a firestorm.

"Easy enough."

His unassuming reaction stunted my blooming shyness.

From there, Lynx took me on a quiet journey through the innards of the castle. We hadn't been walking long when we arrived at a tapestry showcasing the geography of Aurora. He lifted the hem of the coarse material and pushed at the selenite wall behind it. My nose filled with old magic as a concealment spell broke. The rough outlines of an entrance appeared.

Lynx put his shoulder into it, and the fake wall surrendered with an almighty groan.

He sidled through the door first. I slipped into the hidden passage after him. Firelight sconces were brought to life by our movements, illuminating the foot of a staircase tower.

It was cramped enough that when Lynx reached over my head to close the door, his warmth crashed into me and his scent traveled deep into my lungs, moving through my veins like incense smoke. That provoked a dizzying chain of physical reactions. Face aflame, a primal desire nudged at me to bare my fangs, move my hips, and push my wings out. It turned out being alone with him in close quarters was a bad idea. I tucked that knowledge away for the future.

Leaning back, he asked me, "So, what did you want to talk about?"

I wasn't sure if I'd imagined it, but his voice sounded even deeper than usual. In an effort to avoid his eyes, I ended up staring at the prominent stone-shaped lump in his throat. Why in the holy hell was that so attractive to me?

I cough-cleared my throat. "Do you know where Wilder Thorn is?"

Lynx's wings suddenly flared.

I backed up.

Seeing my alarm, Lynx tucked his wings back in. In notes of practiced neutrality, he replied, "Assuming my information is still correct, he's with the legion set to invade the Riverlands."

That added up. I'd seen the moment when Morgan had ordered Wilder to lead the legion. I'd foolishly hoped things might've changed. Hearing that they hadn't only strengthened my resolve to free him as quickly as I could. I didn't want any soldiers from the Riverlands having to fight Wilder. I'd seen him with a sword, after all. I doubted many could stand against my guardian for long and live.

I wrung my hands. "Okay ... I need to ask you for a big favor. I want to break Morgan's bond with Wilder tonight. The way I did with you. But I can't do it alone. I hate asking, but you're the only person strong enough to help me right now. So will you? Help me, I mean?"

Gaze lowering, his face developed creases and shadows. I couldn't tell what he was thinking.

"Please," I blurted out. "He's my guardian. I get that it's reckless to rush off without a proper plan, but there might not be an opportunity to try later on."

"I understand all that," he said, his amber eyes settling on me again. "But why are you keeping this a secret from your friends?"

There wasn't any judgment in his tone. I blushed anyway.

"Because they'd want to come with me. Especially Frazer." I flashed back to all the moments he'd put himself in danger to protect me—to all the sacrifices he'd made. "And I don't have the time or the energy to argue with him."

"You're protecting him." Not a question. An observation.

"He's been through enough." I wet my lips. "And this isn't his responsibility. It's mine."

The sigh came first, then the nod. "I can get you to Wilder. But he's not going to let you break his bond with Morgan—or should I say the magic behind it won't. You need to be prepared for me to knock him out with my lightning. If I don't, he's going to attract a lot of attention fighting against it."

"Okay. I understand. And thank you."

"Are you ready to go?"

"Yes ... well, no. There's one more thing."

"What is it?"

"Can you get me up into the sky?" I asked, picking at my nail beds. "I can fly, but my take offs aren't the best."

As soft as butter, he said, "I don't mind carrying you. We'll get there quicker if I do."

I begged the butterflies mocking my stomach to calm down. "How long will it take for us to get to their camp?"

"About an hour."

"Are you sure?" I frowned, ruminating on the illustrations I'd seen of Aldar. Mysaya was some distance from the Riverlands and Solar border.

Smirking playfully, he flashed me his wings. "What do you think these giant things are for if not for flying faster than everybody else?"

I arched a single brow. "Let me guess; having big wings is a point of pride for males?"

His grin toed the line between innocent and wicked. "Would it thrill you to know that mine are much bigger than Wilder's?"

"You're insufferable," I said without any genuine spikiness.

"So are you." Lynx's blown pupils lingered on my mouth.

He moved into my space, stealing the air from my lungs. "Take my hand."

"Huh?" Gods, I sounded like an idiot.

"Trust me."

I stared at the large hand on offer. It was marked with bold lines, the seat of the thumb was fleshy, his calluses were prominent, the veins of his wrist were raised—masculine, somehow—and his long fingers were artful, quite elegant.

Three loud heartbeats skipped by. I placed my palm atop his.

He guided my hand up around his neck. Quite suddenly, his arms went under my knees and across my mid-back. He picked me up and held me firmly against his granite body. Before I could blink, he'd blown away like dust in the wind, taking me with him.

CHAPTER 36
CLOAK AND DAGGER

We reappeared over a pillow-plump cloud bank and underneath a blanket of stars that burned like distant candles in frost tinted windows.

Lynx was treading air, his darker-than-midnight wings cutting a proud silhouette against the elderberry sky.

I clung to him, disoriented. "What just happened?"

"I shadow-jumped."

"What's that?"

"I can move from place to place instantaneously."

That fit with what I'd heard previously. "But you can't take us straight to Wilder?"

"No," he replied on a lazy downward sweep of his wings. "It's too far."

"Do you know where the legion is encamped?"

"Only the general area." Seeing my expression, Lynx added, "Don't worry. We'll find them."

Without warning, he accelerated faster than a chariot on fire.

"You weren't lying about being fast," I said, squinting ahead.

"I used to sky race when I was younger. And I don't like to lose."

The intensity with which he said that had me quietening and

lowering my head. I didn't know what to say, so I watched the world beneath us pass by.

The desolate moors and tranquil lakes of the valley vanished. But the Metori mountains continued to dominate the landscape. The vicious winds that ruled their peaks sent snow-dusted air howling down their silver-barked slopes. These currents stirred up the dense vapor in the lowlands and dragged an icy mist up into the air like smoke escaping a kettle.

The freezing conditions quickly became a thief, stealing the midsummer heat from my thin clothes and limbs. At the brink of shivering, I abandoned my shyness and stubbornness. I got as close as I could to Lynx, pressing my wind-slapped face against the naked skin of his nape, needing to thaw myself against the heat waves he was throwing off.

Lynx angled his chin over the crown of my scalp. His chest started to vibrate in the manner of a cat stretching out in front of a fire.

"What's that noise for?" I murmured.

"You smell really fucking good."

"What do I smell like?"

I'd tried dismissing his compliment with lightness, but it was impossible to disguise the breathless edge to my question.

His fingers curled into the flesh of my thigh. "It might be better if I don't answer that question."

"Why?"

I almost clapped a hand over my mouth. What the rutting hell was I doing? I shouldn't be stoking this fire. "Forget I said that."

He still replied. "Sugar. There are other scent notes mixed in there, but that's one of the main ones."

Was that a smile in his voice? Was he joking? I looked up to where amber eyes pinned me. They burned through me, warming me from head to toes. Brain blanking, I stuck my tongue out at him.

Lynx studied that pink protrusion. "Are you wanting me to taste that?"

"No," I said, fiercer than I'd intended.

The corner of his mouth twitched. "Shame."

Impossible male.

My gaze dropped to the base of his throat and got stuck there, on the rapid fluttering of his vein. I felt a throb in the air and in my body, as if we were linked by the pulsing.

"Why do you keep getting this panicked look?" He sounded agitated, verging on demanding. "You don't have to be scared of me, you know?"

I glanced up and saw distress written over his features. "I'm not."

"Then why?"

I raked through messy emotions. Honesty would mean saying things that I wasn't ready for. I settled for a half-truth. "I'm just not sure where we go from here or what you're expecting from me. I'm not a normal fae, remember? I didn't grow up coveting mating bonds."

A wall of knotty silence separated us. It was louder to me than the gale blasting my eardrums. I got to the point where I couldn't stand the quiet anymore. As if sensing this, Lynx came out with, "My mother hated my father. They met when he was visiting the eastern continent. She wasn't interested in him, but he still approached her parents for permission to marry her. They agreed, and she was forced into the union." His chest moved in a deep sigh. "After witnessing their disaster of a relationship, I'd sooner cut off my own arm than have you feel obligated to me. If our connection makes you unhappy, we don't have to acknowledge it."

"I'm not unhappy," I confessed.

He waded in, straightforward in his address. "Is it about Wilder, then? You want to be with him?"

I skipped a breath. "Why would you assume that?"

"Wilder told Morgan that he loved you." That turned me inside out. "So, if it's him that you want, I won't get in the way. Our bond isn't a cage."

Those last words of his made my chest feel congested, stuffy. "This isn't about me wanting someone else."

"What is it about, then?" he said, so low that I almost fancied I'd imagined it.

Abraxus's words echoed in my memory. *Morgan and Archon aim for the hearts of those important to us. It's how they control people.*

"It's complicated," I muttered meekly.

Expression fled his face. He grew cold. Almost lifeless.

I swirled my tongue, freeing up moisture in my anxious mouth. "There's something important I've got to do. And if I fail, a lot of people will die. But even knowing that, I risked everything to get my brother back. I would've given myself up if that's what it took. I'm already living with half of my heart outside of my chest. I can't lose more of it when Morgan and others like her would use it against us. It's too dangerous with everything going on."

I tried to read him, tuning into the strain emanating from him. Following my instincts, I gentled. "But I'm not saying I could never ... I mean, I find you attractive."

Oh, gods. Had I really just said that?

His smile was crooked. "Good to know."

I sealed my lips together, afraid of what else might spill out.

"So you think if we get closer, we'll be used against each other? That's why you want to ignore our bond."

"Mm."

"Yeah, sorry, that's not going to work for me."

A drawbridge raised in my mind. "You can't make me—"

"There is no making you," he stressed calmly. "I'll be decent. I'll fly you to save a male who loves you, and I won't argue with you over this. But if you're expecting me to keep my distance and respect your efforts to shut me out, you're going to be disappointed."

I frowned. "But the mate bond doesn't give us a choice to be bound. Don't you resent that after what you've gone through with Morgan?"

A growl thundered through his diaphragm. I shivered, but not out of fear.

Rough words seeped out between his teeth. "Don't compare our bond to what that bitch did to me."

Ashamed, I lowered my eyelids.

"How could I resent you?" He went on, more controlled now. "You freed me from an eighteen-year-long nightmare. To say that I'm grateful doesn't come close to explaining how I feel. I'm terrified to sleep for fear I'll wake up and find this was all a dream."

My heart flew out to him.

"I owe my life to you." In lethal notes, he tacked on, "And if I wasn't determined to be of service and repay you for that, I'd leave and take my chances killing Morgan."

I studied the merciless line of his jaw. That was no empty threat. He'd meant it.

Violent fear mounted in my chest. "She'll pay for what she's done. But you shouldn't do it alone. We can do it together."

"Yes."

I waited for him to go on. He didn't.

In the time it would take for a stick of incense to burn, the intensity of our conversation had been carried away by the numbing wind. Without anything else to distract me, I ended up dwelling on our upcoming mission. On the dangers and difficulties.

Over the next hour, I tried my best to ignore my mounting nerves. I focused outside of myself and watched the great mountains roll back, surrendering to the vast grasslands of the south and the silver seam of a wide, winding river.

Lynx's arm muscles grew rigid.

"We're getting close, aren't we?"

The seed of his throat bobbed in a confirming growl. "We're entering Solar Court territory. I need to call up my shadows now. They'll keep us hidden."

Streams of dark mist flew toward us. They traveled through the night air in the style of shooting stars, encircling us in a bubble. I was relieved to find I could see through them.

"I'll shadow-jump once I've spotted Wilder's tent," Lynx relayed. "Then I'll stun him and get us out of camp. I won't be able to go far. So if you want to avoid him drawing attention, you'll have to work fast. I can only muffle our sounds and scents. If he screams, people are gonna hear him."

Adrenaline kicked at my ribcage. "How will you know which is Wilder's tent?"

"The Prime Sabu is always housed in the biggest tent at the center of camp."

A minute or two later, I glimpsed thousands of neatly arranged shelters bordering a thick evergreen forest. Tension snapped through me.

Please be careful.

Thea's remark made my heart itch. I had a sense she wanted to say more but was stopping herself because of our recent conflicts.

"I can see his tent," Lynx announced.

A surge of nerves brought me out in a cold sweat. "Then let's go," I forced out, peering down at the rapidly approaching encampment.

We *moved*, merging with the night sky.

In the next blink, we materialized beside an imposing tent. Lynx lowered me onto well-trodden grass, sliding his steady fingers through mine.

We sneaked forward, our knees bent, our feet soft.

The entrance to the Sabu's tent was guarded by two straight-backed soldiers, four burning torches, and six black banners emblazoned with a malicious sun painted in the likeness of a drop of blood.

Lynx faced me, a finger pressed to his lips.

I nodded obediently.

He ducked under the half-raised tent flap first. Hand in his, I followed on his heels.

The scene before me almost pulled a gasp out of me. Seven fae were seated around a grand four-sided table. Littering its wooden surface were detailed maps, water jugs, pots of ink, and quill shavings.

Lynx swiftly pulled me into a dingy corner of the tent.

From there, I feasted on the sight of Wilder sitting at the head of the table. He looked every inch the leader of warriors and victor of battlefields, dressed in expensive cloth and fine leather. Half of the officers accompanying him wore similar colors: red and black. The other three donned the night-black armor belonging to the spiders.

I listened in.

"Our scouts have reported the Riverlands army is in the Aurorian forestlands, headed this way," said an elegant female whose countenance reminded me of an ice statue.

My heart lightened a touch. The confirmation that Diana and her people had escaped Kastella was a huge relief.

"How many soldiers does Diana have?" asked a hollow-cheeked spider.

"Around eight thousand."

"And we number ten thousand." A bald and muscled male confronted Wilder. "Diana's forces have just fled their homeland—they'll be tired in body and soul. Why don't we take advantage of their exhaustion? We know their location. I say we go slaughter them all come morning."

I felt the blood drain from my face. Lynx's fingers flexed against mine.

"We still don't know how they escaped Kastella," reasoned the statuesque female. "The Meriden posted to watch over the capital can't make sense of it. Many of the officers fell into an enchanted sleep while the rest were stumbling about as if they'd drunk a gallon of wine. If this is a power Diana can replicate at will, we could lose the entire legion."

Wilder's expression had remained impassive throughout this back and forth. Now, he focused on a hook-nosed male. "Has there been any progress in your investigation?"

"I have a list of possible spells and abilities that match what was done to the Meriden. In my opinion, only three are viable. I'll have more answers soon."

I wasn't sure what it was—maybe that nobody expressed irritation over his lacking answer, or perhaps it was the fact that the male had spoken in notes devoid of emotion while staring into nothingness—but this particular spider brought me out in goosebumps.

"Then I agree with Ziyi." Wilder nodded to the icy-faced female. "There's no cause other than arrogance and pride to abandon our position on the border until we have more information. Let the Riverlands soldiers tire themselves out on the trek here. We'll meet them in battle with well-rested wings."

My stomach rolled to hear him talk like that.

A young, pretty male spoke up. "I don't understand why we're even discussing this. What are our Queen's orders?"

A stout and hairy spider huffed. "You must be new."

Two pink spots appeared on Pretty's cheeks. "I replaced Sabu Kinza two weeks ago. What of it?"

A humorless laugh escaped Bald and Muscled. "That explains it then."

"Explains what?"

"The Queen isn't at court and she isn't reachable," explained Wilder.

Pretty frowned. "Someone must know where she is."

"They do not." Wilder's dignified mask never wavered. "And until our Queen returns and makes her will known, my order to hold our position stands. Return to your posts."

Wilder seized a scrap of parchment and loaded a raven quill with ink. With that, he had dismissed the officers.

A few of the fae sported sour-milk expressions. They still didn't dare raise an argument, and with their departure, I prepared to meet my guardian.

"Sabu, may I have a word?"

I stilled and tensed at that voice.

"Come in."

Hunter entered the tent in the spiders' spiked armor; a thin sword and a short knife were attached to his waist-high belt. The ash-gray wings and fine features were as I remembered them. But his youthful skin had creased and his eyes had sunken, holding burdens that aged him greatly.

"Report." Wilder looked up at the new arrival.

Hunter widened his stance, locking his hands behind him. "As ordered, my team has scouted out Kastella. However, when we arrived we found the Meriden had tried plundering the capital's vaults. They fell into a number of traps set for intruders."

Wilder idly stroked his raven-feather quill. "Any deaths?"

"Six."

"Any gold recovered?"

"No."

"What else?"

Hunter continued as if reading from a script. "The Meriden have decided to raid the Riverlands coastal towns as punishment for Diana's escape."

Horror crashed into me.

Wilder stopped fiddling with his quill. "I trust you informed them that our Queen hadn't permitted that."

Hunter's gaze flickered. "They didn't seem to care."

"Of course not. Any more news?"

A heavy pause.

"What is it?" Wilder frowned.

"Before I came here, I went to update Yeba. There was a fae with her, looking to sell information." A pause, wherein Hunter sipped in a steadying inhale. "He said that his tribe, the Winged Fiends, have set out to attack Mysaya with the aid of a witch called Cai, a red-haired woman, and two females."

Wilder snapped his quill, staining his fingers with ink.

"The informant believes one of the fae to be Adrianna Lakeshie."

"And the other female?" Wilder rose from his chair.

A tiny nod. "The description fits Serena's."

"Why would she go there?" Wilder said as if to himself.

"I don't know, but Yeba wants you to draft a letter to Alexandria about it." Hunter released his arms from their locked position, letting them hang loosely at his sides. "We'll also have to send word to Mysaya. Lynx has to be warned."

Wilder bent at his hips, splaying his hands over the table.

"I know what you're thinking, but we can't protect her," Hunter said under his breath.

Bang!

Wilder palm-slammed the table. Something cracked.

I'd been in a stupor since the mention of the Fiend's traitor. But with that crash, my mind restarted. I was trapped inside a giant encampment, in the chamber of a wicked heart, its walls contracting and closing in about me. We had to leave. All of us.

Looking up at Lynx, I beckoned him closer with a curl of my fingers.

He dipped down several inches so that I could whisper in his ear. "I want to take both of them."

He scanned my face in a silent *Why?*

I shaped my mouth into the word *Please.*

"All right," he murmured. "But I can't shadow-jump more than one person at a time."

I nodded my understanding.

His eyebrows ticked upward in a non-verbal *Ready?*

Again, I nodded.

Hunter's attention was on Wilder's hung head. Neither of them noticed when our veil of shadows dissipated.

I sensed Lynx's lightning charge through our linked hands. Indeed, it rushed through my veins like glittering sunshine.

With his free hand, Lynx struck Wilder in the shoulder and Hunter in the wing. They dropped as hard as stones in a pond.

Lynx and I vanished in a *whoosh* of shadow.

We reappeared in the adjacent forest. The faint glow of firelights and countless watch-fires winked up ahead. The distant murmurs of civilization were also audible.

I faced Lynx. "Why did you move me first?"

"Because you're my favorite." His hand left mine.

"Unbelievable," I grumbled after his disappearing body.

Alone, I surveyed the surrounding glade. The breeze's gentle tides ruffled evergreen needles overhead, creating breaks in the canopy where shafts of moonlight could pass through and pool over the ground in flickering puddles.

Lynx returned, first with Wilder and then Hunter.

"How long before they wake up?" I asked, staring at Hunter and Wilder who were both on their backs, lying side by side.

"You've only got a minute or two," he replied. "I couldn't hit them with a stronger blast; they would've slept for hours, and they still have to fly themselves out of here."

Gods. I hadn't even thought of that.

"I'll keep watch for you." Lynx stepped a few feet out in the direction of the camp. He assumed a guarding position.

My turn. I concentrated on Wilder and Hunter. Their eyelids were fluttering, their fingertips already twitching.

Faced with the reality of freeing them both, I found myself short on confidence and resolve. The energy-sucking pain from my broken wing was gone, but my short nap earlier hadn't refilled my wells of power. What had I been thinking?

Doubt is a poison. Lock it away, Zola urged.

Right. I made my fears as small as I could.

I turned to Wilder first. Then I pulled in waterlight. It flowed in at my bidding, illuminating the malformed bond that squatted in his chest like a black widow spider.

Hatred, revenge, and resentment. I breathed life into these things, sipping from chaotic emotions and nurturing the ugliest parts of myself. When I was brimming with magic, I pointed at Wilder with my index and middle finger.

The darkest string in my magical bow shot into my guardian.

He woke with a wretched gasp. Shit.

As dazed as he had to be, his warrior instincts still kicked in. He propped his upper body up and grasped for the hilt of his longsword.

His green stare latched onto mine. I'd never seen anybody looked so shocked. "Listen to me," I said in a tone that I rarely used. Absolute dominance.

"Serena?" He was doubting me, doubting his own sanity.

"As your charge, I'm ordering you to be quiet. Nod if you understand."

Questions darted over his face. I didn't blame him. I despised the idea of abusing our bond. But in this instance, managing his reaction might save our lives. Mercifully, I got a stiff nod out of him.

I narrowed my worldview, fixating on the twisted thing fastened to his soul. Immediately, I sensed there was something off. As my magic attacked the source of the guardian bond, hellish music played for me. It was a hundred rusty saws groaning, and a thousand people screaming. That vile noise could've stripped the enamel off teeth.

I dug in my heels, refusing to give an inch, working until that perverted bond broke. The last cut went smoother than scissors through a cobweb.

Wilder arced sideways, vomiting up the contents of his stomach. I moved for him.

"Ena," Lynx said sharply. "Hunter's waking. Focus on him. I'll look after Wilder."

I steered my attentions to the right. There, Hunter was already sitting up, bemusement softening his features. "Serena?"

I repeated the steps to channeling my chaos magic. The fuel—the violent emotions—were harder to conjure now. I was wading through mud.

Sweat prickling at my pounding temples, I pushed what darkling magic I could dredge up into Hunter. Already, I sensed his bond hadn't been born of the same wickedness as Wilder's. As a result, it would surely prove as resilient as Lynx's.

"What's going on?" Hunter turned to Wilder and Lynx.

Neither male responded. Lynx was too busy supporting a shivering Wilder.

"Is this a dream?" Hunter said, sounding like a faeling astray in the woods.

My concentration suffered. "Hunter, you need to be quiet."

That was when the magic fueling his bond detected my chaos, and it reared up like an ancient beast bent on revenge. It howled at me, at the intruder threatening its existence. That monster slammed into my chest like a charging ram. It attacked again and again. I gasped, spots speckling my vision.

"Ena?" Lynx's alarm was loud and obvious.

I waved his concern away. "Focus on Wilder."

Legs as weak as straw, I staggered to Hunter's right side.

Seeing my approach, he drew his knees up to his forehead. "It's just a dream. It's a dream."

"It's not a dream. I'm here to save you."

He rocked back and forth, refusing to look at me. "This isn't real."

Face soaked in exertion, I wheezed out, "It's real, Hunter. And you need to help me. Fight it. Fight for your freedom," I pleaded out of hopelessness. I was out of ideas, hanging onto control by my fingertips.

His head rose from his knees. He met my desperate gaze, and in the depths of his clay-colored eyes, I witnessed the quicksand of regret and grief sinking into him, burying him. "Why?"

In that one word, he lost the battle inside of himself.

My magic sputtered and died. I'd failed. I was done. I could've sworn I heard his bond crowing in victory.

A lethal *hiss* sounded. A blow to the gut followed.

Hunter had rutting punched me.

"No!" Lynx shouted.

"Damn you, Hunter," I groaned.

I clasped my belly and came into contact with something wet and solid. Glancing down, I blinked at the knife embedded in my abdomen. I detached from the sight, a kite severed from its line. There was no pain, only the heat of my leaking insides and the cold steel in my guts. It looked absurd poking out of me. Almost funny.

Hunter yanked the blade out, causing my muscles to contract around it. I thought he'd attack me again, but he placed the bloody knife in his lap, staring at it uncomprehendingly.

An animalistic snarl resonated. I glanced up.

Lynx lunged for me. At the same time, Wilder unsheathed his dagger. With a crazed expression and wound up in a reasonless rage, he brought the bright steel down through Hunter's clavicle, straight into his chest.

My lips parted in a silent scream.

Before I could collapse, Lynx reached my side. He braced me against his front and pushed down firmly on my wound. "It's okay. It'll be okay."

It wasn't. It wouldn't be.

Hunter was gasping on the ground, dying in the dirt. He looked so young. Barely older than an adolescent.

I didn't think. I reached out toward him. Lynx seemed to understand and helped me to Hunter's side.

"What the fuck are you doing?" Wilder snapped at him. "Do you want him to stab her again?"

"He can't hurt anybody in this state," Lynx argued. "And she wants to say goodbye. If I don't help her, she'll make her wound worse by trying to do it herself."

I leaned over Hunter, cupping his face. He gaped at me, pupils huge, as if he wanted to cling to my image with everything he had. The stench of terror clawed up my nostrils, imprinting on my memory.

"You're not alone," I whispered to him.

His fingers fumbled for mine. Through fractured breaths, he eked out, "Goodbye, friend."

Memory flashed through a fog of shock and sorrow. I'd whispered those very words to him when he'd left me at Kasi.

The lightest of smiles graced his mouth. When that final farewell slid off his face, his head became a dead weight and his vision glazed over, staring up at a world that had vanished from view.

I was forced to let go of him when Lynx lifted me into his arms.

The thin sheet of shock protecting my mind cracked. Terrible, terrible pain flooded in. I clenched my jaw. Fuck, it hurt. I wanted to black out, disappear.

"Ena, you need to keep pressure over your wound. I can't do it while I'm holding you," Lynx said, low and stressed.

"Mysaya." I pressed a palm over my bloody wound. "Liora. Get me to her. She'll heal me."

Wilder rushed to me, his rough fingers pinching my chin, drawing my focus up to his wild eyes. "Are you still twined to Frazer?"

"... yes."

Being trapped in a prison of pain was bad enough. But he reminded me that my mistake might also cost my brother his life. So stupid. Stupid. *Stupid.*

I sobbed, and the movement wrenched my abdomen. The resulting wave of agony ripped a loud cry from me.

Raised voices sounded from the encampment.

"Gods-damn it," Lynx hissed.

"Soldiers," Wilder confirmed.

"I'll measure my pace to hide our retreat," Lynx told Wilder. "But after we're clear, you'll have to get to Mysaya by yourself."

"That doesn't matter. Just get her there," Wilder demanded, his voice breaking at the end.

Shadows quickly formed around the three of us. That done, we ascended, hidden from view by the dark cloud. Wilder moved into a flanking position. He didn't call out, but I could feel him watching over me. Meanwhile, Lynx held me as if I were made of glass while his wings did all the work, slicing through the night air like giant oars. Despite his efforts, every tiny movement—every inhale—ripped me apart stitch by stitch.

I moved my eyeballs down. That was a mistake. I swayed at the sight of my blood—of my red and sticky fingers. My pulse grew frenzied, as if it had just realized that it needed to work extra hard to keep me alive.

It started to hurt more. How was that possible?

Lynx's cloak of shadows dropped. He accelerated, switching up to a scary-fast speed. We soon left Wilder far behind.

"Lynx." I trailed off as another spasm shredded my insides. My breath shortened, I gasped out, "I have to tell you something. If I die …"

"You're not dying," he growled out. "I forbid it."

"Just listen." I wet parched lips. "Give my necklaces to Sefra. She'll protect them."

Hold on, Ena, Thea said tenderly.

Stop being so dramatic, Zola added, sounding angry-scared.

Lynx's mouth thinned with denial. "You said you were twined to Frazer. Well, he's a stubborn bastard. He won't let you go anywhere. You'll be fine."

I couldn't—wouldn't ignore my duty. "Will you take care of the others for me? Keep them safe from Morgan. And Archon."

His fear mixed with confusion. "Archon?"

"Ask the others. They'll explain."

"You'll explain everything once you're healed," Lynx insisted.

My agitation climbed. "Look after them. Promise me? You're strong —stronger than me."

He shook his head. "Stop it. Stop this. This is not the end."

I cast my watery eyes downward, not wanting an audience for the tears that threatened. "Tell them I'm sorry—"

"All right. That's it." Lynx pinched me on the arm.

I gaped at him. "What are you doing? I've been stabbed, you idiot."

The bastard pinched me on the butt. Even harder. My squeak of outrage had him adding, "If you don't stop acting like a dying person, I'll do that to your nipple next."

Several blinks later, I managed, "You can't say things like that."

"But I can do them?"

"No."

"Why not?"

I eyed him through slit lids. "Because I've been *stabbed*." Even in such a serious situation, he'd reduced me to a sulky brat.

"So, I can do them later?"

I was about to curse him out when his expression stopped me. It was wrung out with poorly concealed stress and panicked fear. Realization crept up on me. He wanted to provoke me—wanted to divert me. "Thank you," I said, calming.

"For what?"

"You know what." I lost my voice after that.

His windblown features hardened. "I'll make it better, Ena."

Before I could ask how, he started to chant. I couldn't decipher the words, but I recognized the melody. He had sung the same song to me when I'd broken my wing.

"What is that?" I whispered.

"It's something my makena used to sing to me, and when it's infused with magic it relaxes the body and encourages healing. It can't do much for a wound like this, and it stops working as a sedative if it's used too frequently. But there's no harm in trying."

Lynx resumed his dreamy melody. The sound turned into the crashing of waves, the swishing of pages, and the crackling of a merry fire, relaxing my mind.

The pain slowly reduced to a dull *thud-thud-thud*. I became a weed in careless waters, and my head slumped back. I eyed the stars hungrily, hoping that this wouldn't be my last night to watch them shine.

Don't give up, Thea urged.

My great-aunts kept up a stream of encouragements, demands, and even threats. They wouldn't shut up, in fact. It didn't stop my vision from dimming.

Ice spikes formed in my blood, spreading to my extremities, numbing them. I lost strength in my limbs, and the hand putting pressure on my belly relaxed. I no longer feared what would happen when the frost reached my heart.

Eyes falling shut, I muttered, "I'm glad I met you."

"Stay with me." Lynx's voice was harsh and rasping in his throat.

I felt a hook under my ribs heave at me, as if I were a fish being hauled up from the ocean's depths. Gasping, my heavy eyelids flew open.

Lynx's arms tightened around me. "What is it?"

"Frazer."

The distance kept me from discerning his emotions clearly. Yet, the ferocity with which he'd yanked at our thread left me in no doubt that he was terrified. It also slapped some sense into me. With renewed determination, I palmed my stab wound. The agony was immense, indescribable. It would've been easier to slip into an eternal sleep.

ENA!

"Argh. Don't shout." I scowled.

"I didn't," Lynx said in a wary way.

Brata—

Where are you?

Lynx is flying me back now. I need Liora.

What happened?

Hunter stabbed me.

After a blip of quiet, he said, *Tell Lynx to land in the courtyard outside the entrance hall of the west wing. Liora will be waiting for you there.*

West wing?

He sent me an image of a large space with a double staircase. I recognized it as the place our group had met earlier, where we had agreed to contact Diana.

I told Lynx where to land, adding, "That's where Liora will be."

"How do you know?"

"Frazer told me." I continued in a slurred murmur. "We can hear each other's thoughts if we're close enough."

He didn't push me for more answers. Minutes or seconds snailed by, then Lynx pressed his smooth lips to my forehead. "We're here. We made it."

His giant wings decelerated, bringing us to touch down in a stately courtyard. I groaned as the slight jostling tortured my body.

"Help her," Lynx demanded, his voice edged with panic. "It's her stomach. She was stabbed."

Liora silently appeared at our side. Lynx was so tall that she had to reach up to me even though I was only pressed against his chest. Her cool fingers enveloped my wrist with surprising strength. Earthy scents and warm feelings flowed into me at a lullaby pace, nudging and assessing damage.

Cai's and Adrianna's presence registered with me in a vague sort of way. They stood nearby, lingering at the borders of my vision.

"Follow me." Liora released me.

"Where are we going?" Lynx asked while walking.

"Healers' ward. Frazer's waiting there, in a private room. If we don't go to him, he'll come to her, and I don't want him exhausting himself."

Liora didn't sound like Liora. She was brisk. Bossy.

The journey to the ward was a meaningless blur. Until, "Siska."

I forced my impossibly heavy head up. Frazer faced me from inside an entranceway. One of his hands clutched at an unwounded abdomen while the other propped his weight against a doorframe. He looked utterly wretched.

Liora reached him first. "I told you to stay in bed."

He backed up, allowing Liora entrance into a room perfumed with sage. But as for the rest of it, he ignored her completely.

"Lynx, put her down there." Liora gestured to a cot in the middle of the space before washing her hands at a ceramic wall-sink.

I was gently placed on a thin mattress. Lynx kneeled at the head of my bed. Frazer closed in on my left, climbing directly onto my cot.

I swiveled my head toward him, and our fevered brows almost touched. His eyes were deep dark pools of reflected pain. My fault.

"I'm sorry," I whispered to him.

"You left because of Wilder?"

A tiny "Yes," passed my lips.

Adrianna positioned herself at the foot of my bed. "What was that about Wilder?"

Lynx answered for me. "She went to break his bond."

"Did he do this to her?" Adrianna asked, gesturing angrily at me.

"No. She managed to free him. He's on his way here now."

"Why didn't he arrive with you?" Cai asked.

Adrianna released a puff of air that could've been called scornful. "He couldn't keep up with Lynx."

Liora placed a stool next to my cot. "Ena, the others are going to have to hold you down."

My insides rebelled, rejecting the idea. "Why?"

"Because healing this amount of damage will take all my concentration. I won't have the energy to numb you while I'm doing it," she said, sitting on her stool. "And if you move around too much, you risk undoing my work."

I pushed out a feeble, "Okay."

"You'll be fine, I promise." Liora slipped her hand into mine. "Cai, Adi, hold her legs down. Lynx, you take the tops of her arms."

I was pinned to the mattress with tears burning up my eyesight.

Liora's magic reached deep inside, manifesting as a white-hot flame, pinching and cauterizing belly tissue. Body consumed in hellfire, I sweated so much that I stuck to the sheets beneath me.

I drew in measured breaths, hoping to relax and to control the shaking of my limbs. It was as effective as propping up a crumbling dam with a stick. My endurance soon tired; my pride broke. I descended into close-mouthed whimpers.

Ena. Frazer pushed at my mental-shield. *Let me in. Let me take some of the pain for you.*

With the last of my strength, I solidified my defenses against him. I locked myself in my own head.

"Let. Me. In." Frazer palmed the sides of my face.

"No." I'd wanted to sound firm, but my voice lacked strength.

"Siska, please." Frazer's hands developed a tremor.

My heart strained. But I refused to give in. The only thing worse than this torment would be sharing it with him.

Lynx lowered his head; his hair tickled my blazing cheek as he whisper-sang into my ear. His powerful voice sent a shiver through me, cooling a little of the fever ravaging my body. It didn't clear my head, though. It didn't stop the pain from closing in on me like a thick fog. Vision dimming, I murmured, "Your makena's song ... what's it called?"

His mouth moved, but I didn't hear him.

CHAPTER 37
THE ROUND TABLE

I was staring at my reflection in the glassy depths of a lake. I couldn't remember the why, the how, or the when, but here I was.

The dark waters rippled, disturbed by an invisible force.

My face changed into Dain's.

I extended my hand toward his visage, and my fingers passed through cool water, nothing more.

Dain smiled sadly at my crestfallen features. "You must wake, tilä. They're waiting for you."

"I don't know how to be what they need."

"Wake up, Ena. That's all you need to do."

That stern, intense expression reminded me of ... *Frazer*.

Awareness happened. I stretched out into the boundaries of my body. Through the sensitive membrane of my skin, I sensed where I stopped and where the mattress beneath me started.

Finally, Zola snapped. *You almost gave me and Thea a heart attack.*

Leave her be, Thea interrupted, her voice sterner than I'd ever heard it.

Both aunts grew quiet.

I propped my eyelids open and peered up at the high ceiling. There, the wooden beams gleamed in the light of the sun. It was a new day.

"She's awake."

My gaze drifted toward the owner of that voice. Lynx was on my left, perched on a stool by my bedside, his hair floating about his shoulders. He was dressed in casual attire. No weapons. No armor. Just heavy-duty trousers, a crumpled shirt with turned-up sleeves, and a piercing that cuffed the top of his ear.

I swallowed, feeling parched.

"How do you feel?"

That voice turned my head to the right. Frazer was there, sitting beside me on the bed. His arms were wrapped around his elevated knees, and his gaze was fixed in the distance.

"I'm fine. Nothing hurts," I said in a scratchy voice, as if recovering from an ague.

"That's good."

My heart twisted at Frazer's deadened voice.

I shuffled up the mattress. Bracing my back against the headboard, I studied my brother's face. That blank mask of his gave nothing away, but the red flush coloring his normally jade-white neck didn't lie. He was furious.

"How long have I been asleep?" I asked.

"Hours." Another monosyllabic response.

Feeling awkward, I picked at the sweater I was wearing. It was massive on me, and I was naked underneath except for my underwear. The traces of a familiar scent had me sniffing the neckline of the black material.

"The pullover's mine," Lynx said before I could comment.

I went rigid. "You put me in this?"

"No. Liora and Adrianna dressed you."

They had put me in his sweater? I didn't dare question that.

"Your old clothes were covered in blood," Frazer interrupted in a near hiss.

Fragments from last night flashed through my mind in pictorial images. "Wilder? Is he—"

"He's here," Lynx answered.

Thank the stars.

I drew my legs up inside the blanket-sweater. Swaddled, I viewed the elegant bedroom. The walls were papered in a print of white blossoms laid over a cobalt background. Pearl-inlaid furnishings were pushed up into the corners, and a fireless hearth dominated the wall opposite me. To my right, a wide window showed glimpses of the majestic mountains. To my left was a closed door.

"How's the wound?" Lynx prompted.

I gingerly laid a hand over my torso. "My skin feels a bit tight, but—"

"Don't ever do that again," Frazer growled out.

My mood plummeted and crashed.

"You lied to me." His bloodshot gaze darted to me accusingly. "Why?"

"Because I had to save Wilder," I said, fiddling with my extra-long sleeves.

I grimaced as Frazer shouted, "I know that! But why didn't you tell me that's what you were going to do?"

Guilt snuck up on me. "There wasn't time to stand around explaining things."

"That's your excuse?" His eyes narrowed. "We can share our thoughts quicker than most people can talk."

My insides shriveled up. For a fae with such cold mannerisms, he could burn with the flame of a thousand suns when triggered.

"I was worried you'd try to come with me," I admitted.

"And why shouldn't I come with you?"

That struck a nerve, shattering my attempt to remain calm. I flared up quicker than wildfire. "Because you spent the last few days in chains. Then you went and stared into some gods-awful mirror that could've broken your mind. That's why! I was trying to protect you."

"Well, you failed," he shot back with a precision that made me bleed. "You almost killed us both."

Haunches up, I snapped, "I didn't know Hunter was going to gut me. I thought Morgan wanted me alive."

Frazer flinched and looked away, his jaw gluing together. Unable to bear the sight of him upset, I grabbed my anger by the throat and silenced it.

"As it stands, Morgan's orders are to capture you by any means necessary," Lynx interjected. "Hunter might've hoped that by hurting you it would force us to stay and seek help from a healer in the legion's encampment."

"That, or his bond forced him to attack," Frazer said, his features clouding with shadows that would've made a tiger tuck its tail and flee. "It might've realized Ena was a threat to its existence and decided that eliminating her was more important than Morgan's orders."

I was flattened. "I'm sorry, brata. I don't know what else to say."

"I'm not upset that you went to help Wilder. But you endangered our lives without even talking to me. You broke the trust between us."

Buried resentment sparked in me. "Trust? Have you ever actually trusted me?"

The flames of his fury blew out, and his inner world grew colder than ashes in winter. I fought a shiver, adding, "I've always been open with you about my past. About everything. You can't say the same, can you?"

"Don't turn this around on me because you feel guilty for lying," he said, his chilly mask locked in place. "I may keep secrets, but lies are the enemy of trust."

Grief bludgeoned me.

Lynx interrupted the strained moment. "Maybe we should take a break? Ena might need to rest again before the meeting."

"What meeting?"

Frazer vacated the bed. "Lynx can explain. I'll set the meet for midday. You've got one hour." He walked to the door and halted, his fingers poised over the handle. "And remember to eat something. My stomach hurts."

He stalked out. I ached all over.

"Why would his stomach hurt if you're hungry?" Lynx asked.

"He'll be sensing it through the bond," I replied weakly.

Lynx's brows wrinkled. "That's unusual."

It actually was. Frazer had never sensed my hunger like that before. Maybe I'd never been this hungry? I hadn't eaten or slept properly since he'd been taken.

"What was this about a meeting?" I asked, wanting to change the topic.

He leaned forward, bracing his elbows on his thighs. "Once you'd stabilized, Frazer gathered us here. He said if we were going to work together, we had to know what was at stake, and we had to understand each other."

"Who was here?"

Lynx used his fingers to list off, "Wilder, Bear, Owl, Ryder, Cai, Liora, and Adrianna."

"What did you talk about?"

"A lot of things," he said, slowly twisting and rubbing his hands together. "I had to explain why I swore myself to Morgan again. Then we discussed the identity of the Fiends' traitor."

I stiffened. "Do we know who it was?"

"There's only one person missing from their camp—a male called Robin. Owl thinks he was an opportunist, looking to gain favor with Morgan's legion." Lynx straightened on his stool, stretching his backbone with a sigh. "After that, your pack told us about the firstborn being real, that the courts are due to open, and that Morgan's working with Archon ... It really scared poor old Wilder."

I pursed my lips. "Just Wilder?"

"That's right." He feigned an innocent smile.

I rolled my eyes.

"Frazer also mentioned your group had been chosen as knights. It was around then I discovered something." Lynx lifted the hem of his dark blue shirt.

Caught off guard, I could only gawk at his body. The lines contouring his torso were graceful, smooth, yet they possessed great strength.

Lynx's smile was pure sin. "You're drooling."

I squint-glared at him. "Liar."

His laugh was a dark purr, bringing my heart to the brink of a shiver.

"Here. Look." He turned sideways, displaying his ribs for me.

The mark of the knights—the same one that adorned my pack—was stamped on his skin. "I got it at the same time as you and the others."

Mentally stumbling, I scrambled to collect my thoughts. Did that mean there were other knights out there—knights we'd yet to meet?

"What did you think it was?" I asked, nodding at the whorl of script, resisting the urge to trace the lettering with my fingertips.

He pulled his shirt back down. "I assumed it was a curse mark, or that Morgan had finally done what she'd always threatened to do and branded me as hers."

A recollection seemed to flash upon him. In the pits of his pupils, I saw a black fire spark and burn with a vengeance.

Change the subject, change the subject ...

I blurted out, "Did you gain any new abilities?"

"No. But maybe it'll happen at some point in the future."

In a blink, his entire face transformed. From avenging demon to mischievous imp; his broad smile made his cheeks shine. "Wilder wasn't marked as a knight, by the way."

My eyebrow bumped up. "Meaning?"

I received a carefree shrug in return. "Just in case you were curious."

Gods give me patience with territorial males.

"Was that the end of the meeting, then?"

"No." He pulled a band from his wrist to tie up his wayward hair. "Adrianna and Liora gave us an account of your fight with Hasan's forces. They also said that you'd allied with Abraxus."

My throat bobbed. *Does Lynx know Abraxus is my grandfather?*

Frazer's response was timely but emotionless. *If he does, he didn't hear it from me. Our pack hasn't talked openly about the stones or your role in destroying Archon either. It's your choice who to share that information with.*

I would tell Wilder and Lynx, I decided. Just not yet.

"Lynx, has anyone told you my real name?"

His head tilted in confusion. "Isn't it Serena Smith?"

"That was my name until I found out who my parents really were." I took a breath. "It's Serena Raynar-Lytir." His gaze flickered. "Sefra's my half sister."

Something linked up behind his eyes. "Dain and Sati—they're your parents?"

I confirmed that with a nod.

Lynx left his stool. He sat opposite me, causing the mattress to dip with his weight. "I've got so many questions for you."

The soft depths of his tone suggested he wasn't only referring to the details of my birth. I forced a small smile. "Same. But can we leave them for now? I'm not really up to reliving my life story. I just felt that after everything you did for me ... I at least owe you my name."

Lynx froze slightly. "It was my choice to go. You don't owe me anything."

"Of course I do," I insisted. "I hadn't even known you for a day before I put you in danger."

"Going there wasn't dangerous for me."

That staggered me. "I can't decide if that's incredibly arrogant or—"

"Incredibly sexy?" he said, his humor showing in the arching of his brow.

That tugged an awkward, stuttering laugh from me. Unable to cope with the cauldron of chaos brewing away inside, I searched for a safer topic. "So, are we still planning on staying in Mysaya?"

His flirty mask slipped. "As long as Diana's army arrives before the legion, everyone's agreed to fight. Even the Fiends."

"And if the army doesn't come?"

"We flee," he said simply. "Frazer ended our talk before we could form an escape plan. He wanted you present for that."

"And there's been no word from Diana or my sister?"

"Not yet."

A hush descended.

"I've been meaning to say I'm sorry about your friend," Lynx said suddenly.

Fresh pain cleaved me open. "That's the thing. We weren't friends. He did some extremely stupid shit, so I gave up on him. He might've fought harder if I'd ..." I lost my voice, the heartbreak choking me.

Lynx kicked his boots off and moved up the mattress. He sat alongside me, his wings up against the headboard, his long legs stretched out in front of him. It was then he took hold of my hand.

"You were there for him at the end," he said, his smoky baritone becoming smoother than antler-velvet. "That's all any of us can ask for."

Do. Not. Cry. Do. Not ... Don't do it.

Lynx nudged my shoulder. "Hug?"

I didn't dare disturb the tears smudging my vision. "No. Thank you."

"Shame. I've missed hugs."

His sweetness undid me. I clawed past the knot in my throat. "Okay then."

With absurd ease, he scooped me up and placed me across his lap. One of his strong arms supported my back, and the other cradled my knees. Tilting forward, he freed his silky black wings and enfolded me in them, too.

Not wanting to risk staring into his eyes, I dipped my chin and relaxed my head against him. It turned out to be the perfect puzzle piece for his shoulder nook.

He traced the length of my spine. Again and again and again. His immense body heat seemed ready to break out of his chest. It seeped into the deepest parts of me, wrecking the shroud of numbness that I'd carried after Frazer's capture. From that day to this, I hadn't really cried. I'd tried to harden myself. To put up a wall between me and my emotions. That choice had prevented me from immediately falling to pieces. But it had only been a temporary support, a beam that had buttressed a leaking roof. Now, the roof was caving in and my emotion was flooding the place.

A tear snuck past my defenses. I lost count of how many escaped after that. When my eyes were almost swollen shut, Lynx used his sleeves to mop my face.

I made the mistake of looking up at him. He stilled.

My toes curled as his breath kissed my lips.

Knock-knock.

"Ena?" Liora called out. "Frazer said you'd woken up. Can I come in?"

I eyed the door, pulse a-pounding. Lynx seized that moment to plant a quick kiss on my cheek. My head whipped around to him. Before I could say anything, he'd vanished into thin air and I landed on the mattress ass-first.

"Thief," I hissed at his echo.

"Ena?"

"Come in," I said, notes quivering like a poorly strung bow.

Liora slipped inside. I rose to greet her.

Quick on her feet, she crossed the distance to me.

We shared a brief hug. Once we'd broken apart, Liora regarded me carefully, her spring-greens creasing into soft-petal folds. "Can I do anything?"

In that single look, an understanding passed between us. In a way, we understood each other better than we did our own brothers. The comfort from knowing that somebody else with the same emotional veins existed eased the misery lining my gut.

"You've already done it. You healed me." I scanned the red in the whites of her eyes, the dryness of her lips, and the disheveled state of her plaited hair. "Did I tire you out?"

"No." Noticing my disbelief, she insisted. "Honestly. Isolde and I realized that she could boost my energy levels in her resting state. It's not much, but it's kept me going. I couldn't have helped so many people without it." Her gaze sharpened. "Speaking of, can I see your wound?"

I lifted the baggy folds of the sweater, inadvertently flashing her my underpants. Liora ducked to examine the pink mark that scarred my bruised belly. The sight of it made me feel funny. I averted my eyes and waited until she was done.

"It looks good. If you feel any pain in that area, let me know." Liora stood up straight and asked, "How much has Frazer told you about what's been going on?"

My answer led us to other questions and different topics. I learned Liora had given the Fiends the spell to connect to their familiars, and a few of them had already done so. Owl had also sent somebody to talk with those in their pack who hadn't come to Mysaya with us. They were to be given a choice. Join us or scatter.

The clock on the mantlepiece showed when time ran short. "Do you know where this meeting of Frazer's is being held?"

A nod. "I can get us there."

"I have to go and change into some actual clothes." I rolled the long sleeves up my forearms. "Then I guess we should head out."

"Your bag's over there." She pointed to a spot next to the bedside table. "And there's a bathroom next door on the right if you want to freshen up."

"Are you staying nearby?"

She confirmed that with a nod. "Frazer insisted that we sleep in separate quarters to the Fiends for security reasons, so we left the west wing and moved into the middle section of the castle. Wilder's down the hall. Lynx is upstairs. And our pack chose a suite of interconnected rooms. Oh, and er, Ryder. He insisted on lodging with us."

Her nose twitch drew a watery laugh out of me. "Let me guess, he wanted to sleep in Frazer's room?"

"He did suggest it," she said, grinning. "But Frazer chose to share with Cai. Ryder's with me. Adi's going to be in here with you. Unless …"

A charged pause.

"Unless what?"

Her lip quivered. "You wanted to be with somebody else, maybe?"

"How subtle of you," I retorted, tone acidic.

Liora rearranged her features into a sheepish expression. "Sorry."

I freed a chuff. "No, you're not."

She worked hard to keep from smiling.

"I'll be quick." Eager to evade any further mention of who might be sharing my bed in the future, I grabbed my rucksack and fled my room in bare feet.

I entered a six-sided foyer with several doors leading off it.

The bathroom turned out to be an ornate space. Rainbow moonstone tiled the floor, and the freestanding tub could've fit five people. The counters also smelled of citrus and cleanliness.

At a vanity sink, I refreshed myself and combed through my hair, leaving the silky strands to drift about my shoulders. Lynx's sweater smelled too much like him. I quickly removed it, packed it in my bag, and chose a black shirt with bell sleeves, slim-fitted trousers, and flat shoes to wear.

I pushed out my wings, bracing for pain. Relief escaped my lungs when I didn't feel anything. Gaining confidence, I splayed my swan-white and gold-tickled wings. I saw no sign of the breakage, not a single bent feather.

Returning to the bedroom, I stowed my bag and belted on my sword. From there, Liora steered us out of our quarters, through a maze of ornate corridors, and down three sets of dusty stairs.

Liora noticed me dragging my feet. "What's wrong?"

Lying to an empath would be useless. "Frazer's angry at me. And I don't know if you've noticed it, but that male can really glare."

Her expression fluctuated between sympathy and poorly concealed amusement. I released a self-conscious breath.

"Ignore the death glares," Liora said after she'd gained control over her face. "He'll come around."

"I don't know. I did lie to him."

She swept that comment aside with a *pft*. "Oh, please. He'd have lied to the gods if it meant protecting you. Besides, why should he expect total honesty when he's a secret wrapped inside of a mystery?"

I couldn't help but feel vindicated by that.

The view out of the windows showed me when we reached the ground floor. It took under a minute to arrive in front of a pair of tall doors. Beyond them, I heard familiar voices conversing.

I couldn't move. My stomach-bees were wreaking havoc. "Wilder's in there," I whispered.

"He's desperate to see you," Liora breathed.

I soaked in her kind smile. It gave me strength.

Squaring off my shoulders, I walked into a circular room. The floor and ceiling were expertly crafted from loula wood. Three windows that were lined up on the far wall overlooked an ornamental garden. These glass panes let in light that hit the crystal wall and made it sparkle like sun-touched snow.

Trifling ornamentations were absent. The sole piece of furniture was a huge round table placed in the center of the room. These design choices discouraged any underhanded plotting in discrete corners. Everyone was equal and accountable and visible here.

Liora and I marched toward the table. It was already ringed with familiar people. Wilder, Bear, and Owl had settled on the left. Lynx, Adrianna, Cai, and Ryder occupied the right.

Frazer stood at the northern compass point, his back to the far wall, and his silvery wings finally out on display.

My footsteps sounded obnoxiously loud as they echoed around the wide-open space. I didn't walk farther than I needed to; I stopped at the southernmost point, which put me directly opposite my brother. In what I felt was a show of loyalty, Liora settled on my left flank.

Abandoning his spot, Cai walked up and pulled me into his arms.

Peppermint, vanilla, and sage. Instant comfort.

"You scared the shit out of me," he said, low and serious. "Don't do it again. Okay?"

I hugged him a bit tighter. "Okay."

Cai prepared to step back; I could feel it in his body, in the stopping of his breath, in the drawing in of his flesh. We released each other at the same time.

"Are you another rival?"

My gaze darted toward Lynx. He stared at Cai without aggression. But there was a definite glint in his eye, a sizing up of the competition.

Cai flashed his teeth in a smile. "Relax, big guy; we're just friends."

"Good."

A string of curses flitted through my mind. I was tempted to confront Lynx about his possessiveness. But at this point, I was intimately familiar with fae nature. His reaction seemed fairly normal for our kind. I had to accept that, at least up to a point.

"I missed you."

My eyes locked with Wilder's. He had said that to me in front of everybody.

I gulped as my heart jumped.

This time, Lynx opened his wings and thunder rolled in the distance. He exuded power and dominance and all the aggression that had been missing in his interaction with Cai. The fae in our group lowered their heads in recognition of the threat he posed. Wilder resisted out of sheer stubbornness. I didn't react because Lynx's performance hadn't affected me.

I'm impressed by your restraint, Zola drawled. *I think if I had a mate like that, I'd have already tattooed his name on my ass.*

Rutting hell.

Wilder pulled my focus by baring his fangs and growling at Lynx.

If they start fighting, would you mind asking them to do it topless? I'm asking for Thea—

No, she isn't!

Nervous laughter threatened. I bottled that and conferred with my brother. *Does Wilder know that Lynx is my mate?*

Frazer deigned to look at me. *Yes.*

How?

Adrianna.

Rut me.

"Stop this." Adrianna flicked her scaled wings in irritation. "We've got more important things to do than watch two males posturing and comparing wing sizes."

"Agreed," Frazer said, attitude neutral. "If you must, work out your aggression in the training ring later on. This isn't the appropriate place for it."

Both males mercifully complied, sheathing fangs and folding wings. Their glares, however, appeared fixed in place.

Frazer went on. "I called us together to decide on what preparations to make in the next two days, and what tactics would best serve us when fighting against the legion."

We discussed the tasks we'd be best suited for in the run-up to the battle. This didn't take long, and in the end, I chose to work in the kitchen. I'd plenty of experience in that area. Frazer was particularly keen on the idea, saying, "Maybe being around so much food will encourage you to eat. My stomach still hurts."

As that topic closed, we moved onto tackling the thorny problem of how to defeat ten thousand fae. Before much could be said on that matter, Ryder announced, "Actually, Owl and I had a splendid idea on the subject of the coming battle."

Frazer side-eyed him. "Are you sure it wasn't just Owl?"

"I am capable of having a good idea, you know." Ryder sulked and pouted in a childish way.

"If you say so," Frazer replied woodenly.

Cai's shoulders bobbed in silent laughter.

"Owl and I think we should call on the Aurorian Sami for help," Ryder announced with no small amount of triumph.

Frowning, Frazer said, "I assumed they'd scattered after fleeing Mysaya."

Ryder nodded. "They did. But our old unit stayed in contact in case one of us was attacked or had information to share." Something hazy drifted through his eyes as he looked at Frazer. "The Sami would join this fight if you asked them to. I know they would."

Frazer was quiet, reflecting on that. It fell to Lynx to say, "It's a good idea."

Ryder beamed at him. "Nice to know somebody appreciates my genius."

"What about the fae who helped you ambush me and Frazer outside Nasiri—would they help us?" Cai asked Ryder.

"That pack has no love of Morgan," Ryder said, concentrating on Cai. "None of the outlaw factions do. But they've lived too long as hired soldiers. They don't know how to live any other way. And we shouldn't invite groups who might betray us for money."

"We'll contact the Sami. Nobody else." Frazer's tone brooked no opposition.

A discussion over battle strategies followed. Wilder and Lynx dominated here. The others pitched in where appropriate. And after being taught by Zola and Thea, I finally felt confident enough to voice my opinion.

Two hours passed, and we reached a point where we had to plan for the worst. The more we talked about escape routes, diversionary tactics, and meet-up points, the more a gloom settled into my soul.

I was grateful when Frazer tried to bring things to a close. "Is there anything left to say before we get on with our tasks for the day?"

"Yes."

Everybody eyeballed Wilder.

He grasped his sword's hilt. That reflex pulled my gaze to his Utemä with its sheath of red and black leather. The sight of him wearing Morgan's trademark colors made me want to snatch the blade and throw it into a bottomless trench.

"Do you recall how Morgan was poaching recruits from Kasi—the recruits that failed in their training?" Wilder asked me.

That was such an unexpected turn in the conversation that it took me a few seconds to catch up. "Yes." I elongated the word, giving myself time to think. "She was going to have them retrained and put in the Solar army."

"I discovered she was placing them in the Kula." Wilder continued, his eyes never leaving mine. "Do you remember what that is?"

"It's a training exercise where fae hunt down human recruits, and if they can find them, they're allowed to torture them," I said bleakly. "I actually saw you arguing with Morgan about it a week or so ago."

Wilder's face slackened in shock.

"I can dreamwalk," I explained. "I've only managed to do it a few times though."

"Dreamwalking, eh?" Cai lifted my mood with a waggle of his eyebrows. "Isn't that one of those gifts that allows you to spy on people? Should I be dressing in the dark from now on?"

I jabbed his arm with my pointy elbow.

"As if she'd want to see your dangly bits," Liora quipped.

"Excuse me," Cai protested. "I've got very nice—"

"Is there more to this story, Wilder?" Frazer asked, raising his voice.

Never losing his dignified air, Wilder nodded. "The fact that Morgan was using weaker recruits for target practice didn't surprise me. But I did find it odd when she kept increasing the difficulty of the Kula. For somebody who's long been obsessed with boosting our numbers should Abraxus invade, it didn't make sense for her to encourage an all-out slaughter on the humans. I poked about in a few holes, literally, and discovered that those who'd died in the Kula were being collected and taken to a hideout outside of the palace."

My feathers itched as if I'd contracted lice.

"Morgan found me out," Wilder said, looking as if he had a bad taste in his mouth. "And instead of punishing me, she told me exactly what she was doing and took great pleasure in it."

Bear proved the most impatient. "What was she doing with them?"

He grimaced, his cheek scars whitening with the action. "She's experimenting on their bodies. Her ultimate goal is to wipe out all the humans. In their place, she plans to raise mindless corpses under her command."

His revelation was a lightning rod: our entire group was shocked.

"Are you certain she was telling you the truth?" Lynx demanded, his eyes flaring with an almost reddish haze.

"I wouldn't say it if I wasn't." Wilder's profile became leonine in nature. Fierce and prideful. "I saw her experiments for myself. She's got shamans trapping traumatized souls in empty bodies, and then her necromancers reanimate the corpses. They haven't yet figured out how to control spirits en masse. But as soon as they do …"

He didn't have to finish that sentence. Horror rocked me.

"That bitch." Cai's chest heaved. "That *fucking* bitch."

I grasped his outer wrist. "We won't let her do this."

"No. We won't." Liora's voice resembled fire and brimstone.

I eyed her shaking form and flickering features. Holy fire. Was she about to shift?

Owl hurried to her side. He spun her toward him and gripped both her arms. The look he gave her was indescribable. Understanding. Knowing. Promising. Whatever it was, it calmed the beast under her skin.

Ears red with rage, Cai went on. "The covens won't stand for this. They can't. There are too many humans in their ranks."

His words were certain, but in his voice doubt lingered. I floundered, feeling sick to my stomach.

"We're getting ahead of ourselves," Frazer warned.

A knock disturbed us.

Bear stepped away from the table. "That'll be one of the scouts. I asked them to report here if there were any developments."

He stalked off toward the doors.

"Scouts?" I posed that question to the group.

Wilder explained. "Owl's got a few people watching the legion for us."

"Cai spelled the Fiends to silence," Adrianna said harshly. "So they can't betray our secrets now, even if they wanted to."

I glanced at Owl for his reaction. His white and brown wings grew rigid against his spine, but his attention was reserved solely for his mate. I tracked his gaze to where Bear met another fae at the entrance. Their brief exchange made my scalp nettle in alarm.

"Well, that's unfortunate," Ryder piped up.

"What is it?" Cai asked, a tad sharp for him.

"Twelve spiders have left the legion and are headed this way," Lynx relayed. "They'll be coming to spy on the situation here."

Bear returned to the table. Not bothering to ask if we'd overheard his conversation, he waded in. "Any ideas on how to handle this?"

Lynx was the first to respond. "I'll intercept them," he said without pride or pleasure. "I can pass on the message that we've taken the castle, and that Morgan's soldiers aren't welcome."

Wilder scowled. "That's like waving a flag under a bull's nose."

"What's the alternative?" Lynx asked, as colorless as the rain.

"I can meet with them," Wilder replied. "I was their leader; their guard will be down around me, enough that an ambush might work. The legion will send more spiders when this group doesn't report back, but it might buy us a day."

"The element of surprise won't last long if you attack them," Lynx pointed out. "And if any of them are combative witches, you'll be shit out of luck."

Wilder glowered at Lynx. "You think it's my first time facing off against witches, *boy*?"

I expected feathers to start flying. Lynx freed a whisper of a laugh instead. "You do realize my mate, the female you're lusting after, is younger than me? Do you call her girl?"

"Damn." Cai sounded almost impressed.

I poked him with my elbow again.

He had the decency to look somewhat apologetic.

Wilder turned positively lethal. "Later."

Lynx nodded nonchalantly. What the rats did that mean?

I was edging near panic when Frazer intervened. "An ambush puts you and others at risk. Lynx should be the one to go. His power level should unnerve them enough that they won't attack. And the news that he's switched sides will create chaos among the leaders of the legion. That's more likely to buy us time than a few missing spiders."

My brother's logic silenced everybody's doubts. Even Wilder's.

Cai spoke up. "He can't go alone, though. What if the spiders are tempted to test the size of their magical balls against the Dark Prince? He can't take on twelve, surely?"

I tensed at his usage of Lynx's less than flattering moniker.

"I'll be fine," Lynx said. Untroubled. Calm.

Adrianna snorted out a noise of contempt. "You always were as arrogant as a cat-loving mouse."

He shot her a half-smile. "And you were always as blunt as a wooden spoon."

That elicited a pursing of her lips. "I'll go with you."

"That's not—"

"That wasn't a suggestion," Adrianna argued. "I'm keeping an eye on you whether you like it or not."

"If you're by my side that sends a message about the Riverlands involvement in reclaiming Mysaya," Lynx pointed out.

Adrianna remained an immovable force. "The time for maintaining my court's image as a neutral party has passed. The legion already knows Diana is marching toward them with her army. If that doesn't say we're rebels, I don't know what does."

I assumed Wilder must've told her about Diana's movements while I slept.

"Fine," Lynx said to Adrianna. "Just don't slow me down."

Surprisingly, Adrianna only rolled her eyes.

"Okay. We've all got jobs to do," Frazer declared, his sudden burst of tiredness seeping through our kin bond. "Let's get on with them."

Wilder was already moving for the exit. "Cai, Bear, you're with me."

Cai gathered me up in another hug. His other arm extended out, beckoning Liora in. She joined our embrace.

"You two need to sleep more," I said to their worn faces.

Cai pinched my cheek. "Stop worrying. You'll get wrinkles."

I batted his fingers away, playing at being grumpy. He freed a chuckle before running after Bear and Wilder. The three of them were to team up and prepare the castle and the Fiends for battle. Adrianna followed them partway to the doors. She stopped and peered over her shoulder at Lynx. "Are you coming or not?"

My gaze skipped to him. Lynx hadn't taken a step in her direction. As soon as I caught him staring at me, I realized he'd been waiting to say goodbye.

Nerves bounced around my stomach, unsettling it. "Be careful."

A lopsided smile answered. "I always am."

How did I know that was a lie?

"I'll see you when I get back." He walked off, lengthening his stride to reach Adrianna.

"They'll be okay," Liora said to me.

Unable to speak, I faced Frazer. He'd huddled together with Owl and Ryder. They were already discussing what they should say to the Aurorian Sami.

Five seconds passed. Frazer didn't look up.

My paper heart crumpled.

"Do you mind if I join you in the kitchens?" Liora asked me as she fired a highly resentful look at an oblivious Frazer.

"No," I said, pushing down the sadness crawling up my throat. "But I thought you were headed to the ward."

"I'm starving," she confessed. "I don't think I've eaten properly in days. And neither have you."

She slipped her hand through the slender crook of my arm.

My eyebrow twitched up a notch. "I see right through you, you know. You're coming with me because you've decided I'm your next patient. What are you going to do? Force-feed me?"

"Will I have to?" she asked, steering me toward the doors.

"No."

She tacked on, "I really am hungry."

"You'll have to fight me if there's any chocolate."

Liora's reply was a pixyish smile.

"I'm being serious."

Her grin widened. "I know, siska."

My heart itched.

At the doors, we quit that stately room having taken our first steps toward war. Neither Liora nor I looked back.

CHAPTER 38
THE CLASHING OF WARRIORS

I spent the afternoon toiling away in the west wing kitchen. Mercifully, I'd two assistants—Squirrel and Fox—to help me cook for the sixty-plus people currently in Mysaya.

Five hours into my labors, Ryder and Lynx walked in.

As I put my knife down on the chopping board, I noticed Squirrel casting a wary glance at Lynx. Judging by that, he hadn't earned much trust, regardless of recent actions.

"We've come in search of food," Ryder said with a wide grin.

That cheerful greeting failed to divert me from the expression on Lynx's face. It was grimmer than a gravedigger's. "How did it go with the spiders?"

He situated himself across from me, resting his forearms on the kitchen island counter that separated us. "They attacked us." Noticing my alarm, he added, "Adrianna's fine. We both are. The spiders fled after they got a few battle scars. I have a feeling that's all they wanted."

"What d'you mean?" I asked, frowning.

"They were probably worried about returning to the legion without evidence that they'd tried to capture me," he said, looking absorbed by recent memories. "They wouldn't want to be accused of letting a traitor go. The Solar Army has whipped people to death for less."

I winced. "Did you get to tell them that we've taken Mysaya?"

A nod. "Of course."

That was that, then. No going back now.

Ryder pointed at the six golden-crusted pies cooling on metal racks. "You're not saving those for anybody, are you?"

"Help yourself." I bumped my chin at them. "There's also rabbit stew warming in the oven."

Ryder stuck his nose up. "Where's the chicken soup?"

"Fox has taken it up to Liora's patients."

A pout. "Oh."

"Did you send word to the Sami?" I asked him.

"Mm," was his only reply.

I couldn't tell if he was reluctant or too occupied by his empty belly to elaborate. Either way, I chose to leave him to it. I went back to slicing up mushrooms.

With his plate heaped high, Ryder raised it to me in a salute. "Thanks for this." He was already shoveling food into his mouth when he left the kitchen.

Lynx filled a bowl with stew and slid it toward me.

"What's this for?"

"For you to eat."

"I ate earlier."

"Not enough."

I shot him a sassy look. "How would you know?"

"I ran into Frazer."

My heart twanged, playing a melancholy note. Even when Frazer was angry at me, he couldn't stop playing the role of older brother.

"He said he could still feel your hunger," Lynx mentioned.

"Maybe he's the one who's hungry." I decapitated a mushroom with a sharp *thunk*. "Has he thought about that?"

"I asked him the same question," Lynx replied temperately. "He said he'd already raided the food supplies in the castle's storehouse and eaten until he felt sick."

Anger burst into my bloodstream. "So he'd rather go to a damned storehouse than come here? He's really determined to avoid me, isn't he?"

"He'll get over it." Lynx nudged the bowl closer to me.

Keen to hide the emotions playing across my face, I turned and strode up to the oven, chopping board in hand.

Squirrel appeared at my side before I could scrape the fungi into the pan. "I'll do this," she offered in her flute-like voice.

I hesitated. "Are you sure?"

"You insisted that we take a break earlier whilst refusing to take one for yourself," she reasoned, taking the board from me before I could think twice. "It's your turn."

Logic paid me a visit. It cooled my frustrations, forcing me to recognize that my feet were heavier than stones and my tongue drier than parchment. The intense heat from the ovens had made me dizzy more than once, even with the fancy ventilation system sucking in fragrant air from the herb garden outside.

I joined Lynx at the island to find him eating from my bowl. "Wasn't that meant to be mine?"

He handed me his spoon with a shameless smile. "I figured we'd share to save on the dishes."

I took the spoon with a sigh. The first bite of the rabbit stew was a surprise. It was good—*really* good. I drank in joy and pride like sunshine-ripened wine.

Over the course of a minute or two, Lynx touched me about a dozen times. A hip bump. A finger graze. A wing clip. I watched his side profile, searching for signs of his intentions, and in turn found myself admiring his sooty lashes, wayward strands of hair, and the natural curvature of his gentle mouth.

"You're staring at me," he murmured, his eyes on the stew.

"I'm glaring."

His lips curled up in a close-mouthed smile. "If you say so."

That irritated me more than a bug bite ever could.

"This is delicious, by the way." Lynx's gaze slid to mine.

His irises appeared brighter in the kitchen lights. More of a honey-brown than a whiskey. I fell into a soft place.

Then, footsteps.

My focus flew to the door as it swung open. Wilder strode in.

The air grew thin. I muttered a tiny, pathetic, "Hi."

His eyes darted from me to Lynx to the lack of space between us. Lastly, he glanced at the single spoon and shared bowl. His jaw stiffened just slightly as he absorbed the scene. He pushed back his shoulders and focused on me. In an even tone, he said, "I've been thinking that we could benefit from a few sparring sessions. Cai, Liora, and Adrianna have already agreed to join us. I couldn't find Frazer."

"Am I invited?" Lynx straightened up to his full height.

Rutting hell. The last thing I wanted was for them to be in the same room together, especially one with weapons and an open invitation to fight each other.

Wilder didn't bat an eyelash. "No, but I doubt that will stop you."

"You're right," Lynx answered in clipped notes. "It won't."

Wilder grasped the hilt of his garish Utemä.

"I have your sword," I blurted out. "You should take it back. I'm sure it cost a lot."

"It's yours," Wilder insisted.

Oh ... "Thanks." I wet my lips. "As for sparring, I've still got work I need to do here."

Squirrel piped up from behind me. "Fox and I can handle the rest. We're almost finished with the dinner, anyway."

I glanced over my shoulder at her. "Why do I get the feeling you want me to leave?"

"It's not you," Lynx said under his breath.

The look on his face was that of a male used to being shunned. My ribs constricted, trying to contain the ache that sparked beneath them.

"I've loved working with you," Squirrel told me, her plump cheeks tomato red. "But you shouldn't miss a chance to train with a Sabu."

Her encouragement tore through my feeble attempts to avoid conflict. Meeting Wilder's stoic attentions, I forced a smile. "Okay."

I retrieved my sword from where I'd stored it and secured it to my hip.

Leaving the kitchen, I stretched out my legs to keep in step with Wilder and Lynx. To call that moment awkward would've been an understatement. I wanted to hide behind my wings.

In strained silence, we walked the length of a corridor, up two staircases, and through a door into an expansive room. Exercise apparatus lined the back wall, and mats cushioned sections of the wooden floor.

Currently, Cai, Liora, and Adrianna were running wall to wall. Our racing one another had been a common occurrence at Kasi. Even without Frazer present, it was a comforting sight. Our pack had undergone a lot of change, but some things remained the same.

I laid down my sword and went to join them.

Once upon a time, Cai would've consistently taken the lead. Now, wings tucked in tight, I pulled ahead of him. That remained the case round after round. The fae strength fueling my lithe frame, in addition to the stamina built from fighting and flying, served me well.

"Take a breather," Wilder called out from the sidelines.

Cai crouched, wiping his damp brow, panting heavily. "This is unacceptable. When did you get so fast?"

I smirked at his incredulity. "Jealous?"

"Very." He hopped up, slapping his thighs and arms to keep the blood flowing. "I'd better get a powerful familiar, otherwise I'll end up being the lame duck in our fivesome."

Adrianna retrieved a water bottle from the edge of the mat. "If that's what you think, why haven't you tried the summoning spell?"

A careless half-shrug. "I will. Just not before the battle. I want to make sure it can defend itself first."

"I'm putting a bet on it being a peacock." Liora grinned.

In a show of false dignity, Cai lifted his chin high. "They happen to be very noble birds."

Adrianna frowned. "We had a few of those floating around Kastella. They always sounded like strangled chickens to me."

Cai's face fell.

Liora laughed freely. The sound reminded me of a branch shaken loose of powdery snow, and in the process of shedding its wintery coat, it found itself lighter.

"I'm going to lead you all in a level four venyetä practice." Wilder strode up and dropped a bag of blunted swords in our vicinity. "Then we'll take turns sparring with one another."

Facing outward, Wilder transitioned into a rising sun position. I willed myself not to get distracted by Lynx, who was standing out in front of us, watching me.

I copied Wilder's movements, which gradually increased in difficulty and culminated in a headstand. While attempting to replicate that pose, I collapsed onto the mat in a heap of tangled limbs.

Lynx approached and offered me a hand. I grabbed it, and he hauled me up.

Amber eyes connected with mine. "Ready to move on?"

My mouth opened in a gormless way. "To what?"

"To sparring with me."

Wilder closed the gap between us. "If you insist on joining us, then partner me."

His words clanged up against my ribcage; the resulting shocks rattled me.

"Later," Lynx replied in a voice that managed to sound provoking, despite its deliberate calmness. "Ena and I should fight first."

"How come?" I asked.

"Magical bouts require more energy than sparring with weapons or fists alone, so our practice takes priority."

Wilder said nothing, unable to find fault with his reasoning.

"Have you done any training in magical combat?" Lynx asked me.

My "Yes," was so definite that it caused Lynx and Wilder to stare.

"Thea and Zola have been visiting my dreams and teaching me there," I clarified. "And by Thea and Zola, I mean the firstborn goddesses."

Their shock paused our conversation. The silence was broken by Adrianna. "Cai, how would you feel about me throwing swords at you?"

"Why?" His tone sounded more curious than worried.

"Because he's right," she added without specifying who "he" was. "We should focus on magical training first."

I side-glanced at Adrianna.

"I'll guide the swords toward you with my metallurgy." She massaged and shook out her hands. "And you can deflect them with your air-bursts."

"You do remember that I can't heal severed limbs?" Liora was stern, her sisterly instincts on display.

"That's why we're using blunt blades." Adrianna picked out four swords of varying lengths from the bag on the floor. "I suppose there's a chance I might break his bones. But you can heal those, and it'll be a good lesson for the pretty peacock."

"Lesson?" Cai raised an eyebrow.

"The memory of the pain will serve as a reminder that you need to practice more," Adrianna replied as if that was a completely acceptable way of thinking.

"That doesn't sound fair," he mused, crossing his arms. "How about when I'm not deflecting swords, I'll attack you and Liora with airstrikes? If you can't dodge them, your bruises from being knocked onto your ass can remind you both to work harder."

Adrianna snorted out a feminine sound of confidence. "Fine by me."

"Mark your words," Cai replied solemnly.

The two of them moved onto the next mat over to begin their training. Liora followed, shaking her head. I could've sworn I heard her mutter, "Moon-mad, the both of them."

"Ena?" Lynx prompted me.

I felt my pulse jump in my throat. "Okay. Let's fight."

Lynx picked up two practice swords and passed one off to me. Avoiding Wilder's gaze, I walked away from him and only stopped when I reached a mat that bordered the wall.

"You good?" Lynx asked, joining my side.

I turned toward him, assumed a defensive stance, and nodded.

The tingling in my spine warned me that his magic was surging. I conjured a hasty moon-shield as he flicked his wrist at me. As planned, my barrier absorbed his lightning. It also shattered, and the strength behind his attack threw me off-balance.

Energy surging through my veins, I quickly stabilized and rearranged my features into a feral look.

He gave me a crooked smile in return. I advanced, swinging my blade.

We crossed swords. The dull steel rang out from the impact, irritating my ears.

Lynx swept his foot out, kicking my legs out from under me. I rotated my body, landing on my front and protecting my wings. Not giving him a chance to seize his advantage, I rolled forward and sprang back up.

Lynx went on the attack. It quickly became obvious I'd have to adjust my tactics and expectations. I'd assumed Lynx would fight as most big males did, relying on strength and superior reach to defeat his opponent. But Lynx could've rivaled Frazer for speed and agility. I was severely outmatched. I couldn't win against a reed in the wind.

Lynx executed a vertical strike. I barely got my blade up in time to block him. As we stood, his sword covering mine, he asked, "Why are you holding back?"

I rolled my weight onto my other hip and spun out of the bind. "I'm not."

"Yes, you are," Lynx insisted.

My secondary canines cut down.

He smiled. "Has anybody ever told you that your fangs are adorable?"

I wanted to smack him with my wing and have him spitting feathers.

Lynx turned somber. "Come on, Ena. You don't have to worry about hurting me. Our magic doesn't work properly against each other, remember?"

It felt as if he was tugging at something deep inside of me, a cage door that he was determined to pry open.

Hesitation will get you killed on a battlefield. Do it, Zola commanded.

I shaped my hand into an eagle's claw and struck outward. At the last second, I splayed my fingers, launching a fireball in his direction. The backdraft was so hot it made my eyes prickle.

My citrine-colored sunlight slammed into his upper half. The sparks flared hungrily, devouring his blue shirt. My heart aflame, I watched him drop his sword and tear his shirt off. He stamped out the flames on the mat.

As expected, the sunstone woke up. If it'd been a dragon, it would've been roaring, snapping its teeth at me, its tail bludgeoning the earth. I summoned a river of waterlight that created a protective barrier in my blood, dampening the sunstone's will.

Lynx tossed his ruined shirt into a corner.

Was getting him to go shirtless intentional or just an unforeseen benefit? Zola asked me.

I pictured a filthy gesture in my mind.

Zola snorted at me. *Weak.*

"Not bad," Lynx said, dusting off his hands. "But we can do better."

No chance to respond. He winked and vanished.

Lynx was hiding in the shadows, and I had to find him.

Darkling magic's weakness was its twin soul, starlight. I channeled that cold brightness through my right palm. It didn't matter that it wasn't particularly strong. Lynx's silhouette appeared no more than a few feet away.

Expanding his night-black aura, he entombed me in darkness.

I tried to throw off the gloom, but it was as immovable as a mountain. Another strategy was needed. Extinguishing my starlight, I tugged in a thread of chaos. I sent it toward Lynx in a snake-like stream.

A chorus of voices rose up, their unintelligible words an itch in my ears. Suddenly, Lynx's darkness dispersed. There he was again, watching me, his expression strained. Both mindful and wary. I wasn't even sure what I'd done.

I stoppered my chaos. With that, the voices faded.

"Do you need to stop?" I asked Lynx.

Face clearing, he shifted into a defensive stance. "No."

Fine.

As he was beyond the reach of my sword, I tossed it aside. Before he could retaliate, I dropped into my hips and performed a double fist punch.

My fireballs barreled into his torso. Those fingers of flame vanished, absorbed by his skin. He straightened up, switching into a relaxed pose. "You're stronger than this."

Sweat and irritation stung my eyes. "You can't know that."

"Yes I can," he said, serious-mouthed. "You're my mate. My equal."

"Meaning?"

"Your power is a match for my own."

I smothered my sunlight, but not my frustration. Baring my fangs, I freed a sound more animal than fae. "Then show me what you think I'm capable of."

His head cocked.

I got blown off my feet by his palm-strike.

Arms cradling my skull, I landed softer than I should have. In my periphery, I spotted a few of Lynx's shadows sneaking away.

Scuffled footsteps. People running.

Adrianna, Liora, and Cai rallied around me.

"Are you hurt?" Liora crouched down to my eye level.

I got up. "No. I'm—"

"What the fuck do you think you're doing?" Wilder growled. "You could've broken her spine or her wings."

My gaze darted to the center of the mat where Wilder and Lynx were in each other's faces.

"I softened her fall," Lynx said coldly.

"I'm fine," I yelled out.

Wilder backed up. A person less familiar with him might've assumed he was conceding. But I knew differently. Sure enough, Wilder freed his fangs.

Lynx nodded, almost formally. "Is this it, then?"

"No magic. No swords," Wilder demanded.

Lynx flashed him a smile designed to aggravate. "I don't need either."

The males began to circle each other, moving in a predatory manner, every step carefully placed, their eyes never leaving their rival's.

In a display of dominance, Wilder flared his fir-green wings. Lynx stretched out his larger wings. His grin seemed to say *Eat shit*.

That action was a stone cast upon loose mountain snow. They exploded forward, colliding with the force of an avalanche. Each blow traded looked capable of breaking bones and severing wings.

As they moved around the mat, I spied dozens of intersecting scars marking the skin of Lynx's back. They could only have been made by a whip, and one wielded by a ruthless and brutal hand. Shock slammed into me.

"By the moons, who did that to him?" Liora breathed.

Adrianna replied, "Morgan, probably." A modicum of pity seemed to touch her countenance.

The sight of his scars had softened my heart. But my sorrow was consumed by frustration; my sympathy hardened into anger upon watching my mate and guardian fight each other. "Are they crazy? They could kill each other."

"They were going to fight eventually," Adrianna remarked, adopting a philosophical attitude. "You can't have two alphas in a pack."

"Don't worry so much." Cai squeezed my shoulder once. "It's better they work this out rather than let their anger fester like root rot."

"Agreed." Adrianna's head did a funny little tilt as she watched them, her long plait swinging over tidy wings. "And in the meantime, you may as well enjoy the view."

Blood rising, I glowered at her. "What does that mean?"

"A match between two famed warriors"—she motioned to Lynx and Wilder—"people would pay good money to see this."

"I think I might be getting a bit turned on," Cai stage-whispered to Adrianna, who snorted in appreciation of his joke.

Liora smacked her brother on the arm.

My next exhale coincided with Lynx kicking Wilder in the belly.

Wilder stumbled. He recovered in a blink, using his body's momentum to twist and raise his leg up into a spinning heel kick, clipping Lynx in the throat. He clutched at his neck, wincing and choking.

Wilder struck out at Lynx again.

Panic fired through my nerves. "Stop!"

Wilder froze immediately, as if I'd jerked on strings attached to his limbs. His forest-greens cut to me accusingly. I'd given him a command, and I'd meant it. Shame sloshed around my belly. "I'm sorry," I said, shaking my head. "I wasn't trying to control you."

He thawed. "It's not your fau—"

Lynx punched Wilder's jaw.

I couldn't watch anymore. Burning with indignation, I exited the room without a destination in mind. I only knew I had to keep moving, or I'd explode.

Leaving the west wing behind, I walked until I stumbled upon a branch of the castle inch-thick in dust, where cobwebs trailed from chandeliers in the style of wisteria tendrils, and countless narrative artworks hung grubby in their frames.

My restless feet brought me to side-by-side doors of ceiling height. One of these heavy doors was slightly ajar, its ancient lock damaged beyond repair.

Just then, the scent of my brother hit me like a hammer to my nose. It wasn't a surprise to learn I'd unconsciously sought him out. It also wasn't shocking that Frazer was already moving off in the opposite direction. I didn't bother going after him. He didn't want to see me.

The question as to why he'd been here niggled at me, though. I slunk through the crack in the doors and discovered a library. And what a library it was.

Breath catching, I tried to take it all in.

A wide path extended outward. On either side of me, rows of bookcases were guarded by pillars crafted in the image of the loula trees.

These flawless statues colored silver and white, adorned with merry firelight lanterns, towered high above me, each of their petrified branches marking the beginning of another mezzanine level.

I wandered forward, drifting deeper into the library's cavernous depths.

Beneath me, the floor was impossibly smooth, with no interlinking cracks. I couldn't have named the material used, but it acted like reflective black glass. On its surface, I could see myself and the artwork above me; the ceiling was a pictorial view of the night sky, speckled with distant stars, glowing constellations, and luminous clouds. The colors were otherworldly in their intensity, masterful in their detailing.

The path opened up into a circular space that served as an axis point for adjoining passageways. Overhead was a large eight-pointed star suspended from a beam. It seemed to be filled with liquid starlight, and as it rotated slowly in midair, it bled shadows and flecks of snowflake-fire.

I twirled on the spot, taking in the view. The higher levels were bordered by brass railings, and accessible via a spiral staircase and several landing platforms, which ensured fae could fly up there if they chose.

Seeing an opportunity to practice my takeoffs without an audience, I spread my wings and took a running leap. My muscles and joints protested from the abuse as I climbed upward.

Idiot, I scolded myself. I should've warmed up my wings.

Lacking control, I stumbled onto the first platform. From there, I got lost in the stacks, passing more books than there were stars in the sky, and staring at numerous wonders. My favorites were a clockwork violin and the countless moths flitting about, their wings shining in the dusky light. I detected trace elements of magic in their origins, but the purpose of such creatures was a riddle.

I came to a natural stop. My heart had grown calm, the chaos from before forgotten. I traced my fingertips along the suspiciously clean bookshelf and the inky treasures it contained. There were scrolls made of bamboo slips, tomb-thick codices, and books so valuable they were chained up.

I sat on the black-glass flooring, my feathers against the bookshelf, and inhaled deeply. That bookish scent tugged on a string from my past.

I was a child again, snuggled in my bed, listening to my mother's voice as she read to me. Amidst these tomes, I felt at home. I could never be lonely here. Not with so many escape hatches surrounding me, each of them a door into another world, a window into a life unlived, and a road that would lead me to new people.

At that thought, I twisted around and scanned for a title in the common tongue. Finding one, I pulled it off the shelf and propped it on my lap. The sharp crack of the spine hurt my internal organs. How long had this book been left unloved, gathering years of neglect on yellowing pages?

I disappeared into a tale of foreign kingdoms, not counting the minutes that sped by.

"Hello?"

I jumped, freeing an embarrassing squeak.

My head swiveled to the right. Wilder rounded a corner, emerging from out of the stacks. He halted, hesitating. "Would you prefer to be alone?"

He sounded uncertain, unusual for him.

I hedged. "How did you find me?"

"Your scent."

I put my book aside.

Taking that as an invitation, he padded over and sat in front of me. I met eyes the color of pine needles under a summer sun—a forest that I'd once gotten lost in.

The silence that separated us hinted at the last breath taken before plunging into deep water. Wilder dove in first. "I can't get used to seeing that."

My lips unglued. "Seeing what?"

"The purple eyes." His expression opened up. "Or these."

He extended a hand toward my downy wing. Feathers prickling and rising, I leaned away from him.

"They're beautiful." His sun-kissed hand retreated, and it seemed to me that disappointment bracketed his face.

I loosened my wings up in a mini flutter. "Sorry. It feels strange to let someone touch them."

A stilted pause. "Are you all right, Serena?"

At the sound of my full name, my past and present collided. He even rolled the "R" in the way I remembered.

I pushed out, "Not really."

The pebble in his throat jolted.

"Why did you attack Lynx?"

"He hurt you." A harsh response.

"His shadows caught me before I hit the floor."

"That's not the point."

My impatience ticked upward. "Then what is your point? Because you can't pretend you've never hurt me during our sparring sessions. If you never went easy on me, why should you expect him to?"

"That was different."

"Why?"

Memories haunted his eyes. "Because I've seen Lynx at full power. The magic he channeled was so wild, he almost lost control of it. If he does that around you, the aftermath could kill you. He's dangerous, Serena."

"The same could be said about me," I admitted.

His lips parted soundlessly. I'd stumped him.

"We've got enough enemies as it is," I reasoned. "If we fight amongst ourselves, we'll lose before we've even begun."

A curt nod. "It won't happen again. But you need to know our bond has changed me." At the sight of my frown, he continued. "I can't sense when you're in danger yet, but my instinct to protect you magnified tenfold when I became your guardian. It's why I killed Hunter instead of injuring him."

Guilt twinged my midsection. "Are you blaming me for that?"

A startled blink. "Gods, no. I just needed to explain that there was more going on with me when I attacked Lynx." He clenched his teeth so hard I half expected to hear them crack. "Although, I freely admit that I hate the sight of him."

Frustration and anxiety clashed within me. "Why?"

"Because he's your mate."

"That's not fair. He didn't choose that."

"Neither did you."

My brain shriveled up. "What are you saying?"

"I'm saying that I love you," he confessed, his whiskey-drinker's voice intense. "And I want you to pick me."

Breathe. "I can't do this right now, with you or with him."

His wings shifted. "Are you trying to let me down easy?"

"That's not it," I said, sharper than broken glass.

Isn't it? Zola questioned.

My palm tingled. I wanted to slap her. Zola countered with a bored cat-hiss.

"Are you confused about whom to pick?" Wilder's tone was composed, and his gaze was steady, almost unlively.

My mood turned thorny. "Don't you get it? I don't want to get closer to anyone."

There. I'd said it.

"You told me once that exploring our feelings for each other would make us vulnerable to people like Morgan. I called you a coward for it." I winced at the memory. "But you were right."

The line of his lip tightened.

"The best way to control me is through the people I care about," I stated plainly. "That's what I'm scared of. It's not our enemies' strength. It's how they aim for your heart and don't stop until they tear it right out of you." I ended thinking about Archon, about how he'd punished Abraxus for his betrayal not by killing him, but by kidnapping his daughter and murdering his wife.

Wilder's head tilted toward the ceiling. He gazed up at an artist's vision of the night sky, his shoulders rising and falling, his nostrils whitening as his lungs pushed out a sigh.

"Losing people we care for is the worst part of life," he admitted, his gaze dropping to me. "It's why elder fae find it so difficult to enter into relationships. We remember the hurts that've gone before, and what it is to have our hearts broken. That's why I couldn't tell you that I loved you at Kasi ... I pushed you away because love is more than a declaration to fae. It's a promise of a future together. And I had nothing to offer you. I was a disgraced Sabu. But when I woke up in that dungeon in Alexandria, I realized how stupid I'd been. Being scared of getting hurt wasn't a good enough reason to avoid the best part of living."

My eyes heated at the corners. His confession had patched an old wound, one made when he'd pushed me away. All the same, it hadn't changed my mind.

Wilder caught me in a straight-on stare. "I'm not giving up on you."

Softly, I said, "And if I choose Lynx?"

"Then so be it," he answered roughly. "But I won't leave you. I swore to protect you, and I will, until the last breath leaves my body."

I struggled with that like a fly in a web. "Why? I've done nothing to earn that kind of loyalty."

"I disagree," he said, taking on a firm tone. "You've the power to do real good in this world, valo. And I want to help you do it."

Valo. That word churned up my insides. He had called me by the moniker before. It meant the light of the heavenly stars.

"All I ask is that if things change, tell me. Even if it's not what I want to hear."

"I promise," I murmured.

"Good." Clean. Uncomplicated.

That unwavering display of loyalty inspired me. "There's something I need to tell you."

I tugged my necklaces out to show him. Wilder's attentions drifted to where they lay on top of my black shirt. I launched into an explanation about the stones' role in destroying Archon, and their locations. When I got to the part about my connection to them and the task ahead of me, it was all I could do to fight past the knot in my throat. As I reached the end of my tale, Wilder slipped into a reflective state, his strong palms cupping his knees, his eyelids lowering to half-mast.

I waited, the seconds lengthening into minutes.

"I'm not sure what to say," he finally said, his voice pitched low.

A feeble laugh left me. "I don't blame you."

His gaze leveled me. "I'll be there. Through all of it."

Language abandoned me.

Wilder joined my side. The scents of pine, pepper, and coffee swept into my lungs. I felt safer.

As we sat together, not saying anything, Wilder's breathing deepened and his head dropped onto my shoulder. He must've been exhausted to fall asleep so easily. Left to my own devices, my brain rebelled, spitting out memories of intimate moments we'd shared. I diligently snuffed them out, one by one, like a candle flame before a breath.

A disturbance of light interrupted my thoughts.

I slowly turned my head, careful not to disturb Wilder. Looking out, I scanned a spot to the left of me. The moths were nowhere to be seen; the hanging lanterns above me were motionless. And still, a large shadow prowled along the bookshelf opposite.

Lynx. It had to be.

Tension and guilt constricted my chest. Lynx was probably viewing this, thinking I'd taken Wilder's side after the fight. I went on the defensive. "I hope you won't use your tricks to sneak into my room. A locked door means don't come in; I could be undressing."

His shadow grew smaller as he stepped toward me and ducked down. My mousy murmur got a response. "I wouldn't violate your privacy like that. But I can't swear to never imagine you naked. Is that a problem for you?"

A flush crept up my neck.

I thought about saying yes, but I could tell his flirtation was a mask for his uncertainty. He wanted to know if things had changed. If I blamed him for the fight. That thought was what made me shake my head.

"Good."

He dropped a quick kiss on my brow. My mouth opened, but I had no idea what to say.

Lynx's shadow vanished, leaving only a whisper of his warmth behind.

After a blank moment, I rested my cheek atop Wilder's head. I'd have to return to the kitchen or the training room soon. But for now at least, I was content to hide from the world in a quiet, forgotten corner of a library.

CHAPTER 39
SCREAMS IN THE NIGHT

Later that day, as night hooded the castle and everyone had retired to their quarters, I fretted that we'd received no news from Diana or Sefra. Long after Adrianna had fallen asleep next to me, I gazed up at the ceiling with only grim thoughts and a solitary lantern for company.

I was considering getting up when spider-tingles scuttled up my spine in a warning. A rumble of thunder echoed distantly above me.

I sat up and peered out the window. The sky was a serene black; its only visitors were the stars.

Adrianna rose to a seated position.

"You're awake," I remarked dumbly.

"I never fell asleep." Adrianna viewed the world outside. "There isn't a cloud in sight."

"I think it's Lynx," I said.

Tension radiated from her side of the bed. "You think, or you know?"

More faint thunder sounded. The thrill rushing through my blood confirmed it was Lynx's doing. His magic already felt familiar.

I threw the covers off. "I'm going to go check on him."

"Not alone."

Too preoccupied to argue over her blatant distrust of Lynx, I shoved my feet into shoes and strapped my sword belt over my stretched-out leggings.

Adrianna approached my flank, her blade secured at her waist.

Knock, knock.

"It's me," came Frazer's soft assurance.

I hurried over and gripped the handle. The anti-intruder spell Lynx had placed on our bedroom doors brushed over my skin, seeking to confirm whether I was somebody it had been made to recognize. Its acknowledgment resonated through me, feeling like the quiver in a web right before it broke.

I opened the door out into the foyer. Frazer and Cai waited for us there.

"I felt your worry," Frazer said by way of an explanation.

It shocked me to find him looking so drained. His lips lacked color, and his under-eyes were marked by exhaustion. My mind flew back to when I'd last seen him at the round table. He definitely hadn't seemed this worn out.

"Are you o—okay?" Cai asked, struggling around a yawn.

Before I could answer, Liora and Ryder joined us.

"Something's wrong, isn't it?" Liora shuddered, pulling on the edges of the blanket she'd thrown around her shoulders. "It feels as if the whole castle's turned against us."

Adrianna's puckered brow hinted at concern. "Is this your empathy talking?"

Liora's nod confused me. Was Lynx angry about something?

"If we're about to be attacked, could we persuade them to try again once we've gotten more sleep?" Cai rubbed his bleary eyes.

Thunder resonated weakly throughout the castle's foundations. That stirred me into action. I marched out into the corridor with the others nipping at my heels.

Wilder approached me in unlaced boots. "I was coming to check on you. Is it Lynx making those ungodly sounds?"

"Yes."

"His room's this way." Frazer twisted his wrist to the left.

Our group followed him up a level and along the fourth-floor corridor.

"Go away!"

Lynx's shout severed me from restraint. I sprinted toward his voice.

Frazer hauled me back before I could crash through a door. "Lynx's apartment is protected by a magical barrier. It has been since he was born. You can't just walk in. You have to be invited."

"Leave," Lynx roared from the room beyond.

Panic spurred my pulse. "Is he being attacked?"

"No." Frazer had a strange look on his face. "Even if an assassin could get in there, he wouldn't be shouting at them to leave him alone."

"Maybe he's yelling at us." A harshness underpinned Adrianna's voice.

"That's not it either." Frazer went on slowly, picking his words. "I wasn't sure what this was before. But now I am. Out of respect for Lynx's privacy, I won't say what's happening in there, only that it doesn't pose a threat to anybody but him, and that he deals with it better when he's got company. Ena and I can stay with him tonight. Everybody else can leave."

Adrianna frowned. "How are you going to get inside?"

"I've got a standing invitation from when I lived in Mysaya. As long as he hasn't revoked it, I should be allowed in." Frazer's night-blues skipped to me. "And given our connection, there's a good chance the barrier won't be able to tell us apart."

I reached for the door handle. Frazer stopped me again. "I can't be sure, though, and if the spell bars you, the kickback will hurt."

"I want to try it," I said without thinking.

"I'll wait here." Wilder assumed a wooden stance.

Frazer regarded him impassively. "We'll likely be in there until dawn."

His eyes hardened. "So be it."

I stifled an unhappy sigh. "Please don't. You should get what rest you can."

Wilder hesitated. The worry that he might come to blows with Lynx again pushed me to add, "I don't want you to stay."

His features flickered.

"Frazer, are you sure about this?" Liora's spooked expression troubled me. "The energy in that room is so dense, it's making me feel sick. It's all violence and vengeance. Even Isolde fears it."

Dragons don't get scared. I am, however, concerned.

"There, there." Ryder gathered Liora under an arm. "You can't be brave if you can't feel fear. There's no shame in it."

Even when consumed by worry, I found a moment to marvel at the strangeness of a fae attempting to mother a dragon.

"Violence and vengeance?" Wilder glared at Frazer accusingly. "You said it was safe for Serena to go in there."

Frazer remained stoic. "It is. The anger that Liora's sensing isn't coming from Lynx."

Foreboding looks were exchanged.

"I don't pretend to understand what's going on, but if you say it's okay, then it is," Liora announced in a show of faith. "I'll see you all tomorrow."

Liora retreated, her pace closer to a jog than a walk. Cai, Ryder, and Adrianna went after her. Wilder gave me one last look before he exhaled frustration. "I'll go, but I want you to promise me not to let your guard down around him."

Wilder eyed the door to Lynx's bedroom as if he wanted to punch it.

"I'll be careful," was all I was willing to offer him.

Jaw clenched, Wilder nodded, then he walked off.

Frazer swung the door open. A dimly lit living space was revealed, complete with a cream-dyed couch, two leather armchairs, and countless shelves lined with books.

I grasped my brother's hand.

Together, we raised our feet and stepped past the doorframe. I braced for pain, but nothing happened. I puffed out my cheeks and released a held breath.

Frazer broke our hand hold and shut the door.

We moved deeper into an area painted sky-blue. Numerous examples of sporting equipment hung from wall-racks, and a fireplace peered out imposingly on the space, its hearth cold and lifeless. Topping the mantlepiece was an embroidered map of Aurora stitched in iridescent silk.

"Shut. Up." Lynx's pained groan stole my focus. The sound had originated in an adjoining room to the right of us. I wanted to run straight in there, but first I had to know what I would be facing.

I rounded on Frazer, hoping the tension between us wouldn't prevent him from giving me answers. "What's wrong with him?"

"Short version?" As Frazer's eyes met mine, the honeyed light from firelit lanterns reflected off his high cheekbones, making his jade-white skin luminous. "Lynx can see and hear spirits who've failed to move on after their death. He seems to be a kind of beacon to them. In the past, he could block them out. But when he's vulnerable—when he's tired, for instance—they overwhelm him so much he can't always control his magic." His gaze darted to the door that separated us from Lynx. "The souls of these spirits have often deteriorated so much that their sole pleasure lies in tormenting the living wherever they can. I think that hatred and resentment was what Liora picked up on before."

My heart dropped to the floor and kept on falling. "How can we help him?"

"Talk to him. Keep his mind occupied. That's all we can do."

Not true, Zola countered bluntly.

Thea talked fast. *Malevolent spirits flee before starlight.*

Relief and purpose fused. I cut across the loula floorboards, shouting out, "I'm coming in."

"Ena."

"Trust me."

With Frazer flanking me, I walked in and found Lynx sitting on a giant bed in loose gray pants. Lamplight and shadows flitted over his naked top half as he rocked back and forth, fingers knotted in his hair, his upper body gleaming with sweat. The sight of that tugged me into a whirlpool of concern and tenderness.

I studied his bedroom, searching for targets. But there were no spirits squatting behind the furnishings or the large drum kit in the corner. Not as far as I could see.

"Lynx, where are they?"

He swiped at the air as if warding off an annoying fly.

I cast a helpless glance at Frazer.

"Lynx," my brother barked. "Look at us. Focus on us."

Lynx's pained gaze drifted in our direction, his face not entirely in this world. "Why did you bring her?" he moaned. "Don't want her to see."

My throat ached. "Too bad."

The temperature dropped as I strode into the center of the space. My breath turned to steam in the bitter air and my feathers ruffled as the feeling of being watched increased. I couldn't see them, but I sensed their gazes frozen on me like a group of predators who'd been fighting over a carcass, only to sniff out fresh meat on the horizon.

Lynx pressed the heel of his hand into the middle of his forehead. "Gods, shut UP!"

I could've sworn I caught an evil little giggle.

"Both of you, shut your eyes," I said.

Frazer obeyed. I wasn't certain Lynx was listening to me or if he was shutting out the sight of the spirits. Regardless, his gaze shuttered.

Looking at Lynx's contorted features, my heart aligned with my magic in clockwork synergy. The elusive power of the stars flowed in quite naturally on a glittering breeze. When I shone like frost under a blue moon, I clapped my hands.

My eyes closed a second before light blasted into every nook and cranny. Remote shrieks that might've been imagined knifed my ears.

I felt the spiteful energy dissipate and a smidge of warmth return to the room. With that, my starlight retreated. It had done what was required of it.

Cautiously, I cracked my lids open.

"Are they gone?" Frazer's manner was so mild, he might as well have been asking me how much milk I wanted in my tea.

"I think so."

Lynx lifted his head, his fingers loosening their grip on his hair. "What did you do?"

"I used starlight to send them away."

"You did this with starlight?" His glassy gaze swept the area disbelievingly. "How? My lightning's never worked on them. Not once."

That's a destructive form of starlight, Thea informed. *It doesn't work as well against innately violent beings. It's like drowning an undine in water.*

I repeated her wisdom. When I was done, Lynx tried for an appreciative smile. "Fate certainly knew what she was doing when she made us mates."

Frazer saved me from awkwardness by stalking to a chest of drawers and pulling out a black nightshirt. He tossed it at Lynx, who slipped it on in one fluid movement.

"How long have you been seeing spirits?" I asked in a tone better used for soothing a child's nightmares.

Lynx froze. Before I could tell him to forget about it, he said, "I was five the first time. I walked into a room and saw a body hanging from the ceiling."

My chest twinged.

"It got worse as I got older." He was on edge, and it showed in his voice. "But I was able to deal with it because the spirits mostly ignored me. Then Morgan bound me, and the ghosts took more notice. I suppose it's easier to haunt lonely souls."

"Are they always this active?" I asked, praying the answer was no. The idea of him coping with this night after night, year after year, was unthinkable.

"It's always worse in places that've seen a lot of violent death," he hedged.

"You could've slept in my room," Frazer said, his sullen eyebrows slashing together. "You always managed better when you were around other people."

"It's too risky." Lynx stared into a corner of the room, wearing a look that made me think he expected another ghost to pop up there. "I already told you, I'm reminding myself of my makena. The spirits wore her down until she couldn't sleep most nights. If she managed a few hours, she'd wake up screaming and attacking anybody who got too close. And she wasn't a powerful witch. Think about what I could do. I could level the whole floor."

At that insight into his past, I bled emotion. "Then I'll stay and chase them away if they return."

I kicked out of my shoes.

"You don't have to do that." Lynx's throat bobbed noticeably. "I've been dealing with this for most of my life."

"It's done." Frazer folded his arms and his moon-dust wings.

Lynx got the look of a deer about to bolt. I squinted my eyes at him. "I'm not leaving. And if you shadow-jump, I'll spend the entire night hunting you down, which means I won't get any sleep and it'll be all your fault."

His tense expression collapsed, and a resigned chuff escaped him.

Leaving my sword beside the bedpost, I climbed under his cotton sheets. My head went up in time to see Frazer and Lynx looking at each other. There was an exchange happening between them, a wordless conversation. I butted in, asking Frazer, "Aren't you getting in?"

He regarded me, his forehead crinkling. "I'll stay to make sure you're safe. But I'm not entering a mated bed. I'll take the floor."

"It's not as if ..." Heat singed the tips of my ears. "I'm only here to protect Lynx."

"He thinks I'll get territorial," Lynx said shrewdly. "And if it was any other male, then my instincts might get triggered. But you're her brother." He leveled an amused look at Frazer. "At the very least, I can promise not to kick you out of the bed."

"I'll pass." Frazer extended his palm toward me. "Pillow?"

"This is stupid," I remarked. "We've slept next to each other before."

"On the ground."

"What difference does it make what's beneath us? A bed made of earth or feathers or straw, it's all the same."

Evidently, he did not agree because he waved his fingers in a beckoning gesture.

Stubborn ass. Resigned, I threw him a pillow.

Lynx left the bed. I watched him retrieve a pile of blankets from a box concealed inside a window seat, and my frustration leaked out of me, lending an exasperated edge to my tone. "Are you sleeping on the floor too?"

He looked at me as though I'd sprouted two heads. "Have you any idea how rare it is for me to spend a night in a bed where my legs don't hang off the end?" He handed Frazer the bedding and then slid into the sheets next to me. "Besides, I don't want to miss out on a chance to outdo Wilder. This beats napping together in a library, don't you think?"

"It's not a competition," I snapped.

That infuriating smile widened. "It most definitely is."

He lay on his front and shut his eyes, ending our conversation.

Maddening. Ridiculous.

Tucking my wings in, I settled down and stewed for several minutes. Feral ghosts and Lynx's flirtations weren't to blame for my restlessness. It was Frazer. I understood his reasons for being on the floor. Yet his continued insistence on maintaining distance between us provoked me. At this rate, we might not resolve things before the battle. That was unacceptable, and the death of my restraint.

Deep in my feelings, I seized the chance to mend things. *Is there anything I could do that would earn your forgiveness?*

The long pause hurt me.

I forgave everything and anything you could do long ago.

I blinked. *Then why have you been avoiding me?*

Because I'm angry, he said, his mental voice cool. *You disappeared and before I knew it, the life was draining out of me. I thought we might die, end up in different courts, and never see each other again.* I heard him sigh. *I needed time to process that. Otherwise, I'd have taken my anger out on you.*

My mind tripped over his confession. *Why would we go to different courts?*

You'd be chosen for the light court. But I doubt that I would. I'm not even sure I'd want to be. I can't see myself floating around on clouds and drinking sunshine all day long, can you?

Zola cackled. *Hilarious. Is that what he thinks it's like here? I could tell you a few stories.*

Forbidden knowledge, Thea interrupted.

You're such a bore, Thea.

Leaving their firstborn drama behind, I mentally climbed into my kin bond. His self-loathing was impossible to miss. The bitterness of it coated my tongue. I couldn't heal that. I could only address his doubt. *If you weren't sent to the light court, then we'd find a home in the moon court.*

And if I go to the dark court?

You won't.

He became a silent wall.

I tried again. *Then I'd storm in and drag you out.*

You know that I love you, don't you?

I melted. He hadn't made his care for me a secret, but hearing the actual words was a first.

His unusually soft voice floated into my head. *I haven't said it before because I put little value in words. And my love isn't a pretty thing. It's an ugly curse.*

My eyesight misted. *That's not true.*

It is. He left no space to argue. *But it's too late to save you from it now. I've left all of my fractured pieces in your care. I just pray that they don't hurt you.*

I blinked, clearing my vision and wetting my skin with dewy lashes.

Don't sneak off again—okay?

I won't.

Show me what happened to you while you were in Asitar.

At his insistence, we dropped into each other's well of memories and entered a state of cross-pollination. Piece-by-piece, I absorbed his experiences trekking through Aurora, experimenting with moonlight, and his conversations with Lynx. It wasn't lost on me that Frazer shielded me from certain things. Like the torture he'd certainly endured when captured, and everything he'd seen in the mirror.

Once our mental pairing had finished, Frazer collected his thoughts first. *We need to sleep, so I'll make this brief. Nobody who matters will care that you're Abraxus's granddaughter. The fact he's your kin is actually an advantage. If he has an attachment to you, we can use that to our benefit. Also, you should've done the familiar summoning at the Shyani camp. I wouldn't have cared if we'd shared such a creature. It might've protected you when I couldn't. That's it.*

I was torn between laughter and tears.

He felt my reaction. *What is it?*

A needle's width of quiet passed as I considered my response. *I find it funny that you can cut through all my crap in less time than it would take me to make breakfast.*

As you say, he mused.

And I'd prefer to wait to summon a familiar until we've got the time to adjust to it. We've got enough to worry about as it is. My mood took a downward turn.

I'm fine with whatever. Sleep now.

I considered protesting. I'd wanted to talk about his foray into magic.

Goodnight, siska.

That term of endearment melted my resistance.

Night, brata.

Sleep gathered on my eyelids. Rest, however, was not in my immediate future. I was hauled into my dreamscape, which today had taken on the form of Mysaya's battlements. Both of my great-aunts stood before me.

Zola broke formation to poke me in the boob. *You've got a lot of catching up to do.*

Startled, I covered my chest and slapped her hand away. Neither of them had touched me before. *What are you talking about?*

Her eagle eyes tapered in judgment of me. *You've spent too long pottering around a kitchen and indulging in romantic histrionics when you should've been prepping for the fight ahead.*

Indignation flared. *I spent hours in the training room.*

Truth. After the library, I'd worked out until I'd become a patchwork of bruises.

It wasn't enough, Zola retorted high-handedly.

I bristled. *Why are you even here? I thought you'd given up on teaching me. You haven't been to any of my lessons since I met Abraxus.*

You were angry at us for keeping secrets, she said testily. *And unlike Thea, I can't ignore it when somebody's upset with me. I thought we'd argue and I'd disrupt your lessons. But I can't stay away when we need to prepare you for a battle. There's too much at stake. If you want to hold onto your grudge, so be it. I'm not going anywhere.*

I stowed my irritated pride and said, *Fine.*

Thea turned to me, her expression bearing the traits of someone suffering from overworked patience. *So, we've designed a few scenarios that could occur based on your group's current battle plan. Our aim is to give you a chance to practice the kinds of counterattacks and quick responses you'll need in order to survive.*

Zola butted in. *And if you hold back with your sunlight strikes, so help me—I will personally see to it that this practice session feels like it lasts a month.*

She would only push me harder if I argued. Zola thrived on conflict. With that in mind, I met each of their gazes, one hard, one soft, and said, *Understood.*

CHAPTER 40
TEMPTATION

I stirred to the pitter-patter of rain hitting the windowpanes. Confusion set in. I couldn't understand what my limbs were doing or why I was pressed up against a hot object.

I unglued my eyes. The cold light of dawn seeped in past breaks in the curtains, illuminating my current situation. At some point in the night, the sheets had been kicked down and I'd become entangled with Lynx. We were pressed up against each other like two pages of a closed book. I stared long at where he began and I ended.

One of his arms supported my head. The other was thrown over my waist and weighed as much as a bag of mill flour. My hands were tucked up against his top half, kissing the cotton of his nightshirt.

Lower down, it got worse. His thigh had ridden up to nestle between my legs, the long muscle flat against my sex. I'd propped my right knee over his hip, as if to keep him there.

I looked up as the rays emitted from a sun barely crowning the mountaintops reached his hair and backlit his face, casting it in a soft glow. He didn't seem real. That sense of illusion emboldened me. I reached for the lock of hair that had fallen forward into his eyes, admiring how the dawn revealed the many shades hidden there: a blueish black, a chocolate-brown, a flaming auburn.

I tucked the wavy strands of his hair behind his ear, taking his masculine scent deep into my lungs. I could've sworn that smell had followed me into my dreams.

"That tickles," he murmured, his breath grazing my lips.

Startled, I withdrew my hand. "I thought you were asleep."

"I am."

"Liar."

He stuck his tongue out. A stud of metal glinted at me.

"Is your tongue pierced?"

"Yes." The delicate skin of his eyelids flitted upward, unveiling amber irises flecked with gold and black. "Does that excite you?"

"Why would it?" I asked somewhat coolly.

"You tell me." His tone was so teasing, it seemed to contain a little hook.

Fearing what would occur if I kept looking at him, I rolled over in bed and disturbed his thigh from my core. I didn't get up, though. I wasn't ready to face the day.

My body was quick to feel the loss of heat. I had no sheets, no Lynx, and the air still clung to a nightly chill.

A violent shudder jolted my wings, bringing them into contact with Lynx. Until that moment, I hadn't thought about the fact that my back was to him.

I waited to feel uncomfortable. It never happened.

Neither of us moved for five loud heartbeats.

Lynx pressed his palm against my left wing, whispering, "Is this okay?"

The truth unsettled me. But I wouldn't lie. Not about this.

I nodded.

Slowly, giving me an opportunity to protest, he swept his fingertips over my feathers. Everything from my toes to my wingtips tingled. It felt nice. More than nice.

Lynx alternated between stroking my feathers and drawing lines up and down my spine. The thin fabric of my camisole didn't provide enough of a barrier. I soaked in everything: the heat from his hands, the gentle scrape of his short nails, the slight roughness from his calluses.

A memory intruded. Wilder had tried to touch my wing in the library. I hadn't let him. But Lynx ...

Shame and confusion built in my blood. My wings retracted shyly.

Lynx paused. Did he think he'd done something wrong?

Something inside of me slipped. I angled my head back, showing him my cheek. That prompted Lynx to pull my back up against his front. He slipped his arms around me and loosed a contented sigh.

Guilt and pleasure bubbled within me. He'd known what I wanted before I had. I'd wanted to be held. I'd wanted the warmth back.

I melted, softening against him. That lasted a few happy seconds, then I shifted back a bit, and as I did, my ass bumped up against a very hard, very proud object.

Lynx froze. I suspected he was waiting for me to react to what I'd felt from him.

The wholly feminine creature inside of me radiated smugness at our mate's equipment. She plagued me with wicked images that made me burn with the heat of a thousand furnaces.

I remained stiff, unmoving, unable to pull away and unwilling to encourage him. Then his cock twitched against my backside.

The instinct to push back against him fought with my convictions like a horse refusing to take a bridle. A needy moan sat on my tongue. I fastened my upper teeth into my lower lip and gnawed until it was a puffy mess.

He pressed his nose lightly to my neck. I wasn't sure why, but I knew he was taking in my scent. His exhale broke over the sensitive skin of my nape.

I arched my back just a little ...

Lynx freed a low growl that shook my entire body, the mattress with it. I held my breath. For what, I didn't know.

A very obvious cough pitched the air. Fuck. I'd forgotten about Frazer.

I buried my burning face into the pillow. Gods, I wanted to flee the room from embarrassment. Lynx, on the other hand, was shameless. "Go back to sleep. We're busy."

A barely audible sigh drifted up from the floor. "If my vision holds true, this is the last day before the battle. I've got too much to do. As have you."

"Yeah, like not being sleep-deprived."

I rolled onto my back and glared at Lynx. A quiver of soundless laughter crossed his features.

"You're not sleeping," Frazer pointed out.

Lynx curved his wing around us. In that cocoon of secretive darkness, I felt an urge to reach up and run a hand along his silky feathers.

"Let's see if he goes away," Lynx whispered.

"Enough." I jostled his shin with my foot.

"Mm." Lynx's short chuckle caressed my ear, causing the hair on my nape to stand up and pay attention. "It's not enough, though, is it?"

No. No, it wasn't. Stars save me.

"Ena," Frazer said, his voice a call for action.

Bringing my elbow up, I nudged Lynx's chest. "Move."

"I'm too comfy," he said, a satisfied smile in his voice.

"Fine. You asked for it." I tickled his ribs.

He pulled away from me with a groan. I seized that moment to shuffle off the bed and slip on my shoes.

Frazer stood up to fold his blankets. Lynx sat on the edge of the mattress with his back to me. His head hung low as he kneaded his neck and stretched out his wings.

I was keen to return to neutral ground. "Where will you go first, brata?"

He placed his bedding on Lynx's mattress in a neat pile, even smoothing out the wrinkles on his pillow. It was only then Frazer met my inquisitive gaze. "To the mirror."

I blanked. "What? Why?"

Tonally, he remained steady. "There may be more that I can learn from it. And the more we know, the safer we'll be."

Fear fired me up. "I'll go."

I got a very firm, "No."

My lips pinched together. "Why not?"

"The mirror isn't meant for you."

I folded my arms, reflecting his obstinate stance. "I command both moonlight and waterlight. I can make it work."

His gaze grew absent. "You can't perceive Fate when you're destined to change it."

"What does that mean?" I asked, scowling.

Frazer's wings twitched. "If we want to survive the coming months, then each of us has to take responsibility for our share of the difficulties.

And wrestling truth from the visions, that's my burden to bear. Not yours."

I checked our bond for more insight into his underlying feelings. But other than disquiet and fatigue, I couldn't get anything from him. He'd locked his emotions down.

A wave of realization and sickness swept through me. "That's why you looked so drained last night—you looked in it yesterday too, didn't you?"

His silence was his confession.

"You could lose your mind," I said, close to pleading. "Thea told me that mental trauma can't be healed—not if the damage is too extensive."

Frazer went for my jugular. "You stormed Mysaya with less than a hundred people to rescue me. Then you snuck into an enemy encampment to kidnap their leader. That was dangerous, but you did it anyway. Don't ask me to do or be less than you. Trust me. Trust that I can handle it."

He waited for my answer, patient and passionless.

I was drowning, my emotional veins stung by a downpour. Amidst the struggle to stay above water—to find an equilibrium—I pushed out, "Okay."

"I'll catch up with you at the pack sparring session," Frazer said, reminding me of what we'd arranged yesterday.

The air thick inside of my chest, I could only hum.

"Before you both go"—Lynx got up and faced us—"thank you for last night."

"We'll be back tonight," was Frazer's response. "No more sleeping alone."

He didn't stick around for a reply. Frazer exited the room.

Before I could follow him, Lynx said, "Wilder plans on outfitting everybody in armor today. But if you're willing, I'd like to take you and your pack to my ancestral vaults. The armor there was designed with leaders in mind." My frown made Lynx add, "It's useful if the key players in a battle are recognizable. For one, it helps the soldiers spot us in the heat of battle and gives them a person to rally behind."

Thoughts of tomorrow squeezed my insides. "How do you know what Wilder's planning?" I asked, my voice thinned by shallow breath.

"He needed to ask me questions about the armories."

I thought for a few beats. "Are you thinking about going to the vaults now? Only I'd planned to spend the morning in the kitchens. And John always started baking before dawn, which means I'm already late."

"Who's John?"

My heart wallowed in memories, aching fiercely. "He was like a father to me. I pretty much grew up in his bakery."

A tiny smile. "He sounds nice."

"He is."

"I can meet up with you and your pack after your training session," Lynx said. "We can go to the vaults then. Is that all right with you?"

"Sure."

Something soft drifted through his eyes. "Bye, then."

"Bye."

I tore my eyes from him and walked out.

Adrianna was already gone by the time I reached my bedroom. No surprises there. Only the lark woke earlier than her.

I dressed in light, breathable clothes, which turned out to be a wise choice because as the day progressed, the humidity and the hot ovens reduced me to a sticky mess. My discomfort was acute enough that Frazer picked up on it via the bond. His suggestion to use my wings as fans wasn't as valuable to me as the knowledge that he'd come through his visit to the mirror unscathed.

By early afternoon, my spirits had taken a severe nosedive. I'd listened with an eager ear to every person coming in and out of the kitchen. There had been no sightings of Diana's army. The reality that we'd soon have to abandon Mysaya inched closer with every tick of the clock and every hour that was lost.

I was laying a malt loaf on a cooling rack when Cai showed up.

He made straight for me. "It occurred to me that it's been too long since our pack shared a proper meal together. So I've come to steal you away. The others are already waiting for us."

"Yes. Take her away." Fox loosed a bark of a laugh. "I'm determined to drown out thoughts of our inevitable doom by drinking that bottle of braka in the cupboards, and I'd like to avoid the sight of her glaring at me while I do it."

Unsure if he was joking, my mouth stalled.

"Don't worry," Squirrel whispered to me from behind her hand. "I'll stop him before he passes out or sets anything on fire."

Well, shit.

"Take this for your pack." With a sweet smile, Squirrel handed me a heavy pot with wooden handles. The hole in the lid released steam that carried the scents of garlic, wine, and sausages.

Cai grabbed bread rolls on the way out. He carried four in his pocket, two in his hands, and one in his mouth.

For practical reasons, the meal halls were accessed via the same corridor as the kitchen. A few doors down, we entered a space large enough to house a few hundred people.

Cai led me up an aisle rowed with tables and benches. We passed a few quiet and unfamiliar fae. Each of them viewed us keenly, without judgment, as if studying people was simply an ingrained habit of theirs. From that, I marked them as Sami. I'd heard they'd been joining us one by one all morning. I wondered now if we'd asked them to come for no reason.

At the far end of the hall, a set of doors opened out onto an overgrown courtyard bedecked with seating that had seen better days. The rest of my pack had already laid one of the circular tables with plates, cutlery, and glasses of water.

I claimed a spot between Frazer and Cai.

During the dinner, within the confines of our soundproof bubble, we went from discussing the problems involved in retrieving the moonstone, to how many Fiends had summoned their familiars, to the current whereabouts of the Riverlands army. Adrianna cursed Danu repeatedly, adamant that if he'd failed to find them and deliver our message, she would pluck and stuff and stick him in a pie.

At such talk, it was probably inevitable that our group would succumb to gloomy thoughts. Adrianna sipped her water slowly. Liora picked absentmindedly at her food, her features sunken in tiredness. As for Frazer, he'd retreated into his mind. Therein I sensed only the vague shape of his thoughts. They darted about like minnows, each one following its own trajectory, each one causing a ripple that impacted the larger pool that they were all a part of.

Cai and I were the only ones to stay present.

"I've actually been meaning to ask you something." Cai leaned toward me, wearing a secret-sharing grin. "What's it like having a mate?"

Adrianna choked on her water.

"Are you all right?" Cai asked, his brow lowering in concern.

She coughed, wiping her mouth on a sleeve. "Fine."

Adrianna glanced at me, her eyes rounding as if to say *Help*.

"It's confusing," I blurted out. "Having a mate."

Cai's hazel gaze darted to me. "How so?"

"I can't really explain it."

Ugh. Lame.

"Well, I like him," Cai said with a toothy grin. "And of course, my opinion is everything."

I leveled an unimpressed look at him.

Liora elbowed Adrianna. Cai noticed and frowned at them. "What's going on with you two?"

"Nothing," Adrianna shot out.

"It's something." Liora's cheeks heated to the color of her burnished curls. I thought she might be about to spit fire.

Adrianna's nostrils ballooned with a stressed breath. "Fine."

I'm guessing this is where she tells him about her mate. Is there still time for us to make a run for it? Frazer's mental voice was dry.

No.

Adrianna just said it. "I met my mate while I was in Asitar."

Cai cocked his head as if sure he'd misheard. When that statement went uncorrected and nobody laughed, his features slackened. A wintery stillness encased him.

My attention skipped to Liora. She dipped her head, sending her springy curls in front of her face. I still caught glimpses of her sorrow and agitation, emotions that undoubtedly belonged to her brother.

"What's his name?" Cai asked stiffly.

"Zeke. He was the contact that got us in touch with Sefra."

Cai's long nose drew up in a minute nod. "Is he nice?"

Underneath the table, Cai grasped my knee. He took care not to dig his nails in, but his grip was firm. I clutched his tanned hand, wanting to put every inch of my support into the touch.

"I don't know if I'd use the word nice." In brisk notes, Adrianna added, "But he's a good male."

Cai's ears tinted pink. "That's ... that's good. I'm happy for you."

"Thanks."

Silence settled in like an unwanted houseguest.

I glanced at Frazer. *Say something. This is painful.*

He viewed me out of the corner of his eye. *Have you forgotten that it's me you're speaking to? You say something.*

Adrianna spoke to me first. "On the subject of mates, I wondered if you'd given any thought to strengthening your bond."

I stared blankly. "What are you talking about?"

Frazer was quick to intervene. "Lynx should be the one having that conversation with her."

"He might assume she already knows about the claiming," Adrianna said.

Curiosity collapsed into trepidation. "What's a claiming?"

Frazer hesitated, remaining tight-lipped.

Adrianna *tsked* at his reluctance. "Mates deepen their connection by biting each other three times in different places. I thought it worth mentioning because if you and Lynx share blood at the neck, you'll be able to speak mind-to-mind. That could help you coordinate during the battle tomorrow, or if you got separated—"

"Why are you trying to talk her into this?" Frazer snapped in a tone made of ice and daggers. "Don't you hate Lynx?"

"This isn't about my feelings," Adrianna countered in a haughty tone. "I want to give her the best chance of surviving. That's it."

I ignored their bickering and focused on collecting information. "What do the other bites do?"

"The one over the heart allows you to sense each other's emotions. I've heard mates wait a while before taking that step, though. Largely because you can't hide your heart in the same way that you can shield your thoughts." Humor glinted in the depths of her azure-blues. "That's what makes empaths so dangerous."

"You can guard against empaths," Liora said. "Sefra's difficult to read. And Frazer's almost impossible to get anything from. It's like drawing water out of a stone." Her eyes flashed to him. "Not that I've tried exactly."

Frazer studied her. He tapped the table once with his index finger.

"I just meant that it's more peaceful around you," Liora babbled. "Tuning into you helps me when we're in a crowded area."

"I see." A delicate reply.

"How are you blocking her power?" Adrianna asked Frazer.

"I repress a lot."

She chuckled. I couldn't smile at that, though.

"What about the third bite?"

Adrianna fidgeted in place. "That's done on the thigh."

Cai tore his hand from mine as if he'd been shocked. "This sounds like a fae thing." As he stood, the feet of his chair screeched against the flagstones. "I'll see you all in the training room."

He released the sound-bubble that protected our pack from eavesdroppers and left at the pace of a deer fleeing a crossbow. Adrianna confronted Liora. "And that's exactly what I wanted to avoid."

"He was going to find out eventually," Liora argued, the color rising in her cheeks.

Adrianna's jaw firmed. Tension rankled the air.

I decided to do them a favor and interrupt. "What's the bite on the thigh for?"

"That's meant to increase your fertility as a couple."

Holy fire. "Well, I won't be doing that one anytime soon."

Adrianna marked me with a wry eye. "You might change your mind when you hear it increases the potency of your orgasms."

"Tempting." Liora's ensuing sheepish look suggested she hadn't planned to say that out loud.

My grin was a crooked thing.

Wearing a look of forbearance, Frazer turned to me. "Just be aware that any step toward claiming your mate is irreversible. It'll also inevitably draw you closer together, which could make things harder on Lynx if you decide not to pursue things with him."

"What does that matter?" Adrianna's azure-blues were frosty snowflakes as she said that. "At least she'll be alive to reject him."

"Don't be a bitch," Frazer retorted. "It doesn't suit you."

Adrianna growled. "What did you call me?"

Frazer lifted his chin coolly. "You've called me a bastard multiple times. I can't return the favor?"

Liora suddenly tipped sideways, her hand fluttering over her eyes.

Adrianna managed to grab her arm and set her back in her seat before she could fall out of it.

"What was that?" I asked, already halfway out of my chair.

"It's nothing." Liora tugged her arm out of Adrianna's hold. "I just got a bit dizzy."

"You've spent too long in the ward," Frazer remarked. "Tending to people in pain and being around so many stressed people must be unbearable for an empath newly come into her powers. It is not weak to admit this."

Liora clasped her hands in her lap. "I know that." That was what she said, but her voice didn't have the ring of truth to it.

"Why don't you find somewhere quiet and do those control exercises that Sefra suggested?" I said, my pulse still racing from watching her almost faint.

Eyes downcast, Liora nodded.

Adrianna stood. "Come on. We'll walk you out."

The four of us abandoned the dirty tableware—somebody would be along to pick it up later—and we strode back inside the food hall. As we moved toward the door opposite, I saw the strangers among us nod their heads at Frazer. That sign of respect confirmed my earlier suspicions. They were Sami.

Liora halted once we'd left the hall and entered the corridor. "I'm going to head to my room. I can meditate there."

"I can go with you," I offered.

A wan smile. "Thanks, but it's better if I'm alone."

I watched her walk away, my heart in my shoes.

"You're going to see Lynx now, aren't you?" Frazer stared, almost daring me to deny it.

"I want to talk to him. That's it."

Frazer pinned me with a knowing look. I had my mental-shield up from an earlier defense lesson with Zola—according to her, attacking my mind while I was wielding a knife in the kitchen was a useful exercise—but my brother didn't need to hear my thoughts to know what I was thinking.

"It's your choice," he said in a tone suggesting neutrality while making it apparent that he didn't approve.

Infuriating.

"I guess I'm headed to our pack's sparring practice alone, then." Adrianna eyed me, her fingers wrapped around her hilt. "Good luck."

She swiveled on her heel and stalked off.

Frazer looked at me, amusement shimmering in his night-blues. "Apparently, I don't count as a member of our pack."

I couldn't let that stand, even though he didn't seem bothered by her dismissal of him. "She assumed you wouldn't go without me."

His eyebrow inched upward. "We're not joined at the hip."

"I know that. But you're not social as a rule."

"I don't know what you're talking about," he replied, straight-faced. "I like everybody."

My forehead pinched in sarcastic disbelief. "Really?"

He freed a breathy cat laugh. "You should try the hot spring." My confusion had him adding, "I came across Lynx an hour ago. That's where he was headed."

"Where is it?"

Frazer fired off directions. I took my leave of him and navigated my way to the central part of the castle, otherwise known as the keep. There, I came to stand before a door of gray-silver wood and intricate hinging.

My heart wavered but my feet did not. They carried me through the unlocked door and down, down, down a narrow shaft lit by glowing crystals.

Minutes passed, measured in hundreds of steps.

A cold breath of air traveled up from below. It carried with it the scent of warm eggs and the sounds of dripping water, strange creaks, and an eerie whistle that reminded me of wind blowing down a chimney.

At the bottom of the shaft, the steps flared out into a cavern lit by glowworms and firelights. I beheld salt-colored rock beaded with condensation, and a turquoise lake—a womb in the earth's belly—that took up the entire middle and back section of the cave. Through a veil of purling steam I saw Lynx briefly surface before diving once again into misty waters. Resolved, I strode toward him.

CHAPTER 41
BITE ME

-LYNX-

My mind relaxed as I swam in the hot spring. I stayed underwater for as long as possible, savoring my freedom. When my lungs screamed at me to surface, I stood up on silty ground and pushed my wet hair off my face.

A very quiet "Hello," sounded.

Tensing, I whirled around.

Ena lingered beside the pool. Alarm bells stilled. "How did you know I was here?"

"Frazer told me."

I studied her nervous stance and tightly tucked wings. Interesting.

"You should get in." I swatted at the water, sending it in her direction without splashing her. "The water's amazing."

A cute wrinkle lined the middle of her serious brows. "How hot is it?"

"Mmm. Like having a very warm bath."

That convinced her to put aside her sword and shoes and to sit on the edge of the hot spring. She extended her leg out long to reach the water below. Her toes grazed the steamy water and with a hiss, she yanked her foot back.

"Not keen?"

"It just surprised me." Ena shifted into a cross-legged position. "Doesn't the heat bother you?"

I cut through the water, heading toward her. From under her lashes, she watched my every move, tracking my approach. "Not even a little. I take after my makena in that way. She was from a hot country and would sunbathe for hours if she got the chance. I figured you'd be the same since you wield sun energy. But I guess your fireballs are no match for our little hot spring."

My teasing made the sides of her mouth lighten. "It's not the same thing," she said, attempting to conceal her amusement behind a tart tone.

I reached the lip of the pool and held my hand out to her. "Want to try again?"

That invitation drew a suspicious look out of her. "Are you going to throw me in if I take that?"

"No." I smiled. "This is so you don't have to jump in."

She eyed the distance from the ledge to the bottom of the pool. I waited, reduced to the role of a flower in the field, a pitiful thing that could only watch as the butterfly floated above, deciding where to land.

Ena's gaze swept over my shorts and bare chest. Blood bloomed in her cheeks and at her swan neck. The redness was glaringly obvious against her porcelain skin, and it made it look as if I'd bullied her in some wicked way. I was about to withdraw my hand when she rested her palm atop mine.

My fingertips kissed her wrist. In those bright blue veins, I felt her pulse racing faster than I could fly. Satisfaction filled me.

I gripped her by her slim hips and lifted her off the ledge. To secure herself, she wrapped her legs and arms around me. In that position, my nose pressed up against her nape. Her scent slammed into me. The top notes were sugar and ocean spray, while the subtler tones reminded me of the air after a thunderstorm. The warmth of the earth after it rained.

Fighting the urge to free my fangs and claim her, I backed up into the lake, not daring to take another breath. I stopped when the water reached my waist and the steam was so dense it cloaked us from the outside world.

"Ready?"

Her nod felt stiff against my cheek.

I crouched. When her thighs met with the heat, her muscles tightened and she retracted her wings. I went slower, giving her time to adjust.

Once I kneeled on the soft floor, Ena inched off my lap. I snagged her hand as she set her feet on the ground. "You should try floating on your back."

We stared at each other for three uneven breaths. She shattered the spell we'd fallen under by asking, "Why?"

I tipped my nose toward the turquoise spring. "There's a legend about this lake that says if you listen underwater, there's a chance you'll hear the earth's heart beating."

Doubt shrouded her face. "That sounds made up."

Laughter drummed against my ribs. "It's not, I promise. I've heard it once or twice. It's like music."

Her skeptical expression was replaced by curiosity.

"Okay. I'll try." Her focus darted to where my hand held hers. "Are you going to let go?"

I grinned. "This is to steady you while you're floating."

Her rosy lips rolled in toward her teeth. She didn't pull away, though. That was enough to make my chest expand with hope.

Ena shut her eyes as she drifted onto her back. That cute crinkle between her brows returned.

I moved to her side and placed my free hand on her back. She relaxed, letting me support her weight. From this angle, it was impossible not to see how her white shirt had soaked through to reveal the two necklaces she bore, and more distractingly, the outline of her beautiful breasts. I tried not to look, but the damage was already done.

Every inch of me hardened, and in turn, her nipples tightened up, saluting me through the cotton, as if determined to grab my attention. It seemed to me that our bodies were linked by the same fevered thread. At that thought, a surge of possession slammed into me stronger than a barrel of whiskey.

I waged war on instincts that made me both tender and fierce. Feral and tame. In a bid to regain control and soften my rock-hard body, I imagined foul things, boring things. Hopeless and pointless. The image of her, prone and naked, kept intruding. Could I explode from sexual frustration? Was that a thing?

"I can hear it," Ena said quietly. "The music ... It's really there."

Her awed smile softened my heart and squeezed my guts. It made my cock and fangs pulse with the desperate need to be inside of her. To make us one.

Ena's eyes fluttered open. Our gazes anchored to each other. I forgot anything else existed as my focus drifted to her parted lips.

She suddenly freed her hand from mine and straightened up. Disappointment punched me in the stomach.

Ena lapsed into distracted silence, staring vacantly at the ripples she created by waving her hands through the water. Something was bothering her. I considered asking her what was wrong and decided against it. I didn't know her well enough to guess whether a question would make her open up or shut down.

"Lynx." Ena looked me dead in the eye. "What would you think about us claiming each other?"

Energy jolted my body. I stood straight up out of the water and spread my wings as far as they'd go.

Ena stumbled back a step. That slapped some sense into me.

"Sorry." I gathered my wings in. "You just shocked the shit out of me."

"I'm sorry too. I didn't mean to be so blunt." She smiled nervously. "It's just Adrianna was saying that if we shared blood at the neck, we could hear each other's thoughts, which would give us an advantage over our enemies."

Anger tapped at me. "Is Adrianna pressuring you into this?"

She came back with a definite, "No. I would've brought it up with you before if I'd known about it."

"Is this something you want to do?" I asked, forcing my voice to remain calm.

"I ..." She paused and frowned. "Yes, it is."

"Why?"

Ena raised her chin, showing determination. "Because the other side has legions of warriors, witches, and a soon-to-be-dead army, and who knows what Archon's got squirreled away in his realm. We need every advantage we can get."

A heaviness settled over my shoulders. "This would be a big step for any bonded pair to take, even under normal circumstances. I thought you were determined not to rush things, or have you decided that you want to be with me?"

The seam of her lips parted in a silent gasp. That show of shock was my answer.

My chest heaved like the Qualari Sea after a high wind. "If this was something you desired for its own sake, I'd already be sinking my teeth into your neck, your breasts, your thighs, and any other parts you told me to." A tiny tremor went through her. I continued, gentling my tone. "I want you to be mine. But by the sounds of it, you only want this for the strategic advantage it might afford us. Or am I wrong?"

"No." Ena concentrated on the tattoo marking me as another knight. "But if reading each other's minds could save lives, isn't that a good enough reason to do it?"

"It's not that I don't respect your reasoning." I slipped on an emotionless mask. "But we shouldn't let the mere threat of Morgan steal away something as important as this by making it all about duty. She's already taken too much from the both of us."

My mood darkened, slipping into unspeakable places. The idea of allowing my slaver to cheapen our claiming made me sick to my stomach. I'd swallowed my desire for revenge to be with Ena—to help and protect her. I couldn't let Morgan have this, too. Not if I wanted to stay sane.

Face clearing, Ena said, "Duty isn't the only reason for doing this. If we have to flee Mysaya, we could get captured or we could lose each other in the chaos. But if we can hear each other's thoughts, I'll be able to find you if we get separated."

My throat convulsed. "And what if you decide to be with Blond and Brooding? Won't it cause issues between you if we've bitten each other?"

Her lips puckered in disapproval. "Seriously? Blond and Brooding?"

I stared at her, unapologetic.

She glanced away. "I've told Wilder I won't be pursuing anything with anyone."

Frustration simmered. "To claim me is to pursue me."

Her whole face fell, and uncertainty dulled her eyes. "Oh."

That response tore at my guts. Gods. I actually wanted this.

"Well, I don't see it that way." Ena balled up her hands. "If Wilder doesn't believe my reasons for wanting this, then that's on him. It's got nothing to do with him, anyway. This is between you and me."

That ironed out a knot in my solar plexus. "Did Adrianna explain what happens when you bite a mate intending to claim them? Things might get out of control."

I was so damned weak. I'd opened a door for her, and she walked right through it. "Meaning?"

I stooped, sitting on my heels. "To be blunt, we might end up in bed together."

Ena squinted at me. "Are you trying to scare me off?"

I shrugged my wings. "You should just be aware it'll heighten our attraction to each other, that's all."

"It won't force us to do anything?"

"Nothing we don't want to do."

Ena hesitated. "I ... I still think we should do it. We only have to control ourselves once. It's not like we'll be biting each other every day."

"If only."

Her stunning eyes cut through me. That *look* was intended to tell me to quit flirting with her, but I didn't miss how her gaze flicked down to my mouth. How it lingered there for just a moment. "And you know that once it's done, it can't be undone?"

She gave me a quiet, "Yes."

I threw my heart to her with no guarantee it would find a soft landing. "Okay. If you're sure, I'll do it."

That final confirmation brought my secondary canines down, and my cock grew another inch. I wasn't even sure how that was physically possible.

Her gaze dropped to my fangs. "Are we doing it now?"

I was burning, burning, burning.

Ena bridged the gap between us. With her this close, I could see her pupils were blown. Unable to resist, I brushed aside the clump of hair sticking to her cheek and her mouth. I ran my thumb along her lower lip, dazed. Her eyelashes trembled at the contact, and I had a moment to wonder at her skin, soft like willow buds.

"Lynx?"

The breathless quiver in her voice almost broke me. Balls aching, I pulled my hand back from her face. "Not yet. Soon."

"Was this to show me what was to come, then?" My insides flipped as she stroked—fucking *stroked*—the length of one of my fangs. "They don't look so bad. Definitely on the smaller side, from what I've seen."

She *tap-clinked* my canine.

"Liar."

I snapped my fangs up, indignant. That sent her into a fit of giggles.

"You asked for it," I said, and I tossed her into the pool.

She hit with a splash that lapped up against my belly. Ena sprang up, coughing, her breasts bobbing. "You ass!"

Laughter shook my chest. "Aww. Poor baby."

She wiped her eyes in a furious motion.

I moved for her and she backhanded the water, spraying me. I didn't break stride or bother to use my wing as a shield. When I stopped a few short breaths away, she glowered at me through wet lashes. "That was mean," she pretend-hissed.

"You were mean first."

Her gaze coyly slid off in a wayward direction. "True."

I lightly scratched the underside of her chin.

She knocked my arm away. "When did you want to do the claiming? Because I was thinking it should be before midnight."

Midnight. That stuck a dreaded cord. It was the agreed-upon time we'd leave Mysaya if reinforcements hadn't arrived. I nodded, suddenly serious. "In a few hours, then."

"What are we waiting for, exactly?"

My smile stretched ear to ear. "You move fast when you've decided something, don't you?"

She lifted a feeble shoulder. "I guess so. Is that a problem?"

"No." I gently rubbed my wings against each other, freeing them of any stubborn droplets that hung onto the feathers' impermeable coating. "But I need to find the right gifts."

Her expressive brows rose to her hairline. "What gifts?"

"We're supposed to exchange gifts before each bite," I said, retreating into my memory, picking out items that she might appreciate.

"Lynx, I don't have much money." She picked regretfully at the hem of her wet top. "I've nothing to give you. Just the clothes I brought with me."

"Then give me a lock of your hair," I suggested.

"That's enough?" She frowned.

"It is to me." I grasped her hand, leading her back through the mist. "I'll make armor my first gift to you. We can head to the vaults for that now."

"I'm soaked. I can't get into armor like this."

I squeezed her hand. "No worries. We'll stop by our rooms on the way."

At the pool's border, she used my hand to boost herself onto dry land. As she climbed out, I got an eyeful of her deliciously round ass.

She pushed out her wings, then she turned and caught my admiring eye. "Were you looking at my butt?"

"Yes. Sorry."

"Don't do that." A lackluster demand.

"Yes, darling."

"Don't call me darling."

My grin widened. "Yes, dear."

She looked away, a reluctant smile creeping up her mouth.

I hauled myself out of the water and grabbed my dry shirt from the floor. Dripping wet, I straightened up before her and gestured toward the exit. "After you."

Her voice dipped, becoming velvet-tipped nails scraping across my skin. "Will you stare at my ass again?"

"Would it upset you if I said yes?"

"No," she admitted softly. A blush, or perhaps the heat from the pool, tinted the tip of her nose pink.

Ena picked up her sword and her shoes before walking away. I angled my head, appreciating the beautiful view. A handful of heartbeats passed.

"Having fun?" she called back to me.

Yes. No. Maybe?

I was straining harder than a rutting mule, my entire body aching to run after her. To tug her into my arms. Strangely, that particular ache made everything else hurt less. It pushed the last eighteen years into the back of my mind, where they would surely live as ghosts forevermore. But I could feel things other than despair now. At that realization, I knew the answer to her question, and it meant everything to me to shout back, "Yes, dear."

CHAPTER 42
LONGING

-CAI-

Steps sounded behind me. "Cai."

I froze at the sound of Adrianna's voice.

"This isn't where we agreed to meet for training," she said.

I gripped my sword hilt tighter and tighter. The blisters sustained from hacking at a prop-dummy for over an hour burst, causing my palm to throb like a nasty toothache. That pain was nothing compared to the gut-wrenching misery involved in turning around to meet sky-blue eyes.

Adrianna's brows narrowed. "What are you doing?"

"I'm working on my technique," I croaked, blood dripping onto the mat below me.

Her beautiful pout thinned dangerously. I braced for an argument, even welcomed it. She denied me that and scanned the empty training room instead. "Why are you in here?"

I took a moment to pick over my next words. I'd always been a moon-touched fool where she was concerned. Those days had to end. The fewer words, the better. "I wanted to be alone. Is there something wrong with that?"

"You never want to be alone."

I shrugged it off. "There's a first time for everything."

She propped her hands on her hips. "Let's get this over with. Before I left for Asitar, you said that you loved me."

Adrianna seemed to take no pleasure in that memory; she could've rivaled a dead fish for apathy. "Forget it. It means nothing now."

"I won't forget it," she said sharply. "There aren't many people I care for and fewer still who I can relax around. You're one of the few. You're important to me, which means I can't pretend that we're okay when we're not."

Her slightly awkward confession stitched up my injured pride. It gave me the courage to ask a burning question. "Did you ever see me as more than a friend?"

Adrianna concentrated on the battered dummy behind me. "No, and it was selfish of me not to set you straight when I realized you liked me. Because I knew I wasn't open to having a relationship with a human."

My magic awakened as anger gut-punched me. I longed to capture and stir the air currents in the room, to give breath to my misery and make the storm inside of me real.

I squeezed my hilt harder, not caring about my bloodied hand. The bite of pain actually felt good. It helped me reach beyond my own emotion and rooted me in something simple, something controllable. "I'd no idea you were a purist."

"I have my reasons."

"Oh?"

Her chin raised in defiance of my sarcasm. "I've only ever loved one male, and that was my isä—my father. His death made a stone out of my heart for years. I didn't grieve, and I didn't move on. I'm not built like that. If I'd chosen a human as my life-partner, I'd have been powerless to watch as they got older and weaker. And when they died, I would've been left to grieve them for centuries, maybe even thousands of years, alone. It would have destroyed me, Cai."

That cut my chest to ribbons. My sword fell to the floor.

"Why did you wait until now to tell me that?" Bitterness burned a hole through my middle. "If I'd known, I would've backed off sooner. Maybe then I wouldn't have made myself so pathetic in your eyes."

She marched up and punched me on the shoulder.

"What the hell?"

I leaned away from her, massaging my muscles. She hadn't put all her strength behind it, but moons, it hurt.

Adrianna pointed a furious finger at me. "Don't put words in my mouth. I never thought you were pathetic." Her hand relaxed. "And I didn't speak up because I didn't—I don't—want to lose you and the others. Like I said, I was selfish."

Mother, have mercy on me. Why did it hurt to breathe?

"Did you think the others would stop being your friends just because you rejected me?" I asked her.

I expected her to say no to that, but she kept her mouth closed and doubt framed her face. That pushed me to say, "You won't lose them, Adrianna."

"What about you? Will I lose you?"

I forced calming air into my lungs. "I'm not so petty that I can't take rejection. I just need some time to sort my head out."

The tension seizing her put me in mind of a bow being drawn, preparing to loose more stinging arrows. "But if you start avoiding me, it'll affect our pack's dynamics. Liora will play peacekeeper. Ena won't take sides. Frazer will go wherever his siska goes. And none of them will want to spend time as a group if it hurts you."

I tried to voice some reassuring words, and they jammed in my throat like gravel. The conversation halted.

Adrianna lasted five seconds before she quit waiting for a response. "I understand it might be difficult for you to be around me for a while, but with everything going on, we can't afford for our pack to drift apart or for us to ignore each other."

All the reasons why I should disagree with her buzzed about my head like flies around a carcass, but her reasoning was sound and her sincerity was clear—and that weighed heavier in my heart. "Agreed."

"Good." Her shoulders dropped from around her ears. "Frazer and Wilder are sparring three doors down, where you're supposed to be. I expect to see you there soon. I'll give you a moment to tend to your hand."

I drew in a ragged and shallow inhale. "Fine."

She stalked off. I couldn't watch her go.

A door closed. It was over.

I slumped to the floor, laid flat on my back, stretched my legs out, and rested my hands on my shuddering chest. I didn't get up for a while.

∽

-ENA-

Two hours later than planned, I walked into the training room with Lynx at my side and took in the view.

Wilder sparred with Adrianna. Every movement in their fight looked deliberate; tempered by grace and ruled by a long-practiced control.

Cai and Frazer were another story. They dueled with swords, dripping sweat, trading blows at a terrifying pace that made me afraid an ill-timed strike would turn a blunted blade into a bludgeon and crack a skull.

I sensed Frazer's acknowledgment of my presence in our bond. He struck as fast as a lizard sprinting across a sand dune, landing a solid *thwack* on Cai's wrist.

Cai lost his grip, and his sword clattered to the floor. "Shit," he spat out between his teeth.

"We're done." Frazer lowered his blade.

Cai shook out his bandaged hand. "I can keep going."

"You're getting sloppy," said Frazer.

That earned a rare scowl from Cai.

"Halt." Wilder stepped back, disengaging from his fight with Adrianna.

She didn't argue with that order. She mopped her brow with a sleeve while dropping her practice sword in the carrying case left at the corner of the mat.

Lynx and I wandered closer to them. Everyone's attention went to us.

Nice haircut, I told Frazer.

A chuff. *Thanks.*

His raven hair had left his shoulders and moved up to his ears, further exaggerating his defined bone structure. He looked more formidable for it—a dauntless warrior.

I motioned to Cai's expertly wrapped-up hand. "What happened?"

"I was just careless." He flexed his fingers self-consciously. "I've already put an ointment on it. It'll heal up in a few hours. You look incredible by the way."

His tone was appreciative but passionless. That didn't prevent the giant beside me from growling.

Cai wasn't the least bit intimidated. "There's nothing wrong with saying she looks good when she does."

Lynx huffed like a damned stallion in heat.

Before I could squash that stupidity, Wilder asked me, "What are you wearing?"

My gaze snapped to where he stood in a sweat-stained shirt and slightly baggy trousers, wariness and confusion written on his face.

"It's my armor."

Glancing down, I ran my palms shyly along the pitch-black fabric. It clung to my body's contours and was like thick silk to the touch. Dark metal feathers protected my shoulders, forearms, and the backs of my hands. That light metal also formed a band of flexible steel that guarded my spinal column and secured the garment in place. The suit came with supple leather boots laced up to my calves, a double looped belt for my weapons, and a detachable hood stored in a hidden thigh pocket.

"That's not armor. It's what a clueless royal would wear when visiting a battlefield." Wilder aimed his leonine glower at Lynx. "Did you pick that out for her?"

"Yes, but—"

"Are you so desperate to drool over her in a skintight outfit that you'd risk her life?" Wilder demanded, his voice strained with anger.

Humiliation scalded my cheeks.

"It's taldävarian armor, you dick," Lynx fired off.

Disbelief rounded Wilder's eyes.

Adrianna strode up and grasped my elbow. She touched the fabric, first with suspicion and then with a reverence that I'd never seen from her.

"What are you doing?" I asked her.

"Did you tell her how rare this is?" Adrianna seemed to address the entire room as she said that, despite the question clearly being for Lynx.

"He said it could turn aside arrows and blades." I side-eyed Lynx. "I'm guessing there's more to it than that?"

His smile straddled the line between mischievous and sweet.

Adrianna released her hold on me. "There are only a few examples of this armor in the world. It's priceless."

Unbelievable. And Lynx had handed it over so casually.

It's the work of the firstborn, Thea said without vanity. *The Smith, to be exact.*

I repeated her revelation aloud.

A stunned silence dominated for a few heartbeats. Lynx was the quickest to recover. "That actually makes a lot of sense. I heard the crafting witches had lost the art of making it, which seemed strange given how valuable it is. They obviously never knew how to do it in the first place."

Wilder confronted Lynx. "How did you manage to keep its existence a secret from Morgan?"

That demand for information yielded a stilted response out of Lynx. "I didn't. But I warned her the armor chooses who wears it, and she ignored me. She maimed seven tailors and six witches before giving up and ordering me to destroy it. When I couldn't find a way to do that, she told me to return it to Mysaya's vaults and bury it so that nobody else could benefit from it."

I glanced up at Lynx in wonder. "Are you saying it chose me?"

A nod. "That's why it conformed to your shape."

"You might've saved her life by giving her that armor," Frazer said, looking at Lynx, gratitude shining in his eyes.

"Forgive me." Wilder's green gaze pinned me.

His hasty judgment and harsh words surged to the forefront of my mind. "I do. And I get why you were confused, but I'm not stupid, Wilder. I wouldn't choose armor based on appearances."

Wilder grimaced. "I wasn't thinking."

The heat of my anger cooled. But the self-awareness, the feeling of being ridiculous, stuck. It irritated and salted memories of when Elain's taunts on my appearance were a daily occurrence—of when the villagers treated me with suspicion and scorn.

Siska. I met Frazer's demanding stare. *Elain was a petty person who would've hated anybody she considered a rival or an obstacle to her ambitions. As for the villagers, they treated you like a threat because you were a white doe living in their forest of fawn. It had nothing to do with you, and everything to do with how small their world was. Things would've been different if you'd grown up in Aldar. For a start, I'd have bitten the brats for insulting you.*

I wobbled internally.

Lynx broke the hush that had fallen. "The rest of you are welcome to whatever armor and weapons you need from Mysaya's vaults. The pieces we own are limited, but it couldn't hurt to look. I can take whoever wants to visit them now if you're done sparring."

"Got anything pink and sparkly?" Cai joked half-heartedly.

Lynx let out a soft laugh. "No. But you're more likely to find something like that in the vaults than in the armories. Most of the stuff in there is black and red and emblazoned with Morgan's emblem."

"Then I'll go with you." Cai crouched at the edge of the mat and placed his sword in the bag with the rest of the practice weapons. Straightening up, he added, "I don't want to dress up as one of Morgan's soldiers if I can help it."

"Same," Frazer added.

Lynx concentrated on my brother. "You should retrieve your sword and your kaskan bow while we're down there."

"You put them down in the vaults?"

A small nod. "I'm sorry I took them off you in the first place."

"You didn't get rid of them," Frazer said neutrally. "That's all I care about."

"What about you two"—Lynx glanced between Adrianna and Wilder —"are you coming?"

"No." Adrianna's face shut down. I sensed her mounting spears—a line of defense—against that question. "I'm wearing the uniform of my court into battle."

There was no point in mentioning there might not even be a fight tomorrow. Adrianna already knew.

"I'll look in your vaults," Wilder declared, standing taller. "I'd like to see what your kin buried down there." He'd said that as if he intended to inspect Lynx's possessions rather than accept a favor from him. Pride, I imagined, was to blame for that.

"Could you give me a minute before you leave?" I asked Wilder. "I need to talk to you about something."

His expression flickered with surprise. "Of course."

I didn't want to delay him, but I wasn't sure when I'd next get a chance to speak with him alone.

Frazer stared at me. *Have you decided to do the claiming? Is that what you want to tell Wilder?*

Yes.

His mouth compressed, not in annoyance but in acknowledgment of my decision. *Fair enough.*

That was it. No criticism. I exhaled relief.

Lynx shared a meaningful look with me. "I'll catch up with you later?"

"Okay." A shiver scurried down my spine like a mouse with cold feet.

Lynx led Frazer and Cai out.

"Before lunch, I was helping the Fiends prepare the battlements for an invasion." Adrianna strapped her very real, very sharp sword to her hip. "I should get back to that since they were short-handed."

I suspected that being on the lookout for the Riverlands army was her real reason for going atop the outer wall. Adrianna left. Then it was me and my guardian.

Nerves tumbled in my stomach. It was now or never.

"Wilder," I said, "I've decided to do a part of the claiming with Lynx."

He became a statue atop a distant mountain. Not a hint of emotion was shown. My lips felt stiff as I explained my reasoning to him.

When I was done, he placed his palm over his fist and pressed down. The *crack* of knuckles punctured the air. It didn't feel like a threat. Just a release of tension.

"I'm not sure what to say." His arms fell to his sides. "It was only yesterday you said you weren't ready to choose between him or me."

The anger and hurt sketched over his brow made my wings wilt. "I'm not choosing Lynx. But I can't ignore something that could give us an advantage in a battle. Believe me or don't, that's the truth."

I waited and waited, guts tightening like a wind-up clock.

Wilder concentrated on a spot over my shoulder, as if to shield me from the wildfire blazing through his forest-green eyes. "I hate the idea, obviously. But I won't try to dissuade you from something that could help you in a fight. And I won't let this come between us."

I expelled a shaky sigh colored with relief. "I thought you might never want to speak to me again."

He looked at me then. "I'm not giving up on us, not until you claim his heart, and he yours."

My tongue grew sticky with unspoken words and weak arguments.

"I don't want to talk about Lynx anymore," Wilder announced, picking up another practice sword from the pile. "I want to check that your skills haven't grown rusty."

He tossed the blade a little way up into the air, caught it by its blunted blade, and offered it to me, pommel-first.

I laid aside my Utemä so that it wouldn't swing and bang against my legs. Then I took up the blade that he offered me.

Wilder widened his stance. I copied him, spreading my feet slightly more than shoulder-width apart, centering my weight.

He charged.

I met steel with steel. A series of actions, reactions, attacks, and counters followed.

My muscles remembered our fights, and a natural rhythm was established. I didn't close in for kill strikes, content to practice my skills and to release some of the pressure trapped inside of me. That pressure had been there for a while, and it only got worse when I thought about what might be expected of me tomorrow.

Wilder seemed to decide we'd danced around enough. He went on the offensive.

I held him off again and again. Block. Dodge. Duck.

Wilder backed up. "Hold."

I halted, glad for the chance to catch my breath and relax leaden limbs.

"Your style of fighting has changed." In a casual flick of his wrist, he lifted his blade and pointed it at me. "You're always on the defensive. At Kasi, you'd do anything to gain the upper hand. You even went after my wings." That memory tugged a corner of his mouth up into a half-smile.

"I changed." I flashed him my snowy-white feathers. "Is it that surprising my style's changed too?"

"As a fae, I would've expected your style to have grown more aggressive, not less so." Wilder tapped his boot thoughtfully with the dulled tip of his sword. "I heard about what you went through in Asitar. You were in a battle—you had to kill people, correct?"

I struggled to hold his gaze. "Yes."

He drew closer until only a few inches separated us. "I might not be Frazer, but I understand you well enough. When you were human, you were physically weaker than almost every opponent, so you threw everything you had at them without thinking about the consequences because in there"—he tapped my temple—"you were fighting for survival. Now you're stronger than most fae, at least magically speaking, and if you met a non-magic user—a d'vainya—in battle, they wouldn't stand a chance." He tilted his head and raised his hands, mimicking surrender. "I wouldn't stand a chance, right?"

My chest shuddered. "I'd forgotten you could do that."

"What?"

"See through me."

Wilder got a forced look about him—that of a male enduring the unbearable. It made the scars stand out starkly on his lightly tanned face. "You've always liked a fair fight. I haven't forgotten the woman who argued against the favoritism shown toward fae at Kasi." He focused on my thought-creased brow. "I also suspect you're worried you'll lose control of your abilities and hurt innocent people."

Violent images infested my thoughts like ivy smothering a tree. "It's not only about wanting a fair fight or being scared to hurt the wrong people. It's how people die when I use sunlight on them. A dagger in the belly is one thing. But seeing somebody blister and char and turn to ash; it's vile. It doesn't matter if they're an enemy—nobody should die like that." A wrathful shadow broke free from the darkest corners of my mind. "Except perhaps Morgan."

He stood there in solidarity. Listening. He knew there was more.

"As for our fight, it's not that I was afraid to hurt you exactly. I'm well aware you could still beat me with both hands tied behind your back. I just forgot about landing hits ... I've missed our sparring matches." I pushed past the lump in my throat. "I've missed you."

Wilder chucked our practice blades into the carrying case nearby. He pulled me into his arms in one fierce motion. I let him hold me, let him breathe me in.

"You'll figure this out," he whispered.

My innards clenched in an effort to hold on to the tears. He'd always believed in me, even when I could barely hold a sword straight.

Wilder landed a quick kiss to the top of my head. He was releasing me, stepping back, when Frazer's stressed voice interrupted my thoughts. *Ena.*

I tensed. *What's wrong?*

He reached for me mentally. I dropped my shield and linked to him. He sent an image of an unknown male and Adrianna landing in a courtyard. They were carrying two bodies. *Kestrel and Eagle were tasked with watching over the legion and reporting their movements back to us. Their bodies were left on the borders of Mysaya for us to find.*

Regret and sadness blended until I couldn't tell which of us was feeling what, only that we were symbiotic. I tore myself from our shared world in order to focus on Wilder. "We have to go. There's been an attack."

A blink, then he paced over to where he'd lain his black and red sword. Using the toe of his boot, he flicked it off the floor and caught it one-handed. "Has anybody been hurt?"

I relayed the news as I returned my Utemä to the belt on my suit.

Wilder and I hurried to the main entrance hall of the west wing. We walked through it and out into a courtyard, one encircled by thick white walls that glittered in the daylight. This fortification separated the castle grounds from the small city beyond.

We spied Frazer, Adrianna, and the unknown male in the middle of the courtyard, standing in front of a statue. The sculpture depicted a kneeling soldier holding his shield up in defense of the castle behind us.

Bear and Owl were there too, crouched beside the bodies of their fallen pack members. Their shoulders were hunched over in grief.

Wilder and I joined their group. The smell of cold blood, fear-loosened bowels, and herbs spilling out of flower beds intermingled in an ugly way. That, plus a closer look at Kestrel and Eagle made me clap a hand over my mouth as bile rose in my throat. Their wings were wrecked and their bodies were missing fingers, noses, and eyeballs. Their foreheads were branded with a Kaeli word: pánu.

What does pánu mean? I turned to my right, to where my brother stood in armor that must've come from the vaults. He wore overlapping pieces of pitch-black leather studded with bright steel. His sword, quiver, and kaskan bow were attached to his belt.

It's a rare sprite that many fae take for a death omen, Frazer replied. *To breathe its name is to utter a threat. Roughly translated, it means you're going to die.*

My stomach dropped away and dread rose to fill the chasm left behind. Violence was already seeping into the cracks of Mysaya. A flood that might soon drown us all.

"Ena. Wilder. This is the leader of the Aurorian Sami, Gaius Rochka." Frazer motioned to the male next to him.

Gaius was taller than me, and much of his powerful figure was obscured by light robes. His features were smooth and handsome; the silver streaking his neat beard and coarse hair were the only indicators of age.

"I haven't gone by that title since the exile," Gaius told Frazer.

"It doesn't matter whether you still use it," Frazer countered, his tone politer than usual. He clearly respected this male. "The host still considers you as their commander, otherwise they wouldn't have picked you to speak on their behalf."

Gaius loosed a growl laced with humility.

Frazer's focus skipped between me and Wilder. "Gaius has led a host of over three hundred Sami here in answer to our pleas for help. He was the one who spotted Kestrel's and Eagle's bodies as he was flying overhead."

Still in a squat, Bear's bent head suddenly went up. "It makes no sense that they were captured. They were seasoned warriors and two of the best shifters in my pack. They wouldn't have lost control over their animals or been careless enough to reveal their fae forms near the legion."

"Had they done the spell to awaken their familiars?" I asked.

Bear rose up as slowly as an elderly person. "No. They wanted to wait until after the battle."

"There is a spider who can sense what abilities and level of power a witch has," Wilder said from my left. "If he saw them in their animal forms, he might've figured out what they were."

"Why didn't you tell us about this before?" Bear demanded, his irises glowing a lighter brown. I wasn't that surprised; Liora had said he'd summoned his familiar.

"Because he wasn't with my legion." Wilder glanced down ruefully at the tortured bodies. "If he's there now, there's only one person who could've ordered a higher-up like him out of Alexandria."

I squeezed my wings together. "Morgan."

He gave me a grim nod. "She must've returned to Alexandria."

"Do we think this spider tortured Eagle and Kestrel for information?" Adrianna said, unusually quiet.

Gaius answered that. "The state of their bodies suggests the disfigurements were done after they were already dead."

That was a small mercy.

"I'm taking Eagle and Kestrel out into the surrounding forest," said Bear, his low voice rough with anger and sorrow. "They should be buried under the trees, not on the grounds of a castle that meant nothing to them."

Owl stood up and signed to the building behind us.

Bear grew gaunt around the eyes. "I want to clean and prepare them for burial before we tell the pack."

Owl nodded sadly.

"Will you come back after their death rites? Or have you decided to leave?" Frazer asked them passively.

"I'm no fool," Bear said. "Thanks to the traitor in my pack, Morgan will know that the Winged Fiends helped capture Mysaya. If I order us to leave, her wrath will follow us into the wilds, and we'll be picked off as easily as tearing the wings from a fly. Our fate, whatever it is, is the same as yours now. We go where you go." His expression was bleaker than midwinter, but his notes were tougher than leather. He sounded resolved. "Let's hope we fly to victory and not to a traitor's death."

Hearing that last bit was equivalent to taking a rock to the skull.

Not the most cheering of speeches, huh? Zola remarked.

Indeed.

Bear and Owl picked up the bodies. They flew south over the wall.

"In your letter to me, you said Morgan would strike the city tomorrow," Gaius said, facing Frazer. "With that in mind, I think we should talk about how the host can best serve you as soon as possible."

"Agreed," said Frazer, "but you should know that our group has decided to flee Mysaya if the Riverlands army doesn't show up by midnight tonight. I'd still appreciate your help whichever way the wind blows."

That received a curt nod from Gaius. "Understood."

"You should call your people inside Mysaya's walls before we discuss things further," Frazer added.

Gaius exhibited shrewdness. "How do you know they're not already inside?"

Frazer coughed a dry laugh.

Adrianna frowned at that. "Three hundred fae couldn't slip past the walls without being noticed. Not even the Sami could pull that off."

Gaius's eyebrow flicked upward.

"It's a joke, Adrianna," Frazer explained.

She grumped. "Oh."

"Tell the host that they can rest their wings in the empty buildings in the inner city," Frazer said to Gaius. "Or you can make use of your old quarters."

Gaius viewed the castle joylessly. "I won't disturb those old ghosts."

"The city, then," Frazer said, settling the matter.

"Why don't you fly out with me?" Gaius eyeballed Frazer's wings with no small amount of awe. "It'll be good to see you in the sky again. I'm still amazed that you got them back. That must've been some healing spell."

Healing spell? Frazer must've lied to explain away his wings. I schooled my features into an unsurprised expression. An unmarked sheet of paper.

"I'd prefer to make my own way into the city," Frazer said smoothly. "I'll find you once you've landed."

"I'll find you first." Gaius's tone suggested that he considered that a certainty rather than a promise.

As he ascended into the late afternoon sky, I bumped Frazer's shoulder. *Healing spell?*

His moon-colored wings twitched. *The truth would've been harder for him to believe.*

Adrianna skirted Frazer and seized me by the wrist. "I'm going to search for the others. They should know about this." She was already tugging me after her when she asked, "Will you come with me?"

"Wait." Wilder's command stopped me and Adrianna in our tracks.

I glanced over my shoulder and looked at him. A question loomed on his brow like a rain cloud as he searched my face for an answer. Tension built in his shoulders, wings, and jaw. Just when I thought he was about to mention the claiming, his features dulled. "Be careful. Don't change out of your armor, and keep your weapon on you at all times."

"Are you worried about assassins getting into Mysaya?" I asked him.

There was a time not so long ago when that would've felt like an absurd assumption for me to make. Now, not so much.

"We've had people dumping bodies on our borders undetected." His expression didn't flicker with worry once. The mask of the cool, calm, and in-control Sabu remained firmly set in place. "So yes, it's a concern. As are traitors."

"We can arrange proper patrols now the Sami are here," Frazer contributed.

"May I come with you to meet with Gaius?" Wilder asked, suddenly turning to him. "I'd like to talk to you both about how we can utilize the Sami's strengths."

"We decided you should lead us into battle at the round table. As our Sabu, you ought to be at any discussion regarding the defense of Mysaya."

Wilder's brow puckered at that lukewarm invitation. "Was that a yes?"

"Yes," I answered for my brother.

Frazer cut toward the gate set into the low wall that divided the courtyard from other parts of the castle. Without a backward glance, he said, "I'm walking down into the city. Are you coming?"

Wilder shot me a parting look that seemed to say *I wish you wouldn't do what you're about to do.*

Adrianna wasted no time in frog-marching me to the double staircase in the main hall. That was where she stopped and faced me. "Did you decide to do the claiming?"

"Yes."

"Are you going to find Lynx now?"

"Y—yes."

A little nod. "Then, you should know that during the process you might feel like you're going into heat—"

"Hold on." I splayed my palms in alarm. "What do you mean by going into heat?"

Adrianna dismissed my concerns with a wave of her hand. "I'll teach you about female reproductive cycles later. All you need to know right now is that if anything happens with Lynx, you don't need to feel guilty about it. Even if you ride his ass into tomorrow, you don't owe him this." With her index finger, she jabbed the spot over where my heart would be. "Understood?"

I was torn between laughter and amused despair. "Lynx has already warned me about what might happen." Curiosity sparking, I added, "But you sound as if you've got personal experience of the claiming. Did you and Zeke … with each other?"

Mouth compressing, her gaze darted off in a random direction. I knew her well enough to see that she wasn't adopting a prim attitude, and she wasn't irritated at my prying. She was fighting back a smile. That, in turn, made me smile.

"We talked about it. That's all."

My grin got bigger, wider.

"Go." She encouraged me with a soft push. "I'll find Cai and Liora and tell them what's happened."

I hesitated, only to ask my brother, *Do you know where Lynx went after the vaults?*

Library.

I went to the east wing directly, entering that temple of paper and ink and coming to a halt underneath the star chandelier.

My nose lifted at the traces of his scent. I cupped my hands around my mouth and cried out, "Lynx?"

That shout *echoed, echoed, echoed.*

I peered up at the many mezzanine levels. It was possible that he hadn't heard me, even with the advantages of fae-hearing.

A faint call sounded from above. "Ena?"

"Yes." My voice pitched higher than usual thanks to the nerves putting pressure on my vocal chords. "Where are you?"

A few moments later, Lynx left the stacks and stepped up to the brass railing three floors up. He extended his silky black wings.

"I'll come to you," I told him.

I ran and jumped into the air.

CHAPTER 43
WHEN GLASS SHATTERS

My movements were clumsy and labored, but I reached the third floor without having an accident. Satisfied, I folded my wings and stepped down to where Lynx was waiting for me at the foot of the landing platform.

"Are you all right?" he asked, brow furrowed.

"Not really."

I recounted recent events. By the end of my tale, Lynx's face was a starless sky. "It's good Gaius has joined us. He's a master of the sword. As for Kestrel and Eagle ..."

Lynx trailed off when I seized his hand. "I think we should do the claiming now."

I felt suspended over a ravine as my words hung in the space that separated us. A short distance that felt like a mile. Only his reply would determine if I fell to the bottom of the ravine or if I made it to the other side.

He nodded, slotting his fingers between mine. "Come with me."

"Where are we going?" I asked, my heart running wild.

"You'll see."

Lynx guided me through the library—the labyrinth of thoughts and memories and expression.

We arrived in a private reading room. It was furnished with a plum-colored couch and velvet cushioned stools. Framing the wall opposite me was a large window with pieces of stained glass arranged to depict a shooting star soaring over a mountain range.

"I learned from Frazer that you love books." He led me over to a table of polished wood positioned below the window. "I thought you might appreciate it if they made up the rest of your claiming gift."

Lynx slipped his hand out of mine and unstacked the three volumes waiting for me on the tabletop. His actions lacked fuss or ceremony. I still felt shy as I studied his gifts to me. Two were leather bound, and the third looked as if it cost a court's fortune. The cover was bordered by jewels; the edges of the pages were gilded.

"This is a famous story among fae." Lynx touched the expensive volume, which was titled *Tristan and Aliya*. "It's about a couple that meet when their kingdoms are at war with each other." He gestured to the plainest book on the table. "That one has a lot of information about mating bonds that I thought might be useful."

I picked up the last book. Its cover was pocket-sized and decorated with a hummingbird.

"That's Kaeli poetry," said Lynx. "I'll translate it for you as soon as I get the chance."

With my fingertips, I grazed the sprig of purple lilac poking out from between its pages. "What's this?"

"A bookmark."

"Odd bookmark."

"I like flowers."

The sincerity in his voice tugged at my heartstrings. I carefully placed the book back on the table.

Zola and I are going to block you out for an hour to give you some privacy, Thea said.

Have fun, Zola added smugly.

I barely heard them as I faced Lynx.

Nerves scrambling my brain, I swept my gaze up over his brown leather boots, sturdy trousers, and the gray cotton top that showed off his arms. When my eyes found his, I was struck by the lamplight quivering there, transforming his amber irises into molten gold.

"As I said before, I don't have much to give you." I plucked a feather from my wing. Ignoring the pinch of pain, I held it out to him. "You told me that a lock of my hair would be enough, but this seemed like something a fae would give."

He stared at the feather, expressionless.

Doubt and embarrassment crowded in. He had gifted me a bejeweled book and a suit of priceless armor. I'd repaid his generosity with a feather. What had I been thinking? "It's fine if you don't want it."

He snagged it from me before I could get rid of it. "This is the best thing you could've given me."

I glowed inwardly at that.

"I'll put it somewhere safe." Lynx exerted his power, vanishing the feather.

"There's some things you should know before we go any further."

He hip-leaned against the table. "Go on."

Neck and cheeks growing hot, I told him about the stones and what I would use them for. He listened with rapt attention, stirring only to shift his wings.

I couldn't look at him when I confessed Abraxus was my grandfather. He could draw the connection between Abraxus and Archon. I wasn't doing it.

"I'm also related to Balor and Freyta through my mother, so it's not all, you know ... bad. That's pretty much it. That's all I wanted to tell you." I pulled my lips in and wet them with a tongue dried with nerves. "I'll understand if you don't want to continue with the claiming."

"If anything, it makes me want to do it more."

Shock made my eyes bigger, rounder. "Why?"

"You've just told me that my mate has to fight the Dark King." He took his weight off the table and straightened up. "You better believe I'll do everything and anything to help you bear that burden. I don't know if forming a mental link with you can help, but if there's even the slightest chance it will, I'll take it." A sly grin hooked his lips upward. "Besides, call me shallow, but I think my mate being descended from gods is hot—even if some of them are evil."

I swiped at his arm.

Lynx pressed the tip of his tongue to his two front teeth in a teasing gesture.

That pulled a disbelieving laugh from me. He was totally ridiculous.

Lynx's expression sobered. "Seriously though, I wasn't exactly proud to be my father's son. There was a reason people called him the Iron-hearted King. But we don't have to be like our relatives, right?"

"That's what people keep telling me," I muttered.

"It must be true, then."

I tucked my hair behind my ear. "If you don't mind, I guess we should ..."

"Start." Lynx's gaze dipped to my sword. "It might be awkward for you to be wearing a weapon when we do this."

Hot-faced, I removed my Utemä and handed it to him.

He rested my sword against the table.

I swallowed hard as he closed the space between us with a single step. My breath hitched as he grabbed my waist, lifting me onto the tabletop.

He curled his fingers into the undersides of my knees and parted my legs. I felt as if corset strings were pulling my ribcage in, in, *in*.

Lynx took his time moving toward me, his outer thighs sliding along the insides of my legs, making me acutely aware of every inch that was lost until our cores met in a gentle bump. That emptied my lungs of air.

Seeing how his height made our positioning awkward, I retracted my wings and lay down on the table to offer him a better angle.

Lynx bent over me and braced his forearm over my head, keeping his weight from crushing me.

I tensed when he ran his thumb along my jaw and dipped his head, but it was only to land a kiss to my collarbone. He moved up to my neck, whispering kisses as he went.

My scalp tingled. "You're not biting me."

Lynx lifted his head up. "This only happens once. We should enjoy it." He rested his fevered brow on mine. His eyes looked almost red, bloodshot. A clear sign of his patience being tested. "I also want to give you a chance to change your mind."

"I haven't. I won't."

His pupils flared. "You'll have me, then?"

"Yes," I croaked.

We shared a shallow inhale.

Lynx linked his free hand up with mine and slid his fangs down. I angled my head, offering up my throat.

He squeezed my hand once. Then, bit by bit, he sunk his teeth into me.

There was no pain, only wave after wave of sensation crashing down my spine. Every part of me, from the soles of my feet to the crown of my head, prickled intensely.

A ripple of pleasure swiftly followed. It sung through my veins, awaking a creature of impulse and desire. I tried to master my fae instincts by taking calming breaths. That only pulled his scent deeper into me. I drowned in jasmine, bergamot, and stormy skies. Those smells tugged at a mental string. As if a memory was struggling to be born. As if I'd dreamed his scent before. At that, my control drained away like sand through a clenched fist.

A treacherous moan spilled from me.

Lynx answered with a sexy-as-fuck growl, causing my toes to curl in their knee-high boots. He relaxed, letting more of his weight sink into me. That aligned our chests, and without a sliver of space between, the hearts caged within revealed themselves to each other. They raced in unison, and our bodies' heat turned me to wax melting in front of a furnace.

His pants grew tight as his cock hardened against my belly. That, combined with the solid wood against my ass, fueled the ache building between my thighs.

Trapped in a dizzying tailspin, my need for release became so demanding, it felt as if I'd swallowed a box of firecrackers. The pressure had to go somewhere, so I wasn't surprised when my magic ignited and embers escaped my fingertips. They wouldn't hurt Lynx, but they could burn the city of paper surrounding us.

"We have to move my books. They might catch fire." I was breathless, almost incoherent.

Lynx removed his fangs from my neck. In a wolfish growl, he said, "Fuck the books," and with a twirl of his wrist, my presents disappeared.

He peppered my pulse line with fevered kisses, soothing the tiny sting left over from his bite. I couldn't take it anymore. I wrapped my legs around his hips and we fitted together like lock and key.

His hips bucked. That was the beginning of the end.

My power exploded outward in a fork of golden sunlight and hit the window directly behind me. The sound of shattering glass filled the air. I closed my eyes as shards fell from above.

Lynx shadow-jumped us out of harm's way.

We reappeared on the couch with him still lying on top of me. He moved off, letting me sit up.

I glanced over my shoulder, gaping at the broken window. The stained glass rendering of the mountains was gone, and in its place was an uninterrupted view of the real thing—of a landscape stained in a loom of dusky light.

"Sorry about the window," I said, turning back to Lynx.

"It doesn't matter." Lynx extended a hand in what seemed to be both a demand and a plea.

He needed this. He needed me to go through with my part.

My heart battered my ribcage like rams at war. I grasped his hand and rose onto my knees. Lynx settled against the couch cushion, pulling me on top of him at the same time. As I sat astride him, my mind went blank. I'd bitten somebody in a fight. This was different. Very different.

I was teetering on a cliff edge, trusting uncertain wings to carry me to safer shores. What if I hurt him?

Lynx kneaded the skin at the top of my hips. "It's all right. You won't hurt me."

I startled. "How did you—"

"Your expression." In the softest of whispers, he added, "I want you, Ena. I want you to—"

I clapped a hand over his mouth and freed my fangs.

His throat bobbed. That shoved me over the edge. And I bit.

Blood slicked my tongue, and my world collapsed. It narrowed to just the two of us and the rolling drumbeat now playing in my head. The noise echoed what I'd heard in the hot spring. It was the earth's heartbeat.

Embrace the storm. Embrace life.

Those words came from deep within and were laced with my magic —the force that connected me to nature. I chose to listen to that ancient power, temporarily releasing my doubts and fears about our intimacy. They were poor companions anyway.

I sheathed my fangs and soothed his throat with a slow stroke of my tongue.

Thunder rolled overhead. That was my only hint of what would happen next.

His power surged, hitting me with a static shock that set my skin tingling.

A golden thread appeared, connecting us at our chests. It shone brighter and brighter, and with it, the heat between us turned into an inferno.

Lynx's long lashes fanned downward. He glared at my mouth as if he wanted to feast on it—to brand it as his.

My thighs clenched against his. That was it.

We met in the middle, kissing with passion, turning our heads, exploring every angle. Through our clothes, I felt his cock twitch up against me. Riding the high of primal energy, I moaned loudly into his mouth.

Lynx swept his tongue past my lips. I opened up to him, and as his tongue slid against mine, his silver stud clicked inside my mouth. I imagined what it would be like if he were doing this to my sex, and my core clenched.

Our hips shifted together, creating a rhythm that mimicked the world's heartbeat still ringing in my ears. The smell, the taste, and the feel of him wound me up tighter and tighter.

Limbs shook, I wasn't sure whose. Lynx tugged at the spine of my outfit. The material resisted. But he knew it would. Taldävarian armor couldn't be removed unless the wearer wished it. I reached around awkwardly and unfastened the fabric for him.

Lynx yanked the sides of my suit down, baring my breasts and trapping my arms. I stretched my spine, signaling him silently.

Leaving my lips, he started to trail kisses down my neck. When he reached my chest, his hot mouth went right where I wanted it, closing over my nipple, sucking at that sensitive bundle of nerves. The cool metal of his stud added another layer of pleasure. He licked and sucked every inch of my breasts. Finally, I couldn't take it anymore. I ripped my hands free of my sleeves and plunged my fingers into his dark hair. "Lynx."

At the sound of my needy pant, his mouth popped off my nipple. I was about to protest when he slanted his lips over mine in a wild, inseparable kiss. I tasted the yearning of his heart, and it pushed me higher and higher.

I gripped his shoulders, and my inner female crowed behind our mental walls, practically swooning at the warrior's strength coiled in his muscles.

Moaning shamelessly, I bore down on him.

He palmed my ass with a strong, firm grip. Helped by his masterful hands, I rocked faster and faster, and my core tightened up in a way that caused my eyes to shut, my brow to pucker, and my lips to part in a gasp.

I was unraveling. And I didn't want to do it alone. "With me," I panted into his mouth. "Together."

"Fuck, yes," he growled, and his face shone with male satisfaction.

Our lips met again as his wings spread to half-mast, awakening in excitement or maybe pleasure. Either way, the female in me loved it.

His eyes danced. "I'm there."

"Mmmm." I nodded. "Me too."

I chased the dangerous fluttering in my belly. The pressure made me squirm until I relaxed into that rising feeling, and into him.

A spasm of white-hot bliss exploded in my core, sending waves of pleasure rushing throughout my entire body. I was gone, flying, floating.

Lynx released a long, guttural groan. My eyes rolled back and fluttered beneath my lids. I took all kinds of strange joy in hearing his blunt pleasure voiced.

The tension in our bodies broken, we slumped against each other, spent and trembling, our breaths disordered.

"Ena." Lynx rubbed his head against my nape, marking me as his.

I held him there for an unknown length of time, feeling like sunlight-warmed snow. The earth's heartbeat quieted, and a peaceful hush replaced it.

A presence loomed at the edge of my mind. It felt like a whisper in the darkness. A voice in another room.

I felt a *tap, tap, tap* against my mental-shield. I reared back to study Lynx's relaxed expression. Lips made puffy by my searing kisses curled up at the corners. Why did I find that so adorable?

I lowered my mental-shield. *Did you just knock to come in?*

Yes. He waved at me. *Hello.*

I huffed a laugh.

Lynx pushed my hair off my sweaty forehead. The happy look on his face hurt my heart. I fell from a high place into the cold waters of reality. What had we done?

He moved to kiss me again as if it was the most natural thing in the world. And it was. That was the problem. I put my hands on his chest, stopping him.

Lynx drew his neck back into his shoulders. From there, he searched my face. That close scrutiny made my exposed breasts feel extremely obvious. I yanked the neckline of my suit up and tried to fasten it at the back.

"Let me."

I ceased my fumbling efforts. "Thanks."

Lynx quietly brought the corners of my suit together at the back and linked the material up to the spine. He seemed to be getting ready to say something.

I braced myself.

Lynx froze, his head cocked, and his gaze cut toward the door that we'd walked in through.

Then we were gone, vanished into darkness.

CHAPTER 44
THE BREATH BEFORE THE STORM

We materialized in my bedroom. Lynx slowly lowered me to the floorboards, reluctant to let me go.

Feet on the ground, I asked him, "Why did we leave?"

"I heard footsteps."

Guilt pitted my stomach. What if it had been Wilder?

"Do you regret it?" Lynx's pained expression wrecked me.

"No," I said truthfully.

He traced the wrinkle between my eyebrows with his fingertip. "What's this for, then? Are you worried about how Wilder will react to our claiming?" Lynx was careful to show nothing in his voice, but his expression was that of somebody preparing themselves for the worst.

"I already told Wilder what we planned to do."

Lynx jerked a little. Surprised, no doubt.

"I'm just feeling guilty. I said I wouldn't pursue anything with anybody." In a self-conscious gesture, I touched my lips. "And then, we …"

I muzzled myself.

"It's not your fault things got heated," he said firmly. "It would've been the same for any mated couple."

My heart lost another inch of ground. "You don't have to do that."

"Do what?"

"I can take responsibility for my actions."

He watched me carefully, as if chewing over his next words. I refused to shy from his gaze and give him more cause to think I regretted our claiming. Still, it felt like a dangerous thing to stare into my mate's eyes. It forced recent images of him into my mind's eye—images that brought me out in a hot flush. The heat radiating off me carried our intermingled scents and my own musk up to my nose. It reminded me that my body still craved him. That it wanted him.

A sense of panic was rising in me. My wings reacted by squirming beneath my shoulder blades. Unable to bear their fidgeting, I pushed them through the slits in my armor—slits that then shaped themselves around my wings, adjusting to their movement.

Lynx cast an admiring eye over my feathers.

"You're staring," I said, my notes tight from breathlessness.

He came back with, "You're beautiful."

The sincerity in his voice punched me in the gut. I wavered, unsure what to do with that compliment.

"Ena, are we all right?" Lynx asked quietly.

I struggled with the knot in my throat. "Mm."

His mouth pursed. But if he didn't believe me, he didn't admit it. Lynx moved to pick my sword up off the bed. I hadn't even noticed he'd brought it along with us.

"Here." He handed me my Utemä.

I gazed down at my sheathed blade, curiosity drawing my eyebrows together. "Can you transport anything? Could you send a person away with a wave of your hand?"

"If I could do that, I would've sent Wilder to the continent."

I pinned him with a withering glare. He appeared completely unapologetic. "I can shift inanimate objects a fair distance. But I can't just send people away, no."

Tucking that information away, I looped my sword onto my belt. My fingers caught on the clasp when I heard, *Open the window.*

I almost jumped out of my damned boots.

Alarm streaked across Lynx's face. "What is it?"

Hurry up. I want to rest my feathers. I'm extremely old, you know.

Excitement exploded through me. *Danu?*

The familiar answered in his usual irritable croak. *Obviously.*

I was already halfway across the room when I said, "Danu's back."

Lynx tailed me. I fumbled with a window latch, and he reached over my head and pushed at the frame. The lock snapped as easily as a flower stem, and the window swung open on hinges that squeaked from disuse.

I peered up at him. "Was that necessary?"

He smirked. "You seemed like you were in a hurry. And we can always fix the latch."

"Not *we*. You."

His smile widened. "Yes, dear."

I whacked his chest.

A squawk pierced the balmy air. I turned to search the evening sky for Danu. He was quick to appear, dropping from on high, pulling up out of his dive with Cora beside him. I ducked as the raven and the eagle familiars sailed into the room. They landed on their own respective bedposts and pointed their beaks at us.

"Cora, is my sister with you? Is Diana with her?"

Turning her head, she fixed a serious yellow eye upon me. *Yes, to both questions. They sent us ahead to tell you that they'll be outside the city walls in fifteen minutes.*

My wings slumped as a great weight lifted off me—a weight that I hadn't even known I was carrying until now.

But the whole army is exhausted, Cora continued. *Danu didn't reach us until late last night, and we had to risk flying over the Metori to get here in time. We've been battling high winds all day.*

I tuned into my kin bond. *Brata?*

What is it?

I shared the news with him.

One moment. There was a break in his concentration, and I got the impression he was talking to somebody. *I'm headed to the outer gate with Gaius and Wilder. Will I see you there?*

I didn't have to think about it. *Yes.*

"Frazer's going to the main gate," I said to Lynx.

"You want to go there too?"

My nod was swift and sure.

"Give me a minute and I'll join you." Lynx vanished.

His unexpected departure threw me. I stalled, unsure of what to do next.

I have to hunt, Cora announced. *If you need anything, think about me and call out my name.*

She spread her six-foot-wide wings. The lamplight highlighted the white, brown, and auburn hues of her feathers, making them gleam and shimmer. Cora flew out the window and disappeared into the darkening sky.

I was left with a sharp-eyed Danu.

You might want to think about washing up, he told me in a wry manner.

That comment had me hurrying out the door. I didn't stop moving until I entered the bathroom and I stared at my reflection in the wall mirror.

Crap.

My lips were swollen from kissing, and the bruising on my neck was as conspicuous as a footprint in virgin snow. I couldn't do anything about the mottled skin, but I could get rid of the dried blood. The puncture marks had already clotted. I wet a towel and scrubbed off the red flakes.

After that, I looked in the neighboring rooms for my friends. I hadn't heard them through the walls, but I couldn't resist checking. A habit from my human days, I supposed. As expected, nobody was around.

I returned to my bedroom to find Danu cleaning his feathers. Lynx was nowhere to be seen. Agitated, I went to the open window and stared out.

My feathers itched at a disturbance in the air.

I whirled around, and my heart caught fire.

Lynx stood before me, looking like a god of war. He exuded a lethal strength, covered head to toe in a suit of ebony steel that flexed with his movements. There were numerous knives attached to his belt, and a longsword beside his hip. The refined silver of the hilt shone brightly —wickedly.

"Ready?"

I shook myself inwardly. "Yes. But shouldn't we try finding Adrianna first? She should know her mother's on her way."

No need, Danu interrupted. *I've already told your friends. They'll meet you at the outer gate. Now, go away. I've been flying nonstop for two days, and I can't sleep with you two chattering.*

Without further ado, he tucked his small head under his wing.

"Want to fly or jump?" Lynx offered me his hand.

My impatience won out. "Jump."

I grasped his warm palm.

In a blink, we stood before the forty-foot-high outer wall. Frazer, Wilder, and Gaius were nearby, facing wide-open doors constructed from steel and embellished with moonstone. Beyond these doors I saw a short tunnel and a portcullis that was lifting, courtesy of some mysterious mechanism.

Lynx and I started toward the three males. The sound of our movements had them turning to greet us.

Wilder stared at me, at the bite mark on my neck. His face was grave, almost unlively. Only the flash in his eyes revealed his inner turmoil.

Gaius was on the far right of their group, his attention fixed on Lynx. "You seem much the same, young prince."

"I wish that was true," Lynx said flatly.

The look that passed between them seemed to indicate a deep understanding, a prior knowledge of each other.

"The winds can't change the mountain, Lynx," Gaius said, the faintest trace of a smile upon his lips.

"Is that so?" A bit of humor had worked its way into his tone.

Gaius nodded.

A hush fell, but it was one of short duration.

"Has there been any sign of the army?" I asked eagerly.

"No." Frazer angled his head, indicating that I should stand beside him.

I did. Lynx settled on my other side.

Bathed in an evening light, we waited. It wasn't long before far-off wingbeats reached our ears. Then another louder noise came into the foreground. I turned around at the sound of hurried footsteps.

Peering up at the city, I scanned the winding streets, the bridges, and the proud and fair buildings, all illuminated by the cold light of crystal lanterns.

Three archways connected the courtyard to the city. Adrianna, Cai, and Liora showed up under the middle arch. They strode over to us at a swift pace.

Only Cai had changed into a battle-ready outfit. For his underclothes, he'd chosen gray trousers and a cotton tunic. His armor was forged from a mysterious metal that had the look of cloud-white marble, but it was pliable enough that he could move with ease. A new sword hung from his waist. The sheath was long and thin with an opaline sheen.

The second my friends reached us, Cai nodded at me, appearing unusually solemn. "You don't need to say it. I know I look great."

I snorted a laugh as Adrianna rolled her eyes.

Liora said, "You look amazing," but the compliment was for me.

If only I could've returned the sentiment. But her cheeks were as red as radishes, her eyes were dull pools, and her curls looked like roses wilting on the stem. "Did you get around to practicing the empath exercises?"

Her papery smile wasn't encouraging. "I tried to meditate, but I kept falling asleep. In the end, I got fed up and went back to the ward."

"I think it's good you rested while you could," Cai remarked. "I doubt any of us will get much sleep tonight."

"In my experience, only arrogant or stupid people sleep well before a big battle," Wilder said. "And neither type lasts long in wartime."

At the mention of war, my stomach, wings, and teeth clenched.

Cai seemed unfazed. "So what you're saying is our chances of survival are better if we're shitting ourselves?"

"Exactly," Wilder said smoothly.

Cai huffed. "I'm safe, then."

Chuckles circled. But it was low energy laughter, the kind affected by a heavier emotion: fear.

"Ena, do me a favor?" In a brotherly move, Cai ruffled Liora's limp curls. "Sort her hair out before tomorrow. She can't go into battle looking like a vagrant."

Liora pushed his arm away. "Quit it."

"I was only thinking of you," he said, wide-eyed.

"Shush," Liora hissed at him.

He did, but that left a gap in the conversation. I had nothing to distract me from restless nerves and a cartwheeling stomach.

Our entire group formed a rough line in front of the open gateway. Together, we watched the stars wink into existence and listened to the sounds of an entire army of fae approach. The noise reminded me of a strong wind blowing through prairie grass.

Gaius was the first to spot the army. "There."

I looked left and followed his gesture toward the eastern peaks. Thousands of soldiers appeared over the Metori mountains.

A horn blast rode the skies. With that, the Riverlands army had announced itself. Now they dove down the slopes in a flawless formation. The only sight comparable to it would've been a murmuration of starlings. Both were a wonder.

The cloud of fae landed half a mile out into the valley.

From behind us came other wings in motion. Bear, Owl, and Ryder flew over our heads and landed in front of us.

"We got your message," Bear said, facing Frazer. "So the Riverlands Court has arrived at last?"

Frazer gave him a tiny nod.

I side-eyed my brother. *What message?*

I asked Gaius to send someone up to the castle with news of the army's arrival. I didn't want the Fiends assuming we were being invaded a day early.

Good thinking.

"Do we go to them? Or do they come to us?" Bear asked, peering out the gateway at the grounded army.

"They come to us," said Wilder, Lynx, and Adrianna.

"At least you're clear about that," Ryder said, his voice lively with amusement.

"We'll have to meet Diana outside the gate, though." Adrianna leveled a stern look at Lynx. "You remember how this game is played? We have to establish rank straight away. Make it clear you're inviting her in."

I held up a hand. "I'm lost. Why is it important to establish rank?"

Adrianna's features stressed. "Because if we don't stand our ground and do things properly, she'll assume authority over Mysaya. Then it'll be her underlings making the calls tomorrow, and trust me, we don't want that happening."

My brows clashed. "She can do that? Just take over?"

"Diana outranks us all," Lynx said. "Under our laws, that gives her the right to take charge. The only thing preventing her from doing that is the fact that this isn't her property—it's mine. So, unless Diana wants to argue Morgan's occupation of my court is lawful, she'll have to accept I get the final say over what happens here."

"Then this is where I duck out," Ryder said. "I'm not a play-it-by-the-rules kind of fae. I'm bound to cause offense if I stay."

"I'm going too," Bear grunted out, cracking his hairy knuckles. "I've no patience for courtly nonsense. Find me when you're ready to discuss something real. Like the battle we're all going to fight and die in soon."

My stomach plunged into emptiness. Stars save us.

Owl gripped his mate's shoulder. I wasn't sure if it was to show comfort, or counsel restraint. Maybe both.

Wilder addressed Bear, Ryder, and Owl. "Don't be hard to find. You should be with us when we discuss our battle plans with Diana."

Owl made the sign of eating to his mate. Bear nodded and then eyed Wilder. "We'll be in one of the food halls."

Ryder snapped his fingers and pointed at Bear. "Great idea. I'm starving."

The feathers on Bear's wings rippled in annoyance. "You've just come from there."

A casual shrug. "So? I'm still hungry."

Frazer marked Ryder with a critical gaze. "You shouldn't take more than your fair share."

"I've brought in three times that of any other hunter sent out looking for fresh meat. And that was my first meal of the day." Ryder sidled closer to Frazer and tugged coyly at his sleeve. "If we're talking about what's fair, I think I deserve a second dinner, don't you?"

Frazer rearranged his features into a nonplussed image. If that wasn't enough of a dismissal, he broke eye contact.

"I'm going." Bear vaulted into the sky.

Owl went next.

Ryder took off last, but not before deliberately tickling the underside of my brother's chin with his russet-colored feathers. Frazer's eye twitched slightly. Otherwise, he didn't react.

"They're coming." Adrianna stepped toward the city gate.

I stared out at the valley. A small company had splintered off from the army and were winging their way toward us. I spotted what I thought might be my sister's blond hair, and excitement fizzed in my belly.

The eight of us strode through the double doors, the gatehouse tunnel, and under the drawn-up portcullis. We stopped on the long, overgrown path that cut across the untamed valley and passed by its three lakes.

Twelve fae landed a short distance away. The soldiers were dressed in scale armor, silver helmets, and blue wraparound capes that would protect them from a high-altitude chill.

The only fae not in uniform were Sefra and Diana. The latter had chosen high boots, leather leggings, and a silver breastplate fitted over a sapphire jacket with sharp shoulder pads. The polite mask of a politician was firmly in place as her gaze swept over our party. I assumed Sefra had caught her up on recent events since she didn't blink twice at the sight of my wings. Her eyes finally settled on her daughter. "You look well, tilä."

Adrianna reeled off a sentence in Kaeli, sounding as if she was reciting a passage from a tedious and boring book.

Diana gestured for Adrianna to join her side. From there, mother and daughter went back and forth in the fae language.

I lost interest and locked eyes with Sefra.

Done with standing on ceremony, she marched up to me, her pace swift and determined. If she hadn't been my siska, I might've been intimidated; she painted a menacing picture in wine-red underclothes, leather bracers, and high-necked chest armor fused with chain mail. Her yellow hair was scraped up into a tight ponytail and secured by a leather cuff, and her eyelids were stained in a strip of kohl that stretched from temple to temple.

When Sefra reached me, she hauled me into a rib-cracking hug. I wrapped my arms under her blue golden-flecked wings and drew in her scent.

"Thank the stars," Sefra whispered in my ear. "Danu said you'd decided to rescue Wilder. I thought I might arrive only to hear you'd been captured."

My conscience twinged.

Sefra stepped back, releasing me from our hug.

I studied her bloodshot eyes and listless wings. Concern rattled me. She was plainly exhausted. If she got no rest tonight, how would she perform on the battlefield tomorrow?

She gave my outfit the once over and smiled. "You look wonderful."

I cringed a little. I feared that she'd made the same assumption that Wilder had. That I'd chosen appearance over function. "It's taldävarian armor," I said pointedly. "Lynx gifted it to me."

Sefra's attention darted to the male standing on my left. Her neck stretched as she stared up at Lynx, who towered above her. "I heard you'd mated to Ena. Is that true?"

Stiff-winged, Lynx said, "Yes. I know you probably don't approve—"

She showed him a palm, and his mouth sealed shut.

"Let me say this first. I'm so sorry for what happened to your court. I'm sorry that I wasn't able to help you back then."

The tension in Lynx's features drained away, yielding to shock.

"Danu explained why you swore to be Morgan's guardian," Sefra said. "It seems our stories are not so different. Both of us made unpopular decisions, hoping we could save more people than we hurt."

Lynx's head hung heavier at that. "I failed in that regard. I've hurt a lot of people."

"On Morgan's orders—orders that you couldn't have refused if you'd tried." Sefra's chin rode even higher. "Or am I wrong?"

"No." He was so quiet that it hurt my heart. "No, you're not wrong."

"Well, then," Sefra said in a final sort of way.

"I knew I was going to like you," Cai said from my far left.

Sefra turned to him. "And you would be?"

"Cai."

"Ah." Her smile was sunshine peeking through the clouds. "Well, the feeling's mutual."

"Obviously."

Merry laughter spilled from my sister. Sefra's gaze then skipped to Liora, who stood between Cai and Lynx. "I'm glad to see that you're safe."

Glancing around the side of my mate, I saw that Liora's fevered complexion had worsened. The pink tint to her cheeks burned more fiercely and had spread to the very tip of her nose. "Same. I mean, I'm happy you're okay."

I guessed that her high coloring was a symptom of exertion—of being around so many people and sensing their emotions. I fought with my instincts, instincts that would have me begging her to return to the castle.

Sefra's focus shifted again. This time, it went to my immediate right. "And you must be my new little brother."

Her teasing was lost on Frazer. Instead, our bond resonated with his surprise and irritation. I felt him retreat into a hard place. "I am Ena's brother."

A pointed distinction.

I waited for Sefra's reaction. I wanted to explain how he was slow to warm up to people. But Frazer would despise that.

Yes, I would, he said, overhearing my thoughts.

"And nobody would doubt that claim." Sefra studied me and Frazer. "You two look a lot alike."

"We know," Frazer and I said together.

Bemusement formed on Sefra's brow. Instead of pursuing the subject, her gaze drifted up our line and stopped on Wilder.

He nodded to show his respect.

She moved to stand in front of him. "It's been a long time, Wilder."

"It has."

"Last we spoke, you called me Queen."

Wilder hesitated.

Sefra held out a hand. "You may call me Sefra now."

Wilder was solemn as he said, "An honor."

They clasped forearms.

"Baz," Diana called out. "Give the princess her sword."

A soldier broke formation and bent down before Adrianna. He presented her with the hilt. The longsword was covered by an ice-blue scabbard inlaid with rivers of silver.

"You left it when you went to Kasi," Diana said in a tone that suggested she'd better take the sword or else suffer the consequences. "It is time it was returned to you."

Adrianna slipped into a skin of bland formality. "Thank you."

The sword had its own belt engraved with the Riverlands insignia—three mountains over water. Adrianna secured the belt to her waist as Diana walked up and halted before Lynx.

Lynx went first. "Queentina."

He didn't bow.

"I couldn't believe it when Danu said you'd rebelled." Her gaze traveled to Wilder and then back to Lynx. "How did the two of you break your bonds to her?"

"That is a conversation for another time," Lynx said.

Many of the soldiers behind Diana regarded Lynx with disapproval; in some cases deepening into dislike, even hatred.

That ruffled the feathers of my inner female. I found myself glaring at them, silently telling them to *back off* with everything except for my words.

"Perhaps you are correct. There are more pressing concerns." Diana peered up at Mysaya's walls, propping a hand on her hip. "If my memory serves me correctly, there aren't enough houses in the inner city to accommodate my company, so we'll set up camp in the valley. In our rush to reach you, thirteen of my soldiers sustained wing injuries. I want them treated in Mysaya's ward."

"I'm willing to overlook the fact you landed your army in my valley without permission," Lynx said, cutting through her speech like sharpened steel. "But if you want to camp here and treat people in our ward, you can pay me and my mate the proper respect and ask."

"You've claimed each other?" Diana crossed her arms, keeping her neutral mask firmly fixed in place.

"We have." Lynx stared her down. There was none of the kindness or warmth I'd come to expect in his expression. "Ena is the Lady of Mysaya now."

My mind stumbled. But for the sake of appearances, I schooled my features into nonchalance. Then I reached out to my brother. *Why is he lying to her?*

He isn't. Your claiming is a formal acknowledgment of the bond between you. In fae law, it entitles you to half of each other's property.

What? I said, my thoughts growing screechy. *Why didn't Lynx tell me that?*

You'll have to ask him. Frazer leveled me with a gaze that demanded calm. *But he was right to reveal it in front of Diana. You're young enough that it'd be easy for people to discount your opinion. Being the Lady of Mysaya gives you a position in our society.*

The Lady of ... Rutting hell. I could feel my racing heartbeat in my fingertips and in the pulsing of the mark on my neck. The mark that would forever be a part of me.

Diana's smoky-blue eyes flashed with a cold light as she said, "I hope you and your mate can forgive me for the oversight, but your message made it seem as if you desperately needed my court's help. Is that no longer the case? Are you able to fight Morgan alone now?"

"No," Lynx replied mildly. "Can you?"

The air was pulled taut by an uncomfortable silence.

There was a *tap-tap-tap* on my mental-shield. I drew aside the curtain of silver light protecting my mind. Lynx swept inside. *I'm sorry. I'm guessing you didn't know our claiming granted you half of my property?*

I kept my eyes on a tight-lipped Diana. *No*

I would've told you. It's just—

Everything happened so fast?

Yes.

"You need us as much as we need you," Wilder told Diana, breaking the impasse. "If you can't bring yourself to accept that fact and show respect, then you're left with two options." He put up one finger. "You can surrender to Morgan."

"That will never happen," Diana said with the strength and smoothness of an iron fist inside of a velvet glove.

Wilder continued as if he hadn't heard her. "Or you can go back to marching south. However, speaking as the former Prime Sabu of Morgan's army, I would strongly advise against meeting the legion on the border. You're outnumbered, with limited resources. A battle out in the open would likely spell defeat for you."

Diana changed tack. "Adrianna told me that you are now the acting Sabu here."

Wilder nodded curtly. "That's correct."

He had barely finished speaking before she added, "And do you remember that you swore an oath when you became a mentor at Kasi—one that makes you answerable to me in wartime?"

My gums itched at her high-handed manner; my fangs were keen to make an appearance. I wasn't the only one struggling with Diana's attitude. Adrianna was rolling and kneading her neck, clearly frustrated with the political games.

"That was before Morgan kidnapped me," Wilder argued without raising his voice. "And since you didn't demand my return from the Solar Court, any prior claim you had over my service has been voided."

Diana went on doggedly. "But unless I'm mistaken, you left Morgan's army without being discharged. That makes you a deserter, which is punishable by death. However, if you promise to honor your oath to me, I'll pardon you and make you Prime Sabu of an actual army, not a band of exiles and rebels."

My anger was a neglected cauldron, close to boiling over. From the depths of my magical well, my sunlight ignited.

Steady, siska, Frazer said. *This is just a tactic she's using to find out where she stands and how much power she has.*

Our emotional landscapes were so interconnected that his cooler temper affected mine. He shadowed the fire in my veins and like a source of waterlight, he helped me quench my magic before it could excite the sunstone.

"I've committed no crime," Wilder told Diana. "I've severed my ties with Morgan, but I didn't swear to be her guardian willingly. I said no words, and I was held down while she forced me to be her bloodsworn. Last I checked, keeping a fae as a slave was still illegal in the Riverlands. Has that changed?"

"No," Diana admitted.

"Even if I were willing to serve you, your authority over me would always be superseded by Serena's," Wilder revealed. "I'm her guardian. By choice."

The slight arch in Diana's eyebrows was the only shock she showed. "I see."

"We should have asked for permission." Sefra joined Diana's side, but she was careful to address me. "For my part, I am sorry, siska. I got caught up in needing to see you were safe."

Everybody's eyes fell on me. That included the fae in Diana's personal guard.

I assumed Sefra had a reason for publicly naming me as her sister. That didn't mean I wasn't blindsided by it. "That's okay. I understand."

That got a light smile out of her.

Diana had watched our exchange wordlessly, respectfully. Then she said quite abruptly, "Will you allow my people to camp here?"

What do you think, my dear? Should we let her stay?

Lynx's mental voice glinted with wicked amusement.

I paid him no attention and gave Diana her answer. "Yes, we will."

"Will my wounded be allowed into your ward?" Another abrupt question.

"I don't have a problem with it." Lynx motioned to the person on his left. "But Liora is the Head Healer here. The decision is hers."

Liora didn't question her new title. "I'd be happy to help your injured, Queentina."

There was no thank you, just a, "Good."

"We need to go over tomorrow's battle plan with you," Lynx added. "Would you like to come inside?" His foot slid behind him, angling his body toward Mysaya. "It couldn't hurt to have thick stone walls surrounding us when we discuss tactics."

"Very well." Diana glanced over her shoulder and barked, "Baz, take the guard and get the camp up and running. Syril will help you."

Baz hesitated for a beat. "I should stay by your side, my Queen."

"I'll be perfectly safe," she said flippantly. "Now go."

"Yes, my Queen." Baz bowed his head.

He led the soldiers to rejoin their army.

Diana viewed me, her gaze shrewd. "Perhaps the Lady of Mysaya would like to lead the way?"

I was halfway to refusing when Frazer intervened. *It's a mark of respect to enter ahead of a party.*

Oh. I hadn't expected that.

"Of course," I said, faking confidence. "Are you hungry? I can stop by the kitchens and order something for after our meeting."

"We'll likely be talking for hours." Diana looked past me, focusing on Mysaya with no small amount of seriousness. "If we're not to go hungry, have the food brought during the meeting, not afterward."

Irritation flared. "The round table's this way," I said as politely as I could stomach.

I turned around and marched back through the gateway. I didn't bother to check my pace. Everybody followed me at varying speeds. Lynx, Cai, Wilder, and Frazer had no trouble keeping stride with me. The rest lagged behind a bit.

"Why aren't we flying?" Diana asked from behind me.

"I don't fly when I'm walking with humans." I kept my voice mild as I added, "I think it's rude."

Cai coughed in a poor attempt to conceal his snort of laughter.

I shot him a warning look. He assumed a contrite expression that was as unconvincing as it was short-lived.

As we neared the castle, I realized that we were closing in on finalizing our battle plan. The cold hand of fear stretched out and clasped my guts, my lungs, and my heart, constricting them and leaving me short of breath and courage. The Riverlands army was here. They had made it. We wouldn't flee.

Tomorrow we would fight. Tomorrow we might die.

CHAPTER 45
BLOOD AND LIGHTNING

The minutes felt like hours, waiting in the darkness for the sunrise. For the day of battle to dawn. For Morgan's legion to show itself.

I stood on the battlements above the gatehouse with Lynx, Frazer, and Wilder. Half of our forces were lined up two rows deep along the outer wall, but I couldn't hear any conversation, not even whispered ones. The air was humid, sticky with the scents of flop sweat and the brewing storm above.

The sun's first light finally crowned the mountains in the east. A crack of thunder greeted it courtesy of the powerhouse beside me. Lynx had dropped deep into his magic in preparation for the legion's arrival. The colors of his violent storm mixed with the dawn: black, yellow, green, and gray. They combined in what appeared to be a bruise, one that had bloomed before the wound had been inflicted. Before the hammer had struck.

Wilder cocked his ear toward the valley. "They're coming." He turned just enough for me to see his cheek. "It's time."

I peered up at Lynx and our gazes met, his look was somber but not fearful. I took heart from that. He tapped at my mental-shield. I lifted it and let him in. *I'll see you soon,* he said, and it felt like a promise.

My next inhale seized in my chest. *Yes. You will.*

A soft smile and a nod. Then Lynx withdrew from my mind. He

glanced up at the gathering storm, his face emptying of emotion, turning pitiless as he lured shapeless shadows toward him.

His feathered wings disappeared, transforming into caged lightning that charged the air with peril. The power lining his body cast his face into a mask of pure-white flame and the darkest of clouds. Such a sight tested the courage of the surrounding warriors. Quite a few of them edged away, giving him a wide berth.

I didn't budge an inch.

In a sweep of shadow and a flash of light, Lynx vanished from my side. I peered up anxiously at the vortex forming in the embattled clouds. Lynx was up there now, hovering right in the center, waiting for the battle to begin.

"The enemy is almost upon us," Wilder said, the volume of his voice amplified by a spelled stone. He whirled around and faced us, his steady gaze running up and down our ranks. "Victory won't come easily. But the legion fights to satisfy the madness of a tyrant. They have no common purpose, no fellowship, no heart. If we break their lines, they will crumble from within."

Every warrior within my sight focused on him. On their commander. In that moment, I understood what made Wilder a great Sabu. Everything, from his stance to his tone to his expression inspired confidence.

It didn't hurt that he looked the part of a mighty warrior. He'd ditched the Solar Court apparel and swapped it for brass-hued armor, an imposing helmet with a strong nose bridge, and a new sword that could fell a troll.

"We stand here united, our minds and hearts as one." Wilder banged his fist against his breastplate. The *thwack* resonated in my bones, enlivening me. "That is what makes us stronger than the legion. That is why we will win."

Thwack.

"We fight for our freedom."

Thwack.

"For our future."

Thwack.

"For the people we love." Wilder looked at me as he tore his monstrous longsword free. "For the light!"

He splayed his wings and raised that brutal steel above his head. Thousands of voices, loud and defiant, answered him. "For the light!"

Wilder faced the valley again, his sword lowering to his side.

Our cheers died. A collective hush followed.

Time slowed, taking on the quality of a waking nightmare.

Over the rumblings of the storm above, I detected a hum similar to that of a stirred up hornets' nest. The enemy host appeared as a blur on the horizon. As they got closer, I spied a great many—too many—tightly controlled lines.

A mortal chill spiked my heart, flushing my veins with ice and sending shudders into my retracted wings. They pushed to be freed, but I kept them trapped. The enemy would likely be on the lookout for a female with white and golden feathers.

Wilder signaled to a nearby fae. "Stand by the catapults," he said, now at normal volume.

The fae leaped into action, pounding out a slow beat on drums that resembled upside down teakettles—instruments that would relay instructions without alerting the enemy to our movements.

"Release," Wilder added to the drummer.

The musician switched to a faster rhythm.

A scurry of activity broke out on the wall. Our people sprung six catapults, firing them at our enemy. The hurled projectiles exploded on impact, showering the legion in iron spikes that would prove poisonous if the metal infected their bloodstreams.

Dozens fell, but not as many as expected. The host moved like a school of lithe fish, twisting and dodging the projectiles. Too quickly, the enemy's front lines re-formed into an archery unit.

"Arrows incoming! Take defensive positions," Wilder cried out and the drummer repeated his warning.

Frazer and I rushed to take cover under the battlements. We crouched along with every other soldier, pressing our shoulders against the wall, making ourselves as small as possible.

I threw up a moon-barrier that covered five people; I wished it was more.

Bowstrings whined. A noise that made my skin pebble and my bones quail.

The deadly volley smattered the walkway. Metal clinked. Wood splintered.

Golden lights flared in my peripheral vision. I assumed they were our warriors' magicked shields. Diana had mentioned her people carried spelled stones into battle, ones that conjured barriers whenever their owners were attacked. The shields were weak—only able to withstand a few hits—but they were better than nothing.

I looked up at Lynx's storm. *Come on,* I urged him silently.

The tingling in my feathers was a warning—a precursor. Lightning wheeled across the storm-beaten sky. Claws of energy forked down and struck at our enemy like scorpion tails delivering the deadliest of stings.

Wilder sprang up. "Catapults, reload. Archers, nock."

My pulse thrashed as the war drums pounded the air. I stood up with Frazer. Without lowering my moon-shield, I unhooked the bow clipped to my belt and swiftly pulled an arrow from the quiver attached to my hip. I anchored my arrow and glanced up.

My jaw swung open. Holy fire ...

Lynx had wreaked havoc on the front section of the legion's ranks. The archer unit had suffered major losses, and their next wave of attack was struggling to re-form. I understood now why so many fae trembled at my mate's name.

"Fire at will," Wilder called out.

Drums. Shouts. Horn blasts.

It was all I could do to focus past the deafening noise and hold my nerve. I raised my bow along with four thousand other soldiers. Together, we loosed a wave of arrows that blotted out the sky.

Our volley slammed into the legion's magicked shields. Hundreds of barriers were destroyed, winking out in a shimmer of gilded light. Those fae dropped to meet a dead end.

Our catapults and bows continued to sing with violence. That, paired with Lynx's magic, stopped the host from using their greater number to overwhelm us. The enemy ground to a halt, deadlocked a few hundred feet from us. I prayed they burned up their strength in static flight.

At the bellow of a horn, the legion shifted and reorganized. I glimpsed fae left and right slotting metal spheres into slingshots.

Frazer dragged me to the ground.

Wilder was yelling, "Take cover," when a sphere landed nearby.

The device didn't explode. It rolled with an ominous *tick-tick-tick*, puffing out poisonous-looking smoke.

Wilder left the safety of my moon-shield and ran over to it, covering his nose with his inner elbow. He seized the ball and chucked it over the wall.

His twisted mouth and clenched hand hinted something was wrong. "Wilder," I called out to him.

He hurried back inside my protective shield. "We have to stop the soldiers with the devices." Coughing, eyes watering, he crouched in front of me. "I need you to ask Lynx to take them down."

I grabbed his hand and turned it over to find his palm blistered. Wilder wrenched his arm away. "Don't worry about that. Can you ask him?"

"Y—yes."

I pushed all other distractions away—the explosions ringing in my ears, the blasts of fire flickering in my periphery, the scent of blood invading my nose—and I threw my awareness into the mate bond. A sense of Lynx grew in my mind until I bumped up against a dark, glittering barrier. I banged my imaginary fists against it.

A crack appeared in his mental-shield.

We need you to stop the fae throwing the metal spheres. Can you do it?

His voice was deeper, rougher than usual as he said, *I'm building up my power. After I strike them, order the next stage of the attack. I can't keep this storm going much longer.*

Understood.

In low spirits, I relayed Lynx's message to Wilder. The next phase of attack would put almost everybody I loved in direct danger.

Lightning breached the pall of clouds, splitting the sky, and saturating the air.

Pained screams rang out from the other side of the wall.

Wilder jumped up and told the percussionist, "Relay my order to ring the bells." He strode down the walkway, waving his hands and shooting out instructions.

I stood up beside Frazer. Looking around, nerves upset the cauldron of my stomach. I couldn't see any more fae with metal devices, but the legion had gained a few vital feet. Our walkway was scarred and scorched in several places, and healers had joined us on the battlements. They tended to soldiers who'd suffered broken bones, nasty burns, and a few cases of poisoning.

Frazer strung his bow. His draw speed was quicker than most, and when paired with the kaskan bow, his aim proved deadly again and again, even against heavily armored fae. That inspired me to lay down my archery. I focused on maintaining my moon-shield to protect those who were better shots than I.

Clang! Clang! Clang!

I clapped my hands over sensitive ears, protecting them from the clamor of Mysaya's chiming bells, the signal for our second wave of attack.

Come on, come on, come on. Where were they, where were they?

Relief buoyed me when I heard the booming roar of a dragon. Isolde headed a five-hundred-strong unit out of caves that riddled the knees of the eastern mountains. Cai was on Isolde's back. When she expelled garnet flames, he manipulated her narrow stream into fire-tornadoes, sending them wheeling into the enemy's flank. Fae fled before the whirlwinds. They fled an ugly death.

It was Sefra and Adrianna's turn next. They appeared leading scores of warriors out of the caverns and hollows that peppered the western slopes. I could've sworn I felt Sefra's sunlight—my sister flame—igniting in the distance. My own magic crowed in response. I wrestled with it. *Not yet. Not yet.*

The legion faltered then, penned in on both sides by our pincer movement.

Scenes unfolded, painful to my eye.

Fae were cooked alive in their armor, run through with steel, and ripped to bloody shreds by the Fiends' counterparts—by their avian familiars. Hundreds of enemy fae fell to the ground, their life cut from them, claimed by death's scythe.

Despite their losses, the enemy lines didn't collapse. They were already adapting, working to fend off the threats to their flanks.

"Time we joined them," Wilder shouted to the right of me.

Drums rolled. Thunder boomed. Wings splayed.

Almost every fae on the wall ascended, swords and spears raised defiantly. Wilder, Bear, and Gaius took point. In a three-pronged attack, they rushed the legion, fangs glinting and steel winking in the morning light.

I watched them go, the strings of my heart stretching taut.

"Ena."

I whirled around.

Lynx swayed in front of me, head lolling, wings sagging. I released my moon-shield and rushed to him as his knees gave out. "You need a healer," I said, placing his arm over my shoulders.

"I'm okay. I just need a minute."

I ignored that lie. Even with my fae strength, I struggled to stand with his weight dragging me down. Until Frazer came to hold up Lynx's other side.

Together we stumbled to a nearby watchtower. We moved through the open doorway into a square room stocked with supplies. It was busy inside, mainly with healers rushing up and down the stairwell that led to the courtyard below.

I stopped a passing fae. "Are you a healer?"

"Yes, but—"

"Can you help him?"

The brunette glanced at Lynx. "Oh. W—what's wrong with him?"

Her fear-wide eyes irritated me.

"You're useless. Leave," Frazer barked at her.

Not needing to be told twice, she hurried away. That interaction caught the attention of a white-haired fae at the top of the stairwell. Frowning, she marched up to us. "What appears to be the problem?"

"She was scared of her patient," Frazer said coolly.

The elder's mouth thinned in disapproval. "I see." Eyes bagged with fatigue landed on Lynx. "Magical drain?"

"Yes," I said as she reached into her shoulder satchel.

The healer presented Lynx with a crystal bottle. "Take this. It's an elixir that will boost your energy levels."

Lynx downed the potion and grimaced in disgust.

I had to ask the elder, "Can the elixir cure magical drain?"

"Not quite," she replied. "This potion forces the body to produce adrenaline, which can fuel more magic. But it's not powerful enough to bring a witch up to full strength."

The healer snatched the bottle from Lynx. "You can drink another elixir in three hours. Take more before then and you're risking a heart attack. Understand?"

"Yes."

The healer shot him a stern parting glance. Once she'd hurried off, Lynx straightened up on his own, his weight lifting off my shoulders. He didn't hesitate to draw his wavy-edged sword. A brute of a thing.

"Are you joining the sky-battle?"

He met my eyes with a nod.

Countless words, tender and grim, flitted through my mind. But all I actually said was, "Don't die."

Eyes softening, his mouth twitched. "Wouldn't dream of it."

I was gripped by a sudden urge to stop him as he slipped away into shadow. I hated not being able to follow him. But at the round table meeting, we'd agreed I lacked the experience to join a sky-fight. As for Frazer, he'd yet to even test his wings.

"We should get back out there," he said, cheerless, the line of his shoulders stiff and burdened by duty.

I forced my head down into a nod. "Ready."

We rushed out onto the walkway, dodging the injured and the healers attending them. Once we'd reached the outer wall, I peered over the battlements.

My gaze naturally landed on the biggest thing in the sky. Isolde. She circled above the battle with Cai, deterring the legion from ascending and swarming us from on high.

I looked for others I cared for. My guts knotted when I couldn't find any of them amidst the fighting, amidst the madness.

Witches blessed with fire, ice, and water had joined the fight, aided by alchemists who attacked with potions that stunned, wounded, and melted skin. With so many wings in the air, it became hard to tell who was with the legion and who was on our side. The individual skill of warriors disappeared, and only butchery remained. The reality of war, I supposed.

Frazer pulled an arrow from his quiver. I raised my hand, readying to form a shield in front of him.

"Don't," he said, gripping my wrist.

"What? Why?"

"Because the soldiers are in the thick of it right now." He bumped his chin toward the battle. "They're not shooting at us. You should save your strength for when they do."

Not if. *When.*

I failed to swallow. "I can't just do nothing."

"You are doing something," he said, releasing my hand. "You're pacing yourself so you've got enough strength to fight the witches they'll hit us with later on."

Not my first time hearing that. Wilder had made it plain that Morgan valued witches more than sword-hands, and her generals wouldn't risk her favorites unless absolutely necessary. That meant I had to be patient. I had to be smart.

I lowered my hand, even though every fiber I had fought it. Fought the idea of leaving my brother unprotected. Guilt set in like root rot. I had to help. To contribute. Even if it wasn't magically.

The drowsy sun inched upward, casting a graying light over a landscape heaving with violence. I helped human healers carry the wounded. I held a screaming fae down while somebody reset their wing. But every blurred second that passed, I was half-delirious with fear that I would lose somebody irreplaceable to me.

I was restocking Frazer's quiver when a battalion of enemy fae separated from the main host and rose up in a formation resembling a sea serpent—a monster that arrowed upward. Toward Isolde.

Panic shredded my insides.

Isolde shot flames at the reckless battalion. Cai expanded and directed her fire-stream, but I could tell his magical strength was diminishing. The fae wove to avoid incineration. Cai couldn't react fast enough and many of them escaped unscathed.

I wanted to do something—anything. But what? I could use sunlight, but taking out dozens of fae at that distance would sink me.

Tipping her wings, Isolde darted toward Mysaya. With a few well-timed swipes of her barbarous tail, she bludgeoned the few fae stupid enough to chase after her.

The legion's soldiers resorted to firing arrows at her as she fled. Gods bless her diamond-hard hide. Cai, meanwhile, had to duck and lay flat against her spine to avoid being shot.

They made it over the wall, coming in to land on the castle grounds.

My lungs kicked, reminding me that I hadn't breathed in a while. I raked in a jerky inhale.

"What is he doing?" Frazer murmured as if to himself.

I turned to my brother. "Who?"

Frazer gestured along the wall. I glanced thirty feet or so away to where Ryder touched down. He approached the war drummer and opened his mouth. "The Sabu ... Diana ... now." That was all I heard over the din of the battle.

Ryder joined me and Frazer once a drumroll had started. "Wilder wanted me to remind you to keep your mental-shields up. The legion's got mentalists trying to break into his and Sefra's minds. Lynx is hunting for them, but he hasn't had any luck."

Alarm punched a hole through me. "Are Wilder and Sefra okay?"

"For now."

Behind me, silvery bells rang out. The sound was surely loud enough to stun every bird in a five-mile radius. I put my hands over my ears. "Is that the call for reinforcements?"

"Yes." Ryder pulled a handkerchief from the underside of his bracer and wiped the blood off his blade. "We need to distract the mentalists. Wilder's hoping Diana's company can make them break off their attack."

The susurrus of wingbeats sounded behind me. I spun around and was met with the sight of Diana's unit, roughly three thousand fae, rising into the sky, abandoning their position in the graveyard of destroyed buildings that skirted the rear of the city.

The unit—our reinforcements—ordered themselves into three vertical tiers. At the spirited blast of a reed horn, they hurtled forward. I spotted Diana leading the top layer's wedge formation, dressed in inky-blue armor, the bright steel of her sword shining like a newly born star.

Her unit soared overhead, pelting our enemies with magic and arrows. Anxiety turned me inside out as the warriors dove into the legion's ranks, fanning out into their flanks.

"We're about to have company," Ryder said from beside me.

I marked his line of sight. My stomach dropped to see groups of legion warriors slipping through the cracks in our lines and rushing toward the city.

Frazer loosed a string of arrows at the incoming fae. It wasn't enough. Our enemies grew nearer and nearer.

It was time. It had to be.

Frazer guessed my intention. "You'll make yourself into a target if you use sunlight. The legion will be on the lookout for light-wielders."

"It was going to happen eventually. Besides, I want to be a target." Gazing out at the people dying, I dug my nails into stinging palms. "If I can bait the mentalists into attacking me, they might make a mistake and give themselves away. Then you can take them out. At the very least, we might distract them from going after Sefra and Wilder."

"You're taking a huge risk," Frazer said, as grim as the battle before us. "But I know you know that."

"And I know you've got my back."

He nodded.

"Aww." Ryder sheathed his sword, grinning. "You two are adorable."

Frazer's expression was one of forbearance. I had a feeling he'd been tempted to roll his eyes, but at the last minute decided it was beneath him. He channeled his irritation into shooting at a group of approaching fae. Ryder backed him up. They struck fae after fae, killing some, injuring others. It didn't stop the tide from drawing in; we still had three units closing in on the battlements. On us.

Thea showed support. *You can do this.*

Don't hesitate, Zola warned me.

I freed my conspicuous wings, spreading them for the world to see. Magic sparked in my blood. Sunlight heated my fingertips.

I conjured a golden bow, drew it up, and aimed it a female who had eyes on me. Exerting my will, I fired and turned a single flaming arrow into ten. They passed through armor, tissue, and organs as easily as a knife through melting butter. The warriors died fast. A small mercy.

The sunstone pushed and irritated me. But cooling its passions with the waterstone was an ingrained response now. Little thought was required.

Enemy fae kept coming.

Ryder and Frazer moved like whirlwinds. Nock, draw, release.

I brought down a few more with sunlight.

Then, the inevitable. A unit of warriors succeeded where their brethren hadn't; eight fae arrived at the wall, splitting up and landing on both sides of us.

I covered Frazer, Ryder, and myself with a moon-shield.

"I'll take the four on the right. You take the four on the left?" Ryder said in a perversely cheery voice, dropping his bow and empty quiver to the ground.

Four of the warrior's outlines blurred. Recognizing the signs of illusion, I grabbed Ryder's wrist before he could throw a knife at a mirage.

"Problem?" Ryder asked, using the same breezy tone.

I pointed to a couple of the soldiers on the right. "Those two aren't real."

The fake fae scowled at me before vanishing.

"And they're under some kind of image distortion." I gestured at two fae on my left. They stood at the back of the unit, guarded by their comrades.

A blond female freed a stark laugh. "She saw right through that. I guess your power's out, Emil."

The male standing across from her scowled and waved a hand. That banished the last of the illusions, revealing the two fae with altered appearances. Both wore black robes and had sown-up lips. Their expressions—their unseeing faces—filled me with alarm.

Frazer growled in warning. *They're mentalists.*

Well, we wanted a shot at them. I guess we've got one.

Indeed.

"Let's try my power next," said the blond on my left. She raised her hand, flashing teeth as white as sun-bleached bones at me.

Frazer shot an arrow at her. Her magicked shield shattered, penetrated by the kaskan's power. With horrified eyes, she gawked at the arrow poking out of her mouth. She slumped to the floor. Her death felt absurd. Oddly anti-climactic.

Given the uneasy looks traded by her comrades, their unit hadn't expected a bow to get past their defenses. Perhaps they possessed stronger shields than the average sword-hand. Thank the stars for the kaskan.

Our enemies didn't hesitate long. A male on our left pulled a potion vial from his bandoleer and threw it at us. My shield took the hit. I felt it flinch and weaken. That potion must be lethal, designed to corrode even magic.

I funneled more energy into my shield. It had to hold. I had to endure.

The male pelted us with potion after potion. Not satisfied with that, a brunette on our right dipped into her pocket and flung out a handful of grit, whipping it up into a sandstorm. The female sent it howling toward Frazer, Ryder, and me.

My moon-shield protected us from the heavy blows of the witch's wind. But the swirling sand blocked our view of the world, blinding us to our attackers' positions.

I need to get eyes on the storm-witch so I can use the kaskan, Frazer told me. *Can you expand the shield?*

I struggled to think, distracted by the attacks on my barrier. *I can try, but—*

It's fine. I'll go outside of it.

Into the sandstorm? Are you mad?

It's not very big. I just have to get past it. And it's not as if she'll see me.

With that, Frazer vanished from my side.

A few breathless moments later, the sandstorm abated. The witch who'd conjured it was gasping, choking on the arrow in her throat. Frazer's invisibility wasn't much use when the sand in the air settled over his outline, revealing him.

Movement flickered in my periphery. I glanced left.

The male—the potion-wielder—swung his arm out, hurling a vial at my unprotected brother.

"NO!" I launched a sun-spear at the witch. The force of my strike shattered his shield and pitched his body off the battlements into the courtyard below.

The sharp drop in my energy killed my moon-shield and weakened my mental defenses. Suddenly, I was vulnerable. A crab without her shell.

Minds bent on domination rammed up against mine. A pain in my skull built and built to an angry throb. I tried to hold up my mental defenses, to keep the damned bastards out. But I couldn't concentrate; my thoughts were consumed by my brother. No longer invisible, he lay on the dirtied ground completely still.

Oh gods, oh gods, why wasn't he moving?

Move, brata. Please.

Ryder muttered, "Help Frazer," before throwing a blade. It wheeled end over end through the air and slammed into Emil's shield. An action that sparked a fight between them.

I drew my Utemä, leveling it at the mentalists on my left. My warning them away didn't seem to register. They stared into blank space, not tracking my movement toward Frazer.

Keeping a wary eye on the witches, I kneeled beside my brother and pushed him over onto his back. His eyes were closed; his harsh features were smooth. Relaxed.

"Frazer?" I shook him with trembling hands. "You have to get up."

Nothing. Not a twitch. Not a murmur.

Panic mounted, pinching my chest, constricting my insides. He couldn't be dead. I'd be fading fast if he was. That knowledge didn't stop me from placing my sword down and pressing my ear to his chest. The second I felt it rise and fall, all the breath whooshed out of me at once. Thank you, thank you.

With the witches attacking my mind, I struggled to think what to do next. The potion could've done anything to him. He might be poisoned. Would I feel that through the twining?

A healer? I had to call for—

The mentalists landed the strongest blow yet to my mental-shield. Pain exploded inside of my head. I doubled over and vomited up bile.

Ena, the two witches before you must've merged consciousnesses with others of their kind. At least twenty of them are attacking you right now, Thea said, the worry in her voice clear. *You can't hold out against them for long. But their linking has left them vulnerable. If Zola and I can break into one of their minds, we can find all of them through their connection—*

And destroy them. Zola's tone promised wrath and ruin.

Thea hurried out, *You need to trust us and drop your shield. When they rush in, we'll be there to ambush them ... But if we do this, there's a price. Our spiritual energy is bound to the waterstone. By reaching outside of those confines and entering other minds, our energy will be expended. We may not be able to contact you again for many months.*

Shock pulsed through me. Despite our conflicts, I dreaded the thought of going months without their guidance. But what other choice did I have?

"I understand," I croaked out.

The waterstone heated, warming the skin of my chest. My great-aunts appeared before me and Frazer. They stood between us and the mentalists in long dresses and leather armor, proud and noble, strong and beautiful.

Thea's sapphire eyes pinned me. *We're ready whenever you are.*

I glanced around, searching for threats to my immediate safety. Ryder remained locked in his struggle with Emil. Other units of fae were fighting tooth, nail, and wing to reach the wall. Only the mentalists were quiet and still. I looked past my great-aunts to study the witches' unfocused eyes, the sweat glistening on their foreheads, and the veins bulging out of their necks.

It was now or never. I peered up at Thea and Zola. "Ready."

Halos of color encircled my great-aunts. Blue for Thea. Gold for Zola. I felt the hum of their power, a vibration like that of a plucked string. It sent a quiver running through me from crown to sole.

The goddesses turned toward the mentalists. I let the wall around my mind fall.

Twenty witches charged inside, trampling on the ruins of my crumbled defenses. Before they could seize control, Zola and Thea struck.

In my mind's-eye, I witnessed the invaders, wide-eyed and terrified, grasp the bars of a shrinking cage. The mentalists searched for a nonexistent door—a way out—but there wasn't one. They shook and rammed the prison bars to no avail.

Thea and Zola made the cage smaller and smaller. I saw the witches' desperation grow, savage and frenzied. The stink of fear suffused the air.

Then, one by one, they were crushed.

I pulled away. I couldn't bear the sight.

The two mentalists in front of me slumped to the ground. Their faces were painted with screams, their eyes were bleeding, but their stitched mouths meant they died silently.

I'd no idea where the other mentalists were. But I felt them struggle to escape our mental link like fish hooked on a line. The goddesses didn't weaken or waver. They showed no mercy.

Soon, the pressure in my skull disappeared. The invaders were gone, crushed to dust, ended.

Exhaustion bit deep. I swayed.

Thea and Zola turned to me.

We'll speak again one day. Until then, be brave. Burn bright. Don't let the world dim your light.

My throat burned to hear Zola say such things.

Thea tagged on, *Stay safe, dear heart.*

Goodbye, I whispered to them. *Thank you ... for everything.*

Thea smiled. Zola nodded. Then their visages burst into white embers.

I touched below my collarbone, and my fingers picked out the waterstone through the fabric of my suit. *Hello?*

No response. That hollowed me out.

I tucked my loss away, refocusing on my brother. *Frazer? Brata—*

Ryder appeared at my side. "Sorry. That fight lasted longer than it should've done. I must be losing my touch." He pointed his bloodied blade at the mentalists' bodies. "Is that your doing?"

"No."

His voice dipped. "Is Frazer—"

"Ena!"

I looked up at the sound of that lilting voice. Cai and Liora left the watchtower at a sprint, not stopping until they reached us.

"Frazer needs you," I told Liora.

She crouched to examine him. Liora had come to the fight in dark green underclothes and tan leather armor that supported light steel rings. Her curls were scraped back and secured in a tight bun at the top of her head.

It didn't take her long to say, "He's just stunned. I've given him a jolt. He should be awake in a few seconds."

The tension in my core collapsed. I slumped, chest deflated.

Liora grabbed my wrist, pressing two fingers to my veins.

She frowned at me. "Your pulse is sluggish, and you're almost drained. Drink this. No arguments." Liora released my hand and extracted a vial from her satchel. Handing it off to me, she said, "It'll restore some of your energy, enough that you can keep using magic."

"It's an elixir?"

She nodded at me.

I popped the seal off and drank the liquid in one foul go. It burned as it went down, making me cough and splutter.

Nose wrinkled in disgust, I passed Liora the empty vial. She stowed it.

The elixir forced my heart to make faster music. It bashed against my ribs, sending more blood throughout my body, flooding my limbs with renewed vigor.

Freshly alert, I concentrated on Cai and Liora. "Are you two all right? I saw the legion's soldiers chasing you ..."

"We're fine." Cai's gaze swept over the sky-battle. He grimaced, adding, "Better than most."

The groggy groan of, "Siska," pulled my focus.

"Brata." I supported Frazer's head. "I'm here."

At a glance, we were connected. In the depths of my mind, he saw flashes of what he'd missed while unconscious.

"We need to move," Ryder said, stepping closer. "Frazer should be somewhere he can recover, somewhere less exposed."

Without delay, I grabbed the kaskan from where my brother had dropped it and clipped it onto his belt. I carried him, cradled in my arms, into the watchtower nearest to us. Cai, Liora, and Ryder moved in behind us.

The supply boxes stacked up in a corner caught my eye. I strode over and lowered Frazer onto a crate.

"Chew on this." Liora offered Frazer a sprig of something leafy and fragrant. "It'll clear your head. You should feel better afterward."

"Can't you just heal him?" I asked, sharper than I'd intended.

Liora treated me with patience. "Healers don't use more magic than is necessary when treating a body, especially in situations when we need to preserve our strength."

I struggled to bite my tongue, to keep my worry from spilling out.

Frazer read me. "Stop fussing. I've only got a headache, and I don't think that was even caused by the stun potion."

"What do you mean?" I asked, head snapping to him.

"I felt the kaskan sapping my strength when I was firing," he said around a mouthful of leaf. "Especially when I hit the witches' shields."

"I didn't know it worked like that." I'd never stopped to think about it.

"Spelled tools are inherently magical, so they won't take energy from their owners unless they're being asked to do something that exceeds their innate power," Liora said, as if she were citing a passage from a book. "That's probably why you didn't notice it taking your energy before now."

"Do you need an elixir?" I asked a frowning Frazer.

"No," he said, his voice gaining strength. "I should save that for when I really need it."

That comment emptied me out. It was a reminder that despite the deaths of the mentalists, the danger wasn't over. It was probably only just beginning.

"I need to go." Liora clutched her bag's strap.

"To fight?" I asked.

"No." Liora was quiet but firm. "My time killing is over. I want to help the other healers." She turned to Cai. "Are you coming with me?"

He shook his head. "I'll be of more use fighting on the wall."

Fear clouded her eyes. "Be careful."

"You too," he said bracingly.

Liora's spring-greens slid to me.

"I know," I said, guessing everything she wanted to say.

She gifted me a feeble smile before hurrying away.

Ryder cleaned his blade. Cai snagged water from a passing healer. I watched Frazer chew on the herb. I didn't know about the others, but I savored the moment to gather my wits and my courage. Seeing my brother hurt, having witches grope about my mind, and losing Thea and Zola had rattled me.

I jumped when another horn bellowed. This one rose above the clamor of the fight, sounding like an enraged ox.

"What do you think that's about?" I asked the others.

"Let's find out." Ryder considered Frazer. "Maybe you should stay here."

"Not a chance," Frazer said, pushing himself up.

He stood straight and didn't wobble. I checked in with our bond and the heaviness on his side had mostly lifted. Relief blunted the edges of my concern for him.

"You always were stubborn." Ryder's critical tone didn't match the admiration in his eyes.

Ignoring him, Frazer grabbed my hand and led me outside. Cai and Ryder came out after us. The four of us stopped and stared.

Beyond the wall, I spied the legion's rearguard leaving the battle. They halted and landed a mile out in the valley. What in the rutting hell?

"Are they retreating?" I voiced, not believing my own eyes.

"No," Frazer remarked darkly. "This is just a break in proceedings before we get back to trying to kill one another."

My mood plunged deeper into melancholy.

More of the legion touched down on the valley floor, allowing our own forces to return to the wall and the courtyard below.

The influx of thousands of soldiers overwhelmed my senses. Fae hurried in every direction, searching for healers, friends, orders, or they were simply collapsing wherever they found space to sit.

I spotted Wilder landing on the wall. Heart in mouth, I picked my way through the crowd to reach him. Cai, Ryder, and Frazer walked with me.

Wilder looked up at our approach.

He'd lodged his helmet under his armpit. His short hair was slicked with sweat, blood splattered his armor plates, and bruises blotched his face.

"Are you okay?"

Before I could answer Wilder's first question, he'd asked another: "Are you injured?"

"I wouldn't say I was okay, but I'm not hurt. What about you?"

"Same."

We were interrupted by a fae needing his instructions. That happened two more times before I could motion toward the legion and ask him, "How long d'you think this'll last?"

"Not long." A stark reply. "These sorts of rests are common in sky-battles. It's the only way that fae can keep fighting in the air."

Black feathers stole my attention away. I skirted Wilder and made for Lynx. He towered head and shoulders above everybody, so it was easy to keep him in my sights while moving toward him.

I reached his side and saw he was holding up Sefra. Her neck struggled to support the weight of her head, her eyelids drooped, and all the color had left her sun-touched face.

"What happened?" I asked, cupping her cheek, staring into her eyes.

"It's my fault." She forced a smile and pulled my hand down. "I overused my magic, then a mentalist attacked my mind. I'm just a bit shaken. I'll be fine once I've seen a healer."

Cora swept down and perched on the battlements. There, she opened her sharp beak and chittered at Sefra.

"Don't scold me," Sefra mumbled at the eagle.

The guys had followed and crowded in behind me. Cai flagged down a nearby healer. My anxiety settled a bit when the witch joined us and took charge. He instructed Lynx to lower Sefra and brace her against the battlements before tending to her.

"Where's Adrianna?" Cai craned his neck to peer over the crowd. "Can anybody see her?"

My insides lurched.

We spent a few frantic minutes searching the faces of the returned fae. Wilder stayed by our sides, but he had to field question after question from the soldiers. Sefra helped us look, once the healer had finished with her.

"I see her," Lynx called out, his gaze centered on a spot farther along the wall. "She's with Diana."

He strode off. The rest of us trailed in his wake, cutting through the crowd.

Adrianna and Diana promptly came into view.

"Adi," Cai shouted, waving for her attention.

She looked up from what appeared to be tense words with her makena. Relief softened her features and lightened the line between her brows.

Adrianna closed the gap between us. "You all look like shit."

I countered with, "So do you."

She huffed a laugh. I didn't miss the exhaustion deadening the noise, a weariness born from both body and spirit.

Diana addressed Wilder. "Do you think there's more behind this break? Could the legion be sending for reinforcements?"

"I doubt it," he said, squinting at the valley and the enemy fae squatting there. "The Sabu in charge won't want to message Morgan with anything other than news of our defeat. He won't want to admit that we've shown more fang than he was expecting."

"Who would've taken command of the legion after you left?" Lynx asked, as if he already suspected the answer.

Wilder's wings tensed. "Balthur."

Lynx swore under his breath.

My gaze darted between them. "Who is he?"

Wilder's jaw squared off. "A powerful witch and a skilled warrior."

"He's a vicious bastard," Lynx interrupted, his face twisted in dislike.

Alarm fired off in my nerve endings.

"I've heard about him," Diana said, frowning. "Isn't he obsessed with Morgan?"

"Yes," Lynx said with dark disgust. "He's wanted to be her consort for years, but she's always refused him because the ladies of the court say his dick's so small, you'd have to look under a magnifying glass to see it."

Cai loosed a harsh laugh. Wilder sidestepped that detour in the conversation by adding, "I think Balthur will lead an envoy here before we return to the battle. He'll likely do it under the pretense of offering us terms of surrender, but in reality, he'll want to assess our situation for himself."

"What information will he look for?" Diana asked.

Wilder replied, "Anything that gives him an idea of our numbers, supplies, and key players. He'll probably try to draw some of us into conversation, so watch yourselves. He's the type that likes to bait people into revealing more than they should."

Lynx seemed to grow in size and menace. But it was Sefra who said, "Then who wants to tell him to fuck off? I'll be happy too. I never was that great at diplomacy."

"Don't remind me." Diana peered out at where the legion's soldiers were recuperating and scurrying about the valley. "I need to prepare my people for the next wave of fighting. Excuse me."

"That's something we should do together," Wilder said as she moved past him.

Diana halted and paused. "Very well," she said, a tad stiff.

Wilder's gaze moved over our group. "If a company of fae approach the wall under Morgan's banners, we'll meet back here."

Everybody agreed.

Diana and Wilder left to organize our soldiers. The others shared what they'd experienced during the battle. I contributed only that the mentalists were dead because of Thea and Zola. Then I exited their conversation and entered a silent one with Frazer.

Do you think we can win? I asked him.

Based on my rough calculations, we've lost about two thousand soldiers. The legion has lost double that. But we started out with fewer people. If I'm right, we're about even.

Frazer trailed off. Not good. *What aren't you saying?*

His troubled thoughts rippled across his features ahead of his words. *Diana has a single trained army. Morgan has five scattered throughout Aldar. The loss of one to her is a blow, but she can afford to lose warriors. The same can't be said for the Riverlands. We might win today, but if we can't end this fight soon, the Riverlands will be severely weakened going forward.*

Neither of us knew how to avoid that. Unless we were to flee.

Sometime later, when the injured were in the ward, the dead were removed from the wall, and every soldier standing was prepared for the fighting to begin again, a company of fae with red and black banners took to the skies. Just as Wilder had predicted.

Shoulder to shoulder with Frazer and Lynx, I stood behind the battlements and watched our enemy approach us. Wilder, Sefra, Ryder, Diana, Cai, and Adrianna stood nearby.

My heart shivered, waiting for what Fate would bring us next.

Life or death. Victory or defeat.

CHAPTER 46
FIRE AND CHAOS

"Stop, or my archers will shoot you out of the sky," Wilder shouted.

The male leading the legion's envoy raised a fist. "Halt!"

Thirty or so fae stopped, hovering in midair. They had dared to come within reach of our arrows, and every archer on the wall had their fingers on their bowstrings, their gazes locked on the V-shaped envoy.

The head of their formation, a bald warrior with bulky muscles, rust-colored wings, and a mean mouth, captured my attention. If he'd been human, I would've put his age at forty. A well-preserved forty. Not the kind seen in the Gauntlet, hunched and haggard from too much work and too little food.

That male waved lazily at the fae beside him. "My chair."

Two soldiers unfolded a canvas seat supported by bamboo poles. The bald male had the fae hold it while he settled atop it like his personal throne.

I sent my consciousness into my mate bond and bumped up against a mental-shield composed of onyx stone. Lynx opened a door for me. *What is it?*

Is the pompous ass out in front Balthur?

That's him.

Wasn't he at the encampment when we rescued Wilder?

Yes.

From the little I'd seen of him, Balthur had struck me as arrogant and ruthless. A terrible combination.

"I had hoped you were dead," Balthur said to Wilder. "Better that than a traitor."

Wilder gave him nothing. No words. No expression.

Balthur sneered at that lack of response. "I wonder how long your self-righteous act will last when you're being tortured for your betrayal. The Queen has cleaved wings and mounted them on the palace walls for less." He ended with a cruel smile.

My fangs nipped my gum-line.

Frazer nudged me with his elbow. *Don't rise to it.*

Anger tested my control. I bore it by linking up with my brother, allowing his cooler emotions to influence my actions. That way, I managed to project indifference and keep my fangs sheathed.

"Why are you here?" Sefra asked Balthur straight. "Tell us so that we can get on with the business of defeating you."

Balthur cocked his head at her. A move that reeked of contempt. "I never thought I'd see the day when Sefra Lytir showed her limp wings in Aldar again. If you're back to reclaim your title, you'll be disappointed." He sneered. "Your name is nothing but a joke at the Solar Court. You're remembered as a wingless worm—a coward."

Sefra got louder. "I suppose being a joke is something you can sympathize with. I've heard the people in Alexandria get quite the laugh out of you and your tiny appendage."

Nobody laughed. The situation was too tense. Too dangerous.

Balthur's expression grew murderous. But instead of rising to the taunt, he turned his meaty face toward me. "You are the one known as Serena Smith—the human whore masquerading as a fae?"

"No," I said without much thought. I wasn't human, and that wasn't my name. Not anymore.

His hand flexed as if he wanted to throttle me. "Let's not play games. I've been shown the memories of somebody who was at Kasi with you. I've seen you in your true form—your human form. You *are* Serena Smith."

"If you say so."

Balthur scowled. "Angelo?"

"She's definitely a light-wielder."

Anxiety pinged beneath my breastbone. My gaze darted to the male who had identified me. His black hair was tied up and streaked with red highlights. A scar stretched from his eyebrow to his leering mouth, and his right eye was gone, replaced by a white orb.

"I've never sensed anything like it," Angelo added. "She's imbued with the four light disciplines, and something else I can't get a read on. She's even stronger than—"

"Silence," Balthur snapped.

Angelo quieted but he kept staring at me, grinning like a jackal demon. A wolf with blood on his lips.

"I'm here to offer you a deal," Balthur told me. "Join the Solar Court, and the Queen will allow these rebels to live." He scanned the battlements, his top lip peeling up off his teeth. "The former Riverlands Queen is the only exception. Her war crimes against the Solar Court cannot go unpunished. Those are our terms."

Low growls erupted along the wall.

"Your queen ordered her forces to occupy our border and invade our lands," Adrianna said, colder than a hailstorm, each of her words a pellet of ice that she aimed at Balthur. "And you're accusing us of war crimes? Are you as stupid as you look?"

His clenched hands were the only sign he'd heard her. "What do you have to say to my offer, Serena?" He raised his voice. "Would you have all these people die just so you can continue living as an outlaw?"

No doubt he'd intended to be heard by as many people as possible so they could judge me. Hate me. Blame me for all the death that followed.

"Give it up, Balthur," Wilder said in clipped notes. "Even if we believed you could guarantee our safety, you're not granting us pardons. We'd be imprisoned or trapped in service to a ruler who enslaves children, forces people to be her guardians, and gets a sick thrill out of raping the males in her court. No person with a shred of decency or sanity would choose such a fate. So what do you say we get back to fighting? And I'll meet you on the battlefield."

My stomach turned inside out. Morgan raped the males at her court? Had she ... with Lynx? Or Wilder?

"You'll get what's coming to you, *valek*," Balthur jeered.

"Not before you, *mŭnta*."

Balthur's thick neck swiveled to me. "I almost forgot. The Queen asked me to give you a message if you rejected her offer." He smiled smugly, and it terrified me. "Han! Show our young witch what we've brought her."

A male dove into his side-satchel and from out of its depths, he produced a severed head.

I tilted under the weight of what I saw. Lifeless eyes and a swollen tongue protruded from a misshapen face, the skin of which was mottled black and green. But I still recognized him. How could I not?

John Baker had been a father to me. He was a dedicated husband, a hard worker, and a kind soul. He'd never caused a moment's sorrow in his whole life. And now he was dead. Because of me.

I blinked, but the image of his severed head remained imprinted on my eyelids. I should have felt something, but my heart seemed to be skipping beats, leaving moments of emptiness in my chest—emptiness that expanded rapidly until the only thing inside of me was a void that howled like a north wind against a frosted window.

Balthur continued, snide and callous. "You were either very stupid or very naive to tell Hunter where to find the people you loved. Morgan sent me to your village as soon as she plundered his mind. I'm afraid I couldn't bring all their heads with me." He mock-shuddered, shaking out his shoulders. "The smell, you know? It was too much. And the woman —Viola, was it? I got carried away with that one. I didn't think there was any point in bringing the sloppy bits back."

I couldn't move. I was locked inside of my own body.

Warm fingers encircled my wrist. I barely felt them. I was numb, my blood transformed into icy waters. Nothing could reach me in such a state—in the big freeze.

Balthur signaled to the fae holding John. "Han, toss it to her. I can't stand the stink."

Han drew his arm up in preparation to throw it.

Frazer twisted me around. His night-blue eyes pulled me into his mind, sheltering me there. *Don't look.*

I only saw my brother. But I heard the murmurs of sympathy and the soft thud as what remained of John hit the walkway.

Adrianna's wildcat growl penetrated my gloom. "You're a fucking monster."

"You're here under the pretense of a truce," Wilder said, fury deepening his voice. "For the sake of the warrior's code, I'll give you twenty seconds to leave my sight before I give the order to have you shot from the sky."

"I'm not going anywhere," Balthur announced. "Edra, now!"

Frazer pushed me to the ground. His blue gaze still held me. "Stay."

My mouth opened. No sound came out.

A shrill screech cleaved the air, penetrating my numbness with the force of a hundred needles. I put my hands over my ears, gritting my teeth against the pain.

"Archers, fire," Wilder shouted.

Drums pounded. Arrows flew with a twang and a whistle.

Frazer popped up. He nocked, drew, and fired.

The high-pitched ringing stopped. Instant relief.

I uncovered my ears as Wilder reeled off orders. "Archers! Witches! Bring their shields down. Don't let them get out of range."

Magic stirred: fire, wind, and darkness.

Through the gaps in people's legs, I saw it. The head.

The skull had caved in from the impact of being thrown onto the stone. Congealed blood, tissue, and maggots filled my vision. Everyone was ignoring it. Ignoring him.

I was underwater, under a sheet of ice, struggling to breathe, starving for air. An unbearable pressure built inside. It had nowhere else to go but out.

Screaming, screaming, screaming. In my head, my throat, my lungs. That smashed the numbness encasing me.

Rage flooded in, fueling my sunlight, sparking a fever underneath my skin. Fire, fire, everywhere. It was all I could see.

I leaped up.

The envoy had retreated to a safe distance. They hovered out in space, waiting for the rest of the legion to ascend and join them.

Before I could jump over the battlements, I was yanked up against a strong body. Frazer caged me in, wings and all, our bond resonating with alarm. "Lynx, take her."

"No." My cry sounded like it came from the throat of a wounded animal caught in a trap. "I'm going to kill him. I'm going to rip him apart!"

"Protect her." Frazer shoved me into unyielding arms. "Go."

We materialized high above the valley. Lynx's wings were already beating, carrying us up and away from the battle.

"Let me go." I flailed and thrashed. Anything to get free. "You can't stop me—"

"I'm not," he said over my shouting. "I'm going to help you kill him."

I stopped raging. "You ... What?"

"Balthur's a powerful earth elemental who can harden his skin," Lynx said quickly, as if worried what would happen if he didn't talk fast enough. "I've seen weaker swords shatter against his hide. Not even my lightning can penetrate it when he's at full strength. If we're to stand a chance of beating him, we need to lure him away from the legion and get him on his own. Then we can hit him with our combined strength and exhaust his magic. Once we do that, his hide will fail and we can finish him off."

"How can we lure Balthur away?" The answer occurred to me the second I finished asking the question. "We're already doing it—aren't we? I'm bait."

"Yes," he said plainly. "And he'll know that. He's a talented Sabu with a sound strategic mind. He'll assume you want to draw him out to get your revenge."

I staved off the grotesque image of John's head. I couldn't give my grief an inch of space, not when it might render me useless. "Isn't Balthur worried we'll beat him?"

"I doubt it," Lynx replied, grim about the mouth. "He's an arrogant prick, and he's ambitious. That combination has a habit of making people reckless."

The din of armies clashing again bounced around my skull. I was tired of trying to think through the noise. "Just tell me that we can do this. Tell me Balthur's the deluded one, and not us."

Lynx's face fixed into granite hardness. "He's already dead."

His confidence comforted me. So did his ruthlessness.

"Is Balthur following yet?" Lynx asked.

I peered down at the ongoing violence. A small unit of fae had detached themselves from the battle. Their wings were aimed at us.

"Yes. Him, and ... nine others," I said, my voice pitching at the word nine. "Why not bring fifty or a hundred?"

"Because he's seen me shadow-jump," Lynx answered, putting on a burst of speed. "He must know that if he makes the odds against us too great, he'll never get a shot at capturing you."

Capturing me ...

Fear leaped up and ensnared me by the throat. *Focus.* I had to focus. Studying our trajectory, I asked, "Are we fighting them on a mountaintop?"

"Not quite."

In less than a minute, we set down inside of what resembled a fae-made bird's nest built upon a natural plateau. It was fixed halfway up a craggy mountainside and backed onto a sheer rock face.

"We're going to need Frazer's help," Lynx said, lowering me.

"I don't want to bring him into this."

"We'll need him and his bow." He grasped my shoulder. "I've used up a lot of energy. So have you. We shouldn't face ten fae without him."

My gut twisted.

"I'll be back." Lynx turned into the wind.

Thud, thud, thud, my heart went.

I went to the railing that was wrought to resemble intertwining branches. There, I watched Balthur and his guard lessen the gap between us.

Lynx returned with Frazer in a swirl of black smoke.

Sensing my wariness, Frazer said, "I only stopped you chasing Balthur because you were ready to fly right at the legion and get yourself caught."

I was hard, graceless. "We've separated him from his army. Will you help now?"

His eyes blazed up like match flames. "Of course, siska."

"Listen." Lynx's gaze fixed on Frazer. "Balthur can toughen his skin. To kill him, we need to batter his hide and drain him, and we can't afford to waste all our energy fighting the other fae. Can you bring them down? As many as possible."

"I'll do what I can," Frazer said, unclipping the kaskan from his belt.

"Start with the third and fifth from the far right." Lynx faced open skies and hostile enemies. "They're elementals."

Frazer strung and released two arrows.

The cloud of fae performed aerial acrobatics, trying to avoid being pierced through. It didn't stop the kaskan from finding a target. The shield of a lavender-haired female shattered. She was struck through the eye and went into free fall.

But the second target, a red-winged male, conjured a wall of flame, burning the arrow to ash before it could pierce him.

Balthur's bellow traveled across the hundred feet separating us. "They're to be taken alive! Alive, do you hear?"

"Yes, Sabu," a chorus of voices sounded.

"Attack!" Balthur ordered.

I sensed a rippling in the world as our enemies channeled magic.

"I'll shield." I stepped back on my right foot, waved an arm out in front of me, and brought up a veil of moonlight to protect the three of us. Just in time. A shrieking wind slammed into it. Smoking potions came after that.

Frazer managed to bring down the air-blessed witch and the potion-wielder. It cost him, though. The flat line of his shoulders rounded forward in exhaustion—the kaskan must have demanded a lot from him.

With our foes closing in, Lynx vanished from my side and showed up behind our enemies, his wings flapping and his mighty sword already freed. His steel glowed in the manner of a lightning bolt, a brilliant, blazing white. Raising his wave-shaped blade, he brought it down in a sweeping motion. Lightning arched off the blade like a scythe.

Three shields collapsed. Three heads rolled. Three bodies fell.

Blood misted the air. Six down. Four to go.

An almighty *crack* resonated through my bones as a female conjured a magical whip and snapped it against my shield, smashing it into pieces.

I flinched, stumbling back.

His expression promising retribution, Frazer sent an arrow straight through her protections and into her neck. As life left the witch, Frazer sunk to his knees.

I rushed to his side.

He pushed me away. "Don't get distracted."

"Incoming," Lynx shouted in warning.

I popped up to find the last female had gained sky-ground, enough that I could see the whites of her eyes. She raised her inked hand. In the same breath, I punched outward, releasing a ball of flaming light.

My fireball crashed into her shield, burning a hole through it, and setting her whole body alight.

A tick later, her power crashed into me in the form of a shockwave, blasting me off my feet.

Instinct retracted my wings. I'd barely shielded the back of my skull with my hands before I slammed into the mountain.

I landed on my side. A nasty crack sounded, and a sharp pain stabbed at me. It hurt to move. To breathe. I still scrambled up and took stock. Eight down. Two to go ...

Outside the bird's nest, Lynx used his steel to batter the magical shield of the fire elemental. "This is pathetic," his red-winged opponent mocked. "I thought you were supposed to be strong. What a joke."

Lynx showed no signs of worry. He was immersed in a killing calm. I wasn't concerned about him. I couldn't be.

Balthur hovered overhead, searching the nest with suspicious eyes. Frazer had vanished from view, causing the brute to hesitate.

I felt Frazer nearby. Lying in wait.

Get him to land, Frazer said.

"What's the matter?" I wheezed at Balthur. "Scared to face us?"

A transparent taunt. It worked, though.

Balthur touched down in front of the railing. "I knew those wings of yours couldn't be real. You're just a worthless meat bag pretending to be something better than you are," he said, leering at the spot above my shoulders where my feathers usually were. "Now, why don't you make this easy on yourself? Come with me, and I won't kill your friends."

Tensed, primed to pounce, I said, "You'll burn in the dark court for what you've done."

He met that with icy apathy. "Stop with the dramatics. You can't kill—"

An arrow shimmered into view, bouncing off Balthur's skull. The brute flinched. That was it.

Fuck.

Balthur turned and jumped twice, kicking thin air. Frazer reappeared as he hit the ground on his back, the impact making him drop the kaskan.

"Pathetic worm." Balthur dog-growled, bearing down on Frazer.

Ribs aching from my injury, I staggered over to them. Balthur got to my brother first. He yanked him up by the neckline of his black, steel-studded armor.

Stay away, Frazer warned through our link. *Let me handle this.*

My footsteps faltered.

Frazer spat hawthorn-colored blood in Balthur's eyes. When he screwed them up, Frazer moved as quick as an eel twisting through water, slamming a knife into the underside of his chin.

The blade broke off at the hilt. Oh shit.

Balthur threw my brother out of the bird's nest. I watched him disappear. The moment stretched; disbelief held me in a stasis. Then I snapped.

A single blast of sunlight exploded out of me. The world turned red.

In the space of a breath, my attack knocked Balthur into the metal rail and slammed into Lynx and his opponent as they fought in midair. The fire witch burst into bloody chunks; Lynx was hurled backward. Before I could see where my mate ended up, I collapsed.

Fired by terror, I flung myself into my kin bond. I jumped into the other half of my heart.

Our minds fused. I felt the pain in our chest from being kicked by Balthur. I sensed our wings beating frantically as we fought to slow our descent. I saw Mysaya's smallest lake rising up to meet us right before we slammed feetfirst into its waters.

Agony splintered through our legs. We'd definitely broken something. But our arms were fine, they were strong, working to drag us up, up, up.

Our head broke the surface; our lungs quivered in relief as they pulled in air.

Concentrate on killing that bastard. With that, Frazer ejected me from his mind.

I returned to myself in a blink.

Balthur lumbered to his feet, seemingly dazed by my sun-blast. His skin was chapped, resembling the earth after suffering a drought, and his armor hissed, melting, glowing white and bright orange in places.

I reached for my magic, but it was slow to answer my call. The sunlight within had been reduced to embers. It needed time to recharge, to burn with a might and a fury once again.

Luckily, I wasn't alone. Lynx reached the nest in a few hurried wingbeats, sword raised, his gaze fierce and focused. He swung at Balthur while still in the air.

With a turn of his body, Balthur freed his blade and blocked the strike.

Lynx disengaged and somersaulted, landing lightly on the ground.

"Finally." Balthur smirked. "I've wanted to cross blades with you for some time, Dark Prince."

"Be careful what you wish for."

Their swords went to war with an almighty clang.

Afraid of distracting Lynx, I crawl-shuffled to the mountainside. There, I cradled my side, forcing air into too-tight lungs, ignoring the pains that accompanied my inhales.

Back and forth, Balthur and Lynx dueled.

Dodge. Feint. Lunge. It was hard to say who was better. Their swords appeared mere extensions of their arms.

I couldn't bear it. I was about to risk drawing magic from the sunstone when Danu showed up on the railing and interrupted me. *Why haven't you killed him yet?*

I glared at him. *What do you think we've been trying to do?*

You haven't used chaos. He eyeballed me. *I've been watching you.*

That halted the furious path my mind was on. *It's too unpredictable.* Thinking of how I'd failed to save Hunter, I added, *And it doesn't always work.*

A sharp, *Ena,* came from Danu. *There isn't time for you to wring your hands over this. Chaos can disrupt energy, and that reptile is channeling huge amounts to sustain his invulnerability. Use your magic to turn his own against him. Unmake him. Now!*

Gods help me. I concentrated on Balthur, who was snarling like a mad dog when cornered. He looked ready to rip Lynx's throat out.

That threat against Lynx stoked the flames of my anger. I dwelled on the rage and let it build, reeling in the darkness birthed from such feelings. But the chaos was reluctant to come.

You can't create chaos when you're holding onto control, Danu groused. *Your ghosts are pounding at the windows. Let them in. Feel the pain.*

My ghosts ... I really didn't want to go there. Those bleating thoughts met a swift end when Lynx ducked under a blow that would've taken his head off.

I looked inward. There, John's kind smile and flour-stained cheeks waited for me. We worked side by side in comfortable silence, rolling out pastry. Viola toiled in her small garden, her hands covered in dirt as she taught me my weeds from my remedies.

Years of memories followed. Countless moments wherein John and Viola had made a lonely child feel safe and loved. I'd repaid that kindness by getting them killed. The last of my parental figures were gone. Dead. Ripped apart.

Such thoughts had me drowning in a sea of grief and anger. I turned that choking, wrenching, sickening feeling into a corrosive hatred that burned in my stomach like acid.

Night-black smoke appeared, drifting through my fingertips. With a grimace, I stood and arrowed that silent poison at Balthur.

He only noticed my chaos when it invaded his nostrils. Distracted, he failed to block Lynx's blow to his abdomen.

The metal of Lynx's sword rang out as if in pain. Balthur wasn't injured. But he backed up quickly, withdrawing from the duel. "What is this?" he snarled at me.

"Your end," I promised him softly.

I felt the heat of Lynx's gaze on my cheek. He stayed silent, though.

Balthur's face contorted. "You think you can kill me? You're nothing. You're worth less than the dirt—"

He choked on his words when I extended my hand, willing my chaos to corrupt his magic. To make it revolt. To harden his insides.

Face a nasty red, he took a step toward me.

I raised my other hand and stopped him in his tracks. Balthur steeled his jaw against me as if his stubbornness could save him. It couldn't. I brought him crashing to his knees, eyes bulging, his muscles straining.

"Bitch," Balthur spat.

The magic surging through my veins, darkening my soul, laughed at him. At his struggle. "This bitch is the last thing you'll ever see."

Mercilessly, I forced my smoke to wrap around his heart. That vital organ which pumped life and spiritual energy throughout his body.

His tough mask cracked. Balthur blurted out, "Stop this."

"Why? You didn't." I curled my fingers into my palms: squeezing, disrupting, unmaking. "You murdered two of the best people in the world without a second thought. You even enjoyed it. You're a heartless monster."

"You aren't like me." He gasped and coughed. Blood showed on his teeth, even trickled down his chin. "You don't want to be like me."

"Go to hell."

With that, I finished him. I turned his magic against him and transformed his heart into a lump of charred coal. He fell forward and hit the ground with a final thud.

I felt no triumph or relief. His death hadn't fixed anything. It wouldn't return what he'd stolen from me.

"Ena."

Lynx. That was Lynx.

He moved for me. "Are you with me?"

I flashed him my palm. "Stop. Just give me a minute."

Gathering the threads of my sanity, I focused on how I had to help my brother. That stitch of love kicked earth over the darker emotions and severed me from the chaos. The magic—the madness—dissipated peacefully. An irony.

I forced myself to meet Lynx's waiting eyes. They flickered with sadness or understanding. I couldn't tell which. There was no disgust or fear. No care or interest in the dead body lying a few feet from us.

"What can I do?" he asked, projecting a calm air. A calm that I knew was for my benefit.

"You need to help Frazer." I checked in with my kin bond again. "He's hiding in a gorse bush next to the smallest lake. And he's injured. I think one of his legs is broken. Can you get him into the city?"

"I can't shadow-jump. My magic's almost exhausted." Lynx's gaze darted to where my hand clutched my side, supporting my cracked ribs. "But I'll fly faster than the whole damned legion if it means getting him to safety. What are you going to do?"

"I don't think I can fly with my ribs like this …"

An unsurprised nod. "I'll be back for you."

Gratitude welled up within me. "Thanks."

Lynx exchanged a meaningful glance with Danu. I suspected they were conversing silently. Whatever it was, it ended when Lynx leaped over the railing.

I'd no desire to stare at the male I'd just killed. I kept Balthur in the corner of my eye only so I could give his body a wide berth as I hobbled forward. Every movement triggered short bursts of agony in my right side. The pain reached into the joint of my hip and even my teeth.

At the rail, I watched Lynx dive for the small lake in front of us.

Lynx is coming for you. Make sure you're visible to him.

What about you?

He'll come back for me.

Is Balthur dead?

Yes.

A savage, *Good*, was his response.

I stared out at the battle of the thousands. Less magic was on display now. The witches must be drained. It came down to sword against sword. Steel against steel.

I attempted to riddle out who was winning, and how many warriors each side had left. My observations led me to sink into the depths of despair. It appeared to be a tie.

Danu flew over and perched on my shoulder. *So.*

"So?"

You've realized the problem?

Frazer had already made me aware of it. "Even if we eventually defeat the legion, the cost to the Riverlands will be too high."

That's right.

The muscles of my chin trembled. Why couldn't I make this right? How could I defeat Archon if this was the limit of my abilities?

Danu fanned his feathers, brushing my cheek with them. *There's only one way to win. You have to tap into the sunstone and use its power to push the legion into fleeing or surrendering.*

My breath stalled. "The amount of magic that would take ... I wouldn't survive it."

Why not? The stone is a concentrated source of magic. You won't have to tap into your own power reserves to use it, and it won't be as complicated nor as tiring as pulling magic from the world.

I swallowed what felt like a handful of thorns.

Danu peered down the length of his crooked beak at the violence.

The only danger lies in losing control of the magic once you've started. But you should have some idea of your limitations by now. When you feel yourself struggling, just pull back.

"It isn't that easy." Anxiety broke my voice.

He ruffled his tail feathers. *Fine. Just give up then.*

His sarcasm was not subtle.

Frazer interrupted my bout of self-doubt. *What's wrong? You're terrified.*

During my conversation with Danu, I'd kept an eye on Lynx and Frazer. At present, they were landing on the city wall.

I hedged. *Have you found a healer?*

Answer my question.

Reluctantly, I shared a short version of my talk with Danu.

Frazer grasped it all easily. *Have you decided what to do?*

No. And it can't just be my decision. We could die if I do this.

We could die if you don't.

His reply seemed interrupted. Likely he was having to speak to somebody else. A healer, hopefully.

Are you saying you're all right with this?

Acceptance traveled through the bond. *The stones were meant for you to wield. If anybody can handle their power, it's you. And you're not alone, remember? We were twined for a reason. I can help you bear magic that might be too much for one witch.*

But how many people would I have to kill before the legion fled? How many lives could the stone take? Hundreds? Thousands? The possibility capsized my stomach and stung my throat with bile. If I lived past today, I'd be plagued by nightmares. Sleepless nights would become the norm.

The selfish part of me wanted to keep my soul intact, to return to the castle, to never use the sunstone. But that wouldn't stop the battle or all this death. It would weaken the Riverlands—the only army willing to fight against Morgan.

I couldn't let that happen. If I survived the doing of it, I'd just have to learn to live with myself afterward.

Frazer sensed me arrive at my decision. *I'll be with you. To whatever end.*

Chest aching, I sent love through the bond.

I pointed my chin at Danu. "I'm going to use the sunstone. You should leave."

An old-man croak flitted into my mind. *Good luck.*

He disappeared in a flash of feathers.

Wiping damp palms down my front, I sucked in a shallow breath and steeled my nerves. Then I reached beneath the neckline of my armor and tugged out the sunstone. In my hand, the citrine flared to life.

This time, I didn't yank my hand out of the figurative fire. I walked straight into it. Big mistake.

Trapped in a burning room, I found myself in the grips of an ancient power that reduced my barriers to ash. Courage-sucking pain seized me when sunlight rushed in, pouring into every spiritual channel—every vein.

Bones groaned. Skin heated. Blood hissed.

An intense pressure grew behind my skull. I thought it would fracture and my life would end with a crack. Even as that thought flitted in and out, the flow of magic slowed to a drip, then to a drop. The image of that last glowing ember flared in my mind's eye. I saw a golden seed rush through me, putting down deep roots somewhere beneath my ribs as if it could grow there.

The citrine turned cold; the agony in my body subsided.

I felt full and weightless. Connected and detached.

In that state and with the enemy in my sights, I sensed the sunlight's true nature. Aggression. The desire for power and control. They were a part of it. But the fierce need to protect burned brightest. The sunstone was the warrior's spirit born again. A lioness seeing off a threat to her pride—her family.

My magic roared inside of me. It wanted out.

A vision came to me of my sunlight melting the bars of a cage. Bars that I had placed there. Bars to imprison the wildest parts of me. I couldn't be contained anymore.

Freeing my wings, I drifted up and over the railing like pollen on a breeze, supported by the currents of fire escaping from my hands.

"We can't hit our own." I didn't know who or what I was speaking to. Either way, an acknowledgment resonated in the very marrow of my bones.

Force and intent, together as one, I extended my inked hand. With a flame-painted heart, I sent a chariot of wildfire across the dim sky. I pulled back on the reins when it passed over the rearguard of the legion.

Thousands of fae lifted their faces heavenward.

Curling my fingers inward, I turned wildfire into golden lightning. Deadly forks of sunlight descended, hitting the soldiers again and again. I lost count of the lives lost. But I felt each of their deaths as if we were connected by a thousand strings, and one by one those strings were being severed. As each thread was cut, I gained another nick on my heart, another chip from my soul, another ghost that would haunt me.

Seconds or minutes passed.

Warriors broke rank to escape death by sunlight and to avoid the hell waiting for them below. For the dry undergrowth in the valley—the gorse and the heather—had caught fire in several places.

Sensing victory, our side rallied. Morgan's forces fled. Yet the fever in my soul did not die.

Another mind touched mine. *Siska?*

A distant cry. Unimportant.

Ena? Let them go. We're safe now.

A strong tug around my middle brought me to my senses. I recognized my brother calling to me, struggling to ground me.

It wasn't enough. The energy within me was too potent and powerful to ignore. It had to be depleted. That was the only way to be free of it.

Lynx will be with you soon.

I blinked. Lynx?

Somehow, my eyes knew where to find him. He'd left the city; his wings were straining to get to me. No. No. *No.* I could hurt him.

"Get out of me," I pleaded with my magic. "Get out!"

It was stubborn. It didn't listen.

Desperation pushed me to choose an area at the end of the valley. That was where the fae were fleeing, but they hadn't gotten there yet. I performed a palm-strike, releasing a colossal wave of magic.

Forks of sunlight struck the valley floor like the many branches of a burning tree. Morgan's soldiers beat their wings madly, trying to slow and avoid my cage of lightning.

Our forces caught up to them, capturing some, killing others.

Now, it was over. And I was extinguished.

My eyelids sagged as I crumpled and fell toward angry flames that licked the earth, devoured fallen fae, and birthed plumes of black smoke.

Hair flying wild in winds of stormy heat, I collided with something hard. Instinctually, I retracted my wings to avoid damage.

Black feathers glinted in my fading vision. "I've got you."

"I know," I whispered before my spirit fled the world.

CHAPTER 47
A MIND OF FLAMES AND WATER

-LYNX-

I paced up and down, feeling helpless, watching Liora tend to my unresponsive mate in what had to be the longest examination in the history of the healing arts.

Scraping my fingers through my grimy hair, I checked the crystal clock on the mantlepiece again.

Had we really only been in this room for fifteen minutes? It felt like I'd sought Liora out hours ago. With no cots available in the healers' ward, we'd taken Ena to her own bed, followed closely by Sefra and a limping Frazer.

I halted at the sound of approaching footsteps.

Still tense from the battle, my hackles rose.

The door swung open, banging against its frame. Wilder, Cai, and Adrianna stalked in.

I willed my overworked muscles to relax.

"What's wrong with Serena?" Wilder spoke in a strained rasp, courtesy of the battle most likely.

"She's been unconscious since she used the sunstone on the legion," Sefra said from where she stood next to the bed, staring down at Ena.

Wilder coughed and rubbed at his throat. "Is she drained?"

Sefra smudged her war paint as she kneaded the pressure point between her brows. "Liora hasn't said. But it can't just be burnout, otherwise she wouldn't be running a fever."

I caught the alarm rounding Cai's eyes as he gazed down at Liora, quietly holding Ena's hand, and then at Frazer, propped up against the headboard, clutching his sister's back against his front as if his life depended on it.

"Are you okay, Fraze?" Cai asked.

Frazer's ashen face lacked expression. He stared into empty space, appearing catatonic.

I palmed my nape, massaging out the tension there. "He hasn't spoken for a while."

Wilder rounded on me. "Can you reach her mind?"

"Her mental-shield's changed." I arrived at the brink of Ena's mind. "All I see is a wall of fire. I can't get past it."

"What does that mean?" Adrianna demanded.

"I don't know."

"Then what good are you?"

Her expression was accusatory, burning with ferocity. It snagged and aggravated emotions that were already making it hard to breathe.

Sefra turned on Adrianna like a tiger. "That's enough. You're not helping."

Being chastised didn't suit Adrianna. Stifled anger compressed her lips and embarrassment painted her cheeks a darker shade of brown.

I handled the awkward air by pacing the floorboards again. Another five miserable minutes passed before Liora stirred. I came to a standstill when she released Ena's hand and pushed herself off the bed.

That movement snapped Frazer out of his trance. He must've been waiting for this moment to interrogate her. "Well?"

Liora faced him, hands trembling a little. "I've fixed the injury to her ribs."

"And?" Frazer dead-eyed her.

"Her energy levels are low, but with treatment and time, she would've recovered normally," Liora said, sounding hoarse, looking cheerless. "The problem is her temperature. I haven't been able to bring it down using the usual methods, and the longer it continues unchecked, the more damage it's going to do to her body."

I gripped the footboard of the bed. Anything to keep me steady.

"Are you saying she'll stay like this until she dies?" Wilder asked, strangling the pommel of his sword.

The slender line of Liora's throat convulsed. "I'll give her potions made for patients suffering from heatstroke to see if that helps." Her next words were whispered. "But there's only so much I can do."

That blew the heart out of my chest.

Just then, a tiny whimper escaped Ena. Everybody froze.

Eyes shut, she scowled as if in pain. "Brata."

That soft groan was a merciless fist squeezing my innards. Frazer rested his chin on the top of her head. "I'm here, mina sydä."

My Heart. That was what he'd called her.

Wilder and I traded a short glance. I saw my thoughts sketched over his bruised face. Both of us wanted to be the one she called out for in these moments. We wanted the right to hold her.

Thirty frustrated heartbeats skipped by. When Ena didn't speak again, I ground my teeth and fought the urge to break something.

Liora freed a sigh tinged with worry. "I'll get the potions."

"I'll come with you," Cai said, quietly falling into step behind her.

Leaden silence was left in the wake of their departure. Wilder slumped to the floor, his spine and green wings braced against the wall. Adrianna peered out of the window and watched the Riverlands army round up the dregs of the legion.

And I stared at Ena. To stand by unable to help her was unbearable. At the hands of Morgan's torturers I'd been force-fed salt, suffered hundreds of lashes from an iron-tipped whip, and had my nails ripped out. I thought I knew a thing about torment. But this—this was worse. I'd sooner have my wings stretched out on the rack than endure the sight of my mate bedridden. Dying.

My bruised hands got pinker at the knuckles; the footboard creaked ominously under my grip. All eyes went to me.

I loosened my grip on the wooden frame before I broke it.

Sefra shook out her wings. "Ena will wake up." Her voice was lined with command, with every bit of power she'd accumulated over the centuries, both as a witch and a queen. "But in the meantime, we've got work to do—work that will ensure her efforts to protect us won't be in vain. There are bodies to be buried. Fires to be put out. Letters to be written. And transport to be arranged for those needing safe passage to Mysaya."

"Safe passage?" Wilder questioned from his spot on the floor.

"For the citizens of Kastella," Sefra explained. "They fled the city with Diana, but she couldn't drag them into the fighting, so she left them on the northern coast, guarded by two thousand of her soldiers. But now we've secured Mysaya, we should bring the rest of her people inland. Indy won't stay and protect them from the Meriden forever."

"Have we secured Mysaya, though?" Adrianna turned away from the window and the sight of the burning valley to confront Frazer. "You said Morgan wouldn't send anymore legions in the foreseeable future—has that changed?"

"No," he said from the bed. "But the lack of a vision isn't a guarantee."

Adrianna's brow furrowed at that noncommittal response.

"Morgan won't attempt another direct assault so soon after today's display of strength," Sefra said, folding her arms. "But that doesn't mean she'll leave us alone. And we must be ready for any eventuality. Liora will tend to Ena. The rest of us—"

"I won't leave her," I said, already resolved.

Wilder stretched his neck, lifting his chin. "Neither will I."

Sefra challenged Wilder. "You are our Sabu." Her hard stare landed on me. "And you are the Lord of Mysaya. As such, you are both responsible for the people within Mysaya's borders. By abandoning that duty, you disgrace your names, and as her mate and guardian, you disgrace Ena's, too."

There was too much truth in her admonishment to be denied or fought.

At a sigh, my wings drooped. "Fine."

Wilder grunted his surrender.

"Frazer—"

His haunted eyes pinned Sefra. "Mysaya could burn to ash and the world with it before I left her side."

A nasty pause punctuated the conversation.

"I only wanted to ask you to take care of her," Sefra said, a newfound wariness in her tone.

Frazer's gaze slid away from her in a clear dismissal. "I was taking care of her before you even knew her."

Sefra replied before I could tell Frazer he was being a prick. "I know that, but don't make the mistake of thinking you're the only one who loves her."

He ignored her. Her chin didn't lower. "I should go and find Diana. Adrianna, do you want to accompany me?"

Adrianna glanced at Ena, appearing conflicted. I thought she might refuse to leave. At the next tick of the clock, her hesitation broke. She strode toward the door, her gait determined. Sefra went after her without a word.

Wilder, however, made no move to leave. Neither did I.

Frazer drifted off, succumbing to exhaustion. Ena's eyes rolled under their delicate lids in what had to be fitful sleep. It wasn't until Liora returned that Wilder stood up and confronted me. "We should go."

That set my teeth on edge. How did he make a prompt sound like an order?

"After you." I waved a pissed-off hand toward the exit.

He marked me with a *look*.

I cocked a brow.

Wilder glanced off to the side, huffing in irritation. Then the brooding bastard turned on his heel and marched outside.

Liora ignored me as she set up a mobile healing station beside the bed. That forced me to see sense. She needed to concentrate. I shouldn't be disturbing her.

I stole one last look at Ena. That proved a mistake; my feet seemed to grow roots into the earth.

My hands and jaw clenched. I had to rip out the roots and move. Because I wasn't doing her any good like this. I wasn't honoring what she'd done for us. But I might if I left to help others.

With that in mind, I walked away. I didn't dare look back.

∽

-FRAZER-

I pushed up against my siska's mind, only to be blocked by sky-high flames and interminable silence yet again.

Ena had fainted hours ago. And I had failed to reach her countless times. Old enemies—fear and frustration—clawed at me.

"Frazer."

I retreated from my kin bond to meet Liora's gaze. "What?"

"Didn't you hear what I said?" Seeing what must've been a blank expression, she clarified. "I should examine your leg."

"Not necessary. Another healer fixed the bone and warded me against infection."

She perched on the edge of the mattress, tucking her foot underneath her thigh. "You were limping before. I need to check for damage to your muscles."

I dragged my eyes over her, studying her closely.

Liora had tried to look tidy and professional: clean hands, scrubbed face, and she'd pinned her hair up in an attempt to tame the untamable. But her exhaustion showed in her bloodshot eyes and clumsy movements. She had tended Ena from morning to afternoon. Always there, burning herbs for wakefulness, wetting her lips with potions, and dabbing her face with cold compresses.

"Save your energy."

Quite calmly. "I have strength enough for this."

I raised a skeptical brow.

"You're not doing Ena any favors by refusing me." Liora sat a bit straighter, squaring off her shoulders. "And you're not helping her by sitting here like a block of wood. You need to take care of yourself. Let me check your leg. Eat something. Please."

Guilt irritated my skin like a mash of nettles. "Fine. Just don't cry."

"I'm not crying." She brushed a tear off her cheek. "And if I was, it would be because I'm angry you're not looking after yourself. I care about you, too, you know."

"You'd make an excellent politician," I said with a flat look. "You're quite proficient in emotional blackmail."

She adopted a haughtiness in both tone and countenance. "I'd prefer to think of it as applying pressure where needed."

"Do what you will," I told her.

With care and diligence, she inspected my leg. Liora mentioned something about bone calluses being formed, but that she had to fix nerve damage. I hardly listened.

When finished with me, Liora left the room. Gone to get food.

I turned inward again. Thinking it might jolt Ena out of her coma, I yanked viciously on the cord connecting me to her. I shouted into her mind and demanded for her to wake. When that failed to work, I pleaded with her.

Liora and Cai's arrival put a stop to all that.

"We brought food." Cai raised the tray he was carrying, showing me the various snacks on display. "And you're eating with us. No arguments."

Liora placed her own tray, complete with coffee pot and cups, on the rug beside the bed. When I hadn't moved, she straightened up and eyed me. "You said you would."

I carefully moved out from under Ena. "I'll be back."

On stiff but pain-free legs, I exited the room.

I relieved my bladder, scrubbed the battle off my skin, and switched my armor for clean clothes. That done, I returned to find Ena much the same. She wouldn't have woken without my sensing it, but it still proved a bitter disappointment.

Liora and Cai now sat side by side, resting their backs against the bedframe, engaged in an argument over a basket of pastries.

"Stop hoarding them." Liora jostled Cai with her elbow.

Cai's speech became muffled when he shoved a cinnamon roll into his mouth. "I don't know what you mean." His credibility was rendered null and void by the sweet-smelling pastry he held in each hand.

Unable to ignore the hunger clawing at my belly, I joined Cai and Liora on the floor and made up my own plate of food. I spent a few minutes picking at fruit, cheese, and bread before Adrianna and Lynx's raised voices reached me.

"And she didn't tell you that she was planning this?"

"My makena doesn't tell me anything."

I stared expectantly at the door, dusting my hands free of crumbs.

"Somebody's coming?" Liora guessed.

"Mm."

Liora put her plate down. Cai continued inhaling pastries.

Adrianna and Lynx soon walked in. They looked at Ena first. Seeing her still sleeping, gloom clouded their expressions.

"What *is* Diana planning?" I directed that question at both the arrivals.

"At least let me get in the door," Adrianna snapped.

She sat next to Liora and opposite me. She appeared worn through, and a throat-catching scent of smoke clung to her clothes. Based on that, I suspected she'd been helping the team tasked with putting out fires in the valley.

Lynx dropped down between me and Adrianna. He reached for the tray closest to me, grasped the handle of the coffee pot, and poured out a cup that he placed in front of Adrianna.

Impatience ballooned within me, causing my fingers to tap atop my knee.

Adrianna absentmindedly picked up her cup and blew over the coffee to cool it. "We just had a meeting that was supposed to be about making plans for the next few days. Diana decided to take it over and announce her plans to sail to Mokara."

Cai and Liora were stunned into open-mouthed silence.

I recovered fastest. "Why is she sailing to Mokara?"

Adrianna looked at me over the rim of her steaming mug. "Because over two thousand of our warriors died today, and there are a lot of people injured who might also be destined for the pyres." Her strangled notes stirred pity even in my cold heart. "Diana thinks she can secure more soldiers for us in the place she grew up. Thousands, if she has her way."

"Mercenaries?"

The flash in her eyes suggested the distaste in my voice hadn't been missed. "No. She intends to seize the soldiers from her parents."

Cai stopped his hand en route to his mouth, leaving a honey bun hanging an inch from his lips. "Am I missing something? Why do your grandparents have an army?"

Adrianna explained that her grand-kin were rich nobles who maintained a standing army to protect their many businesses from rivals and thieves.

I asked the obvious: "Why would your grand-kin's soldiers follow Diana, and to another land no less?"

"The soldiers are paid next to nothing," she replied. "Diana plans to offer them land in the Riverlands if they fight for her."

"Did Diana say when she'd be back?" Liora asked.

Adrianna slumped, her shoulders rounding forward. She sipped at her coffee in a way that made it apparent she desperately needed the pick-me-up. "She thinks it won't be until next year, sometime in the spring or early summer."

Glances were exchanged.

Cai popped his sugar-dusted thumb out of his mouth and said what we were all thinking. "That's a long time to wait for reinforcements."

"Yes, it is," Adrianna muttered.

My interest in the continuing conversation waned. I moved on to dissecting the information about Diana, attempting to place it within the context of my visions.

Liora's voice trickled in through my musings. "Who is Diana leaving in charge of the court while she's gone?"

That recaptured my attentions.

"Me," Adrianna said shortly. "But I haven't said yes yet."

"Why wouldn't you?" Cai asked.

"Because it requires me to be her heir apparent, which means consenting to be the next Queen."

"And that's a problem?" Cai ended on an uncertain high note.

Adrianna's jaw and wings tensed.

"Even if you were crowned, you could still visit Asitar," Liora said gently.

Adrianna flared up. "Who said I wanted to go to Asitar?"

There was a stiff pause. In that handful of seconds, Liora seemed to realize her mistake. She continued tentatively. "I just assumed ... because of Zeke."

"This has nothing to do with him." Adrianna's nostrils whitened with the strain of drawing in a steadying breath.

Nobody contradicted her. I certainly wasn't about to. I'd no wish to insert myself into the troubles of others.

Adrianna glared out into space. "I don't want to be the heir, because I hate politics. I always have." Her voice lost strength. "But I know if I refuse Diana she'll appoint one of her advisors, and given what's at stake, we can't risk someone outside of our circle taking charge. So ..."

She left it at that.

Everybody handled the lingering tension differently. Adrianna tore chunks off a bread roll, chewing on it as if it had personally offended her. Liora and Cai snuck glances at each other but seemed committed to a path of non-confrontation.

Lynx was the only one who dared confront the unpleasantness. "Well, I'll feel safer knowing it's you in command of the Riverlands Court rather than some power-crazed politician."

Adrianna didn't reply, but her features seemed to ease.

A sharp *tap-tap-tapping* caused my shoulder blades to contract and smart. I pivoted toward the source of the sound, which turned out to be an eagle-sized bird hovering outside the window.

Liora gasped. "Is that ..."

"It's a phoenix," Lynx said, awed.

We all scrambled to our feet and went to investigate.

Lynx opened the squeaking window, and without hesitation, the phoenix fluttered in and settled on the sill. I'd seen illustrations of the species in books. This one was a fine example. It had wine-red plumage and a mane of golden feathers collaring its neck.

The bird stuck its foot out. It had a pouch tied to its leg.

"God's tooth," Cai breathed out. "Who the hell gets a phoenix to deliver a letter?"

"Morgan?" Liora gazed at each of us in turn.

The phoenix in question squawked and wiggled its clawed foot at me.

"It seems to like you best." Lynx sported a faint grin. "I guess that means you should open it."

I retrieved a sheet of parchment from the phoenix's pouch. Once I'd unfolded it and smoothed out the wrinkles, my eyes skipped to the bottom of the page. "It's from Sandrine."

The stress melted from Liora's and Cai's limbs.

I frowned. "It's addressed to me."

"Read it out." Adrianna urged me on with an impatient gesture.

I read:

. . .

Dear Frazer,

I know this will reach you while Ena is still sleeping. I wish I could've written with news of when she will wake, but my power has failed me in this regard. However, I feel certain that if she truly were in danger of not waking, the undines would've foreseen it.

I realize this will be of little comfort to you at present. Yet, I must beg you and your pack to look past your concerns for Ena and start to plan for the future. For there is much to be done.

Taking Mysaya was a good move. Morgan won't send her legionnaires there again—not in the foreseeable future, anyway. Of course, that does not mean she will stop trying to retake it. I, and others, have reason to believe she'll force people she deems less valuable to attack Mysaya. In doing this, she hopes to keep your forces occupied, wear down your morale, and exhaust your resources.

I'm sure you're aware Morgan controls dozens of settlements throughout western Aurora. These outposts will be the first places she'll turn to when looking for soldiers to strike Mysaya. But if you can remove the officers at these outposts, you can free the settlements' inhabitants—people she would otherwise use for evil ends.

From there, you should head to the Crescent. If you can't secure the witches' allegiance, I see only failure before us. The covens are notoriously difficult to deal with. Luckily, someone is already there, working on your behalf. After our time at Lake Ewa, Hazel traveled to the witches' court to ascertain who might be sympathetic to your cause. She wishes to be of service to your pack and waits for Ena to join her in the northeast of the Crescent at an estate called River-Willow House.

I saw myself at said estate this coming autumn. I hope this means we'll meet soon. But for now, I entrust the care of my niece to your Sight. You have always looked three steps ahead, Frazer. You will be a magnificent seer.

Love to everyone,
Sandrine.

—You can be sure this message hasn't been read by our enemies. The phoenix is a longtime friend and trustworthy messenger. However, it would be prudent to burn this letter.

. . .

The moment I finished reading, the phoenix flew off and became a dash of color amid the mellow tones of late afternoon. It must've decided it had done its job.

I folded the letter up, reflecting on the words written there.

"I understand we need the witches' help." Adrianna propped a hand on her hip. "But what happens to Mysaya if we leave? Too much blood has been spilled here for us to abandon the city."

"We don't all need to go to the Crescent," Lynx said. "Moving through enemy territory and stirring up rebellion is a task best suited to secrecy."

"Then you shouldn't go." Adrianna flashed him a barbed look. "You're too recognizable."

"Agreed," he said, viewing the charred remains of his valley. "But I'm not missing the opportunity to go to the western settlements. Morgan's kept my people penned in such places for years. The last of Mysaya's citizens are being held in several of those gods-forsaken places." Anger deepened—roughened—his voice. "And they've suffered long enough. All Aurorians have."

"Maybe you can finally bring them home?" Liora said.

Lynx gave her a thin-lipped smile.

"I hate to say it, but I need to stay too," Adrianna announced. "I have to be where the court is, and my people are safer here than they would be in the Crescent."

I decided to make my own stance clear. "Just in case it wasn't obvious, I'm going wherever Ena goes, which I suspect will be the Crescent."

"Don't worry," Adrianna said dryly. "It was obvious."

Cai expelled a ridiculous piggish-like snort.

I dead-eyed him. He pretended to look contrite.

"It makes sense for you to go," Liora said fairly. "You would've always had to travel to the Crescent with her anyway."

True. I bobbed my chin.

"To retrieve the moonstone?" Lynx voiced.

Our pack swapped looks of uncertainty. Lynx guessed at the reason for our silent exchange. "Ena told me about the stones."

I wasn't remotely surprised.

"Yes." I looked up at Lynx. "We would've traveled there for the stone."

Liora chimed in. "Sandrine's advice is actually pretty similar to Abraxus's." She stared down at the letter in my hand, her eyebrows nudging together, almost touching. "The only difference is that he said Ena should go to the Crescent so that she could challenge Morgan for the right to rule there."

Lynx's chest deflated in a surprised laugh. His expression shifted between pride and concern.

"Why haven't I heard that Abraxus wants her to be the next High Witch?" Cai asked, frowning. "Did you just forget to tell me?"

Guilt rippled across Liora's face. Adrianna went on the defensive. "Yes. And given what we've gone through since returning to Aldar, it's a wonder we haven't forgotten more."

Cai looked a tad mollified by that.

Adrianna pivoted the conversation. "I assume you'll both be headed to the Crescent?" She had directed that question at Cai and Liora.

"You assumed wrong." Liora's bright eyes dimmed. "Isolde should stay here."

I had to admit that surprised me. "We might need your healing skills in the Crescent."

"There are other healers here," she said firmly. "I'm sure one of them will agree to go with you."

Her resolve struck me as altogether strange.

"Is there a reason you don't want to return?" I asked.

Her furtive expression told me there was. "I'm staying because we need somebody who can protect Mysaya in Lynx's and Ena's absence. Sefra's the only other witch whose reputation might make our enemies think twice before attacking. And I doubt she'll want to be separated from Ena or miss out on seeing Sandrine after so many years."

"Take it easy, Li." Cai leaned away from her, palming his chest to signify an emotional blow. "You keep on like that and my pride will never recover."

Liora winced in sympathy. "Sorry. I just think keeping a dragon around here might not be such a bad thing."

"Fair point," Cai admitted, his smile forgiving.

"What about you?" Liora asked him. "D'you think you'll go back?"

Cai's chest expanded in an uneven breath. "I don't know. Maybe."

His uncertainty spurred Liora to respond with, "You only left home because of me. You gave up your dreams to look out for me. But I'm not afraid of my power anymore, and I can protect myself."

"I didn't give up anything that mattered," Cai said sharply.

"Yes, you did," she insisted, her eyes softening around the edges. "Whether you admit it or not, you wanted to take over from Grandfather as coven leader. And you were the most popular candidate to replace him. If anybody can convince the scholars to fight against Morgan, it'd be you."

My neck stiffened. *Grandfather?*

"Are you trying to guilt me into doing what you want again?" Cai asked Liora, his voice sounding like both flint and spark.

"That wasn't ..." Her freckled cheeks looked freshly slapped. "I'm sorry."

An annoyed growl resonated in Adrianna's chest. "I'm getting dangerously close to bashing your heads together." She motioned between Cai and Liora. "What are you two talking about? I thought you both belonged to the healers' coven."

Cai slipped on an unfeeling mask. Unusual for him.

"Our parents were sworn to different covens." Liora's tongue swiped across her lips, wetting them. "But after our mother died, our father raised us to be healers like him. It was only when Cai got older that our maternal grandfather approached him about transferring to the scholars' coven. He was their leader—still is—and he thought Cai should be their next one."

"Your grandfather is Atticus Vox?" Lynx asked, his eyebrows raised.

"Yeah. Unfortunately," Cai muttered.

Adrianna smacked him over the head.

"What in the moons was that for?" Cai glared at her, clasping the back of his skull.

"Why are we just hearing about this?" Adrianna demanded.

"Because I've no reason to talk about the old bastard," he snapped. "Atticus cut off contact with us the second he heard that we were leaving the Crescent."

The cold fires of rejection flickered in the back of his eyes.

Cai faced Liora. "I get where you're coming from, but you don't know the scholars like I do. I could tell them about Morgan allying with

Archon and her plans for the humans, and it wouldn't matter. They would demand a mountain of proof." His hand waved about our group. "Something we can't get. Even if we could, getting them to act on it would be harder than herding cats. Their coven's gained a lot under Morgan's rule."

"You're underestimating yourself." Liora's face shone, hopeful. "You convinced Grandfather to teach you spells forbidden to outsiders. If you can do that—"

"Like the twining, you mean?"

Liora nodded earnestly. "That's right. And without that—"

"He didn't teach me anything, Li." Cai grimaced as if in remembrance of an evil memory. A wound that had festered. "I stole those spells."

I watched Liora's face slacken. "W—what?"

Cai's exhale was blunted with irritation. "I asked the crotchety bastard for them. I told him that we'd be in danger in the Riverlands. That we might need spells to survive there. But he wouldn't even consider it." His top lip twisted up off his teeth. "He said only high-ranking scholars could be trusted with those spells. So I snuck into their library and I took them. I also sent them to the other covens."

"Why?" Lynx asked.

"Because fuck him. That's why."

Lynx nodded, acknowledging that, understanding it, respect glinting in his eye.

Liora was quick to rally and hide her feelings. "I still feel you're our best shot at gaining allies in the Crescent. If not among the scholars, then inside the healers' coven." His flexing jaw had her adding, "I believe in you. That's it. I'm done. I won't mention it again."

Cai hesitated. "I'll think about it."

"Then do it somewhere else," Adrianna grumbled. "All this emotion has worn me out worse than the battle, and I need to get some rest if I'm not to keel over." Her day-blue eyes flitted over to Ena, who continued to sleep, oblivious to everything. "I'll sleep on the floor. You're all welcome to do the same."

She broke from us and stalked off.

"Where are you going?" Liora asked her retreating back.

"To get a mattress from one of the other rooms." Adrianna gripped the door handle. "I'm not sleeping on hardwood floors if I don't have to."

Cai and Liora both hurried off after Adrianna.

I slipped Sandrine's letter into my trouser pocket. Lynx caught the movement. "Aren't you going to burn it?"

"I will. After Ena reads it."

My feet carried me to her bedside again. I picked up a washcloth from the healers' station and dipped it into the bowl of water. After wringing it out, I sat on the quilt and bathed the fine bones of her face. Caught in the rose-gilded light streaming in through the open window, her porcelain skin stood out as translucent, tender, and fragile. I could see where the fever entered her face through certain blood vessels, making her cheeks two bright spots of color on an otherwise fair canvas. The contrast was glaring and unforgiving.

"You see it too, don't you?" Lynx walked up to my side. "Her mind's in flames."

The fear in his voice hurt my ears. "I see it."

Lynx didn't push the subject. Maybe he was like me, struggling to fight off the parasite of despair.

Ena's forehead crinkled beneath my attentive hands. I quit dabbing at her brow and dropped the washcloth into the basin to look at her twitching lips.

I got the sense she was talking to somebody.

Am I right? Is somebody with you? Are they keeping me from you?

Her silence made my insides ache.

Where are you, siska?

∽

-ENA-

Floating, staring up at the night sky, I thought how well it resembled my mental state. Darkness veiled my mind and blotted out recent events. But a scattering of glittering lights remained. Those stars were my dearest memories, alive and well, giving context to my innermost being.

A masculine voice reached my water-clogged ears. "Tilä?"

The stars above shone brighter and brighter.

Interesting.

I angled my head slightly. The change in perspective showed the stars were actually getting closer, falling to the earth in will-o-the-wisps. They sunk into the lake that cradled me, barely disturbing the waters as they went.

Memories flitted in, banishing the shadows in my mind.

The battle.

John. Viola.

Chaos. Fire. Death.

Those recollections tore strips off me.

I floundered, only to discover solid ground underfoot. It soothed my jagged pieces to feel something as normal as the soft squish of sand between my toes.

Standing in chest-high water, I peered down at my outfit. The taldävarian armor was, inexplicably, bone-dry. I touched the silky sleeves, the metal feathers on the shoulders, and even the steel spine that guarded my wingless back. Not a drop of moisture was to be found.

The strangeness didn't end there. The small lake surrounding me didn't mirror me or the world above. Instead, random images rippled across its surface: ancient times, foreign lands, strange faces. As if I had landed in a pool of memory.

"Ena?"

My head went up.

I viewed the landscape with an eye to its barren beauty. An endless stretch of sand dunes drifted, moved by a warming wind. The horizon was crowned by pale, thin clouds courting an orb of silver-cream.

But none of that could compare to the sight of the male who stood upon the shore. He showed me his palm in greeting.

Excitement exploded inside of me. "Dain?"

I waded to the shore as fast as I could. In my haste to reach him, I stumbled and fell to my knees near the lake's edge.

The sound of water kicked up, then a hand marked by strong fingers, smooth nails, and alabaster skin extended toward me. I grabbed it and Dain pulled me up to join him on the shore, at which point the taldävarian boots appeared on my feet. Another weird occurrence.

Dain swept me into his arms, almost knocking our heads together in his quickness. I found comfort in his embrace. The action felt natural, familiar. But his closeness also forced me to recognize my situation for what it was. Because if we were together, didn't that mean I was dead?

And if I was dead ...

"Where's Frazer?" I pushed out of Dain's grasp. "He has to be here. I promised him that we'd end up in the same court."

Panic cracked my voice, made it shrill.

Dain clasped my upper arms, fixing me with a steady eye. "Frazer isn't here because you're not dead. Not yet. Your spirit is hovering on the brink. That's why we can meet here."

My knees wobbled. "And where is here? I feel like I've seen it before."

"You have." His hands left my biceps. "Your spirit traveled here after fighting Goldwyn. This is where you saw your makena."

I nodded. "I remember. I also remember her saying it was forbidden to speak to me in this way."

"The situation has changed," he said. "Balor found proof that Morgan and Archon were using the moon court to communicate with each other. He took the evidence to Persephone and Poltaris, the rulers of this land, and while they claim to know nothing about it, they agreed it would only be fair to grant Balor's request and allow me access to their court. Your makena wished to join me, of course, but when she came here to speak with you, she did so without permission. As punishment, she's been banned from returning."

Loss and disappointment. My emotions didn't stop me from tweezing several questions out of his words. I chose the most obvious one to ask. "Why did Balor send you here? I can't imagine it was just to say hello."

"No." A rueful smile. "I'm to act as his messenger. But before we get into that, why don't we sit down?" He jerked his chin at the boundless stretch of desert before us. "We may as well be comfortable while we're talking."

Stress whetted my tone into a sharp point. "Sit where? On a sand dune?"

He cast his gaze across the landscape as if searching for something. "That wouldn't be my first choice."

As if in answer to his silent questing, a large tent materialized not far away. Its structure was simple: wooden poles provided the framework, white canvas created four walls, and soft carpets served as the flooring.

My lips parted in a tiny gasp.

"Perfect." Dain walked up to the tent, his stride long, his gait quick.

I hurried after him. "Where did that come from?"

"Something or somebody conjured it for us," he said, passing through the open doorway which was just a gap cut out of the canvas. "I can't be sure of what or who, though. The celestial courts operate by their own rules."

I ducked into the empty shelter.

A phantom breeze blew sand in from the outside. This dust formed shapes in the middle of the room: a low-to-the-ground table, a glowing lantern, a tea pot with a wooden handle, and two small cups appeared.

"It seems 'something' also wants us to have tea," I said.

Dain's lips twitched, giving the illusion he was about to smile. "Indeed."

Tucking his magpie-like wings in, he settled in a cross-legged position. I sat on my own side of the table, at a right-angle to him, with a view to the desert landscape.

Exuding cool grace, he rolled his sleeves up to his elbows and poured fragrant tea into the cups provided.

I couldn't help studying him. I'd seen him before, but not without the limitations of time and distance working against us.

He wore a gray robe that ended at the ankles. It was secured by a belt and designed with a cross collar that showed off his black undershirt. He'd tied his hair up, but the strands were loose and falling down his neck to his shoulders.

Stomach awhirl, I summoned my courage. "So what does Balor want to tell me?"

"Two things." Dain slid a cup of white tea across the table to me. "First, he thought you'd want to hear news of Zola and Thea."

My back straightened. "I do."

A pale smile. "They're well. Just exhausted. It may be a few months before they can contact you again."

"I know. They told me before they left."

His flat eyebrows bunched lightly over his straight nose. "My second message relates to the sunstone." I lifted my hand to where the stones usually resided. My fingers touched the silky fabric of my armor and nothing else. "The seers of the light court saw you using it in the battle. They believe, as Balor does, that you've drained the sunstone permanently."

Horror and panic clashed like two cymbals within me. "I've doomed us?"

"No, tilä," he said softly. "The stones are conduits to source energy, so the magic inside would've always regenerated. But it seems when you drew energy from the sunstone, you also imbibed its connection to the source."

Confusion fogged up my brain. "I don't understand."

"In short, you've become the new sunstone."

Stunned, I struggled with my response. "What does that mean—is that bad?"

A frown marred his noble brow again. "By taking in, well, for lack of a better word, the sunstone's spark, you've thrown your magic out of balance. If you don't correct the equilibrium, the sunlight will destroy you." He gestured ahead to the lake. "That's your path back to your body. You'll need to put your head underwater, and waking up might feel like you're trying to escape a dream. But you must wake, and the second you do, draw in energy from the waterstone. That should neutralize the sunlight long enough for you to recover from being drained."

Fear clunked through me. I was weak, near death. What if I couldn't call up more magic?

My doubt might've shown on my face because Dain laid his hand on mine. "Have more faith in yourself. You were powerful enough to absorb the sunstone—something that even Balor wasn't sure was possible. You must trust in that strength now." He squeezed my hand gently, then released it. "You'll need to absorb a bit of the waterstone every day until you're powerful enough to consume its essence. That should bring your spiritual energies into alignment for a time."

His last sentence constricted my throat. I sucked in shallower inhales and my voice thinned. "For a time?"

"Sunlight and waterlight are natural counterparts." He continued in that careful tone that people used when they hated to impart bad news. "They'll harmonize each other for a few months—maybe. But there will come a point when you need to absorb the energy of the other two stones as well. That's the only way to maintain an overall magical balance. If you don't, you'll end up here again."

Dain lifted his teacup to pursed lips, cooling the surface with a few breaths. He seemed content to sit with me. To let me work through things.

Questions popped up in my head faster than weeds in the grass. I picked the one pressing on me most. "I know you hid the moonstone in the Crescent and used its power to create the barrier between the fae and human realms. But it'd help if we got an exact location—can you give me one?"

His head lowered in a placid nod.

Relief swept in, then confusion at the stilted pause.

Dain cleared his throat. "A little help?"

Quill, ink, and parchment appeared on the tabletop.

"Just the thing," he said. "Thank you."

Our helpful "friend" either couldn't hear him or didn't care to reply.

I watched Dain sketch out a sickle-shaped landscape. His hand proved skilled, his lines were masterful, and when the illustration was completed, he wrote instructions on the back.

He presented the map to me. I studied it, concentration creasing my forehead.

"You can look at it properly when you wake up."

My gaze flicked up to him. "I can take it with me?"

"You can carry back whatever I give you." He sipped at his tea. "I made sure of that."

"Did you know I'd ask for this?" I said, raising the map and showing it to him.

He gave me a sly smile. "I figured you'd be smart enough to ask. You are my daughter, after all."

My heart stumbled, falling into a warm place.

I tucked the map inside a hidden breast pocket.

"You have more questions." He seemed certain about that.

Bringing my cup up to my lips, I breathed in the mellow fragrance before sipping. By the time the fresh, floral taste cleared from my tongue, I'd decided what to ask him next. "Why didn't you tell me who your father was?"

That remark sent ripples across the temperate waters of his face, reshaping his expression into something murky and troubled. "Because I was worried if you met him knowing you were related, you might not treat him with the kind of caution that somebody as dangerous as him deserves."

The distrust ringing in his voice drove me to confess. "I inherited his magic."

He dipped his chin in a small nod. "Zola and Thea said."

"I've already killed somebody with his magic." My palms tingled, remembering the power that had recently flowed out of them. "Then I used the sunstone ... And a lot of people died."

I peered down at my twisting hands, almost expecting to see blood there. Just how much more life would I have to take before this was over? What if this war lasted for years?

"Do you recall what I told you when you were becoming fae?" Dain said kindly.

Mind in a muddle, I shook my head.

"I said that the lives lost in this fight belong to tyrants like Morgan —people who would set the whole world on fire if it benefited them."

"My magic killed them." I fidgeted and picked at my nails. "Not Morgan's. And some of them were probably innocent, trapped into serving her—"

"That's right." Dain's glacial tone silenced me. His twilit-blue eyes burned. Not with fire, but with the harsh winds of winter. "She sent slaves to fight the people who want to free them. It's a sick wheel that must be broken. I know you don't want to hurt others, nor should you. But today you showed Aldar that it doesn't have to accept Morgan's cruelty as the norm. And in the process, you saved a great many people."

Intense grief struck me unexpectedly, like a lightning bolt in broad daylight.

"I didn't save them. I got them killed." That whisper choked me.

The cold anger left his features. "Who, tilä?"

I set my elbows onto the table, letting my head drop into my hands. "John. Viola. Hunter. Everybody in Tunnock. People in Asitar." I sucked in air and it was like inhaling through an ever-narrowing tube. "They're all dead because of me."

I slid my fingers into my hair, grasping at the roots there, hoping to hold onto the remnants of my control. But when I tried to hide behind my defenses, I found they were eroded by turbulent emotions. Like the sea weakens the cliffs.

My vision blurred. It was no use. I had nothing left. My inner fortifications were crumbling and images, real and imagined, invaded my mind.

Hunter dying in my arms.

John's mutilated head.

Balthur tormenting Viola. The villagers. The children.

A sob clawed at the back of my throat. I pressed a hand over my mouth to try to stop it from coming out. Ancestors help me.

Dain shuffled to my side and placed a hand at my back. "Their deaths don't belong to you, Ena."

Lies. Lies. I dug my nails into my cheek as hot tears crashed to the table.

"Here." Dain showed me a white blob.

I clumsily reached for what turned out to be a handkerchief. Clearly, the being that conjured the tent was also witnessing my breakdown. That tiny kindness destroyed what self-control I had left. I wept openly; the cries that escaped me were broken and disordered, as if my lungs were punctured by shards of glass.

I unstrung anxiety, grieved loss, and suffered guilt. Flooded with emotion, my spine bowed and my teeth chattered. I dabbed at my swollen eyes, streaming nose, and tried to master scattered breathing. But I was fighting a losing battle.

Sometime later, the jaws of exhaustion ensnared me and the salty tide ebbed. I became a wrung-out sponge, boneless and leaning against Dain.

He held me against him, anchored me. "You are equal to this, Ena."

My tongue unglued from the roof of my dry mouth. "Doesn't feel like that."

Everything tasted of ash.

His chest fell in a sigh. "It rarely does."

I gathered my remaining strength and lifted my rock-heavy head off his shoulder, dislodging his arm from my back. "I'm just scared of losing more people. And I'm terrified that this war will end up turning me into the thing we're fighting against." I looked at my father and forced out more listless words. "You know, Atlas warned me about the sunstone?

He said I'd want to use it to protect people, but then I would be tempted to control them with it. Now that magic is inside of me forever. What's to stop me from becoming the next Morgan?"

Dain gave me a stern blue look. "Atlas and Morgan were always drawn to power, always resentful of what others had inherited. I've had visions of you since before you were even born, and you are nothing like either of them ... But you are like me." His eyes shuttered. "I spent my whole life worrying I'd become as ruthless as my father. That fear bound me tighter than any shackles. And because of it, I hesitated to end Morgan's life when I had the chance of it." His slim shoulders shuddered in a regretful breath. "It was why I lost everything."

My vision grew watery again. But the tears didn't fall. They froze in the corners of my eyes, and my mind became a house in a snowdrift. Silent with darkened rooms and a suffocating weight hanging overhead.

"Doubting yourself can lead to self-destruction as easily as arrogance." The tips of his fingers moved up and stopped an inch from my temples. "I want to show you something. It's a vision of what'll happen should Morgan and Archon win. Will you let me share it with you?"

From the look on his face, I could tell this was important to him. That he thought it might help me. Stomach cramping, I slowly nodded.

At the touch of his fingers, a grisly battle flashed in front of me.

Countless corpses. Monstrous sprites. Foreign creatures. All of them were hacking, slashing, and biting. Fae and human were dying in droves.

The earth was stained with blood, the skies were riven with lightning, the world had become a wasteland, devoid of life.

Those nightmarish pictures faded, and Dain's grim face swam into view. "That is one possible future—one that we cannot allow to happen." His fingers lowered from my temples. "That is what you're fighting to stop."

Black dizziness bolted through me. I gripped my knees for support, thoughts scattering like beads across an uneven floor.

"Let me ask you this," he said, his gaze challenging but not unkind. "If you hadn't used the sunstone, would you regret not saving more of the Riverlanders? Or your friends if they'd been hurt or killed?"

I ruminated on that, even though my heart knew the answer to be yes.

Dain drank his tea until only leaves remained and set the cup down with a final-sounding clunk. "Sometimes, there is no good or right choice. Only the choice we can live with."

That and the vision he'd shared lightened something in me. Grief and guilt remained, but he had tempered it and made it bearable.

"It's time, tilä."

With a regretful smile, Dain shifted onto his knees and held his hand out to me.

His words, gesture, and expression carried countless meanings.

Our moment was over. I had to go back. I had to keep fighting.

I sucked in a deep, tearing breath and nodded, not trusting myself to speak.

Hand in hand, we stood.

The tent, table, and tea vanished, returning to the lonesome desert.

I linked my arm around Dain's. Together, we walked toward the lake, our moon-cast shadows slinking before us.

Sadness pulled at my heart's cords when we toed the water's edge. Dain drew me into one last hug. A gentle one.

I listened for his heartbeat, hoping to preserve it in my memory. It was then I realized he didn't have one. I felt a vast chasm opening up between us, separating our souls, even though we were still locked in an embrace. "Will you wait until I've gone before you leave?"

"Yes. I'll be right here."

The muscles of his arms relaxed. I followed his example and we parted.

My mouth opened. Then closed.

"What is it?" he asked.

"Can you watch out for John and Viola in the light court? Mama will know who they are. She'll recognize them." I had said that without a shred of doubt that my friends would end up there. How could they not? "I don't know if you can do anything for their spirits, but it would make me feel better knowing you were looking out for them."

He gave me a sad smile. "Of course."

"Also ..." Stars. This felt awkward. "Have you seen my father in the light court? Halvard, I mean."

A pause, in which his throat bobbed. "Sati has seen him. His soul is resting now. He's at peace."

I didn't ask him to clarify or elaborate. The questions springing to my mind would likely take hours to answer, and the exhaustion from earlier continued to weigh on me, as did the dizziness. At first, I thought it had been an overflow of emotion that had caused my symptoms. Now, I wasn't so sure.

I felt unstable, close to floating away.

"My greatest regret will always be that I couldn't raise you." Dain continued, his eyes burning with sorrow and pride. "And my greatest joy will always be that I helped create you. I hope you remember that."

Loss and love flickered in the same chamber of my heart.

"We'll see each other again, tilä." His gaze flitted over my face, tracing my features. "But don't let it be too soon."

I wished I could promise him that. "One last thing—what should I call you?"

Both his eyebrows lifted. "Call me?"

"Dain? Father? Isä?"

His forehead relaxed, smoothing out in understanding. "Just call me Da."

"Da ... Okay. Well, when you see my mother again, tell her that I love her."

He nodded, wearing a bittersweet smile. "I will. Goodbye."

Steeling myself, I waded into the lake.

Chest-deep in water, I wheeled about and looked my last upon his face. He raised a palm in farewell.

Goodbye, I said silently.

I pulled in a long inhale, pinched my nose, and took the plunge. Dark water flowed in overhead.

A faint heartbeat sounded in the distance. Kicking off from the bottom of the lake, I swam toward the sounds of life, leaving the moon court behind.

It was only when I heard, "Siska," that I dared to surface. As I broke through that thin film of water, I passed through the veil separating worlds.

I woke up with a gasp, returning to a body that had a tropical storm raging in its blood and wetting its skin. Thunder rolled through my head. It made everything ache and turn cloudy. Lightning struck my nervous system, setting off stabbing pains behind my eyes and causing my joints to burn.

"Ena?" someone cried out.

"Fuck. That scared the shit out of me."

My addled brain ran on one word. *Waterstone.*

I clawed under the neckline of my armor with shaking hands.

"What's wrong with her?"

Couldn't answer. Had to focus.

I clasped a rough and cold object. No, not that one. My slippery fingers moved, stumbling upon a cool, smooth stone. That was it.

I dove into its depths, desperate to flee the raging fever. That was how I found myself standing knee-deep in a slow-flowing river. The water lapping against me started to steam, hissing and spitting like a campfire being rained upon. Pain and relief combined.

Lynx's voice resonated in the air surrounding me. "Elämayen, can you hear us? Can you tell us what you're doing?"

I wasn't the one who replied to him. "I've seen memories of her pulling magic in from the waterstone to counter the effects sunlight had on her. She must be hoping it'll help her again."

Hearing my brother was heartrending. I smothered the temptation to speak with him and concentrated on drawing in more waterlight. It was the boiling sea. I was the reluctant tide.

Alarm rattled me when the river swelled. It went from trickling past me to running wild, as if snowmelt and rainfall had rushed in from an unknown tributary.

The white horses—the rapids—swept my legs out from under me. Taken by the current, I fought to keep my head above water.

Magic flooded into my veins faster and faster. Panic seeped in alongside it. This was what had happened with the sunstone. That couldn't happen again.

Then I spotted a waterfall up ahead. Shit.

I tried to swim for the shore. To escape the currents of my power. Next thing I knew, I lost my stomach. I was free-falling.

The second I crashed into a pale blue pool, I kicked for the light glinting on the surface. But no matter how hard I fought, I couldn't reach it. I slowed in both thought and movement.

Lungs deprived, spots flashed in my vision. Help, I thought. Anybody. Somebody. *Please.*

Two different hands plunged into the water, stretching down to me.

That was my hope. I must gain it. I kept going. I kept fighting. I didn't stop.

My head finally breached the surface. I gasped in glorious air and the magic pushing its way into me stoppered.

Thank you, thank you, thank you.

In a blink, the pool faded and the real world crept back in. I'd just enough sense to realize I was lying in bed. Frazer and Lynx sat on either side, staring down at me with wrecked expressions. Everything behind them was blurred out, characterized by static and moving smudges.

I met the night-blue eyes looking at me from under raven lashes. Frazer glanced at the waterstone clenched in my palm. His hand covered mine. "You did it."

Every bone, muscle, and organ hurt. All I could give him was the tiniest nod.

Lynx pushed out a wobbly sigh. "Thank the light."

Another wave of tiredness stole over me. I wanted to sleep for days. Weeks. But ...

I kept my eyelids propped up through sheer will. "Keep them safe."

"We'll take care of everybody, siska," Frazer's smooth voice answered.

"We will, as long as you promise to wake up," Lynx's deep voice added.

"Mm."

"Hey." Lynx shook my shoulder. "Is that a yes—you'll wake up?"

"It's a yes," Frazer said, releasing me from the obligation to answer.

At that, I embraced oblivion.

CHAPTER 48
THE WANDERING STARS

I spent five days and nights in bed, dozing most of the time, recouping my energy. By the sixth day, I managed to stay awake for a few hours. By the seventh, I rose with the dawn, clearheaded and alert.

Liora checked in with me as she had every morning. I got her approval to end my confinement on the condition that I didn't start training again.

From there, Frazer and I walked around the city. It had become a hectic place courtesy of the many people taking refuge here. We kept to the gardens, alleyways, and quiet corridors as neither of us wished to be in crowded places or stared at by strange people.

The morning blurred past in this way. Frazer dominated the conversation—a rarity for us—and spent his time entertaining me with tales of what life had once been like in Mysaya. I heard about the sky races in the summer, the month-long star festival that had been held in the autumn, and how people would skate on the frozen lakes in winter.

At noon, I couldn't resist stopping by the kitchens. It became clear within seconds that I wasn't needed there anymore. The influx of Kastella's citizens had brought proper cooks into Mysaya, along with tailors, tinkers, butchers, and nobles, all of whom were trying to pick up the pieces of their wrecked lives.

After seeing how busy they were in the kitchens, I felt uneasy about my aimless wanderings. Frazer, sensing my restlessness, suggested we join Cai in studying the Crescent's ruling hierarchy—their rules and procedures—in preparation for our journey there.

We found Cai on the ground floor of the library, where the comforting scents of worn leather, ancient paper, and warm amber drifted through the air. He sat at one of the wooden desks that lined the aisle between bookshelves, his face half-hidden behind piles of books, large and small.

Wilder was also there, standing next to the row of desks, holding leaves of parchment in his hands. "Serena." He walked over and halted before me. "How are you?"

I exhaled a weak laugh. "You've asked me that question every time you've seen me. The answer is the same as before. I'm fine. Better."

That failed to lift the concern from his face.

"Why aren't you wearing your armor?" He cast a disapproving eye over my blush-pink jacket and high-waisted trousers.

"I needed a break from it."

His mouth thinned.

"I've slept in it for a week, Wilder. It was starting to smell." The heat of embarrassment spread across my chest, up my neck, and into my cheeks. "I haven't gone anywhere without my weapon, though."

"You should still have a bodyguard," Wilder insisted. "Perhaps somebody from among the Sami?"

I held in a sigh. "I'm not a porcelain doll. Don't treat me as if I'm about to break."

His expression grew heavier, older. "I know you're not weak. But thousands of strangers have joined us in Mysaya. Any one of them could be a spy or an assassin. It's only right and prudent that somebody watches your back."

"I was with her all morning," Frazer said.

"I meant when you're not there."

"Danu and Cora are looking out for me," I countered, trying to find common ground. "We spotted them when we were walking outside."

Disapproval bracketed Wilder's face. He plainly didn't think much of me having avian bodyguards.

Frazer lost interest and stalked over to Cai. "How's the research going? Learn anything new?"

"Yes." Leaning back in his chair, Cai stretched out his long legs and massaged his nape with ink-stained fingers. "Some of it's outdated, pointless crap." He pointed his chin at the tower of books beside his right arm. "That's the stuff that might prove useful to us later on."

Frazer pulled a book from the top of the stack. He was already speed-reading the first page when he slid into the seat next to Cai.

"Have you absorbed the waterstone's magic today?" Wilder asked me.

"Yes."

He persisted. "Are your sunlight levels stable?"

Gods, give me patience. "Yes." I cut myself off before I could add *For now*.

"But you're not up to full strength yet, are you?"

A cold shiver prickled my spine. I'd already told the others that I hadn't regained all the magic I'd imbibed from the sunstone. It would regenerate, though, and when it did, I would get stronger and stronger. More and more unbalanced.

"No. I'm not." I raised a palm when I saw him opening his mouth. "I don't want to talk about this anymore."

He shot me a look, seeming to say *I know you're not telling me something*.

True.

I concealed my feelings: the sense that a meteorite had struck me and created a chasm—a new well of power—in its wake. I sensed magic at the bottom of the well, but I couldn't tell how fast the sunlight would fill it up. I was in the dark. Ignorant and scared.

"I know I'm being overprotective." The stone in his throat quivered. "But I am your guardian. Your safety is everything to me."

Tongue-tied, unsure what to say, I simply nodded.

Wilder drew in a wide inhale that stretched the stitches in his leather cuirass. "So, Cai and I have written up a list of names." He glanced through the sheets of parchment in his hands. "These are the coven and clan leaders that Cai and I could remember, as well as the status of their relationships with one another and how closely they're allied with Morgan."

He picked out three pages and handed them to me. I passed an eye over the copious amounts of notes that were written in bold script.

"I'll take you through them," he said, responding to what had to be an anxious look from me.

I nodded.

The four of us passed the afternoon in pockets of discussion and study. The latter was only disturbed by turning pages, creaking wood, and scratching quill-nibs.

I decided I'd had enough of research when various rules, titles, and allegiances blurred together, and my belly grumbled from lack of food.

"Do you think it's time for us to meet Adi and Li?" I voiced.

Yesterday, our pack had agreed to eat together. We intended to make it a tradition for as long as the five of us remained at Mysaya.

Directly opposite me, Frazer glanced up from his reading. The light of the table's lantern reflected off the blade of his nose, warming his cold features. "You're hungry."

I saw little point in denying it since he knew the answer. "Yes."

He scraped his chair back. "Let's go."

Relieved, I vacated my own spot.

Cai stood up, but he was quiet, listless.

"I'll walk with you for a bit," Wilder said, coming out from behind his desk.

"Don't you want to eat with us?" I asked him.

"It's not a question of want." He half-smiled at my frown. "It's better if I eat with the other officers. We need to become familiar with one another."

That made too much sense for me to try to persuade him otherwise.

Wilder accompanied us to the central block of the castle. We parted with him at the foot of a staircase that led up to the higher levels—to my bedroom.

I reached the third-floor landing, accompanied by Cai and Frazer. Adrianna's velvety timbre and Liora's singsong notes sounded in the distance. I made my way toward their voices and stepped through my door to find them spread out on the floor.

"You're late," Adrianna said, but she didn't look up at us. She remained focused on the documents fanned out before her.

"Have you already eaten?" was Cai's only concern.

"No," Liora answered. "We were waiting for you."

Adrianna called out, "Wanda."

A four-foot-something sprite popped up beside Adrianna.

I stifled a pinch of alarm. I'd yet to become comfortable with Adrianna's new maidservant and her abrupt entrances, having only met her yesterday.

"What do you want now?" demanded Wanda.

Wanda's gentle face, her cute horns, and the delicate flowers in her hair were a sweet mask—a lie concealing a personality that, based upon my first impressions, was as coarse as it was brattish.

Adrianna frowned at Wanda. "Servants aren't meant to complain this much."

"If you'd desired a fawning toady for a maid, you wouldn't have picked me," she said smugly.

Adrianna didn't deny this. Instead, she got straight to it. "We need a hot-pot and assorted platters. Drinks too. Sparkling water is preferable. And bring us some maple buns and cinnamon swirls. Ena and Cai love those."

Wanda crossed her short arms. "You shouldn't eat so many sweets. Your teeth will rot, and you'll get too fat to fly."

"I didn't ask for your advice." Adrianna assumed a dangerously calm tone. "Now, do as I ask before I hang you up in the dungeons by your fingernails."

"That's disgusting." Wanda scrunched up her pert nose. "What's wrong with you?"

Wanda exited the room via a twirl, never giving Adrianna the chance to respond, which I supposed was the point in her quick exit.

"Is she coming back?" I asked, bemused.

"Yes," Adrianna said. No doubt.

"You've got a very odd relationship," I observed.

A shrug. "Insults are how we communicate."

"Sounds healthy," Frazer deadpanned.

My chuckle skipped through the air, scattering quickly.

Frazer, Cai, and I settled on the floor with the others. Our pack formed our usual circle.

Just then, refreshments materialized one after the other. Wanda didn't show her face again, but as an air sprite, she could transport objects across short distances, so she didn't need to come herself.

I transferred meat slices, leafy greens, and fungi from the platters into the hot-pot's bubbling broth. Once the ingredients were cooked, I plated up and tucked in the second my tongue could bear the heat.

Fifteen minutes into our meal, Cai set aside his newly clean plate and confronted Adrianna. "Aren't you eating?"

"I'm not hungry," she murmured, her attentions absorbed by a lengthy scroll.

Cai heaped what was essentially sugar and dough onto a plate. He slid it toward Adrianna's knee. "You skipped breakfast."

"I'm fine."

Cai arched an eyebrow. "I can hear your stomach rumbling from here."

"No. You can't." Adrianna peered up at him, scowling.

"I'm pretty sure I can hear it too," Liora said, adopting a serious look.

I joined in. "Same."

"Mm," Frazer grunted.

Adrianna expressed an annoyed sigh. She nibbled at a sticky bun in a distracted sort of way, as if she had no time or stomach for it. I suspected that her lack of appetite was caused by stress. Her mother's recent departure from Mysaya had forced Adrianna to assume all the burdensome duties of a queen during wartime.

She was yet to look comfortable in her new role. It required her to wear a silver and sapphire diadem; I'd noticed her adjusting it several times. Then there were her clothes: trousers woven from pristine cotton and a sky-blue top spun from embroidered silk. Despite the quality of her garments, she couldn't stop fidgeting and pulling at them.

Those observations made me gesture to the documents piled up like molehills in a field, and say, "Is there anything I can do to help you with this stuff?"

"No, not really." A blunt but not impolite refusal.

Liora brought her legs up, wrapping her arms around her knees. "I've no idea how you're managing all of this."

"What do you mean?" Adrianna spoke too sharply. She was searching for the insult.

Liora served her a placating look. "Don't get spiky. I'm giving you a compliment. I'd be tearing my hair out if I had to organize food and clothes and homes for thousands of people."

Adrianna made a face. "I'd much rather that than dealing with the nobles and their stupid demands."

Cai patted his trim but slightly swollen belly. "Speaking of annoying tasks, I better head back to the library."

My eyebrows nudged together. "You haven't had a very long break."

Cai staggered up. "Well, we can't take the library to the Crescent. I've got to memorize what I can while we're here."

"You could've brought your reading materials with you," Adrianna said, frowning up at him. "I did."

Cai's shrug came off as dismissive. "It didn't occur to me. Next time, maybe." He waved limply. "Later."

I didn't miss the sigh slipping out of Adrianna as Cai walked off. His abrupt exit was swiftly followed up by another. "I'm going too." Frazer stood, deliberately brushing his wing against mine. "See you soon."

He strode out of the room without another word. I was left staring at the closing door, a tad dazed. "Bye, then."

Adrianna returned to studying her documents. Liora also seemed preoccupied. Her eyes were glazed, and she ate her food without care or interest. I wondered at that—at whether her job interrogating the legionnaires was taking its toll on her. Giving a voice to my thoughts, I said, "How's it going with the prisoners?"

Liora shrunk before me. "Honestly? Hard. Messy."

"Messy?"

Her chest rose in a shuddering way. "They're just really difficult to read. Sure, there are some soldiers who'd spit on Morgan's wings if given the chance, and a few who'd cut their own throats if she asked them to. But most don't fit into either category. Those are the ones who might abandon the legion or even vow allegiance to us, but it's not guaranteed they'd remain loyal to us. Isolde thinks we should keep them imprisoned. Better safe than—"

"Betrayed." Adrianna's tone mimicked the chilly darkness of caves.

A curt nod was Liora's reply.

"How many of the soldiers share bonds with Morgan?" I asked.

Liora's expression didn't tell me anything good. "I haven't read them all yet. But out of the ones who want to be freed from her control, I'd say forty? Maybe a few more."

An undertow of doubt swept me out into uncertain seas. I'd

committed to try freeing the prisoners as soon as I was able. But I wasn't convinced I could break forty or more bonds. I hadn't saved Hunter ...

"You lied," Adrianna said to Liora.

"About what?" Liora questioned.

"You said you'd be tearing your hair out if you had to do my job." Adrianna gathered a few papers together and tapped them on the floorboards to align them. "But what you're doing is just as hard, if not harder."

Liora's eyes flared in surprise. "Thanks."

"See?" Adrianna assumed a smug, cattish air. "I can give compliments too."

Amusement brightened Liora's face. I glanced away, laughing under my breath.

Incoming footsteps distracted us.

The sound of a familiar voice had me hurrying to the door. I wrenched it open as my sister appeared in the foyer dressed in a wine-red top featuring billowing sleeves, wrist cuffs, and a fabric belt. Her sword and dagger glinted at her hips, and her daffodil-colored hair was braided into intricate knots off her face.

Two males walked into the foyer after her, each hauling wooden trunks that smelled of old wardrobes and mothballs.

Sefra motioned to the chests. "Can I put these in your room?"

"Sure."

I stepped back from the door, letting the fae through with their burdens.

Sefra strode in after them.

"Where should we put them, vénhin?" one of them asked.

"Beside the bed."

The males did as they were bid. Sefra thanked and dismissed them.

They bowed to Adrianna and left. The deference felt odd to witness, although it would likely become an ordinary sight in the future.

"Have you both finished eating?" Adrianna directed that question at me and Liora.

"Yes."

"Yeah."

"Wanda?"

She reappeared, scowling heavily.

"Take everything away, please." Adrianna rose onto her knees, shoving scrolls and documents into the satchel she'd brought with her.

With a snap of Wanda's fingers, the dinnerware and water jugs disappeared. "Am I done being your fetcher and carrier for the day? Because I want to dye my hair."

Wanda preened, stroking her green locks.

"Go away," Adrianna replied, standing and shouldering her satchel.

The air sprite flashed her an insincere smile. Then she was gone in a whirl. With her departure, Adrianna turned to me. "Now that Sefra's here, I should go."

"Are you leaving because I've arrived?" Sefra said, dry humor tickling her notes. "That doesn't make me feel very wanted."

"It's got nothing to do with you." Adrianna frowned as if she couldn't understand why my sister would think such a thing. "I have to prepare for an audience with the nobles. If I arrive late, they'll pout like overgrown faelings. I haven't wanted to leave Ena alone after what she's been through. But you're here, so Liora and I can get on with our work."

Her words both warmed my heart and kicked me in the gut.

Adrianna addressed me. "I'll see you later."

She strode out, satchel swinging at her side.

Liora stood, fixing her reticent gaze on me. I could've sworn she was silently apologizing for something. "I should probably get back to my interviews."

I nodded.

Liora came over and hugged me. "Love you."

"Love you too," I whispered as she pulled away.

Liora flashed Sefra a strained smile that doubled as a grimace. "Bye."

Sefra nodded, smiling politely—warmly. Liora hurried out, head down.

"I know you haven't seen much of me since you woke up." Sefra neared me. "I have been visiting, but you were always asleep."

"I know. The others told me."

"Did they tell you what I've been doing?"

That stirred up a memory. "You went to get the money you'd left on Indy's ship."

"That was actually a few days ago." Sefra lowered her voice. "Since I got back, I've been on a retrieval mission." Seeing my bemusement, her face lit up with a sly kind of glee. "Before Morgan could invade the Solar Court, I smuggled our family's belongings out of Alexandria. I couldn't take everything to Asitar with me, so I buried our things in trunks all over Aldar. I've only managed to retrieve a couple so far because I haven't wanted to roam too far from Mysaya. I'll get the dragon's share of our inheritance back once we're in the Crescent—that's where I hid most of it."

I stared at the trunks. "What kind of belongings?"

"Money, mostly." Sefra crouched, unbuckling the trunks. "But I filled these with keepsakes and heirlooms. I want you to have them."

She flipped the lids of the chests.

I kneeled beside her, viewing the contents. The trunks contained books and expensive jewelry: crystal tiaras, gemmed necklaces, ornate daggers, and dozens of hair pieces.

"You could sell the jewelry, but I thought it might be useful for when you meet nobles in the future. They tend to be the most dreadful snobs." She rooted inside a trunk, moving objects around until she found a leather bound book with a gilded rose etched onto the cover. "This one belonged to Mama."

I detected lavender and orange blossom in the vicinity. Logically, I knew my mother's scent couldn't linger after so long. My heart yearned, nonetheless.

Sefra handed the book to me. I took it without a second thought.

"What is it? A story or ..."

"It's a very old, very famous collection of short stories."

Gratitude swelled, and my chest felt too tight to fit it. "Thanks for this. I never expected to own anything of Mama's again."

Sefra's kohl-lined eyes dipped into grief. Not wanting to follow her into sadness, I blocked out every memory of my mother and focused on the book instead.

I flicked through the pages, savoring the crinkle of aged paper and becoming increasingly frustrated at my inability to understand Kaeli. It served as another cold-hard reminder that I was bound to a destiny I was wholly unprepared for. I'd had enough. With care, I returned the book to the trunk.

Sefra and I stood up. I faced her, resolved. "Can you teach me Kaeli?"

A startled blink. "Yes, if you'd like."

"And will you help me with my magic?" I swallowed, clearing the thickness in my throat. "Sunlight's always been hard for me to control. But I think as difficult as it was before, it'll be a lot worse now I've absorbed the sunstone's power. I need somebody to help me control it ... Be my teacher?"

She smiled, clearly pleased. "I've been hoping you'd ask me."

"Thanks." I felt compelled to add, "I should warn you, though. I might accidentally set you on fire."

"You won't."

That dismissive tone worried me. "I might."

Her gaze traced the fear on my face, and she sobered. "I know sunlight is aggressive. If it doesn't get what it wants, it acts like a restless stallion biting at the bit. But you should have more faith in yourself. When I was eighteen, I was still setting my curtains on fire."

Sefra pointed her chin at my perfectly intact curtains. "From what I can see, you're already doing better than I was at your age. But even if you weren't, I can deflect sunlight." In a maternal move, she tucked my stick-straight hair behind my ear. "So you can stop worrying—you're not going to hurt me."

My jaw fell. There were precious few witches skilled enough to deflect sunlight. At least, that was what I learned when I was with Zola and Thea.

"Now, what would you say to going for a walk?" she asked. "We could decide on a lesson plan on the way. Or we could just talk."

I could tell she preferred the idea of conversation. Her tone told me as much.

"I passed by an orchard earlier," I told her. "I was planning to go back and visit it."

"Perfect—"

"I'd like to walk there together. But I want to go into the actual orchard alone." Her expression faltered. I hastened to explain. "Frazer said fae carve the names of the people they've lost on stones or trees, anything they consider more immortal than themselves. I thought a tree from the orchard could be a good grave marker. I wasn't sure what else to do. John's remains were burned, and I don't have Viola's body."

The loss of them felt like a barbed arrow in my gut, and remembrance only thrust it deeper inside.

Sefra paled, but her voice remained steady. "I think that's a wonderful way to honor them."

I strengthened my body with a breath. "Do you still want to go? Walk with me, I mean?"

With a faint smile, she replied, "Of course."

We went at a leisurely pace down the staircases, out of the back of the castle, and through a courtyard under the changing sky. There was some light conversation between us, but when we turned onto a meandering path that bordered overgrown gardens matured by summer's touch, we grew quiet, distracted by the beauty that surrounded us.

Everything was alive. Everything was in bloom. And my fae senses brought me closer to nature—they made me a part of it. I lost time, transfixed by the early evening light as it bathed the land. It sent silken cobwebs glittering, and lengthened the straight-backed shadows of sunflowers, foxgloves, and hollyhocks.

I became immersed in the sounds of bees humming among the lavender bushes that fringed our path, in the croaks of frogs occupying a pungent pond nearby, and in the flitting of butterflies as they danced about, fickle in their attentions, only consenting to rest their wings upon the cones of flowering lilac. The only noise that disturbed nature's song were our footsteps and my own sneezing; my nose was tickled by the feminine scents of white jasmine, rambling roses, and honeysuckle.

Our slow walk ended once we reached an archway sprayed purple by wisteria with a view to the apple orchard beyond. The gateway was the only intact part of an old wall, a boundary line that was crumbling, vanishing behind an invasion of moss and ivy.

"This is where I leave you, then." Sefra didn't look happy at the idea.

"Before you go, I want to give you this."

I tugged at the leather lace holding the sunstone. It snapped easily under my strength.

Her forehead puckered. "The sunstone was meant for you."

"The magic inside, maybe." I held it out to her. "But it's just a crystal now. And you dedicated years of your life to searching for it. You should have it."

A bit hesitant, she took it from me.

I smiled. "Besides, you gifted me keepsakes from our family. I should do the same." I nodded at the necklace. "Atlas carried that for a long time, which I think makes it an heirloom of our kin."

"I suppose it does," she admitted.

Sefra tied the necklace at the nape of her neck. I tucked my chin in, viewing the shard of citrine that hung an inch below her collarbone. It looked right there, suiting her sun-burnished coloring.

"Are you sure you want to be alone?" Sefra studied me with worried eyes.

My eyebrow tugged up as if by a shepherd's crook. "I'm not alone though, am I? Or are you saying that Cora's stopped following me?"

She had the grace to look sorry with her eyes. "To be fair, that wasn't my idea. She was worried ... and, well, she cares about you too. Are you angry?"

"No. To be honest, I feel safer knowing she's around."

Sefra's shoulders dropped an inch or two. "Oh, well, that's good." A pause and a glance at the orchard. "I'll leave you to it."

I nodded. "See you soon."

Sefra clasped my shoulder as she passed by me. A quick squeeze, and she was gone, striding back up the path we'd come down.

I moved under the archway. The wisteria vines drooped low enough that they caressed my scalp with their petal clusters. The plant's sweet fragrance stayed with me as I walked on.

My feet carried me over wood garlic, upturned roots, and meadow grass. I meandered past crisp-scented apple trees, unsure what I was looking for.

A discordant squawk pitched the air. I jumped. "Danu?"

He gurgle-croaked again, sounding like a crotchety old man compared to the other birds and their merry chorusing.

I went to the tree I suspected his call had come from. And there he was, perched on a low branch weighted with fruit.

"What are you doing here?"

He cocked his head. *You needn't look so annoyed. I'm only here to pass on a message from Abraxus. He wishes you to know he's laid siege to Casatana. So far,* everything is going according to plan, and he still hopes to join you at the start of the new year.

"Okay. Is that it?"

No. Danu wagged his tail feathers irritably. *He says he's pleased you've decided to go to the Crescent, but he wishes for you to be careful when visiting the River-Willow House. Abraxus's spies say that the owner has always acted neutral in matters related to Morgan's rule. Keep your wits about you. Don't trust anybody at their word, only their deeds. That is all.*

I mulled that over.

Since you clearly don't want me here, I'll go back to stalking you from afar. If it was possible for a raven to appear snarky, then that was how Danu looked. *You really need to think about summoning your familiar. I'm watching over you as much as I can—*

"I never asked you to do that."

Irrelevant.

I rolled my eyes.

Your familiar might have the ability to protect you better than I could. I can't fight armed assassins for you. At best, I could peck a few to death.

Gods. I did not need that visual in my head.

"I might not have a familiar, you know," I argued. "Adi didn't. And Liora said Cai tried the summoning a few days ago and he doesn't have one either."

Danu opened his beak, emitting a rapid clicking noise. *Your obstinance is becoming boring.*

He vanished, leaving behind a tiny feather that floated down and passed in front of a name carved into the trunk before me. I hadn't noticed it before, but now it was as plain as the bright blue sky.

I reached up, tracing the letters carved into the gnarled bark: G R A C E.

This tree belonged to somebody else. To their grief. To their memories.

I should've walked away. But I couldn't. If I never returned to this spot, maybe whoever had carved Grace's name would. I hoped if they did, they would take my names into their care too.

I picked up a jagged stone and stared at the knotted wood. Suddenly, it wasn't enough for me to honor two people. I wanted to memorialize as many as I could.

Eyes clouding with salt and memories, I etched the names of the Tunnock villagers into the hard bark. Everybody that Balthur had murdered because of me. Every person remembered chipped off another piece of me. I had no numbness to shield me and no anger to hide behind. That ice had melted. That fire had burned out. I was reduced to blistered palms, bleeding fingernails, and a heart made of broken glass.

Nearing the end of my list, I paused.

I hadn't written Elain's name yet. I'd already realized and acknowledged that my stepmother would've died along with the others. But I hadn't wanted to think about it, to dwell on it. She'd helped murder Halvard. She'd gotten me exiled from my village. I couldn't find it within me to feel guilty over her death. Maybe that made me a savage. So be it.

Staring at the tree, I imagined Elain's face. "I don't forgive you, and I'm not carving your name. But since I got you killed, it doesn't feel right to hate you either. That's the best I can do."

I made Elain small in my mind, and I moved on.

Only a few names were left.

Sati. Dain.

Hunter.

John. Viola.

That was it. I was done. The stone tumbled from my shaking hand. Head bowed, I used my sleeves to wipe away the fiery trail of tears staining my skin. When my cheeks were dry, I steeled my spine and faced those names. "I'll remember you."

That promise was an important one. I was all that remained of John and Viola. The only one who in years to come would recall their voices. Their faces. Their kindness. The world was poorer for not having them in it. I was poorer.

The murmur of flapping wings reached me.

I grasped my Utemä and glanced upward. Lynx was coming in to land, his large shadow moving over me, cooling my sweat-slicked skin.

I released the pommel of my sword.

Lynx touched down, tucking his large wings in against his spine. He stood before me in an oversized gray shirt and black trousers. His dagger was connected to his belt by a chain. *Annoying.* Why did he have to look so good?

Lynx's attentions lowered to my scratched-up palms. Concern touched his face, and his fingers moved for mine.

I shifted my arms behind me, out of his reach. "I'm fine."

His jaw flexed. He didn't believe me. And he shouldn't. I'd lied.

Lynx's gaze skipped to the tree's tattooed flesh. He stepped up to the trunk, his expression turning remote. I watched him, wondering if he'd traveled somewhere else in his head, contemplating a thing faraway or forever lost to him. Then his long fingers drifted up and skimmed over the "G" in Grace. That soft, reverent touch ...

Rats. "Did you know her?"

"She was my makena," he said low-voiced.

Double rats. How could I explain this?

"I'm sorry. I shouldn't have—"

"I'm glad." His eyes snapped to me, pinning me in place. "She'll watch over your people for you, and they can keep her company in return."

I held his unwavering stare. I wasn't sure if I should ask ...

"When did she die?" I said, barely above a whisper.

"I was fifteen. She killed herself."

Hearing that felt like taking a physical blow.

"The spirits got louder and louder as she got older," Lynx elaborated, heartache showing up in the lines under his eyes. "I suppose she just couldn't take the noise anymore."

He exuded quiet despair, a sense that he shared her fate. No, no, no. *No.*

I invaded his space, grasping his forearm. "That's not going to happen to you."

Lynx's grimace seemed to say *Don't give me platitudes.*

"They can't haunt you if I'm here." My hand slid down his arm, feeling the solidness of his muscles beneath his gray sleeve. "You're not alone anymore."

I gripped his wrist tightly. Determinedly.

"Is that right?" Lynx's pitch deepened, and the amber in his irises darkened to scalding whiskey hues. His blistering gaze searched my face, branding every inch of skin that it touched with heat and want.

"Don't make this into something it isn't."

I released his wrist, but he caught my hand and linked it with his. "Is that what I'm doing?" Lynx angled his head in a manner that made me think he was daring me. Challenging me. That movement had his locks drifting about his face.

My fingers twitched with an urge to push his hair back. To touch him. I expelled those treacherous thoughts. *Shoo!*

"Just so you know, what you said goes both ways." He waved between us. "I'll always be here for you—no matter what."

I didn't resist when he drew me into a hug and held me there. His closeness caused my pulse to do funny things.

His chest moved against mine in a sigh. "I almost forgot that I came here to tell you something. It's not easy to focus around you, you know."

"I could say the same about you." The second that confession tripped off my tongue, I mentally slapped myself. I may as well have thrown a rock at a beehive.

His breastbone vibrated with a rumbling *purr*.

Dangerous. This was dangerous. I withdrew from his embrace, getting a safe distance away from him. "What was this thing you wanted to tell me?"

The fire in his eyes banked. "Did Frazer mention he was going up into the mountains?"

"What? No."

Lynx didn't seem surprised at my ignorance. "I was scouting the area for enemy movements and I saw Ryder flying him up there—"

"Ryder flew him up there?" I parroted. "And Frazer let him?"

"Yes ... But now Frazer's just sitting up there."

Turning inward, I tuned in to my brother's feelings. I felt as if I'd landed in a narrow corridor with shaking walls, the cold winds of a nightmare nipping at my heels.

I retreated from our bond, stomach upending, mind racing.

There were very few things that could've caused him to feel such terror. That strand of thought tripped me up into a series of memories that, when combined, brought illumination.

"His father threw him off a cliff," I blurted out.

Lynx shook his head in confusion. "What ..."

I waved my hand about, agitated. "That's how Frazer learned to fly. He's going to force himself to jump. You have to take me to see him. Please."

If Lynx had questions, he didn't ask them. He spread his wings out, and the falling light struck his feathers, making them gleam, highlighting the subtle indigo tones in them.

He lifted me up into his arms. I'd barely settled against his chest before we exploded upward, ascending into cooling skies washed in autumnal colors.

Lynx tipped his wings, angling west.

As we passed over the valley, I dared myself to look. To not be a coward. But the second I glanced down, I wished I hadn't. The moorland undergrowth was gone, and only ashen filth and black earth remained. That was what my magic had wrought.

Guilt kicked me in the teeth. I swallowed it, and it was more bitter than vinegar going down.

Once Lynx had climbed to the same altitude as the mountaintops, I caught sight of Frazer. He sat on one of the lower peaks, on a flattened section of the summit. It didn't take long for us to get to him.

Lynx touched down softly, lowering me onto nutrient-starved earth.

Frazer didn't acknowledge our arrival. He was a picture of loneliness, facing away from us, gazing out at the horizon, his elbows on his elevated knees. His wings were out and tucked in tight. I couldn't help but admire his feathers and the many shades hidden there: the shiny pewter, the cool slate, and the heavy gray that reminded me of rain clouds.

Lynx stepped up to my side. His thoughts bumped up against my shield.

I let him in. *Yes?*

Should I leave?

I considered that. Lynx had known Frazer longer than I. Their shared history might offer a fresh perspective, a way to reach my brother that hadn't occurred to me.

Unless he asks you to leave, I'd prefer it if you stayed. Maybe you can help.

Lynx's nod was small, a bit doubtful.

We approached Frazer.

"Brata?"

No answer.

"Lynx and I were worried ..."

Silence.

Following my instincts, I slunk to the ground. "I'm sitting behind you."

With that warning given, I shuffled up to him until our spines and wings met. A tremor traveled through Frazer's body. I sent my consciousness into our kin bond, letting him feel me there, too.

His discomfort slowly faded. But his frustration and anger continued to build and build. I sensed it all. It felt like standing underneath a waterfall with all of that immense pressure falling on top of me, the water invading my nose and throat passages, making it difficult to breathe.

I thought my lungs might burst from the lack of air—

Frazer was about to explode.

"FUUUCCCCCKKKK!" His scream was blunt rage and red agony.

I refused to block it out. I refused to cry.

His shout ended abruptly. A wordless silence stretched out, interrupted only by the noise of air heaving in and out of his chest.

I desperately wished to cure his pain. But I remembered what Thea had said. That only time and courage could heal his wounds.

"I'm sorry," he said, after his breathing had evened out. "I kept avoiding flight training, and it almost cost us our lives during the battle."

Frazer rarely lost control to the point of projecting his thoughts without intending to, and yet that was exactly what happened next. *Broken. Useless.*

I almost choked on the self-loathing that bled into our bond.

"You're not broken or useless," I said, a fire igniting in my core. "You survived something horrible, and you don't want it to happen again. That doesn't make you anything except normal."

"I am terrified of losing my wings again. That's true," Frazer admitted roughly. "But that's not the only reason I don't want to fly."

I waited anxiously for him to continue.

"It took me a long time to adapt to being wingless, and even longer before I could look at the sky without wishing I could rip my own heart out. And now I can fly again, but I don't want to do it; not when it feels like an invitation for more pain. It's always the hope that hurts the most."

He'd ended on a droll note. I could tell he wasn't joking, though. He was being serious and cloaking it in the guise of dark wit. That knowledge made me cold and hollow and sad inside.

"You told me once that the only time you ever felt at peace was when you were flying," Lynx said from Frazer's right. "That if you were having a bad day, you could lose yourself in the sky and the motions, and the world would fade away."

"I remember," Frazer said dully.

"Life isn't long enough or certain enough to deny yourself something that makes you that happy."

I sensed Lynx's eyes on me. There was no doubt in my mind that he was thinking about us, about my refusal to take things further. So I didn't voice agreement for what he'd said. It would've been useless, anyway. Frazer remained despondent.

I cracked. "You don't have to fly, brata."

"Yes, I do," Frazer said, sounding like he was destined for the hangman's noose. It killed me. "Staying grounded makes me an easier target. And I refuse to keep being your weak spot."

Frazer rolled up off the ground. I stood with him and kept my wings folded to stop the blustery weather from unbalancing me.

Turning around, I came face-to-face with his fear. It showed in the tightness of his jaw and the dampness of his brow. In his eyes, I saw the battle raging in his soul. I couldn't fight it for him. But I could be by his side while he did.

"Then fly with me," I said.

The faint tinge of pink in his cheeks brought about by the mountain winds drained away, leaving him paler than usual.

"We can jump together," I added.

Frazer raised his chin, not in defiance but in acceptance. "All right. Let's do it." He side-eyed Lynx. "You can go first."

"Fine by me." Lynx's lip hooked up in a teasing manner. "You never could keep up with me anyway, even when I gave you a head start."

Frazer lifted an eyebrow, and that was it.

Lynx didn't lose his smile. He put his back to Mysaya and casually walked out ahead of us, stopping at the precipice. Then the crazy male whirled around and fell off the edge. Not leaped. Not dove. But *fell* backwards.

I raced forward a few steps and looked over the edge.

Lynx plummeted toward rocks, ridges, and instant death.

Panic hit me.

At the last second, he flipped over and beat his mighty wings. He gained air and momentum quickly, leveling out over a valley—a wedge that sat between the surrounding mountains. It was a pristine wilderness, untouched by the weed of civilization, unmarked by the ravages of war; nothing like the wasteland behind us.

Frazer joined my left side. "Idiot. He never could resist showing off."

I glanced at my brother. "Our turn?"

Fear flashed through him. I could taste its sourness on my tongue, feel it in the nervous butterflies in my belly, and hear it in how loud my heartbeat echoed in my eardrums.

I didn't know who reached for who, but our hands linked up. My brain registered something strange about the positioning. I peered down to find my hand was on the outside. I was leading us. A first, maybe.

"I'll countdown from five, and then we'll jump," I said, unsure if I was asking him or telling him.

Frazer's mouth never moved, but he gave me a tight nod.

We backed up. Then stopped.

I stared straight ahead at the thin chain of dimming light that gilded distant mountain peaks in timeless beauty, softening their craggy points into pillow creases. "Five. Four. Three. Two. One!"

Frazer and I rushed forward. At the precipice, our hands parted and we leaped into the unknown.

The fall only lasted for a few seconds, enough time for the rapidly approaching ground to sear into my eyeballs in excruciating detail: barren slopes ended in a loula forest that covered the valley floor. A gossamer-fine mist wreathed the canopy of white blossoms in a spectral cloak, giving the impression that the clouds and stars had descended. That the sky had visited the earth.

Frazer pulled out of the dive. At the same time, I splayed my wings, capturing the breeze like the sails of a ship. The abrupt tug on my joints and shoulder blades made me grind my teeth. I breathed through the pain and flapped my wings.

I let Frazer pull ahead of me. All the better to watch him without being spotted.

His flying was far from smooth, and that shakiness mirrored his mental state. I sensed his mind skipping the same way a hare would flee a predator, bounding across the land, never slowing for fear of the fangs, talons, or claws that pursued it.

Lynx looped back around to us. He settled on my left side but maintained enough of a distance that Frazer emerged as the apex of our V-formation.

Gradually, the fear gripping my brother ebbed. As a consequence, his jerky movements leveled out.

I also began to unwind. The muscles in my jaw unglued. I settled into a rhythm, enjoying how the fresh air moved through my feathers, setting my blood singing and my scalp tingling.

"Where are we going?" Lynx asked lightly. "Should we do a circuit?"

"Have you forgotten your house's motto?" Frazer said, sounding a bit thin, a bit breathless.

"What motto?" I called out.

"Aruk valo myrskei ja tivita tähde," Lynx said, his voice clear and strong. "Let the stars guide you to safer shores."

I smiled, my spirits carried higher by those words.

The sun winked its last before vanishing below the skyline. It might've only been a fanciful imagining, but as the world went from waking to dreaming, my bonds with Frazer and Lynx strengthened, heightening my awareness of where they were in relation to me. In the gathering dark, I realized I didn't have to look at them to stay in alignment; our formation had become a fixed configuration—a constellation.

For an uncounted length of time, we flew like wild geese over the earth, our swift wings kissed by faint moonlight, each of us riding a chilling wind that carried whispers from far-off lands yet to be visited.

My reverie was interrupted by a shooting star. It set my heart on fire as it arced overhead, cutting a swift but dazzling path through the night sky. As it disappeared behind the western mountains, I longed to follow it, to see where it crashed down. A strange knowing gripped me then. That the wandering star wouldn't land. That it would simply go on forever, a divine light that refused to fade away, a rare sight that would visit every kingdom under the heavens, serving as a beacon of hope, uniting all.

The horizon suddenly held endless possibility in my eyes, and it was on reflection of that thought that I left behind the guilt and pain of the past. I forgot the enemies that plotted against us in the present. I released the doubts and fears I carried for the future. In that moment, I felt unbound from earthly woes and cares.

In that beautiful second, I felt free.

Because the lovely little flower is free
Down to its root, and, in that freedom, bold.
—William Wordsworth—

ABOUT THE AUTHOR

If you want to keep in touch with Nova, you can do so through her social media accounts. If you'd like to receive book updates, you can visit sbnova.com and sign up to her newsletter.

DID YOU ENJOY THIS BOOK? Please consider leaving a review on the site you purchased it from. Reviews can make all the difference to an author. Thank you!

facebook.com/sbnova1
twitter.com/sbnova1
instagram.com/sbnova1

ACKNOWLEDGMENTS

A big thank you to my editor, Linda. You went above and beyond to help me.

To Beren. Thank you for believing in me. For being there when I needed help. Love you lots.

To Ross. Thank you for the laughs. The hilarious pictures. For always listening and encouraging me.

To Tom. Thank you for the phone calls. The cat updates! The constant support.

To Dawn, my own alätia. Thank you for always cheering me on. Love you!